UPON A
BURNING THRONE

The Burnt Empire Saga

Book 1

UPON A
BURNING THRONE

Ashok K. Banker

A John Joseph Adams Book

HOUGHTON MIFFLIN HARCOURT

Boston New York

2019

For information about permission to reproduce selections from this book,
write to trade.permissions@hmhco.com or to Permissions,
Houghton Mifflin Harcourt Publishing Company, 3 Park Avenue,
19th Floor, New York, New York 10016.

hmhco.com

Library of Congress Cataloging-in-Publication Data
Names: Banker, Ashok, author.
Title: Upon a burning throne / Ashok K. Banker.
Description: Boston ; New York : Houghton Mifflin Harcourt, 2019. |
Series: The Burning Throne saga ; book 1 | "A John Joseph Adams book." |
Identifiers: LCCN 2018043600 (print) | LCCN 2018044776 (ebook) |
ISBN 9781328916259 (ebook) | ISBN 9781328916280 (hardback)
Subjects: | BISAC: FICTION / Fantasy / Epic. | FICTION / Fairy Tales, Folk Tales,
Legends & Mythology. | GSAFD: Fantasy fiction.
Classification: LCC PR9499.3.B264 (ebook) | LCC PR9499.3.B264 U66 2019 (print) |
DDC 823.914—dc23
LC record available at https://lccn.loc.gov/2018043600

Book design by David Futato

Map by Carly Miller

Printed in the United States of America
DOC 10 9 8 7 6 5 4 3 2 1

for bithika,
yashka,
ayush yoda,
helene,
and
leia.

~

this gift of words and swords,
this forest of stories,
this ocean of wonders,
this epic of epics.

Dramatis Personae

The Burnt Empire

Kr'ush (deceased)	Founder of the Krushan dynasty and the Burnt Empire
Shapaar (deceased)	Descendant of Kr'ush; emperor of the Burnt Empire; king of Hastinaga; father of Sha'ant and Vessa
Sha'ant (deceased)	Son of Shapaar; emperor of the Burnt Empire; king of Hastinaga; father of Vrath, Virya, and Gada; husband of the goddess Jeel and of Jilana; cousin of Jarsun
Vrath	Son of Sha'ant and the goddess Jeel; uncle to Adri and Shvate; prince regent of the Burnt Empire
Jilana	Dowager empress of the Burnt Empire; dowager queen of Hastinaga; wife of Sha'ant; mother of Vessa, Virya, and Gada; stepmother of Vrath
Vessa	Seer-mage; son of Jilana; biological father of Adri, Shvate, and Vida
Virya (deceased)	Son of Sha'ant and Jilana; husband of Umber
Gada (deceased)	Son of Sha'ant and Jilana; husband of Ember
Ember	Wife of Gada; mother of Adri; sister to Umber
Umber	Wife of Virya; mother of Shvate; sister to Ember
Adri	Prince of the Burnt Empire; son of Ember and Gada (legally) and Vessa (biologically); grandson of Jilana; nephew of Vrath; half brother of Shvate and Vida; husband to Geldry

Shvate	Prince of the Burnt Empire; son of Umber and Virya (legally) and Vessa (biologically); grandson of Jilana; nephew of Vrath; half brother of Adri and Vida; husband to Mayla and Karni
Vida	Son of Vessa; half brother to Adri and Shvate
Mayla	Princess of Dirda; wife of Shvate
Karni	Princess of Stonecastle; wife of Shvate
Geldry	Princess of Geldran; wife of Adri
Kune	Prince of Geldran; brother of Geldry

Subjects of the Burnt Empire

Prishata	Captain of the imperial guards
Adran	Charioteer of Adri; husband of Reeda; adoptive father of Kern
Reeda	Wife of Adran; adoptive mother of Kern
Kern	Foundling son (adopted) of Adran and Reeda
Sauvali	Maid in the royal palace

The Reygistan Empire

Aqron	King of Aqron; father of Aqreen
Aqreen	Princess of Aqron (capital of the Reygistan Empire); daughter of Aqron; wife of Jarsun
Jarsun	Descendant of Kr'ush; nephew of Shapaar; cousin of Sha'ant and Vessa; husband to Princess Aqreen
Krushita	Daughter of Aqreen and Jarsun; cousin of Shvate and Adri
Hasar	Aide to Jarsun
Vidram	Aide to Jarsun

The Gods

Jeel	Goddess of water; former wife of Sha'ant; mother of Vrath
Artha	Goddess of land; the Great Mother (a.k.a. Mother Goddess); protector of the mortal realm; sister of Goddess Jeel
Shima	God of death and duty
Sharra	God of the sun
Inadran	God of storms and war
Grrud	God of winds and birds
the Asva twins	Twin gods of animalia, health, and medicine
Shaiva	God of destruction
Coldheart	Spirit of mountains and high places; forebear of Jeel; grandfather of Vrath

Other Royals and Rulers of City-States

Belgarion	King of Darkfortress; lord of the mountain tribes
Anga	King of Anga
Vanga	King of Vanga
Kaurwa	Princess of Kanunga
Pundraki	Queen of Pundar
Vindva	Prince of Keyara
Vriddha	King of Virdhh
Ushanas	King of Ushati
Usha	Ushanas of Ushati's successor
Druhyu	King of Druhyu
Sumhasana	King of Sumha
Karta Mara	King of the Hais

Ripunjaya	King of Avant
Drashya	King of Dirda
Baal	King of Bahlika
Shastra	Chief of the Longriders clan
Stonecastle	King of Stonecastle; adoptive father of Karni

ARTHALOKA

MOUNT
COLDHEA

COLDHEART
MOUNTAINS

THE BURNT EMPIRE

LITTLE
ARANYA

HASTINAGA

JEEL

FO
SIST

•VIRDHH

•SERAPI

RAVINES
OF BEEDAKH

•MADRI

STONECASTLE

•DIRDA

TEARS OF
THE GODDESS

ANGA •

• AVANT

• VANGA

USHANATI •

• KANUNGA

USHATI •

•KEYARA

FEET OF THE GODDESS

•SUMHA

GREAT
DWARF

DRUHYU •

•BIRDDHA

•BAHLIKA

ISLE OF
ABANDONMENT

BAY OF
BEWITCHMENT

TEETH
OF DEMONS

FANGS OF
THE SERPENT

ARANYA
FOREST KINGDOMS

MOTHER OF SEAS

COLDHEART SEA

THE MOUNTAIN KINGDOMS

•DARKFORTRESS

BIG MESA

THE BROKEN LANDS

PLATEAU OF DESOLATION

SEA OF SORROWS

GREAT PLAINS

SEA OF GRASS

BAY OF BARREN HOPE

THE ISLES OF HONOR

THE REYGISTAN EMPIRE

RED DESERT

GAR

AQRON

KEY	
🌲	Forested Area
	Red Desert
	The Burnt Empire
•	City
✦	Capital

PROLOGUE

The Test of Fire

1

THEY CAME TO WATCH the children burn.

The royal criers had gone about the city the night before, calling out the news that Dowager Empress Jilana and Prince Regent Vrath would appear before the royal assembly at the auspicious hour to issue an important announcement. One that they had all been waiting to hear for over a year.

That was the official word.

The unofficial word, passed shivering through the body of the great metropolis like a fever through a favela, was that there would be a Burning.

The imperial palace would not confirm this; they did not deny it either.

People believed the rumor. They always do.

They came from far and wide, high and low, leaving work unfinished, doors unlocked, food half eaten, eager for entertainment.

Who could blame them?

After all, it isn't every day one gets to see princes and princesses burned to a crisp.

People packed the avenues and roadways, sat atop rooftops and terraces, crowding every dusty field, every mud-tracked street, every bylane leading to the palace. Children sat on their fathers' shoulders or on their mothers' hips. Caste was ignored; class, forgotten. Merchants and traders, hunters and farmers, priests and soldiers, all stood jostling one another. Two million perspiring bodies anxiously awaiting the royal proclamation. Runners awaited, the reins of their mounts in hand; horses, camels, elephants, wagon cart trains, and other transports all ready to depart for cities across the known world, for the outcome of a Burning could change the course of history, influence the rise and fall of empires, or launch a thousand wars.

Inside the magnificent palace stronghold, the great Senate Hall was thronged from wall to wall with kings, princes, ministers and merchant lords, preceptors and traders, as well as ambassadors from a score of distant foreign lands. Even the sentries posted at each of the thousand and eight pillars of the vast hall were pressed back against the cold stone by the crowd of humanity. The influence of the Burnt Empire extended not only to the far corners of the continent, but the entire civilized world. Traders and priests crossed oceans and deserts, mountain ranges and war-torn regions, braved barbarian hordes and bandit bands, to visit Hastinaga, City of Elephants and Snakes.

There were ambassadors with ebony complexions as dark as Dowager Empress Jilana's as well as pale-skinned foreigners with yellow hair, strange garb, and stranger tongues; men from the East with long beards and drooping mustaches; allies, tributes, and even royal emissaries. Some were of dubious loyalty. A few had warred, allied against, or otherwise opposed the expansion and growth of the Burnt Empire, before being compelled by force, expedience, or simple economic necessity to join its ever-burgeoning expansion. Many of those present had ancestors who had been present at the legendary founding of this capital city. More than a few had lost ancestors in battles or rebellions against the Krushan.

Former enemies or past rivals, they were all as one on this historic occasion. In place of poison-tipped daggers, they brought honeyed words. In lieu of arrows and legions, they offered rich tributes and exotic gifts.

All present, without exception, bowed their heads with humility before the fabled and feared Burning Throne.

2

At first glance, it looked like nothing more than a big rock.

As first impressions go, this was a perceptive one.

If seen in a different setting, in the high rocky mountains of Kalimeru perhaps, or the desert wilderness of Reygistan, or even the inhospitable forests of Jangala, one would have passed it by without a second glance.

It was just a rock.

Yet it was not a rock at all.

The jet-black substance perfectly emulated the appearance and texture of a rock.

Yet unlike any ordinary rock, it was imbued with deep, powerful sorcery. For one thing, it evaded the human gaze. The obsidian-dark surface drank light as parched earth drinks rain. The jagged texture made it deadly to touch: a passing graze could strip the skin off one's arm with the ease of a shredder.

Most importantly, if touched by living flesh, it burst into flame instantly and did not cease burning until the unfortunate limb or individual in possession of said limb was completely and conclusively consumed.

Stonefire, as it came to be known, did not simply burn you.

It devoured you.

A stonefire boulder in the wild could lash out with a tongue of fire reaching several feet, or yards, to snare its victim, yank them back into its fiery core and devour the unfortunate one, alive and screaming.

It emitted sounds as it ate its victims, terrible, inhuman noises comparable only to mythic beasts, and those who witnessed a Burning never forgot the sounds or the sight of the fire as it cavorted, frolicked, leaped, and laughed whilst consuming its prey.

It was no ordinary rock.

Yet little was known about it beyond these observed behaviors and qualities. For one thing, stonefire did not lend itself to examination but reacted to any living gaze. One indication of its presence was the utter absence of any fauna in its immediate vicinity. Even the fiercest predators gave it a wide berth. Those foolish few who sought to unearth its mysteries were consumed by its fiery flame, their ashes scattered by the wind.

All that was left then, as with most of life's mysteries, was speculation.

The gurus said it came from the celestial void, the emptiness between stars. A fragment of time and space, hurtling across unimaginable distance to strike our planet like a stone hurled by a disorderly god.

Its arrival upon our planet caused a cataclysm that disrupted the natural order for millennia, led to the extinction of most life, displaced continents and oceans, raised new mountain ranges, erased entire civilizations, and brought a million years of geologic turmoil and volcanic changes.

When the ash clouds finally settled, those few mortals who had survived the million years of cataclysm emerged, tempered by fire, to repopulate Arthaloka.

Of those few, the Krushan blazed the brightest.

The gurus claimed that Kr'ush, the forebear of the dynasty, was formed of the burning rock itself, a fragment of that celestial substance that took the shape of a man and walked Arthaloka. Ten thousand years later, it was impossible to separate myth from reality. The truth, be it as it may, was forever submerged in the ocean of lost knowledge.

What was true then, as it was today, was that Kr'ush and all those born of his seed were possessed of a symbiotic link to the stonefire.

This link manifested itself in different ways with each individual, but there was one thing all Krushan had in common:

They did not burn.

3

The crowds had grown restless, the gossip more spirited, by the time the tall, dark, stately form of Dowager Empress Jilana appeared upon the dais of Senate Hall. Her appearance was met with instant silence as every pair of eyes turned to her, every pair of lips quieted, and every pair of ears awaited her proclamation.

She began with the customary homilies, made the usual ritual declarations, and honored the ancestors, gods, and all those required to be acknowledged by tradition. Priests surrounded her like a swarm of bees around their hive queen, prompting her with suitable quotes from Krushan scriptures, performing the ritual consecrations and other religious rites with efficient economy, condensing what would have been a ceremony lasting an entire moon-cycle into a sprightly three hours.

When all the formalities were over, she took to the dais, a raised, circular platform of polished marble with veins of gold and silver. Sunlight descended through the painted skylight dome a hundred yards above her head, pinning her with a shaft of brilliant gold.

Behind her, the brooding stonefire seat loomed.

The dais turned slowly, presenting her sharply angled features to all the thousand and eight rulers present in turn. Each represented a kingdom or a nation. Each was accompanied by only one armed aide and watched over by one armed Krushan guard.

From the periphery of the great circular hall, acolyte priests observed and recorded every detail, passing along a running commentary that was then repeated by royal criers to the perspiring people outside.

The ritual formalities ended, Dowager Empress Jilana came to the crux of the matter. Not one to waste breath, knowing she already had a captive audience eager to receive her words, she voiced the name of Prince Regent Vrath.

The man in question stood in full court armor, gleaming and resplendent, the most magnificent specimen of manhood in the entire assemblage, the symbol of power of the entire Burnt Empire and pillar of the dynasty.

Vrath approached Jilana with a bow and a kneel that displayed a son's respect, though, as a demigod, he was far more powerful than she. Yet that show of humility was significant, intended as a message to all who observed them both, this unlikely duo of stepmother and stepson. For it was by Vrath's leave that she ruled Hastinaga and through Vrath's power and influence and reach that she maintained that post. This kneeling and show of respect was to convey to the world at large that all was well between the dowager empress and her stepson, the steward and regent of the Burnt Empire. All was well and as it had been since the demise of her husband, the late emperor Sha'ant.

A thousand wagers collapsed on that look alone.

A thousand fortunes were won and lost because of that kneeling and the angle of Vrath's bowed head.

The Krushan Empire, better known as the Burnt Empire, was, as it had been, ruled by the late Sha'ant's widow, Jilana, and protected by his son Vrath. Let no one doubt or question that status quo, on pain of death.

This message conveyed, Vrath took his place beside his stepmother on the dais. After a few gruff formal words — the prince regent was not fond of public speaking — he bowed again to Jilana, leaving it to her to make the proclamation that all were waiting to receive.

"It is a great day for the Krushan dynasty, a great day for Hastinaga and the dawn of a new epoch," she said with a regal tone and manner that belied her origins as a fisherman's daughter who had spent her youth ferrying pilgrims across the sacred Jeel River all day long, clad in scanty garb and stinking of fish. Now, as she stood before the diamond-bright eyes of the world's most powerful and wealthiest monarchs, she was the very image of what a widowed queen should be, proud and dignified, the gold tiara on her head and gold scepter in her hand leaving no doubt of her authority.

"The Krushan dynasty has two male heirs," she said. "The princesses Ember and Umber have each given birth to a son. Both boys are healthy and well."

The cheer that exploded from two million throats buffeted the humid air and filled the metropolis. In the great hall, the thousand and eight were equally vocal in their exuberance, each vying to outdo the others in expressing their joy — and, more importantly, to be seen and heard expressing that joy.

After the deafening uproar finally died down, Prince Regent Vrath took over again, announcing in his military commander's bullfrog voice, "In the name of my father, Emperor Sha'ant, and all the ancestors back to Almighty Kr'ush himself, I call upon the new heirs to undergo the Test of Fire."

4

A double row of Krushan fire maidens had entered the great hall during Jilana's speech, forming a long path from an inner palace doorway to the foot of the dais. Every last one was armed and held her weapon at the ready. The fire maidens favored the bladed weapon called a Flame, held by a fist-shaped grip from which protruded four inches of layered razor-sharp steel that curved in a semicircle with a flame-shaped tip at the top. They each held two Flames in the resting position, the flat of the blades overlapping to form a shield against their navels, and stood facing the dais.

As the princesses Ember and Umber emerged from the inner palace, the fire maidens let their mistresses walk past, then turned smartly to face outward, forming a wall of blades that only one intent on suicide would dare challenge.

Despite having given birth only days earlier, both young women walked with the regal dignity that was expected of them. If there was a bead of sweat on one's brow or a queasiness in the other's belly, it was only to be expected. Their lives, their reputations, their futures, as well as the fate of their birth nation, rested upon the outcome of the next few moments.

The gathering in the great hall and in the city outside observed the approach of the princesses, hawkishly seeking any show of nervousness. The biggest bets were now being placed on which of their offspring would be the lucky one today and which the less fortunate.

They reached the dais together, but Princess Umber, being the elder, permitted her sister Ember to precede her up the steps.

Upon the dais, both turned the tiny bundles that they held against their chests so that the audience could see with their own eyes the children they brought to the test.

The difference in the two babes was striking.

One was dark as pitch, with eyes as white as alabaster.

The other was white as alabaster with eyes as colorless as glass.

The thousand and eight monarchs gasped.

A blind prince and an albino?

Murmurs of unease began at the corners of the great hall. Darting looks of doubt.

In the streets and avenues, the news caused consternation.

Envoys and dispatches wanted to ride at once, for this very news was enough to draw doubt, suspicion, even anger down on the Burnt Empire. What good, after all, many would say, were two such heirs? How could either of them prove worthy of the Burning Throne? How could a blind prince or an albino prince rule the Burnt Empire? Were Jilana and Vrath seeking to enrage the thousand and eight kingdoms? How could a dynasty as powerful as the Krushan possibly expect to command the world's greatest empire with either of these two on the throne? Surely they were not fit to even be put to the Test of Fire? What mockery was this?

The mood turned mutinous; the air thickened with the possibility of violence.

Vrath sensed this sudden turn of mood and stepped forward.

"Does anyone here challenge the right of these two boys to undergo the Test of Fire?" he demanded, his voice edged with steel, his grey eyes the color of frost, his hand resting on the hilt of his sheathed weapon.

Eyes that had sparked defiance softened at once, voices stilled.

The city grew quiet.

None dared challenge the son of the late emperor Sha'ant and the river goddess Jeel.

Vrath held his posture and gaze a moment longer, to suppress any further thoughts of rebellion.

Then, when he was satisfied, he stepped back, offering a clear path to the throne to the princesses Ember and Umber.

"Let the test begin. As the younger, Princess Ember's son will go first."

Princess Ember walked the dozen steps across the dais to the massive throne, the eyes of the world upon her slender form.

She stopped a full ten yards from the stonefire and held up the tiny bundle of life with both hands, displaying the child to the black rock. She kept her eyes low, her posture obeisant, and her tone prayerful, as she had been taught and made to rehearse a hundred times.

"I, Ember, daughter of the Serapi nation, wife of the late prince Gada, daughter-in-law to Dowager Empress Jilana and the late emperor Sha'ant, submit my son, Adri, flesh of my flesh, blood of my blood, life of my heart, to your keeping. I pray to thee, bear him with grace, guard him with fire, empower him to rule the great Burnt Empire."

The last echoes of her words faded, leaving a pall of silence.

The great black throne loomed, five yards taller than the princess, two yards wide, a cold, malformed darkness in the center of the vast chamber that was not human, yet brooded with sentient life.

With a roar as savage as a vyag in the deep jungle, a tongue of fire shot out and grasped the tiny infant held aloft by his mother.

Princess Ember cried out as the tongue of flame enveloped her newborn babe, took hold of him in a fiery grasp, and snatched him out of her arms. She fell to the gleaming dais, her fingertips scorched and smoking from the mere brush with the fire.

The fire curled with tortuous slowness, drawing the infant to the great mass of black rock.

The child himself was either too startled or too terrified to make a sound. The boy Adri stared, his arms and legs flapping wildly in consternation, but remained silent.

The flame formed fingers that caressed and stroked the baby's soft cheeks and round face. The fire reflected in his milky white eyes, but there were no pupils to contract, nor any reaction to the searing heat that must surely have been produced by that intense flame.

The fire spoke to the boy in its own savage voice, whether threatening or cajoling, it was impossible to say which, for none of those watching spoke its language, and the only grown person who did understand, namely Vrath himself, showed no inclination to offer a translation.

The babe calmed, his limbs slowing, his agitation ceasing.

The fire murmured again, and perhaps this was just a fancy of their imagination, but the monarchs thought it sounded . . . *pleased.*

Either that or it approved of the meal it was about to enjoy.

Without further delay, the flame lowered the babe to the flattened part of the rock, the seat of the fabled throne.

Held by the fist of flame, the babe appeared to be sitting upright of his own accord, caped by fire.

Then: a slow growl, deep and rumbling as if from the bowels of Arthaloka.

The throne burst into flame.

A conflagration to match a giant bonfire.

Yet a hundred oak logs ignited at once could not have produced a fire so intense.

The thousand and eight gasped and stepped back, no longer eager to be close to the dais.

Those who stood only a few dozen yards away swatted at their hair, their eyebrows, their mustaches, their fine robes and shawls, sweat popping out on their faces as they stared in amazement.

The Burning Throne burned, and as it burned, it sang.

You did not need to speak the language of fire to know the meaning of that song.

It was a song of fire and fury, war and blood, death and glory.

It blazed fifty yards high and ten yards wide, the throne itself disappearing, lost in a blaze too intense, too searing to look upon directly.

Hands shielded eyes, the desire to witness overpowering the fear of fire. One ancient urge dominating another ancient need.

Upon the dais, Princesses Ember and Umber, Prince Regent Vrath, Dowager Empress Jilana, stood unscathed and unharmed by the heat and the flames. If they felt the scorching fire, they showed no sign. Though the three women were only wedded to Krushan men — not Krushan by birth — they too were protected by the power of the stonefire.

Vrath — as the child of both fire and water, on his father's and mother's sides, respectively — was both Krushan and immortal, and as such, doubly protected and empowered. He looked into the heart of the blaze and saw all, though he said not a word to anyone else. He listened to the savage song of the stonefire and understood every word and sound — and of these too, he said nothing.

The monarchs assembled in the great hall, the fire maidens, and the royal guards were neither impervious to the power of the stonefire, nor were they immune to its appetites. Many recalled the terrible tale of the Great Devouring, when a false aspirant had angered the stonefire with his disrespect and arrogance. The throne had responded by lashing out and burning not only the aspirant himself, but every last monarch present, reducing them to a thousand and eight piles of ash in moments. Even the fire maidens, the guards, and the aides had not been spared, and the gurus said that the floor of the vast chamber was a foot deep in ash by the time the throne was finally done burning. Only the Krushan family members had themselves been left untouched, but that was only to be expected.

Fear of a recurrence had some of the thousand and eight turning to look toward the exits, but none were permitted to leave or enter once a Burning began, and the ready spears of the royal guards outside would end their lives as surely as the fire. The fire maidens were unafraid, having been raised from birth to serve the Burning Throne; every last one expected to end her life in sacrifice to its service. If that end came today, so be it. It would be as much an honor to be taken by fire as to fall in bloody battle.

But the Burning Throne did not seek any other prey.

No tongues of flame darted out to yank nervous monarchs.

The blaze, intense and white-hot though it raged, remained confined to the throne itself, and within the perimeter of the dais.

Slowly, by degrees, the blaze subsided.

The terror of the crowd abated.

The thousand and eight heaved a silent sigh of relief, glad that they would not perish today.

Their fear was replaced by their desperate desire to know the fate of the aspirant, the young prince Adri.

They lowered their hands and stared at the Burning Throne.

Almost to the last, all in attendance expected to see a tiny pile of ashes, no more than a handful or two perhaps, thus ending the foolish ambition of a mother who dared to suggest that a blind prince could rule the Burnt Empire.

The flames diminished, soon relegated to but a few wisps and licks shrouding the throne, though the black rock from which the seat was carved now glowed crimson — or in some places white-hot — from the searing heat.

Smoke, thick and white as fog, then dissipated with frustrating slowness, revealing at last, with tantalizing coyness, the result of the Test of Fire.

5

Prince Adri sat, held by gentle fingers of flame, upon the Burning Throne.

A roar of excitement rose from the great hall.

It was echoed by the crowds outside.

The Burning Throne had chosen a new heir for the first time in a quarter of a century.

Prince Regent Vrath silenced the gathering with a mildly raised voice. "Princess Umber may now offer her son."

The gathering stilled again, befuddled. What was the point of testing another aspirant? The throne had already chosen. Even the gurus were puzzled. There was no precedent for such an event. Never before had two aspirants been born on the same day. Krushan tradition demanded that once an heir was chosen by the stonefire, he or she ruled until their death. Yet it was true that, in the rare event that twins or triplets or multiple siblings were born, the eldest of them would undergo the test and, if accepted, would rule. By that same logic, it also followed that Princess Umber's son, being the firstborn of these two boys, should have taken precedence.

Later, it would be speculated that it was Dowager Empress Jilana and Prince Regent Vrath's joint decision to put the younger boy to the test first, thereby giving him an opportunity to prove his legitimacy. Had they simply called upon Princess Umber to offer her son first, she being the eldest and her son the firstborn of the two, the point would have been moot. Princess Umber's son would have passed the test and been accepted as the rightful heir of the Burnt Empire, destined to rule till his death. There would have been no call for Princess Ember to place her own son upon the Burning Throne.

On such decisions are empires built, dynasties founded, and wars waged.

But at that instant, in the great hall, none dared challenge the right of the elder princess to offer her son to the fire test, not while Vrath stood by and endorsed her.

So the assemblage watched in silent wonder as a second child was offered to the Burning Throne.

"I, Umber, daughter of the Serapi nation, wife of the late prince Virya, daughter-in-law to Dowager Empress Jilana and the late emperor Sha'ant, submit my son, Shvate, flesh of my flesh, blood of my blood, life of my heart, to your keeping. I pray to thee, bear him with grace, guard him with fire, empower him to rule the great Burnt Empire."

What followed was a reenactment of what had gone before.

The Burning Throne took Shvate, son of Umber, and embraced him in its fiery heart, sang its savage song, blazed with as much fervor and delight, and accepted him as rightful heir of the Burnt Empire.

This time, when the flames died down and the white smoke cleared, the exultation that met the sight of the living infant was no less enthusiastic — for to show anything less than complete ecstasy over the anointing of a Krushan heir would have been unforgivably disrespectful — but there was also consternation and confusion amongst the monarchs as well as the people.

What did this mean?

How could there be *two* heirs?

And what of their afflictions? One was born blind, the other an albino. In their own kingdoms, neither boy would have been deemed fit to rule.

But there was more to come.

After Princess Umber had retrieved her little bundle of flesh and stood proudly beside her sister, both now equal in their roles as the mother of an heir of Krushan, and therefore in line to be future Queen Mother of the Burnt Empire, Prince Regent Vrath made a final announcement.

"As each of the two princes is gifted with special needs, and since both have been anointed by fire and proven fit to rule the Burnt Empire, it is the decision of the elders that they shall rule jointly for the time being."

The questions had been answered. The confusion had been cleared. The reasons for the dual Burning explained.

There was some relief among the monarchs and the people.

Perhaps this was tenable.

The cruel consensus was that a disabled prince, on his own, was hardly a worthy ruler by the measure of tradition.

But two princes, working together, well, perhaps they would be able to compensate for each other's shortcomings.

But there was one more surprise still in store.

The Burning was not yet over.

6

A monarch stepped toward the dais.

At once, the guards moved to stop him, weapons drawn.

The monarch ignored them and called, "Prince Regent Vrath, Dowager Empress Jilana, I ask your leave to approach."

Vrath and Jilana exchanged a glance.

Jilana spoke. "The court recognizes King Aqron. Speak. What is your purpose?"

"By the law of the Krushan, I demand the right to submit my grandchild to the Test of Fire."

This was met with such deafening silence that even the earlier roars of exultation could not match its impact.

On a day without precedent, here was yet another unprecedented event.

Vrath said, "The throne has chosen its heirs. Prince Adri and Prince Shvate shall rule the empire jointly. The test is over."

King Aqron replied, "Nevertheless, by Krushan law, I demand that my grandchild be permitted his test."

Vrath's thick brows beetled. He was not known for his patience. Before he could speak again, Jilana spoke. "King Aqron, you are not of Krushan blood. Neither is your wife, nor your daughter. How then do you claim the right to test your grandchild?"

King Aqron gestured toward the nearest entrance. A young woman stood there, bearing an infant child. At his gesture, she held up the child proudly.

"My daughter, Princess Aqreen, bore a child of Krushan blood six months ago. We have traveled here from the kingdom of Aqron, far beyond the white deserts of Reygistan, to submit to the test. We were set upon by dacoits in the Ravines of Beedakh and held captive for months until my aide could ride back home and fetch our ransom. When we finally arrived here in Hastinaga and sought to present ourselves to the court, we learned that there was to be a Burning. It was such fortuitous timing that it cannot be a coincidence. Only the gods themselves could have planned it thus. Pray, command your guards to let my daughter enter the great hall, that we may submit to the test."

Eyes flicked from King Aqron to the dais, watching and drinking in every word and gesture, nuance and intonation. This was turning out to be quite a day.

Quite a day indeed.

Now it was Jilana's turn to frown. Her slender, artfully plucked brows arched as she asked, "You say your grandchild is of Krushan blood. Who, then, is the father?"

King Aqron offered a peculiar expression, neither a smile nor a scowl. "My daughter has not confided that to me, and refuses to do so to anyone. She says it is a woman's business whom she chooses to take to her bed, and I cannot argue with that."

Jilana and Vrath put their heads together briefly to consult, and neither looked very pleased when they parted.

Vrath asked with obvious irritation, "You understand what it means to fail the test?"

"I do," Aqron said. "As does my daughter. I sought to dissuade her, but she is as stubborn as I am when she sets her mind to something. She will not rest until her child is tested."

With obvious reluctance, Jilana said, "Let Princess Aqreen and King Aqron approach the dais."

The sentries at the door parted, the princess entered, watched by all eyes.

She wore the head-shawl of the Aqron people, a mark of their faith, and her finely carved features were as delicate as a profile drawn in desert sand. Like her father, and like most Aqron, she was taller and thinner than most of the grown men in the great hall, except for Vrath, who was the tallest by far. Accompanied by her father, she strode to the dais, bowed gracefully to the dowager empress and prince regent despite the burden in her arms, and ascended. The two princesses Ember and Umber glared at her without any attempt to conceal their disapproval. If their resentment could have been expressed with fire, Princess Aqreen would have been burned to a cinder right there and then.

She approached the stonefire and raised her child, offering the thousand and eight their first clear view of the infant. It was a handsome girl of some six months of age, her tiny features a miniature of her mother's but with a high, flat forehead. She gazed with intelligent eyes at the vast hall filled with men and women in garments of every color and style, and gurgled happily, stuffing a fist into her toothless mouth.

"I, Aqreen, princess of Reygistan, child of my father, Aqron, and my mother, Aqreela; and servant of the prophetess Aquirella; unwed mother to my daughter, Krushita. I submit this flesh of my flesh, blood of my blood, life of my heart, to your keeping. I pray to thee, bear her with grace, guard her with fire, empower her to rule the great Burnt Empire. In the name of the prophetess, namas!"

More than a few brows other than Vrath's were raised at this dramatic deviation from the traditional words of offering, but none objected or intervened.

The child's fate was now in the hands of the stonefire.

Moments later, the Burning Throne delivered its verdict.

It embraced the child with fire and warmth, and when the smoke and flames cleared, the little girl sat of her own accord, chubby arms splayed, patting the razor-sharp black rock as affectionately as if it were a beloved pet. Where her tiny fingers made contact with the jagged stone, sparks flared. She laughed at the phenomenon and clapped her hands together in approval. Her laughter echoed around the great hall, for words spoken upon the Burning Throne were amplified by its power.

Vrath and Jilana exchanged a stormy glance. It was clear to everyone present that they were furious at this turn of events. Tradition and Krushan law demanded that they acknowledge Princess Krushita as the rightful heir and yield the throne to her, with her mother and father managing the empire until the girl was of age. This meant, in effect, that both Jilana and Vrath would have to relinquish their roles and step down. Neither appeared willing to do so.

Vrath was renowned for his adherence to Krushan law. Those who knew his expressions and body language read the telltale indications. Despite his resistance to relinquishing the reins of power, Vrath was prepared to step down because it was the right thing to do.

He spoke. "The law of my ancestors is clear. King Aqron, your grand-daughter has passed the test of fire. She has proven her right to sit upon the Burning Throne and rule the empire. Under the circumstances, I have no choice but to —"

"One moment, Vrath."

The prince regent frowned at the interruption.

He glanced at his stepmother.

Dowager Empress Jilana's face was as stormy as a monsoon cloud, her sharp tone of voice leaving no doubt about her refusal to accept the situation. "There is still the question of succession. Before we can accept this aspirant as our future ruler, the people of the Burnt Empire have the right to know from what bloodline she is descended. Princess Aqreen, I demand to know the name of this child's father."

Princess Aqreen, her baby safely in her arms again, lowered her chin to the shorter, older, woman, completely unabashed by Jilana's imperious tone and manner. "Among the Reygistani, a child is known by their mother's name. We are a matriarchal society. A woman may take as many husbands as she wishes, or bed a hundred men, it matters not. Her children are her children."

Though Jilana had to raise her head to look at Aqreen directly, she did so in a manner that made her seem the taller and more threatening woman. "This is not the white desert. You are not in Reygistan. Krushan law is pa-triarchal, paternity is determined by the father. You must name the father of this child."

Aqreen set her jaw defiantly, showing Jilana her long, delicate neck. "The stonefire has proven her legitimacy. She is of Krushan blood. That is all you need to know."

"Stepmother," Vrath said cautiously, for once in the unlikely role of intermediary, "what she says is true. Under Krushan law —"

Jilana responded with a tone as scathing as the stonefire. "I am Krushan law. As dowager empress, I still hold the reins of power in my fist. I will not relinquish ten thousand years of greatness to a desert rat and her bastard daughter!"

Aqron's face turned dark with blood. "You insult my daughter and grandchild and our people! Prince Regent Vrath, will you stand for this? Is this how the great Burnt Empire treats its own heir and her family?"

Vrath, for once in his life, looked as if he would rather be anywhere else than upon this dais at this moment. He raised both hands. "Clearly, we are not all in agreement. I recommend we convene in chambers to discuss the matter further. It is not seemly to continue a family dispute in the public view."

"It is hardly a family dispute," Jilana countered, breaking with tradition again by publicly correcting her stepson. "These people are not family by any definition."

"My father told me you would not accept the stonefire's test," said Princess Aqreen, cradling her daughter. "He told me that the only way to force you to let us take the test was to make our demand publicly, during the Burning. I am sorry that he was right. Had we approached you privately as I wanted, you would not have accepted us. I see that now. I was foolish to ever think that the high and mighty Jilana would ever loosen her iron grip on the reins of power. But my daughter has no part to play in your politics and your bigotry. She is of the same blood as Prince Vrath, the same blood as your late husband, Emperor Sha'ant, and the princes Adri and Shvate. That makes us family, whether you like it or not. For my daughter's sake, and for the sake of this family's future, I ask you respectfully, Dowager Empress Jilana and Prince Regent Vrath, is not her claim upheld by Krushan law? Is not her seniority over Adri and Shvate evident to anyone present here today? She is elder to them and has passed the test of fire. The Burning Throne has accepted and embraced her. She is a daughter of queens and champions, a proud inheritor of the great tradition of Reygistani warrior queens for seven hundred years. She will make a great queen, a fine empress, and the worthy successor to great Kr'ush himself. Give her her rightful due, and I predict the Burnt Empire will flourish. But deny her, and you will bring down the wrath of the gods themselves upon this dynasty."

Prince Vrath spoke into the heavy silence that followed. "Krushan law —"

It was as far as Jilana allowed him to go. "Krushan law demands that the lineage of any successor be made known to the world, that there be no doubt about the parentage and right of any aspirant. This law was laid down by Krushan himself to prevent any counterclaim or dispute. By failing to identify the father of her child, Princess Aqreen has forfeited her claim under Krushan law."

King Aqron spoke, tempering his obvious outrage for the sake of his daughter. "The Burning Throne has identified the father's bloodline. If little Krushita were not of Krushan blood, she would not be alive right now. She passed the test of the stonefire. She has been declared fit to rule and a worthy successor. That is also Krushan law."

Jilana turned to address the king of Reygistan. "Then we are in conflict, and as dowager empress, I have the sole right to break that conflict with my decision. And I say that your granddaughter is unfit to rule. That ends the matter. Now take your bastard grandchild and whore of a daughter and return to your desert rat hole."

King Aqron's fist clenched the hilt of his scimitar, the knuckles whitening with force. "Jilana, you dare speak to us in this manner? Why, you yourself are nothing but the daughter of a fisherman! You ferried travelers across the Jeel River for pennies a crossing! And your own son Vessa was born out of wedlock, from a casual night spent with an anonymous stranger of Krushan blood. And yet you, the pot, are now presuming to call the kettle black! My daughter is a princess and the daughter of queens. You were nothing but a common fisher caste. They say your skin reeked so much of fish no man would touch you. It was that Krushan stranger who magicked away that smell, making you desirable and seductive. It was with that magic that you seduced Emperor Sha'ant when he happened to board your ferryboat, and enticed him into taking you for his wife. From a ferryboat to the Burning Throne! What a long way you have come, Jilana. How dare you criticize the morality of my daughter when you yourself had your own first child out of wedlock. Indeed, when your two sons by Emperor Sha'ant died tragically in their youth, you summoned your own bastard son, Vessa the mage, to force himself upon your two daughters-in-law, seeding their wombs with offspring of Krushan blood. Did you announce that today? You presented Princes Adri and Shvate as the heirs, but you did not name their father, did you? Such hypocrisy! You did not name their father because that would have meant acknowledging the fact that he was your son, and of Krushan blood. Moreover, it would have meant naming the Krushan stranger who fathered Vessa himself upon you, even before your marriage to Emperor Sha'ant. Who was that stranger, Jilana? The mystery has been kept for decades. You will not name him, yet it is of his son Vessa that these two heirs apparent were seeded. And yet you have the audacity to claim that my daughter, an honorable and brave warrior princess who is a shining exemplar to the women of our nation, has no right to take your place as Queen Mother? Your hypocrisy and duplicity are an insult to Krushan law and an affront to the people of the empire! You, Jilana, are the one who is not fit to stand where you stand today. By the same token that you dismiss my daughter Aqreen, I dismiss you!"

"*Enough!*" Vrath thundered.

The thousand and eight staggered back, their ears ringing from the deafening bellow. For when Vrath spoke in anger, it was with an impact to match a thunderclap. While Jilana could only posture and pout, Vrath was the real power. It was not for nothing that his name kept any dissenters across the vast and unruly span of the empire in check. A demigod in full temper is not something any mortal can withstand and still survive.

"I will not tolerate anyone speaking to my stepmother in such a manner," he said, his eyes dribbling fire. Behind him, the dark throne glowed a deep scarlet, sensing the mood of one of its own. "She has already communicated her decision. Her word is final. If you wish to complain or protest, you will follow the usual protocol. There will be no more mouthing of cheap insults by anyone." At this he paused and turned to glance briefly at Jilana, including her in his stricture. "The Burning has concluded, and this matter is over. The people expect a jubilee, and they shall have it."

7

"The people expect a lot, but they get very little."

The words came from the entrance, spoken by a voice as quiet and smoldering as a banked fire. Heads turned to see which new character had entered the stage of this imperial drama. The figure that stood there resembled a life-sized version of a child's stick-figure drawing. Tall, a whole foot taller than seven-foot Vrath himself, and with angular shoulders and bony limbs jutting at sharp angles to the rake-thin torso, he loomed above the imperial guards who held their short spears pointed at him. By some trick of the light, his features remained clouded, shrouded by a miasma that seemed to move when he himself moved. All one could see was the *impression* of a face, and there was clearly something not quite human about those features, yet one would be hard-pressed to say what it was exactly that it lacked. Though the figure's face was a mystery, his mouth and tongue were very visible and constantly motile; indeed, his tongue flickered in and out of his thin lips, punctuating his speech with sibilance.

"Least of all, justice," he added. "This reputation you have earned, Vrath, of being the great pillar of Krushan law, upholder of the great tradition of Kr'ush himself . . . it is ill-deserved. Today, you put the lie to the claim that Vrath the Oathtaker always upholds the law. Today, all of Hastinaga witnessed firsthand that Vrath was confronted with a clear matter of law and even voiced his agreement, only to then dissemble, bluster, and bully his way out of his own decision. Does your father's widow have such sway over you that you forget your first loyalty is to the law? Has Empress Jilana completely corrupted your moral code? Has your legendary vow of celibacy weakened your adherence to law? Are you too distracted by your unfulfilled lust for the three beautiful widows with whom you share a household?"

"Silence!" Vrath thundered, fire spilling from his eyes and mouth now. Tiny motes of flame fell from his eyes and lips, turning to bits of coal as they cooled. His boots crushed them underfoot, smearing the pristine white marble. "You are out of order, stranger. Sentries, clap him in irons and drag him down to the dungeons."

The sentries moved to comply, a half dozen strong men with short spears converging on the insolent speaker.

One sentry, in his zeal to comply with his prince regent's command, put the point of his spear to the waist of the stranger.

Like a coiled whip unleashed, the tall man's hand shot out and struck the sentry's forearm. The sentry collapsed, gagging as froth welled from his open mouth, eyes rolling up to reveal their whites. Before he had touched the ground, the stranger's hands had whipped around, striking at each of the other sentries in turn. The strikes were minimal, barely a pinprick; the effect, instantaneous. All six sentries fell to the polished floor of the great hall, writhing and kicking in their death throes.

The stranger stepped over their flailing bodies as he approached the dais. Kings and queens parted to let him pass, eyes wide with awe.

A name rustled through the air like a dry leaf in an autumn breeze.

"Jarsun."

Jilana's voice was quiet, her temper banked now, her face guarded.

As a hundred more sentries sprang forward, willing to die rather than let a stranger trespass, she gestured sharply. "Let him pass."

They paused as one man, and retreated to their posts.

"It has been a long time, brother-in-law," she said, visibly regaining her composure as the tall stranger reached the foot of the dais. Even standing three feet lower, his eyes were at the same level as hers. "But I don't seem to recall inviting you to this occasion. Why is that?" She snapped her fingers in a mocking pretense of absent-mindedness. "Because you were banished from Hastinaga thirty years past! It was my own father-in-law who banished you, as I recall."

"You speak as if you were there when it happened," Jarsun said, placing a foot on the lowermost step of the dais. "You were still a ferrywoman on the Jeel River at the time. I sat in your rickety little boat once, though you had no idea who I was, and to be fair, I had cloaked my identity to appear as a Gujwari merchant. What King Aqron said was true. You reeked of fish. It was difficult enough to endure the river crossing. If my father had not used his power to eliminate the odor at your request, I doubt my brother Sha'ant would have endured it when he sat in your boat. Let alone have wooed you. More likely, he would have jumped overboard."

The stone-dead silence that met this drew a smile from the visitor.

He turned to look at the assembly.

"Why? Did you not know that the Krushan stranger that your Empress Jilana dallied with on the banks of the Jeel was none other than the former Emperor Shapaar? Does that shock you into silence? I see even Prince Regent Vrath looks a little taken aback. Vrath, were you not aware that your beloved and highly respected stepmother Jilana first mated with your grandfather Shapaar and bore him a son, before mating with and then marrying your father Sha'ant and bearing him two sons? Of course, she probably knew you would react thus when you knew the truth, which is why she kept it a secret for all these years. It must be a terrible shock to you personally, Vrath, to learn that Vessa is in fact your uncle as well as your half brother."

Vrath's face gave no hint of his inner turmoil. Aloud, he said only, "By Krushan law, you are banished from Hastinaga."

"Krushan law." Jarsun's laughter was as sibilant as his speech. It filled the chamber and spilled out into the crowded streets, making mothers draw their babes closer and causing even the least religious to make signs of appeasement to their gods. "Krushan law is a joke. Your stepmother here has made a mockery of Krushan law. She violated Krushan law when she slept with one Krushan, then went on to bed and marry another Krushan. That is unacceptable, and you know it."

"The veracity of that allegation is as yet untested," Vrath replied stiffly.

"Listen to yourself! You speak as an officer of the court, using your formal legal language. But it's all a sham and a show for the sake of the world. The truth is, my daughter Krushita has proven her right to rule the Burnt Empire. She has been tested and has passed the test. I am here now to demand that you comply with the law. Step down from your office as prince regent. Ensure that Dowager Empress Jilana steps down as well. Accept and acknowledge Princess Krushita, daughter of Princess Aqreen and myself, Jarsun Krushan, as the legitimate heir to the Burnt Empire and let her claim her rightful place upon the Burning Throne. Do this now and without further prevarication and prove that you are truly a man who abides by the law of our ancestors."

Vrath was a man torn apart by loyalty and law. Despite his demigod self-control, he could not conceal the war within himself. He turned to look at the parties named: Jilana. Aqreen. And lastly, the cheerful babe, Krushita, now contentedly asleep at her mother's breast, the nipple still in her puckered mouth.

Finally, he turned back to Jilana again. But before he could speak, she shook her head slowly from side to side. "No, Vrath."

"Mother . . ." he said.

"Do not listen to Jarsun's forked tongue. It spills only poison. He seeks to finish what he started thirty years ago when he defied his father and attempted to kill his brother, Sha'ant. He is a being filled with hatred and venom. He wants nothing more than to see the Krushan dynasty fall into ashes and dust. Do not let him poison your mind with his talk of law."

"But the law favors his argument," Vrath said. "You demanded that Princess Aqreen name the father of the child, and he has presented himself. On what grounds do we deny the child her inheritance now?"

"On the grounds that she is the daughter of a banished criminal. One whose name was stricken from the annals of Krushan history. Go look through this palace, through all our thousand and eight palaces and fortresses across the empire. Search all your life. You will not find a single bust, portrait, etching, or document that mentions his name or bears his likeness. He has been erased from history. He is no longer Krushan, and as such, any offspring he may bear, legitimate or otherwise, are not Krushan either."

Jilana turned and pointed to the sleeping babe in Aqreen's arms. The mother had moved the child to her shoulder and was adjusting her blouse; she glared at Jilana through half-lidded eyes. "That bastard child is not Krushan and will never be Krushan. It is forever cursed by the sins of its father."

Vrath turned back to Jarsun, still standing with his foot on the lowermost step of the dais. "You have your answer."

"All I hear are the prattling words of a power-hungry widow who has not accepted the fact that her husband died a decade ago. These are the desperate ravings of a woman who refuses to let go the reins even though they are no longer hers to grasp. Break her fingers, pry them apart. It is the only way. If you will not do it, Vrath, then I will."

Vrath stared down at the man who was still his uncle by blood, if not by law. "Is that a threat?"

Jarsun took a second step up, then a third, then a fourth and final step. He stood upon the dais now, towering a full head higher than Vrath, and above the entire room. "Why threaten when I can simply *act*?"

"You cannot take the throne by force," Vrath said, the fire in his eyes showing itself. Smoke trickled from his pupils, curling around his blue-tinged locks.

"I do not need to," Jarsun replied, his multiple tongues slithering in and out of his mouth, lingering at the corners of his lips. "The throne has already chosen. My daughter Krushita is the rightful heir."

"You heard my mother. The child is no longer Krushan by our laws."

"Laws are mere words. The stonefire speaks a tongue older than language itself. You heard what it said when it tasted of each of the three children. Only my daughter is whole and capable of governing this empire. A whole that is superior to *those* two halves." He indicated the two newborn boys in their mothers' arms on the far side of the dais. "It is called a Burning for good reason. The throne knows who truly deserves to sit upon it. It has delivered its decision, and its decision is the oldest law of all among our clan. *That* is the true seat of the power of the Krushan. Respect it, Vrath. Respect it and uphold it."

Vrath was silent for a long moment.

In that silence, the world hung in the balance. History forked. Time bifurcated into multiple pathways, each leading to a different possible future.

A deep growl sounded from the throne, like the rumbling from the belly of a volcano.

Hastinaga waited.

Then, with a single word, Vrath changed everything, dismissed the alternative futures, aborted the possibilities before they could even be conceived fully.

8

"No," Vrath said.

Jarsun hissed.

"No," he repeated. "You tried to kill my father. My grandfather banished you. You are no longer Krushan. Your child is not Krushan. She will never sit upon the Burning Throne."

"You deny your heritage," Jarsun said. "You deny the test of fire, the voice of the stonefire."

"You denied them all the day you tried to bring down the House of Krushan. You left here swearing hellfire and destruction upon my father and his descendants. Today, you come back here asking to place your own daughter upon the throne? What about the time you swore you would break the Burning Throne into pieces with your own bare hands? I was not born then, but my father and grandfather told me all I need to know. You only sought to destroy us, to destroy everything, and now, after thirty years, you come back to claim it all? You are the hypocrite, Jarsun. You are the one who makes a mockery of your own claims."

Jarsun raised a clenched fist, and beneath the fabric of his robes, the arm that held that fist appeared to writhe and wriggle, like a dozen separate cords moving individually. "The blood that moves in me moves in you as well, Vrath. The power of the stonefire is as much mine to command as it is yours. I ask you one last time, give me what I demand peacefully or face the consequences. I can still fulfill my threat. I can tear apart that throne with my own bare hands. If you will not permit my daughter to sit upon it, then I will bring it all down, and the world will fall with it."

Vrath's eyes flared fire then, great gouts of burning coals that skittered and fell, steaming, at Jarsun's feet. Flames began to seep from his arms, his corded muscles, his coiled back, his every pore. The throne blazed red-hot and flamed, answering his demand for power. "Not while I still stand."

Jarsun's robes writhed, his head flattening, his voice shrill, his very shape changing into something other than human.

Before he could change completely, Princess Aqreen stepped forward and placed a hand upon his shoulder — or the place where his shoulder had been a moment ago.

"Husband," she said.

Jarsun's body stabilized and grew still. He stood as a man again. He turned his eyes to his wife. Multiple nictitating pairs of eyelids opened and closed, revealing triple, slitted pupils.

"Let us take our leave," she said.

He stared at her. A soft questioning hiss escaped his lips.

"What will you do?" she asked. "Fight your own family? Kill, maim, burn? Destroy your daughter's legacy? How will that help anyone? This is not the way. Let us return to Reygistan. In time, Prophetess willing, we will find a way. Krushita's claim will not be denied forever. Her time will come. When that day comes, these will be her cousins, her aunts, her great-aunt. She will play at their feet, she will clasp their hands, and she will dine with them. This is her family too. For her sake, we must leave now without spilling any blood. You promised me when we first lay together that you would forsake vengeance. Fulfill that promise now. No good can come from killing one's own, Jarsun."

Jarsun looked at her for a long, hard moment.

Then he let her lead him away, down the steps of the dais, and back to the entrance he had entered through. King Aqron followed after them.

After an appropriate pause, during which throats were cleared, feet shuffled, and the thousand and eight waited, Vrath exchanged a glance with Jilana, who nodded once, curtly.

Vrath addressed the great hall.

"The stonefire has chosen, and the elders have spoken. Princes Shvate and Adri shall rule jointly. There is a new heir upon the Burning Throne."

He gave the prearranged signal to the waiting courtiers.

"Let the jubilee commence!"

9

The celebration that followed, enhanced by a royal edict granting free access to the granary reserves and soma stores of the palace to one and all for the entire duration of the traditional feasting period, was as lavish as befitted the greatest dynasty of the known world. Runners leaped aboard their wagons and carriages and mounts to carry the news to the farthest ends of Arthaloka. Men dueled in the streets. Gamblers won or lost fortunes. Men conjoined with their wives in the hopes of fathering princes themselves. The wives countered, mischievously, that they had better, or else Mage Vessa would have to come and do it for them!

Few stayed to hear the shocking afterword to that proclamation, delivered by Jilana to a select inner group of trusted familiars after the main assemblage had departed. These select few could be depended upon to spread the news cautiously, with care and empathy, among the people at large, downplaying the unfortunate defects of both newborn sons and emphasizing the fact that they were, nonetheless, heirs to the Burnt Empire and destined to sit upon its throne. A throne still defended and protected by none other than Vrath. Jilana was a wise enough stateswoman not to harp on the specific limitations both boys had been born with, mentioning them in passing as if it were quite natural for one son to be born blind and the other son to be born white-skinned in a race of dark-skinned people.

What she did emphasize, in that iron tone that had made her a formidable figure in Krushan politics, was that Vrath remained firmly in control of the kingdom itself and would continue to steward it for as long as he was alive. The same held true of her, maintaining her position and influence over the governance of the kingdom for as long as was foreseeable. She was at pains to ensure that everyone understood and spread the message clearly that nothing had changed in the balance of power, and regardless of the afflictions of the two newborn heirs, Hastinaga itself remained as powerful as ever. Let none challenge that power, or they would face the fury of Vrath himself.

The message was understood and passed on, through the circuitous routes that political messages traveled, reaching the bejeweled ears of every king, emperor, tribal chieftain, bandit lord, and horse master in distant kingdoms.

Hastinaga had two newborn sons that day, both destined to follow the line of succession.

One was born blind.

The other was malformed in appearance.

It was questionable whether either one would be fit to ascend the throne and, even if he did, whether he would be capable of staying seated.

Yet the essential balance of power had not changed.

The reins of power still remained firmly in the hands of the son of Sha'ant, Vrath.

The seat of power was still occupied by the wife of Sha'ant, Jilana.

Nothing had changed that day in Hastinaga, she insisted.

And yet, as those who knew politics well understood, *everything* had changed.

10

The empire was already prosperous, powerful, and growing by leaps and bounds. The arrival of two new sons invigorated it. In many ways, a new age had dawned.

But too many chieftains, traders, kings, farmlords, and other ambitious allies doubted the dynasty at crucial times, thinking that without a king, it was a leaderless horse team that would go astray or stumble over a cliff.

"Hastinaga is an elephant without a head!" some said and plotted to secede, cheat, deceive, steal from, deny, or otherwise dupe the dynasty of the Krushan. Some thought that without a king upon the Krushan throne, a few years' failure to pay tribute would not be noticed; others presumed that they could use it as an excuse to raid their neighbors' grazing pastures and steal their water and horses and kine at will. Some chose the opportunity to declare themselves as rajan — kings in their own right. An astonishing variety of transgressions were committed in those early years after Sha'ant's demise by those who believed that the power of the dynasty had waned and they could now do as they pleased.

They were all proven wrong, bitterly wrong.

Even when young, Vrath was a formidable prince and administrator. He was no young spoiled scion, seeking pleasure in wine, women, and princely pursuits. He considered the kingdom's welfare to be his foremost mission, and put his entire energy into upholding it.

After he became prince regent, he served only that purpose. And he did so with the single-minded determination of a demigod on a mission of Krushan law.

There was a popular saying: *Greatest of mothers, Jilana. Greatest of empires, Krushan. Greatest of cities, Hastinaga. Master of law, Vrath.*

Even priests feared his austere vows, for while priests were sworn to celibacy, they were permitted to make exceptions to sire heirs upon childless warrior caste women. Some seers even took the forms of other creatures in order to perpetuate species: in one case, a seer took the form of a deer to balance the population depleted by the growing human density in the Krushan forest. The great mage Vessa had emerged from his decades of solitary meditation to further the Krushan lineage.

But for Vrath, the word was the law. His interpretation of Krushan morality was literal and uncompromising. When he had sworn himself to lifelong celibacy, he had meant it. Such unwavering adherence to a vow only added to his legend. Some believed, incorrectly, that it was the source of his indomitable prowess in war.

Celibacy had nothing to do with Vrath's prowess as a warrior and general, however. It was his fierce nature that had caused him to take that vow and, more importantly, adhere to it without once straying; that fierce nature did in fact reflect the ferocity of his will.

Vrath was a force of nature unto himself.

He rode down cattle thieves, trampling them into the very dung of the cows they had stolen. Land thieves were buried alive in the soil they had presumed to encroach upon. Water polluters were treated the worst: for to Vrath, water was the mother of life itself. They were fed, piece by living piece, to the giant turtles and crocodiles and gharials, while their kinsmen watched. Terrible was his vow, and terrible were his punishments, which no wrongdoer escaped. No transgressor received mercy. No quarter was given to any lawbreaker. No excuse accepted for the very rich, the powerful, or even the pious. He treated — and punished — all equally.

Those who assumed that the young prince who had been away with his mother for all his childhood and youth would surely be as soft and relenting as the very water of the Jeel River (which he worshipped daily) learned the truth the hardest way imaginable. Even when young, Vrath was formidable. But after Sha'ant was gone and the foolish ones began to presume that the demise of their king was an opportunity for personal gains, Vrath soon corrected any misimpression that the kingdom was kingless.

As immovable as his grandfather Coldheart and as relentless as his mother, the river goddess Jeel, he soon demonstrated that he was like no king anyone had ever known. A king would at least take time to tarry with his queen or his concubines, go hunting every now and then, travel for pleasure or to accept social engagements in other kingdoms; at the very least, he would fall ill every once in a while, or require a respite from kingly affairs.

Vrath, however, seemed never to rest. His vow was upheld so strictly, no woman was permitted to come within reach of him: even serving girls scurried to move out of his way when he strode the long, vaulting, marble-floored corridors of Hastinaga palace. The question of dalliances never even arose. He took no holidays, went on no hunts for pleasure, never accepted social engagements unless they were combined with Krushan business.

He never once fell ill and remained in robust virile health, needing barely any time to recover even from the most grievous wounds received in battle, to the consternation of the royal healers. He seemed hardly to require sleep, or rest, or nourishment. Like a relentless juggernaut, he roved the kingdom, unstoppable and incorruptible, dispensing terrible unmitigated justice to the transgressors of Krushan law.

Thereafter, Hastinaga became renowned as the kingdom which had virtually no crime or transgressions. For no matter where a crime was committed or what manner of transgression it might be, the terrible Vrath would somehow arrive there and ensure that justice was meted out without mercy or delay. Yet, to those who committed no crimes and applied themselves to concerted efforts for growth, he was magnanimous to a fault. Those whose conduct proved their loyalty to the Krushan dynasty he rewarded with lenient taxes and a share of any new bounty they assisted in procuring, whether by means of invasion of other kingdoms, or through the exploitation of natural resources.

By the time the two sons, Adri and Shvate, were born to the princesses Ember and Umber, every caucus of power in Hastinaga was unambiguous in its loyalty. Every last denizen of the land, even those sworn allies in farflung corners of the empire, raised their voice in celebration and joy. For the greater prosperity of the Krushan meant the greater prosperity of them all. Such was the promise of Vrath's regency and administration. Having two additional heirs to the throne could only mean that this prosperity was now guaranteed even after Vrath's eventual demise, if and when such an event ever occurred.

Even those who secretly resented the power of the Krushan throne and wished and hoped for their downfall were effectively shut up by Jilana's announcement. The last vestige of hope for the naysayers and dissenters was crushed.

So they all did as any sensible player in the game of kings must do: they bowed down to the Krushan dynasty, celebrated its continuance with the birth of the two new male heirs, and occupied themselves in building their own fortunes, setting aside for now all thought of secession or rebellion.

The period that followed the birth of the two boys was a golden one in Krushan history.

The kingdom of Hastinaga, the vast holdings of the Burnt Empire, all grew in prosperity and repute. The gods showered their blessings, spawning bountiful crops and rich harvests. Flowers and fruit colored the landscape, providing fragrant garlands and sweet nectar. Beasts of burden undertook their labor without complaint; animals mated and littered and were content; birds filled the air with cheer. Traders prospered; artisans found ample work; bards were rewarded well enough that they composed odes of joy.

Prosperity, gainful employment, and the absence of local unrest changed the character of the citizenry. Even the commonfolk of the kingdom gained a reputation as being honest, fair-minded, jovial. Soldiers were brave; gurus more learned than ever; students better behaved and eager to gain knowledge. People respected one another and upheld Krushan law. Rites were performed as prescribed; charity was given without complaint; robbers and thieves found more opportunities to earn lawfully than through criminal acts. Pride receded, anger was quelled, greed was shunned: when all was plentiful, no man had reason to covet another's wealth, possessions, or stature. People aided one another in their rise to success. What use was competition when partnership benefitted both parties more profitably?

Across the country, it seemed as if the Age of Prosperity had dawned anew. It was as if the sun of history had traveled backward in time and the world was young and fresh and full of hope once more.

It was only as the boys grew old enough to be seen and heard by one and all, once the public ecstasy at the royal issue had faded, once the heirs stepped out into the public view, that the kingdom and the world realized to their shock that the rumors were true after all.

11

Prince Adri, the younger of the two princes, was as blind as a stone. He was gifted from the outset with an extraordinary number of compensatory abilities. He could hear, smell, sense, and feel far more sensitively than most. With the help of Palace Guru, he learned from a nascent age to develop these abilities and use them to cast a kind of sensory net around his body, moving and maneuvering with astonishing grace and agility in the trickiest of settings. He was even able to fight in this fashion against sighted warriors, and often offered up worthy opposition.

But his opponents soon learned that while his senses and training could compensate for his blindness, Adri had a fatal weakness: his temper.

All an opponent had to do was whisper the word "blind" in any combination of insults — "blind fool," "eyeless wonder," and "owl prince" were among the less offensive epithets — and Adri was lost. Overcome by anger at first, later by frustration, then by despair, and finally by a crushing, debilitating paralysis of mind, will, and body, he would lose the bout. This weakness grew into a canker, which in turn blossomed into a condition in its own right. One day, the blind prince threw his weapon aside with a clanging finality and went to his chambers, from whence he did not emerge for either food, water, or conversation for a whole seven-day. After that, he was never the same, reduced to a rail-thin, dark-souled shadow of his former self. He never touched a weapon again or tolerated being asked, however kindly, to consider taking up arms again.

12

Prince Shvate was, just as his name suggested, "white colored": an albino with milky pale skin and colorless eyes that could not withstand bright light. The light of the sun was so torturous to him that from a tender age, he fell into the practice of sleeping by day and emerging at sundown. This in itself was regarded as scandalous, and indeed was even considered by some to be against Krushan law. Yet he was a prince of Krushan. And no one dared speak ill of this or any other habit of the princes of Krushan. By night, his milk-pale complexion seemed to glow in pitch-darkness, frightening many a soul that glimpsed him in the hours of the owl watch. His condition rendered him able to see sufficiently even in the dark, like a predatory animal, and so he trained under cover of night, requiring only the faint gleam of shielded lamps for the benefit of his instructors and sparring partners. In time, this disadvantage turned into his keenest advantage, enabling him to fight when no other warrior could. Even so, the stricture against raising weapons after sundown rendered even this unusual skill a fault, and armed the bows of his detractors who spoke ominously of Krushan law being violated. The fact that the stricture against fighting after sundown was intended for those who could not see by darkness meant nothing at such a time; to most, the letter of the law was more important than the intent of the law.

In a world which scrutinized every facet of a royal heir mercilessly, accepting nothing less than the most rigorous standard of genetic perfection, neither prince was fit to rule. How could a blind king face an attacker, let alone lead an army into battle? How could a paleskin command respect from his opponents? Strong though he was, and sound of body and mind, the very sight of him would undermine his regal stature, people argued — and, also, how could he fight effectively when the bright light of morning was unbearable to his sensitive eyes? A weakness of any kind was unacceptable. And thus both princes were deemed unfit to rule by Krushan standards.

And yet, they *were* Krushan princes; sons of Virya and Gada under Krushan law, regardless of the fact that they had been surrogate-fathered by Vessa — he was, after all, Jilana's son and a renowned seer-mage and, as such, acceptable as a sire under Krushan law. They were conceived, carried to term and successfully birthed by the late kings' wives, Ember and Umber, in the presence of hundreds of palace faithful and preceptors, who monitored every stage of the process as custom demanded, confirming the biological lineage beyond the shadow of a doubt. Nobody could dispute their legitimacy.

For their naysayers, it was a quandary.

And one that would lead to a dangerous spiral of events.

If the seeds of war had been sown when Vessa fathered progeny upon the princesses Umber and Ember — and also, incidentally, upon their maid — then the coming of age of the princes Adri and Shvate represented the first green shoots of that seed, poking their way up thornily to emerge from the rich soil of Hastinaga into the gloam of the northern sun.

The seeds of war were about to sprout a great tree of violence, one that would tower above hundreds of millions of lives in the Burnt Empire. And the fruit of that great tree would be a terrible dark and cankerous thing, bitter as heart's blood.

Part One

Adri

~

1

ADRI'S EARLIEST MEMORIES FROM boyhood were of a voice and a hand. His brother's voice and hand.

He did not recall the specific details of the first time, but he recalled one particular time when he, a little toddler, had stumbled and fallen.

Falling was something he did often early in his life. Skinned knees and bruised elbows were such frequent occurrences that his were always scabbed. But there were falls and there were falls. Some resulted in more than skinned knees and bruised elbows. He suffered a string of injuries, none too serious, but each sufficient to deliver more lasting damage than mere bodily harm alone.

In most cases, it was his self-confidence that was really hurt. To be able to run, to play, to gambol, or even to simply walk without constantly falling or colliding was something even the most ordinary of children enjoyed. Yet he, a prince of Hastinaga, heir to the great Burnt Empire, could not take more than a few dozen paces without injury. Could not play with the other children he heard laughing and squealing and running about with such abandon. Could not do as his growing, energetic little body desired. There was no outlet for his boundless energy. No cure for his problem.

The royal household did everything possible to ensure his safety and comfort. There were wet nurses and maids everywhere. But he was a child, a strong, robust boy with a growing body and eager, questing mind. He wanted to run, play, yell, jump, tumble, to unleash the dog of youth.

These luxuries were denied him.

He had to sit and listen, merely listen, as other children did all those things. When he tried, as he often tried, to join them, it would always end the same way, with him falling or colliding, injuring himself, bleeding and cut, or bruised and battered. And each time, his self-confidence diminished, along with his zest for life.

A bitterness took root in his heart.

Questions arose: *Why me? Why deny me this most basic of abilities? Why punish me in this manner — and it is a punishment, is it not? For what crime? What was my karma in past lives that I need suffer so in this one?*

Though everyone assured him that it was neither karma nor punishment, simply an accident of nature, he could not believe it. A wet nurse, the very one who had nursed him from birth, always told him that he had been handicapped because otherwise he was too strong, too brave, too intelligent, too powerful. *The gods feared your might,* she told him as she dressed his injuries and wiped his tears. *They feared that you would come to the afterworld one day and challenge them in their own abodes, so they took away your sight that you might never find the way.*

I don't want to challenge the gods, he cried. *I don't want to go to Swarga, I just want to see.*

Ember said nothing. She was barely present in his life.

A shadow, a presence, a physical body that offered no warmth, comfort, or affection, she only saw him at bedtime, when he was brought to her after his bath, after he had been cleaned and dressed and made presentable, to bid him a good night. Even then, she did so absently, with strange formality and a sense of distance. Even when he hugged her, she would start by patting him on the back, as if admonishing him for something he had done, then, if he continued holding on too tightly or too long — which was almost every night at first — she would speak to the daiimaa, and the wet nurse would gently untangle his little hands from around her neck and separate mother and son.

Adri could not recall a time his mother had fed him, dressed him, bathed him, washed his cuts, dressed his wounds. Telling her about the day's accidents only seemed to elicit the same response from her: a stiff silence followed by a curt "I see." No offer of sympathy, no words of reassurance, no gentle caress or any other show of support. Simply that vaguely disapproving "I see." Even the choice of phrase seemed designed to belittle him. *I see . . . and you don't, you silly little blind boy.*

She never said anything more hurtful than that; she simply never said anything that showed affection, or love.

Adri heard other children with their mothers, the way they spoke and laughed together, played together, ate together. He heard babes suckling at their mothers' breasts. Heard the female voices cry out with alarm when they saw their children injured or about to come to harm, heard the distress and concern in their maternal voices.

Adri never heard such emotions in *his* mother's voice.

And on that day, the day when he fell, and a hand reached out and took hold of him, a voice spoke and strengthened him, it was not his mother's hand or voice.

It was his brother's.

2

"Adri!" Shvate cried.

Adri gasped as he felt his feet swing out over emptiness.

He scrambled backward, trying to find his footing on the edge of the riverbank. The heels of his feet slipped on the loamy mud. He felt himself falling, heard the roar of the water below, and absurdly thought, *At least I can't scrape my knees or elbows on water.*

Then his brother's strong hands were grasping him tightly beneath his armpits, surrounding his chest like a vise. Shvate's breath was hot on his left ear, grunting and exclaiming as he too seemed to struggle with the wet muddy ground, then he yanked hard on Adri, and both of them fell on their backs.

They both lay there a moment, the mud yielding and cool underneath.

Adri could feel the soft evening sunshine on his face, and on his arms and legs. He knew his special silk anga garment and dhoti must be soiled from falling in the mud, were perhaps even torn. He could hear the voices of the wet nurses and the younger maids from behind him, calling out his name, then came the sound of footfalls slapping the damp riverbank. A mo-

ment later, he felt the presence of people all around him, helping him up and
fussing.

"He was about to step off the edge!"

"Into the river!"

"He could have drowned!"

"The water flows so strongly here, he would have been taken downriver
in a flash."

"He would have been a mile away before we started after him."

All this was said and more like it.

Adri was used to it.

He had been the center of many such scares and alarms.

But he knew this was different.

It was the anniversary of his naming day, for one thing.

Then there was the river: he had never fallen into a river before.

And of course, there was Shvate's voice, right beside him.

"Adri, are you well?"

He turned his head toward the sound of his brother's voice.

He attempted a smile.

Then, remembering what one of the children had told him — *You look
like an urrkh when you do that!* — he spoke aloud.

"Shvate."

"Yes, Adri?"

"Brother."

It was all he could think of to say at that moment.

Gratitude, affection, respect, adoration, all packed into that one word.
Brother.

The moment was interrupted by the wet nurses, who then began fussing over Shvate as well. As did, before long, Uncle Vrath and Grandmother
Jilana.

"You saved your brother's life, young Shvate."

Adri recognized the smooth deep tones of his uncle's voice. They always
reminded him of the roar of the river itself for some reason. Though that
was hardly possible: for how could a man's voice resemble the sound of rushing water?

"Had he fallen into the river, he would have drowned, or been dashed against the rocks downstream," Grandmother Jilana said, her husky, sonorous tones unmistakable.

Adri heard Shvate snort, a dismissive sound. "That would never happen," he heard his brother say. "Not as long as I'm nearby."

There was a brief silence. Adri sensed that the elders were looking at each other in that moment, then at Shvate. He knew this from similar silences during conversations with other adults. People always did that if you said something unusual or unexpected. They looked at one another. He wondered why they did it. What would they see, after all? Each other's faces? Surely faces did not change from instant to instant. Only voices could convey emotion, as far as he knew. But he also understood that there was much that he did not yet know.

He heard in that silence their pride for his brother, and heard that pride reflected in Shvate's reply. *Not as long as I'm nearby.*

Adri felt a surge of emotion rise in his chest, then tears rolled down his cheeks.

That was the first time in his life he had a sense that there was someone in the world who actually cared if he lived or died, and who would risk his own life for him.

Brother.

Shvate

~

SHVATE HAD A DEEP sympathy and love for his brother.

Ever since he could run and play, he had wanted to play with his brother, run alongside him, team up with him against the other children. He was proud to know he had a brother, a fellow heir to the great Krushan throne. It made him feel as if he was part of something bigger than himself. An empire, a dynasty, a tradition . . . a family.

It had been difficult accepting that Adri was not like him — or like any of the other children. Sight was something that Shvate, like most people, took so much for granted that he could not truly understand how anyone could not see and yet live. How could you not see all the colors, the shapes, the light, the people, the places, the things? It was unthinkable to him.

When he was younger, he had thought that maybe someday this would pass, that one day Adri would wake up and suddenly be able to see. Everything would be fine then. Then he and Shvate could run and play, and be kids together.

Shvate even dreamed of this, happy dreams in which he and his brother had wild exotic adventures together — fighting urrkh, battling the enemies of the Burnt Empire, besieging enemy forts, quelling rebellions, squashing troublemakers. These were all things he had heard of their uncle Vrath doing, things he dreamed of doing himself someday soon, once he was old enough to fight.

In these dreams, Shvate was different, too. His skin and eyes were normal, the same dark shade as other people of his race. He could see and fight and do as he pleased — bare-naked if he wished — in full sunlight, with no need to always clothe himself in layers to protect his skin and vision from the sun, no need to wait until sunset to roam outside freely.

They were a formidable pair in these dreams, Adri and he. They were princes of the world. They traveled the kingdom, did as they pleased, and no one who challenged them survived. It was so wonderful, he would wake up smiling from these dreams and jump out of bed, eager to go to his brother and tell him.

Then, as he grew a little older, he understood that such a day would never come. He did not stop hoping and dreaming — indeed, he dreamed of it all the more after that — but a part of him *accepted* that it would never happen. Adri's blindness was as permanent as the old sword guru's missing arm.

"Arms don't grow back, blind men don't see," the old man had said gruffly to Shvate, swatting him on his backside with the wooden practice sword. "Hoping don't make it so, just as dodging my sword don't make you a better swordsman. Stand and fight. You're a Krushan, act like one."

Still, Shvate felt bad for Adri. He was always falling, colliding with things, hurting himself, getting into accidents. Always forced to sit and listen while the other children played. *Listen! Paagh!* Where was the fun in *listening* to other children playing? It was as if Adri were being punished for something. Which was entirely unfair because Adri was the best behaved child in the entire palace.

Shvate would, from time to time, try to involve Adri, try to make him get up and join them at play. He couldn't help it; he wanted to share the fun, the joy, with his brother. These attempts almost always ended with Adri falling, or knocking heads, or taking a tumble, and after a while, Shvate stopped encouraging his brother, not wanting to be the cause of him sustaining further injuries and humiliation. Yet he missed him.

As more time passed and they both grew a little more, Shvate started to feel a different way toward his brother: *protective.*

He began to accompany Adri around wherever he went, watching him, calling out his name to warn him if he saw Adri about to fall or trip or dash into something. The wet nurses were there for that, of course, and they did their task admirably well, but Adri had taken to ignoring them and deliberately walking where he pleased, as an act of defiance. When *Shvate* called out a warning, however, Adri always responded. He would stand still and wait until someone provided him guidance or instructed him to walk the other way.

Shvate was watching Adri the day of his brother's naming day celebration.

The family had a tradition of spending naming day celebrations on the banks of the Jeel, always at the same spot, under the great banyan tree. It was the place where Grandfather Sha'ant had met his first wife, Grandmother Jeel. It was also the place where Uncle Vrath had first been seen by Grandfather Sha'ant, when he, Vrath, returned from *his* grandfather Coldheart's abode. There were other things that had happened at this spot as well, something to do with babies and the river and Grandmother Jeel, but these were things that the wet nurses did not speak of to the children.

The family spent all naming day celebrations there, bringing cooks and tents and servants and throwing a grand feast for hundreds and thousands of the highest nobles and aristocrats and ministers and diplomats. There were dancers and musicians and lavish feasts, along with colored banners and horse riding displays and wrestling matches.

None of which could Adri see, even though it was his own naming day celebration.

When Adri wandered away from the festivities on his own, Shvate noticed. He saw also that the wet nurses and maids were busy gossiping. It was not their fault. They assumed that Adri was listening to the music. But Shvate was sitting nearby and he could tell that Adri was *fed up* listening, and who wouldn't be, when all you could *do* was listen?

So when Adri got up from his comfortable silk-cushioned seat and wandered away, Shvate followed him —

And thus saw when Adri was about to step off the edge of the riverbank.

He leaped forward, grabbing hold of his brother and pulling him back to safety. He banged the back of his head on a small rock when he fell, but he didn't care. He was happy he was able to save his brother from falling into the river. He couldn't have borne it if Adri had fallen and drowned, or even just been hurt badly. Shvate *had* to look out for him.

They were brothers after all.

Jilana

~

JILANA AND VRATH WATCHED Adri and Shvate playing from the terrace of the palace.

It was some weeks after Adri's naming day. Ever since that day, Shvate and Adri had become inseparable. Even now, Shvate was teaching Adri how to wield a sword in the courtyard. They were using wooden practice swords, and Shvate never let his swings connect with his brother's body, but Adri could not help striking Shvate occasionally. Vrath saw Shvate wince when the side of Adri's sword caught him on his collarbone. But Shvate did not lose his temper or admonish his brother. Instead, he congratulated him on a "kill strike."

"They love each other very much," Jilana said.

"Yes."

Jilana glanced at Vrath. He was her stepson by marriage, but he was, after all, a demigod. It lent their relationship a curious edge. Nominally, Vrath deferred to his stepmother, and by law, she was the dowager empress of the Burnt Empire. But Vrath, as the eldest living Krushan male and son of Emperor Sha'ant, was prince regent. And because he ruled and governed the empire, controlled and oversaw every aspect of its administration — and of course kept it safe and prosperous — he was regarded with the same respect as she. Somehow, the balance of power worked. They had never been seen to argue or heard to disagree. The mother-son bond between them thwarted any political attempt to divide and conquer. They were a perfect pair, and together they ran Hastinaga and the empire as smoothly as a pair of charioteers ran a sixteen-horse team.

But they were nothing alike.

The young princes, though, despite their physical differences, were, in their hearts, *very* alike, and when Jilana watched the growing bond between them, it made her feel good. She had been so disheartened when the sons of the princesses Ember and Umber had been born blind and albino. Shvate had found ways to overcome his disability, by dressing to protect his sensitive skin and eyes in sunlight, and training twice as hard to overcome any questions of his talents as a prince. The boy had a big heart.

But while Adri was stout of heart as well, his disability was harder to overcome for the role he wished to play. With his heightened hearing and other senses, he could function well enough to live comfortably the rest of his life, even perform certain princely tasks that only required listening and delivering judgment. But how could he be expected to ride into battle, to go to war, to confront enemies or suppress rebellions, survive assassinations —all the warring and marauding that was an integral part of being an heir to the most coveted throne in the world?

It did not help that Adri's mother had turned her face away from him. Since the day he was born, she had not demonstrated any affection or concern for his well-being. In a sense, it was as if, when it came to her own son's existence, it was she that was blind.

Shvate's mother was only a little better; she, too, clearly resented the way she had been impregnated. Her head understood that it was necessary for the kingdom and the lineage; her heart rebelled. Jilana had seen her look at Shvate with a clear expression of distaste for his pale, colorless features, his white hair and white eyebrows, his inability to endure bright light or sunlight. But there was still some affection there underneath the distaste. Umber did not hate Shvate the way Ember hated Adri. She, at the very least, tolerated her son, though Jilana knew that this was more than partly because Umber understood that with Adri's disability, it would most certainly be Shvate who eventually ascended to the Krushan throne, despite the public proclamation of a joint rule. That conviction itself made her albino son appear tolerable in her eyes. *Vain woman,* Jilana thought, but then sighed, for was she not herself vain as well? Would she have reacted so differently had she been in Umber's place? It was easy to judge from afar.

Vrath was watching the two boys now with a strange expression; his striking grey eyes were directed at them, but his gaze was so distant he might have been looking at the horizon.

"The talk among the citizenry concerns you?" Jilana said.

He turned that thousand-yojana stare upon her, and Jilana had to force herself to meet it without flinching. One did not easily match stares with Vrath. She could not even imagine what it must be like to meet this giant of a man on the battlefield, with his enormous strength, knowledge, and ability to defeat seemingly any opponent. The sight of him alone was known to send warriors fleeing — and those that did had good reason.

"The citizenry always talk. It is what they do," he replied.

She sighed. "Nevertheless, it concerns me. Because there is some truth in their talk."

He kept his eyes locked with hers. "If it is true, then it cannot be helped. Let the people talk."

"This kind of talk could lead to trouble. Even an uprising."

"Uprisings can be quelled."

"It would better if we do not have to kill our own people." She thought for a moment, then amended her statement: "Any more than we absolutely must."

Vrath did not seem perturbed. "I can find out who seeks to foment rebellion. Root them out in their nests, wipe out any uprising before it raises its hood and slithers out to attack us."

Vrath said the words as if he were speaking of the extermination of pests — and that was how he differed from other men: it was not that he was cruel or cold, but that he simply saw things as they were, harsh and dangerous, saw no need for any euphemistic softening of the jagged edges.

Jilana, meanwhile, had never been able to regard crises with such dispassion. She felt strongly, intensely, and did not hesitate to express herself in like fashion. Her mother had been a hot-blooded fisher princess whose clashes with Jilana's father had been legendary. She had not been born of a glacial river as Vrath had, but she knew when to fight and when to *fight*.

"I do not doubt your ability to maintain order, son of Sha'ant. But if we acted against every king, noble, and warrior who spoke against Hastinaga, we would soon have no one left to govern." She shook her head. "No. Violence will not resolve this problem. We must do more than simply crush the poison tongues. We must silence them."

Vrath said nothing for a moment before responding. "I do not comprehend your meaning, Mother. Do you wish me to use violence to quell the unruly or not?"

Jilana thought before answering. "I wish you to do nothing at all," she said. "It is elsewhere that I seek the resolution to this dilemma."

She gestured with a small raising of her chin, pointing to the two boys in the courtyard below. "It is to the future generation that we must look to silence their own detractors. They are the cause of the gossip and unrest. They must answer their critics by their own actions."

Vrath regarded the boys below. His expression did not change, but his words betrayed an uncharacteristic lack of conviction. "And you believe they can do this? Bear the weight of the Burnt Empire and my father's legacy on their slender shoulders?" *A blind boy and an albino* was what he left unsaid.

"They are Krushan," she said simply.

He had no answer to that.

They watched the two boys continue their swordplay long past their mealtime. By the end, she observed, Adri was actually able to parry and counter Shvate's strikes at least a third of the time. She watched thoughtfully. Vrath was right about one thing: the fate of the empire would rest on these young shoulders, whether she liked it or not. For better or worse, they were Krushan princes. She decided then that she would not make the mistake that so many others had: she would not prejudge them. *At least let them be blooded and then we will see.*

"Perhaps," Jilana said, "it is time to take them to Guru Kaylin."

Vrath

~

VRATH DROVE THE FOUR-HORSE chariot with the ease of a master charioteer.

He and the two princes were on their way to the guru's hermitage. Before they left, Jilana had fussed over them endlessly, giving them so many instructions that he was sure they would forget them all the instant they arrived. The wet nurses had wailed and cried their hearts out as he rode away with their beloved boys. Soon, the palace complex was long behind them, the city's rear sally gate their last glimpse of the City of Elephants and Snakes.

The chariot rumbled over the kingsroad, fields of crops rolling past on either side, succeeded in time by the open ranges of dairy, cattle, and poultry farms. Some of it fed the bottomless appetite of Hastinaga, but the larger part was sent off to other parts of the empire by wagon trains, or to foreign kingdoms across the spice route by ship or by land. Vrath noted that the boys were being much quieter than usual, and so he contemplated reeling off some figures — quantities of grain harvests, efficiency of cattle production, and the like — to make conversation, but then decided that the last thing two young boys about to be separated from their homes for many years wanted was a lecture on economics.

Vrath glanced back at them. Shvate and Adri were both standing in the well of the chariot, staring out at the passing countryside. The chariot was designed to shield grown men, and so the two boys could only just barely peer out over the edge. They were both of a good height for their age, physically strong and well built. If not for their respective handicaps, they might have made fine warriors, Vrath thought, but then corrected himself: *They may yet still.*

That was why he had agreed with Jilana that they be taken to Guru Kaylin. Vrath and Jilana, as wardens of the empire, needed to know sooner rather than later if one of the two could someday serve as emperor of Hastinaga. And if not ... well, that was a fjord he would bridge when he came to it. For now, all that concerned him was putting the heirs of his father's legacy to the test. And none could administer that test better than Guru Kaylin. If they were of good mettle, the guru would surely hammer them into fine swords.

They were finally past the long line of farms just outside the city, and now passing the lumberyards. The scents of grain and barley had given way to that of buffalo and fowl, and now the aroma of fresh sap and timber overtook them. Men working in the yards saw them passing and paused to watch them go by. Shvate and Adri took in every sight and sound as if their lives depended on it.

"It is a long ride," Vrath said, turning his head so the wind would carry his words to them. "You may lie down and rest if you desire."

Vrath had rugs laid on the floor of the well for just that purpose. Refreshments too. The latter were the wet nurse's doing.

Neither Ember nor Umber had come to see her son off, as was the usual custom. He assumed they had said their goodbyes in chambers. He knew that neither mother doted on her son, but was still somewhat surprised at this seeming lack of parental emotion.

Vrath did not feel human emotions the way most mortals did, but he did understand what was appropriate under certain circumstances, and what was not. It was unfortunate that the wives of Gada and Virya did not love their sons as they should have. A mother's love, especially a queen mother's love for her princely son, could give a boy a great boost. Vrath knew that he himself would not be the man he was today if not for his mother's strength.

Jeel had a heart of ice, it was true, and felt even less emotion than he did; if he was half mortal, she was no mortal at all, even when she assumed the physical form of one. But she loved him deeply in her own way, and he knew that he could always count on her support. He still recalled how hard it had been for him to accept that he was to leave his mother's embrace and take his place in the mortal world by his father's side. It was a long time ago, but to Vrath the pain was as a fresh prick from a thorn.

The memory of his own separation from his mother made him empathize a little more with his two young wards. They were still standing, leaning their chins and hands on the rim of the chariot well as the world went by.

The chariot had left the lumberyards far behind, crossed the first low hills, and was now rumbling through the relatively sparse wood before entering the formidable jungle for which Hastinaga was named.

It had been more than half a watch since leaving Hastinaga. The boys ought to have desired rest by now, or nourishment. Children always seemed to require one or both of those two things long before Vrath himself ever would. They still remained unusually quiet, especially in light of their last day in the city, when they had been quite loud and boisterous during their sword practice, clearly enjoying their newfound activity.

The answer came to him late, but it came nevertheless: *They are feeling anxious and scared of what lies ahead. Like minnows out of their depth, without the comforting presence of their usual caretakers.*

But Vrath could divert their minds from their homesickness. It was something that had worked for him, years ago, when he himself had left his mother's grasp and first gone out into the world on his own.

There was no reason it should not work on the young princes as well. For did not the same Krushan blood run through their veins?

Adri

~

ADRI WAS SURPRISED WHEN he felt the chariot wheels slowing and heard the creaking of the taut leather reins as Vrath steered the horse team to a halt. He had not expected to arrive at their destination this soon. He sniffed warily. It smelled like forest, but it had smelt of freshly cut lumber only a few hours before. Surely Guru Kaylin's hermitage could not be such a short distance from the city?

"We are stopping in a clearing," Shvate's voice whispered in his ear. "I don't know why."

Adri felt a rush of warmth for his brother. Shvate had been entertaining him since they left Hastinaga, speaking softly in his ear, informing him of the places they were driving past, sketching in details that Adri could not have guessed at from scent and sound clues alone. That act of kindness had enriched the journey considerably.

Until this trip, Adri had hated traveling. It invariably meant a bewildering profusion of smells and sounds, most unrelated to one another, leaving him with disturbing mental pictures of what they might mean. And so Shvate's commentary was extremely useful: it helped him make sense of the world. It was not just a meaningless jumble of smells and sounds; he could form a sensible image of what lay out there. Farmers harvesting crops. Grazing cattle. Clucking fowl. Timber being cut and prepared for transport downriver.

But why were they stopping now? And what place was this? Shvate didn't know either.

"We have arrived." Vrath said, his voice smooth and clear as always.

Shvate's hand on Adri's arm advised him that they were to disembark from the chariot.

"Jump down," Shvate said, and Adri jumped from the chariot without hesitation, followed shortly thereafter by his brother.

They stood before their uncle, awaiting further instruction.

Vrath

~

VRATH NOTED THAT THE boys were standing close together, shoulders touching. He had observed Shvate whispering to his brother in the chariot, and dwelled momentarily on the wisdom of allowing Adri to grow up dependent on his brother's eyes and presence. He pushed the thought aside. Such concerns would be the domain of their guru soon. Vrath had only a day or two remaining to spend with the boys; he did not intend to use that time correcting them. Let brother lean on brother. If Guru Kaylin wished to separate them, let him do so.

"We shall take a short holiday before proceeding to Guruji's hermitage," he said aloud.

The looks of surprise on both brothers' faces were nearly identical. For once, even Adri's usual slack-faced expression was replaced with something akin to a happiness.

"You will both be away for a long time. As your uncle, I wish to spend time with you pursuing activities that bring you delight. Tell me, Shvate, Adri, what would you like to do?"

There was a brief moment of utter silence. Then the responses clambered over each other, as enthusiastically as if he were confronting a whole squad of young boys, rather than merely two.

"Hunt!"

"Fish!"

"Climb!"

"Dive!"

"Fight lions!"

"Stay the night in the forest!"

"In a cave!"

"Track wild boar!"

"Build a machaan!"

"Climb Coldheart Mountain!"

"The desert!"

"Spear snakes!"

"Drive the chariot!"

"Hunt urrkh!"

"Besiege a fort!"

"*Build* a fort!"

"Attack a —"

Vrath laughed.

The sound was unusual enough that it silenced both boys at once. He laughed and laughed, the rolling tones of his laughter echoing through the forest.

Both Shvate and Adri watched and listened in astonishment. They had never seen or heard their uncle laugh before.

In all likelihood, no one had.

Vrath himself could not recall the last time he had laughed — not since he was a boy, probably. When he lived in the river, with his river friends, swimming and hunting and playing underwater like any fish, in his mother's embrace, truly, completely happy. He had never been that happy since, and, he thought, would never be again. It was the way of life. Babes cooed, children laughed, men smiled . . . then learned to smile without meaning it, and finally, death laughed *at* men and ended their humorless lives.

But death was not laughing yet; Vrath was.

He was happy again. He had remembered what it was to be a boy again. To be innocent, carefree, the whole world before you, all of life lying ahead, unexplored, undiscovered, filled with wonders and treasures, adventures and secrets.

He came forward, spreading his arms as he crouched down, startling them both, and he put his hands around both of them and swept them up into a great, happy, bone-crushing hug.

The boys were surprised at first, then understanding washed over them, their uncle's action speaking more eloquently than his words. Giving themselves over to him, both of them broke out laughing as well.

Vrath stood up, still hugging the boys, carrying them as easily as a crane lifting a pair of young salmon, and laughed on.

The forest filled with the sound of the three Krushan laughing.

Shvate

~

THE NEXT FEW DAYS were a blur of activity.

Shvate and Adri learned more in that time than they had in their entire short lives until then. They learned to track, to hunt and kill, to fish, to skin and clean and cook, to start a fire, to keep it going, to bank it so as to reduce telltale smoke. They cut sapling boughs, carved them into bows and shafts, cured and stretched strips of sinew to string the bows, then learned to use the weapons.

They hunted deer, and in doing so, Adri learned how to still his body and senses and how to breathe until he became one with the jungle and its patterns, to distinguish the soft sounds of the deer snorting or stomping or chewing, to aim and loose by these sounds alone, and by the end of the trip, to regularly hit his target.

Shvate learned to stalk the deadly but very delicious spiny boar, to corner and kill it without risking it ripping open his abdomen and spilling out his bowels — though it tried mightily, and came close enough to leave Shvate with a small crescent-shaped scar for life — and then to skin and clean and cut and cook the animal, wasting no part of it.

They ate what they caught, and they ate very well indeed. Vrath did no hunting himself, restricting his role to that of a mentor. It was terrifying at first to the boys, but also exhilarating. To be given such responsibility, thrust into such an adventure, face-to-face with snorting, smelly, whiskery-faced death, yet knowing that if it came down to it, their uncle would surely step in and protect them.

Or would he?

He said he would not, and they took him at his word, which made them try harder, and perhaps that was what made the difference in the outcome.

To play at hunting while Uncle watched over them was a challenge.

To actually hunt while Vrath watched — but did not intervene — was a *responsibility.*

They learned the difference in those days in the jungle.

Shvate found it even more exciting because the dense jungle afforded him cover from the cruel sun that tormented his sensitive skin. Unlike in the open environs of Hastinaga, here he could roam and range at will under the shady canopy of the woods. He was overjoyed when he realized this at first. The sense of liberation from the tyranny of sunlight was thrilling. Even in the chariot, he had had to keep a burlap cloth over his head to protect his skin. Back home, he always dressed in attire that kept his entire body covered, even in the hot season. Now, for the first time in his young life, he could be free of such encumbrances. He could swim and play in a pool fed by a waterfall by day, the dappled patches of sunlight robbed of their intensity by the time they reached him; he could hunt and run and practice and play all day without having to wait for sundown. And when sundown *did* come, he could lie down to sleep like other people did, as people were supposed to do.

The nights were a different matter.

Accustomed to the soft silk cushions, army of servants, their every need catered to, the two heirs of Hastinaga had never experienced true survival.

That first night, both were unable to sleep for hours.

Their straw pallets were prickly and uncomfortable. The darkness was absolute, a living thing that pressed in around them, squeezing, throttling, suffocating.

And the jungle was *alive.*

It was on that night they realized that the jungle was, in fact, a city.

Inhabited by countless denizens, each of whom had their own agenda, cutthroat ambitions, goals and targets, occupations and duties, all going about their work under cover of darkness. Not merely selling, trading, buying, serving, as in Hastinaga. But killing, hunting, raiding, squealing, roaring, growling.

Oddly enough, Adri suffered more than Shvate. He had been born in darkness; it was his natural state of being. He did not fear it in itself. But the living jungle that enveloped him and its inhabitants were all the more terrifying because he could not see any of them, and was compelled to imagine their nature from their sounds and smells alone. To him, they were all monsters. He slept with his handmade rough-hewn bow clutched tightly in both fists, and he did not sleep deeply or long.

Shvate, on the other hand, had been unnerved at first, but as the first watch passed and he grew more accustomed to the sounds of the jungle, he became intrigued, and then fascinated by the savagery of the life-and-death game being played out all around him. He knew what several of the animals looked like, and what sounds they made, and so even if he couldn't see them, he could form mental images of what was transpiring most of the time, or make a reasonable guess at it. A lion bringing down a deer. Two spiny boars tangling tusks. A herd of deer passing through on their way to the pond. The mental pictures that formed in his mind were informed by the sights he had seen.

Shvate slept eventually, and dreamed of the animal city going about its business, taking strange pleasure in the inevitability and unending cycle of life and death. To him, the jungle was a city of animals. Was that not why they called it the animal kingdom? Yet he felt more at home here than in his own princely chambers in Hastinaga. The jungle awakened some ancient powerful impulse within him, a race memory of a time when all creatures lived together in the forest, and the forest was their entire world.

He slept and dreamed of a world where he roamed as freely as a lion, a tiger, a bear, a wolf, and ruled his own ranging ground armed only with his wits and brute force.

In contrast, Adri tossed uneasily all night, unable to break free of the nightmare world where teeth, fangs, claws surrounded him, and only pain and agony lay in wait. He wanted nothing more than to go back home, to the seclusion and safety of his chambers in Hastinaga, to be able to call for a wet nurse and lose himself in her large, warm, soft maternal embrace.

The jungle was one brother's paradise, the other's nightmare.

Vrath

~

BY DAY, THE BROTHERS were as one being. They did everything together, as a team — Shvate communicating with his brother via a whispered word or a combination of sound and deft touch; Adri moving confidently, secure in his brother's presence and support, allowing his instincts to guide him, catching sounds that Shvate could not even hope to hear, his acute hearing a tool that enabled him to "see" without seeing.

Shvate's hand was impressively steady, his ability to draw back a bowstring and loose in a single fluid motion markedly superior to Adri's. By the eve of the third day, he could, if he desired, stalk, hunt, and down game entirely on his own. He had an instinctive understanding of the jungle that Vrath found intriguing. It was like Vrath's own symbiotic relationship to water bodies: to Vrath a river was a living highway filled with teeming life. He knew every creature, plant, and rock that inhabited that bustling intercourse and could traverse that watery world as easily as any finned denizen.

Shvate was like that in the jungle: it was as if he was home, had been born and brought up there, and knew it like the back of his hand. He knew things without being told: like which side of a tree moss grew upon in a season, or that a doe that grazed in a certain pattern was heavy with child, or that the claw marks on a sala trunk were not from a sloth bear but from an aging half-blind lion that used it to clean and sharpen his claws.

The speed and efficiency with which he picked up the essentials and then graduated directly to far more advanced skills was astonishing even to Vrath. He had brought his half brothers Gada and Virya to the forest at around this same age, and while they had been fearless and eager to learn, they held no candle to Shvate. This young boy was born to the hunt. He was not merely highly skilled: he was a *prodigy*.

Vrath took pride in the thought that his nephew could not be anything *but* a prodigy. By the second day, he had to acknowledge that what Shvate possessed was beyond normal mortal ability. As the son of a mortal man and a goddess himself, Vrath knew *he* possessed senses, knowledge, and abilities that were not within the reach of mortals, but Shvate, being born of a mortal mother, could not compare to Vrath. But he was definitely a notch or three superior to most mortals.

Shvate was seeded by Jilana's firstborn son, Vessa. The sage was a child of the forest himself, a being greater than mortal but less than divine. Born of a union between a sage who was in fact Shapaar traveling incognito and Jilana years before she met and married Emperor Sha'ant, Vessa grew to adulthood within hours of birth, and after taking his mother's blessings, departed for unknown destinations. From his mother and his river relatives, Vrath knew that Vessa had gone into the deep woods, into the heart of the jungle, to a place where even the most self-flagellant tapasvi sage would not venture.

There, in a place where the jungle itself did not permit mortal intrusion, Vessa abided. He subsisted on infinitesimal molecules of nutrition derived from air alone; inserted vines into his veins, merging sap with blood; inhaled the color of the leaves, the dark energy of moonlight, the sinews of the wind, the songs of the birds, the storms stirred by insect wings. From water drawn up through the soles of his feet he slaked his thirst. From the whispering of butterflies he came to know the intimate secrets of the forest. The jungle fed him as one of her own, and in return he fed the jungle with his own energies and fluids, forming a symbiotic bond that was beyond the capacity of human understanding or belief.

Shvate had inherited his father's intimate relationship with the jungle. Clearly the forest herself recognized her brethren and welcomed him, opening her secrets to his mind and senses.

But that did not explain why Adri lacked the same bond.

Where Shvate was completely at home in this verdant environment almost at once, Adri remained uncomfortable, anxious, even afraid. At crucial moments, he would err and fail to loose the arrow that would have downed his prey, or fail to follow through on an easy kill.

His senses were no less acute than his brother's. He possessed the same uncanny level of intimacy with the jungle as Shvate. But where Shvate thrived and reveled in this habitat, Adri did not wish to be there at all. Vrath could see the signs the very first night; while Shvate slept peacefully, all but purring in his sleep, Adri thrashed about, started at sounds, and was drawn into the clasp of nightmares that sucked his energy dry. So long as Shvate was beside him, guiding and encouraging him, Adri was in fine form — and he did his part exceedingly well, capable of matching any sighted boy his age. But time and again he sabotaged himself, hesitating at crucial moments, pulling back or otherwise disengaging when it came to the nub.

Vrath felt sympathy for the boy. He clearly feared the jungle; even though he could have been as much at home as Shvate, he *chose* not to let himself trust the mother forest. Why or how was something Vrath could not quite fathom. They were both birthed from the seed of Vessa, after all, and possessed of similar skills and abilities. Yet they were developing in very different ways.

He wondered if it was merely Adri's lack of sight. Perhaps, but he sensed it was something more. He recalled that their mothers had reacted differently when Vessa had come into their respective chambers. Shvate's mother had been horrified by the sage's wild appearance and had turned ashen white. That seemed to have resulted in Shvate's lack of skin color, as Vessa had prophesied. But after her initial fright, she had kept her eyes open and undergone the seeding. That showed great courage on her part: to have seen a man who physically repulsed her and still consented to take him to her bed, for the dynasty. Adri's mother, on the other hand, had shut her eyes from the start, unwilling to even look at the sage. Perhaps that accounted for Adri's weakness: not the blindness itself, which did not diminish his ability, but his imagination. Like his mother at that crucial moment of conception, Adri feared the unseen, and because it was unseen and therefore unknown, it loomed as something far more terrible than the reality.

That was it, Vrath decided. Adri suffered from his mother's flaw: a last-minute failing of will.

It was a dangerous flaw in any man, but a fatal one in a warrior or a king.

It meant, Vrath mused sadly, that Adri could never rule as king. To be emperor of Hastinaga required fortitude. A king who hesitated at a crucial moment could cause the downfall of the empire.

As the holiday drew to an end and he began preparing to resume their journey to Guru Kaylin's hermitage, Vrath decided he would not judge the boys just yet. They were still young and about to be delivered into the tutelage of a great master. He would delay judgment until they had graduated from the hermitage and achieved manhood. A great deal could transpire in that period. Boys become men. Princes become kings. And life has a way of surprising you.

But in his heart of hearts, he knew the die was already cast.

Of the two brothers, only Shvate was fit to rule.

All that remained was for time, and the guru, to prove his assessment right — or wrong.

It was with this thought on his mind that he finally delivered his two wards to the guru's hermitage.

Shvate

⁓

GURU KAYLIN'S GURUKUL WAS nestled in a clearing deep within a forest even denser and lusher than the one in which Shvate and Adri had spent the past few days with Vrath. Here, the trees were so tall, Shvate could not see the top of them, however hard he craned his neck. Their branches formed a canopy so dense that the only light that filtered through was greenish in hue. Not a single bar of direct sunlight passed through here, except in the clearing, where, from the angle of the light, he guessed that the sun would shine down for a only few hours each morning. A brook they came upon was nestled between stands of trees that only gave a few yards of space, as if the wood was reluctant to let even the water pass.

He felt a thrill of anticipation at the thought of all the animals that must drink here all day and night long, of the wealth of game that would be ripe for the taking. And this was further north and higher up the foothills, which meant there would be bigger game here, larger predators, much bigger leaf-eaters. Vrath had told them stories of past hunts with his own father, of sighting a blue stag the size of an elephant. Surely there would be some like that here in the mountains. And tiger, bear, lion, panther, leopard, and wolf too.

The jungle pressed in from all sides, like a crowd of spectators eager to touch the hems of the two great princes of Hastinaga. The sounds of birds, insects, small game, the babbling of brooks, the shirring of wind — all rose like a symphony of music and voices raised in a hosanna to greet their arrival. Shvate imagined spending days and nights in this wilderness. Years, even. The prospect thrilled him beyond words. He felt as if the jungle had been waiting for him all his life, eagerly anticipating his arrival. And now he was here at last: home.

His heart sang and resonated in chorus with the song of the forest.

Adri

~

ADRI FELT RAW PANIC as Vrath released his hand and began speaking with the other adults who had joined them from the hermitage.

He had heard and smelled the jungle, and the overwhelming sensations he felt now were despair and terror. The past few days had been tolerable, even enjoyable at times, because of his uncle's and brother's presences. But though Shvate would remain with him at the hermitage for the duration, he already sensed that his brother did not share his fear and loathing of the wilderness; if anything, he heard and sensed joy in his brother's voice and words when he spoke of it. Shvate *loved* the forest. Adri very much did not.

On their journey to the hermitage, Uncle had said he would not intervene to help if he and his brother encountered trouble, yet on at least two occasions, Vrath had either aided Adri or prevented him from harming himself. And, now, in a few moments, Adri would be left here in this desolate, forsaken wilderness, and the last adult protector in his life would leave him. Leave him and go back to the city, to the palace, where he would reside in comfort and security. While Adri stayed here, in the stark, savage clutches of the jungle, this living, breathing thing that pressed in on all sides around him, like a herd of wild fanged beasts wanting a closer sniff to gauge the weaknesses of this blind two-legged prey.

A moment of utter despair washed over him.

He turned to Vrath, sensing his uncle preparing himself for departure, and said in a voice half-choked with desperation, "Please, Uncle, please, take me home to the palace. Don't leave me here. I want to go home with you. Please take me."

He heard the startled silence that followed his pleas, the sharp intake of breath from his side, and knew that everyone, including Shvate, was surprised and disappointed at this outburst. Most of all Vrath, who had repeatedly urged them to always show restraint of emotions and reactions, as a warrior and a king always kept his true feelings to himself lest they be used as weapons against him. But Adri couldn't help it. He couldn't bear the thought of staying here for days, nights, months . . . maybe even *years*? Impossible.

"Adri . . ." He heard the patient tone in his uncle's voice and knew that he was supposed to understand from that single syllable that this was no way for a prince to behave, that he was a Krushan, heir to the great dynasty of Hastinaga, inheritor of a great legacy and responsibility, ruler of the civilized world — an emblem of Krushan law. The world looked to him for guidance and governance. He could not burst out begging and crying thus.

And yet, for the next several moments, that was all he could do. He was, after all, barely nine years of age, suddenly removed from all the comforts and luxuries to which he was accustomed, sent far away from home, and was now being forced to live the life of a warrior hermit.

He begged, he cried, he screamed, he howled, and finally, when Vrath reluctantly but firmly tore him loose from the leg he had latched onto, he heard the pain and sorrow in his uncle's voice as he said, not without sympathy, "Be strong, child. All things are hard in the beginning. Give it time. You will adapt."

And then, with a strong stride and without a backward glance (Adri sensed, for he could sense such things without the benefit of sight), his uncle was gone. Back to the pathway several miles away where they had left the chariot to negotiate the densest part of the forest on foot, and thence back to Hastinaga, a good three full days' and nights' ride from here. Five hundred miles? A thousand? Two thousand? He did not know. It did not matter. He was far enough from home that he may as well have been in the netherworld, among the Nagas, or in the lower realms, where urrkh roamed like mad demons eternally. His family had left him here.

He was forsaken.

"Adri," said his brother's voice in his ear as he stood, desolate and bitter of heart. "Adri, do not fear. I am with you, brother."

But in that moment of black despair, bitter-hearted at being abandoned in this desolate forest against his will, Adri felt a sudden surge of anger at his beloved brother.

Without thinking about it, he shoved Shvate away with a fierce push.

"I don't want you! I want to go home!"

He regretted the action and the words as soon as they were committed. But he knew that there was truth in them too—his heart's pure naked truth. He did not want a brother's help. He wanted his home, his family, his protection and security.

He wanted his mother.

But she had abandoned him long ago.

She had let go of his little hand even before he could walk on his own.

She no more cared what happened to him than she cared about what happened to a deer roaming these jungles.

She was the first to forsake him. Uncle Vrath was the next. Soon, Shvate would forsake him too.

In time, everyone would.

It was what people did. They made you want them, need them. Made you trust them, love them. And then, when you needed them most, they turned and walked away, shaking off your hand.

In that moment, Adri's handsome face coiled and twisted, his tears stopped, his sobbing ceased, his heart drank its own bitter juices, and he vowed that if the world could be this cruel to you, if even those whom you loved most, the woman who had birthed you herself, could forsake you, then he would learn to be cruel as well.

He would show them.

He would show them all someday.

And he let the hermits lead him into the hermitage without another word of protest.

Jarsun

〜

1

THE CITY OF REYGAR rose above Jarsun, climbing level by level up the slope of the mountain that loomed like a stone god amidst the endless dunes of the desert kingdom of Reygistan. *His* kingdom, now that his father-in-law, King Aqron, was deceased, the unfortunate casualty of their last battle, a particularly brutal clash with three different tribes of Reygistan; the heir —Jarsun's wife, Aqeela — had quit the campaign trail to nurse her own severe injuries.

All things considered, his campaign of consolidation had gone well, considering how many warring factions and desert tribes resisted the very concept of a Reygistan Empire.

Unlike the pitched battles and methodical campaigns of the Burnt Empire, there was no Krushan law to govern conflicts in this part of the world: even the word "Reygistan" simply meant "desert." Since time immemorial, the Reygistani desert tribes fought as they pleased, whom they pleased, when they pleased. It was common for allies to break ranks with each other in midcampaign or even, on one recent memorable occasion, midbattle. That last clash had been nothing but a melee undeserving of the word "battle," and Aqron's savage demise had been only one of many casualties the Reygistani forces had suffered.

Aqeela had not taken her father's death well, and had opted to stay home with Krushita after that, which suited Jarsun. For Sandeaters, as he still disparagingly thought of these desert dwellers (though never out loud in the presence of his wife or late father-in-law), the Reygistani were far too moral

69

for his taste. As far as Jarsun was concerned, the universe was inherently chaotic, and war was chaos personified; in the dust and heat and bloody froth of battle, everything was clear and meaningful. Like the inhabitants of many longtime desert settlements, Aqeela's people had stayed in one place for far too long. City life encouraged the illusion that the world could be governed by order and patterns. With that came the delusions of morality, justice, and law. In reality, Jarsun thought, a city was nothing but a jungle inhabited by clothed beasts with sheathed talons.

Take this present specimen, for example.

Reygar, the oldest city of the desert kingdom. First settlement of the desert tribes. Site of a great mountain oasis. The last stop on his campaign and now, apparently, the hardest to conquer.

The city had thus far withstood the siege of Jarsun's army for six full moons, the longest any city had resisted him. It was hard to imagine that the inhabitants of this isolated mountain city-state were stubborn — and resilient — enough to withstand such massive assaults. As he gazed up at the mountain city, Jarsun mused how this could be even as he pondered how to break the siege once and for all.

Perhaps he had been too complacent in his first approach, sending his usual emissaries with the standard missive advising the liege of the land to lay down his arms and accept Reygistan's superiority. He had even sent a white ass ahead of the emissary, his own little attempt at satirical commentary on the Krushan practice of sending a black horse ahead of their army. In the Krushan ceremony, any land that the anointed black horse stepped on became the domain of the king who had sent forth the stallion. If the liege of that land failed to surrender his kingdom as was mandated under Krushan law, the occupying king was justified in waging war until he conceded.

Jarsun's twist upon that arcane Krushan ritual was meant only to confound and confuse the receiving kings and their armies. By his interpretation, any place the ass *shat* was his to possess. It was both an insult directed at his own estranged bloodline as well as a message that the Reygistan Empire was nothing like the Burnt Empire. In place of law and order, taxation and roadways, he offered chaos and pillage, plunder and lawlessness. Instead of the black horse sacrificed to appease the stone gods, he butchered an ass and defaced the most sacred shrine of each kingdom he conquered, defying their gods and dispelling any notions of righteous rebellion the conquered people might harbor.

Unable to see the satirical wink he intended toward the Burnt Empire, they invariably responded with contempt at the outset, rejecting the emissary outright, laughing off the white ass as evidence of Reygistan having lost its collective mind. It was only when the screaming and the fires and the slaughter began — always starting from the back end of the city, which Jarsun's intrepid assassins infiltrated discreetly even as all attention was focused on the emissary and the ridiculous white ass with its colorful anointments — that they realized the white ass was meant to represent *them*, the victims of that lethal jest.

But none of his usual ploys and tactics had worked on Reygar.

He had tried frontal assaults, stealthy infiltration, siege engines raining fire, storms of arrows, poisoning the fresh water supply, slaughtering children from the desert tribes that dwelled in the city, and a variety of other devilish devices. But the walls still stood, and armed defense met his soldiers when they attempted any assault, and the gates still rose up proud and unwelcoming. He had inflicted great damage and fatalities upon the people of Reygar, enough to bring any other foe to their knees.

Yet Reygar still resisted. Battered, broken, bleeding . . . but not yet under his power.

He beckoned. His trusted aides, Hasar and Vidram, always near, came up at once.

"Give the order to withdraw," Jarsun said without preamble.

They both gawked at him. "*Withdraw, sire?*"

"Pull out all our troops. Leave not so much as a dying man or a ragged tent behind. Take everything. Sound the retreat and take all siege machines and support works as well. Move out within the day and move on."

The men exchanged a brief glance, then nodded slowly, turning to go. Jarsun laughed darkly, giving them an excuse to look back and stare questioningly. "You're wondering why."

Like all those close to him, Hasar and Vidram spoke rarely and only as much as was needed. Jarsun was no Krushan to depend on words. There were more efficient ways of communication: swords spoke loudest of all.

"You're thinking that if Jarsun of Reygistan retreats without conquering this city, it will dent my heretofore unmarred reputation. Especially because of the historic and religious significance of Reygar, the holiest of cities. Word will spread that the forces of Reygistan can be resisted. They will say we are not the demons we claim to be. That we can be stood up to and bested. Then the rout will begin. Even those cities we have already subjugated will rise up against us. And those we intend to conquer in other regions will resist us with renewed vigor. We shall have to fight twice as hard and ten times as long to conquer the same territory and will always have desert wolves at our back, nipping and testing us."

They did not have to nod to show agreement: Hasar and Vidram agreed with everything their lord said or did. It was implicit in their existence. The first thing they disagreed with would be their last. Dogs to their master, there was no room in their cognition for anything other than total obedience. That was why they had survived this long and brutal campaign while so many of his other aides lay putrefying alongside the corpses of their enemies.

Jarsun smiled. "You are right in thinking these thoughts. I cannot afford to let Reygar go unsacked and unpillaged. In fact, I must now make an example of it. I must demonstrate to the world what happens when anyone defies me too fiercely. It is one thing to put up the show of a fight or a brief siege in order for the local chief or king to maintain his honor in his people's eyes. That I can accept and condone. But this" — with a contemptuous arm, he indicated the city towering above them — "this is unacceptable. This is open defiance. A challenge to the death. I cannot let it stand and walk away. So you wonder why I give the order to retreat. Fear not. I intend to give the inhabitants of Reygar exactly what they ask for. They shall have death. They shall have destruction. I shall give them a fate so terrible that the world will know and retch violently at the mere mention of the city's fate. I will make Reygar an example of what happens to those who dare to oppose us."

He grinned, revealing his teeth in an expression that made even his most trusted generals want to step back uneasily. Rarely did they see their master this infuriated, this bloodthirsty, but often enough to know to be wary of him, of his power, of what he was capable of unleashing.

"But how can I achieve all this if we withdraw our forces and retreat, you wonder? I shall tell you how."

He clapped his hands around both men, dwarfing them with his freakishly long arms and size in his attempt to make a show of camaraderie. He felt both of them stiffen instinctively, fearing his touch; they were wise to fear it, but fortunately for them, his ire was not directed at them. "In order to set an example, I have decided not to use the army for this special case. Instead, I shall accomplish this personally."

Jarsun sensed the men's powerful shoulders tensing involuntarily.

"*You*, sire?" Vidram asked, unable to help himself. "You will take the city yourself . . . *alone?*"

"Yes, my friends," Jarsun said with a grin. "Both I and myself shall do it together."

2

The people of Reygar rejoiced. It had been over four days since the invaders had departed, taking every last piece of siege machinery, weaponry, and booty; not a living being stirred outside the city walls. The siege was over, the threat had ended; they had triumphed! It was an incredible success. "We withstood the might of Jarsun and survived," said one of the wise old Maatri women who ruled there. Reygar was a matriarchal society governed by the Maatri. No male had ever ruled here, nor ever would. Women were better at governing, running things, administrating, keeping the peace, maintaining the cities, and doing all the things that made up the daily business of ruling a kingdom. And if anyone dared to think that men might perhaps, possibly, just maybe, be better at warcraft, the person had certainly not faced the Maatri in battle.

The citizens emerged now, resplendent in their armor, which was specially polished and cleaned for the occasion. During weeks of hard siege and withstanding brutal intrusions and assaults, there had been little time for food or rest, let alone polishing armor. But with the enemy having retreated, and a celebration called for, the Maatri were proud to adorn themselves in their finest. And for a Maatri, no garb was more resplendent than battle armor. Glimmering with gold, silver, and flecks of colored stone cleverly sewn into the chain links of the mail, the metal garb clung to the bodies of the hard-muscled warrior matrons who were the mainstay of the country's army. Nor were they all young specimens; there were grandmothers among them, white-haired and noble in their aging pride, as well as women scarred and maimed from combat. They were nonetheless resplendent in that moment of glory.

The environs of the city had been scoured thoroughly over the past four days. The moment the last wagons of the so-called Reygistan Empire had departed, fading into a faint trail of dust on the horizon, the spies had been sent forth through underground tunnels to scour the countryside. They went hundreds of miles in every direction, seeking any sign of a ruse. They found nothing. The enemy had truly withdrawn. Not a single Reygistani soldier remained anywhere.

They took down the rotting corpses of the unfortunates who had been tortured and left to die before the city gates, interring them with due honor along with their own dead, those who had fallen to the many assaults by Jarsun. These numbered in the thousands, and disposing of the corpses was a considerable exercise but a necessary one, to avoid the outbreak of disease.

And then the celebrations began.

The celebrations were still ongoing when the team charged with disposal of corpses gathered up the final batch of bodies. If they could even be called bodies: they were mostly bits and pieces, severed limbs and grisly parts, left to rot in the unrelenting Reygistani sun. The stench from these gathered bobs and bits was even more offensive than from the whole corpses. From across the city, sounds of revelry filled the air. The Maatri tasked with this duty were eager to finish the chore, clean up, and join the celebrations.

As they approached the pile, the volunteers made various sounds of disgust, mostly imitating retching.

"Let's just throw on as much oil as we have and burn the whole lot where it lies," said one Maatri, her voice deeply nasal due to her pinching her nose to avoid the stench.

"Can't do that," said another woman apologetically, wincing as the wind changed, bringing the full richness of the aroma to her. "Our orders are to bury them. Oil supplies are short enough as it is."

The women looked at the pile doubtfully. "We could bring dry brush and wood and use that to burn them."

The Maatri in charge snorted. "Do you know how much it would take to burn this lot? A hundred wagonloads! Maybe more. And without oil . . . Besides, the smoke and ash would carry across the whole city." She gestured at the city behind them and indicated the direction of the wind. "And the outer ones would burn, but it would be a putrefying mess on the inside."

They were all silent for a moment, considering the idea, then, one of her companions said in disgust, "Oh, thank you, Suverya, for that wonderful thought. Excuse me while I go relieve the contents of my belly."

"Get to it, then," the Maatri in charge ordered. "Let's start digging a pit. And remember, we have to make it large enough and deep enough to take the whole of this sorry bunch. Maatr intends to plant an orchard over it afterward."

"An orchard?" someone asked, incredulous.

"Yes," said the woman in charge sourly. "To commemorate the siege. Besides, fresh corpses underground give good fruit. Come on, get to work, you lazy bunch!"

The pit was dug and almost all the body parts thrown in when someone exclaimed loudly.

"Maatri!" she called out. "Come take a look at this."

The Maatri in charge and several of the others within hearing range came out of curiosity. They looked down at the male body split perfectly from the center of the bald crown of its head right down to the waist. The cut was blade-smooth, immaculate, as if it was an apple that had been sliced into two halves rather than a grown man.

The Maatri in charge frowned and wiped the sweat and grime from her brow before asking irritably, "And what great vision am I supposed to be looking at, Naranito?"

"It's as good as new," replied the young woman who had discovered the anomaly. "It hasn't rotted at all. How is that possible?"

And it was true. Apart from the fact that the body was split down the middle, it was pristine. No decay had occurred as yet, nor were any maggots or putrefying flesh visible. The women examined the body curiously and all agreed that its skin and flesh resembled that of a living man.

"It's almost as if . . ." Naranito said, then stopped.

"What?" asked Agmindesh beside her.

"Well, it's almost as if you could put the two halves together and they would fit perfectly, with barely a seam visible."

"What do you know about seams, Naranito?" her wife called out. "You've never touched a sewing needle since we were married." That drew a burst of laughter. It was good to have something to laugh about after the miseries of the past months.

Out of sheer curiosity, three or four of the women actually picked up the two halves of the severed corpse and placed them together.

"Look! They fit together like a whole body!" said Naranito, the one who had thought of it.

One of the Maatri holding the halves together felt movement beneath her fingertips. She frowned, assuming she had only felt some reverberation or other movement, and looked down.

The eyes of the severed corpse opened.

The Maatri screamed and let go of the body, backing away, scrambling away. She tripped and fell over another body. "It's alive!" she cried out.

The erstwhile severed corpse got to its feet, causing the other women around it to back away as well. It looked around. The thin red line running down the center of its bald head all the way down its naked chest and body glowed brightly for an instant, then faded away.

The severed body was now a whole man. A living man. With no trace of a seam, as the wit had remarked.

As they stared in stunned incomprehension, the Maatri in charge reached for her sword. "Kill him!" she cried. "Kill—"

That was as far as she got. The severed man's tongue shot out of his mouth and lashed out at her with whiplike ferocity, covering a distance of over two yards to strike her across the chest and waist from shoulder to hip. The Maatri in charge felt a moment of scalding heat, as if she had been struck by a red-hot scourge. Then the acid saliva from the figure's tongue ate through her armor, garb, flesh, and bone with instant efficacy, and her body split into two at the diagonal cut. She fell open like a ripe fruit and instantly perished. The two halves of her body hissed and sizzled as they parted, the exposed flesh and organs corroded by the acidic saliva.

Stunned but stalwart, the other Maatri recovered quickly and began marshaling their forces against this unexpected enemy. But the severed man moved amongst them with lightning speed, swinging around in a half circle to strike cobra-like at the more than half a dozen Maatri in rapid succession. He would be *here* one instant, his whiplike tongue lashing out to sever one's arm before she could slash out with her sword, then *there* in the next, yards away, decapitating another woman. Many died screaming in agony and without even lifting their weapons; others, shocked and stunned, died not understanding what had killed them.

It was an astonishing display. Within moments, the entire burial crew lay butchered, the dissected bodies of its members steaming and hissing.

Then the figure moved into the city. And then began the slaughter.

There, he met a great deal of resistance. Relaxed and reveling though they were, taken by surprise, caught off guard — the Maatri yet were fierce fighters.

But it made no difference. The devil was in the gates and nothing could stop him.

The severed man passed through Reygar all like a force of nature, like a hurricane through a sugarcane field, like a tiger through a flock of lambs. By the time he was done, there were many, many more corpses to cremate and commemorate, but no one left to do the needful.

3

When he was done with Reygar, Jarsun turned toward his true goal: the Burnt Empire.

Jilana and Vrath had denied his daughter, Krushita, her rightful legacy, while insulting his wife, his father-in-law, and the people of Reygistan. They had denied him, Jarsun, a born Krushan, his claim to the bloodline of the Burning Throne. Even stonefire had screamed in protest at the injustice; he had heard and felt it in his Krushan bones. The people of Hastinaga would have accepted him. The army too. It was only Jilana and Vrath and their newly minted heirs, Shvate and Adri, who stood between his daughter and the Burning Throne. Once he eliminated those two boys, he could take Hastinaga by force. Jilana and Vrath would have no pompous arguments or legal citations to hurl at him then. His beloved Krushita would be the only rightful heir capable of sitting upon the Burning Throne. Whether they liked it or not, the Reygistan Empire and the Burnt Empire would be allies, linked by blood.

And the world would be his to command.

Part Two

The Guide

~

1

THE CONSPIRATORS CAME FROM every direction.

The marg each traveled converged at the great kingsroad of Madhya De-sha, where all roads united. With their entourages, they were the size of a small army and could have been mistaken for an invading force. Their de-meanor was grim enough, but after further observation, it was evident that they were here on a cooperative venture, not at loggerheads.

As they joined together and proceeded farther north, approaching the jagged rises of the mountain ranges, the marg they now traveled dwindled to a path and, before long, was nothing more than a fading scar across the stony face of the land. Nothing grew easily here, except small game and predators. There were shapes moving in the gathering shadows as dusk fell, and a peculiar odor in the air. On the tiny scratch of a path, the company trundled along together until even that unwelcoming trail dwindled away to terrain dotted with rocks large enough to break the hooves of any carriage horse. A ridge rose steeply from this point, cutting off the view of the moun-tains that lay beyond.

The irritated travelers dismounted and then debated how best to pro-ceed. Their awkward pleasantries were interrupted by a piercing whistle from above. Several of them reached for their weapons. They were foreign-ers here, after all, and the mountain folk were notorious for their lack of love for outlanders.

A wizened old woman looked down on them from the peak of the ridge. She leaped down from her perch, hopping and skipping as easily as if she were playing a child's game, all the thirty yards down to where the company stood.

Landing with a broken-toothed smile, she rattled off a stream of words in the mountain tongue. A few of the travelers understood enough to translate for the others. But it was hardly necessary to know the language to understand her message: she was to be their guide; they were to follow her.

She instructed them to leave their valets and accompanying guards and, without waiting to see if they had heeded her instructions, disappeared behind a cluster of large boulders nearby, reappearing shortly after with a pack of ugly-faced mules with too-large ears. She handed each traveler the reins of a mule.

The travelers looked at one another, then at the flea-bitten, ragged-eared creatures with open repulsion.

"We are royalty," one of them pointed out haughtily. "We expect royal treatment."

Their guide looked up at him — she was short enough that the withers of the shortest mount reached as high as the top of her grey head — and chattered a comment in her tongue.

The two or three travelers who knew the language sniggered or laughed in response.

"What did she say?" demanded the pompous one.

"To put it in more polite words: she said you could park your royal ass upon a mule and follow her or you could bugger it royally for all she cared."

The pompous one glared but said nothing further.

There was much grumbling and some cursing from the others as well; the indignity of riding a mule was something few of them had suffered until now. But their own selectmen and valets advised them that it was in their own best interest to endure this minor indignity. These mountains were notorious for claiming more lives than any enemy they had faced in battle. The mules were the only way to navigate the harsh and dangerous pathway to their destination.

The cursing and grumbling continued. But the wizened old guide led the way and the company followed, their royal asses mounted uncomfortably on the ugly mules. The woman cackled in her own tongue that it was hard to tell which were the bigger asses, the ones riding or the ones being ridden!

The pompous one stared at the others who knew what she meant, but they stifled their laughter and did not translate.

As the path wound steeper, the ridge grew more brittle, and the chance of falling more likely. Even the protests died out. It is a peculiarity of mortals that only when confronted by their mortality do they realize life's value. After a few hours of teetering over sheer falls, the only sound on that knife-edge pathway was the chuffing of the mules.

Apparently unconcerned with the mortals astride them, the mules would deign to pause wherever the fancy took them, here to chew on a tiny patch of weeds, there to fart noisily and violently, or a few yards farther, to defecate the well-digested remains of an earlier meal, without any consideration for the royal noses and constitutions being assaulted by these frequent bodily purges.

The wizened guide glanced back from time to time, and chuckled at the discomfort of her unlikely followers. Occasionally, she would pause to stroll back, walking as easily on an inch of dubious ridge as a royal carriage rolling by on the kingsroad of Hastinaga. The travelers could hardly bear to look at her as she went past, swinging out over a sheer drop without a downward glance.

A touch of a saddle here, a stirrup there, a twitching tail further on, and she was by, handing out savories suitable only for mule constitutions. The animals made gleeful chuffing noises at each of these feed stops, and the travelers grew accustomed to a marked increase in the passing of wind and feces for the hour or so following this ritual. The woman winked at the pompous one as she went by, slapping his mule's backside affectionately. The creature chuffed happily in response; the pompous traveler remained as stony-faced as the cliff beside him, not with his customary arrogance but with stone-cold fear. He had discovered in the course of the journey that he was terrified of heights, but his royal pride prevented him from admitting it. And even if he had confessed, surely he would not relish the thought of turning around and going back the way he had climbed, alone.

The guide fed with the mules, chewing at regular intervals on the odd-looking (and odder-smelling) contents of her hemp sack. She did not offer a share of her repast to her followers, nor did any ask for it. Accustomed to their every need being met the very instant such a need arose, none had thought to bring any nourishment for the journey.

By the midway point in their trek, around the time the sun began declining on the late afternoon of the first day, the grumbling and whinging had ceased altogether.

Now only the mules spoke. Chuffing, breaking wind, doing what they did routinely. The mortals mounted on their back endured silently.

There was absolutely no doubt who was in command.

Viewed from a great height, as by one of the floating silhouettes high in the sky above the snowcapped peaks, the procession appeared as nothing more than a worm wriggling its way up the mountain. It proceeded with agonizing slowness, reminding the travelers at every curve in the narrow pathway why the Mountain Kingdoms had never been successfully invaded by any mortal army.

The pathway was barely narrow enough for a large man to stand facing forward — and only just sufficient for the mules to remain afoot with all four hooves pressed close together — there was no room for privacy or modesty. Though the royals protested even more vociferously, they all ended up relieving themselves in like fashion. If you wished to survive the mountain, dignity was an unaffordable luxury, no matter who you might be. They rested on their mounts too, sitting on those high, windy, bone-chilling mountain path ridges, one misstep away from permanent sleep. Most were barely able to doze more than a few moments at a time; for all, it was a harrowing night.

By dawn of the second day, they were almost as indifferent about falling as about reaching their destination: they just wanted this nightmare on hooves to end.

It was with a great sense of relief that they came into sight of their destination.

The late morning sun illuminated it as they rounded yet another curve, all but hugging the mountainside with fingernails to aid their mounts, some of whom, at long last, now displayed signs of tiring. With bleary, sleep-deprived — yet irritably curious — eyes, they gazed, finally, upon the place that they had endured such hardship to reach.

The remote, desolate, snowcapped, stony peaks of a place so rarely visited and perpetually feared by all who had heard tell of its terrors, that none dared but whisper of it in the dark watches of the coldest winter nights.

Darkfortress.

2

The mountain fortress bore the ravages of a recent siege and assault. Toppled towers, demolished ramparts, great gouges and pits in the sides of the stony slopes themselves, all marked the terrible conflict that had been waged here not long before.

Yet despite these ravages, the keep was still magnificent. A haunted capital city of a kingdom of mountain fortresses ranging for hundreds of miles in an interweaving maze of stone and rock and black ice. Its rugged roughhewn beauty, carved from the very rock of the mountain with chiseled artistry, was an achievement to be admired. All of the travelers had heard of the great city. None had had the pleasure, dubious though it might seem at this moment, of having visited. Its very remoteness and inaccessibility was its strength. But what none of them had expected was its extraordinary beauty. Beauty of a piece with the mountains that it stood astride. Not a thing made by mortals that had been set upon this landscape, but a thing *drawn* by mortals, inch by painfully carved inch, out of the landscape itself. It was organic to the mountain, as much a part of it as these mules were to these impossibly narrow pathways. That was its true beauty.

There were fewer abuses and insults voiced during the remainder of the journey. As each hooved step took them closer to that vaulting masterpiece of stonecraft, their thoughts turned finally from the discomforts that had plagued them the past day and a half, and toward the invitation that had summoned them here.

When the visitors finally reached the sloping paved approach to the gate of Darkfortress, they heaved a sigh of relief. Some had traveled for the better part of a fortnight to reach this remote keep. Even the closest had been on the road for several days. And then the tortuous path up the mountain on the backs of the mules, to whom their rear ends now felt wedded after all these painful hours.

All swore a silent vow they would never visit this wretched place again. Some swore not-so-silently, not caring if they offended their hosts. The king of Darkfortress was just a mountain lord, after all. Not true royalty like themselves. None of the Houses they represented would ever think of making a marital alliance with him or his family.

Their guide hand-fed savories to the relieved mules and cackled merrily, shaking her head as she led them beneath the giant draw-gate. One of the travelers was so large that the instant he dismounted, his mule teetered for a moment, then fell over on its left side. The guide bent over it, fussing briefly. But the unfortunate creature was dead, its heart burst from exhaustion. The old woman remained crouched, her cackling giving way to a single silent moan. The pompous one passed her by, grinning down at her and the dead beast as he trundled past heavily. He said something to her that only she heard. Whether or not she understood his words, she did not look up immediately, but after he had gone by, she looked in the direction he had gone, and had her gaze been lethal, the pompous one would have dropped dead as suddenly as the mule.

Barely had the last of the company passed through when the gate slammed down with a boom that echoed across the mountains.

Belgarion

~

1

THE LORD OF THE Mountain Kingdoms was no hirsute savage. No doubt, he had ancestors who lived up to the reputation expected of a mountain king: great bearish hulks of men spending their lives carousing and whoring, interrupting these vital activities occasionally to wage war against anyone nearby, notorious for their brutish ways and indomitable fortresses.

But Belgarion was cut from a different stone.

The current king of Darkfortress was a handsome figure clad in a cloak of snow leopard fur that suited his catlike gait as he rose from his seat to welcome his royal guests. He was young, perhaps the youngest of them all, but then again, as they each reflected silently, he had not won his throne by challenge or war, as was the mountain custom.

He had been enthroned by none other than the liberator of Darkfortress himself: Prince Regent Vrath.

To have the backing of Vrath was to be untouchable by any and all foes. Mere knowledge that Vrath's hand was above his head was sufficient to silence any challengers to Belgarion's claim. Those few that dared to murmur dissent were pulled back by their own clans and soon grew silent, changing their murmurs to politic praises for the new One King.

The sixteen hundred mountain clans were too occupied repairing and rebuilding their own homesteads and fighting forces after the battle for Darkfortress and the debilitating occupation that had preceded it. Even the most cantankerous of them reluctantly agreed that it was no time to be fighting amongst themselves. Perhaps later, much later, when the clans had rebuilt all that had been destroyed to some semblance of its former strength, they would raise the issue again — if the One King lasted that long.

For now, Belgarion was, for the first and only time in the citadel's history, the undisputed master of Darkfortress. This young smooth-cheeked man — a boy, really, since he was barely within reach of his third decade — was set to rule with an authority that had not been enjoyed by his predecessors for ten times a thousand years.

And because of the consolidated power he represented — the sixteen hundred clans united for the first time in that long history — he was the strongest lord of the citadel that had ever sat the stone throne. Which made him a powerful man by any measure. Even ravaged and debilitated, the mountain state was a force to reckoned with, and its unassailable location itself made it impossible for any invading army to threaten — or, rather, any *mortal* army. The suscrufa summoned from the realm of urrkh to serve him had been a shocking interruption to the unassailable dominance of the clans. While they had since been sent back to their demoniac realm, everyone knew they could be summoned again were Darkfortress under threat. For mere mortal enemies, unaided by supernatural means, the stone citadel was a city which could not be broken by war.

It was this impregnable reputation and might which brought the royal travelers to Darkfortress.

Belgarion stood at the doorway of his aerie, greeting the dusty, road-weary, battered-bum arrivals as they strode haughtily in. This itself took them unawares. No king stood at the doorway of his throne room; it violated every royal protocol. They themselves would have sat on their thrones upon a high dais and loftily acknowledged their guests. To see this young fresh-faced man with the neatly cut beard and charming smile welcoming them at the vaulting doors was disarming. More than one of them returned his cheerful yet respectful greeting with a measure of warmth themselves, caught off guard. Weary though they were from the travails of the road, backs and bottoms aching from the bumpy ride up winding mountain paths, they found themselves responding to his charm and graciousness.

Perhaps it was his easy smile, clean-cut good looks, or good manners, but even the most hardened among them relented to his hospitality. Within a short time after arrival, they found themselves intrigued, even attracted, to his curious mixture of craggy but handsome mountain features and noble-folk manners.

Belgarion apologized for the customary mountain rituals of welcoming, helped them endure the small army of gaily decked women and outlandishly attired men who presented to them a seemingly infinite variety of food, drink, and entertainment.

They were washed, bathed, scented, fed, relieved, and otherwise comforted in every way available to royal mortals. They slept that night in luxuriant surroundings. A bit too much fur and stone for some tastes perhaps, but then again this was the high Mountain Kingdom, and there had just been a great occupation and siege. After the backside of a mule, it was Swarga on Arthaloka, heaven in every sense of the word. Appetites were indulged, bile was purged, intoxicants consumed, and a very pleasant night was had by all.

The company was woken the next day at dawn by the gentle pealing of a distant bell. They were given ample time to see to their individual morning needs, including the ritual sandhyavandana prayers. Purges were consumed to remove excess intoxicants, overindulged appetites were appeased by healthier consumptions, and by the time the sun had leaped the ridge of the eastern horizon to show his full brilliant face to the world, every one of the travelers was eager to meet their host and start the day.

Once again, Belgarion surprised them by visiting each one's chambers personally, inviting them to join him in the day feast room for the morning repast. Warmed by the eastern sun streaming in through apertures cut horizontally in the fortress walls, they shared a sumptuous banquet of a morning meal that earned even the pompous one's grudging approval. By the time their stomachs were full, their mouths were bursting with the question on all their tongues:

Why had they been brought here?

The handsome young mountain king took them into his own den. This, again, was unusual and defied protocol. To be welcomed and plied with all manner of comfort, to that they were accustomed. But to be invited to share a host's most intimate personal space on a first visit was unusual.

The One King of Darkfortress was an unusual man.

Belgarion shut the door of his den himself, the large wooden slab carved with the motifs and totems of his clan booming shut with a heavy finality. The ease with which he did it implied more strength than seemed likely with his compact physique. More than one of his guests reflected that he did it precisely to show off his unexpected strength.

Turning back to the gathering, he invited his guests to seat their battered backsides on furry cushions beside crackling fires and brimming flasks of mulled wine. And it was then, as the high morning light through the vaulting arches illuminated the chamber with brilliant clarity, that the gathering came to its true business.

2

Belgarion sat comfortably upon a black and red cushion embroidered with the sigil of his clan, a pitcher of wine beside him, as he gazed around at his guests. The flickering light from the large log fire beside his seat highlighted his sharp, strong features. His voice was soft but authoritative, the voice of a young man groomed to rule.

"Thank you for coming," he said. "You honor my aerie with your presence."

"You left us no choice," said a man with distinctive Far Eastern features, clad in the garb of the land that lay beyond the Redmist Mountains of the northeastern reaches of the Burnt Empire.

Belgarion acknowledged his guest with a polite nod. "I ask that we each introduce ourselves. We are somewhat informal here in the high mountains."

"Informal?" said the pompous one. "Bloody savages!"

Belgarion acknowledged the man with a patient glance but did not retort. He turned back to the first speaker.

"Anga, King of Anga," said the Northeasterner.

"My brother Anga speaks truth," said a man some years younger but a measure taller than his brother. The resemblance was unmistakable, as was the irritation creasing both their faces. "I am Vanga, King of Vanga. We are here only because you sent us each a message threatening to reveal our secrets to Vrath of Hastinaga."

A tall dark woman with a profile so precise and sharp it could have been carved from basalt, spoke in a strong voice: "I am Kaurwa, a daughter of

UPON A BURNING THRONE · 91

Kanunga. I speak for myself as well as my five brothers. We of Kanunga have no secrets. We are not intimidated by your threats."

Belgarion inclined his head respectfully, acknowledging her status. "It grieves me that you too viewed my missive as a threat."

"How else could it be interpreted?" Pundraki frowned suspiciously. "Were you not threatening to reveal our secrets to Hastinaga if we did not attend this . . . gathering? How else could that be interpreted if not a threat?"

The pompous one spluttered around a mouthful of wine, deliberately spitting it out on the luxuriant fur underfoot, right on the snarling head of the white tiger. "Don't try to dodge us with your petty wordplay. That was a threat. You sent it knowing it would force us to come to your godforsaken ass-in-the-sky pile of stone." He did not bother to introduce himself.

Belgarion spread his hands, smiling disarmingly. "It was never my desire to antagonize any of you. I apologize if the method of my summoning indicated otherwise. It is with friendship and alliance in mind that I have sent for you all."

"Alliance?" said a lean, muscled young man with the metal studdings and piercings of a yoddha, a master warrior — and the arrogance to match. "I am Vindva, prince of Keyara. What kind of alliance can the lords of the civilized world, of which Keyara is the highest in stature, possibly wish to forge with" — he pointed with his sharp jaw — "a mountain goat?" His almost colorless grey eyes threw Belgarion a mocking challenge.

Several others made similar mocking comments.

The pompous one had held his tongue while the others spoke. Despite his earlier outburst, he appeared to have no compunctions about partaking of his host's fare. This was not surprising, considering he was by far the most ample of all present. Prodigious of girth as well as height, he was only a foot shorter than the king of Virdhh, but almost as broad in the torso. The difference was that while Vriddha was all muscle, with not a gram of flab visible, the pompous one appeared to be all fat, with not an ounce of muscle visible. His entire body shook and trembled as he continued feasting, arrogantly oblivious to the fact that everyone else had finished slaking their thirsts and satiating their appetites and was staring at him. He glanced up, a meaty chop in one hand and a fistful of fruit in the other, and froze. The realization that they were all waiting for him to speak dawned over his consciousness, warring with the impulse to continue feasting.

Scowling, he gestured with the food in hand, waving the roasted chop bone at Belgarion like a weapon. "Outrageous. Unacceptable. Your insolence will not go unanswered. You may call yourself king of the mountain in this godforsaken place, but in the civilized world, we don't treat Krushan thus. *Barbarian!*"

Vriddha made a sound of disapproval. "Now you go too far, Ushanas of Ushati. To use such a term is not warranted. The mountain kings may not marry or commune with other Krushan tribes, but they are still Krushan. Even Lord Vrath of Hastinaga blesses their continuance. To call them savage barbarians unschooled in Krushan law is too much."

Ushanas tore a mouthful of meat from the chop in hand, glaring over the large haunch bone at Vriddha. "Barbarian is too good for him. King of the mountain indeed! And speaking of that Krushan you call *Lord,* he and his cowardly brother Gada huddled in their island fortress while Reygistan wrought havoc across my kingdom. Far as I'm concerned, any ally of his is no ally of mine. I intend to leave for home at once, as soon as I have refreshed and nourished myself after that wretched journey. Mules!" He spewed a mouthful of obscenities in the Ushati dialect, all apparently directed at his host. Particles of meat and fruit and other edibles spewed with the abuses. Finally he came back to his host. "I leave at first light. I need a decent night's rest. Since I am here anyway, go on then, barbarian. Spin your mountain tale and be done with it!" With that, he resumed his feasting.

Vriddha muttered something too softly to be heard but said nothing further.

Belgarion looked around at all present, giving the others a chance to speak if any still desired. It appeared that everyone there had had a chance to speak their minds. Even the menacing Druhyu was listening with narrowed eyes. Nobody objected or commented.

"Very well, then. I will start with a confession." Belgarion spread his arms wide, smiling. "It was not I who summoned you all here."

3

Belgarion continued in a genial, conversational tone as if he were discussing pleasantries with friends.

"Nor was it I who claimed to know your treasonable secrets. That too was the suggestion of my sponsor. This gathering and the proposal that will be made here is all the work of his great mind. I consider him my mentor and spiritual guide. Not only is he an emperor among kings, he is the only yoddha amongst us all who has never been defeated, either in single combat or in pitched battle. Only Vrath can match that. The two of them have never confronted one another, but were that to occur, I would place my coin squarely on my guru. I introduce him now by his title as God-Emperor of Reygistan . . . *Jarsun*."

Belgarion indicated not the door, as might be expected, but a wall.

Perfectly on cue, a figure stepped forward.

One moment there was a wall with nothing upon it except a richly detailed tapestry depicting some great ancestor of the mountain king. The next moment, an impossibly thin, tall man was standing before the tapestry, his hatchet face as familiar as feared.

Some of the gathering reacted.

All present had coins in their possession minted with the Reygistan lion seal and the profile of this same man. If indeed he could be called a man. Some believed him to be a sorcerer only partially of human origin. Others regarded him as a being from another species altogether. Such was his reputation and the legends linked to his name.

His entrance could be easily explained: the tapestry concealed a hidden doorway. Any royal residence worth its name had such secret doorways, chambers, passages, stairwells, tunnels, ingresses, and egresses.

But his presence was shocking nonetheless.

Whatever the gathering had anticipated or guessed at, this was not even a part of their wildest surmises.

Aware of their shock, reveling in it, relishing every dilated pupil staring at him, every racing heart, each mind leaping — the most dreaded man in all of the Burnt Empire looked around at the gathering without smiling.

"I know what you have done," he said.

His voice was neither deep nor sonorous, yet it carried to every last ear. His manner was not threatening or aggressive, yet his words, his face, his mere presence, struck fear into the hearts of all present.

Even the pompous Ushanas finally stopped his feasting and dropped the denuded chop bone, wiping his greasy hands on his own anga garment. Instinctively, he gestured for a servant to bring him fresh apparel to replace the soiled top garment. But of course, none came. He started to call out. It was then that Jarsun glanced in his direction, a casual, almost genial glance. Ushanas choked on his words before they could be formed. He swallowed them with the last morsels of unchewed meat, the food untasted and already turning to acid bile in his belly.

The God-Emperor of Reygistan met the startled gaze of each visitor, his impossibly thin face slashed by a razor-sharp smile. He completed his survey of the visitors and glanced at Belgarion, still ensconced on his seat. Belgarion smiled back at his guest, but even those who were farthest from him could see the tightness of his smile, the widened eyes, the fists clenching the wooden armrests of the throne. Still, he smiled and acted as a king would be expected to.

Jarsun appeared satisfied by his survey. He resumed in the same pitch as before: "I know you have sought, each in your own way, to separate yourselves from the Burnt Empire."

Again he glanced around at the visitors, this time lingering a moment longer than before; there was nothing genial about his survey this time. The smile was in his eyes, not on his lips. Each person looked upon by Jarsun felt that the God-Emperor was gazing into his or her soul, reading its innermost secrets.

Ushanas felt the hastily imbibed contents of his copious belly rumble, a familiar storm warning. Sweat popped on the pores of his wispy top hairs, rolling around the girth of his rounded face to disappear into the folds of his soiled anga garment. When it was his turn to be looked upon and into by Jarsun, he avoided meeting the God-Emperor's gaze. The gaze lingered a fraction longer on his massive bulk before moving on to the next guest. Sweat-snails raced down Ushanas's flesh.

"Did you think your treason would go unnoticed?" Jarsun asked. His voice dropped at the end of the question, instead of rising, turning it into a declaration of simple truth. Ushanas quivered. Others in the chamber sat so still, the entire assemblage could be mistaken for a diorama of statuary.

Jarsun stepped forward, stalking the aerie on silent feet, bridging the distance between himself and the guests of Belgarion. There was a jungle-like menace in his motion, the sense of a predator marking his territory.

"Vrath sees all, knows all," he went on. "What knowledge is not gleaned from hearsay, he gains from simple observation."

He paused momentarily before each ruler, addressing them each in turn. The first were the Northeasterners King Anga and his brother King Vanga. "Redmist bandits waylaid your tithe due to Hastinaga last summer?" Jarsun smiled his thin smile. "Vrath knows that the bandits ply their pillage under your protection and would never touch the tithe wagon."

The brothers glanced at one another, eyes hot with temper, but kept themselves in check. They had the legendary swift rage of the Northeast, but also the wisdom. They cast their gazes downward, not meeting the eyes of the God-Emperor.

Jarsun stopped before Kaurwa. The Kanungan displayed no emotion as she gazed coolly back. "A sea storm delayed the arrival of the Grekos trade ships?" he asked, then tch-tched sympathetically. "Hastinaga spies sighted them sailing homeward. They could hardly have made the hundred-day voyage only to have turned back *without* bartering their cargo at Kanunga port."

The Kanungan's cheeks flushed the shade of rotten fruit beneath her dark skin. She looked away. Jarsun moved on.

Sumhasana's face was lowered as if to conceal his gaze from the Reygistani. Only his boxy bulk, flaming red beard, and bald head were visible: the bald head gleamed with perspiration. Not the flowing rivulets of Ushanas, but a light misting that suggested nervousness.

"Sumhasana," Jarsun said. "Are your fists missing the comfort of cold vengeance?" Without waiting for an answer, he went on. "Or are they longing for the cold weight of gold? The rich vein of old gold that Sumha unearthed almost by accident deep within an overworked mine far beneath the bowels of Great Dwarf?"

Jarsun continued in this manner, listing the treasonous secrets of each of the conspirators. By the time he was done, every face was flushed with anger, embarrassment, shame, or guilt, some with all of the above.

Finally, Jarsun stopped before the last guest. The quivering wobbling mountain of a man was already in motion even before the Reygistani turned his attention.

It was remarkable to watch that prodigious bulk move with such speed.

In mere moments, Ushanas of Ushati had reached the door of the chamber. He threw arms as meaty as the haunch bone on which he had gnawed earlier, striking the strong timber.

"Let me out, let me out!" he cried in a shrill, hysterical voice. "I wish to leave at once! *Open these doors!*"

The doors remained sealed.

Ushanas turned to Belgarion, his several chins quivering with outrage. "Mountain goat! Oaf! I command you to open these doors at once! How dare you imprison us? Do you know who I am? I am Ushanas of Ushati! I have enough wealth to buy anyone in this room ten times over! I am the wealthiest merchant-king in the Burnt Empire. Open these doors at once, or I will see to it that nobody trades with the Mountain Kingdoms for the next thousand years. You inbreeding goats who call yourselves kings!"

Belgarion's face revealed its first trace of displeasure. The ruler of Darkfortress turned to look at Jarsun, who was standing in the center of the chamber, watching the performance with his thin head cocked to one side.

Jarsun smiled at Belgarion, who grimaced once, in the semblance of a response. Something passed between them that did not require words to be understood. Belgarion nodded once, but kept his eyes lowered and his head averted, studiously ignoring Ushani and everything that transpired thereafter. His aspect made it clear that even though this was his aerie and his kingdom to command, he deferred to Jarsun. Had any one of those gathered in that chamber needed any confirmation, that one silent exchange between the Reygistani and the king of Darkfortress made their relationship crystal clear.

Jarsun began walking with slow deliberate steps toward the Ushati king. "Ushanas of Ushati."

The quivering mass that was the "wealthiest merchant-king in the Burnt Empire" turned hesitantly, reluctantly, agonizingly, to look at the approaching Jarsun.

"Had you chosen to ignore the invitation to come here and taken your chances with Vrath and the might of Hastinaga, that would have been your right."

Jarsun was some twenty yards from the doors before which Ushanas stood in quivering fear.

"Had you turned back at any time during your arduous journey up the mountains, that too would have been your choice."

Ten yards now, and closing.

"Had you paid your respects to your host during the introductions being made, partaken of some refreshment, and started back before the doors were sealed, that too might have been acceptable."

Jarsun paused some five yards away, cocked his head, reconsidered.

"Perhaps not then, that might have been too late, but it was still a possibility, if a dim one."

Jarsun looked at the Ushati king.

"But to hear our entire plan, to listen to all I had to say, to hear me hint with sufficient detail at the secrets of your fellow conspirators gathered here to provide you with fodder enough to feed the hungry ears of Hastinaga spies, to eat our host's feast, to guzzle his wine, to partake of his hospitality and our fine company, and then to act thus. Demanding. Abusing. Insulting."

Jarsun shook his head from side to side.

"Unacceptable."

Ushanas appeared to be melting with terror and sweat. His face shivered as rivulets poured down. Stray morsels of food stuck to his chin and cheeks were dislodged by the streaming perspiration and fell to the floor, a tiny pile of food crumbs in a growing puddle of sweat. "I heard nothing!" he screeched. "I know nothing of your plans against Hastinaga! I have no knowledge of your stupid secrets. Let me go. I will not say a word to Vrath. I am not a fool, you idiots!"

Jarsun tch-tched, wagging his long index finger.

"In that case, allow me to enlighten you. We are gathered here today for one reason and one reason only. To discuss our mutual interest in ridding ourselves of the Krushan dynasty and dividing up the wealth and territories of the Burnt Empire amongst ourselves. That much was obvious from the time you received the message. Otherwise, why would any of you have come at all? Even an idiot or" — Jarsun chuckled — "a mountain goat would know that merely to respond to such an invitation would be regarded as a treasonous act against the Burning Throne."

Ushanas shook his head. "No. NO! I know nothing of any conspiracy. I am not part of any treason. Let me go. I will never speak of this as long as I live."

Jarsun smiled his slash-mouth smile. Even though the others could not see his face now, as he was standing with his back to them all, facing the door, every last one of them shuddered or reacted with something less than pleasure at the thought of that horrible smile.

"At last, you speak the truth," Jarsun said. "You will never speak of this as long as you live. Because you will not live long enough to speak any more."

And before Ushanas could speak another word, Jarsun moved.

With a flash, his body split. Like a wood chip struck by a powerful downward axe stroke, Jarsun's body divided down the middle. The two halves separated from each other with a sticky unguent tearing, producing a sound like that of live flesh being ripped apart. The twin sections, still living, stood momentarily, each as steady on its single foot as any man on two.

Had Jarsun been a man cleaved by a razor-sharp axe stroke, it would have been a feat to rival the tales told by Sumhasana Longaxe's ancestors. Had he indeed been sliced into halves, the inner part of each half would have oozed and bled, blood and flesh and inner organs visible.

But Jarsun was no man.

He was in fact, two men — named Jarsa and Sunna — that chose to unite and exist as one. If you could call such creatures *men*.

Each half now stood individually.

Not on feet, for these creatures, this *being*, had no feet in the mortal sense.

Each stood on a base that was fluid and mutable, coiling and uncoiling as it prepared to make its next move.

The effect was not unlike that of two snakes, pythons perhaps, standing upright prior to a strike.

However, it would be a mistake to term these creatures, this being, a snake, or anything allied to the snake family.

It was far, far older than any serpent that had swum through the primordial ooze on this world.

And far deadlier.

The exact features and limbs of each part was not clearly visible to those gathered in the aerie, for Jarsun had his back to them all and was facing the door where Ushanas of Ushati still stood, cowering and relieving himself involuntarily of his bodily fluids, the yellow stain spreading under his massive tree-trunk-like feet.

The only one who could have seen what the two divided beings looked like from the front was King Belgarion, and he was studiously examining at the pattern on the floor of his own aerie. Only the tenseness of his features and the tautness of his hunched shoulders suggested his own state of . . . fear?

Terror, more likely.

The two creatures coiled into themselves for a brief kshana, not like any snake anyone had ever seen. Their flesh seemed to grow tighter, condensing, pressing into itself. Like a muscle tightening.

Then, with a motion as sudden as a whiplash, each half *flew* across the distance that separated Jarsun from Ushanas.

Both halves of the Reygistani's body snapped around Ushanas's considerable bulk.

There was nothing snakelike about this motion either.

It was as sharply executed as the winding of a lash around its target.

Ushanas screamed, entwined by this unthinkable *thing*.

His fat, rolling face was striped diagonally in both directions by the two halves of Jarsun.

The effect was like two thick pythons had coiled around the man's corpulent body in a criss-cross diagonal pattern.

And like two thick pythons, both halves now tightened themselves with unimaginable force.

Parts of Ushanas's flesh bulged from the gaps between the diagonal strips.

The Ushati king made one final attempt to scream, but even the last breath had already been squeezed out of his body.

Then, with a suddenness that was shocking to all present, despite their familiarity with the many forms in which death acted on a battlefield, the Ushati's body simply . . .

Exploded.

It disintegrated into a hundred chunks of bone, flesh, organs, blood.

Like the morsels of meat Ushanas himself had been tearing apart earlier.

It was all over in a flash of a whipcrack and a breath.

What lay on the ground before the doors of the aerie was no longer a man, or even a semblance of a man.

It was a scattering of morsels and chunks of raw flesh, in a puddle of gore.

The dismantling of the Ushati king took barely a few kshanas.

Belgarion still kept his eyes downcast and head averted.

Perhaps the mountain king had viewed similar actions by the Reygistani before, and had no desire to view it again.

Like a whiplash returning to its wielder, the two sinuous halves flew back through the air to the spot where Jarsun had been standing.

Each half merged seamlessly with the other, the joining taking place in a single motion. Like clay pressed into clay, merging to form a single piece, seemingly inseparable and unitary.

Jarsun turned around to face the gathering, his smile slashing his face like a knife cut. Was it their imagination, or were his lips redder than before?

"Now," Jarsun said, "I shall tell you how I intend to destroy the Krushan dynasty and take Hastinaga."

He paused and looked again at each one in turn individually. "Unless anyone else has an objection?"

There were none.

Crow

~

CROW SAT UPON A window.

The window's chamber was large by mortal standards, but by Crow standards, all chambers were small, since Crow's home was the world entire, her roof the endless sky.

Crow had no interest in the goings-on within the chamber.

She knew there were mortals there, she could see them, arrayed like a murder of crows, keeping distance between them as if in anticipation of a quarrel. Had Crow been curious, Crow might have wondered if there was a pecking order among mortals, and if that mortal sitting on the larger perch at one end of the tiny chamber (tiny to Crow's sky-accustomed eyes) might be the leader. But there was also another mortal standing near the one on the large perch, and all the other mortals seemed to be staring at this standing mortal. Perhaps the standing mortal was the leader. He looked hawkish enough to rip them to shreds should they question his leadership.

None of this actually interested Crow.

What did interest Crow was the thing the standing mortal had just done.

He had pounced, hawklike, upon another much fatter mortal. And torn that mortal to shreds.

Crow could not quite understand how the standing mortal had done this: he appeared to have no claws or beak. But Crow had seen the standing mortal split into two sinuous halves, and each half had then *flown* through the air to attack the fatter mortal.

Now, that had been a sight worth seeing.

Crow was a bird; birds feared serpents more than anything else, even other birds. Crow had seen serpents kill crows. They moved and killed in a similar manner. Some swallowed their prey whole from the beak, or whatever it was that serpents' mouths were called in their language. But other serpents wound their slimy sinuous bodies *around* their prey and squeezed them to death. Crow had seen this done too, once to a field mouse and twice to rabbits. After the prey was squeezed to death, *then* the squeezing serpents had uncoiled themselves and swallowed them through their beaks/mouths.

But this mortal had not swallowed the prey.

Crow could still see the remains of the fatter mortal, not simply choked and crushed to death like the field mouse and the rabbit had been. The fatter mortal was not merely crushed to death. It was . . .

Destroyed. Torn apart. Shredded. Like the remains after a cat attacked a pigeon.

Looking at the remains, Crow began salivating.

The thought of that tasty feast was what kept her here, on this window. Waiting. Watching.

Just a morsel. Or a chunk. That nice big juicy red chunk right there, with just a bit of white gristle and yellow fat, and oh my, Lord of Birds, a bit of broken bone with pink marrow peeking out.

Crow wanted that chunk.

But Crow was frightened of the standing mortal. The one who had killed the fatter one and turned him into a mess of shredded chunks.

Oh my, Lord of Birds, that mortal was a scary one. He could split himself into two, turn from a mortal into a kind of serpent — a *pair* of serpents — and move like no serpent Crow had seen before, then tear his prey apart like a hawk, or a cat, or some combination of bird-snake-animal that could not possibly exist, and then simply *leave* the prey. Not even eat it or carry it off to eat later.

What arrogance. What waste. What terror.

Crow could not comprehend such behavior. Or such a creature.

But that did not matter.

There were many things in this world Crow did not comprehend.

This was not something that kept Crow awake at nights.

All that mattered was that juicy chunk of flesh.

And how to get it without incurring the wrath of that scary man-animal-bird-thing.

Crow saw a flock of her fellows fly past in a ragged formation, part of the murder to which she belonged.

She would usually have cawed to attract their attention. The more crows stealing morsels, the better a chance she would have of getting her feast. Always better to steal from another bird, even another crow, than to steal from other animals or mortals. It was a challenge, and if she succeeded, as she often did, it made the food taste better.

But this was not a crow feast.

This was serious, a matter that required Crow to forgo a tasty opportunity and do something other than scavenge.

So she did not caw.

Instead, she waited.

Inside the chamber, the man-animal-bird-thing continued to caw at the other mortals. Or whatever it was that mortals called cawing.

The cawing continued.

Crow watched as the day wore on.

The sun reached its apex then began its downward slide.

Crow waited.

Crow watched.

Crow did not caw.

The afternoon wore on. Crow began to tire.

Crow dozed for a bit, a kind of awake dozing that only crows did to overcome tiredness. Crow even had a term for it in Crow's language: a crow nap.

Crow watched with semi-interest as pigeons mated on the stone battlements of the mortal structure. The pigeons were vaguely nervous because Crow was watching, but went ahead and did it anyway. Thrice. Shameless. But they were pigeons, what did Crow expect? Not civilized, like crows.

Then, when Crow was starting to feel the pangs of hunger gnaw her belly, the mortals all rose up suddenly and exited the chamber.

In moments, they had all flown the coop.

The chamber was empty.

Only the remains of the dead mortal lay where they had lain the past few hours.

The blood was now congealed, the flesh too, but that didn't matter to Crow. If anything, a little time made food riper, tastier. It was seasoning for the feast.

Crow watched as other mortals began to peer into the chamber, pointing at the remains of the dead mortal and cawing to one another. Crow knew that mortals usually liked to clean up fallen food and cart it away, to be thrown out. Such a criminal waste! But mortal waste was what supplied Crow's feasts. Crow knew that once the mortals carted away the remains of the dead mortal, she might not find them again easily. She would have to search all over again.

Her best chance was to snatch it now and fly.

She saw her chance when the mortals left the room, no doubt to bring back objects suitable for carting away fallen remains.

Crow hopped down from the window to the stone floor of the chamber.

Crow hopped quickly across the floor, all the way to the remains.

My, Lord of Birds, they did smell delicious.

Crow looked about quickly, craftily, wary of being seen by a mortal.

Or worse, being seen by a cat.

Dogs were not a problem, silly funny creatures that cawed loudly but could never catch a crow.

But cat? Oh my, Lord of Birds. Cats were deadly.

Not as deadly as hawks, or serpents, or, above all, the mortal who could turn into a snake-animal-bird-thing.

But still deadly enough.

Crow stood still and waited for several long moments, making certain that no enemy was present and close by.

When Crow was certain the coast was clear, Crow pounced.

In a flash, Crow had the morsel in her mouth and was flying across the chamber, through the window, and out, out, out to freedom, away from the mortal house, across the mountains, and as far as she could get from that scary man-animal-bird-thing.

The chunk was heavy, and usually Crow would have stopped and rested on one of the windows or ledges, shooing away those silly pigeons, perhaps even have tasted a bite or two of the delicious flesh. Easier to carry in Crow's belly than in Crow's beak.

But so frightened was Crow of the man-animal-bird-thing that Crow didn't stop until she had flown clear across the valley and the river that ran through it.

A drop fell from Crow's mouth on the way; it hardly mattered. It was not Crow's job to clean.

Crow didn't slow until she was across the valley and in the safety of a grove she knew well. She had been birthed in this grove, and it was always the place she felt safest.

She perched upon a high branch and examined the morsel briefly before tearing into it with great enjoyment.

Oh my, Lord of Birds, mortal flesh was tasty flesh! Where could she get some of this every day? Oh my. Oh my.

Crow raised her head high and cawed happily, not caring if any of her murder heard her now.

Crow lowered her black head and feasted.

Jeel

~

RIVER FELT A DROP.

It was a single drop, fallen from the beak of a passing crow.

That was common enough.

What was unusual was that the drop was human blood.

River disliked human blood, or blood of any kind.

River tasted her share of blood, mortal and otherwise, especially during times of mortal war. Which seemed to be almost always. Sometimes, it came in great quantities.

At those times, she avoided tasting it as best as she could manage. Too much pain, anguish, rage still lingering in that blood.

But it had been days — perhaps weeks or even months, for River did not measure time as mortals did — since she had tasted any mortal blood. And a single drop was unusual. So when this drop fell, she couldn't help but taste it idly.

It intrigued her.

There was information in this blood, something of import. Something new. Something frightening.

She would convey it to her Mother. Not merely *her* mother.

Mother of all Rivers, all water on Arthaloka.

Jeel.

She encased the drop in a bubble and put the bubble into the mouth of a fish.

Fish swallowed the bubble, which did not burst inside its mouth because River had made it impossible to open except by Jeel.

The bubble went into Fish's stomach, where it remained as solid as a swallowed pearl.

River pushed Fish up to her surface as a flock of cranes flew by.

Sure enough, one of them swooped down greedily and snatched up Fish.

River caught hold of Crane's tail.

Crane gave a cry of alarm, dropping Fish.

Fish plopped back into River.

River spoke to Crane, telling him her errand.

Crane listened, wide-eyed, and did not argue.

Crane gathered Fish in his beak and flew away.

Over fields and forests and hills and valleys.

Until Crane came to another smaller river, a tributary of Mother River.

Crane dropped Fish into Smaller River, passing on River's message.

Smaller River carried Fish dutifully, passing Fish up through several other tributaries, streams, rivulets, until Fish was conveyed finally to Mother River herself.

Jeel examined Fish, removed the bubble from Fish's belly. (A simple burp was sufficient to accomplish this.) Jeel burst the bubble and tasted the drop of mortal blood carefully.

Jeel neither liked nor disliked mortal blood. Part of her Krushan law was to absorb the mortal remains of all those who cast them into her waters. To cleanse and recirculate them.

She knew how to read a mortal body and its secrets as well as a saptarishi could read a Krushan scroll.

Jeel read the entirety of the information contained in that drop of mortal blood.

When she was done, she knew what she had to do with the information.

She had to go to her son and warn him.

Vessa

~

IN THE DEEP FOREST, Vessa opened his third eye.

The jungle pulsed crimson.

Every tree, trunk, branch, leaf, appeared to be suffused with the opposite of its natural verdancy.

It was as if the green blood within their veins had turned red.

A disturbance agitated the forest, coming from nowhere and going no place. It was not produced by wind or any natural force. It was the agitation of the forest itself, expressing its fear.

It shook the high trees, caused the great trunks to shudder, made insects scurry out from their crannies, filling the air with a sense of chaos and terror.

Vessa's long white beard rippled.

He smelled the fear of the forest.

It was also the fear of She Who Birthed All Forests.

She spoke to him in agitated voices of wind, leaf, insect, animal, all the beings under her protection and in her care.

Vessa listened.

Yes, Mother, he said. *I felt it too. The Twice Born is at work.*

She said more to him, which he heard patiently.

He is growing powerful, Vessa admitted. *And will grow stronger yet as time passes. But it is not yet time to confront him.*

Trees swayed without wind, branches bent with no hand forcing them, leaves shirred of their own accord.

The forest spoke to Vessa.

He listened.

But each time his answer was the same.

Not yet, Mother. It is not yet time.

The forest asked one final urgent query.

Vessa mused on it a kshana or two.

When the Five are born, he said. *Until then, we must endure. It is all we can do.*

The forest stopped its agitation and was still for a moment. Then, with a single keening voice, it sang a song of sorrow and hope.

It was a song not meant for mortal ears. Even Vessa did not comprehend its entire meaning. But he understood its emotion:

The Great Mother of the Forest, of *all* forests, of Arthaloka itself, was crying out for help.

Vessa listened for a great length of time. Eventually, he gave in reluctantly. *Perhaps there is a way. Perhaps.*

The forest cried out in hopeful excitement.

Vessa sighed.

If Light and Dark unite. It is the only way. But, he cautioned firmly, *it is nigh impossible.*

The forest waited, shirring, pleading.

Vessa rose to his feet, took up his staff, and draped his anga garment over his arm.

Very well, Great Mother. I shall make an attempt. I shall go to Hastinaga.

He walked out of the hut, across the clearing, and into the dark woods.

Jilana

~

SOMETIMES JILANA THOUGHT THAT being a dowager empress was easier than being a mother-in-law. *Anything* was easier.

Seated on a comfortable cushion in a silk merchant's tent, she tried to get some relief from the heat by sipping a cooling drink while her attendants fanned her, as she watched her two daughters-in-law arguing over a length of silk.

Ember and Umber were pretty girls. Beautiful even, if one liked coy, petite girls with the bodies of women and the brains of sparrows. Jilana herself appreciated women who had some substance to them, both physically and mentally. But then, these two were princesses, and little more than that. What could one expect from the products of entitlement and royal privilege?

Jilana herself had worked her hands raw as a young girl. First as a fisher, treated no differently than the other village children, all of whom were expected to earn their daily meals. It mattered not a whit that her father was the chief of the entire tribe. Fisher King to outsiders, but plain fisherman to his family. He worked hard alongside his people, cutting himself no slack. He believed that work defined a person. Not just fishing, anything one did to ensure one's survival. Anything that made one useful to one's family, one's people, the world in general. To old Chief Jael, doing a job that mattered, doing it as well as it could possibly be done, and doing it for as long as one could do it, until the fishes ate your eyes, that was the only purpose to existence. That was the way of the fisherfolk and had always been, since the Jeel had descended to Arthaloka from Shaiva's hair.

Even when Sha'ant, king of Hastinaga, had first met Jilana, she had been working, ferrying travelers across the Jeel. The king of the greatest empire in the world, attracted to a fisherman's daughter!

She had once asked Sha'ant teasingly, years later, "Did you want to bed me because of my strong limbs and supple rowing? Because you had never had a fishergirl before?" He had surprised her by replying, "I wanted you as my wife, because I wanted a wife who was *someone*. More than just a daughter, a sister, a wife. A person in her own right. Watching you work, the pride you took in your ferrying, the way you spoke of your people, of what they did, pointing out the children doing the baiting of the nets as you had once done in younger days, I saw that woman. You had a life, an identity, a job that mattered, not only to you, but a real task, something that affected people, helped people, enabled them, added value to their lives. That was why I fell in love with you." He then added, teasing, "It was only *much* later that I even felt any urge to bed you." She had exclaimed, "Oh, really!" and slapped away his probing hand — but almost immediately, she had caught the same hand and put it back where it had been.

She sighed now, handing off the half-consumed beverage to an attendant. It was refreshing, but no drink could slake the thirst she felt inside, the parched heart she carried within. She *missed* Sha'ant. She missed him as much now as she had the day he had died. Not just his probing hand and sly wit, but his authority, his wisdom, his keen insight, deep knowledge of people and cultures, and above all, his uncanny ability to immediately know what the cause of a problem was, and his ability to then divine a solution.

She wished he was here now.

She had no ill wish for either of her daughters-in-law — well, nothing that she would ever act on at least.

But sometimes they could be so, *so* tiresome.

Now, for instance.

Here they were, in a traveling bazaar that set up its tents once every year or two in Hastinaga, conditions permitting. The bazaar was made up of merchants who traveled the length of the Masala Marg from one end to the other, endlessly. A polymorphous collection of men and women of all races, colors, creeds, cultures, they spent their entire existence traversing the rough route along which the civilized world sent its spices — masala, as it was colloquially known in the capital of the civilized world — silks, trinkets, and salable items of every description. They bought, they sold, they traded.

Sometimes, they stopped while on their way back from the West, en route to the East. Other years, they stopped on the way from the East to the West. It depended on what they had to offer and where they thought those items would fetch the highest prices.

This time they were traveling from West to East. Which was why they were almost out of silk. Silk came from the East and went West, where the lesser civilized kingdoms considered it to be a marvel or a miracle, depending on the culture and belief system. By the time the traveling bazaar returned from the West on its way to the East, all the silks were sold, and sold for small fortunes.

The only reason they had any silk left at all was because Jilana's daughters-in-law had given standing orders to bring them silks each visit. The merchants complied more out of fear than greed. Any price Jilana offered could easily be matched by the kings and queens of Western kingdoms. But the might and power of the Burnt Empire could not be matched.

And so indeed the merchants did comply this time as well. The problem was, they had only a single bolt of silk left.

It was exquisite stuff, the red of sealing wax, that deep rich shade that the Easterners achieved so brilliantly. The fabric felt like an upseer's wings between Jilana's fingers, the individual grains distinguishable to the touch. So diaphanous that she could see the whorls of her own fingerpads through the cloth. It was material to be caressed, desired, worn with abandon, the touch of it like a baby's breath on one's skin, the sensation as delicate and ethereal as the first cool touch of the Jeel when young Jilana had plunged in on a hot afternoon after a long day's work.

It was the most sensuous thing she had ever felt. It would look beautiful on any woman, and both Ember and Umber should be ecstatic to have it.

Instead, they were fighting.

Because there was only one bolt of red silk. And each wanted it for herself. Exclusively.

Jilana had already suggested that they could both make garments out of the material. There was enough, considering these young ones barely used much anyway.

But neither wanted to wear the same thing that her sister would wear.

Naturally.

Jilana sighed.

Her daughters-in-law argued on.

The afternoon grew hotter.

The bazaar busier.

The air dustier.

The bickering louder.

And she thought, for the thousandth time since the daughters of Serapi had come to her, that being a dowager empress was easier than being a mother-in-law.

Especially this day.

Jilana turned and saw the merchant standing beside her. He was a kindly fair-skinned middle-aged man with the high cheekbones and epicanthic folds above his eyes that were characteristic of Far Easterners.

He bowed, speaking softly.

She frowned and looked at him. "Here?"

He inclined his head, indicating the rear of the tent.

Jilana looked back, but all she could see was a partition separating the public area of the tent where all the goods were displayed from the merchant's private space at the back.

She looked at the merchant again, quizzically. He inclined his head again. Jilana frowned.

This was quite unusual. It occurred to her that she was a target for enemies of the Burnt Empire, and that this could well be some kind of ploy.

She glanced at her guards, indicating the rear as the merchant had. They went at once, returning with surprising quickness to bow their heads and confirm that there was no danger.

Jilana stood and accompanied them to the rear of the tent.

One of her attendants held up the fold of the partition so she could pass into the private area. Her guards took up unobtrusive positions to grant her some privacy.

She saw the person waiting for her.

Jilana's face crinkled with a smile that lit up her entire middle-aged face, a smile that only appeared for one person in the whole world: her son.

"Mother." Vessa bent his wild-haired head and touched his mother's feet.

Jilana touched her son's head, offering the ritual maternal blessing. She let her hand linger a moment, feeling her heart stir with a long-dormant emotion. She had never been able to raise Vessa as a mother usually raised a child. That was because of his supernatural nature: though born as normally as any mortal babe, he had matured to adulthood within the space of a few hours, before her awestruck eyes.

She had always been aware of his extraordinary powers and abilities. But somewhere within her heart, there still remained the secret yearning to have nursed her babe, nurtured, guided him on his first steps, gone through all the miraculous stages of growth and maturation. Vessa was a supernatural being, fathered by a great mage and endowed at birth with powerful magic, but Jilana was just a normal woman, a mother who had never had the satisfaction to watch her own firstborn child grow as mortal children grew.

She buried her long-dormant desires, with an expertise born of years of self-control. "It must be important, for you to leave your meditation and come here thus."

"It is, Mother," Vessa said. "I have a message of great urgency to deliver."

Vrath

~

VRATH WAS BORED.

The court of Hastinaga was not officially in session. An official session would have required the presence of Dowager Empress Jilana. This was simply a conference of the kingdom's ministers regarding sundry matters. The majority of these matters concerned administrative and procedural issues. The hows and whys of the actual business of political governance. There was a time when Vrath would have sought an excuse, *any* excuse, to recuse himself from such a conference. Such things bored him at best, infuriated him at worst. What was the point of making up endless rules and byrules for every single thing? Why not simply use one's judgment as each matter arose?

He knew the answer: a king overlooking a small kingdom could afford to be autocratic. A large kingdom like Hastinaga could not be overseen by any one man, even a man as omnipresent and sleepless as Vrath. And the Burnt Empire was a hundred times — nay, a hundred times a hundred — the size of an average kingdom. It required a small army of administrative staff just to keep pace with the endless procedural, diplomatic, and trade oversight matters that cropped up on a daily basis. Each of those many departments themselves required oversight, by a competent *honest* minister, and each minister had questions, doubts, problems, challenges, that needed to be answered and dealt with on a regular basis. For the entire empire to function smoothly — or as smoothly as any large juggernaut could manage — it required a system. Checks and balances. Protocols. Procedures. Rules. Byrules.

Which meant conferences like this one. Someone had to oversee these overseers and ensure that nobody amongst them or farther down the line was attempting to get rich at the empire's expense. Or worse.

And because Vrath was the prince regent of the empire, this onerous responsibility was his burden. Dowager Empress Jilana was an important symbol of the late emperor Sha'ant's rule, especially since Vrath had sworn a life vow to never himself sit on the Burning Throne. Her presence authorized every court session as law, even if she didn't speak a word, as was often the case. The actual burden of governance fell on Vrath's broad shoulders.

After decades of enduring such sessions, he had come to accept it as his lot. It didn't make these conferences any easier, or less tedious. But it helped him restrain himself from reacting to every irritating debate over irrelevant matters of protocol. Like the present debate over whether a feather-hatted emissary of a foreign kingdom with a title that had no correspondent in the Burnt Empire should be met by a minister, a secretary, a clerk, an ambassador, or even, as one bright spark suggested, a *courtesan*.

This last was presumably suggested as a way of eliminating any possibility of giving offense and providing a warm friendly welcome at the same time. Did these idiots even remember that he was a sworn celibate? Could they be deliberately dragging out the discussion *because* he was a celibate? He dismissed the thought at once. Fools they might be, but not foolish enough to risk angering him.

Vrath was listening to this bizarre and quite pointless debate with the growing suspicion that his ministers were deliberately prolonging the discussion because of its greater entertainment value rather than because it genuinely merited such a long discussion, when he felt the change.

It began as a rippling in the air. The scent of lotuses. The cool breath of the glacier that birthed her.

The far wall of the sabha hall, fifty times the height of a man, shimmered and dissolved like vapor.

Like a tidal wave, Jeel burst through the high wall and into the great chamber.

The great river roared into the heart of Hastinaga, raging torrentially across the throne room, washing over the royal dais and disappearing behind it. The Burning Throne, simmering with its usual banked red glow when a Krushan liege was not seated upon it, hissed and gave off a cloud of steam that was instantly suppressed by the rushing torrent.

The ministers, the guards, the assorted palace staff and servers, all remained unaffected, as if they noticed nothing amiss. This was a sight meant only for Vrath, not intended for mere mortal eyes.

As Vrath watched, the cascading water sculpted itself into the shape of a mortal woman. The shape coalesced into a liquid statue. The statue of living water glistened and gleamed wetly in the afternoon sunshine as it stepped on the royal dais.

Jeel, clad in a garment of shimmering translucent white, touched the back of the Burning Throne with fingertips formed of water. Droplets coalesced on the glistening stone and remained there, a divine blessing.

Vrath went at once to her, bending to touch his mother's feet. "Mother."

"Vrath. I have grave news for you."

Jilana

⌒

1

VRATH AND JILANA MET shortly before midnight.

They were the only ones present, by mutual decision. Vrath shut the doors to the throne room behind himself, securing it to ensure that nobody entered, even at this late hour. The torches burned low in their sconces. The rows of empty chairs, the dais with empty thrones, the deserted hall with row upon row of polished pillars, all served as reminders that they were completely, unquestionably, alone. Whatever decision was made tonight, it would have to be made by the two of them and none else. There was no question of bringing this before the Council, the ministers, or even discussing it in open court.

"Do we know who the conspirators are?" Jilana asked, seating herself not on her throne but upon the nearest convenient seat. Vrath continued to pace restlessly along the length of the approach to the throne dais.

"Belgarion, the One King of the united Mountain Kingdoms, hosted them at his palace in Darkfortress. Those in attendance were Anga, king of Anga; Vanga, king of Vanga; Kaurwa of Kanunga; Sumhasana of Sumha; Pundraki of Pundar; Vindva, prince of Keyara; Vriddha, king of Virdhh; Karta Mara; Ripunjaya of Avant; Drashya of Dirda; Druhyu of Druhyu; Shastra of Longriders; Ushanas of Ushati." He paused and looked at her with an unusual show of emotion. "And Baal."

Jilana sucked in a deep breath. "But the Bahlikas are —"

"Blood kin to me, yes," he said. "Nevertheless, they were present as well."

"Ushanas of Ushati was killed. That eliminates him from the list."

"Yes, but his successors, whichever of his sons or daughters it is, will very likely fall into line. The execution of their father and king is a powerful motivator."

Jilana shook her head slowly. "The audacity of these kingdoms. How dare they even contemplate going up against the might of Hastinaga?"

"Contemplation is one thing. I don't care if they *contemplate* open rebellion or worse from now till the end of time. It is forming an actual alliance against us that rankles. This cannot be allowed to stand, Mother. If word gets out that some of our most powerful kingdoms have allied against us, who knows how many others will join with them. At least a dozen that I can name. And several dozen more smaller kingdoms will rush to join in as well, if only to ensure that they back the winning side."

Jilana frowned. "Are you not overstating the danger? Strong as this alliance seems, these kingdoms you named could not possibly field a host to match our own Krushan armies. Besides, we have many allies that we know we can count on if such a situation arises. Together, we will easily outnumber the forces of this alliance."

"So you would think," he said, "but you are forgetting one more conspirator. The ringleader himself: Jarsun of Reygistan. It was he who summoned these fence-sitters to Darkfortress. His own Reygistani forces are almost two-thirds of our own. Combined with those of the alliance, that would give them an armed force twice the size of our army, and even more than the combined forces of our allies."

Jilana clutched the solid band of gold that ringed her throat, as if feeling the metal noose tighten. "That is a formidable alliance. I cannot deny that. But even so, we can still prevail in an open battle. Hastinaga will always prevail with you leading our armies, Vrath. No force can withstand you in battle. However strong their armies may be, whatever their numbers, they lack our secret weapon: you. You yourself are an army unto yourself. You balance all ledgers and tip the odds in our favor."

Vrath shook his head sadly. "I am flattered by your faith in me, Mother. But even I cannot be in a dozen places at once."

"What do you mean?"

"I have studied Jarsun of Reygistan's battle strategy for years. He does not engage in pitched battles except on rare occasions — usually when his numbers far outreach those of his enemy and victory is certain. Instead, he divides and conquers. He has not summoned an open council to appeal to these kingdoms. He has summoned them in private, and used force and intimidation — even murder — to press his will upon them. He means to use each one's individual strength against us. He will fight a war of attrition, attacking us on all sides at once, over and over again, until the garment that is the Burnt Empire is shredded with holes and rips. Only then, when he sees the opportunity, will he throw all his forces against us in battle, and finish what his allies began."

Jilana sat without speaking for several moments, absorbing Vrath's words. "Then we will fight him on those terms. We will divide and defend. We will use our allies to counteract his allies, fighting them one-on-one, on as many fronts as he chooses to open. Better yet, we shall go on the offensive and attack him as well. We shall rip the fabric of his own empire to shreds. And when we see fit, we shall attack Reygistan openly, crushing it without mercy. We are not merely another of the thousand and eight kingdoms. We are Hastinaga. We have overcome tyrants and despots, invasions and upris-ings by the hundreds. We shall overcome these challenges as well. We shall prevail."

"Your strategy is shrewd, your spirit indomitable," Vrath said. "But I still fear it will not be sufficient, Mother. There is a risk to being the aggressor. Jarsun will use our own allies against us as proxies. He will not show his own hand until much later in the game. By pitting us against our allies, he makes it difficult for us to retaliate or to take the aggressive stance. Each enemy we crush is an ally lost, and it demoralizes our other allies as well. Already, I am given information that there are rumors spreading across the empire."

"Rumors of this rebel alliance?"

"No. Rumors of our wrongdoings. Of atrocities committed in the name of Hastinaga. Of tyranny and oppression in Hastinaga. Of slavery. Abuse. Genocide. Assassinations by our hand."

Jilana clutched her choker tighter. "I do not follow. These are all untrue. What purpose does it serve anyone to spread such vile lies?"

Vrath looked at her without answering.

"Ah," she said, "I see. Jarsun is the one fomenting these rumors."

"He is building an image of us as tyrants. He wants the kingdoms to be-lieve that we are cruel and oppressive, that even our own people want to be free of our tyranny. He paints himself as a liberator of slaves, a friend of the oppressed, benefactor of the disenfranchised. He seeks to turn our own people against us over time, so that he and his allies will be seen to have just cause and we to be in the wrong. He is waging a war of the mind and spirit, as well as of the body."

"We will fight him on that front as well," Jilana replied, undaunted. "Two can play at that game. We can spread word of his actual atrocities and tyranny. Tales of his cruelties to his own people, his family, his homeland. We will bring him down off his high pedestal."

Vrath nodded approvingly. "These are all sound strategies, Mother. But they are not endgames. Jarsun does not play for the love of war. He plays to win. He will not stop until he has achieved his endgame."

"And what is his endgame?"

"To split Hastinaga into pieces, back to the thousand and eight kingdoms that we united and now call the Burnt Empire. He does not seek to defeat us in open battle, or even to wipe us out to the last Krushan. He merely wishes to destroy our empire. To take away our ability to hold the original coalition of kingdoms, now grown to one thousand and eight, that consider themselves as a single great empire."

"But what will he gain—" Jilana began, then stopped. "Of course. That will leave Reygistan, his own empire, as the largest empire in the subcontinent."

"Indeed. And once he achieves that, he can incorporate all his allies, present and future, into the Reygistan Empire, and rule the civilized world undisputed. He means to destroy Hastinaga not by facing us and defeating us in open battle. But to outdo us by building the larger empire. Once he achieves that, the very fear of his size and power will make kingdoms bow before him and concede his superiority."

"As they do now to Hastinaga, without even so much as a debate or a fight," she said. "He is an evil genius. A demon not to be trifled with. Yet we cannot simply stand by and let him win the day by any means. One way or another, we must prevail. The future of the civilized world is in our hands. Hastinaga stands for Krushan law, for law and order, for truth and justice. While Reygistan stands for slavery, oppression, tyranny, genocide, chaos, and anarchy. It is the antithesis of Krushan law, the apotheosis of evil to our way of thinking. The good people, the little people, the kingdoms too small or too foolish to stand up to him, even those allies who have allowed them-

selves to be seduced by his lies and promises, his intimidation and threats
— all of them need our help. We are the only hope humanity has against this
demon tyrant. We must stand against him. We must defeat him. We must
find a way."

"I believe there is a way," Vrath said. "But it will not please you."

"Speak, son of Jeel."

When Vrath did, Jilana blanched.

"But to do such a thing," she said, "to thrust such responsibility upon their
shoulders . . ."

"The war of the mind is always greater than the war of the body," Vrath
said. "If Jarsun stands against them, everyone will renounce him as an im-
moral tyrant. No matter the outcome upon the field of battle, we will win
the battle of the mind and heart. It will give us the upper hand, and that is
all we need."

"But we will win the literal battle as well, of course," she said, still pale
from the shock of his proposal. "Upon the literal field of battle."

He hesitated a moment. "I will do everything in my power to ensure a
victory on all fronts."

She did not like his answer. She did not like his suggestion. But he was
right. Desperate times called for desperate measures. This whole problem
had been caused by the perception of their own weakness. The vacuum left
by Sha'ant's demise had barely been filled by her sons Gada and Virya when
both had been taken from the world too soon, much too soon. One of them,
Gada, had in fact fallen in single combat against Jarsun himself. That had
been a terrible blow against the Krushan dynasty.

The only way to silence all detractors and doubters was to deal a strong,
decisive blow, and the only way to do that was through a military victory so
great that nobody could doubt the power of Hastinaga.

And right now, that meant sending her two grandsons into war.

2

With the births of Ember's and Umber's sons, the return of honor she had
anticipated had not come. Shvate's skin and sensitivity, Adri's blindness
— these things had all but taken both boys out of contention. It was this

weakness in the armor of empire that Jarsun had exploited. So long as Hastinaga had heirs who were deemed unsuitable, the restless would continue to consider other options.

If an albino prince and a blind prince, both barely old enough to sit a throne, could confront and defeat the empire of Reygistan in battle, it would silence all their critics. If they could do so and win back the allies that had been lost to Jarsun through the same use of force, intimidation, and seduction that the Demon-Emperor had used, it would decisively answer the question of Hastinaga's future. If two boys with such severe physical challenges could achieve a great victory, then imagine what they could do later as grown men — to say nothing of their heirs, and the heirs of their heirs.

Unlike the game of kings, the game of emperors was not about merely winning a single seat and crown. It was about proving that you were capable of sustaining your position over a hundred, two hundred, a thousand years. Empires were built through fear and power. Today, the world perceived Hastinaga as a fading power because its true future, its heirs, appeared incapable of ruling. Vrath was proposing that they prove once and for all that this was false. That the two princes were not only capable of ruling as ably as any full-bodied man, but of doing so better than most men could. And his plan was to throw them into battle and launch a swift, decisive strike against the heart of tyranny itself.

It was the boldest, most audacious plan she had ever heard. If they succeeded, they would remove the strongest argument their rivals and detractors had against them. It was a compelling, brilliant tactic.

"But," she asked, rising to her feet to face her stepson, "what if we fail?"

She did not need to spell out her meaning: *What if Shvate and Adri prove inadequate to this challenge? What if they are truly weak and inferior to other able-bodied men? What if, being mere boys, they are not ready to take on such a task — which would be an immense challenge even for the bravest of kings or generals? What if Jarsun grabs hold of them, tears them into shreds, and chews up the remains while laughing through bloody teeth?*

"If we lose," Vrath said, "we will lose knowing that we were doomed to lose anyway."

Jilana nodded. Vrath was right: if Shvate and Adri could not face Jarsun and defeat him now, it would likely mean they would not be able to do so in future either. A prince could not wait to grow older and wiser to face his enemies in battle; he had to fight when the time came to act. "That is true," she said sadly.

"And by acting first, we will have the element of surprise. Jarsun will not have anticipated this move. Not now, not when he has barely begun his secret alliance. He is unprepared for war with us. We will have the upper hand. We will strike first, and hard. We will force him to face us in open battle. And his allies will be too shocked and uncertain to know whether to support him or to continue supporting us. Their indecision, his unpreparedness, the shock of facing young Shvate and Adri in battle, of being forced to fight against a blind boy and an albino, these are all factors which are invaluable to us in battle. We only gain these advantages if we strike first and strike now. Either we act now or stay on the defensive."

"And yet," she said, "if we lose . . ." She looked away for a moment. "We lose not only the empire, and the reputation of the Krushan dynasty, but also the future of both. Shvate and Adri are all we have, Vrath. Would you sacrifice them for the sake of victory?"

"No, Mother," he replied. "I would prove their ability to lead our empire, our dynasty, to victory. I would silence their critics once and for all. I would ensure that everyone in the civilized world believe beyond the shadow of a doubt that Hastinaga is the greatest empire in the history of humankind."

Jilana was silent a long time. She knew now that Vrath had already made his decision. He intended to go through with this. All that remained was for her to agree or to oppose. Yet, even if she opposed him, he might still proceed. He had the authority as prince regent and military commander of the empire. He had every right. But she could still oppose on principle alone. As a dowager empress. As the reigning matriarch of the dynasty. As a grandmother.

"They are just boys, Vrath," she said at last, unable to find any other argument to counter his implacable logic. "Just boys."

Her stepson shook his head slowly, his proud, craggy face betraying an empathy he rarely displayed, and in that moment, she understood that he felt as deeply as she did, cared as much as she did, loved them no less than she did. And yet, this was the only way. "They are Krushan."

She had no argument to counter those words.

She put her hands on Vrath's broad, powerful shoulders, looking up at his face.

"May the gods forgive us," she said.

He bent and touched her feet, taking her blessings, which she gave with a heavy heart.

Vrath rose upright again, his face betraying the same heaviness of heart that she herself felt.

"If there were any other way . . ." he said.

She touched his cheek gently, reassuring him. "But there is none. What must be done must be done."

Vrath put his own hand over Jilana's, pressing it to his cheek. He held it there a moment longer, then released it. He stood there, then, taking in the dais, the proud throne, the banners, the carved motifs of empire and dynasty, the great portraits and frescos, all the symbols and trappings of a great lineage. All now in the hands of two young boys who probably slept the sleep of the innocent in their distant forest hermitage even at this moment.

"My mother once told me," he said, "that like all noble dynasties, the Krushan line is touched with both tragedy and greatness. She said that where there is great power, there is always great tragedy as well. She said this was proven by the fact that all the children of the Krushan line had been born in the darkest watch of night."

Jilana nodded, acknowledging the wisdom of his birth mother's words. "This is true. They have all been born at night."

"The children of midnight are fated to face the worst terrors of the dark and the arcane," Vrath said, releasing a long breath. "While all mankind sleeps, we awaken and put on our armor and go forth to battle the forces of darkness. It is our Krushan law. We fight evil by night that the world may awaken to see the dawn tomorrow. That is the Krushan law that awaits young Shvate and Adri. They must do this not because I decree it or you approve it. They do this because it is their destiny. They are the swords of Krushan law. It is their duty to go forth in battle. Whatever the outcome, victory or tragedy, or some of both, they must act. That is their Krushan law. The outcome is not theirs to anticipate or expect."

Their eyes met, and Jilana nodded once, giving him her complete and unconditional permission. He nodded, acknowledging and accepting her support.

Then, without another word, he turned and strode to the doors, flung them open, and set off to save the empire.

Jilana knew that he would go directly to the stables, board his chariot, and ride for Guru Kaylin's ashrama that very minute. That was Vrath's way. Do now what must be done, without hesitation or delay. It was what made him indomitable. She prayed that the same indomitable spirit would serve her grandsons as well.

She clasped her hands together and knelt on the cold stone floor, praying for hope, victory, a miracle for herself, her family, her dynasty, her empire, and for the children of midnight.

Adri

~

How did we get here? Is this really happening? We can still stop this, can't we?
Three questions that seethe up in the gullet when you first confront the
armed forces of your enemy. The sight of that great host, thousands upon
thousands of armed soldiers, horses, chariots, war elephants, lancers, spear
throwers, archers, all gathered in this field for the sole purpose of your destruction — to kill you, in other words — will strike fear into the heart of
even the bravest of the brave.

For young Shvate and Adri, it was the most terrifying sight of their lives.

Adri, who couldn't actually see the field of battle or the armies arrayed
upon it, was even more terrified than Shvate. However terrible the reality
of a situation, imagination can always find a way to make it seem worse.
To him, the strange sounds and smells of the enemy forces, the raw animal
stench and peculiar noises, the very theatricality of the entire enterprise,
all merged into one contiguous nightmare following on from the horror of
his weeks in the forest hermitage. He had thought *that* was the nadir of his
short life. But this was worse, *much* worse.

For him, the three questions that rose in his gullet like acid were desperate pleas to escape this situation. The inevitable panic that strikes every
warrior head-on when faced with the stark reality of war.

How did we get here?

*By grandfather Vrath's chariot, yes, but how did we get here? All of us, Krushan
and enemies, on this field, in this situation, facing mutually assured destruction?*

Is this really happening?

*Denial. The refusal to believe that anyone could be foolhardy enough to actu-
ally go to war. That I could actually be here today, on this field, spending this fine*

summer day trying to stab, puncture, hack, and otherwise injure other warriors while they attempt to do the same to me and my fellows. Surely it's just a bad dream. Or a hallucination. Or . . . Sacred Goddess, it isn't really real, is it?

We can still stop this, can't we?

Bargaining. There must be some way out of this that doesn't involve me killing or being killed? There has to be. Because. I just. I can't. Stop it. Somebody, please, stop it. Before it's too late.

But of course, it was already too late.

The three questions were moot.

The field was set. The armies were aligned. The blades were drawn. And blood would be spilled.

All the three questions really did was force you to confront the ugly truth of your situation. After that, you really only had three choices: Panic and run. Die. Or endure.

Shvate endured.

Adri . . . struggled. But he managed to endure too.

They were crown princes of Hastinaga. They were the future kings of Hastinaga. Their entire army was looking to them for leadership. They couldn't run. Dying was not a preferable option. They had no choice but to endure.

The Conspirators

~

THE LEADERS OF THE enemy forces were neither boys nor physically disadvantaged, yet they were facing some doubts and questions of their own.

Jarsun of Reygistan was a terrifying being. What he had done to Ushanas of Ushati was horrific enough, but the tales of his atrocities were legendary. Every one of the kings, queens, princes, and princesses who had gathered that fateful day in Belgarion's aerie in Darkfortress knew the tales; many had witnessed firsthand the results of those atrocities, and none dared risk incurring the Reygistani God-Emperor's wrath.

But that was then, and this was now.

And today, they were confronting not Jarsun the Atrocious, but Vrath the Terrible. Vrath, whose name conjured countless tales of awe-inspiring feats of combat prowess. In his own way, the prince regent of Hastinaga was as terrifying if not more so than the God-Emperor of Reygistan. And it was he they would be shortly facing on this field of battle. This, needless to say, was causing no small amount of consternation among the enemies of Hastinaga.

The allies sat upon their horses and chariots on a hill overlooking the field of battle, close enough to converse with one another. All who had met that day at Darkfortress were present.

Anga and Vanga, kings of eponymous neighboring kingdoms, were dressed as per the custom of the Redmist Mountains. Stripped down to loincloths girded with diagonal leather harnesses to carry their weapons, their bodies were shaven of all hair, oiled, and painted with red, black, and yellow dyes. The marauders of Anga and Vanga were notoriously aggressive. They would pick a fight with nearly anyone for no other reason than to prove their prowess. This attitude had led over time to their altering their appearance when going to battle and thus contributing to the legends of their vanar-like ferocity in combat.

"What are we waiting for?" Anga demanded, flexing his painted biceps. "Let's kill some Krushan!"

"Aye, brother," said his sibling Vanga. "I have my heart set on killing a Krushan prince today."

Both raised their hooked spears, designed to pluck down vanars from overhanging branches, and brandished them aggressively, ululating the An-ga-Vanga war cry.

Kaurwa of Kanunga looked down upon this display of machismo from the back of her mare, a magnificent white beast some twenty hands high. In the Kanungan style, the mare was unsaddled; Kaurwa rode her bare-back, contrasting her mount's absence of accoutrement with a swaddling of tightly wound fabric that encased every limb, leaving not one inch of her dusky skin uncovered. Even her face and head were wrapped in strips of cloth, only her eyes peering out hotly from a visor-like gap. She made no comment on the display of testosterone from the Northeastern brothers but her attitude of haughty disdain spoke for itself.

Beside her, the short squat form of Sumhasana of Sumha openly gri-maced through his flaming red beard. "We of the cave cities believe in show-ing respect for one's foes. Kill them we must. Crow about it, we need not. It is ill luck to behave thus before the start of battle." He hefted his longaxe, its shaft and blade carved with a fine filigree of symbols; this was the legendary weapon Cold Vengeance, forged and hammered over three hundred years earlier and responsible for the deaths of many hundreds — nay, thousands — in the hands of his father and forefathers. With his free hand, he wiped the top of his bald pate of the fine sheen of perspiration that seemed omni-present.

The powerful arms of Pundraki of Pundar flexed as they swung twin long-swords, each a gleaming length of scintillating steel and gold-inlaid handles. With smooth, fluid actions, she sheathed both weapons crosswise on her back. Her back, torso, legs, even her neck, all bulged with massive slabs and ropes of muscle, exposed by her lack of garments. At a glance, she appeared to be a naked mass of muscle, leather, and metal, the crossed sheaths upon her back extending in similar strips of leather inlaid with metal around her limbs, breasts, and vulva. In contrast to her bulk and musculature, even the two Northeasterners appeared slender.

"You expect too much of those two, if you expect civilized behavior," she said. "The men of Anga and Vanga are not known for their intelligence or their sense of duty. But even so, in a brawl, I would rather have them on our side than against us. They can fight dirty, and that may come in useful when facing Vrath."

Vindva of Keyara's cold grey eyes took in Pundraki's appearance and garb, lingering a moment longer than necessary upon her feminine areas. His face and body were shaven clean like the kings of Anga and Vanga, but his lean, muscled body was only oiled for battle, not painted. Metal studdings and piercings decorated a substantial portion of his body and face, adding an odd contrast to his sharp jaw and clean, handsome features. There was a sense of menace and suppressed intensity to his seemingly slow, cool exterior; the metal decorations inserted in his skin echoed that sense of threat. He wore a number of blades around his waist, a broadsword, a shortsword, a thin needle-pointed dagger, and several others of varying sizes, thicknesses, and curvatures.

"If this were a brawl, you would be right. But for a pitched battle against the likes of Vrath of Hastinaga, their bravado will be short-lived. I wager they will not last the morning. If they do, it will only be by scuttling from the field with their tails between their painted arses the instant they see Vrath's ivory chariot racing toward them."

Pundraki considered this for a moment, returning Vindva's lingering gaze with a like appraisal of her own, openly viewing the Keyaran's masculine parts with sexual curiosity. "I will accept that wager," she said casually, "the winner earning the right to bed the other."

Vindva returned her gaze with a matching look. "A very equitable wager," he replied. "I accept."

Vriddha of Virdhh snorted in amusement. "What point, this wager? Win or lose, the outcome is same!" A giant of a man, he sat astride a young bull elephant with eyes that danced with madness. His face, a map of battle scars, severed left ear, and two missing fingers on his right hand all testified to his veteran experience in the business of warfare. The enormous weapon he carried, a lance-like object with an end shaped like a butcher's chopping blade, looked like it needed an elephant of its own to ride into battle. Both

Vindva on one side and Karta Mara on the other gave the Virdhh and his elephant plenty of space.

Karta Mara was the most unusually mounted of them all. He sat upon a wooden litter of unusual size and dimensions. It spanned about a yard in width, some three yards in length, and was over a yard thick. None of the other leaders of nations had ever seen or heard of such an unusual litter before. Even more unusual were the number of litter bearers. Some two dozen Hais stood beneath the litter, bearing its weight upon their shoulders, with another two dozen standing on either side of them. Six dozen men and women to carry one man? There was more to the contraption than met the eye, but no one wanted to ask, and Karta Mara was not the sort to chat pleasantly about such things. He sat comfortably upon a cushioned sedan seat, his flabby belly and gelid torso shivering with every movement. His arms, unnaturally long for his height, hung down by either side of his chair.

"Where are the Reygistani and his sycophant, the mountain king?" he asked of no one in particular. He was chewing on a plug of some intoxicant-laced betelnut preparation and from time to time leaned his head to spit a wad of blackish-red effluvium, not caring if it splattered his own litter bearers. "It is almost time for the battle conchs to sound, and they are not yet here. What is our strategy to be? In what formation and order are we to attack and defend? What tactics will we use to outmaneuver the great Vrath?"

He ended his litany with a hawk and purge that coated the back and neck of a litter bearer, who stood stoically.

Kaurwa shook her head, visibly disgusted at the display of arrogance. To a Kanungan, such overbearing behavior was intolerable. This was why Kanunga had dissolved its monarchy and become a republic, so that rulers like Karta Mara could not assume the mantle of entitlement.

Ripunjaya of Avant chuckled genially. "It would be a fine thing if they were to abandon us here. Why, it would even make one suspect that perhaps this whole exercise is the connivance of Vrath himself, designed to lure us into showing our hostility and justifying him quashing Hastinaga's enemies in one fell swoop." He slapped his leather-gloved hand against his leather-trousered thigh, his purple neck and face tattoos quivering as he laughed at the thought. "That would be quite brilliant, tactically speaking."

Drashya of Dirda made a sound of despair, grimacing at Ripunjaya of

Avant. "Speak auspicious things, liege of Avant. Our leaders will arrive at any moment. My stomach is already churning from my fasting of the past three days and nights, I cannot bear to contemplate such inauspicious thoughts."

The next person, Druhyu of the eponymous kingdom, fingered the ugly web of scars across his throat, glaring with inexplicable fury at everyone around, contributing not a word to the conversation. His compact two-horse chariot was as ugly as he himself, cruel rusty spokes and barbs poking out at every angle, threatening to rip open anyone, man or beast, unfortunate enough to come in its path.

It was Baal who responded next, tossing back his flowing grey hair. "Vrath needs no stratagems or undharmic tactics. If he desired to punish us for our transgressions against Hastinaga, he would simply have mounted his chariot and come to our front gates, meting out the harshest penalties under the law. My blood kin does not resort to trickery or subterfuge to achieve his ends. He is a man of Krushan law."

Pert-nosed, flat-faced Shastra, chief rider of the Longriders horse clans, nodded in agreement without saying a word to her fellow allies, but bent her head to the twitching ear of her sleek, muscular stallion and whispered continually to him. The stallion shuddered with pleasure and anticipation, pawing the firm earth to show his eagerness to carry his mistress into battle.

The last of the allies was the only person who had not been present at the gathering in Darkfortress. Her squat, broad physique and wide features revealed a strong family resemblance to her father, Ushanas of Ushati. But Usha betrayed neither of her father's loquaciousness nor his gluttony. While broadly built, she was more solid than corpulent, and the way she stood upon her four-horse chariot suggested practice and experience belying her youth. She was clad in unusually festive colors and accoutrements, rainbow-hued shawls and robes swirling around her stocky form. The clutch of javelins standing in the well beside her were equally colorful and bejeweled as well. Clearly, though she had inherited her father's genetic makeup and his kingdom, she was very much her own woman and queen.

There was no time for further discussion. The sound of cloven hooves from behind the motley group caused them all to turn their heads just as Belgarion and Jarsun appeared from over the rise. The One King of Darkfortress and his mentor, the God-Emperor of Reygistan, were dressed much as they had been that first day in the aerie, which was to say, they were dressed for court, not for battle. This fact did not go unnoticed by any of the allies, but none remarked on it. Whatever questions or doubts anyone had until this moment were dispelled by the appearance of the two men responsible for this military campaign. It was with their ears rather than their mouths that they paid service to the new arrivals.

Jarsun

~

JARSUN AND BELGARION DREW up their mounts at an angle that afforded them a view of all the allies. Belgarion smiled casually at each of them in turn, unfazed by the scowls, grimaces, and even outright hostility (this from Druhyu) that met his attempts at friendly greeting. He said not a word.

Jarsun sat silently, his back to the enemy lines, staring down at the reins clutched in his thin bony fist. Several moments passed. The first gloaming appeared on the eastern horizon. The Krushan lines straightened up into perfect formation, not a man out of place, then fell completely silent, ready for the imminent start of battle. Several of the mounts dropped the inevitable loads of manure and steaming hot streams of pungent piss, filling the brisk morning air with two of the many odors of battle. The stink of human urine, offal, blood, vomit, intestines, bowels, and other bodily parts would join it as the day progressed, but for now, these twin animal odors were the strongest smells. A flock of cranes flew by from west to east, calling out mournfully. Higher in the sky, carrion birds had begun to gather in anticipation of the feast to come.

Jarsun spoke without raising his head, his voice barely loud enough to be heard. "You fear Vrath." Even the horses pricked up their ears and tilted their heads in his direction. He had the complete attention of all present. There was no grumbling now, or wayward comments. Even the perpetually angry Druhyu lowered his flaming eyes and listened.

"But it is not Vrath you will fight today."

Slowly, after another long pause, the God-Emperor of Reygistan raised his head. He swiveled his skull, taking in every one of the allies. Even though he did not linger on any one, each and every man, woman, and beast felt his gaze sear their minds. Pupils widened. A horse whinnied nervously and had to be restrained by its rider.

"It is the crown princes of Hastinaga whom you face on this field today. Adri and Shvate. One blind since birth, the other crippled by his inability to withstand direct sunlight. Both boys, barely on the cusp of manhood, extracted from their guru's hermitage before they could complete even a full season of learning."

Jarsun raised an arm and held it at an impossible angle, pointing behind himself at the Krushan frontline across the field. "There they stand, about to enter the first battle of their lives. No experience in single combat, armed or unarmed combat, horseback, chariot, foot, or melee. No experience at all, in truth. Only a few score practice rounds, mostly with each other, with virtually no supervision or expert guidance. Why is that? When even a little boy or girl born in the Krushan line is an expert at all varieties of combat by the age of nine? Because Adri and Shvate were born crippled and deemed incapable of achieving the high standards demanded of their lineage. Yet, because they are Krushan, and because they are the crown princes, tradition demands that they lead today's battle."

Jarsun lowered his hand and moved his horse, riding the line of allies slowly, looking each one in the face as he passed. Each one felt an uneasy prickling in the back of their head, at the base of the skull, as if the Reygistani's gaze penetrated through their eyes into their brains all the way to the command centers of their bodies.

"Vrath believes he is achieving several things with this ruse. By bringing the crown princes to lead this battle, he creates the illusion that they are capable of ruling someday. Naturally, he intends to lead the actual fighting himself, using his mastery of warcraft and his own prowess as an unsurpassed yoddha to crush our rebellion. He intends to win the battle almost single-handedly, then credit the victory to young Adri and Shvate. Thus ending our uprising, crippling our armies, and proving beyond a doubt that the two grandsons of the late emperor Sha'ant are true heirs to the Krushan dynasty. It is a brilliant plan, but it is this very plan itself that will be the Krushan's undoing today."

On the field, the conchbearers on both fronts raised their white conchs to their mouths, lifting their heads to prepare to issue the first call. Jarsun glanced in their direction but did not react. He continued speaking as calmly as if they had all day to discuss the matter at hand.

"Vrath's plan depends on the two boys merely being figureheads, seen by all, present in action, perhaps even tossing a spear or loosing a few arrows, drawing swords for effect mayhap, but not actually engaging in full combat. Our plan is simple: engage the boys. Focus our entire attention upon them, and them alone. Attack them with every cadre and weapon at our disposal. Assault them relentlessly, ruthlessly, and do not stop until both boys are lying dead and maimed beyond recognition."

The conchbearers sounded the first call, a short, sharp burst that filled the early morning sky as the first rays of sunlight crested the eastern mountains. The allies responded with hastened breath, flared nostrils, and quickened pulses. But in their eyes was a spark of hope that had not been there before. In some eyes, there was even . . . excitement. In one pair of eyes, there was malevolent glee. Druhyu grinned broadly, rising to his toes and peering down at the field as if to mark out the two young lives he looked forward to ending this day.

"Vrath has anticipated this stratagem, of course. He anticipates everything, knows all. But he will have no choice. While every last one of you attacks the two Krushan boys, he will be forced to leave them to fend for themselves. Because he will be occupied with a more pressing threat, locked in a fight which he will neither be able to win nor end quickly. Because he will be facing me personally, in a fight to the death, and if you think Vrath is a warrior to be feared, then know now that Jarsun is one foe even the stone gods of Krushan would fear to face in battle."

The second call sounded, the mournful lowing of the conchs lingering longer than the first, but breaking off just as abruptly.

Jarsun stopped. He was now in the same place he had been when he had begun his pre-battle speech. He scanned the allies once more with the same intense gaze. More than one shivered as if the warm summer day had turned unexpectedly chill.

"When we win the day — and win we shall — I shall ask something of each of you. Nothing too precious. Yet not trivial either. You will give it freely of course, without hesitation or question. And in case you need reminding, our pact remains in effect even in the unlikely event that one or more of you should fail to survive the battle." Jarsun's gaze paused upon Usha of Ushati. "Your successor will inherit your part in this alliance. We are bound, not merely until death do us part, but until Vrath and the Krushan dynasty are completely destroyed."

Jarsun looked at the assembly in one wide, sweeping glance and smiled, showing thin long teeth. "*To war!*"

Jarsun turned his horse to face the battlefield, gathering the reins in a preparatory stance as the third and final call began to sound.

As the conchs finally faded away to a grim silence, the Reygistani spurred his horse onward and galloped down the hill at a blistering pace, blazing a trail down the hillside, aimed as straight as an arrow at the legendary white chariot of the war marshal of the Krushan forces: Vrath.

The battle had begun.

Vrath/Shvate

~

VRATH SAW THE LONE rider galloping straight toward him and narrowed his eyes. The gesture was not to enable him to see more clearly: the son of Jeel could view the individual barbs of each feather of a crow from a hundred yards. He was reacting to the tactic. At the pace the Reygistani was setting, he would be at Vrath's chariot momentarily.

"Adri! Shvate!"

At the sound of their names, both boys turned their heads. Their young faces were drawn and taut, raw with anticipation and a heightened state of awareness close to panic.

"Do as I said, and all will be well," Vrath said. He had unslung his longbow and gripped it in one hand; an oddly shaped missile was clasped in the other hand. "In my absence, protect each other. Remember, you are sons of Krushan. Fight bravely and tirelessly. No retreat, no parley, no surrender. Those who rise against Hastinaga must be taught a lesson."

Vrath raised his longbow above his head and roared, "*Jai Jeel Mata!*"

His chariot lurched forward, the reins wrapped around his waist and controlled by deft movements of his torso. Picking up speed with lightning swiftness, the fabled white chariot raced ahead of the Krushan frontline, heading not directly at the oncoming rider, but at an angle designed to draw him away from the two princes.

Adri and Shvate swallowed nervously, throats thick with terror, hearts pounding in their bony chests. Shvate wiped an errant drop of sweat from his forehead and glanced at his brother. Adri was standing with that odd stiff stance that meant he was scared and frozen into inaction.

"Adri," Shvate said softly, "I am here with you, through thick and thin. We will stand and fight together."

Adri's throat worked. He turned his sightless eyes toward his brother. His voice was gruff and unlike his usual speaking tones. "I can take care of myself."

Shvate blinked. "Vrath said we are to protect each other."

Adri sucked in a deep breath and released it. "Protect yourself. I will protect myself."

Before Shvate could say another word, Adri slapped the back of his charioteer who obeyed the command and urged the chariot's horse team forward.

Shvate watched in dismay as his brother's chariot rode away from him, toward the frontline of Krushan chariots, preparing to make their first charge. Vrath's instructions had been for them to remain here in an observer position until he said otherwise. But Adri's action left him no choice. He could hardly remain here while Adri rode into battle. Besides, Vrath's last instruction had been to protect one another, and whatever Adri might say, Shvate intended to ensure his brother's well-being.

"Forward," he instructed, and his charioteer chased Adri's chariot.

Jilana

~

JILANA WATCHED FROM THE high platform off the field. A select guard and entourage surrounded her and the other ministers and courtiers who enjoyed the privilege of viewing the battle from this vantage point. The platform itself was no less than a throne podium, bedecked with embroidered carpets, comfortable seating, attendants with food and drink, and all the luxuries that royalty commanded. The courtiers and ministers feasted and drank as they discussed the battle formations and the odds and tactics as if viewing nothing more than a sporting event. Which, in a sense, was true: war was indeed a sport. A sport of kings and queens.

Only Jilana was not entertained. Those were her beloved grandsons down there, riding their chariots to the frontline despite Vrath's assurances to her that they would only observe from the sidelines and not engage in actual combat. As for Vrath himself, he was already halfway across the field, racing to meet one of the enemy riders, a madman galloping as if in a race — a race to the death, she hoped.

"Who is that?" she asked.

The ministers closest to her broke off their discussion of tactics at once. "Why, Maharani, that is the wretched Reygistani who has plagued the world so much of late. The two-faced Jarsun. The barbarian who considers himself an emperor and a god, both at once. Such hubris deserves a most painful death at the hands of Vrath!"

Jilana leaned forward, gripping the cushioned arms of her royal seat. Jarsun himself. And it looked like he was racing to challenge Vrath. Forcing Vrath to leave both Adri and Shvate unprotected. This was not an auspicious beginning. Not auspicious at all.

Vrath

~

WHEN VRATH ESTIMATED THE distance between his racing chariot and the oncoming chariot of Jarsun to be seven hundred yards, he raised his bow and loosed his first volley. The arrows he used were bunched tightly together in a packed sheaf, each long arrow segmented. The full sheaf of 108 arrows rose into the sky. As they reached the zenith of their arc, the 108 split into ten times that number, each yard-and-a-half-long arrow separating into ten darts with pointed metal tips. As they fell, the natural force of the easterly blowing wind and the angle and trajectory used by Vrath caused them to spread in an umbrella-like formation. Except, of course, an umbrella was supposed to protect those beneath its shade; this umbrella consisted of 1,080 pointed metal-tipped darts of six inches each, each now falling with a velocity and force sufficient to punch through metal armor and bone and pierce the vital organs of the human body. The formation was so precisely aimed that no two darts were more than a few inches apart. The entire umbrella had a diameter of three hundred yards, with Jarsun's chariot precisely at its center at the time of groundfall.

Both armies and their leaders saw the volley and drew in breath. Those who had enjoyed the privilege of witnessing Vrath deploy this same missile in the past knew that such a volley was capable of bringing an entire company of a thousand foot soldiers to a painful halt, killing a tenth of them instantly, wounding most of the others.

The person for whom the volley was intended did not even look up at the descending umbrella of death. Instead, he pointed a finger at Vrath and grinned, displaying his divided teeth. Even across the six hundred yards that now separated them, that skullhead grin was easily visible to all the thousands of watchers.

Then Jarsun disappeared from sight.

The volley made groundfall with a metal shirring. Darts embedded themselves into the hard-packed dirt of the field, the shafts almost disappearing into the ground from the force of impact; they embedded themselves into the wood and metal parts of Jarsun's chariot; they pierced the flesh of Jarsun's unfortunate horses, penetrating the innocent hearts of those unfortunate beasts. The horses stumbled, broke their forelegs, and collapsed in a cloud of dust, the chariot upending and somersaulting over their broken, dart-pierced bodies to crash and tumble over and over on the field, coming to rest almost a hundred yards further on. During this chaos, of Jarsun himself there was no sign.

Only Vrath's demigod eyes saw what actually happened.

At the moment when he raised his finger to point at Vrath, Jarsun split himself into two.

His two halves separated as precisely as a wood chip cut by the sharpest axe and stood independently for barely a fraction of a kshana.

Then, in a movement so fast it was a blur to the mortal observers, the Reygistani divided himself again — and again — and yet again. A hundredfold.

Each segment of himself was so thin, it was barely a sliver. Yet every portion of his body, organs, hair, skin, bone, vein, blood, bodily fluid, remained perfectly intact and functional. Each sliver of his body existed and survived independently, an organism unto itself.

As the volley of darts fell, the slivers easily avoided being struck — not a single dart so much as nicked any part of Jarsun.

As the horses died and the chariot upended, the hundred slivers of Jarsun flew up into the air, as slender as gossamer wings. In midair they conjoined once more, assembling themselves into a perfect whole. To the watching mortals, it seemed Jarsun had disappeared a moment before the volley struck, then reappeared in midair, miraculously; only Vrath knew the truth.

Jarsun landed on bent knees, lithe and easy, his slender, axe-like face still retaining the same grin, his finger still outstretched, his eyes winking at Vrath . . . who was now less than five hundred yards away and bearing down fast.

The watchers gasped in astonishment.

Never had anyone present seen an assault by Vrath so successfully thwarted. Even without knowing how Jarsun had survived the volley, what was clear was that he had indeed survived it.

Vrath pursed his lips and acknowledged his enemy's hardiness. So Jarsun was every bit as difficult to kill as legend claimed. Very well, then. He would use harsher tactics. It was a long time since the son of Jeel had faced an adversary with supermortal abilities. But it would take a lot more than such tricks to survive Vrath.

He raised his bow to loose his next assault.

But before he could attack again, Jarsun made his move.

Jilana

~

JILANA REACTED WITH DISMAY as Jarsun survived the deadly volley. Everyone around her expressed shock as well. The war minister, a curmudgeonly old man who had spent more time in the drinking taverns of Hastinaga than on battlefields, was the only one who expressed admiration for the Reygistani's survival. "It looks like Vrath finally has a fight on his hands." The old minister had little say in a kingdom where the war marshal, Vrath himself, was a one-man army undefeated in his entire lifetime. Jilana dismissed his smug comment as the frustrated bitterness of a once-famous warrior overshadowed by the greatest yoddha of all time, but she couldn't help wondering if there was even the slightest truth to his words. *If Vrath has a fight on his hands, then what of Adri and Shvate? Who will look out for them?*

She turned her head to look at the place where Adri's and Shvate's chariots had been stationed moments earlier. Distances being so vast on the field of battle, she had to search to spot them. Finally, she found them. There they were, their bone-white chariots and purple-black flags standing out amidst the red-ochre chariots and leaf-green flags of the other charioteers. They had moved from the sidelines to the frontlines, and that was worrying enough. But at least they appeared to be standing in one place, not entering the fray. And perhaps being with the rest of the chariot lines was safer than being isolated on the sidelines.

Jilana knew very little about warcraft and battle tactics; unlike most queens, she did not come from a warrior-royal background. Her father was a fisher chief, not a warrior king. But as Emperor Sha'ant's queen and later as his widow and dowager empress of Hastinaga, she had viewed enough battles and heard enough war campaigns planned to have picked up some ba-

145

sic knowledge of the ugly business. However many rules and warrior codes people talked about, the brutal truth was that the entire purpose of war was to kill, maim, wound, destroy. It was all very well for Vrath to assure her beforehand that so long as the princes did not engage any enemy on the field, warrior caste Krushan law prohibited from anyone attacking them. In the heat of battle, with persons such as Jarsun and Druhyu and some of those other rebels involved, she would not put it past the enemy to bend the rules, or even break them.

Now she raised her gaze to the enemy lines and saw her worst fears realized. "Jeel, Mother of Rivers," she said, clasping her hand to her chest as she rose to her feet.

The alliance of enemies of Hastinaga were descending from their hilltop vantage point, charging downhill at the Krushan frontlines. Elephants, chariots, cavalry, foot soldiers — they appeared to be making a concerted all-out assault on her army. There was no attempt at any formation or finesse: they were simply pouring everything they had into a full frontal assault.

And their intended target was clearly the chariot lines where the two young princes of Hastinaga were stationed.

Jilana pointed at them, raising her voice. "They are violating the code of battle. They have no right to attack our princes unprovoked. Someone, send word to Vrath at once. They must be stopped!"

But no one heard her; no one paid heed to her voice or noticed her shock and alarm.

Everyone was too busy gaping and gasping at what was happening at the other side of the battlefield.

Shvate

~

SHVATE HAD WATCHED WITH amazement as Vrath loosed his first volley, then with shocked disbelief as Jarsun survived the attack. Now he watched gobsmacked as Jarsun pointed a finger at Vrath, then disappeared into the earth.

Or not disappeared . . . not exactly. Shvate could see a flurry of movement just before Jarsun vanished: a blurring of the man's outline and shape, as if his body had . . . disintegrated? Not quite, but it was a close enough description of what he'd seen. The fragments or pieces or whatever they might be then sank into the earth like worms burying themselves in the ground. The speed with which they burrowed raised a hundred tiny puffs of dust.

How was such a thing possible? Shvate had heard a story about Jarsun, and the person telling the tale had implied that the God-Emperor of Reygistan was not human but some kind of demon. Shvate had laughed at the time. He had been raised to think rationally and scientifically. He had studied the scriptures, and it was known that there were no more demons or urrkh or any of the demon races left on Arthaloka. They had all been exterminated long, long ago.

This was not the age of stone gods, or the age of Krushan. This was the modern age. The time of the Burnt Empire. Jarsun could not be a demon. It was probably a superstition spread by those he had defeated — spread to explain their loss, rather than admit their own failure, Vrath had told him and Adri. At the hermitage, only a few weeks ago, Adri had asked one of their gurus, the teacher of hand-to-hand combat, if there were still urrkh in the world. The guru had told him to focus on the assignment at hand and put all irrelevant thoughts out of his mind.

But the question seemed very relevant now. For how could a mortal man disintegrate into pieces and burrow into the ground like a nest of worms?

Shvate watched as Vrath's chariot slowed its forward advance. Even at this distance, he could see Vrath lowering his raised bow to point at the ground, then fitting a new set of arrows to the weapon. That meant Vrath also had seen Jarsun go into the earth, and so Shvate knew he had not been seeing some cheap illusion. Jarsun had, in fact, somehow disintegrated himself and tunneled down.

As Shvate watched, Vrath loosed the new clutch of arrows, releasing this second volley not into the air, but *into the ground itself!* Shvate felt a thrill of anticipation: Vrath was the greatest warrior who had ever lived. Surely he would outsmart and outfight the Reygistani.

The volley of arrows struck the ground with an impact that exploded like a thunderclap. The sound and the vibrations caused by the impact rippled through the air and rolled across the field, reaching Shvate a moment later.

His chariot lurched. The entire line of chariots shuddered. Horses neighed in alarm, elephants trumpeted, soldiers cried out.

Shvate reeled, gripping the side of the well of his chariot to retain his balance. His charioteer reached out a hand to help him, but Shvate managed on his own.

He turned to the chariot beside him, concerned for his brother. Adri was standing upright, his charioteer's hand on his shoulder to steady him.

"Adri! You should have seen it —"

Adri turned his head in that way he had when he was listening to something approaching. Suddenly, Adri cried out and raised his hand, pointing to the west.

"Brother!" he cried.

Shvate turned to see what Adri was pointing at.

His heart thudded.

The entirety of the enemy forces were charging straight at them. Tens upon tens of thousands of foot soldiers, horse cadres, elephants, chariots, all in their own akshohinis, all heading directly for this part of the field. They would be here in mere moments.

And the only person who could help defend them against such an assault was a whole mile away, far across the field.

Vrath

~

VRATH WATCHED AS HIS second volley struck the ground and burrowed deep within. The tremors and thunderclap of the impact were deafeningly loud this close, but he did not need to brace himself. The son of Jeel was capable of standing upon still water. This was solid earth. His horses whinnied in distress, and he spoke to them gently, reassuring them.

He watched the ground carefully. It was impossible to tell exactly where Jarsun had burrowed to. The speed with which the Reygistani had achieved that feat was impressive. In a mere blink of an eye, he had split himself again into segments, this time burrowing down instead of flying up. But Vrath had countered the move with that second volley. The snake arrows he had used had penetrated the surface and were now crisscrossing the ground beneath the field in a widespreading pattern impossible to predict or to avoid. This time, no matter how thinly Jarsun divided himself, or how cleverly and quickly he wriggled, he would not escape harm. The snake arrows would turn even the smallest pebbles underground into grains of sand. No living thing could avoid being destroyed by their progress. They would burrow fifty yards deep then be still. By now, Jarsun was probably reduced to a million infinitesimal parts.

Vrath allowed himself a grim twist of his lips to show his satisfaction —

When suddenly the ground beneath his chariot erupted.

A wave of wetness drenched his entire form, and metal shards exploded through the air, flying in every direction.

He himself was thrown up, up into the air forty, fifty, sixty ... a hundred yards high, savaged by a series of ripping, bone-deep cuts and stabs and punctures, spurting blood and precious fluids from a hundred wounds all at once, pain coursing through his entire being.

Jilana

~

"VRATH!"

Jilana's anguished cry silenced the entire royal assembly. Everyone turned to stare at her, their own eyes wide with shock and terror, before returning to the horrific scene unfolding upon the battlefield.

Vrath was under assault, his chariot and horses shattered to fragments by the force of Jarsun's attack from beneath the earth. Jarsun's hundred slivers had emerged with the intensity of a horde of rampaging elephants, smashing up through the surface of the field, shattering Vrath's chariot, cutting his unfortunate horses to shreds, and flinging Vrath himself up into the air a hundred yards like a hollow doll.

Now, as Jilana's cry faded away, all assembled watched Vrath's punctured body spatter blood from a hundred wounds, the snakelike segments of Jarsun's divided body attacking him from every angle, sinuously winding around his limbs, his torso, even wrapping around his face and neck, cutting, slicing, stabbing. The level of damage being inflicted upon the son of Jeel's body was beyond human tolerance. No human could survive such an assault.

And yet still Jarsun continued to press his attack and inflict more and more damage to the prince regent's horribly disfigured and abused body. The two great warriors hung in the air above the field, the spurts and sprays of blood vividly visible against the clear blue sky. The writhing snakes and worms that were Jarsun's body worked their vicious assault relentlessly, both attacking Vrath while carrying him higher and higher. Two hundred yards, three hundred . . . Vrath's writhing body resembled a rabbit attacked by an entire nest of vicious serpents. It was a horrific sight to behold for even the hardiest war veteran. Even if Vrath somehow broke free of that deadly assault, he would fall to certain destruction. Five hundred yards now, the spinning, writhing mass continuing its relentless assault unabated. How much longer could the son of Jeel survive — if indeed he was alive still even now?

Another cry burst from Jilana's throat.

"Adri! Shvate!"

A turn of the head, a glimpse of the scene unfolding on the eastern side of the field, and everyone gasped and blanched again, reacting to an equally horrific sight.

The entire enemy army had encircled and engulfed the chariot company of the Krushan forces.

A thousand Krushan chariots were a formidable force — when in motion, charging at an enemy, loosing arrows by the thousands, flinging deadly aimed javelins and spears, wreaking havoc in the ranks of the enemy army.

But caught thus unawares, stationary in a lowland position, boxed in on all sides by enemy forces, not only enemy chariots as the rules of war specified, but even elephant, cavalry, and foot cadres, there was very little the Krushan charioteers could do. They could fight back — and were, using their arrows, javelins, and spears, defending themselves with everything they had at their disposal. But deprived of the ability to move, to maneuver, to fight in motion . . . they were like a hobbled and blinded horse. A chariot is not meant for defense: it is an assault vehicle. By attacking the Krushan chariots en masse, by breaking the rule that specified that only like cadres could challenge like cadres — chariots versus chariots, horse versus horse, foot versus foot, elephant versus elephant — the rebels had gained the upper hand.

And by throwing the entire might of their army, all their akshohinis against a single chariot company, they were ensured not merely a victory but a massacre.

Vulture

~

VULTURE HUNG MOTIONLESS IN the sky.

She looked down upon the beautiful carnage below.

What a feast! What a spread! What a cornucopia of carnal delights!

Her sons and daughters, brothers and sisters, continued to arrive from all points of the compass, now in the hundreds, soon in the thousands. There would be no infighting amongst their own today. Today, there was plenty for all. Everyone would feast and satisfy their most gluttonous appetites. *Eat all you can! Carry what you will! Come back for second and third and even tenth helpings. Eat till you cannot fly. Sit and digest and then eat some more.*

It was heavenly.

Vulture loved battles.

If only the humans could host a battle every day, vultures would feast all their lives.

But not only their kind — even the other scavengers, both winged and on foot, would have ample repast. Even those who did not usually scavenge could not resist such a festival of savories.

Vulture could spy them gathered at the edges of the battlefield. Hyena, rat, wolves, even lazy lions and panthers and leopards and wild dogs . . . In the sky there were crows and jackdaws and even a few gulls who had somehow come this far inland and stayed to feast.

But what was this, now?

Rising up in the sky like a pack of squabbling birds, a mortal fighting a nest of snakes?

No.

Vulture knew snakes well. She loved snakes. They were a fine delicacy and one of her main sources of nourishment. She could spot a snake from a mile high. Those were not snakes.

These furiously writhing things were shaped more or less like snakes, but they were something else entirely. She smelled a peculiar odor from them. Somewhat mortal, yet something other than mortal too. Urrkh, then? Naga? Pisaca? One of the other snakelike demon races? She had thought they were mostly extinct, but who knew what lurked in the far corners of Arthaloka. Those rabid monsters had a way of coming back when least expected.

She could not tell precisely what manner of demon this creature was, but it was a demon, no doubt. And yet it smelled of mortal blood too. A crossbreed, then. Vulture had eaten a few of those in her time. They did not taste good. She cried out to her flock, cautioning them to avoid the crossbreed that flew like a bird and moved like a snake. There was plenty of better fare to enjoy without spoiling one's appetite on urrkh flesh.

But what was this, now?

Clearly, the crossbreed was winning the unequal fight. He had picked up the mortal male from the surface of Arthaloka and carried him high above, much as a carrion bird would do with prey. Using his unnatural crossbreed abilities, he was raking and cutting and puncturing the prey with furious energy in midair. Already, from the smell and sight of the mortal blood spilled, Vulture could see that the mortal could not possibly survive this assault. It was an unequal battle whose outcome was a foregone conclusion.

But there was something unusual happening now.

For one thing, the mortal blood that Vulture smelled was again not solely mortal.

It was something else.

What, then? Was the mortal also a crossbreed like his attacker?

Hmm, yes. But not a demon-mortal crossbreed. This was a different species of being.

A demigod.

Part god, part mortal.

And he was not succumbing as any mortal would have long before now. He was fighting back.

Adri

~

"PROTECT THE PRINCES!"

The call went out from the captains of the chariot cadre, across the ranks of the chariot company, repeated and carried forward a thousandfold. Adri heard it even above the rising thunder of the oncoming army. The unexpectedness of the enemy tactic had caught everyone by surprise, but being blind gave Adri one advantage: he relied on his other senses more than the sighted did, and his ears had warned him of the approach of the enemy long before anyone had fully comprehended what was happening. Perhaps the chariot captains had assumed the enemy forces would change direction at some point, moving into different formations or positions across the field.

But Adri had sensed the single direction and unity of those thundering hooves, wheels, and sandaled feet. They were all headed here: directly here. Every last elephant, chariot, horse, and foot soldier. Not just intending to attack in a full-frontal assault, but to surround this position completely.

By the time the Krushan chariot captains had realized what was happening, it was too late to escape — they could have retreated, but how would it appear if the leaders of the Krushan army began the battle by turning around and running away?

That was, naturally, unacceptable. So they had done the best they could, moving line upon line of chariots in a circuitous action, ringing the two white chariots occupied by Adri and his brother, protecting them by multiple ranks of Krushan chariots. By the time the first lines of the rebel forces struck their frontlines, Shvate and Adri were buried fifty chariots deep in an island of over a thousand Krushan vehicles.

But that island was fast being eroded by the ocean of enemy forces.

The rebels were not merely deploying a tactic here. Adri could tell from the mayhem and screams and shattering of wood, screaming of metal, howls of agony from animals and humans alike, that the assault was an endgame with no intention of giving quarter or allowing retreat. They meant to get to him and Shvate today, here on this field, within the next few hours. And to snuff out their lives like one of the elephants pounding the skull of an unfortunate Krushan charioteer fifty yards away.

When one has not the benefit of sight, hearing becomes a form of seeing. Adri's preternaturally alert senses, already honed by his time in the jungle, were sharpened and heightened by the mortal peril of battle. He could make out individual sounds and events in the cacophonous melee that enabled him to know things that no sighted person could observe through vision alone.

There, seven hundred yards east: a horde of armored elephants smashing through a line of Krushan chariots, demolishing chariots and horses and charioteers altogether. Elephants were wounded, injured, impaled, pierced, and killed, their screams provoking their fellow gaja to panic and stampede with even greater ferocity.

Five hundred yards west: several dozen wooden wagons ramming into the Krushan chariots. The wagons laden with pots of oil. As they smashed against the wall of Krushan chariots, the pots broke open, spilling oil everywhere. From the far side of the hill, rebel archers loosed burning arrows that went high, arched, and fell, igniting the oil. Krushan charioteers and horses went up in a blaze of fiery torture. Barely had the fires died down, and a company of rebel chariots were already rolling downhill to smash through the smoking debris and finish the job.

Behind his right shoulder, four hundred yards northeast: an entire battalion of cavalry attacking the chariot wall with every weapon at their disposal. The brave Krushan charioteers were fighting back furiously, but the sheer weight of numbers worked against them. Their numbers were reducing by the hundredfold while the enemy could afford to lose twice as many and still have enough left to keep attacking all day.

All around him, swirling like a miasma, the screaming chaos of an unequal battle.

Krushan forces all across the Krushan lines were converging here, attempting to support their besieged chariot company and rescue the princes.

But the enemy's action had been too swift and unlawful to have been predicted or countered in time. Even now, to engage the enemy, the Krushan army too would have to forgo the rules of war.

But that was not possible. The rebels were already at fault for defying the might of the Burnt Empire. If Krushan armies *also* started breaking the law, then the empire would lose all respect in the eyes of its other allies. No matter how the battle proceeded, Hastinaga must abide by Krushan law and restrict their actions to the permissible limits, lest Hastinaga lose all respect among the Krushan people and thus sow the seeds of their own undoing.

That meant only pitting like against like: elephant against elephant, foot soldier against foot soldier. Which was a tall order since the rebels had smartly spread their foot soldiers around the periphery of their circle. This meant that by rule of war, Krushan elephants and cavalry could not attack that outer circle directly. Even now, Krushan foot soldiers were battling the rebel foot soldiers, trying to break through, and by concentrating on driving wedges through certain points, the Krushan generals were succeeding in making inroads. But that outer circle was almost a mile away, and by the time they broke through and sent the heavier cadres into the fray, it would be much too late.

Adri estimated that it would take perhaps several hours for the rebels to reach him and Shvate and engage them directly. But due to his lack of experience in battle, he couldn't be sure; they could break through in as few as four or five hours for all he really knew. This battle could easily be over before the sun reached its zenith.

He was surprised to find that he himself was not as panicked or scared as he ought to have been. If anything, the sheer odds confronting him and his fellow Krushan made him feel angry. A surge of self-righteous rage was building inside him. Who were these rebels to resort to such low tactics? How dare they stoop to such means? Even if they succeeded, did they really think the world would cheer their victory?

He was, of course, too young and immature to understand that history favors only the victors. Once the rebels won the day, they would be joined by other disgruntled allies of Hastinaga. The rebellion would grow into a nationwide — perhaps even worldwide — phenomenon. With Vrath gone, and the only two heirs to the empire dead, there would be no line of succession left in Hastinaga. Chaos would erupt across the length and breadth of the empire. Pocket rebellions would occur. Allies would fight allies. Everyone would tear the Burnt Empire to shreds, and feast on the remains. And in a hundred years, the Krushan dynasty — Vrath, Shvate, Adri himself . . . all would be half-forgotten names, tragic footnotes in history.

Adri could not see that far ahead. He could only view the events of the present hour. And those events were both terrifying and soul-crushing, but also so desperate that taking any action, no matter how brash, seemed preferable to merely standing there in a chariot and waiting to die.

"Shvate," he said.

He had to repeat himself twice more, raising his voice the third time to be heard. Shvate was enraptured by the horror of the battle raging around them, visible only in violent glimpses but shocking enough to have hypnotized him into rapt fascination. Adri could sense Shvate's own fear and rising anger, the suppressed frustration and outrage he shared with Adri. Neither of them had actually expected to have to fight that day. Both had feared the prospect but had not seriously believed they would be under any real threat. That situation had changed abruptly, shockingly. The person they had assumed would lead and win the battle on his own was no longer here by their side to protect or advise them. They were now left to their own devices, with only each other to turn to.

"Brother," Adri cried out, his deep tenor voice loud and commanding.

Shvate turned to gape at his brother. "Adri?"

Adri held out his hand, reaching toward Shvate. "Brother, are we Krushan or are we cowards?"

Adri heard Shvate's sharp intake of breath, the moment of stunned silence, then the slow release of breath that told him Shvate was smiling.

He felt Shvate's hand grasp his own, squeezing it in response.

"We are Krushan!" Shvate shouted back in answer.

"Good," Adri said in a normal voice. He smiled in Shvate's direction. "Then let's show them who we are."

Jilana

~

JILANA RUSHED TO THE balcony's balustrade, leaving behind her comfortable, cushioned seats and fan-turning attendants to view the horrific events unfolding on the battlefield below more clearly. That was her family out there, facing terrible, shameful deaths — her grandchildren and her son by marriage. She loved them all dearly and could not endure the thought of losing them. But that was only part of her anguish. To lose them would be terrible enough; to lose them like *this* was unbearable. The great Krushan line could not end thus, driven down to its knees in the dust of a nameless field, overcome by treacherous allies and illegitimate tactics. This could not be the end of her beloved Sha'ant's legacy. She would not allow it.

She was a breath away from rushing down from the pavilion and taking to a horse herself to join the battle. She would rather have died here today than stand by as her family line was destroyed. Though a fisherwoman born, Jilana was Krushan by marriage, and she would fight, even if only for a few desperate instants, rather than let this travesty stand.

But just when all seemed lost, something miraculous happened.

Vrath

~

JARSUN AND VRATH WERE almost a thousand yards in the sky.

Jarsun's assault continued unabated, his hundred segments attacking Vrath's body without respite, constantly cutting, stabbing, piercing. Vrath's body was covered with so many wounds that it now appeared entirely red. There was not an inch of whole skin left upon his frame. His limbs were brutalized, his torso cut to shreds, his muscles and tendons hanging like torn ropes, skin dangling in patches and flaps, his face a single mass of bloody pulp. He was no longer recognizably human or male or even a living organism in any sense of the term.

Yet his grievously punctured lungs still wheezed and hissed, drawing agonizing gasps. His battered and stabbed heart still pumped blood. (Though most of it spurted into the air and fell, pattering down, wasted, upon the dusty field far below.) His other organs likewise still struggled to perform some fraction of their normal function. Thus Vrath was alive only in the sense that he was not yet completely dead. But to call him a living being, let alone a man, would be an abuse of language itself.

And yet still he struggled, feebly now, for there was barely enough blood left in his body to carry energy to work his limbs. His arms and legs flailed. His back spasmed. His eyes struggled to see, his ears to hear. His brain functioned, but barely.

Two bloody limbs that vaguely resembled hands, with a few appendages that might once have been fingers, grasped one of Jarsun's snakelike excrescences and attempted to twist it like a rope, seeking to wrench it, or tear it. But the strength that had once brought innumerable mighty warriors to their knees was now fading fast, and the body that had won a thousand battles and challenges was decrepit and brutally damaged, and Jarsun slipped out of his grip easily, slicing open the last tendons that enabled Vrath to use his hands at all. Now those once formidable limbs hung limply down, useless as the skinless limbs of a butchered beast at a feast.

With his every attempt at breath, Vrath still fought, as he would continue to fight, to the very end. But it was a lost cause now — for Vrath had nothing left to fight with, and Jarsun was still so powerful, still so ferocious, and had every advantage remaining.

Jarsun

~

JARSUN SENSED THE IMMINENT end of his prey, and his frenzied movements slowed; his various components twisted and writhed until they were entirely wrapped around Vrath's body like a pattern of ribbons. He allowed himself and Vrath to hang suspended in midair for a moment, then began to squeeze.

The rebels on the field below, those not wholly engaged in pushing home their own certain victory at this moment, glanced up and knew what was about to come next. As he had done to Ushanas of Ushati at Darkfortress, Jarsun would now squeeze the last vestige of life out of Vrath's body as easily as two fingers squeeze a ripe grape.

But before he could accomplish this end, rain began to rise up.

Strictly speaking, to be described properly as rain, it must be said to be falling. Yet *this* rain fell upward, not downward, rising from the ground to the sky.

The rain seemed to come out of the earth itself, from the groundwater beneath the earth, from the great water table that lay like a vast ocean under the surface of the land. It burst out of the pores of the field and rose like raindrops, falling upward as rapidly as a heavy rainshower.

It gathered speed as it rose, rising faster and faster, and converging upon the place where Vrath struggled feebly, entrapped by Jarsun, a thousand yards high. The sound it made was like a hissing. It gained speed until, by the time it reached Vrath and Jarsun, it was only visible as a blur. Enough rainwater to fill a sizable lake gathered from miles around to converge upon a space barely seven feet long and three feet wide —

And crashed into the demigod and the demon with the force of a cloudburst.

Jilana

～

THE SOUND CAUSED EVERYONE on the battlefield below to pause and stare upward at the incredible sight: a cloudburst of water, large enough to drown a village, exploding on contact with the body of Vrath a thousand yards high. Jilana gasped at the sight.

The brunt of the impact was borne by Jarsun.

For by wrapping himself around his prey's body, he had encased Vrath in a protective layer of his own flesh. The force of the water striking his thinly spread form was so intense that it caused Jarsun to lose bodily cohesion completely. His flesh was smashed into a thousand tiny droplets.

He exploded like a cloud of spray in midair.

The cloud of spray drifted down like a red mist, carried eastward by a current from the southwest.

As the cloud was borne away by the wind, those below watched to see what had happened to Vrath.

Vrath's body remained floating in midair, no longer entwined by Jarsun, but now entirely encased in water. The water was several yards deep, forming a giant block roughly rectangular in shape. The edges and sides of this block were not smooth or perfect; they were wavering and fluid, rippling in the current of wind, but the water cohered into this shape and remained thus. In the center of this rough shape was Vrath's body, now only blurrily visible but somehow still intact.

As all watched, the block of water began to harden and grow more blue in hue.

Despite the morning sun shining down, in just a few moments, the block had frozen solid, and remained where it was, hovering in midair, a thousand yards above the blood-soaked battlefield.

The Charioteers

~

"Krushan!"

The battle cry tore loose from the throats of the two young princes. The cry applied equally to children of Krushan of any gender, but in this particular case, it was used to mean, literally, "Sons of Krushan!" Shouted by both Shvate and Adri together, at first it was noted only by the Krushan charioteers. They turned their astonished heads to see the two young princes raising their voices — and their swords.

It was a miserable morning for the charioteers of Hastinaga. What should have been a battle with a foregone conclusion had turned out instead to be an unwinnable fight. The enemy's unlawful violation of the rules of war and their cowardly tactic had turned the balance against the Krushan. The sheer mass and speed with which the rebels had attacked the Krushan chariot lines was unheard of. No one could have anticipated such a move. To start a battle with such skullduggery! But any outrage had been swiftly replaced by dismay, then alarm, then outright panic as the odds mounted against the charioteers.

Now, barely an hour into the battle, the sun only a hand's breadth above the eastern horizon, the brave charioteers were already facing not just their own imminent deaths, but also imminent total defeat. Both of these ignominious outcomes were galling, but the knowledge that the heirs of Hastinaga would be killed also was unbearable. So long as there was even a single Krushan charioteer alive and standing, they would fight the enemy tooth and nail.

The princes must not die.

The rebels would win this day, but they would pay a price for that victory.

The captains had sent out the word: ten for one. That meant simply, kill ten enemies for every single Krushan felled.

And that was what they were doing until that moment: selling their lives dearly. Fighting with whatever they could, using every means at their disposal, against impossible odds, to make the enemy pay as expensive a price as possible to achieve their goal. The charioteers of Krushan had fallen into a fighting spell, a hypnotic state wherein all they saw was the enemy and all they sought was the means to kill that enemy. The world fell away and reduced to that narrow purpose. Even the fantastic battle raging in the sky between Vrath and the Reygistani Jarsun was only an occasional distraction. They could do nothing to help their prince regent. And for once, Vrath could do nothing to help them. They were each fighting their own battles.

"*Krushan!*"

The sound of the princes' battle cry had startled the charioteers out of their collective reverie, waking up a part of their minds that had shut down in anticipation of the looming defeat.

"*Krushan!*"

Prince Shvate and Prince Adri shouted again, their young eager voices a stark contrast to the gruff older voices of the other charioteers.

The charioteers turned and paid heed to their princes.

"*Krushan!*" the charioteers cried in chorus with their lieges.

Prince Adri and Prince Shvate were standing on the rims of the wells of their chariots, each with a hand on the flagpole that carried their house colors. They were waving to attract their fellow Krushan's attention.

Now that they had that attention, they delivered their message. It was a single-word order, yelled with the same furious youthful intensity as the battle cry.

"*Attack!*"

Both princes pointed in the same direction.

The charioteers turned their heads to look —

And saw their opportunity at once. Every charioteer's nightmare is to be stuck and rendered immobile, whether by an obstruction, a broken wheel, a dead horse, or by the worst of all calamities: a chakra — a ring of enemies so dense that even the most skilled of Krushan charioteers could not find a way to break through.

They found themselves in the midst of the worst chakra imaginable right now. Ringed in on every side by layers upon layers of enemy forces — not merely chariots, but also cavalry, foot, and even elephants. It was impossible to escape such a chakra, and even if they could, they had had their hands full until now merely surviving and protecting their princes, which meant creating a chakra of their own, circling their own chariots to prevent enemies from reaching their lieges — but at the same time preventing themselves from breaking out.

But now Shvate and Adri were pointing to something that every charioteer recognized instantly.

The place where the wagons had breached the Krushan wall of chariots was a scorched patch of earth. Because of the fire and hot ashes, the enemy was tactically restricted. Elephants and mounted horses might panic at the smell of fire and cause havoc. Foot soldiers would be useless too. Only chariot teams could brave that fiery breach and attack the Krushan lines. So they had sent chariots through, many of whom were still there, fighting and killing more Krushan on every side.

But chariots *moved* . . . which left a gap in the wall.

Yes, there was a vulnerability in the chakra at that place. Not a very great weakness — and one that the enemy could fill in a moment once their leader entered the breach with more chariots — but for the moment, the spot was weak, and the opportunity was there for the taking. And the two princes had spotted it and were calling to their army to act.

And the charioteers of Krushan did.

Jilana

~

JILANA CLAPPED HER HANDS together and drew in breath.

Above the field, the cloud of red mist that had been Jarsun dissipated, blown away by the wind.

The block of ice that remained marked Vrath's location. Though he lay still as death within the block, she could not believe he was dead.

He could not be.

She knew that the water that had finally defeated their enemy and saved Vrath's life was no ordinary water.

It was Vrath's mother herself — Jeel come to save her son: it was a powerful reminder, as if she needed one, that although Vrath lived among them as a mortal, he was yet the demigod son of the divine River Goddess Who Nourished the World. Jeel had felt her son's life blood pattering down through the ground, soaking into the dirt of the field, and had risen up to come to his defense.

And destroyed the demon Jarsun.

And in doing so saved her beloved Vrath.

And helped the Krushan draw victory from the jaws of defeat.

Even now, Jilana knew, within that block of ice, Vrath was likely being healed by the powerful magical properties of Jeeljal, the precious sacred water of Jeel herself, descended directly from heaven to Arthaloka, purest of the pure, most blessed of all fluids, the water of life itself.

Upon realizing the miracle that had occurred, Jilana had clapped her hands together and shouted, "Jai Jeel Mata!" and had heard herself echoed by everyone on the royal platform.

Then she had turned her attention to her grandsons.

And that was what had caused her to clap her hands together and draw in a breath.

Adri and Shvate were leading a charge!

The two brave boys had somehow managed to rally their Krushan chariot cadre and had ordered them to change tactics. The defensive wall the charioteers had built to protect the two boys would not last long, and so it made sense for them to change from a defensive to an offensive approach; in the absence of Vrath or another senior leader, the charioteers could not undertake such a change of tactic . . . but the princes of Hastinaga could. Ordering the chariots to attack, they were now leading them through a very narrow breach in the enemy lines, barely wide enough for a single chariot to pass through at a time.

She watched with rapt attention and hands clasped in silent prayer:

Jai Jeel Mata.

Jai to all the stone gods who watch over us.

Protect and bring home my grandsons safe.

Adri

~

"Krushan!"

Adri's heightened senses informed him that the breach he was seeking lay directly ahead.

It was he who had found the breach and informed Shvate of its existence. Even though Shvate had eyes as sharp as an eagle's, he had not been looking for it, while Adri, not needing to look with his eyes, had heard the absence of sound in that one particular spot that meant an empty space — a small but vital empty space.

Adri was now using that same heightened sense to race his chariot toward that breach. Yet even Adri's own charioteer could not see the breach himself — there was too much debris and smoke still in the air in that area to see the narrow gap. It was only Adri's acute hearing sensitivity that enabled him to guide his charioteer via a series of taps and touches on his back and shoulders, indicating which way to turn.

For several agonizing moments, they drove through dense smoke so thick and foul smelling that even Adri suffered a moment of self-doubt. If they continued through this and found a line of rebel chariots waiting with drawn bows beyond the haze, this would be his first and last battle tactic ever executed.

But then, with a sudden thrill, he sensed that the smoke had cleared and they were on the other side — and most importantly, that there were no enemy chariots waiting to greet them with arrows.

Adri heard his charioteer shout, "We are through, my prince!"

And then he heard his brother shout from behind.

"Attack!"

And the message was passed on from mouth to ear to mouth as the Krushan charioteers followed their princes' lead and drove their vehicles through the breach.

Moments later, they were spotted.

Adri heard the sounds of enemy captains shouting at their forces, ordering them to "close that breach!" In another moment, he knew, the enemy would realize that the Krushan penetrating the breach were none other than the princes themselves — their main target. And then, the entire might of the rebel forces would descend upon this part of the battlefield. They would be assaulted on all sides by insurmountable forces and would go down in a hail of arrows, spears, javelins, elephants, cavalry, and the stone gods knew what else.

But for now, they were heroes.

They were princes.

They were brothers-in-arms.

They were Krushan.

"*Krushan!*" Adri yelled forcefully, drawing his bow and taking aim. He let loose, directing his arrow by sound at the thickest cluster of enemy he could sense.

He heard the *thwa-thump* of the arrow punching through armor and piercing flesh and bone, heard the startled cry of the man, and heard him fall to the ground, crushed under the wheels of the chariot behind him.

My first kill.

"*Krushan!*" he cried again, and loosed a second arrow.

Adri heard Shvate echo the battle cry and loose an arrow as well, at the same instant as Adri's second arrow found a home in the throat of another rebel charioteer. The man emitted a gurgle and fell back in the well of his own chariot, spasming as his heels drummed out the rhythm of death. Adri was already loosing a third arrow before the man died, then a fourth, and a fifth, as rebel charioteers converged on him from all sides.

Then he was in the thick of battle, being shot at and attacked and fighting back and loosing arrows and yelling until he was hoarse and his fingers bled from the bowstring and his hand found only an empty quiver as it reached over and over, instinctively, for the next arrow that was no longer there.

Shvate

~

"*Krushan!*"

Shvate loosed arrows in rapid succession, feeling a thrill of satisfaction each time he saw an arrow find its mark and an enemy fall. His gurus had taught him that the taking of life was a serious matter not to be glorified or gloated over. But to him right now, it was not the satisfaction of killing that thrilled him; it was *surviving*. His first battle, his first actual experience of mortal combat — surrounded and overwhelmed by enemies more numerous than any yoddha could ever hope to overcome, unsupervised and without his protector to shield him . . . and yet here he was, not only surviving this calamitous turn of events, but actually fighting back, eliminating enemy charioteers by the fistfuls.

He had loosed almost his entire quiver already, close to threescore arrows, and he had counted more than half as many strikes. It was impossible to tell if those thirty men had been killed instantly or merely wounded, but even so, that was thirty rebel warriors that he himself had taken out of the fight. What had the charioteer captain said earlier to his cadre? "Ten for one"? By that measure, Shvate had already done the work of three charioteers, and if he only had more arrows, he could yet continue to bring down many more.

Even as this thought occurred to him, his arrows ran out. His hand continued to reach into the empty quiver, feeling the rim of the container, desiring just one more arrow. But there were none to be found.

"More arrows?" he called out to his charioteer.

The man glanced back, noting Shvate's empty quiver. His eyes flashed up at his prince, and in that look, Shvate saw respect, admiration, pride.

"I'm sorry, Yuvraj," he said. "I did not expect you or Prince Adri to engage the enemy, or I would have stocked more. But we have those." He jerked his head at the back of the chariot as he maneuvered it past a rebel vehicle turned on its side, wheel spinning. The rebel charioteer lay half crushed beneath the car, an arrow through his throat.

My arrow, Shvate thought proudly. He felt a twinge of remorse for having taken the man's life, but in battle there was no time for such humane consideration. Kill or be killed. Besides, the enemy had violated the rules of war. Shvate was only doing what he had to in order to survive.

He looked in the direction his charioteer had indicated. At the back of the chariot, hooked to the well rim, was a clutch of spears and javelins. Shvate unhooked a spear and hefted it.

Around him, the chaos of battle reeled and screamed.

Chariots of both sides were driving every which way, the rebel forces tripped by their own ingenuity. Their attempt to ring in the Krushan forces had left their numbers relatively thin at the outer ends of the chakra. Shvate saw that he was barely two or three hundred yards from clear ground. If he could fight his way through the last lines of enemy chariots, it might be possible to break the chakra altogether, enabling the Krushan chariots to turn back and attack the enemy from the other side, forcing them to fight on two fronts at once — inside and out.

"Dhruv," he said to his charioteer, "do you see yonder flag?" He pointed with the spear.

"Aye," his charioteer replied, turning the heads of his horse team to dodge a volley of arrows from a cluster of chariots racing toward their position from the east.

Shvate ducked down behind the well of his chariot, feeling the *thwack-thwack-thud* of the volley striking the outer wall. One arrow fell into the well itself, skimming his shoulder and drawing a tiny spurt of blood. "Make for that flag, but don't let the enemy see that we're making for it."

The charioteer, a middle-aged man with a bristling red beard flecked with grey, furrowed his lined brow. Abruptly, his battle-experienced mind glimpsed the tactical significance of Shvate's order. He grinned, displaying yellow teeth with a double gap in the lower line. "Prince, you are a born warrior. A brilliant maneuver! I will pass the word along to the rest of the company."

"Do that," Shvate said as he sought and found a target for his first spear. A rebel chariot cutting out of line and racing toward them at a sharp angle, the man aiming a longbow straight at Shvate. There was an instant when Shvate was taking aim at the same time as the enemy charioteer and their eyes met across the expanse between them. Shvate saw that the arrow was aimed directly for his throat, and from the intense calm of the archer, he sensed it would hit its mark. He heaved the spear a kshana before the archer loosed his arrow and watched his missile fly through the air, quivering and shuddering as all spears do when thrown with such force, as the arrow shot toward him — and Shvate *shifted*, twisting his head and neck just a few inches to the right, and saw and heard the arrow *whick* past with deadly accuracy, passing through the empty space his throat had occupied just an instant ago. Still bent over, Shvate saw his spear strike the chest of the archer, punching through his breastplate and driving the man back against the well of his chariot. The mortally injured archer gazed across at Shvate, and Shvate saw the Look in those eyes — that look that acknowledged that the better warrior had won the bout, before the man tumbled backward, falling out of his chariot and into the dust of the field, dead.

Shvate heard the pounding of the blood in his ears as he reached for another throwing spear. The man he'd killed had been a veteran from the looks of it, a man who had trained and fought and survived many battles before this, yet one who now lay dead on this very field, less than seventy yards away, felled by the first spear thrown by the hand of a young boy in his maiden battle. Shvate was humbled by the knowledge of what he had just done, saddened by the thought that he had taken yet another life, and simultaneously also proud that he had survived yet another brush with death — not by hiding behind walls of soldiers dedicated to protecting his life, but by looking another man in the eye and matching his weapon with his own, by fighting and winning the right to live. What a privilege it was, this life — to breathe, to walk Arthaloka freely, simply to exist here and now. Freedom was a privilege dearly won by the brave and the unbowed. Compared to most, Shvate knew he had paid but a fraction of the price of his own freedom and right to live. He vowed then and there that he would earn the right to the rest of his life *himself*, by fighting for it every minute of every day.

He aimed his second spear at a chariot racing alongside him, the archer aboard it aiming a shortbow at him and loosing a series of arrows in quick succession. Shvate dodged the arrows easily—the archer's aim was wide, and his speed too desperate—but then saw the man's true intent was not to hit him but to distract him while two other chariots came at him from the other direction. Shvate smiled to himself, acknowledging the ingenuity of the tactic, yet now he had three enemies racing at him from different directions, all loosing arrows, and closing in fast.

Shvate contemplated the situation for a kshana, ignoring the whistling arrows flying past, the cacophony of battle all around, the dust and heat of the battlefield, and focused on the problem at hand. He closed his eyes and saw himself and the other chariots as if from a great height, three-dimensional miniatures moving on a tabletop field. Everything else faded away to a white drone.

Without thinking, he picked up another spear and a javelin and kept them in his right hand as he hefted the first spear in his left. He aimed and threw the first spear, and then, in the same motion, and without waiting to see if it struck true, he spun about and threw the second spear and then the javelin, both in quick succession. As the javelin left his hand, he heard the sound of his first blow and turned to view the result.

The first spear struck the wheel of one of the two chariots coming at him from behind. The chariot upended and tumbled end over end, causing the one behind it to collide with it. Both vehicles went crashing in a jumble of shattered wood and screaming horses and men, the driver and archer of the first chariot lost in the crush, the driver of the second also killed instantly. But the archer of the second had time to see the disaster coming and leaped off his chariot, rolling with the expertise of a veteran and returning to his feet, shortbow and arrow ready to loose. The javelin struck him through the belly—not the chest as Shvate had intended, but then, the man was shorter than he had appeared when standing in the chariot—and the archer crumpled with a shocked look on his face. He had seen the spear and the crash and anticipated it; he had not anticipated the javelin to come so soon after, nor the accuracy with which it was thrown.

The second spear had been aimed at the archer of the other chariot, the one trying to distract Shvate. That bowman lay slumped over the rim of the well of his vehicle, Shvate's spear through his chest, as his charioteer raced pointlessly alongside Shvate's battle car. He registered the death of his officer and veered away, useless without his archer.

Shvate was reaching for another spear when he felt a piercing agony in his eyes. He moaned and crouched down in the well of his chariot, shielding himself. He had been so caught up in the success of his first combat, he had completely forgotten his primary weakness: light. Until now, he had been able to fight without any restriction because the day was young and the early morning sunlight was soft and slanted, but now, as the sun rose a hand higher in the east, the light was growing stronger, brighter — too strong and bright for Shvate's sensitive colorless eyes. He realized now that his skin was also feeling the effect of the stronger sunlight. Soon, the light would be too strong for him to function at all. In the hermitage he had been shielded by the dense jungle. Here on the open battlefield, he was naked and unprotected.

"My prince," Dhruv asked with concern, glancing back at him, "is all well? Are you struck?"

Yes, I am crippled by infirmity, and wounded by light, Shvate wanted to tell him, although it was well known and fairly obvious to see that his albinism was his great weakness. Instead, he held his tongue. Mother Jilana had cautioned him against talking about it openly to anyone: *Not anyone,* she'd said. *Let your enemies and detractors say what they will. Never acknowledge or comment on it yourself.*

"I will be fine," he replied to Dhruv. "Continue with the maneuver."

The charioteer did as he was told, glancing back only occasionally to check on the well-being of his prince.

Shvate suddenly realized that in the excitement of his own first combat, he had completely forgotten not only about his condition, but also about his brother. It was as if, for the past half hour, his entire world had been reduced to himself and the enemies trying to kill him. He had not even thought of Adri for that entire time.

He stood up in the well, ignoring the shooting pain from the intense rays of sunlight that struck him in the face. He raised a hand to shield his eyes from the direct light. "Where is my brother?" he said. "*Where is Prince Adri?*"

Adri

～

ADRI LISTENED FOR THE sound of his javelin hitting its mark: not the charioteer nor the archer, but the ground immediately before the rolling wheel of the enemy chariot. The javelin bit the ground at a sharp angle, obstructing the oncoming wheel just enough to force the vehicle itself to veer sharply. That brought it into the path of the half dozen other rebel chariots coming at Adri's. The charioteers all struggled desperately to control their teams and avoid a collision, as Adri's charioteer urged his team and drove them forward through the outermost gap. Adri felt a thrill of excitement as his senses told him that they had done it, they had broken through the last line, they were now outside the enemy chakra!

"Breakthrough!" his charioteer shouted.

Adri heard other voices taking up the cry and passing it on. "Prince Adri has broken through!"

He felt a sensation of deep pride. Today, he had shown the world as well as himself what he could do. Not merely something that a blind man could do just as well as any *normal* person, but that he, Adri, prince of Hastinaga, heir to the Burnt Empire, could accomplish, even in the heat of battle, fighting an overwhelming enemy against impossible odds. He had shown them that he did not need to be compared to other boys his age who were sighted. *If you want to compare Adri, then compare him to the warriors lying dead on this field, the ones killed by his arrows, spears, javelins, and — most of all — his tactics. Match that, if you can!*

"Prince."

His charioteer's voice was suddenly anxious. Gone was the joy of a moment ago.

"Yes, Adran?" Adri did not share the man's concern. Whatever the situation, he was ready to deal with it. He was Adri, the Krushan prince who had led the Krushan chariot cadre to what now seemed likely to be a miraculous comeback, if not outright victory. And the day was yet young. The sun barely two hands above the eastern horizon. There was much left to be done today, and he, Adri, was ready and able to accomplish it.

"From the north and west, my lord," said the charioteer, his voice deathly serious. "We cannot outrun them, and we are out of weapons. I was not given to expect that you would be required to engage in actual combat, my prince. I only stocked a single supply of arrows and spears."

Adri tuned out the man's voice and focused instead on the approaching rumble of vehicles from the north and west. Yes, there was indeed a small force approaching from that direction. Two chariots. The rest on horseback. Why did they concern Adran so?

He listened carefully to the sound of the men and women in that group. He could form a picture of the men and women themselves from the sounds they made by interpreting the complex interaction of sounds and effects in and around the actual persons — the displacement of the air that passed over their bodies, the impact of their horses' hooves in the dirt, the sounds of their grunts and their voices when they spoke.

There were only five of them. Just five. What was there to be so concerned about?

Then he felt it. It was a quality not merely in the sounds themselves, but also in the spaces between the sounds. These were not ordinary soldiers, or even officers. They were master warriors, yoddhas, kings and queens, princes and princesses, or champions of royalty. Master artists of the art of war.

And they were all approaching with the sole intention of killing him.

Suddenly, the bravado of the past hour left him as rapidly as water from a sieve. Five yoddhas approached, and Adri was without weapons.

The pride he'd felt at his kills; the joy at his arrows, spears, and javelins hitting their mark; the exultation of his first tactical victory — all of it faded away, leaving only a stark realization: He was weaponless. Alone. And about to be attacked by the real enemy.

Not the soldiers, captains, generals, or even the champions of the enemy army. The enemies themselves, the rulers who had united in the alliance against Hastinaga.

And from the grimness he felt in their hearts even at this distance, he knew that they meant to kill him by any means, whatever it took.

Suddenly, in a single moment, he was little Adri again, blind, lost, and forsaken in his cold dark world, grasping and groping for someone, *anyone* — spurned by his own mother, laughed at by his play companions, sneered at by his peers. Alone in a jungle of frightening beasts who would rip his flesh apart without a second thought.

"Shvate?" he cried out, suddenly afraid. "Shvate, where are you? I need you, brother!"

Shvate

~

"SHVATE!" ADRI CALLED.

Shvate heard his brother's shout and tried to peer over the rim of the well. Another shaft of sunlight struck him directly in the eyes, causing him to cry out with pain. To his sensitive eyes, it seemed like the entire world had caught ablaze, the field burning with white hot sunlight. To even peer at it through half-lidded eyes, through the gaps in his fingers, was agonizing. Shards of pain shot into his eyes, piercing his brain. He could not think, move, act. Mere breathing was an effort. His skin was afire. His insides, too, were burning. Gone was the Shvate who had stood and loosed an entire quiver of arrows, flung spear after spear and javelin after javelin. Here was Shvate, a little albino boy who could not withstand direct sunlight for a moment without experiencing a subsequent day and night of acute, head-splitting agony.

Even through the agony, he could hear his brother's voice, calling.

Even through his pain, he knew that he had to do something.

Adri was in trouble. His brother needed his help.

But how could he? He had no weapons left. He could barely stand up in the well of his own chariot. He could not open his eyes or see for the intensity of the sunlight beating down upon the field.

At the moment, he was as blind as his brother, and his skin was on fire, his insides ablaze.

Shvate crouched down in the well of the chariot, hugging his own knees, trying to push past the pain and the sense of utter helplessness he was feeling.

He could not help Adri. He himself needed help — and who was there to help *him*? Not his mother, who would not even hug him as a child, who was repulsed by his white skin and pale eyelashes and colorless eyes. She regarded him as a freak of nature, a curse upon her life. A blight upon the world. Even the other children looked at him differently, treated him differently. Other adults too — speaking with extra care around him as if he was not merely albino but slow of mind as well. Everyone treated him like he was different, damaged, undesirable. And nobody came to his aid when he needed help, comfort, and protection.

He was alone. And so was Adri.

Brother, forgive me. We are each alone in our own private hell. Live through this. If you can.

Vrath

~

IN THE BLOCK OF ice floating a thousand yards above the battlefield, the body of Vrath lay suspended.

The miracle waters of the Jeel had worked their magic, healing the many hundreds of wounds inflicted by Jarsun — repairing the damage and destruction to organs, limbs, flesh, blood, muscle and sinew, bone and gristle.

The process was not yet complete.

Almost, but not quite.

A little while longer, perhaps another hour or two, and the reparation would be complete. Vrath would be restored to his perfect self.

But the voices of his nephews were audible to him, even inside his cocoon of ice.

He could hear their agony, their suffering, their terror.

They needed help.

They needed *him*.

The enemy was bearing down upon them. They were weaponless and isolated, exposed and helpless. The enemy was strong and ruthless. Druhyu of Druhyu was eagerly racing toward them, grinning at the thought of driving his blade through that young flesh, maiming and butchering the young princes of Hastinaga. The others were not as savagely inclined toward killing young ones as was Druhyu, but they were equally motivated to kill the princes. Killing them would end the battle, win the day, and secure a triumph for the rebellion. The world would rise up against Hastinaga and tear the empire apart, sharing the spoils among themselves. And they, the first to defy the might of Hastinaga, would enjoy the lion's share. They would be emperors and empresses in their own right. Everyone would fear and be in awe of them forever after.

All they had to do was kill two frightened young boys and show their chopped heads to the world, displaying them like prizes of victory.

Inside the cocoon of ice, Vrath knew all this and more. He had to act now, before it was too late. It was not merely his responsibility, it was Krushan law.

And Vrath always upheld Krushan law.

With a sudden explosion, the giant block of ice *burst apart* —

It shattered to fragments in midair, which fell to the battlefield below as a shower of tiny chips, none large enough to injure anyone and indeed already melting in the late morning sun as they descended toward the hot earth below.

Vrath hung in midair, his skin still scarred and bruised, his reparation incomplete, not fully restored to his former strength.

But he was still *Vrath*.

He fell from the sky, falling to the earth with blistering speed, like the great eagle god Grrud bearing down upon the army of Nagas, and landed upon the field with an impact that shook every last mortal and beast for miles. The dust from his impact rose fifty yards in the air. When it cleared, he was visible there on bended knee, powerful shoulders hunched, head lowered.

Slowly, he raised that great head, his mane of grey-white hair falling back over those mighty shoulders and arms, and turned his withering gaze to stare down the oncoming chariots and horses of the rebels who were racing toward the princes of the Burnt Empire.

Vrath rose to his full height, standing astride the field, naked and weaponless, body still oozing blood from a dozen unhealed wounds. The oncoming rebels slowed, awestruck at his appearance and the sheer majesty of his presence.

Behind him, Shvate and Adri still cowered in their chariots, aware that their guardian and protector had arrived at last, but still suffering from their respective conditions.

Vrath spread his arms wide, gesturing to the rebels confronting him.

"You wish to kill the princes of Hastinaga?" Vrath said, folding his arms across his chest. "Then you must kill me first. If you can."

Jilana

~

AFTER THAT, IT WAS a rout.

Without the demoniac Jarsun to keep the flame of rebellion stoked, the alliance fell apart. Confronted by the legendary Vrath, their morale as badly dented as their shields, the remaining rebel leaders surrendered with varying degrees of reluctance. There would be punitive measures placed upon each of their kingdoms, but all that was for later, in the messy aftermath of battle.

For now, all that mattered was that the Krushan had won the day.

Jilana wept.

She fell back into her chair and sobbed tears of joy and relief.

Once more, Vrath had fulfilled his word.

He had protected her grandchildren.

The House of Krushan was safe once more.

Part Three

Karni

~

1

KARNI EXECUTED A PERFECT swan dive from the top of the rock, her graceful body hanging suspended in the air for just a moment before slicing the surface of the lake with barely a splash. She emerged more than a dozen yards away, smiling.

Her companions laughed and applauded. "Another perfect dive as always, Princess!"

Karni tossed back her lustrous dark hair and swam strongly across to the far bank. It was a good fifty yards away, and even the strongest swimmers in her company did not dare try to race her. Karni was in the habit of swimming one hundred breadths daily, and could still race them all home to the palace afterward. They contented themselves with playing at swimming on the shady side of the lake, the more boisterous ones splashing water at one another and squealing, the vainer ones braiding flowers into each other's hair to make the merchants' sons in the marketplace turn their heads as they passed.

It was a lazy afternoon, the sun slipping to the western sky, songbirds calling in the trees, flocks of geese and ducks flying overhead; butterflies flitted over the flowers, deer grazed on the soft kusa grass nearby, and at one point in the slow, indolent afternoon, a young lion crept down to the lake on the far side of the glen and drank his fill, keeping a wary but unafraid eye on the cavorting maidens, before slinking back into the shadowy depths of the jungle.

Karni was on her eighty-ninth lap when she paused in midstroke, treading water.

Something was different. It was hard to pinpoint, but there was for certain a ... *change*. The lake was suddenly quiet, and likewise the songbirds were silent, and the bees had ceased buzzing, and the dragonflies that had been humming over the water were now no longer anywhere to be seen. The ducks, too, had ceased their quacking in the rushes, and even the birds flying overhead now did so silently, the angled shadow of their passing the only indication of their presence.

Across the lake, she could hear the faint sounds of her companions playing and laughing, but they too seemed to sense something was wrong, and hushed one another.

From the forest, a lion emitted a single dismayed roar, as if protesting, and then he too fell silent.

Karni turned in the water, frowning.

A shadow began to grow in the center of the lake.

The sky was clear blue, the sun dipping in the west but still half a watch from sunset. There was not a cloud in the sky to cause the shadow. Yet, as Karni watched with puzzlement, the center of the lake began to grow darker.

Could it be fish? No. The shadow was circular and concentrated in the center of the lake, not moving the way a school of fish might move.

As Karni watched, the shadow deepened, turning the sallow surface of the water black as pitch. The pitch-black circle of water then began to swirl.

Karni was closer to the far bank of the lake than to the center. But even here, a good dozen yards or more from the edge of the strange pitch-black circle, she could feel the pull of the water.

The swirling black water began to turn round on itself, swirling faster and faster. In moments, it became a churning, the water breaking and producing waves that should have been white-tipped but instead were dark. Now, Karni could feel herself being drawn in by the force of the churning, pulled toward the center of that swirling vortex.

Strong swimmer though she was, she had to strain against the pull. Grabbing hold of a willow root that dipped into the water, she wrapped the tendril firmly around her arm, standing on the muddy floor of the bank in waist-deep water, and watched with rising alarm.

The center of the lake had become a whirlpool.

The whirlpool churned and spun faster and faster, like no vortex Karni had ever seen or heard of. It was as frenzied as a whitewater rapid, roaring now with great force. Across the lake, she could see her companions standing on the shore, backing away in fright as they watched this freakish display.

Karni could not believe this was a natural phenomenon. She had been swimming in this lake with her friends ever since she first learned how, which was not long after she was able to walk. She was a young woman now, fourteen summers of age, and as such she no longer needed nurses to accompany her. Nor bodyguards, for the kingdom of Stonecastle was at peace and had been at peace for decades. The nearest neighbors, Dirda, Avant, and Hais, were not at war with Stonecastle or with each other. But for the first time in her life, she wished she had both bodyguards and a blade of her own by her side.

Yet what good would a sword do against a water demon? she wondered.

Nothing, probably. But it was all she could think of. That, and the realization that she should do as her companions had done and get away from the lake at once. Even if she ended up on the wrong side, and would have to walk all the way around the bank to get back to her companions and the pathway that led back to the palace. She had to get away from this thing, whatever it was.

Yet some part of her resisted.

She could not bring herself to turn and climb up on the bank, to run away from the churning maelstrom that was now roaring and spinning in a dervish-like frenzy, sending water spraying across the tops of the trees that surrounded the lake.

Karni watched, compelled by a fascination she could not explain. The whirlpool swirled now in a descending cone, the dark water of the lake foaming white. The roar of the water drowned out all other sounds, but at the edges of vision, she glimpsed birds flying, animals fleeing, and underfoot, she felt creatures of the under-earth scurrying away from the waterside.

Then something began to rise from the center of the maelstrom: a man.

A holy man, clad in the red-ochre garb of the forest hermits, hair matted and piled overhead, possessed of the aging, withered limbs and wasted body of the lifelong penitent engaged in bhor tapasya.

Yet there was nothing withered or aged about his eyes. They shone with a ferocity that was unnerving. Large and bulging, in a bony angular face, their irises were a unsettling grey. That penetrating gaze scanned the shore of the lake in such a way that Karni got the sense he was searching for landmarks to ascertain his exact location.

Had he come from the underworld? How did a man emerge from a whirlpool in a lake? What force was at work here, raising this man up above the water, so as to make him float in the air?

As Karni watched with open amazement, the old hermit lowered the point of his raised staff, pointing down at the whirlpool. At once, the maelstrom subsided, settling suddenly into a calm, unbroken surface. Likewise, the wind that had howled a moment earlier died away, and the ripples and waves caused by the disturbance ceased. So too did the cries of the agitated birds, the sounds of animals in the forest, and the scurrying of insects all subside.

The lake was as calm and still as it had been before this holy man's arrival.

The hermit now stood on the surface of the lake, as comfortably as a man standing on solid ground. He began to walk across the lake, the soles of his feet dipping into the water lightly, merely breaking the skin of the water, hardly disturbing it otherwise —

Heading directly for Karni's side of the lake.

As he neared the bank, he caught sight of Karni, seemingly registering her presence for the first time. This sent a sudden chill through her heart. All at once, the balmy summer sunshine felt icy cold. She wrapped her arms around herself, realizing how wet her garments were and how little she wore. Her outer garments lay on the other side of the lake, where her companions and she had discarded them. She wished her friends were beside her; they likely would have been screaming in alarm or excitement, but Karni was not given to outbursts of emotion. She stood her ground, remaining calm.

The hermit was almost at the shore.

He was staring straight at her now, his piercing gaze taking in her lack of proper attire, her disheveled and damp condition, her shivering posture . . . What must he think her to be? She looked far from a princess right now. As she glanced up anxiously, she saw his eyes darken visibly, turning from grey to jet-black. A darkness swirled around him like a cowl, exactly in the way the water of the lake had. A miasma enveloped his face and head; she could see his dark eyes shining from inside the miasma, directed only at her as he reached the bank at last and then stepped ashore.

For a moment, the thought struck her that this man could be a Naga, one of those denizens of the nether realms who were said to rise, at their whim, to the surface of the world and assume any form they pleased. The man who emerged from the lake could well be such a creature — a snake in a man's body. His eyes were as fierce as any snake's venomous gaze. The darkness of the water could be caused by his venom, Karni reasoned, and perhaps this human form was just a disguise to enable him to approach unsuspecting humans.

The hermit was still approaching, now mere yards from her.

Those piercing dark eyes continued to bore into her, his concentration intense, and as he walked, his hand gripped the wildwood staff hard enough to cause his knuckles to turn white, every aspect of his posture suggesting a predator about to attack.

Remember who you are, she told herself firmly. *You are no ordinary young girl. You are Karni of the Mraashk, daughter of Karna Sura, sister to Vasurava, adopted daughter of King Stonecastle, princess and heir to the Stonecastle kingdom. You will not let yourself be intimidated by anyone — or anything.*

She released the breath she had been holding.

Gathering her errant emotions, Karni bundled them together, tied them in a tight knot, then tucked them away.

With perfect self-control, she joined her palms in a namas, bowed her head low, and intoned, "Greetings, Great One. Welcome to our humble kingdom of Stonecastle."

2

"Who might you be, young doe?" the hermit said.

The intensity of his gaze seemed not to lessen even when she greeted him. His bony face and penetrating eyes remained as fierce, his posture still one of attack. Yet his voice was surprisingly pleasant, a startling contrast to his wild appearance.

Karni inclined her head. "May it please your holiness, I am the adoptive daughter of Stonecastle, king of the Stonecastle nation. I go by the name of Karni, after my birth father, Karna Sura."

The holy man continued to regard her with the same severe scrutiny. She waited, unnerved inwardly but determined not to let it show.

He then raised his staff and strode toward her. Karni resisted the urge to flinch, cry out, back away, or run, though all these presented themselves as desirable actions. The hermit reached the spot where she stood, still dripping from the lake, and passed her by without pausing, working his way up the path.

And before long, he was gone. She could see him, striding away through the glade, his tall bony form moving through the trees. Away from the lake, away from her. Karni heaved a giant sigh of relief and all but collapsed to the ground, and there she sat, just breathing for several moments as she collected her wits.

From across the lake, she heard the faint sound of voices calling. She looked up and saw her companions on the far bank, shouting and gesturing frantically. She raised an arm, acknowledging them.

They gestured back, calling to her to come across the lake. Karni had never been so glad to see her friends, and got to her feet slowly, amazed to still be alive. When that old hermit had come striding toward her with his staff raised, she had been certain he was going to attack her. Now, of course, it seemed silly to have thought it. Why would an old hermit attack a helpless young girl?

Then again, the old man had emerged from a maelstrom in a lake, a maelstrom that he himself seemed to have caused, then walked on water. He was no ordinary itinerant holy man, that was for sure. Who knew what else he was capable of? She shook her head, trying to rid herself of the sense of dread that lingered after his passing.

Karni took two steps into the lake, then stopped in ankle-deep water. She wanted to rejoin her friends, but suddenly, she had no desire to swim. Not right now. Not today.

Perhaps not for a long while.

Perhaps never again in this particular lake.

She waved and gestured to her companions on the far bank, pointing to the west. They waved back, acknowledging that they understood.

She turned and ran around the lake, through the trees. The opposite of the route the old man had gone, the long way around. She didn't mind running an extra mile or two, so long as she did not have to face that fierce visage again.

She covered the distance in record time, startling a pair of weasels back into their holes along the way. The forest was slowly returning to normal, the sounds and ambiance resuming now after the unnatural event at the lake.

Finally, Karni saw her friends through the trees and sprinted to meet them. They met in a clamor of cries and embraces and tears.

"— saw you in the lake and then —"

"— thought you were sucked in —"

"— what would we tell your father —"

"— the king would have our heads for —"

"— what was that *thing* —"

"It was a Nagdevta, wasn't it?"

This last came from Ramyakumari, a sweet but simple daughter of a cowherding family. Ramya was terrified of snakes and prayed daily to Grrud, Lord of Birds and archenemy of all serpents.

"It was an old hermit, that's all," Karni told them. "He asked me who I was, then walked off down the path."

"Did you tell him you're the queen of this realm?" asked Jaggatpuri indignantly.

"I'm not the queen, Jaggi," Karni replied.

"You might as well be, since King Stonecastle doesn't have any sons."

"Did he say who he was? I bet it was Seer-Mage Nrudam!"

"He didn't say, and I didn't ask." Didn't *dare* ask, she added silently. She gestured past her friends. "Let's go back. I have to collect my clothes."

"Oh, I have them!" Sunidhi said, producing a bunched bundle she had been squeezing anxiously with both hands.

"Thanks for keeping them unwrinkled," Karni teased as she shook out the crumpled garments. She slipped them on quickly. "Now, let's go home. This lake makes me nervous. That old rishi could come back anytime."

3

The girls chattered excitedly as they walked. Most of their speculation was about the rishi's spectacular arrival. Karni, having seen the event up close, had a theory.

"I think he used the water of the lake to travel from another plane to this one. The water is runoff from the sacred river, after all. These old hermits have the power to ask River Goddess Jeel to transport them through other worlds, don't they?"

"But why come *here*? There are no gods here to visit. What possible business could he have in our world, let alone our kingdom?"

They were still exclaiming and debating over the rishi's identity and mission when a young man slipped suddenly through the trees behind them and began to follow. He stayed close enough to hear what they were saying but avoid being seen. His attention was rooted on Karni most particularly. He watched her every move, took in her every gesture and word, admired the way she shook her wet hair, bumped her hip against a friend's to make a point, laughed with her head thrown back and hand raised to her chin. There was no question that he was besotted with her beauty and her personality. More than besotted, he desired her. His longing was evident in his look, the way he smiled at her laughter, the wry shakes of his head he gave when she said something tart to her companions and they squealed in delight.

This man was head over heels in love with the princess of Stonecastle.

He finally made his move a mile outside the city.

Coming upon them from behind, he fell into step barely a yard aft of Karni herself, matching pace with them.

The other girls noticed him first, their eyes widening as they saw him, then relaxing and smiling as he touched his finger to his lips to shush them. They kept his secret, but their own amusement at his presence undid them. Karni noticed their unprovoked giggling and frequent glances behind and stopped suddenly, spinning around with her hands on her hips.

4

"What do you think you're doing!" Karni asked, in a convincingly indignant tone.

The young man shrugged. "I thought I was coming to the lake to bathe with you," he said, "but you were already gone by the time I arrived. So I was coming to visit you at your father's house."

She cocked her head. "And what would you have done there? Marched into his court and asked him for permission to visit with his daughter?"

"Perhaps I would have asked him for permission to do more than visit," he replied with a grin.

Her friends gasped in mock outrage at this comment.

He glanced at them with an innocent expression. "I meant I would have asked him for her hand in marriage. What were you girls thinking?"

They laughed and flapped their hands at him.

Karni relented and let her face relax in a smile. She glanced over her shoulder. Her companions teased her, and she rolled her eyes. They were accustomed to Karni and her boyfriend's antics, and she was accustomed to their teasing.

"You girls go on ahead. I'll catch up with you."

"Don't be late or we'll tell your father *the king!*" they called out, then ran away laughing.

"We were supposed to have a rendezvous on the north side of the lake under the ashoka tree after you finished your swim," he said as they walked leisurely together through the woods in the late afternoon light.

"I never finished my swim today," she replied. "Something very strange happened." She told him about the maelstrom and the strange snake-eyed hermit.

He stared at her. "You aren't making fun of me, are you? This really happened?"

"I swear to you on my ancestor's name," she said, reaching up to touch the lower boughs of apple trees as they walked. The apples were still tiny and green at this time of year, and she was careful not to jostle or break them free.

He whistled. "Who does that? I mean, who comes out of a lake like a snake god rising from the underworld?"

She turned to him with a gleam. "That's what I thought too! He even *looked* like a snake god, his eyes dark and so intense, I thought he was going to open his mouth and show a forked tongue and then —" She crooked her forearm at the elbow and thrust her hand forward like a cobra striking. "He was scary!"

"Probably just some old hermit-muni on an urgent mission to save the world," he said. "You'll probably never see him again. It was a good thing you didn't get sucked into that maelstrom yourself."

"Why? Would you have jumped in to save me if you were there?"

He grinned. "Of course. I have to protect the future mother of my future children, don't I?"

She giggled, covering her mouth with her hand held upright. "First you joked about asking my father for my hand in marriage, now you're talking about motherhood and children. Aren't you forgetting one important thing before either of those things can happen?"

"What's that?"

"I have to decide if I'm *ready* to get married," she said, ticking off the first point on her finger, "then I have to decide *who* I'm going to marry."

"Oh, is that all?" he asked, "Well, the second point is already decided. As for the first, how about this summer? If you could decide by then, we could be married late autumn, the perfect time of year." He gestured northward. "The cherry blossoms will be in full bloom by then. I know how much you love cherry blossoms, Karni."

She smiled. "I do love cherry trees in bloom, it's true. That does sound very tempting. I will have to give it serious consideration."

"Well, don't consider it for too long," he said. "Otherwise, my father might pack me off to Dirda to attend a swayamvara."

She stopped short, hands on her hips and a frown on her face. "A *swayam-vara*? In *Dirda*? Whatever for?"

"For the same reason all princes go to swayamvaras, my sweet. To compete in the contest and try to win the favor of the princess. And if she approves, then to marry her."

"In *Dirda*, of all places?" Karni asked scornfully. "Those Dirda princesses are older than the mountains and more wrinkled than old prunes!"

He looked at her with a half smile on his face. "Sounds like someone's more than a little jealous of Dirda girls."

"*Jealous? Me? Of Dirda girls?* Why, I —" She realized he was laughing at her and stopped herself. "You're teasing me, you scoundrel. You know Stonecastle and Dirda always compete with each other, so you're just trying to make me angry."

He laughed. "Of course I'm teasing. Mayla of Dirda is my sister! Though she is pretty, at that, I hardly think I'd be seeking her hand in marriage. On the other hand, there *are* other princesses in Dirda who would be worth competing for!"

She shoved him hard enough to send him sprawling. He was still laughing as she began striding purposefully toward her home.

"Hey," he called, jumping to his feet and running backward to keep pace with her, "I was just teasing about Dirda. But I am serious about my parents. They are getting restless, and the invitations to the swayamvaras are starting to pile up. I will have to start attending a few so other kingdoms don't start thinking that the prince of Mraashk is afraid of competing."

"You can do as you please," she said, walking faster. "What's it to me?"

"Hey," he said, "slow down. Now, don't go off in one of your foul tempers. I did say that I intended to approach your father and ask for your hand. Not right now, not so casually, of course, but with proper protocol, in a few days."

She slowed her pace a bit. "I don't like to be rushed. You know that. I will make up my mind in my own way, at the right time. It could even be this summer, and then you could approach my father in the proper way, and it's even possible we could set a date for late autumn. But it has to be my decision in my own time. I thought you understood that."

"I do, I do," he said, "And I know that it's not done for the boy to seem too eager. Marriage is a woman's decision, and it's your right to make that choice when you please. But can I help it if I'm so madly crazy in love with you, Karni of Stonecastle, apple of my eye, that I can't bear to wait another year, another season, or even another night, to make you my wife?"

She slowed even further, her face beaming with pleasure at his tone and his words. "I am eager too," she said softly, almost shyly. "To make you my husband, young Baron Maheev of Mraashk."

"Then what's there to think about?" He stopped and spread his arms. "I love you, Karni Stonecastle. We've known each other since we could first talk. We played together as infants in your father's castle in Mraashk. Our families know each other well and are good friends. Even after you left Mraashk to come live here at Stonecastle, I followed you and changed my entire life to be near you. I love everything about you, from your quick temper to your stubborn will, to the way your back arches where it meets your hip, to how you toss your hair when you walk, plus your strength, your beauty, your love for fried tapioca —"

She giggled.

"— your prowess at weapons and combat, your sense of Krushan law, your refusal to give up on any chore no matter how demanding until it is done to your satisfaction." He then continued in this vein for several more moments, and Karni realized with a start, *He loves me. He really, truly loves me. This is not mere lust or youthful infatuation. He genuinely loves me and will care for me as long as he lives. This is a man I could spend the rest of my life with and be happy.*

She started to go to him, then stopped herself, realizing where they were. The spires of the palace tower were within sight, and the rumbling of wagons reminded her that they were within view of the busiest road leading out of the city. And so instead of going to him and reciprocating his expression of love right then, she pushed him away playfully. "Nice speech! Now, go home. I'll see you tomorrow by the lake as usual."

If he was disappointed by her failure to return his eloquent declaration, he did not show it.

"I'll be there," he called out. "And I'll make sure there aren't any Naga men stirring up the lake into a frenzy!"

Karni had already turned and begun running; she waved over her head without looking back. She could imagine the look on his face without seeing it: sweet and wistful and handsome. She laughed to herself as she ran, and allowed herself the freedom to blush deeply and rosily at the thought that she might actually be planning her own wedding in a few weeks.

That afternoon, she reached home a very happy girl.

It would be a long time before she felt as happy again.

5

The royal compound was abuzz with excitement, men and women rushing to and fro on various errands, the guards looking more alert than usual. Even the horses and elephants and dogs felt the excitement, whinnying, stamping their feet, and barking in their kennels.

"Princess! Your father wishes to see you at once. He has a visitor!" said Shatabdi, a round-faced palace staple who ran the royal household like it was her own fiefdom.

Karni frowned. Her mind was still filled with thoughts of an autumn wedding, and she hadn't quite registered the hustle and bustle around. "What, why?"

Shatabdi took in Karni's appearance with a look of horror. "You can't go before him like that! What have you been *doing?*" She flapped her hands. "Never mind. Shrutakirti! Mandakini! Take the princess and get her changed into suitable attire. *Now!*"

The flustered maids hustled Karni away. She glanced back helplessly at her companions, who all wore worried expressions. Their gaiety after the swimming excursion had vanished completely; none of them even inquired after her rendezvous with Maheev, which was quite unlike them.

"This visitor . . ." she asked the maids as they dressed her hurriedly in her chambers.

"A very important seer-mage," Mandakini sang out as she pulled Karni's left arm through a sleeve, "His name is Pasha'ar. They say he's the same one who cursed the king of the gods for letting his elephant Airavon trample a garland he had gifted him."

Shrutakirti, who was a mite slower-witted, blinked as she fitted the last bracelet on Karni's wrist. "He gifted a garland to an *elephant?*"

"No, silly, he gifted the garland to *the king of the gods, Inadran.* That's why he was so angry when the god gave it to his elephant, who then trampled it." Mandakini finished adjusting the garment and began combing Karni's hair over an urn of smoldering sandalwood, fanning it out to catch the scented smoke.

"What was the curse?" Shrutakirti asked round-eyed. Stories of sages and their curses were a frequent topic of gossip around the palace. Such men were known for losing their temper, and for their penchant for spewing curses at those who provoked them.

"He decreed that the gods would fall from popularity, just as the sage's garland had been allowed to fall, and that Inadran would one day become as insignificant as dust." Karni spoke the words by rote, recalling her itihasa lessons with the royal guru. "That led to the great war between the gods and the urrkh, and the start of the eternal enmity between the two groups."

Shrutakirti paused in the act of fixing a diamantine necklace around Karni's throat. "Goddess save us! He is *that* sage? He's supposed to be the worst of them. What if he takes offense with something in Stonecastle and curses us all to turn into asses?"

"It wouldn't make the slightest difference to you then, would it?" Mandakini snapped. "Come on, finish up before *Shatabdi* curses *us!*"

Karni saw the younger maid's hands were shaking. She smiled and took the necklace from Shrutakirti's hands, fixing it around her own neck. She put a reassuring hand on the maid's arm. "Whatever you do, don't act nervous or scared around him. That will just make him more angry. Be calm and keep your head down, and you'll be fine."

Shrutakirti nodded but wrung her hands nervously as Karni turned to leave her chambers.

She soon forgot the maid and everything else as she strode quickly toward the royal hall, wanting to run but knowing it would not be proper for a princess to be seen running in the halls. She reminded herself to take her own advice. *Stay calm, Karni. However terrifying the stories, he's still just a man.*

A man who had the power to travel through vortexes of air and water and had ruined the king of gods with a single uttered curse.

6

The royal court of Stonecastle was as silent as a tomb.

Even the court jesters, who were paid to keep people amused and entertained at all times, were uncharacteristically silent . . . because they weren't present at all, Karni saw. Her father must have ordered them sent away, to avoid causing any offense to the sage. Many priests frowned upon court entertainers. On the other hand, some, like the frequent envoys and merchant ambassadors who traveled the several hundred miles southwestward from Hastinaga, had a taste for Stonecastle's cultural delights, which might not be as risqué as the hedonistic excesses of the Krushan imperial court, but could be quite titillating in their own unique way. *Especially the serapi and harva dances!*

Her adoptive father, King Stonecastle, was seated on his throne, uncharacteristically somber. That itself was strange: she was so used to hearing either boisterous laughter or his cheerful voice in this room. But now his face was composed in a neutral expression, displaying no outward emotion. His ministers, courtiers, and nobles all imitated his example, seated around the hall like wax effigies in a display gallery. The only movement came from the servants gently fanning the sage, who was seated just beside the king's own throne.

Karni's first thought was that the visitor really did resemble the friezes and paintings of snake gods she had seen, as Maheev had so astutely pointed out earlier. She tried to suppress the lighthearted mood that still buoyed her heart after the earlier encounter with her beloved. It simply would not do to offend this man!

But she couldn't help thinking that he was quite a character.

The sage's long, angular face was set in a perpetual scowl. His bush of matted hair, overgrown eyebrows, and wild beard looked like they had never seen a comb. *I bet he doesn't scent his hair with sandalwood incense!* He was seated with one leg crossed over the other, staring at nothing in particular. With his stick-thin limbs, bony torso, and long neck, he reminded Karni of a perched grasshopper. He continued to stare into the middle distance, contemplating goddess knew what. Karni felt sorry for the servants standing by with trays laden with various offerings for the guest's refreshment. She could imagine how terrified they must be, though they stood ramrod straight and barely even blinked.

She wondered why in the world one man, any man, should have the power to terrorize so many. *Just because he is a priest?* It seemed so unfair.

The inequity of it outraged her sense of justice, but she sat as still and patient as the rest.

At last, the visitor raised his head.

"King Stonecastle," he said in a voice as harsh and unconcerned with civility as his appearance, "I shall partake of your hospitality. Kindly ask your firstborn to attend me during my stay, as is customary."

Karni saw her father's eyes widen.

"Great One," he replied with unctuous care, "I have no progeny of my own. However, by the grace of the stone gods, my cousin Karna Sura of Mraashk saw fit to grant me guardianship of his firstborn daughter, Karni. I have raised her as my own, and she is my sole heir. If it please you, I shall have her attend to your every need during your stay."

Karni felt herself flush, knowing that every pair of eyes in the court turned toward her. Her parentage was no secret. If anything, it gave her a certain status: not only was she sole heir and princess of Stonecastle, but she was also sister to Vasurava, prince of Mraashk, the capital of the Yadu nation. That made her a bridge between two nations. But right now, she would have given anything to have an elder sister, a brother, a half dozen siblings, a hundred even!

She sensed the sage's intense scrutiny on her and kept her own gaze demurely downcast.

"So be it," said the sage Pasha'ar.

7

It was the only time Karni's foster father had ever appeared nervous and uncomfortable when addressing her.

"I need you to play a more modern role," he had said, and she had laughed at his choice of words.

"Do you wish me to perform an entertainment for the sage, Father?" she asked, making light of the hermit's notorious dislike of such vulgar pastimes.

"Sage Pasha'ar . . ." He paused. "Is notorious for his temper. It would not do to make him irate. He is a powerful sage. A *seer-mage*. Stonecastle needs to please him and gain his blessings, not his curses."

She nodded, matching his serious tone. "Say what needs to be done, and I shall see to it, father."

"You must stand service on him yourself."

She raised her eyebrows. "Myself?"

He rubbed his leathery face. "I am asking too much of you, daughter. You are a princess, a queen-in-waiting, not a —"

"I can be a serving woman, if that is what the good sage requires. A royal serving woman. I have seen how these sages expect to be treated during such visits. I have heard the stories, read the itihasas. I know what fury their curses can bring. Besides, I have with my own eyes seen Guru Pasha'ar's powers at work. He is formidable. I would not want him to become irate with our good kingdom."

He looked up at her. "Thank you, daughter. Our nation's good name and future depend on how well you serve the sage."

She lowered her chin, all merriment gone. "You can count on me, Father. I will make sure he has no cause for complaint."

8

The following nights and days were a blur of endless chores. While the entire palace staff was kept on its toes by the presence of the venerated sage, none were worked as hard or as relentlessly as Karni. Pasha'ar would demand anything he pleased at any hour he pleased, with no thought for her need for rest, comfort, or nourishment.

In the beginning, his demands were not impossible, but were unusual and difficult.

"Go fetch me white marigolds," he said one night at an unearthly hour.

Karni bowed her head without hesitation and sent her maids running to pluck the flowers from her own personal garden. But before the girls had left Karni's chambers, she was summoned to the guest chambers again.

"They must be plucked by your own hands," the sage added, "otherwise they are of no use to me."

Karni bowed her head without argument and backed out of the guest chambers. Once out, she ran faster than her maids and fetched the choicest white marigolds from her own garden. She ran all the way back to the sage and set them before him.

He did not so much as glance at the flowers. "I desire sabudana vadas," he said, using the local term for fried tapioca. Prepare it with your own hands and make sure it is neither too hot nor too cool when you serve it to me."

Karni backed out of the chamber and went to the royal kitchen, where she prepared the sage's favorite repast. She carried it in a silver dish covered with another silver dish, removing the top only when she laid it before the sage. He took a bite of one of the tapioca balls and ate it without compliment or comment.

"I also desire buttermilk flavored with mango," he said. "I would like to partake of it the instant I have finished my snack."

Karni's eyes widened, but she dared not question his wishes. She backed out, and this time she sprinted to the kitchen, where she shouted at a cook to fetch her buttermilk at once from the cooling pit, while she herself ran to the fruit pantry and selected the ripest, juiciest mango she could find. She poked open a tiny hole, tasting it to make sure it was in fact ripe and juicy. She didn't bother with slicing, instead she rolled the mango in its skin between her palms until the flesh inside was reduced to a dripping pulp. Motioning to the cook to set the silver bowl before her, she squeezed out the mango pulp through the hole, and stirred it with the handle of a wooden ladle.

She took but a moment to wipe her hands clean on a kitchen cloth, then she raced back to the guest chambers, where she slowed to a formal walk as she approached the sage. She entered the chamber just as Pasha'ar was finishing the last tapioca ball. She offered him the bowl and waited, heart still pounding, as he sipped of the treacly concoction. He made a sound that could possibly have indicated approval — or it might have just been him clearing his throat.

When he set down the bowl and she saw it was empty, she almost beamed with relief. He, on the other hand, did not communicate in any other manner that he had enjoyed the proffering. But it did not matter. The empty bowl was enough of a sign that it was a job well done.

9

Over the following days and nights, Sage Pasha'ar ran Karni ragged.

The worst nights were the ones where he would summon her and ask her to prepare one of his favorite items and then, after he was done eating it, sink into one of his meditative trances. She would wait in the expectation of further requests, not knowing if he would summon her again in an hour, half a watch, or even a whole watch later. She barely slept. The man seemed to spend almost all his time in chambers, either meditating or discoursing with other priests on a variety of philosophical matters.

Oftentimes, he would ask her to fetch refreshments for himself and these guests, many of whom seemed discomfited at having the royal princess herself wait on them. Pasha'ar seemed to either not notice or not care about their discomfort.

Once, he summoned Karni and asked her to wait awhile. She stood unobtrusively to one side while he and his cadre continued a discussion of some inscrutable passage in the scriptures. Suddenly, he asked for her opinion on an obscure aspect of the passage in question. "Which interpretation do you favor?" he asked.

She blinked rapidly. "Your own, Gurudev."

"Yes, but why do you favor my reading over the excellent interpretations of these venerated priests?"

All eyes in the room were on her.

"Because of the context, Gurudev," she replied. "It is evident that the reference to storm in this particular instance refers specifically to the king of gods, Inadran, personified as a storm."

"It does not say so at all," said an elder hermit, looking angry with Karni. "The language refers only to thunder, lightning, and a flash flood. There is no indication of personification at all."

"But there is, Great One," she said, inclining her head to show respect for a superior mind. "In the third line of the second verse of the fourteenth parva, the text specifically uses the masculine when referring to the fury of the storm and the feminine when referring to the river, which clearly indicates that the river in question must be the Jeel, since none but River Goddess Jeel could stand before the masculine arrogance of Inadran."

Everyone stared at her. Even the elder hermit looked gobsmacked. Sage Pasha'ar leaned back with a gleam in his eye.

"Any reference to a storm would be masculine, surely," the sage said.

"True, but in this case, the Krushan word used to describe the masculine fury of the storm is one that is associated with Inadran's notorious tendencies. 'With what thunderous fury does he strike . . .'" She quoted the rest of the verse from memory, then quoted three others that used the same phrasing to refer to the king of gods.

All the white-haired heads in the room were nodding by the time she finished the last quote.

"Hmmph!" said the sage, clearly perturbed. "I concede the point. However, on the matter of the river being the sacred Jeel, that is a highly perceptive deduction." He turned his gaze to Karni. "You are King Stonecastle's daughter? Commend your guru for me."

She bowed graciously, avoiding mention of the fact that since only male warrior castes were expected to be educated, she had read and mastered the sacred texts on her own, aided in private by a like-minded group of older women — much older than she, for the most part — who believed in the maxim that if women could fight, women should also be able to write and become educated. Had she enlightened the guru on this point, he would likely have choked on his sweet potato savory.

10

Shortly thereafter, the guests departed. Karni waited patiently for Pasha'ar to say something, to acknowledge her contribution in some way, if not outright praise her.

But he said nothing, except to ask her to prepare more fried tapioca, this time with groundnuts.

As the days and weeks passed, this familiar pattern continued, with Pasha'ar frequently calling on her to clarify some point of controversy or to break a deadlock, but never again acknowledging her scholarship or memory. If anything, he made it a point to always ask her to perform some completely mundane chore immediately after — clean his chambers, wash his garments, fetch him a particularly difficult-to-obtain item from the far end of the city — as if to remind her of her place. Intelligent, well-read, endowed with scholarly gifts — yet still a serving girl.

She accepted all this with good grace. She toiled all hours without protest. Endured outbursts without a plaint. Yet the one thing that galled her was his stubborn refusal to permit her to handle the scrolls.

Pasha'ar frequently requested a particular text — or several texts all at once — often at a most inopportune time, such as during the evening meal or in the middle of the night. Karni was tasked with going to the priest quarters, which was situated a good five miles outside the city walls, disturbing the brahmacharya novices on night rotation — the round-the-clock verbatim "pad-a-pad" recitals — and asking one of them for the text in question. She would then wait while the novice fetched it, check that he had fetched the correct scroll (more likely than not, he had not). She would then have to accompany the novice back to the palace, bring him up to the sage's chambers, and present Pasha'ar with the requisitioned scroll. After he finished with the text, Karni would accompany the novice back to the hermitage, and finally, of course, make the long trek back to the palace.

In between, she would of course be asked to perform her usual tasks: fetching refreshments for the sage and his guests, sweeping and swabbing his chambers, or performing other chores he asked of her. But all this she endured without complaint. As she endured the dismissive looks that even the most hairless, green-eared novices gave her when she came to collect the scrolls, asserting their superiority of sex, scholarship, and caste all in a single sneer. Knowing the import of keeping the sage happy, she said nothing.

What she could not brook was the fact that she was not permitted, at any time, or for any reason whatsoever, to so much as touch or breathe upon any of these sacred scrolls. The logic being that as a woman, subject to womanly foibles and monthly leakages, she was inherently impure and unfit to partake of the domain of Aravidya, the sacred lore of herbal and healing knowledge.

I can be as intelligent as any man, as well read as any priest, as insightful as any scholar, yet because I am a woman, I have no right to any of those things? Hmmph! River Goddess Jeel, grant your worshipper patience to endure such absurd bigotry.

On one occasion, the novice insisted (twice) at the hermitage that he had retrieved the exact text she had named — and indeed seemed incensed that Karni might question him — so Karni returned with him to the palace without double-checking the scroll. Yet when they arrived and presented the scroll to Pasha'ar, and the sage immediately fumed and raged at being given the wrong text, the novice had the audacity to immediately pin the blame on Karni. He claimed she had asked for this one and so it was the one he had brought, and of course he could hardly be blamed for an ignorant, illiterate, impure *woman's* faults.

Of his words, the one that stung the most was the accurate one: that she was a *woman*. Yes, she was a woman and proud of it. Did this young upstart think he had emerged wholly formed out of the stone god's egg? Did he speak to his own mother and sisters with the same tone? He knew very well that she had requested parva 231, canto 89 — not parva 89, canto 231, which he brought.

She said none of these things aloud, merely bowed her head and endured the hailstorm of outrage and insults the sage heaped upon her while the novice looked on, smirking, even though her heart raged with the injustice, the unfairness, the sheer *bigotry* of it all.

But none of these or similar incidents were the worst.

No, the worst was yet to come.

11

It was a cold rainy day in the first half of winter. Stonecastle did not get snow, but it was far enough north and within blowing range of the Cold-heart Mountains to get bitterly, dangerously cold. Cold enough to freeze water and deliver the occasional shower of hailstones the size of a man's fist. And when the winter winds blew through the city, Shaiva help any unfortunate who happened to be out of walls. The daily count of travelers and drunks who froze to death from exposure was in double digits at this time of year.

Pasha'ar had been in a particularly benign mood these past days. There was a rumor that the sage was planning to take his leave shortly, a rumor perpetrated by Karni herself, based on a conversation in which the sage had been asked by another priest if he would be there in the spring. "Distinctly not," he replied, "I must be in Uttarkashi before the winter snows set in."

This alone had made Karni want to yell and throw her hands in the air, perform several somersaults and tumbles around the chamber, then dance a very unprincesslike caper, hooting and cheering all the while. She did in fact perform all these antics, but only much later that evening, when she was safely in the privacy of her own chambers with her friends.

"Finally, we shall be able to see you again daily as we used to," they said happily, once the initial euphoria had died down. "We shall go swimming in the lake, picking berries, climb to the top of the rookery, and do all the happy things we used to be able to do together."

She was about to correct them by saying that since it was winter, they could hardly do any of those things, but she realized it didn't matter. The point was, she would be free soon. Free to resume her girlish ways and indolent, carefree life as a young princess. She would rather dive into a frozen lake than serve the sage Pasha'ar another season!

So it was with sunshine in her heart that she waited on their honored guest over the next few days. The passes to the Coldheart Mountains were generally snowed in during the third month of winter. They were already at the start of the second month. That left less than a fortnight before the sage would have to leave if he meant to reach his destination before snow closed the passes; ideally he should leave within the week.

Karni was wandering in her mind, daydreaming about resuming her sword-fighting training again. She had been so consumed with her round-the-clock duties for the sage that her fight guru — a crusty old woman veteran who had served in the Stonecastle army and trained three generations of royalty — had squirted a mouthful of betelnut juice with disgust at Karni's irregular appearances, wiped her mouth with the back of her hand, and told her in her characteristically vulgar fashion to come back when she was able to extract her "head out of the elephant's backside." Karni missed the physical exertion of swordplay, the world reduced to just the edge of the blade, one's opponent's eyes, and the elegant dance of death.

The first time Pasha'ar spoke that morning, she thought she had misheard.

Karni stared blankly at the sage, not wanting to commit the sacrilege of asking him to repeat himself, yet not able to believe she had heard him correctly.

He gazed up at her patiently. He had been in a relatively less intense mood these past days. Less intense for Pasha'ar, of course, was like saying a hawk was less intense after he had eaten a full rabbit. It was not something that was easily evident to a casual observer, but Karni had learned to tell a great deal from his most minor gestures, vocal patterns, body language. One might even say that she could read Pasha'ar almost as well as she could read Krushan. Though Krushan rarely lost its temper and flew into a flaming rage if your tapioca cakes were a tad less crisp. Right now, though, he was calm, and he proved her right by doing something he rarely ever did: he repeated his request without a trace of irritation.

"I require an item fetched from Dirda."

She stared at him without response for several heartbeats. She was too taken aback to simply bow as usual and acquiesce.

"From Dirda, Great One?" she said.

He named an item. Something so trivial that it could be found in any marketplace anywhere, or even right here in the palace itself, perhaps in this very guest wing. A paper fan, the kind that visitors from the Far Eastern kingdoms brought with them and traded for local spices or silks, the kind that Eastern women apparently held before their painted faces and smiled coyly behind.

What in the world could a celibate guru want with an Eastern woman's paper fan? Surely not to gift to a lover! Which was what those exotic items were rumored to be most commonly used for: as gifts from rich men to their concubines. Obviously, the sage had no women in his life, so that could not be its purpose.

She dared not ask the next question, but he read it in her eyes anyway and answered it aloud. Apparently, he had learned to read Karni almost as well as she had learned to read Pasha'ar.

"It must be from Dirda, specifically," he said, "from the shop of the merchant Gutap. It will be easy enough to find. It is the largest store in the town market, with a substantial stock of fans decorated with baby elephants and lion cubs on display at all times."

He glanced at the window. "If you leave right now, you should be back here before the full moon."

She was dumbstruck. She had no words. Did he realize that Dirda lay beyond the hill ranges? That this was winter, and one of the coldest winters in recent memory — the coldest since before she had been born, apparently? Even the royal couriers and courtiers ferrying information to and fro between the two neighboring kingdoms had reduced their biweekly trips to once a fortnight, and then only if the news was urgent. Wars had been postponed to avoid crossing the Dirda ranges in winter. Marriages called off. And he expected her to go all the way to Dirda now, at the start of the coldest winter in memory, to fetch a *paper fan*?

He was still looking at her, as if reading every thought that passed through her mind.

"Tell Merchant Gutap I send my blessings and tell him that he may send his eldest son-in-law to Hastinaga next spring, as I shall be present at the Krushan court by then, and the imperial permit he desires will be issued. I have spoken to the appropriate authorities, and they have assured me it will be done."

She stood there, simply staring at him in utter disbelief.

He added mildly, "The message must be delivered in person by you alone. No one else must accompany you, or he will suspect betrayal. Once you deliver the message successfully, he will give you the fan. Bring it directly to me."

Delivered in person and by her alone? And no one else must accompany her? Asking one to travel over the Dirda hills in winter, during the season of hailstorms, when the bandit gangs, the bears, and the predators virtually ruled those hills, was insanity. Even the most seasoned courtiers went with a cortege of at least eight armed guards, and no woman, princess or not, went without a full company as well as a team of elephants. Yet Pasha'ar expected Karni to ride alone, risk death by exposure, by hail, by bandits, by predators, riding day and night without halting for food or shelter, just to fetch him a paper fan? She had suspected it all along, but now she knew for certain: he was a torturer. An assassin. A murderer. A ruthless barbaric killer who cared nothing for the lives of the daughters of his hosts. He had probably left a trail of dead princesses and noblemen's daughters in his wake, scattered across the thousand and eight kingdoms like chaff from grain.

And he asked this of her even though, as Karni herself had witnessed, he had the ability to travel from place to place through magical means, the way he had simply appeared from a maelstrom in the lake, a season and a half ago.

She wished that he had drowned in that lake, in that maelstrom of his own creation, drowned and choked and been washed up on the shore of the lake, pale, bloated, and half eaten by fishes.

She saw by his face that he had read her thoughts, or divined the gist of them at least. He read it in her pauses, her stance, her wider eyes, her clasped hands, her slightly furrowed brow. Just as she could read his every change of mood and direction of thought in the way he breathed, inclined his head, or sat.

That was when she thought, *I can't do this anymore. I can't go on.*

But then she remembered her foster father, King Stonecastle. How sad and desolate he had been when she first came to live here, broken by the loss of his wife and son in childbirth. How entranced he had been by her every word, gesture, and action — not just in those early days, which she barely remembered, but as she grew and got older as well. How he had doted on her every deed. How he lived and breathed by her. She could not bear the thought of doing him wrong.

He had spoiled her more than her birth father ever would have, or even her real grandparents. Although they had loved her dearly, King Karna Sura and Queen Padmeen were both preoccupied with matters of governance. Whatever attention Karni had received in her birth father's house had come mostly from her brother, Vasurava. But a brother's love was different. Vasurava was kind and gentle, but he was also mischievous and prone to teasing: he was but a boy too back then, after all, and she was his sister — and if there was one universal familial truth, it was that a brother will tease a sister.

Nothing and nobody came close to providing Karni with the warmth and affection, the lavish helpings of love and care and tenderness that King Stonecastle had showered upon her. She had quickly come to realize how precious she was to him, how much he regarded her as a gift from the gods themselves, a ray of hope in the darkness of his soul. Unlike many kings, he did not seem to care that she was a girl rather than a boy, that he had no son, that she was not actually of his blood and therefore his line would only continue through her in the most indirect way possible.

He had encouraged her every wish, however unusual, be it learning to master the sword, or learning battle strategy from the most expert general of his kingdom — and even allowed her to choose her friends without regard for class, ethnicity, caste, or social level. Karni was her own woman, and unlike many fathers, especially rajas and maharajas, he had never sought to clip her wings or make her feel that her freedom was anything less than a natural birthright. Likewise, he had been completely accepting of the old Krushan tradition of matriarchal governance, a tradition that had been mostly abandoned these days by those whom it did not benefit. No one in Stonecastle had any doubt that it was Karni who would inherit the throne and kingdom if anything were to befall her adoptive father; nor did anyone doubt her ability to rule as effectively as Stonecastle himself.

Asking Karni to attend Pasha'ar was the one and only time King Stonecastle had asked her to perform the duties of a modern, fashionable girl of high birth. She had not feared the stories she had heard of Pasha'ar's legendary temper and terrible curses, or the power he had displayed when emerging from the maelstrom in the lake. She only knew she could not bear to break her adoptive father's heart, or to cause distress to the people and kingdom she cared for so greatly. She loved them too much to let this awful, self-centered man throw a temper tantrum and use his powerful gifts to cause misery to innocent souls.

It was that love and concern that made her grit her teeth, bite back any reluctance, and bow as gracefully as she could manage under the circumstances.

"As you say, Great One."

12

People stared at Karni when she returned from Dirda three weeks later. Nobody could believe she was Princess Karni. She looked like a ragged forest hermit, emerging from the deep woods to ask for alms.

When she paused for a moment to catch her breath, relieved to be breathing the spice-scented air of the marketplace again, a passing noble on a horse even tossed her a copper coin.

She let it lie where it fell and made her way wearily but with growing enthusiasm toward the palace.

Even the gate sentries stared with astonishment as she greeted them and passed through. She went through the kitchen and maids' quarters to avoid causing a scandal among the courtiers. The maids and serving girls who caught sight of her gasped.

"Princess!" one exclaimed. "How —" She broke off, eyes filling with tears as she looked Karni up and down with knowing eyes. "My dear, shall I fetch the royal healer?"

Karni shook her head, throat filled with an emotion she could not name. "It is not my blood. I am well."

That last was not entirely true. She was far from well. But it was no sickness or ailment she suffered from, nothing that Aravidic herbs and ointments could cure or treat. It was a fever of the soul. There were things in the world that could affect a young woman in ways more damaging than a physical assault or a disease contracted.

She felt a great deal better once she had bathed, partaken of some nourishment, spent some time drying out and combing her hair over a scented sandalwood brazier. She was humming to herself as she finished, unaware that she was doing so, or that the tune she was humming was the same one her mother, Padmeen, would sing to her and her brother Vasurava to put them to sleep. It put her in mind of the gentle, comforting caress of her mother, of that warm maternal embrace, the softness of her cheek upon Karni's, the scent of her. It was hard living apart from one's family, to be separated as a child, knowing that every one of those people — father, mother, brother, cousins, uncles, aunts, grandparents — all still existed, that whole enormous circle of warmth, comfort and filial affection, but that she was now *outside* the circle, a satellite moon destined to live in her own lonely orbit. What did it mean? Why did such things happen? She had brought comfort, warmth, and joy to her foster father, Stonecastle. But what of her own comfort, warmth, and joy? Did she not deserve as much also?

She put these thoughts out of her mind as she finished her toilet, shook them off and breezed out of her chambers and all the way to the rishi's apartment. Sentries, courtiers, maids, running boys, everyone who passed her by could not help but look at her twice — and some stared, others whispered — but she ignored them all. She walked tall and strong, and did not stop for any distraction.

"Gurudev," she said, bowing to Pasha'ar.

He looked up absently from the scroll he was perusing.

She offered him the paper fan, presented upon her open palms.

He glanced at it with a frown, as if about to ask her what this object might be and why she was troubling him with it. Then he shook his head irritably and said, "Put it anywhere."

She placed it beside other items she had fetched for him during his long stay, each of which represented some arduous effort or sacrifice on her part. None of them had been touched or moved from their original position as far as she could tell. She did not dwell on this fact but simply turned back to him and stood politely waiting until he looked up again, questioning.

"Merchant Gutap of Dirda sends his gratitude and says he will surely send his eldest son-in-law to Gajapura next spring as instructed, and will ensure that the boy does not squander this priceless opportunity."

It was clear the sage had stopped listening halfway through her recitation. She waited for some acknowledgment, some response. Anything.

There was none.

That night, her friends came to see her, eyes wide and hands clasped to their chests with concern.

"Your face!" they said, taking her chin gently and turning her face this way and that, and then exclaiming in dismay. "Your arms, your legs, such bruises! These are purple and fresh. How did you come by them?"

Karni was silent for a long moment, emotion choking her. "Hailstorm," she said at last. "On the road to Dirda." She added after a moment, "*And* on the way back."

They asked her a thousand questions, fussed and fretted about her like mother hens around a solitary chick. She smiled wanly at their fussing, allowed them to redo her hair, to beautify her as best as was possible with a bruise-covered appearance. They then insisted on bringing Karni her favorite savories and invited her to go to the son of the grain minister's wedding the following evening.

She went along with everything except the last.

"I must remain here, to serve our guest."

They made pooh-pooh noises, waving their hands in disgust. They tried their best to convince her to sneak away for a few hours at least. The handsome son of the Jamadgura war minister was expected to attend, stoking gossip about his former steamy romance with the bride-to-be. Scandal and fireworks were expected.

She heard it all as if from a great distance, viewed her friends as if she were meeting them for the first time, as if all this was strange and faraway, from another time, another Karni.

She stayed in the palace the next day, making tapioca savories and almond buttermilk for the sage, fetching scrolls, cleaning his muddy wooden cleat slippers, and performing sundry other chores. The sound of the wedding music was faintly audible from the kitchen floor, plaintive and sad as a dirge to her ears. She wondered how people did such things as dressing up in finery, wearing jewelry, and attending weddings, when the world was such a hostile place. What was the point?

She woke up that night and found her pillow soaked; she could not understand how. It occurred to her as she was drifting off into a restless asleep again: *Could I have been crying?*

But she didn't remember crying.

The sage Pasha'ar left the next day. But not before he gave her a parting gift. If, that is, you could call what he gave her a "gift" at all.

13

"Memorize this mantra."

Karni looked up at Pasha'ar. They were at the egress of the guest chambers, the sage about to depart.

King Stonecastle had come to touch the sage's feet and ask for the customary blessings, which Pasha'ar gave freely. The king thanked him profusely, then hesitated before asking the traditional host's question: "I trust everything was to your satisfaction?"

Karni had felt no trepidation during the long pause before the sage responded. She had passed the point of anxiety a while ago. During that trip to Dirda, perhaps. Or even before. It did not matter. She no longer feared Pasha'ar's curse or anything he may say. She was long past all that.

"I have no complaints," he said finally.

Karni was looking at her father's face when he heard his guest respond and observed King Stonecastle's delayed reaction: clearly he had been expecting the sage to say more. Some small words of praise perhaps. A compliment. Maybe even a lavishing of admiration for his daughter's impressive attentiveness and diligence.

But there was nothing, of course.

Sage Pasha'ar did not praise, compliment, or lavish admiration.

That single sentence was all he had to say.

It was enough.

Coming from him, it was the equivalent of a thousand effusive praises. Many of his courtiers, noblemen, priests, and other seers would say as much to King Stonecastle in the months and years to come, expressing their admiration for his daughter's extraordinary dedication to the most feared priest visitor. There would be an abundance of compliments later — from others. But none from Pasha'ar. Not now, not ever.

Karni waited at the egress with the customary earthen bowl of yogurt, which she offered to their departing guest, and which he partook of without comment. He returned the bowl to her palm, and she thought that he would then begin walking, and continue walking — out of the guest chambers, the palace, the city, the kingdom, her life. He could not walk fast enough.

Instead, he paused.

And said to her, "Memorize this mantra."

Then he recited a very brief couplet.

The instruction, and the mantra that followed, were delivered quietly, barely loud enough for Karni to hear.

Nobody else was close enough to hear.

The words were intended for her ears alone.

He spoke the words, then began walking.

She stood there a moment, expressionless, holding the earthen bowl with the dregs of the yogurt upon her palm, as his wooden cleat slippers sounded on the steps leading down from the guest chambers, rang out as they crossed the stone floor to the archway, then grew softer, then muffled, then finally faded entirely as the sage left the palace complex and was gone, out of her life forever.

She never saw him again.

Her father came to her and embraced her warmly, releasing an immense sigh of relief.

"Daughter!" he cried out. "Daughter, you have done us all proud. All Stonecastle thanks you today."

People crowded around them, smiling, laughing, moving about and talking normally again, abandoning the stiff, somber attitude they had assumed in the past several months of the sage's visit. She saw her father's gratitude and relief reflected in all their faces. King Stonecastle was only saying aloud what they all felt.

She knew she should smile at him, so she did. But there was no mirth in her heart. She did not see what she had done that was so special. She had been given a task, and she had completed the task to the best of her ability. Whether or not the task had been appreciated and had earned her the recognition of their guest did not matter at all. She had performed her duty, as was the modern custom.

It was what any young daughter of a decent noble household would have done.

14

Karni went through the rest of that month in a daze, unaware of when she ate or rested or slept or participated in the activities her friends managed to rope her into.

She did everything expected of her, said all the right words, dressed the right way, but those close to her knew she was not herself, that her heart was not into anything she did.

Her friends expressed concern for her. Her father showed sympathy for her "exhaustion" and suggested she might wish to visit her hometown, Mraashk, to recover from the ordeal she had been put through.

Everyone was sympathetic and supportive, effusive with praise, but none of this what she wanted or needed.

What *did* she want, then?

She did not know.

15

It was a whole season later, in the spring, that she woke one night, to a mercifully dry pillow this time, and remembered the sage's parting words.

Memorize this mantra.

She had indeed memorized it. Memorizing mantras by the rote method was something little toddlers were taught to do, and something Karni had been doing her entire life. It was the way all knowledge was learned, passed on, stored over generations. Memorizing one mantra was like storing a drop in that vast ocean of knowledge.

But for the guru to call such special attention to it, the timing of his giving it to her, the solemn tone with which he had imparted it, the way he had stopped her from repeating it back to him — told her that this was no ordinary mantra.

She mused on its possible purpose. She sensed now what she had not realized at the time: that this mantra was meant to be, in some way, a reparation for all that she had endured during her long service to the guru. A payment, a reward of sorts. She had heard stories of priests imparting mantras to hosts who treated them with special grace. Gifts from the gods, they were called.

How a simple couplet of rhyming Krushan verse could be a gift, a payment, a reward, she did not know. But the stories said that reciting those mantras produced magical results. The results differed from story to story, but all concurred on the mantra being magical. The poor became rich. The sick became healthy. The lovelorn were united with their lost loves.

She stopped herself short.

She had been pacing her chamber, sweeping from end to end ceaselessly, a practice she had fallen into in the months since the guru's departure.

It was often the only real exercise she took. Her old habits of running, swimming, horse riding, hunting, archery, swordplay, and javelin had all fallen by the wayside.

She had barely seen her friends for a whole season and a half. Two had gotten married, she had heard, and all of the others were now betrothed. Girls their age did not stay single long. Girls *your* age, she reminded herself. She knew her father had been showered with requests from kings and emperors, asking that she host a swayamvara and permit suitors to vie for her hand as was the custom of the land. She could still refuse them all at the end of the tourney, if none pleased her. But they all wanted a chance at impressing and catching the eye of the legendary Karni of Stonecastle, she who had served the irascible Guru Pasha'ar and kept her house safe from the ill favor of his cursing tongue. Because of that duty she had performed, she was the most desirable bride in fifty kingdoms.

Her father had reminded her, gently, that the longer she waited, the more young princes her age would find other brides, less suitable than she but still good brides nevertheless. Princes must have wives, just as princesses must have husbands. It was simply the way of the world. But she didn't care about age or availability. Though the thought of marriage once pleased her, now it sickened her to her stomach.

King Stonecastle had sensed this, and also that somehow, her dislike of the topic of marriage was related to the sage's visit. "Did Gurudev say something to you about your future prospects?" he asked her one day after she had staunchly refused yet another request for a swayamvara. "Did he perhaps foretell your husband-to-be and your life together?"

She frowned at her father. "He said not a word of such things."

He blinked. "Then what is it, my child? What ails you? Do not deny it. I have seen you these past weeks. You take no pleasure in the things that once delighted you. You spend all day sequestered in the palace. You go nowhere, see no one, and have turned in against yourself. You are like the ghost of the laughing, active, happy Karni you were before the guru came here. I cannot believe that your change has nothing to do with the sage's visit. If he said something to you that put fear into your heart, that made you dread marriage or your future husband, please, daughter, tell me now. Men such as he can often make stark pronouncements that terrify us mortals, but their intention is often to caution and help us prevent future calamities, not prevent us from living altogether."

She shook her head slowly. "Sage Pasha'ar said nothing about such things. Or about anything to do with me personally or my future, nothing at all."

And this was true. Guru Pasha'ar had barely paid her any heed except as a vehicle to serve his needs. Bring this, fetch that, go there, summon so-and-so. She was nothing more than a glorified servant to him. What did he care about a servant's future prospects? All he cared about was having his needs fulfilled.

"Then what is it, daughter?" King Stonecastle asked her, his face lined with anxiety. "Something ails your heart. I see it in your every aspect. It festers like a sickness in you. It is poisoning your zest for life. Tell me what it is. If it is within my power to give you what it is you desire, I will give it to you, no matter the cost and the effort. Speak but once, and you shall have your heart's desire."

She hung her head in shame, for she heard the concern in her father's voice. She knew he cared greatly for her and could not bear to see her unhappy. But even so, there was nothing he could do. "I am sorry, Father. Thank you for your concern, but there is nothing you can do."

"There must be *something!*" he said, and Karni could see in his face that he flailed about mentally, searching for something to appease her. "Would you wish to go home to your father's house? Would spending some time with your birth mother and father set your heart at ease? Is that your plaint? Does your heart ache for home? Say the word, and I shall drive you there myself in my own chariot this very day."

"No, Father," she said sadly. "I would love to go home someday, in the summer perhaps, when the orchards of Vrindavan are lush with fruit, and Mraashk's markets are bustling with foreign traders after the ships return from western ports. I would love to see my beloved mother and father and my brother, Vasurava, again. But that is not what ails me."

"Then you admit something *does* ail you?" he said, grasping at this dangled thread eagerly. "Tell me, then, what is this canker in your heart that robs my beloved Karni of her happiness and youth day by day? Is it some bauble? A place? A song?" He could not think of anything further to suggest and threw his hands up in the air. "*Speak!* I beg you."

Karni bowed her head for a long time. "It is nothing within your power to give, Father. There is nothing I desire. I am content here in your house. You are a good father, and I bless the gods for delivering me here."

He clenched his fist in frustration. "There must be *something*."

She stood up, sighing softly. "Permit me to leave your presence. I am tired and wish to rest awhile."

As she departed, she heard him calling, irritably, for more wine. She wished she could tell him everything, to put his mind at ease.

But she could not.

16

Memorize this mantra, the sage had said.

Karni paced the floor of her chambers, tracing the same route endlessly, as she went over every detail of the guru's last instruction to her.

But what *was* the mantra? What did it do?

She was certain now that it did something. But how to find out what that was without actually *using* it. From the way the guru had stopped her from repeating it, she had understood that merely reciting the mantra aloud would achieve some result. But surely there must be a way to know what that result was *before* reciting it?

Surely Guru Pasha'ar would know what the mantra did, of course. But he had not told her, and she had not thought to ask at the time. All she knew was that he had intended the mantra to be some kind of gift to her — that was the tradition, after all. Her father had not thought to ask her if the guru had given her any gift in parting because he had simply been too relieved that Pasha'ar had not cursed them. The thought that the rishi had actually attempted to reward her for her services had not occurred to King Stonecastle at all.

The mantra was her secret. She had told nobody about it. She had spoken to no one about her ordeal, though many had asked. Everyone was curious and awestruck at how a princess of Stonecastle — a presumably spoiled, pampered, self-centered, rich, powerful, beautiful young woman — had served a notorious priest for so long and so arduously, enduring such hardship and deprivation, without once giving offense. It was the talk of fifty kingdoms, as evidenced by the requests from those realms for an opportunity to win her hand in marriage. There were stories and tales she had heard snippets of, most resembling the truth not even remotely; she had heard of them from the wet nurses, who had themselves been fishing for the true story. But even then, she had said nothing. The torture of those months serving the guru was locked in her heart, and she had thrown away the key. She did not intend to speak of it to anyone.

Because speaking of it would have meant speaking of the other thing as well, the thing her adoptive father had tried so desperately to pry from her. The pain of what had happened on that fateful journey to Dirda. And that pain she could not bear to speak of to anyone.

But now she thought that perhaps the mantra was the key. Perhaps the guru had given her the mantra as a means of appeasing her heart. Perhaps even, if she dared think it, the mantra would bring her that which she had lost.

Now *that* would be a true reward. *That* would serve as reparation for all the hardship Pasha'ar had caused her.

It would be a gift of the gods, truly.

Could it be possible? she wondered.

Could he really have been that insightful — and that powerful?

He was a great guru, after all. She had seen him use his powers with her own eyes, the day he had risen from the lake. Surely he could do much more than simply control nature's elements in order to travel from one realm to another. He must wield true power.

Perhaps the mantra really was magical. Perhaps it really could set right what had gone wrong in Dirda.

Bring back what she had lost.

Repair the damage to her shattered heart.

Reward her troubled soul.

There was only one way to find out: she had to recite the mantra aloud.

She paced for hours, trying to decide, to work up the courage to actually do it, and it was late that night by the time she arrived at a decision.

The night watch had completed their rounds, and even the servants and staff had long gone to sleep. Except for the occasionally restless horse, hound, or elephant from the royal stables, the palace complex was quiet.

She stood on her balcony, breathing in the cool, bracing air of early autumn, and — at last — recited the mantra, once, carefully, enunciating each Krushan syllable perfectly, without a single error or repetition.

17

The night blossomed with light.

It began as a slow lightening, like the soft flush in the eastern sky at dawn, announcing the imminent arrival of the rising sun; except that it was near midnight now, and dawn was a whole watch away. The gloaming grew to a glow, and then suddenly the darkness was dispersed with a flash so bright, Karni was momentarily blinded. She felt a surge of heat so intense that she cried out, expecting to be seared to death. But the heat receded as quickly as it had arisen, reducing to the intensity of a crackling blaze in a fireplace across the room.

Her eyes were still dazzled from the flash of light. She rubbed them and blinked several times, trying to regain her vision.

When she did, she saw that there was a presence in her chamber.

She took a step back, her hip touching the stone balustrade that enclosed her balcony. There was nowhere else to go.

Karni blinked again, trying to focus her blurred vision. Yes, there was definitely someone there, and the figure — which she could now make out as a man — was the source of the intense, banked heat she felt, as powerful as any fire, that exuded from the man's body. His face glowed, as if illumined by flame, making his features difficult to see clearly.

"Who are you?" Karni asked, hearing the tremble in her own voice. *Where was her sword?* She scanned the chamber frantically. It was hanging beside her bed, behind the stranger. Her eyes searched the room quickly for a more accessible weapon, as she edged sideways into the chamber.

You summoned me, the figure said.

She started. The words had come not from his lips but from . . . *his being.* Like a thought projected into her. She felt the heat of his mind touch her own and then dissipate at once. It felt like a tiny pinprick of intense warmth had stabbed her in the forehead. She forgot her search for a weapon and clutched at her forehead, feeling sweat break out at once. She cried out from the pain.

Have I caused you . . . discomfort? I did not intend to. I do not often assume mortal form.

The pinprick was more painful this time, the heat more searing. She cried out again, and thrashed around until she found a staff she used for stick fighting. She took hold of it and pointed it at him. "Stay back. I can call for a hundred guards in a moment."

It is illogical of you to fear me. I am merely answering your summons.

She cried out at the sharp pain in her head, clutching her temples. Sweat was popping out across her face now, rolling down in rivulets. "Stop *doing* that! It *hurts!*"

He was silent a moment, then she sensed the heat emanating from his presence reduce in intensity, banking to a mere warm glow, like a fire that had burned down to the embers.

When he next "spoke" into her mind, the sensation was like an uncomfortable warm prickling in her brain rather than the searing, stabbing pains she'd felt initially.

Am I endurable to you now?

She wiped the sweat off her brow with the back of her hand. He had the glossy ubiquitous appearance of all the gods and goddesses depicted in statuary and art, an almost inhumanly smooth, unblemished perfection of limb, symmetry, and facial features that made it impossible to describe exactly what he looked like except that he was a perfect specimen. "Who are you? How did you appear in my chambers?"

Did you not summon me? I recognize your voice. It was you who recited the Mantra of Summoning.

The mantra. Pasha'ar's mantra.

"Who are you?" she asked.

He gazed at her steadily. "I am known by many names in your tongue. The most commonly used one is Sharra."

She stared at him. The intense searing emanating from him, the sudden appearance out of thin air, the ability to project thoughts into her mind. Could it really be . . . ?

"Sharra?" she asked in wonderment. "The . . . the sun god?"

He inclined his head. **At your service.**

At my service? "I don't understand. Sage Pasha'ar did not explain what the mantra does. I recited it expecting . . . something else."

What were you expecting?

She hesitated for a second, then blushed.

"A friend," she replied.

I sense turmoil within you. You were expecting a lover. Someone dearly beloved to you but now lost . . . Am I correct?

She said nothing.

I am sorry to have disappointed you. But you did summon me specifically.

She frowned. "I did *not!* I was thinking of someone completely different."

The mantra summons any god of your choosing. But yet I am here. There is a reason for that: you intended me to be the one.

"I wished for my friend Maheev of Mraashk . . ." She stopped, her throat choking at the use of his name. She shook her head. "I was a fool. I should have known my wish would not be fulfilled."

This Maheev of Mraashk, he was dear to you. A lover, perhaps?

She shook her head. "We never consummated our friendship. Any intimacy between us was only emotional. I was resistant to the idea of a permanent bonding. He wanted marriage. The last time we saw each other, he wanted to vie for my hand in a swayamvara."

And you did not give him this opportunity. Because you were busy serving the priest Pasha'ar at the time?

"Yes. And in the interim, to uphold tradition and family honor, he was compelled to attend the swayamvara of another princess. In Dirda. By chance, I happened to be traveling through Dirda at the very time."

He moved across the room slowly, seeming to glide rather than walk. **Why do you assume it was a matter of chance?**

She had no answer to that. It was a possibility that had never occurred to her, but now that it was suggested, it seemed obvious.

Pasha'ar was the one who sent you to Dirda, was it not? And he sent you at precisely that time?

He was right. It was an odd coincidence that she happened to be dispatched to Dirda at the very time that Maheev was also there for the swayamvara. In fact, when she heard in the marketplace that the princess was hosting her swayamvara, the first thing she had thought was *Maheev must be here.* He could not refuse the invitation because it would reflect badly on his house. And when she went to the tourney grounds, there he was, handsome and resplendent in his golden armor on his gold-paneled chariot, as beautiful and perfect as the first day she had seen him on his first visit to her father's palace.

"Yes, I see what you mean," she said slowly. "It was as if Pasha'ar sent me on that pointless errand to Dirda only so that I could be there in time to watch Maheev . . ." Again she felt her throat choke, and she shut her eyes.

To watch him die competing in that chariot challenge. An unfortunate mishap when a stray arrow struck one of his horses and caused his chariot to overturn. You ran to the spot where he fell and cradled his head in your lap and cried as the light passed from his eyes.

The god's words sparked a flaring light in the dark corner of her mind where she had buried the memory, illuminating the jagged edges of the pain she had felt when she saw it happen. She relived the shock and disbelief she had felt that day in Dirda as she saw the chariot tumble and shatter before coming to rest in a cloud of dust.

She lowered her head. The staff felt like a leaden weight in her hand. She leaned it against the wall and clutched her face in both hands. "He was broken and bleeding and beyond help. He recognized me and was happy to see me. He said he had wished to see my face one last time before he died, and there I was, a gift from the gods. He told me he loved me . . ."

And he wished you much happiness in your life ahead. Before he died in your arms.

"Yes," she said, weeping openly now, "yes. And I told him I loved him too — but I was too late, he was already gone." At this, Karni became overwhelmed and could not go on.

Sharra waited patiently as she cried the tears she had held back since that day, the pain she had banked and hidden from Sage Pasha'ar, her father, her friends, the wet nurses, everyone, even herself.

Finally, she could cry no more. There would be more tears tomorrow. And the day after. And for many days to come. But for now she was drained. She wiped her face with the hem of her garment.

You mortals have such brief existences. It is always sad to see you fail to achieve your desires and die unfulfilled. Maheev's end was unfortunate. But you have a great and fulfilling life ahead of you. His dying wish is prophetic. You will achieve much happiness in your life — as well as great sorrow. Both are inevitable, I am afraid. Your place in the mortal world is a special one, your life and times extraordinary, and your sons —

"I don't want to know," she said brusquely. She paused and tempered her tone. "Please. Do not reveal my future. I know that as a god you have sight of all things past and future, seen and unseen. I do not wish to know what lies ahead for me. I want to live my life myself."

He was silent for so long she thought she had offended him. But when he spoke again, there was no rancor in his voice. **So be it, Karni of Stonecastle. I will speak of it no more.**

"Is that why you came to me? To show me my future? Is that the purpose of the mantra?"

He smiled. She saw a flash of his teeth, which gleamed with the brightness of a rising sun. Light exuded from his eyes, his body, as he smiled, and she felt warmth emanate from him in a small wave. It passed through her with a stimulating frisson. Such power! Just from a smile.

I am not a fortuneteller, Karni of Stonecastle. I do not appear when summoned to show mortals their future. I am Sharra, Star of the Sky, Light of the World.

She smiled back despite her emotional state. There was something dangerously charming about him. Like the sun itself, you could not take your eyes off him, even though you knew that staring at him too long would burn your eyes blind. Charismatic yet deadly.

"Then why did the mantra summon you?" she asked.

He took a step toward her. He had mastered his emanations now, and she felt none of the searing heat that he had been emitting earlier. Now it was but a genial warmth that Karni found oddly comforting. His features blurred again, and she braced herself, expecting another blast of heat. But instead of the bright flash, his features rearranged themselves to form a new face, a new body, one that was so familiar, so desirable to her that she gasped involuntarily.

He smiled at her now with the face and form of her dead sweetheart, Maheev. Exact to the last detail.

The purpose of the mantra was to grant you your wish, Karni of Stonecastle. To give you the wedding night with Maheev that you desired.

The sun god paused as Karni's beleaguered mind tried to process what he had just said. Was he truly saying what she *thought* he was saying? She felt herself as the memory of her last embrace with Maheev returned. He had wanted her so much, and she had denied him, as any young woman in her position would have, not because she didn't want him with the same intensity — River Goddess, how she had wanted him! — but because she wanted to wait till they were wed. She had been so filled with the confidence of youth that death was not even a distant possibility.

She tried to speak now, but her throat was choked with emotion.

The wedding night that you were so cruelly denied. And the child that would have been produced from that union.

18

"No!" Karni cried out, aghast. She backed away, her heel striking something. She heard a clattering sound as the staff fell to the floor. "I did not ask for this."

Sharra, the sun god, in the form of her dead sweetheart, Maheev, moved closer to her in the same gliding motion.

Maheev of Mraashk was of the Solar dynasty. My direct descendant. When you used the mantra to attempt to summon him, it was only natural that I, the sire of his bloodline, should appear.

She shook her head, still backing away from him. "I did not ask for you, or any god. I thought only to use the mantra in order to see Maheev again one last time, if only for a few moments, to speak to him freely, to pour my heart out and say the things I neglected to say while alive."

To feel his touch, to press your lips against his, to hold him close and to melt in his arms . . . Do you deny that these desires were also in your heart when you uttered the mantra?

She looked down, embarrassed, but unable to lie. "We were to be wed this season, to be husband and wife. I had every right to feel those emotions, those desires."

As you have every right to live out that desire now, with me.

She was shaking her head before he finished the sentence. "No. I cannot. It is one thing to desire, quite another to succumb. I am an unwed girl, and I am not ready to be wed yet by my own choice. Someday I will find a husband whom I believe I can love as much as I loved Maheev. I am willing to wait until then. What you are proposing is impossible."

His eyes — Maheev's eyes — glowed brightly for an instant, reacting to her refusal. She felt the heat emanating from him again. You are mistaken, Princess Karni. This is not an offering. This is inevitable. Once the mantra has been uttered and a god is summoned, the summoner will birth a child. The question of choice does not enter into it. The mantra compels me to instill myself within you and ensures that you will bear a child of our union. All the mantra allows one to choose is which god to summon, and what qualities one wishes the resulting child to possess in life.

She gasped, raising a hand to cover her mouth with her upright palm. "But I do not wish this! Will you assault me then? Against my will?"

Nay, Karni of Stonecastle, he said. I am a god and need not impregnate a woman in the mortal way. I do not wish to possess you by force. I am sympathetic to your situation. Your intelligence and strength of will impress me greatly. If you do not wish to accept my gift in the usual way, through the union of man and woman, then I can plant the seed in you through the force of godhead itself.

She swallowed. "What does that mean?"

He raised a hand, the palm beginning to glow at once, producing a tiny ball of heat and light, a spinning fireball the size of an almond. **By passing my seed to you through the medium of my energy. Just as I engender life within the womb of Great Mother Artha, the goddess of Arthaloka, through the life-giving power of my sunlight.**

She hesitated. "And if I do not want this method either? If I refuse you altogether and bid you leave this instant?"

Do not test the patience of a god, young woman. You will have more interactions with my fellow gods in your life. And your offspring —

He paused, recalling her earlier admonition.

You would do well to keep good relations with any of us. You will have need of our aid in your life to come.

She reflected on that, her heart racing. Why had she uttered that mantra at all? Sage Pasha'ar had brought her nothing but hardship and discomfort. She should have known he would never give her a simple gift. The man clearly cared nothing for anyone but himself. He had given her this mantra out of some patriarchal sense of tradition: men bestowing offspring upon women as though children were things to be given and taken, rather than mutually created expressions of one human being's love for another. She wished now that she had put the mantra out of her mind and never used it. But it was too late: wishing would do her no good. She was a realistic woman. What was, was. What had to be, had to be.

There was also the practical matter of there being no alternative. She could not fight a god. And even if she tried and failed, what would that achieve? If what Sharra said was true, she would require the aid of the gods in her life ahead. And not just she. *Your offspring,* he had said. That tantalizing fragment suggested that her future children would need the aid of the gods as well. She could not act now out of pride and willfulness and risk endangering her unborn children. Besides, she *had* uttered the mantra, and in her heart she did indeed desire all the things Sharra had named. Maheev *had* been of the Suryavansha line. She *had* wanted one night with him, if only to give herself the satisfaction of showing him how much she loved him, expressing all that she had failed to express in life. To give him the gift of herself. To give herself the gift of him. She needed it . . . nay, she *wanted* it.

"I have one last question," she said.

Sharra waited, Maheev's handsome face set in that same wistful, longing gaze that had always won her heart.

"Will Maheev . . . wherever he may be now . . . be able to hear what I say to you?" She hesitated, trying to find the right words. "I suppose I'm asking if he will, in some way, be able to sense the feelings I express here and now? Is there some way to make that possible?"

The god did not answer her immediately. She thought she had finally crossed a line, given offense to a powerful divine entity.

But when he looked at her, it was with Maheev's face, Maheev's eyes, and, she could have sworn, Maheev's spirit.

"Karni," he said, in that same gentle, respectful tone of Maheev's she had loved for its contrast to the loud, boisterous voices of most rich young men, "Marriage is a woman's decision, and it's your right to make that choice when you please. But can I help it if I'm so madly crazy in love with you, Karni of Stonecastle, apple of my eye, that I can't bear to wait another year, another season, or even another night, to make you my wife?"

She raised her hand before her chin, shocked speechless. It was not merely a mimicking of Maheev. It *was* Maheev. By the grace of the gods!

The incarnation of Maheev spread his arms. "I love you, Karni Stonecastle. We've known each other since we could first talk. We played together as infants in your father's castle in Mraashk. Our families know each other well and are good friends. Even after you left Mraashk to come live here at Stonecastle, I followed you and changed my entire life to be near you. I love everything about you, from your quick temper to your stubborn will, to the way your back arches where it meets your hip, to how you toss your hair when you walk, plus your strength, your beauty, your love for fried tapioca —"

Karni shook her head in amazement, tears rolling down her face again. She began to walk toward him.

"— your prowess at weapons and combat, your sense of Krushan law, your refusal to give up on any chore no matter how demanding until it is done to your satisfaction."

She put her upright palm over his mouth, cutting off the rest.

"Maheev, oh, Maheev," she said, her heart tearing apart and filling with unspeakable emotion both at once. "I love you, my beloved. I love you more than anything else in this world. Would that I had told you when I had the chance, that last day we met, after the lake. I wanted to tell you, but I was too proud, too stubborn, too willful, to admit that I wanted you as much as you wanted me. I was young and arrogant. I thought we had all the time in the world. I thought we had forever. I was wrong. I know now that all we have is the given moment. The here and now. There is nothing else. The future is uncertain, the past unreachable. We only have tonight. I should have told you how I felt; I should have held nothing back. Nothing would have given me more joy than to have taken you as my husband. I wanted to spend my life with you. I want to be with you, my love."

She paused, knowing she could not stop herself now. "Tonight."

The god opened his arms and embraced her. She crushed herself against his body and felt a rush of emotions, of love, lust, desire, sorrow, joy, that she had never felt before. For once in her life, she stopped controlling and let herself go completely. She surrendered to the given moment. The heat grew within her and took her by storm. She allowed it to consume her. It blazed through her veins like a flood of fire. She let herself catch fire and burn. And he burned with her.

Together, they gave themselves over to the blaze.

Part Four

Shvate

~

1

SHVATE LOOKED UP AT the city of Reygar and felt his heart sink. How could he hope to defeat such a mighty place? How could anyone? Surely all the armies of Hastinaga could not accomplish this task. His first impulse was to turn the whole army around and ride back home to the blessed leaf-shaded palace of his ancestors, where he could spend even the hottest summer afternoons basking in honeyed splendor with his two beautiful wives. What madness had possessed him to invade Reygistan? Look at their capital city! Nothing he had ever seen, studied, heard, or experienced had prepared him for such a sight.

The city rose in layers, tier upon tier rising up so high that even when he craned his neck, he could not see the peak of it. He had carefully approached the city from the west in order to have this one glimpse before sundown. The sun was behind him, and his men were diligent in keeping the canopy above his head, keeping his sensitive skin out of direct sunlight at all times. But it was not his albino sensitivity to bright sunlight that was causing him distress. It was the sheer scale and height of what lay before him.

Reygar was *gargantuan.*

The city was like nothing else he had ever seen. Built into the side of a granite mountain, the grand metropolis comprised levels upon levels, not a few dozens or a score, but hundreds upon hundreds of levels ranging from the height of a man to ten times the height of a man, with no discernible pattern or uniformity. The whole was a densely packed mass of housing and humanity that rose hundreds of yards high. Reygar was a mountain, and the mountain was the city. The two were one and the same, and the whole was formidable.

"How does it all stand?" he heard himself whisper, awed.

"The mountain supports it," the man standing beside him said. "The shelves of rock you see jutting into the city act as beams and pillars of support, holding it up. It is carefully engineered to lean into the mountain, even if struck by an earthquake or the strongest of desert windstorms. That is why it has stood so long without mishap. So long as the mountain stands, Reygar stands. Do you see those shelves of granite and basalt rock jutting through the layered masses of human construction? The city's vishwakarmas carved out the mountain itself, cutting away the softest parts, leaving the hardest, most indestructible shelves and spurs of hard rock. Then, they built human platforms, houses upon houses, mansions upon mansions, castles upon castles, all piled in a maze of incredible complexity, myriad materials and substances intermingling until it was all one endless mosaic of brick, stone, wood, fired clay, marble, even shaped metal and raw ore. This occurred over centuries, piling layer upon layer of houses, streets, aqueducts, bridges, chutes, and other complex constructs that are unique to Reygar. It's quite extraordinary. There's nothing like it anywhere else in Reygistan, let alone the rest of the civilized world. Though I have heard of a city named Petrak in the West . . . but that's quite different, being cut out of the rock itself. Reygar is like no other city that I know of."

Shvate turned to look at the man who had spoken. The great seer-mage Vessa, who had fathered Shvate and his half brother Adri upon the princesses Umber and Ember respectively, had also given his gift of seed to their maid, whom they had sent in their stead in a misguided attempt to avoid lying with the uncomely sage themselves. The progeny of that maid and Vessa was Vida, and because of his mother's social stature, or rather her lack thereof, he was not considered part of the imperial lineage.

Shvate had been slightly resentful when Vrath had insisted he take Vida along on this campaign, but over the course of the long journey to Reygistan, Shvate had come to appreciate having Vida by his side. The young man had a keen mind, an alert eye, and an ability to analyze and anticipate that was quite exceptional. He was already Shvate's favorite minister, a far sight more useful than any of the tiresome gurus who sat and argued all night in the war tent about how great emperor Sha'ant or great emperor Shapaar or some other great king of the Krushan would have done this or that. When Vida looked at a situation, he gave crisp, pertinent suggestions on what Shvate could or could not do. One of these suggestions had saved them half a day's march through the waterless wasteland of a desert, and many of his other pieces of information had proved very useful to Shvate. That was why he had asked Vida to come along on this scouting trip, leaving everyone else behind.

"How do you know all this of Reygar?" Shvate asked.

Vida, who had been gazing up at the great mountain city, turned and faced Shvate. His features were perfectly aligned, perfectly formed, yet despite that symmetry and balance, he was neither handsome nor remarkable to look upon, merely plain and ordinary. His physique was the same: neither tall nor short, not fat nor thin, not muscular nor skinny. He was plain, ordinary, average. But his mind? His mind was extraordinary. That average, ordinary appearance concealed what Shvate now believed to be a genius intellect. His capacity to acquire, store, and process information was unparalleled. Shvate had heard stories around the palace of Vida winning debates with the gurus, but had always assumed these were exaggerations or that the "debates" in question were nothing more than meaningless displays of rote recitations. He now knew that everything he had heard was true. Vida was a genius thinker and analyst, and having his prodigious memory by your side was like having a hundred priest scribes available at your beck and call, ready to recite whatever fact or statistic was required, at a moment's notice. Shvate now found that he depended completely on his half brother's vast store of knowledge.

"After Jarsun of Reygistan rallied a conspiracy of allies against Hastinaga and led the uprising against us, I made it my business to dredge up everything I could learn about the Reygistani Empire. Mind you, a lot of it is folklore and even superstition. Of course, Jarsun himself is no ordinary mortal — the very fact that he somehow survived that battle with Vrath is proof enough of that — and some of the other things I learned are not in the realm of the plausible, or even the possible. But I've learned that all knowledge is useful, even if it's an exaggeration or a misquote. Even myths have their origins in legends, and legends in truth."

Shvate raised an eyebrow and shrugged. "When it comes to Jarsun, even the myths are probably true. What he did at the Battle of the Rebels, the way he attacked Vrath and kept him out of the battle, that was the stuff of superstition and myth. He is no ordinary mortal, that much is clear. I don't know what he is, but he's not human. His powers are unlike any Krushan I've heard of before."

"He is Krushan but actually two separate beings, Jarsa and Sunna, joined together by a mage guru through the use of powerful maya," Vida said matter-of-factly. "His mother was so grateful that after the guru brought him home —"

Shvate held up a hand. "Vida, we can discuss Jarsun's origins another time; for now let us focus on the city of Reygar. I have a very large army camped out in the middle of a very large, very hot desert, with virtually no water, no food, and no way to retreat or regroup, and we need to invade and capture this city — which is a mountain, or mountain which is a city — and we have to do that *right now*. It looks more or less impossible to me, but I'm hoping that you can help me find a way to make it plausible if not possible, to use your own words."

Vida nodded slowly and squinted his eyes, staring up at the city towering above them. The man was nearsighted, Shvate knew, but despite his inability to see clearly across long distances, he was still somehow able to draw conclusions and insights that even Shvate, with his eagle-eye vision, could never have reached in a thousand years. "Taking Reygar seems daunting, even impossible."

"You don't say," Shvate said sarcastically. "I was planning to simply stroll up to the front gates and say I was visiting my third cousin on my mother's side."

Vida blinked. "But your mother, Umber, is from Serapi, and all her siblings —"

Shvate sighed. "Vida. My brother. I was jesting. Please put your mind to work on the problem at hand. How do I invade a city that rises vertically above the desert for miles?"

"It's not *miles*, plural. I estimate its height at a little more than one mile but less than two miles."

Shvate slapped his brother on the back. "Brother, brother. Never mind the calculations. I need strategy, not figures. And I can't come up with a strategy unless I understand what I'm up against."

Vida nodded slowly. "You want Jarsun, and you want to know how to take his capital city and kill him once and for all."

Shvate grinned. "He's a genius!" he said, raising his eyes briefly heavensward as if speaking to the gods. "Yes, brother dearest. That is what I want. Jarsun dead, Reygar taken, Reygistan conquered. How do I do it? Can your brilliant mind solve that problem?"

Vida looked up at the piled layers of humanity rising above them. "Any city can be taken. Every army defeated. It's only a question of finding their weakness and then exploiting it."

"Good," Shvate said. "Let your genius brain work on that while I deal with other business. When you have something for me, do interrupt whatever I'm doing. And remember, brother, we are in a desert and running low on supplies. An army without food and water is an army doomed to failure. Whatever we do, we have to act soon. Soon means days — not weeks or months."

Vida nodded. "I understand, Shvate. Give me a little time and let me see what I can come up with. May I use your authority to deploy our resources?"

"Of course. Everything is at your disposal. What do you need done?"

"Spies sent into the city. To gather information. Better yet, if I could go myself . . . There's nothing like seeing things firsthand to gauge the lay of the land."

Shvate raised an eyebrow. "You expect to go traipsing into the city of our archenemy, while our entire army has surrounded and besieged it?"

Vida frowned; clearly he had not given any thought to this circumstance. "You have a point. They will be on the alert at such a time, won't they?"

"Just a little bit more than usual," Shvate said, his tongue firmly in cheek. He was frequently amazed by how Vida could spew out scrolls of information on an arcane subject, but when it came to viewing the bigger picture, he was often clueless. "But you do know we already have spies embedded in Reygar, and if there's anything useful to be learned from them, it's likely to come through those usual channels. Besides, your life is too valuable to risk on such a mission. I need you right here, thinking of a stratagem that will enable me to take that damned mountain of a city without a long, expensive siege. And by expensive, I am not counting the value in gold or taxes. I mean to lose as few lives as possible, *if* possible. If not . . ." He didn't need to complete the sentence. Vida knew as well as he how much depended on the successful completion of this campaign.

"I understand, Shvate," Vida said solemnly. "I take this responsibility you have entrusted to me very seriously. I will not disappoint you."

Shvate slapped Vida on his back, then regretted being so forceful. Vida lurched forward, almost losing his balance. "I know you will, brother. You are my most valuable asset in this campaign. My secret weapon."

He thought of adding a wish that Vida would build himself up more through regular exercise and simply by eating more generously, but left that part unsaid. Vida's true strength lay in his mind, not his body. Shvate himself had expanded and developed his own physique considerably in the past few years. As he walked back to the large tent that served as his command center, he flexed his arms and chest, stretching them out. He had always taken pride in being fighting fit, but he had now surpassed even that and had bulked up into a truly formidable figure. He could see the difference in the way his soldiers looked at him as if with a greater respect, and could feel it in the ease with which he was able to heft even the heaviest maces and other weapons of war. He had sacrificed some speed and agility, but he was no foot soldier who needed to march a hundred miles a day; he was commander in chief of the armies of Krushan. He had not had to participate in actual combat for months now, barring his practice sessions. But he had come to enjoy building himself up, the way it made him feel stronger, more confident, more in control.

He also enjoyed the way his coital partners responded to his new build, both when they saw him and when he took them to bed. Shvate made no secret of the fact that he loved women, and loved loving them even more. He had heard his erotic appetites compared to those of his late father and uncle. Apparently, Virya and Gada were legendary even among Krushan princes for their proclivities. This pleased him too: even though he knew his true biological father was the seer-mage Vessa, by the law of succession, he was the titular son of Princess Umber and the late prince Virya, and it was as Virya's son that he was officially known. It pleased him to hear that he had "inherited" his late father's legendary prowess at lovecraft. It was the one thing in common he shared with the father he had never known.

Shvate reached the command tent and entered its blessed shade. He dismissed the shade bearers and gestured to his personal servants to sprinkle cool, perfumed water while fanning him. The cool, moist air relieved the burning sensation on his exposed areas of skin, and he relished it. His eyes and face were the most heated and reminded him briefly of the agony he had suffered that day when he had fought the Battle of the Rebels. The afternoon sun had caught him full strength, piercing him like an insect speared by a red-hot needle. It had taken him weeks to recover fully from that trauma, both physically and psychologically. Still, he *had* healed, his burnt albino skin repairing itself with the aid of cooling lotions of the royal healers. His brother Adri, on the other hand, had withdrawn so far into himself that everyone feared he would never be the same again.

Shvate sighed. He loved his brother and was his keeper, but he also had a duty to the empire. And if Adri would not go to war again, then Shvate could hardly stay home in Hastinaga, rolling dice with him. Besides, they were both grown men now; they chose how to live their lives. Adri chose to stay home, wasting away his precious youth. Shvate wanted more, much, much more.

He motioned to the servants to cease their fanning. Attendants gently dabbed away the excess moisture with soft absorbent cloths, careful not to rub his sensitive skin too roughly. They left him only his langot to dress in, the thin strip of undergarment that covered his maleness. As he stepped out into the cool silk-shrouded shade of his palatial tent, he was met by an unexpected sight.

A beautiful young woman lay on his bed.

Shvate's breath caught in his throat. Even after the heat and harshness of the desert, after a day spent on the march, scouting the enemy capital and instructing his generals, after weeks of marching through hostile territory, skirmishes and minor battles on the long march from Hastinaga to the inland kingdom of Reygistan, his carnal appetite had not diminished.

"Mayla?"

The vision stretched out on his bed smiled up at him; the thin sheet covering her slipped away at this movement, and Shvate saw that she was nude. "My love, are you pleased to see me?" She glanced down at his langot. "Oh, I see that you are. *Very* pleased."

"I am," he said. "Of course I am! But what are you doing here in Reygistan, my love?"

She arched her back as she rose to her elbows, and Shvate's breath caught in his throat. "There was a supply train. A thousand wagons . . . or was it ten thousand?" She tossed her long, lustrous hair. "It didn't seem like a few more wagons would make a difference. After all, there are all kinds of supplies. Just as an army must eat, drink, clothe itself, and receive medical treatment, it also has other needs that need taken care of." She stretched out one long bare foot toward his waist, her toes searching. "*Essential needs.*"

Shvate watched her bare foot, only inches from his groin. "So you brought" — he swallowed, suddenly parched — "essential supplies for my army?"

"What good is an army if its commander is not nourished? I brought something you need, my love. Something I know you cannot function without for long. Is it not better that I, your love, brought you this vital resource instead of forcing you to go in search of . . . *supplies* . . . in the arms of some Reygistani princess?"

Shvate chuckled at the thought. "Do you see any Reygistani princesses here? All my attention is focused on breaking this siege before the summer heat intensifies and our supply lines are stretched beyond endurance."

"Then you must be starving. Come, feast with me."

Mayla undulated her shapely body in a way that made Shvate flush. That sinuous body and its charms had kept Shvate confined to her chambers for weeks on end after their marriage. That was only a few short months ago. This campaign had been their first time apart since they had been married, and he was suddenly wondering how he could have set off on this expedition leaving this beautiful woman behind. All the ministrations of the fan attendants had been negated now as he felt new sweat pushing from the pores of his heated skin. He found himself drawn toward her step by step.

She reached out and grasped the cotton string of his undergarment. "It's too hot to be clothed. Unencumber yourself."

He unencumbered himself with a single tug.

He fell onto the bed, onto her.

After that, there was very little left to be said.

As Shvate and Mayla sought bliss in each other's arms, the sun dipped below the horizon, bringing lengthening shadows, and allowed the fevered desert to cool to more habitable temperatures. With the suddenness of a scorpion's sting, night fell upon the Krushan camp.

2

"My lord, forgive the intrusion."

Shvate rose from his bed of furs, sword already in his fist, rubbing the sleep from his eyes with the knuckles of his free hand. "What is it?"

The soldier bowed low as Shvate emerged from the sleeping area, letting the curtains fall behind him. "Sire, we have captured some of the enemy."

Whatever vestige of sleep had remained in Shvate's body suddenly fled. "Take me to them at once. And send someone to rouse the quartermaster and bring him to me."

"He is the one who sent me to fetch you, my lord." The soldier started to rise, then bowed again, lowering his eyes to the ground. Shvate frowned then sensed movement behind himself.

"What were they doing?" Mayla asked, strapping on her sword as she emerged from the sleeping area. "The enemy soldiers who were captured?"

The soldier kept his eyes lowered, but Mayla seemed unconcerned by her nudity. She had picked up a garment belonging to Shvate and carelessly draped it about herself, concealing some but not all of her assets.

"I know nothing more, Princess, forgive my lapse."

"It's all right," Mayla said, stepping past the soldier. "You did your job. Shvate? Are you coming?"

Shvate chuckled and exited the tent, the startled soldier following him when he should be leading. "Why not?" he said. "The more the merrier."

The camp was relatively quiet and still. The fires had been banked hours ago, but in the faint light of the coals, he could see the shapes of several men still sitting around, talking softly. The soldiers of Hastinaga were un-accustomed to idleness. These were men who joined to fight; they wanted to see action. They could only sleep a full night after a hard day's combat. Shvate had given orders for the wine ration to be restricted severely, using the excuse of extended supply lines. In fact, he was concerned about fights breaking out amongst the restless troops. The wine would be supplied in full rations once the battle started, for his men as well as for himself. He too had restricted his intake to just a few watered-down cups for the same reason.

Watching the shapely silhouette of Mayla moving easily through the tents and lines and assorted gear of the war camp, he smiled to himself. He, at least, had a way to while away the idle hours now that Mayla was here.

She was not just a fine woman, but fine a soldier as well — easily the equal of the best Krushan champions. The kingdom of Dirda was a fighting nation, constantly at war for its entire existence. They made no distinction between women and men when it came to training fighters. Dirda women fought better than the men, by and large. The theory was that they had more to lose: apart from the usual rape and impregnation which was a common byproduct of wars, Dirda's enemies were known to kill all infants and children even if they were too young to fight — going so far as to cut the unborn out of pregnant mothers' bellies. This gave Dirda's mothers even more reason to fight, and all the more reason to win.

Shvate was glad that it was Mayla who had chosen to visit him on this expedition. His first wife, Karni, was no less beautiful and desirable, but for reasons he had never been able to fully understand, she chose not to fight alongside him unless it was deemed essential. Mayla, on the other hand, loved every opportunity to see action, and while he considered his own amorous prowess to be considerable, he knew that it was the promise of battle that had seduced her into making this long journey.

She was all business now, leading both him and the soldier as she moved briskly enough to make them both have to jog to keep up.

The soldier ran ahead, and Shvate followed. They caught up with Mayla, who had finally paused at the eastern perimeter. The soldier pointed. "This way, Princess Mayla, Prince Shvate. It is about half a yojana in that direction."

Half a yojana? A yojana was nine miles, so that meant the enemy soldiers had been captured four or five miles out of camp, and since their camp itself was a full yojana from the city of Reygar, that meant they were —

"Almost fifteen miles away? What were they doing so far from the city?"

"Running away, what else?" Mayla kept pace easily with both of them, her movements out-of-doors as fluid and economical as they had been languid and generous in bed, although she had snatched up a cloak and tied the sash as she had left the tent. She was clad for fighting now. Because of the night-cool sand, they had no need for footwear, and made better progress barefoot than if they were booted.

"Why would they be running away from their own capital city?" Shvate asked. The desert air was cool and refreshing. He realized he actually liked the climate here. At this time of year, Hastinaga would be sweltering by night and deadly hot by day. The dreaded Lu would be blowing through the capital city and leaving the usual death toll in its wake. He was glad he was out of the city and out here instead. It was actually quite beautiful by night, though by day, he felt very differently about the desert, especially with his condition.

"What else?" she said. "They saw the size of our forces and knew they didn't stand a chance. So they tried to run for it, like rats leaving a sinking boat on the Jeel."

"I can believe that, but I can't believe that Jarsun would simply allow them to leave. To desert a city under siege is treason. I'm surprised they even made it this far without him cutting them down."

"Perhaps you overestimate Jarsun. The so-called God-Emperor has had his run. His end is in sight now, with the might of Hastinaga camped outside his capital city. I wager even he is thinking of running at a time like this."

Shvate didn't agree with her but decided not to say so. Mayla could be trenchant with her opinions, and he didn't want to get into an argument. On the other hand, she did make a good point. Even glancing back over his shoulder, he could see his camped army sprawled for tens of miles, tens of thousands of tents encircling the mountain that rose in the middle of the desert. Vrath had insisted he bring the whole of their main force into play, to make a point.

Shvate had command of just over two million fighting soldiers, divided into the usual four cadres: elephant, chariot, horse, and foot. The smell of unwashed horse, human, elephant, and dog must carry all the way up to the mountain city, stinking up Jarsun's nostrils. The sight of such a vast force, almost twice the size of Reygistan's entire army, must drive some fear into even that megalomaniac's brain. Or so Shvate hoped. But he had learned enough about Jarsun's past exploits from Vida and other informed sources to know better. It was unlikely that the God-Emperor would be quailing in his boots before even a single arrow had been loosed. And this business of Reygistani fleeing from a besieged city just didn't make sense. He felt the familiar unease of intuition curling inside his belly like a serpent. Something was *off* here.

And with an urrkh like Jarsun, that could mean anything. Shvate still recalled the Battle of the Rebels with less than pleasant emotions. It was frightening to witness *anyone* take on Vrath and do to him the things that Jarsun had done at that battle. And that was in enemy territory; this was Jarsun's home ground — the Heavenly Capital of his Divine Empire as he called it; who knew what forces he might unleash to defend his home?

Shvate saw the cluster of silhouettes as they approached. The site was unlit, but there was more than enough starlight to see by. There were more than he expected. At least a full company of his own soldiers, with a general in command. The general was also the quartermaster of the camp, Prishata of Panchala, an old veteran and staunch supporter of the Krushan. Vrath had appointed him personally, and Shvate was glad to have him in charge of what was a very large and unwieldy army, leaving Shvate free to think strategically without worrying about day-to-day operational issues. The large grey-haired head turned to watch Mayla and Shvate approaching.

Prishata inclined his head respectfully. "Princess Mayla, Prince Shvate, apologies for interrupting your respite."

Shvate bowed to the senior man. "Time enough to sleep in Swarga, General. Pray tell, what brings us out in the desert at this late hour?"

Prishata's long grey mustaches bristled as he glanced back over his shoulder. The elder warrior's face never revealed any emotion, but Shvate sensed something in that backward glance and in the prickling of those whiskers. Whatever it was, it was enough to worry Prishata.

"I have never seen anything of this ilk." Prishata shook his head. "Damned urrkh maya . . ."

Shvate and Mayla glanced at each other. "What is it, General?"

"I thought it best to send for you so you could see for yourself and form your own opinions." Prishata glanced at the cluster of Krushan soldiers. "This way, please."

Shvate and Mayla followed the much taller man as he led them through the lines of soldiers. The soldiers parted to let them pass through, then closed ranks again. Shvate noted that they were standing in a shield formation, except that the shield was turned *inward*. From a distance, he had assumed they were simply guarding the captives. Now he saw they were actually guarding a declination in the desert floor itself. The smooth, flat, sandy ground suddenly yielded here in a curiously circular pattern, somewhat like a spiral staircase, except that these were steps seemingly cut into the sand itself, leading . . . where?

Prishata stood at the top of the decline, looking down. "I had been receiving reports of Reygistani approaching from the east and the south, apparently coming toward the camp, but always disappearing before they reached us. I put special scouting parties to watch for the next group, and they finally spotted several stray individuals coming across the desert at irregular intervals. It took longer to discover them because they were all creeping and crawling."

Shvate saw Mayla's head swivel toward the general. "Creeping and crawling? Across the desert?"

General Prishata looked at Mayla. "Yes. Even at the height of the afternoon heat, when the sun is hot enough to scald and scour the skin right off the body."

Shvate said nothing. He was trying to imagine what could possess anyone, even a soldier, to crawl across open desert for hours or presumably days . . . And at what cost?

When neither of them said anything, Prishata went on. "They keep coming, through the night and day. Based on my observations of the past few hours, I estimate that a few dozen arrive each hour, and they all converge at this site and two other similar sites further east and south, all of them along the perimeter." Prishata pointed to indicate both.

Shvate glanced down. "I don't understand. These Reygistani, they come crawling across the desert and do . . . *what* exactly?"

Prishata grimaced. "They go down these ingress points. These steps lead to some kind of a tunnel that travels beneath the desert, right under our camps, and all the way to the base of the city. At least they appear to be going in that direction. I cannot say with certainty because I have not been able to send any scouts down the tunnel to test that hypothesis."

Shvate frowned. "Why not?"

"It is best if you see for yourself, Prince Shvate. It is difficult to describe."

Shvate studied the elderly man's face for a moment, then looked down at the steps cut into the sand, a pattern as neat and perfect as stairs shaped out of iron. He failed to see how steps could be cut into sand at all, or how they could retain their shape and solidity. Even the desert dunes shifted constantly, and any footprints one left in the sand would disappear within the hour. Yet these steps appeared to be as solid as metal or stone stairs.

Mayla was also examining the strange stairwell, then glanced up just in time to catch Shvate's eyes. He exchanged an unspoken agreement with her: *Let's go see for ourselves what all the fuss is about.*

Mayla moved before he could, putting her foot onto the first step, then the next. Her feet left no impressions in the sand, and even after she stepped off each stair, the pattern remained as perfect and solid as before. He followed, marveling at how solid and perfect the steps felt under his bare feet. Yet they still felt like sand, gritty, grainy, coarse.

The steps led down much deeper than he expected. He counted several score steps, then a hundred, then a few more . . . At precisely 107 steps, the spiral staircase ended in a flat, even surface.

Mayla glanced over her shoulder, eyes flashing in the darkness. Shvate nodded, acknowledging what she had also noted. The auspicious number for such things was 108. To stop a single digit before that auspicious number was not an accident. Someone had deliberately flaunted the auspicious 108 and stopped at 107, which meant a total sum of eight instead of nine. And eight was the number of urrkh, just as nine was the number of divinity.

Whatever these sand steps were, they were no natural formation. Someone had carved exactly 107 of them with a singular purpose.

Prishata descended the steps behind Shvate and Mayla with a torch in his hand. The torchlight flickered and flared as he descended, disturbed by the desert wind, but when he reached the bottom, the flame somehow rose vertically and then stood still. The general's face remained as expressionless as ever, but Shvate saw his beard bristling again and sensed his unease. Shvate shared his discomfort. Something about this place made him wish to be elsewhere.

"The tunnel proceeds all the way under our camps," Prishata said, indicating the darkness ahead. The torchlight threw about thirty or forty yards into view, and as far as Shvate could see, there was nothing there. Just a perfectly cut tunnel some seven or eight yards in height, and as many feet wide.

Eight yards. It will be precisely eight yards in height as well as width.

"We need not go all the way. Only up to . . ." The general left the sentence unfinished. He was not the kind of man who left a sentence unfinished or lacked a word to express himself. He began walking, holding the torch by his side as the ceiling was only a foot above the top of his head.

Shvate and Mayla followed him.

For the first hundred yards or so, there was nothing to see or hear. Just the smooth, immaculately cut sand walls, floor, and ceiling. Shvate reached out and touched the walls and saw Mayla do the same: a few grains of sand came off between his fingers if he pinched, proving that it was indeed sand, and not sandstone or something similar. How could a tunnel carved out of sand maintain its integrity? He could see no pillars or beams, no other means of support. Yet the tunnel was a perfect square cut into the ground. He shook his head. There were more important things to focus on than architecture of this strange tunnel.

After another hundred yards or so, he began to sense a *change*.

First, there was a smell. A familiar odor.

Shvate recognized it at once.

It was the charnel house stench of corpses. The battlefield stink of freshly butchered human bodies cut open, eviscerated, and slowly putrefying.

He breathed through his mouth as the stench grew worse.

Mingled with the battlefield stench was the even more familiar army camp stink of living flesh — sweating, oozing oils and acids, and the residue of whatever foods and drink the bodies had consumed. But there was a sourness to this odor, an underlying layer of some bilious smell that was neither human nor animal. The mixture of odors made for a sickening, gut-churning cocktail. Shvate felt the remains of the haunch of meat and the watered-down wine he had consumed hours earlier stir uneasily in his belly. He resisted the urge to cover his mouth, knowing it would not staunch the smell. He suddenly experienced a powerful urge to turn and run back down the tunnel, out into the open desert air, away from whatever horror lay ahead at the end of this dark descent.

"It would be best to stop shortly," Prishata's voice said, giving Shvate a measure of reassurance. "I would not advise going much further. I have lost a few men already to the . . . phenomenon."

The phenomenon.

Shvate was watching the general when he slowed to a complete halt, the tall man's body mostly blocking his view of the tunnel ahead. But once he stopped, General Prishata moved to one side to allow Shvate and Mayla a better view, holding the torch out to light the way ahead.

Shvate drew in a breath through his mouth and dared to look at what lay in the tunnel.

3

The light of the torch washed over the thing that lay in the tunnel ahead, illuminating it well enough for the first several yards, then dimming the detail as it progressed, until, around a hundred or two hundred yards ahead, it faded into a featureless mass. The thing writhed and moved restlessly.

Mayla had remained a step or two ahead of Shvate, and she turned now to look back at him. Her face was lit fully by the light from the senapati's torch, and her eyes glittered with confusion and a mix of other emotions.

"How . . . ?" she said, then was unable to complete the question.

Shvate could not even begin to form a question.

He stared at the monstrosity in the tunnel and felt all words, language, reason, leave him, fleeing as rapidly as he wanted to flee back up the length of the tunnel. He had no desire to be here, in this dark, cool tunnel shaped by invisible mysterious forces underneath the desert, in the middle of the last watch of the night, staring at something that was an affront to nature and creation, at something that could not possibly exist, and yet *did* exist, writhing and wriggling in front of his very eyes.

People.

The thing was made up of people.

Reygistani, he guessed, though it hardly mattered what nation or tribe they were from.

It was made of people who had apparently been drawn in from all points of the compass, all ends of the Reygistani Empire, to converge on the capital city, Reygar. Crawling across the desert on their bellies, using their hands and knees to cross the searing hot sand in the height of summer. Once they reached the mouth of this tunnel, they presumably crawled inside, up the tunnel, until they reached . . . this. Whatever you called such a thing.

"The one you see at the end there," General Prishata said, his voice echoing eerily in the enclosed space, "is the most recent arrival. As you can make out, he has yet to be assimilated fully. The two others arrived a few hours ago, they appeared to be mother and son."

The man he was referring to was the figure at the extreme end of the *thing*. His body was still recognizably human. Shvate could make out his legs and lower body, still more or less intact. His upper body, though, had already started to merge with the monstrosity. From Shvate's perspective, it looked like the man had crawled up to the thing and pressed his head into the back of the woman who had immediately preceded him. From farther up the tunnel, some kind of whitish ichor was seeping down continually, like sap oozing from the bark of a tree. This ichor was probably acidic to some extent, because it seemed to be dissolving the bodies of the people who inserted themselves into the abomination. In this case, the head of the man had begun to meld with the back and torso of the woman in front, to the point where it was impossible to tell where his skull ended and her spine began. The man's hair and features had dissolved, melted really, and the flesh of his face and neck had *merged* with the flesh of the woman's back and shoulders. At other places, wherever the man's body touched the bodies of those in front of him, the whitish ichor had seeped in and filled the cracks and crevices between the bodies, melding them together, like ants glued together by sap oozing down the trunk of a tree. But sap would only swallow and cover the insects; this ichor dissolved and joined them together, flesh and hair and bone and organs all fusing to form a living continuum.

Shvate allowed his eyes to travel up the length of the thing, past the man, the woman, the child, then to the other people who had come before, then further up . . .

"Hundreds," he said, startled at the hoarse sound of his own voice in the tunnel. "There must be hundreds, thousands even . . ."

"Nay, Prince Shvate," General Prishata said. "What you see here is only a few hundred yards. This tunnel travels for at least fifteen miles as far as we can tell, then turns upward to enter the underside of Reygar Mountain and the city itself. Surely, there would be thousands in this tunnel, perhaps even tens of thousands. But remember that there are probably dozens of such tunnels all around the desert. We do not claim to know how many exactly. Even if you assume threescore or fourscore such tunnels, each filled with two- or threescore thousand hapless souls, that would make . . ."

"Hundreds of thousands, even millions," Shvate said, shocked.

Mayla turned to stare again at Shvate. "But *how . . . ?* How can such a thing be done? And by whom?"

"He is not called *God*-Emperor for nothing, Princess," the general said. "We know he is an urrkh, a demonlord of the highest order. I have heard many tales, including a few from a prince of Mraashk himself. But I have never heard of anything like this. It is something new. Something never seen or heard of before, even in the annals of urrkh history. This is urrkh maya on a gigantic scale."

"These are truly *people?*" Mayla said. "People joined together . . . to form . . . *what?* What is the purpose of it, this thing, this worm or snake or whatever it is?"

Worm and *snake* were apt names to call the monstrosity. It writhed and squirmed just like a gigantic sandworm or python. Except that the individual people who made up the whole were still not wholly melded or digested by the whitish ichor, and their arms, legs, heads, and assorted body parts stuck out unevenly along the squirming length. And each of those individual body parts *also* squirmed and writhed, and appeared to retain some independent volition.

"I don't know," Shvate said grimly, "but I have a feeling we will find out soon."

Mayla's face distorted with an expression he knew well. She was disgusted by the sight. "It is inhuman, monstrous," she said. "I cannot bear the sight of it."

Shvate understood just how she felt. He was disgusted as well — any right-thinking person would be. The writhing mass of melded bodies in the tunnel — coated with that sickly whitish ichor and hair and bone and organ, with faces joined to stomachs, legs jutting out of throats, torsos intertwined with thighs and buttocks, a nightmarish, writhing horror — was an abomination, an affront to Great Mother Artha and all her creatures, an insult to the stone god and the Priapratis, a slap on the face of creation itself. People were not meant to be treated thus. Human beings were not ants or bugs. They were not slaughter beasts to be stitched together through use of urrkh maya into a slimy length of flesh and bone, gristle and sinew. Whatever vile purpose Jarsun intended for these Reygistani, it was inhumane and torturous to the living people he was abusing to serve his ends. These Reygistani, no matter how patriotic or loyal to their emperor they might have been, could not have voluntarily agreed to serve his cause in this manner. They had to have been mesmerized or brainwashed somehow, by his evil sorcery, and forced to crawl across the desert, into these tunnels, to join this awful experiment. It was the people Mayla was feeling sorry for, their plight that disgusted and horrified her, and Shvate agreed.

"I have to do something, Shvate," she said. "I cannot stand aside and watch."

He nodded slowly. "Neither can I."

He took a step forward, forcing himself to walk toward the horror in the tunnel. The first two or three steps were very difficult, his mind resisting his command to approach that terrifying sight. But once he was moving, it became a little easier. Momentum carried him forward, determination caused him to reach for the sword at his waist, and a cold hatred of injustice made him draw the shastra and raise it.

Beside him, Mayla was walking as well, and she unsheathed her sword when he did. She looked as scared and determined as he did.

"Shvate?" she asked uncertainly.

He nodded. "The only way to stand up for what one believes in is to act." And with that, he raised his sword and struck down hard at the awful thing.

The sword struck the last man at the end of the monstrosity. It hit him in the chest, which was coated with a layer of ichor. As the ichor seeped into the man's body, dissolving and melting flesh and bone, the slimy substance hardened into a congealed mass of pinkish brown. As Shvate's sword stabbed the thing, he felt as if he had just struck a very soft tree, one that was rotten in the center, but still dense and damp. The sword stuck in the mass, and though he pulled at it with all his might, he could not get it free.

Mayla raised her sword and struck at another spot on the man's torso — resulting in the same wet soft sound, like an axe striking the trunk of a damp, rotten tree. Like Shvate's, her sword also held fast.

"Shvate, my sword . . ."

"Yes, mine too."

They both struggled to free their swords but could not.

Suddenly, a shudder rippled down the length of the monstrosity.

Shvate felt the vibration through his sword, up his arms and into his body, down to his bones, to the soles of his feet.

A deep rumbling echoed down the tunnel, setting off oscillating echoes.

The ground trembled beneath his feet, and loose sand fell on the side of his face and left shoulder from the ceiling of the tunnel.

The man's torso burst open, spewing out ichor, blood, pieces of flesh and gristle, stomach acids, offal . . . the horrible mixture of foul fluids and viscous slime splattered Shvate and Mayla. Mayla cried out, letting go of her sword and reaching for her face. Shvate released his sword too, covering his eyes and face instinctively.

A tiny head emerged from the gaping hole in the man's chest, pushing past the shattered ribs and the throbbing lump that Shvate realized — with horror — was the man's still-beating heart. The tiny head was that of the child that had accompanied the woman, a little boy no more than nine or ten years of age. His face and neck had been melted down and disfigured by the ichor, though his head and features were still recognizably human. But when he opened his mouth to speak, he revealed a mouthful of blood. There were no teeth, no tongue, no throat. Just a hole filled with dark, thick blood. The sound he made next appeared to be formed from the blood itself, gurgling and bubbling. There were things in the boy's throat, Shvate saw, tiny moving things like insects, and they bubbled and squirmed in the blood-filled throat as the voice emerged.

Shvate of the Krushan!

Mayla turned and clutched at Shvate's arm. He caught hold of her and pressed her close. From behind, he glimpsed General Prishata with the torch, staring and reacting with the expression of a man who had just seen the door of the underworld, Nrruk, thrown open and the face of the lord of the nethermost demon-realm revealed.

Your line has plagued me too long —

The creature that spoke through the boy's throat spoke with liquid sounds, the words somehow forming and bubbling through the frothing blood in his open mouth. His lips did not move, nor did his throat muscles, and as far as Shvate could tell, the child had no tongue to speak of. Whatever this was, it was no longer human. Merely an instrument of some arcane force.

And now you dare to invade my sacred sanctum? You lay siege to my homeland? I will have done with you. Today is the day I will send you back to the womb from whence you came. Begone, spawn of Vessa!"

And before Shvate could move or turn away or do anything at all, without even a twitch of warning, the boy's throat released a spume of blood as wide around as Shvate's own arm. The blood struck Shvate full in the face, drenching him from head to foot in an instant, cold and viscous and foul-smelling as a cesspool. So cold that it was like ice water, freezing cold. Mayla cried out as the freezing foul blood washed over her as well, drenching them both and spattering in all directions, for yards all around.

You!

The rumbling began again, this time loud and fierce enough to dislodge entire chunks and showers of loose sand from the ceiling of the tunnel. Shvate felt the sand stick to the disgusting bloody mess coating his body.

Will!

He forced himself to move, back down the tunnel, toward the torch held by General Prishata. He pulled Mayla with him.

"Our swords!" she gasped, wiping away the blood from her face.

"Leave them!" he cried.

All!

The tunnel shook and rattled from side to side, shaking like a wagon rolling at full speed down a sharp incline. Shvate felt the vibrations in his bones. A keening sound rose from behind as he reached General Prishata. The general was shouting something, but the rumbling was so loud that he could only see the general's mouth move without hearing a word. The senapati's crisp white uniform was also splattered with the foul blood. The whole tunnel was drenched with it, the ceiling dripping. Sand was falling from the walls in pieces. The ground shook beneath Shvate's feet, and he felt loose sand heaving underneath as he began to run.

Die!

"Faster!" he cried. "Run faster!"

Mayla and he sprinted up the way they had come. Soldiers were holding torches and shouting their prince's name. Shvate glanced back over his shoulder and saw the general following them, sword drawn, guarding their rear. Behind the general, Shvate saw the monstrosity writhing and lashing like a snake in a frenzy, spewing blood and ichor, smashing into the sides and ceiling and floor of the tunnel, breaking the perfect rectangular form of the tunnel.

The tunnel itself was dissolving around them. Whatever force had held the sand in its impossibly immaculate shape had released its power, and the sand was now behaving like sand again, collapsing, raining down like a monsoon shower on them all.

Shvate saw the light of several torches ahead and, beyond them, the blessed starlight of the night sky.

He pushed Mayla ahead of himself, turning back to reach out a hand to the general —

But the tunnel collapsed in upon itself.

The senapati's torch was extinguished as the sand tunnel closed around him, capturing him from the waist down. The elderly warrior cried out and flailed.

Shvate grasped hold of his hand. "Hold on!" he cried out above the deafening noise.

The desert was filled with raging wind and sand, like a sandstorm risen out of nowhere.

The tunnel closed like the maw of a snake upon the senapati's body, pulling him down into the earth.

Shvate pulled. He felt Mayla's hands beside his, grasping hold of the senapati's arms above his elbows pulling with all her might.

Both of them pulling together, they exerted all their strength. The general burst free, flying out of the sand to tumble and fall beside them on the desert floor.

They lay gasping, shielding their faces and eyes against the sand and the wind.

They were safe, and whole, and alive. For now. Shvate thanked his ancestors —

Suddenly, everything fell silent and still.

The wind died out completely. The sand stopped swirling. All sound was extinguished. The reverberations and noise from the tunnel ceased, and there was a moment of deafening silence and stillness.

Shvate saw the soldiers who had been waiting aboveground rise slowly to their feet and look around fearfully.

He rose to his feet as well, helping up Mayla, while she helped General Prishata to his feet. The general appeared to be shaken but unharmed. They were all unharmed, except for the vile stuff that had drenched them. Shvate rubbed at his hand and saw a patch of pale white skin emerge. He bent and picked up a handful of sand and rubbed at another bloody patch. "The sand scours it off," he told Mayla. She began doing the same.

They were almost clear of the awful blood when the rumbling began again. This time it was a long, slow sound that rose from somewhere to the south and west, the direction of the camp . . .

No, not the camp. The city.

It was coming from Reygar.

The rumbling grew and grew until the entire world seemed to be vibrating and shuddering, on the brink of some terrible calamity.

4

The reverberations died down, the desert stopped shuddering, and the wind ceased blowing.

There was a brief period of utter stillness during which Shvate realized that he didn't have a sword, and neither did Mayla.

"Soldiers!" he snapped. Half a hundred faces turned at once to look at their commander and prince. "You and you, give me your swords!"

They complied at once.

Shvate tossed a scabbarded sword to Mayla, who caught it deftly with one hand and drew it with the other, all in a single motion.

What they had seen in the tunnel would have unhinged any person, soldier or civilian. Yet here was Mayla, with that horrifying experience already shaken off and ready to fight. But *what* were they fighting? Shvate didn't know and didn't care to guess. All he could do was be prepared for the worst. A sword in hand helped.

As the silence drew on, the sound of approaching hoofbeats grew louder. Shvate glimpsed the silhouettes of riders approaching from several different directions. In moments, they resolved into couriers seeking out the general.

They all had the same message: strange movements in the other tunnels.

General Prishata had started to give orders to the couriers when suddenly the desert exploded. Sand flew everywhere.

"*Shaiva!*" Mayla cried.

Something suddenly rose from the desert, erupting from below and into the air. It was as thick as an elephant, and as sinuous and long as a thousand elephant trunks in a line, and it emerged from under the sand dunes, rising up into the air higher and higher, until it stood almost vertical, like an undulating pillar a thousand or more yards — perhaps even a mile — high. Sand sloughed off its length, falling in a shower so dense that for several moments it was like being trapped in a monsoon downpour. Shvate felt the weight of the sand and immediately pulled his anga garment over his head to cover his eyes, ears, nostrils, and mouth. He held his breath, keeping his eyes squeezed shut almost completely, only peering through the thin fabric in brief glimpses. He saw that Mayla had done the same. They waited out the shower of sand until it had died away, leaving only a powdery dust billowing across their numbers. Shvate coughed and hacked out the dust and sand that had gotten past his defenses and struggled to make sense of what he was seeing.

It was the abomination from the tunnel. Ten thousand human bodies mashed together, merged into a single long, continuous monstrosity, swaying slowly, like a king cobra considering its prey. Shvate heard distant cries and screams, of men as well as animals, and saw that other monstrosities just like this one had also erupted from the desert and now stood swaying around the Krushan camp. There were dozens, perhaps hundreds of them, each with tens of thousands of people joined together in that inhuman chain, like gigantic sandworms.

Shvate felt something cold and wet splatter on his head and reached up to rub at his scalp. It was the same disgusting ichor-and-blood mixture that had drenched them in the tunnel. The swaying sandworm above him was dripping the combined fluids of its unfortunate participants.

"Shvate? Are you seeing this?" Mayla asked. Her voice was steady, but underneath the calm resolve of a Dirda warrior caste princess was an undertone of horror.

"I think —" Shvate began, but was cut off by a gigantic groaning.

Shvate strained to see in the darkness. It was shortly before dawn, and while the starlight was sufficient to make out the features of his wife and the general and soldiers nearby, he could only dimly glimpse the outline of the jagged mountain and the city that rose alongside it. But even in silhouette, he could tell that something extraordinary was happening. The entire mountain was juddering, shaking like a loose rock in an earthquake. He could see bits and pieces of it crumbling and tumbling down its length, then heard the debris land with resounding thuds on the desert floor far below. The groaning grew louder and deeper, into a kind of keening vibration that hurt his ears and made him grit his teeth.

Then, abruptly, with a great gnashing and grinding, the entire mountain itself broke free of the ground and lurched away.

"Mother of gods!" Shvate heard himself say.

Around him, a hundred voices mouthed a hundred different praises to diverse deities. Many were to Shaiva the Destroyer, favored deity of most warriors, especially in times of calamity. It was appropriate to call upon the Destroyer of Worlds when one's own world appeared to be on the brink of destruction.

The city of Reygar staggered away from the place where it had stood for some thousands of years. Shvate saw that the mountain and the city that had been built into it were both one entity now, and that entity was sentient, moving of its own volition, standing like a giant in the desert.

No, it *had* legs, but not legs in the human sense. Even in this darkness, across this distance, Shvate could see that the city-mountain was standing erect upon *something*. It was supported by some means, though he could not tell what or how.

With an earsplitting *shirring* sound, the city jerked one way, then another way, then another, turning and twisting, lurching and bending. It was an extraordinary sight. An entire mountain with a city built into its side, over a mile high, stumbling around the desert like a drunken man on shaky legs.

Then it kicked up its legs.

One, two, three . . . a half dozen, a dozen, a score of flailing long shapes rose and fell in the darkness, breaking free of the sand, falling back with dull thumps, rising again, falling, sand flying everywhere, the city-mountain lurching and staggering around in a wide arc. Shvate saw the Krushan camps being struck by the flailing limbs of the enormous thing, heard the screams and yells and terrible chaos of the soldiers and animals crushed or struck by the long wavering stalks, by the city-mountain itself as it staggered to and fro.

Finally, Reygar seemed to find its balance, swayed upright one last time, then began moving again, this time with more purpose and intent.

"The things in the tunnels," General Prishata cried, "they are its legs!"

If you could call miles-long tentacled limbs made up of tens of thousands of human bodies joined together "legs," then yes, they were its legs. That was what the tunnels were for, he realized. They served to gather enough bodies for the city to use to support itself. Once it had sufficient strength to walk upright, it had torn free of its moorings, breaking the mountain and the city itself free of its earthly roots. And now, here it was, stomping around the desert, crushing thousands of his soldiers, horses, elephants, chariots, into the desert sand.

"General!" Shvate cried, raising his sword. "Sound the call to arms. We are at war!"

The general turned to stare at him for one brief moment. His bearded face betrayed his shock clearly even in the dim starlight. Then his decades of training and experience snapped him back to his senses. He began yelling orders to his soldiers. An instant later, several of them drew out conch shells from their pouches and raised them to their mouths, lifting their heads, and the sound of the conchs filled the desert night, rising above the mayhem and cries of dying men and beasts.

It was answered a moment later by other conchs, from a mile away, then five miles, ten . . . In a few moments, hundreds of conchs were sounding out across the desert, filling the air with their mournful plaintive calls. Shvate saw the city-mountain pause and hold still, swaying slowly, as it heard the sound of the war conchs.

"Krushan!" Shvate cried, raising his sword high. "To battle!"

"To battle!" cried Mayla beside him.

General Prishata raised his own sword and roared, "Krushan, to battle!"

The war cry was echoed by the soldiers, taken up by others, then echoed across the desert, at first in ragged patches, then together, as a single great voice.

The sound of half a million voices raised together rose from the desert.

"*Krushan! To battle!*"

With a roar, Shvate's army began to charge. Whatever it might be, however alien and bizarre, however indomitable and gargantuan, Reygar still represented their enemy, the enemy they had come here to fight and conquer. No speeches were needed to remind them of that, no lashes to bring them back into order, no threats or challenges to force them to fight. The armies of Krushan lived to fight — and for a challenge. Now they had both.

A giant mountain city tottering about on tentacles made of intertwined living bodies. Incredible and horrific as it was, this was their enemy.

And they had a job to do.

Elephants were brought into control. Horses reined in and mounted. Chariots wheeled about and lined up in order. Infantry resolved into ranks and ready to charge.

"Sound the charge!" Shvate cried.

General Prishata seconded the order.

The conch shell trumpets sang out again, this time issuing shorter, terser appeals, booming bursts that set all the cadres to readiness, then followed with a final single sustained note that broke off abruptly, signaling the charge.

The army of Krushan attacked.

Reygar loomed above them, swaying from side to side as it considered these puny beings, the size of ants to a human. Elephants as small as a man's thumb, horses the size of a fingernail, chariots as small as bugs . . .

The city reared, its tentacles flailing, lashing out.

It struck down, sending elephants flying, smashing chariots and the men and horses with them into a bloody pulp, crushing a hundred horses and riders with a single blow. A hundred tentacles struck in a hundred directions, killing soldiers and animals alike by the thousands. The city lurched and cavorted, turning and swaying as it danced the dance of death.

The Krushan threw spears, loosed arrows by the hundreds of thousands, hacked with swords, axes, blades of every size and description; elephants charged, horses kicked, men lost their lives at the flick of a tentacle or the crashing down of an elephant or a chariot; bodies were cut in half by flying debris. Tens of thousands died. More rushed to take their places.

The sands of the desert were washed red with the blood of the Krushan. Again and again the conch trumpets sounded and resounded, rallying the forces to attack and attack again, and yet again.

The new sun rose over the eastern horizon, illuminating a grisly scene. The golden sands, stained red with the blood of a hundred thousand dead, another fifty thousand brutally maimed or fatally wounded, tens of thousands more injured but still fighting on. Over a third of the army that Shvate had brought to Reygistan was destroyed, the rest in shambles.

And still the city of Reygar stood, tall as a mountain, indomitable, undefeated.

"Shvate!"

The voice rose above the cries and moans of dying men and suffering beasts.

Mayla saw the approaching horse and rider and pointed them out. "It's Vida!"

Shvate reined in the horse team. At some point in the chaos of the battle, Mayla and he had commandeered this chariot, the better to ride around the theater of war and issue such commands and instructions to the troops as were needed. None of his tactics or attempts had succeeded, alas, and he was exhausted from fighting, from riding and dodging the tentacles and flying debris himself, from watching his soldiers and animals die. And he was no closer to victory than he had been the night before. Soon it would be day and the sun would rise . . . and with the sun, his skin would burn, his eyes be pricked with needles of fire, and his strength diminish. Yet how could he withdraw at a time like this? Against a foe who did not even obey the normal rules of war and chose to attack in the dead of night. An enemy that defied the very laws of nature. No matter how bad he had thought it might be, he had never expected it to be *this* bad. This was a disaster.

"Shvate!" Vida drew alongside their chariot and forced his mount to a halt. The poor horse was frothing at the mouth and wild-eyed. All the animals were terrified by the supernatural nature of their enemy. Battle alone was terrible enough for animals; this was the stuff of nightmares.

Vida dismounted from the horse and climbed onto the chariot. He was bloodshot and wild-haired, face and body splattered with blood, clothes ripped and filthy. He had sand in his hair. He looked much the same as they all did on this mad morning when nightmares came true and entire cities came to life and attacked.

"I think there might be a way." Vida pointed up at the mountain hovering above them. It had taken to pausing for several moments at a stretch, as if resting from its attacks. These brief periods were the only respite the Krushan forces had received during the past several hours. The moment it began to move its tentacles and lurch forward again, a collective cry would rise from the battered troops.

"There might be a way to get into the city," Vida said, still pointing up at Reygar, but looking at Shvate and then at Mayla.

Shvate sighed. "What good will that do? Yesterday, we needed to get into the city. Today, we need a miracle. Unless you have a miracle in your pocket, Vida, there's nothing more to be done here."

"But that's it. That's what I'm saying."

"What do you mean?" Mayla asked sharply.

"If we can get in and get to its heart, we can kill it. I'm sure of it."

Vida sounded so sure, so confident. Shvate blinked and rubbed the sand and blood from his eyes to stare at his half brother. "What heart? What are you talking about, Vida?"

Vida pointed up at the city reeling like an inebriated fool leaning against an invisible wall during a moment of semiconsciousness. "Jarsun got an entire city to come alive and fight us like a living thing. To mimic a living being, it must have a heart. Or a brain."

"Yes — a command center," Mayla said frowning. "Go on."

"That abomination is not randomly staggering around. If that was the case, it would go wandering off in any direction. It moves like it has eyes, ears, senses similar to a living creature. I think that's because it *is* a living creature." Vida paused, pointing now at himself. "It's using people as its legs . . . or limbs. Whatever those things are. It bends and turns this way and that before attacking each time. I have been watching it for hours now, and it acts exactly like any bipedal organism."

"A *what*?" Mayla asked.

"A person," Shvate said, sharper now, "or anything that stands on two legs. Go on, Vida."

"I believe that Jarsun is in there somewhere, controlling it, using his people as eyes, ears, senses, limbs, similar to the way we use our organs and senses." Vida pointed at his own face, sense organs, head, and heart. "He is the city's heart. Or brain. Or both. The control center."

Shvate turned to look up at the city. The top of the city-mountain was already awash with full daylight, the sun having reached the upper parts of Reygar several minutes ago. Now, as the sun topped the horizon and morning sunlight washed across the desert, the whole formidable length and bulk of the city was lit up. A thousand houses stared blankly, streets and buildings rose and twined around its mountainous half, sunlight reflected off thousands of pieces of glass and metal, glittering and sending refractions in all directions. Shvate felt the familiar sinking feeling he experienced each time he saw the sun rise, but now there was also a spark of hope in his heart, kindled by Vida's words.

"A command center," Shvate said. "Like a brain, controlling the whole thing. That makes sense. It is sentient. It is aware. It sees and hears and reacts to our attacks, it counters our every move, it knows where to strike and how hard, when to sweep, when to turn or lash out. There is some measure of precision in its movements, or as precise as anything that large and clumsy can ever be, like a lumbering elephant learning to walk for the first time, but still an elephant. It makes sense, what you are saying, Vida. There must be a brain in there, and that brain has to be Jarsun himself. It's the only thing that would explain this impossible abomination."

Mayla stared at him, then at Vida. Her beautiful dark face was smeared with blood and sand and dirt, but her eyes shone brightly, full of fight and anger. "So it can be brought down, then?"

Vida sighed. "As much as Jarsun himself can be brought down. Though only the gods know if such a thing is possible."

Shvate knew what his brother was thinking. The Battle of the Rebels. Where Jarsun had proved a match for even the mighty Vrath. If Vrath had been unable to kill Jarsun that day, then how could he, Shvate, do what the mightiest Krushan warrior of all could not?

"We will do it," Shvate said. "We will go in, we will search for Jarsun, we will kill him."

Both Vida and Mayla regarded him.

"Shvate," Mayla said, "are you sure?"

He shook his head. "I have never been less sure of anything in my life, dearest. But I am sure that if we continue the way we are fighting now, we will be defeated."

"We could retreat," she said softly, very softly. He knew that to a warring nation like Dirda, even the mention of retreat or surrender was dishonorable. The fact that she even suggested it showed how much she loved him.

He clutched her shoulder. "My love. Better to die honorably than live dishonorably."

They were her own words, her own nation's motto.

She looked at him. "Aye. But if you mean to do this, Shvate of Hastinaga, then I am going in with you as well."

"No," he said firmly. "I need you to stay here and command the army in my absence."

"To hell with that!" she said forcefully. "Let General Prishata do it. That's what he's there for, isn't he? My place is your side, living or dead. Say one more word or argument, and I will cut off your tongue right here and now."

Shvate laughed. "If you cut off my tongue, Mayla of Dirda-desha, then how will I be able to tell you how much I love you? Very well, we go in together. And you, Vida, you go with us."

"I?" Vida said, face cringing.

Shvate grasped Vida with both hands, by his shoulders. "Brother, if Jarsun is the brains of that monstrosity, then you are *my* brains, *my* command center. I need you to guide us. Come now, let's move before the damn thing begins to slaughter us again."

Mayla raised her whip and cracked it, urging the chariot team forward. Smiling impishly at her husband, she said, "I have always wanted to visit Reygar."

Reeda

~

1

REEDA KNEW THERE WERE deadly predators in the Jeel.

Mother River, though she was holiest of holy waters, goddess of the people, was also a habitat — and like all natural habitats, she harbored predators as well as prey. While most of these river-dwelling creatures were content to dine on their natural prey — fish, water mammals, and the occasional turtle mostly — a few older ones did lose their ability to hunt and were tempted to attack easier prey such as animals who came to drink from the river. And once in a rare while, humans. Most denizens of Hastinaga foolishly believed that Mother Goddess Jeel could never harm them. She was the patron deity of most of the commonfolk, after all. But Reeda was not that naive. She had heard stories from the other charioteers and their spouses over time.

So when she sensed the rippling movement out the corner of her eye, she did not ignore it and continue washing clothes. She froze and watched it without turning around.

There was definitely something moving under the surface, approaching from the river itself, through the ring of rocks that diverted a little of the river's flow to create this pond. It was downstream from the city and only a couple of miles' walk from the palace quarters, an ideal place to wash clothes. The only living things that she had seen here were small fish.

Whatever this thing was, it was no fish.

She put her bundle of clothing on the rock on which she had been beating it clean, and turned to face the ripple.

It was within yards of her now.

She couldn't tell what creature it was, precisely, but there was definitely something alive under the surface. And it was heading straight for her.

Reeda climbed onto the rocks, stepping up to the largest one, well out of the water. She let her clothes stay where they were: Adran and she were not well-off by any standard, but they were not poor enough that she would risk her life and limb for a few garments.

As she watched, the ripple reached the spot where she had been standing only seconds earlier.

And stopped moving.

Nothing happened for a heartbeat.

Reeda thought that perhaps it was only a turtle that had lost its way, and that in a moment it would turn around and swim back toward the river. Perhaps it had been confused by the absence of a current.

Or perhaps it's a crocodile, or a gharial, or even a shark. Better safe than sorry. She remained where she was, watching the spot intently, barely letting herself blink.

Suddenly, the water heaved, startling her.

"Mother Jeel," she exclaimed.

Something rose from the surface of the river up to her eye level and hovered in midair, streaming water. For a heart-stopping instant, Reeda thought she was done for. Not a warrior by nature, she was no shrinking violet either. She braced herself to fight, scream, defend herself as best as she could. Crocodiles emerging from the Jeel to snatch and drag were slow, lumbering beasts that could be frightened away by loud thrashing and screaming, and by the goddess, she could thrash and scream.

What hovered before her was no crocodile.

It was no predator at all.

For a moment, her eyes struggled to focus on the object as her brain fought to comprehend it.

It was a large bubble of air, raised up by a pillar of water.

Inside the bubble was a newborn babe, no more than a day or two old.

And the babe was alive.

She gaped at this extraordinary sight for a moment, hands still raised in a defensive stance, mouth wide open in readiness to release a scream.

The pillar of water curved toward her, bringing the bubble-encased baby within reach, and remained still.

A hush fell over the river.

All the natural sounds ceased.

For a moment, there was nothing else that mattered in the world except she, Reeda, and the child being offered to her.

By Mother Jeel, she thought. *This is a gift from the goddess herself. She knew that Adran and I have been trying to start a family for years now, without success; I have prayed often enough to her, asking her to bless us with a child. And she has finally answered our prayers.*

Reeda reached out, and as if in response, the bubble was lowered gently into her hands. It felt unusually warm, even though the river water streaming from it was as could be expected at this time of year. The bubble seemed to melt away at her touch, leaving the sleeping babe cradled in her hands. The pillar of water collapsed, the water streaming back into the river.

She stared down at the child, marveling at the tiny features, limbs, the sheer perfection of creation. There was something unusual about the boy — for it was clearly a boy: a kind of shell-like covering grew seemingly naturally over his chest and abdomen. There were similar growths on his ears as well. They appeared to be natural extensions of his flesh, but rather than appearing gross and abnormal, they looked quite fitting somehow. As natural as hair on the head, or nails at the tips of one's fingers and toes.

The growth resembled a warrior's armor breastplate. But unlike a brass or iron cuirass, this was golden in hue, like a perfect golden coat of armor over his naked skin.

Like a shell protecting a kernel, Reeda thought. A natural shield of protection.

And: *Gods, he's a beautiful child,* she thought as well.

As she stared down at him, the baby opened his eyes and gazed up at her. He seemed perfectly healthy and blessedly content, as if traveling underwater down a freezing river for who knew how many miles was a perfectly natural thing for him.

He is so beautiful, in his plate of golden armor. Reeda thought. *What a beautiful baby boy. Surely he is a gift from the goddess. Why else would I be chosen to find him here and now, floating in the river? Me, an ordinary charioteer's wife.*

She reached down and offered the baby her finger. He grasped it at once, squeezing with a grip and strength that astonished her.

"My, but you're a strong one, you are, little Kern."

The name seemed apt to her ears: *kern*, as in the seed of grain protected by its natural shell.

She came to a decision then, bending over and picking up the handle of the basket.

"You're coming home with me," she said quietly. "Mother Goddess Jeel has gifted you to me, and so I am your mother now."

Reeda picked her way across the rocks carefully and started for home. She was halfway there when she remembered her abandoned laundry. She didn't care. The goddess had answered her prayers. It was a blessed day. Laundry could wait.

2

The sun was to Kern what water was to most people.

Ever since he could walk, he had loved its hot embrace. As he grew, he took to spending his days out in the open, finding reasons to be out-of-doors until dusk. Even in the searing summers, when the dreaded Lu wind kept everyone indoors and the city lay still and lifeless, he would walk through the streets bare chested, raising his face to the gilded orb of Arka, which was what the charioteer caste called the sun god, drinking in every drop of honeyed light.

Even when the deadly killing Lu blew through Hastinaga, as searing as a blast from a furnace, leaving dogs, cattle, horses, elephants, and the occasional unfortunate citizen in its path, brains baked dry and bodies leached of life and moisture, six-year-old Kern still went about his daily tasks. While a thirsty person was limited by his stomach capacity, little Kern could absorb unlimited amounts of sunlight. Other children who occasionally played with him would, before long, begin avoiding him, encouraged by their mothers, who thought the boy — as well as Reeda herself for adopting him — must be mad. They watched him running and playing in the blazing heat all afternoon without a care in the world and expected him to drop dead of sunstroke at any time.

Kern was unconcerned by what everyone thought. He missed not having friends to play with but soon grew to accept the fact that they were weaker than he. He was considerate enough to leave the horses and elephants in their shaded stables, rather than taking them out into the sun with him all day — even fetching water and daubing them to help them keep cool in the deadly heat wave. But he himself trained and practiced with fierce discipline, going through the martial exercises and asanas, the weapons practice, the running, swimming, leaping, climbing, and other physical challenges that were part of his grueling regime. Even the waters of the river grew hot enough to kill fish at such times, but Kern swam his miles without respite.

His skin had never been what one might call fair even at birth, but under such relentless exposure it became the color of reused charcoal. Reeda worried that he would suffer heat stroke, that someday he would push himself beyond his own limits.

But that day never came. Little Kern played and went about his business as if the weather were cool as autumn. The deadly Lu took a serious toll each year across this part of the Burnt Empire; in the capital city alone they counted the deaths by sunstroke in the triple digits. It was nothing to be scoffed at. But after witnessing Kern's ability to endure even the most debilitating heat in the heart of summer, both Reeda her husband, Adran, agreed that his ability to withstand exposure to sunlight was well beyond typical human capacity.

"The heat of Arka is no enemy to his well-being," Adran had said. "He is beloved of the sun."

Ever since he had come to Reeda, she and Adran had noted that the boy tended to sleep almost the entire duration from sundown to sunup, almost as if in compensation for the exceptionally long hours of exposure he spent in the inhospitable heat.

Reeda said, "I knew he was no ordinary boy from the day I found him on the river. He had the mark of greatness upon him, my Kern."

She still favored the use of that affectionate name, even though they had named the boy Vashta at his naming ceremony, claiming him as their own. Abandoned infants were not uncommon, and the priests had decreed it likely that the child had been the illegitimate product of some noblewoman's indiscretion or a nobleman's unwanted bastard. No one minded if a childless charioteer and his wife wanted to adopt him, and from that day, everyone simply regarded little Vashta as Adran and Reeda's boy.

But they never forgot the truth. He was not their natural-born child, and the unique markings on his body were unlike anything they or anyone else had ever seen. Kern had distinctive bumps on his ears, head, chest, shoulders and back. Reeda had touched them curiously, worried that they were some kind of disfigurement. Instead, she had found the bumps hard — as hard as, or even harder than, bone spurs. Not only were they not tender or sensitive to the touch, they actually served as some kind of protective shield to the boy.

When Kern began to creep and then crawl, he was unaffected by the usual bumps and scrapes that every infant suffered: the growths on his upper body protected him so effectively that he would simply bang or bump into objects without a care, even chuckling at times. Surprised, Reeda had designed a special yoked garment for him to wear during those early weeks, hoping to conceal his uniqueness from prying eyes. Little Kern looked quite cute with his head and torso covered, peeping out from under the hood. But only a few hours later, she found him bare-topped again, the garment lying in shreds, cast aside. Every time she tried to cover him up again, he would simply tear off the clothing. It took her some time to accept the fact that he not only abjured protection from the harsh sun of Hastinaga, he actively desired exposure to it. He appeared to thrive on sunlight from his earliest days, and as he grew, his need to be out in the sun grew as well.

Now Adran looked at her affectionately. "Kern," he said, softly, though they knew that nothing would wake the boy except the first rays of sunshine through their front door — which they had taken to leaving open at his urging. "His name is *Vashta,* my sweet."

Reeda smiled. "I know, but I can't help it. Those . . . growths on his body, whatever they are, they are so unique. And have you noticed? They are becoming stronger and harder as he grows. Their pattern is also taking shape, joining together, almost like . . ."

"Armor. Like a suit of armor."

"Yes. Exactly. A suit of golden armor, with matching earrings and a helm. What does it mean, Adi? What is his fascination with sunlight? Why does he not suffer heat stroke or sunstroke like other people?"

"He is special, our Vashta," Adran said. He smoked his chillum, sucking lightly on the ganja pipe. It soothed and relaxed him at the end of a long hard day. Reeda took an occasional lungful as well, keeping her husband company as they enjoyed the relatively cooler evening air — if you could call a sultry stillness *cool.* Outside, the city settled down to another summer's night, the streets and markets still bustling as people used the sunless evening hours to complete their chores and shopping . . . . and, of course, the drinking and revelry that was an essential part of city life in this rich, diverse heart of the Burnt Empire. People said Hastinaga never slept. Perhaps it would be more accurate to say that Hastinaga never slept . . . sober.

"He is no ordinary mortal child," Adran continued. "His natural body armor and markings aside, there is the matter of his unusual resilience to heat and sunlight. But that is nothing compared to his martial skills."

"What do you mean?" Reeda asked. "What martial skills? He is barely a boy, only just out of infancy!"

Adran looked at her through the ganja haze, his grey eyes sleepy, the smoke weaving into his dark mustache and beard. His ropelike muscles knotted as he held out the chillum to her. "He watches the master warriors training and then goes to a field on his own and imitates their movements. This itself is not unusual. Many of the poorer warrior caste children of the city watch the masters during their open sessions and learn by simple observation. But what Vashta does is unique. He watches them all morning, then goes to a place where he can be alone — usually an open field away from the city or a clearing in the woods. There he repeats the movements he saw the masters make, perfect in every respect, then does them over and over again, completing entire circuits without a single error. His form, his skill, his body control, his mastery of the movements and the asanas, they are all immaculate. It is better than the best students achieve even after months of rigorous practice. Better by far than even Prince Shvate or my own master, Prince Adri. It is quite astonishing to watch him."

Reeda smoked silently for a moment. She blew out a small stream of blueish smoke. "All this just from watching them once?"

"Yes. I have never seen anything like it. I have never even *heard* of anything like it. I don't think any warrior caste in Hastinaga could claim such perfection. At any age. Mind you, these are not simply beginner's asanas. These are the masters' own exercises, the most advanced circuits of physical endurance and skill by seasoned veteran warriors with a lifetime of training, experience, and knowledge. It is quite extraordinary, yet I have seen it with my own eyes more than once."

Reeda considered his words. "What does it mean, then?"

"This is not just talent, it is something else. This, coupled with his affinity for sunlight . . ." Adran shook his head slowly from side to side, his lined face appearing and disappearing in the haze. "It is something beyond human capacity. He is no ordinary mortal."

Reeda felt both pleased and anxious. Pleased, because Adran was speaking of little Kern, *her* Kern. Anxious, because he was not truly hers. Still, she took pride in the knowledge that she had been chosen to mother such an extraordinary child. "What are you saying, Adi? That he is blessed of the gods?"

Adran stared at the far wall for a long time before answering. "All children are blessed of the gods. I think our little Vashta is something more than that. I think perhaps he is a god himself. Or at the very least, a demigod."

Reeda stared at him. "You mean . . . his parents were gods?"

"One of them at least. And it doesn't take a great mind to guess which god that might have been."

"Arka. Sharra. Surya. Call him what you will. The sun god." She stared across the tiny hut at the still form of her little boy. Kern slept without covers in both the hottest and coldest seasons. Neither cold, nor heat, nor wet appeared to affect his health. He had never fallen sick for even a day, never showed any weakness of any kind — was always fresh, alert, and energetic, even when he forgot to eat for most of a day (which happened frequently since he went out at dawn and rarely returned before evening).

These had all been signs, Reeda saw now. Signs of his extraordinary birth. She had wondered often, but this was the first time that she had heard the possibility mentioned aloud. Once Adran said it, she knew he was right. Her little Kern was a demigod, offspring of the sun god himself. That would explain everything.

"We are blessed," she said. "Our humble home has been graced by the presence of a god in human form. We must have done some great karma in past lives to have earned such a distinction."

Adran raised his hand to wave away the smoke. His sharp features looked at her intently.

"What?" she asked, "Why do you look at me this way?"

"Having a demigod in one's house can be a blessing, yes, but it can also be a curse."

"A *curse?*"

"Gods rarely cohabit with mortals without a purpose. There must be some intent behind Sharra God fathering our little Vashta on a mortal woman. Some larger purpose. A great mission for which a demigod was required. Some future plan."

"So, what of it? When the time comes, he will fulfill his purpose. If that is his destiny, so be it."

"What *is* that purpose is the question, Reeda. When the gods descend on Arthaloka, it is not always to the benefit of us mortals. Time and time again, as our puranas tell us, we become collateral damage in their great wars and missions. When elephants do battle, insects are crushed underfoot."

She tried to think through the implications of her little Kern being a demigod. "But he is our Kern. He will never do anything to harm us."

"How do you know that? How can we know anything for certain? Even he knows nothing of his fate or destiny now, for he is merely a child. But one day, when the time comes, he will awaken and rise, and go about his divine purpose, and you can be sure when that day comes, he will not be 'our little Kern,' as you call him, or even our little Vashta anymore. He will be his own man. His own *god*. And what he does then will impact lives, of that much you can be certain."

"How can you be so sure?" she asked.

Adran toked on the pipe. His long exhale resembled a plaintive sigh. "I have worked with kings and queens all my life. As did my father and forefathers. We have served the kings of Hastinaga for generations. The kings regard the game of chaupat as a window of insight into life itself. Whenever a great game is played out, the pieces are put on the board years, or even decades earlier. I once watched Shapaar play a game with his brother-in-law that lasted fifty-seven years and employed tens of thousands of moves! Shapaar finally won by using his elephants in a move that I have never seen rivaled since, but he had to prepare for that move thousands of moves earlier, and had to be prepared to sacrifice most of his other pieces in the meanwhile. The appearance of that little infant in the river, here in Hastinaga, was no accident. He is a piece in a great game, brought here for a purpose. I do not know whether his move will be made in ten, twenty, or even fifty-seven years from now, but I suspect it will be a game-changing one, and when it happens, it will cost many, many other lives. *Mortal* lives. Because gods play out their games of chaupat using us mortals as pieces on the board of Arthaloka. And our little boy is an elephant among those pieces."

Reeda continued to regard the sleeping child, thoughts and emotions swirling through her like the hemp smoke swirling through their hut. She couldn't bring herself to think like Adran did. She knew he had been to battle and seen terrible things, things he could never unsee — things that had changed him forever. He was wise and knowledgeable and knew whereof he spoke. But Reeda too was wise, and she too knew things that he had never thought of, had seen and heard many stories, many true accounts, of mothers and children, of special or gifted children. Not different in exactly the way that her Kern was different, but each unique in their own way.

Above all else, Reeda was a mother, while Adran was a father. A woman, while he was a man. There were things she knew instinctively that he could never know, not because he was incapable of knowing them, but because he had been raised and taught to *think* like a man, while Reeda herself simply thought as she thought. And her mind, her *heart*, told her that whatever Kern's purpose in life might be, it would not involve harm to her or Adran. She knew this as surely as she knew it was now night and that the sun would rise again when it became morning again.

"Elephants are beautiful creatures," she said, looking at her little Kern, so beautiful, so perfect, so *special*.

Adran raised one eyebrow, gazing at her. But he said nothing further.

They smoked the rest of the chillum together in peaceful quiet.

Kern

⁓

KERN WAS IN A clearing behind the elephant preserve practicing his asanas as usual. He liked this clearing. No one else ever came here because of the stench of elephant dung. He didn't mind the smell. Hastinaga literally meant "City of Elephants and Snakes," and the smell of elephants and their offal was the smell of home to him now.

He liked spending his days away from other people, especially other children, because they were too puerile and immature for him and were always obsessed with things that made no sense to him, like playing pointless sports and engaging in useless games. To little Kern, *this* was play, being out in the bright summer sunshine, wielding his wooden sword, repeating his asanas, perfecting them.

He was dressed in only a dhoti, exposing as much of his body to the sunshine as possible. The feeling of the sun's heat penetrating his pores was wonderful. He felt energy seeping into him every hour he spent in the sunlight; after a whole day, he felt almost . . . powerful. If only the sun could shine all day and night, *every* day and night, he was sure the energy it gave him would make him stronger. For now, the long fifteen-hour summer days were a godsend; he intended to spend every possible minute out under the sun, and he could feel the rays invigorating him, empowering him.

He had learned an interesting new asana that morning, after watching the yoddhas on the practice field, and was trying it out. He used a wooden sword he had made himself, deliberately shaping the shastra from tough, heavy sal wood instead of the usual balsa wood, to make it feel and weigh more like a real sword.

He had completed his warm-up exercises and was now putting himself through niuddham, concentrating on the movements. He was accustomed to spending several hours this way, repeating a sequence of asanas, then varying them in subtle, minute ways to account for a variety of factors: wind direction and force, ground, temperature, the possible height and bulk of his imagined enemy, the enemy's angle of approach, force, intensity, the number of opponents, their weapons, their ages, their sizes . . . He repeated each of these variations over and over until he was certain that in *those* circumstances, against *those* opponents, using *those* weapons, *that* angle and force of attack, he would be able to counter and overcome. He was focusing mainly on defensive moves because that was what the masters had been practicing this week. He hoped they would move on to offensive asanas soon. He liked offense better than defense. Anyone would defend themselves when attacked. A warrior's purpose was to attack, overcome, conquer.

He was so absorbed in his asanas that he didn't notice the others until they were only a dozen yards away. It was careless of him and ironic in a way; here he was, practicing defensive asanas, but when an actual threat approached, he failed to heed to it. He observed the figures and made a mental note to never let such a lapse occur again in the future.

The intruders on his privacy were several young men, about a dozen of them ranging in age from eight to fourteen. He had seen some of the older ones before, engaged in activities that his father called "nefarious." Kern wasn't sure what the word meant but knew it didn't signify anything good. He knew that Adran used words like that when he didn't want Kern to know what he really meant, but just by using such words, he conveyed to Kern that it was something that elders considered bad.

The boys approached across the open field in leisurely fashion, sprawling out in a wide, irregular formation. Some of them were smoking that odd-smelling stuff that his father and mother also smoked at night — what they called ganja. The boys were smoking it in the form of little tubes of tobacco leaf rolled tightly and lit at one end. They were passing the tubes to one another in a certain pattern, the older, bigger boys keeping them longer and sucking for longer before passing them to the younger, smaller boys. At least two of the boys didn't get to smoke any at all, and hung back behind the others, looking beaten down and miserable, their clothes even more ragged and filthy than those of the others.

The leader of the group was easy to make out. He was not the largest of the boys, nor the eldest, yet everyone deferred to him. He had a small chillum all to himself which he shared with no one, his clothes were new and of richer material, and he wore gold jewelry on his ears, around his neck, wrists, and arms. He also carried a *real* shastra: a shortsword with a jeweled hilt that he wore on a special leather belt around his waist. The two biggest and oldest boys — men, actually — walked on either side of him, both armed with longswords, plainer and without any jewels or decoration, their muscled bodies dressed in clean, crisp anga-vastras and dhotis, not as rich or fine as their master's but not like the dirty rags of the other vagabonds with them.

Kern observed all this in a single sweeping glance. He lowered his "sword" and returned his breathing to a waiting pattern as he had seen the masters do between sessions. This kept the body anticipatory and capable of being brought into play quickly, but not at full alert — somewhere between a resting heart rhythm and an active one. He said nothing. He spoke as little as possible to strangers, so little that at times he had been assumed to be mute by people unknown to him. From the very beginning, he had known that most arguments could be resolved by silence: if you did not engage, you could not lose. You only engaged when you wanted to destroy your enemy. This was true of arguments as well as physical combat. Never start a fight unless you intend to win it. And winning for a warrior could only mean the destruction of your opponents. Anything less was a fool's victory.

"The little cub that thought it was a lion."

This came from the rich boy. He was holding his little ivory chillum cupped in both hands, sucking on it every now and then, puffing out little circles of smoke. He was as stout around the waist as anyone Kern had ever seen, plump in the way a poor boy could never be: corpulence brought on by sheer excess. Kern stared at him with frank curiosity. *How much must one eat — and how rich must one be — to become so large? And doesn't all that bulk hinder him when moving, running, jumping, fighting?* Despite the beautiful sword at his waist, Kern suspected the rich boy was no warrior caste. A warrior would never treat his body thus. *The body is your first and greatest shastra,* the masters taught. It was a warrior's most valuable weapon.

"What are you doing here, little cub?"

Kern knew the question was directed at him but did not answer. He was used to strangers asking him questions. He never listened to the questions themselves. The words were irrelevant: it was the question behind the question that one had to listen for — the meaning and true intent behind the words.

This rich boy wasn't interested in what Kern was doing here. He was interested in Kern himself.

The rich boy stopped about three yards away. The two muscular young men stopped too, one on either side of him. One of them eyed Kern's wooden sword, assessed it to be of no significant threat, then ignored it. The other one kept looking around, sweeping the surrounding area. Kern liked their single-minded efficiency. They were both of a warrior caste for sure, and both clearly had experience with violence.

Kern glanced at the other ten boys; they all bore the marks and signs of fighting, both from recent encounters and older ones, both with and without weapons. He observed all this in a single glance, as easily as other children his age might notice other children's ages and toys. He saw, too, that at least five of these boys — three of the bigger ones and two of the smaller ones — were seasoned fighters, with their numerous scars and bruises suggesting frequent conflict. They had seen things as well; they had a look about the eyes and in the way they held themselves that spoke of hard lives, struggles endured, hardships suffered, and abuses inflicted, both upon and by themselves. All of the boys had some part in the "nefarious activities" his father spoke of, but it was those five, as well as the two seasoned fighters, who were the main threat. The rich boy's sword ought to have qualified him too, but he appeared so unfamiliar with actually wielding the blade that Kern discounted him. That was a mistake, as he would soon learn, for everything and everyone was a weapon, and not all weapons were deployed physically.

The rich boy finally realized that Kern was not going to answer. He lowered the chillum and glared at Kern.

"I asked you a question, boy. Answer." Except he didn't say "boy," he used a vulgar word that Kern didn't fully understand but which he knew was not a polite word to use for anyone, especially not a son of a respectable charioteer, a charioteer to royalty. The use of the abusive word didn't upset Kern, but it did tell him something about the character of the rich boy. Only a weak person hurled abuses without provocation.

Kern didn't answer. He maintained his breathing pattern while watching the other boys. They were moving away, almost casually, but he was watching them out of the corners of his eyes and could see them circling around him on both sides. They were cutting off his retreat. In a few moments, he would be surrounded, with no place to run. He didn't mind that. He had no intention of running. This was his clearing, and it was late morning, so he had a full nine or ten hours of beautiful sunshine left. He wasn't going anywhere.

The rich boy handed his chillum to one of the other boys with a sharp look that Kern interpreted as a warning not to partake. The boy held the chillum in his cupped hands the way Kern had once held a sparrow with an injured wing that he had picked up to examine out of curiosity — as if it was fragile and would break if held too tightly. The other boys were milling about with apparent aimlessness, but their eyes kept cutting to Kern, and he saw the growing curiosity in their faces as they tried to intuit his true nature: Was he a boy playing with his elder brother's practice sword, perhaps? A little thief who had stolen the wooden shastra? An acolyte from a forest gurukul who was playing hooky?

"How old are you, boy?" Rich Boy asked. This time, he didn't wait for Kern to answer — or *not* answer — and turned to one of his two bodyguards. "Farsha? What do you think? Five? Six?"

The bodyguard shrugged his powerful shoulders. "The way he holds that shastra, at least seven or older. But his size and height make him look younger."

"Younger."

Rich Boy turned his gaze upon the boy who had spoken. It was one of the older boys, one of the five big louts that Kern had identified as a potential threat. He had circled around to Kern's left side, and was standing about three yards away. "He's the son of a charioteer. No more than five, if that."

Kern tilted his head sideways to look at the boy who had spoken. He did this for two reasons: it gave him a deeper peripheral perspective of the space behind himself, where several of the boys had drifted around to close the circle, and because dogs did it.

Kern liked dogs; they couldn't concentrate on one thing for long, slobbered a lot — especially on your face — and would eat just about anything, but he liked them all the same. They had a drive and intensity when excited about something that he admired. He liked the way they tilted their heads when you spoke to them as if asking, *Huh? What was that you just said?* Kern liked talking to them. They *listened* even though they didn't understand most of what you said. It was by watching dogs that he had learned that it was the tone used — the emotional state and body language of the person speaking — that was more important than the actual words spoken. Dogs listened and understood far more than most people. People, on the other hand, only *pretended* to listen, but really they were just hearing whatever they wanted to hear, busy listening to the voices inside their own heads. If they'd actually *listen*, as dogs did, they wouldn't need to talk so much. Dogs conveyed most of what they needed to say through looks, expressions, and brief sounds. People, on the other hand, could use scrolls of words without saying anything useful. Even his father said so. *"Courtiers . . . all they know is talk!"*

"A charioteer's son? This ruffian? You must be joking."

"I wouldn't jest with you, Masher. I saw him going back to the charioteer quarters just the other day, at sundown. He was carrying that same wooden sword."

Masher, the rich boy, looked at Kern with new interest. "A charioteer's son? What is he doing with a practice sword, then? Hey, boy? Who did you steal that from? You're a charioteer, aren't you? Your kind aren't allowed to handle shastras."

"Except to pick up and hand to their masters," said another younger boy. This one had a mean look to his pale features. They were all pale and fair-skinned, several with light colored hair too. This one had eyes as blue as the sky above. Kern saw the way Blue Eyes touched a long object he had tucked into his dhoti. A blade of some sort. He guessed they all carried shastras of some kind, though only the rich boy, Masher, and his bodyguards carried proper swords. One of the smaller boys carried a makeshift bow made of balsa wood with a few reed arrows, which would hardly bring down a crow, but at least one of the bigger boys (standing behind his right shoulder) had a small throwing axe, and one of the others (directly behind him) had a long chopping knife. Two of them had slingshots, one the kind that you held in one hand and pulled on with the other, the second the kind that you swung around with one hand then let go.

Kern only had the practice sword.

And himself.

Masher grew impatient of waiting for Kern to answer and gestured to the bodyguard who had spoken. "I don't see any master around, do you? This charioteer boy shouldn't be carrying that sword. This is why Hastinaga is going to the dogs. These lower castes all think they can do whatever they please. As if we all exist to serve their whim and fancy. Farsha, go take that from him."

The bodyguard frowned. He looked at Kern. "It's just a wooden sword, sire."

"I don't care if it's an elephant's stinking penis. If I say go get it, then you go get it." Masher turned to the boy to whom he'd entrusted his ivory chillum and took it back from him. The boy's tense expression dissolved in a look of such abject relief, it made Kern smile. "What in the name of the gods are you smiling at, charioteer? Did you see that, boys? He's an arrogant one. I tell you, these low castes should be whipped every day just to remind them of their place in society. Because the Krushan don't enforce the ancient customs, the world is going to hell. My father says that in Emperor Shapaar's reign, every low caste who didn't fall to the ground and kiss the earth when a higher caste passed by was executed on the spot. That's how you keep these bastards in line. When I become king, I'm going to make every one of these wretches sport a mark, carved into their foreheads the day they're born, so they never forget that they were put on Arthaloka to serve and suffer, not smile and strut about playing at being warrior castes like this insolent charioteer. Farsha, go get that boy's sword, or I'll put my sword up your backside and push it out your face!"

Farsha grimaced, sighed, and moved toward Kern. His sword remained in its scabbard at his waist. He must have felt that this little charioteer needed no more than a little physical intimidation. Probably felt sorry for him. Kern could see it in his eyes. He had intimidated, bullied, beaten, abused, broken, and even killed too many times for his spoiled young master before. Farsha was starting to feel that maybe he should change his employer, but Masher's father paid him well, and he had access to the boy's well supplied wine and ganja stock. (Not to mention the *girls*.) Kern read all this in the young man's eyes and in the way he reacted to his master's threat. It was like seeing *into* the man's mind.

Kern raised his face, looking up at the sun, which was almost directly overhead now. He felt the blessed heat of the noonday sun wash over him, *into* him, and drank its energy with every pore, every inch of his skin, through his eyes, his nostrils, his mouth, his ears, sucking it in as avidly as Masher was sucking in the intoxicating smoke from his ivory chillum. Kern drank in the energy of the noonday sun and felt his body sparkle with energy.

He was ready for the first bodyguard when the man reached out, intent on violence.

He was born ready.

Jilana

~

1

JILANA AND VRATH WERE holding court when word came of the events in Reygar. They listened intently to the courier's description of the city that had come alive, broken free of the mountain, and attacked the Krushan forces. From the courier's appearance and her expressions, it was evident that she was making a great effort to suppress her own personal reactions. Her tone was even, her vocabulary impeccable, her manner immaculate.

Jilana admired the woman's strength of character even while her heart sank with each successive description. When the courier came to the part where Shvate, Mayla, and Vida had decided to attempt to enter the living city and confront Jarsun themselves, Jilana could not help but clutch her throne arm tighter. She had seen what Jarsun was capable of, in his stunning display of power at the Battle of the Rebels. On that occasion, he had been up against no mere mortal adversary, but Vrath himself, and so the thought of her all-too-mortal grandson and his wife confronting that demon with nothing but their skill and steel was terrifying. She managed to restrain her own emotions till the courier had finished speaking, then thanked her for her service and dismissed her. The moment the woman had bowed and backed away from the throne dais, Jilana signaled to the prime minister to call for a brief interval in the proceedings. The elderly statesman formally announced that the court would take a brief recess but would resume very shortly.

Jilana turned to her stepson. "Vrath, you must go to Reygar at once."

Vrath acknowledged her use of his first name with a very slight nod. His greying whiskers, beard, and mane of greying hair framed a face that looked as always as if it had been carved from the ice of Mount Coldheart, then weathered on the same high slopes. "That would not be wise, Mother."

"You have seen what that demon is capable of."

"And so has Shvate."

"Shvate is mortal, a young man. You, with all your power and experience, were hard-pressed to overcome Jarsun. Shvate will surely not survive such an encounter."

Vrath gazed at the eastern wall, lined with elegantly shaped windows carved from the stone itself. The afternoon sunlight shone through the gaps between the numerous pillars that lined the length of the enormous sabha hall, lighting up the gold inlay and precious gems embedded in the pillars and ceiling frescoes. It was a grand, ostentatious chamber, built to display the might, power, and wealth of the Burnt Empire. Vrath's ice-grey eyes reflected the glittering grandeur with an aspect of stony fortitude. "He will do what he must to succeed."

"What if he does *not* succeed?"

"He is a prince of Krushan in line to be king. He must prove himself."

"What if he does not *survive?* Then he will never be king."

"What will be will be."

"Jarsun is no mere enemy. He is a being of enormous power . . ." She stopped. "You already know all this. You know that Shvate is outmatched. He stands no chance of surviving this encounter."

"You knew the odds when we sent him on this campaign." Vrath's voice was mild, unemotional. He continued to gaze at the sunlight streaming through the hall. His face was as implacable as one of the many statues placed around the chamber and palace.

"I thought he would wage a pitched battle against a mortal enemy." She heard the lie even as she spoke it. "No, it's true, I admit I feared that something like this might come to pass. But I thought if things got too dire, you would step in and assist your nephew."

"I will not."

"You did so at the Battle of the Rebels."

"He was but a boy at the time. It was his first battle. He was inexperienced and unprepared, unblooded. He has fought many battles since then. He is a man now, married twice over, well blooded, well seasoned. He has our finest fighting akshohinis at his command, an in-depth knowledge of the terrain and of Reygistani military tactics and strategy. He has a great general in General Prishata. It is time for him to prove himself as capable of facing an enemy and emerging triumphant. It is a necessary stage in the long journey from princehood to kingship."

"What use is the journey if he never achieves his destination? If he dies in Reygar, he will never be king!"

Vrath contemplated a palace cat, stretching out languorously to sun itself in a quiet corner behind a pillar. He turned to look in Vrath's direction, eyes glittering. "If that unfortunate day comes to pass, then Adri will ascend to the throne."

"We both know that Shvate is the best suited. He is the best choice to be king."

"Then he shall be."

"That is why you must protect him, to ensure that he survives to be king."

"If he requires constant protection and oversight, then he is not the best suited. He must be independently capable. That is Krushan law, as you know."

"I am not talking about law, I am talking about my grandson. The hope of Hastinaga, as he is popularly known, and for good reason. Shvate represents hope, a bright future, the legacy of your father, Sha'ant, upheld honorably. It is our duty as his elders to watch over him."

"What use is a king who cannot face his enemies in battle without the help of his elders? What will people say if I rush to fight Shvate's battles every time he is in trouble? How long will that popularity last if he cannot turn hope into triumph, intent into accomplishment? There are things he must do on his own in order to prove himself capable. This is the most important of them all."

Jilana seethed in frustration. She knew Vrath was right, but she could not bear the thought of young Shvate all the way in distant Reygar, battling against a foe who was a thousand times as powerful as he, facing certain defeat and death. "Vrath, I am not asking you as Dowager Empress Jilana. I am asking you as your mother. As the widow of your father, Sha'ant. The woman for whose sake you took the very vow for which you were dubbed "Vrath." You gave up so much so that your father could marry me and find happiness. I know you care for me, and for Shvate. Go to him discreetly if you must. Go in secret. Go incognito. But go and help him defeat Jarsun, aid him in his moment of need. The world need never know you had a hand in Jarsun's defeat. Let Shvate take all the credit, let him be the hero of the hour. You must do this to ensure his survival — and the survival of your father's lineage. Otherwise, what purpose did your vow serve? What of your father's legacy? What of Hastinaga's future? I entreat you, Vrath, do this for the sake of your family."

It took every ounce of Jilana's strength to keep her voice pitched low, so only Vrath would hear her. It was hard enough having such a conversation in front of a courtroom filled with people, all the dross and dreck of the empire's politicians, courtiers, nobles, aristocrats, ministers, and the small army of servants and sentries as well. She had to keep her face composed, her manner calm, her tone controlled and soft. Yet she had to make Vrath see reason. He *had* to see reason.

Vrath looked at her with eyes as distant as that of the palace cat in the corner. Her passion had not melted his ice or whittled his resolve by even a single chip. "It will not be necessary," he said.

Jilana met his gaze, trying to interpret that cryptic remark. What did he mean by that? Was he saying that Shvate could succeed on his own? Surely that was impossible! She already knew that it was impossible, or else she would not have begged Vrath at all. Or did he mean that something had happened that made the whole discussion irrelevant? Something... so decisive that there was no point in him going to Reygar now? But she had received the same news that he had, only moments ago. There had been nothing else since then, no other courier or communication.

But then she recalled that Vrath had his own sources of information, just as she herself did. Before the Battle of the Rebels, when she had received word of the imminent threat from her firstborn son, Vessa, and brought the news to Vrath, he had already been informed of the same threat. She had guessed at the time that he had learned of it through his true mother somehow. Gods and goddesses communicated in ways mysterious to mortals. She had assumed that Jeel Goddess had somehow communicated the threat to her demigod son. Was that what had happened just now? While they had been sitting here arguing, had Vrath received a communication of some kind from his mother? Something that told him ... *what* exactly? That it was too late? That Shvate was ... already dead? A dozen terrible thoughts raced through Jilana's mind. She clasped her throne arms tighter, sitting up, staring rapt at Vrath, searching for answers in his stony sculpted face and icy grey eyes.

Before she could ask him any of these new questions churning in her mind, the prime minister of Hastinaga stepped forward, bowing formally before the dais.

"Dowager Empress Jilana, Prince Regent Vrath, forgive my interruption. There is an urgent matter that has just been brought to the court's attention. I beg your leave to present it at once."

Jilana forced herself to turn her head and look down at the elderly man standing before the dais. Prime Minister Shakra was an intelligent and astute man. If he said something was urgent, it must be so. But she had no patience for regular matters of court right now.

"Unless it has bearing on the campaign in Reygar —" she began.

"Forgive me, Mother," Vrath said quietly. "But we need to consider this matter at once. It cannot be delayed or postponed."

She was taken aback. Rarely had Vrath interrupted her, or anyone else. His manners were perfect to the point of pedantry. For a second, she was too startled to understand the what or why of the words he spoke. Was he doing this deliberately so that her attempts to convince him would be curtailed?

No, she knew Vrath too well. He did not snub or insult people, least of all her. He was the very epitome of good grace and perfect poise. She saw something new in his face: even though his granite features had not shifted, there was a sense that he was trying to say something beyond the words. He genuinely felt this matter was important enough that they must hear it here and now, without delay. Yet how could he know? The prime minister had already explained that it had just been brought to the attention of the court. She realized that once again she was trying to scrutinize the inscrutable, to understand things that could not, would not be explained. Whatever Vrath's reasons, he meant exactly what he said and said exactly what he meant.

"Very well," she heard herself say, the strain in her voice audible to her own ears. "Present the matter."

The prime minister beckoned to the court sentries. A surprisingly large number of them came forward, moving in a block as they usually did when guarding a particularly dangerous criminal. With Vrath present in court, the precaution was unnecessary: Vrath was a more effective deterrent than an entire regiment of soldiers — an entire army, actually. But it was protocol, and she assumed it was some band of murderers or sellswords who had been foolhardy enough to commit their acts of mayhem within the precincts of Hastinaga. Whoever they might be, they had committed their last crimes. She was in no mood for clemency today. They would receive the harshest sentence possible under law.

Accompanying the quadruple quadrant of sentries — sixteen armed and armored soldiers moving noisily in unison, their captive boxed into the center of their square formation — was another quad of soldiers accompanying a man she vaguely recognized by appearance, but could not name. One of many high families of the city, a rich merchant or trader, among the oldest settlers of Hastinaga, loyal in their support to the Krushan dynasty for generations, ever since the great Krushan himself had settled this northern wilderness. He was extremely obese, his corpulent bulk weighted down even further by the kilos of jewelry he wore on his neck, ears, arms, and wrists. She assumed that the nobleman had been the victim of a burglary or dacoity and braced herself to listen to a tirade about rising crime rates in the city and the need for stricter policing, perhaps even a rant about the importance of segregation and the need to "remind" the lower classes of their "place." While she didn't recall his name, she recalled similar encounters in the past, and knew more or less what to expect once he began speaking.

The group came to a halt at the prescribed distance from the throne dais. Her own private bodyguards, all female, had already moved in to form a tight but casual semicircle, ensuring Jilana's safety. But that was not a concern at all to Jilana. No fool would dare to attempt an assassination with Vrath present; none would survive such an attempt.

"Your Highness, this is Lord Mashkon the Eighth of House of Mashkon. He appeals to the court on behalf of his son Young Master Mashkon the Ninth of House of Mashkon."

So this time it was to complain about some slight his spoiled brat of a son had received. Jilana fumed. Why had she agreed to hear this case? From Vrath's appeal, she had assumed it was something of national importance. Surely this was not the reason why he had brushed aside her appeals to go to Shvate's aid? She glanced at her stepson sharply, but he was in prince regent mode, attention directed fully at the prime minister. She scowled in his direction anyway, knowing that he would sense her extreme disapproval.

"Where is Young Master Mashkon the Ninth?" she asked. "If he is the complainant, he ought to be the one bringing the complaint to the court's attention."

Prime Minister Shakra looked at Lord Mashkon, who spoke in a tone of outrage, his voice rising shrilly. "Your Majesty, my son is on the verge of death. My wife prays at the shrine of our deity for his survival today. And it is all the doing of that villain!" He pointed a quivering finger at the quads of sentries surrounding the accused. "He all but killed my son! I demand that he be sentenced to immediate execution. I demand justice!"

Vrath replied. "Prime Minister, remind the complainant that only the court decides the sentence and delivers justice, not he."

The prime minister spoke quietly but sharply to the nobleman. Lord Mashkon glared at him and muttered something under his breath.

"Prime Minister, give us the facts of the matter quickly," Jilana said. "And ask the complainant to be quiet until you are done."

"Your Highness, the complainant says that earlier this morning, his son and several of his companions were enjoying a leisurely stroll when they were brutally attacked by this assassin, who injured several of their number and left Young Master Mashkon at death's door. They summoned the city watch, who dispatched guards to arrest the culprit. When the guards sought to arrest him, he resisted violently, injuring almost a dozen guards as well. It was only through the intervention of his mother, who arrived on the spot, that further violence was avoided. She appealed to him to cease the violence and allow himself to be apprehended."

Jilana frowned. "And he agreed?"

"He did. It would seem that the accused has deep affection and regard for his mother and obeys her without question."

"And is the mother present here as well?"

Prime Minister Shakra beckoned, and Jilana saw a woman coming forward, clearly agitated. "She is, Your Highness. This is she."

Jilana, still irritated, said, "This appears to be an instance of unruly behavior, or street violence at most. The city magistrates could have handled it. Or even the city guard themselves. Why do you trouble the court with this matter?"

Prime Minister Shakra looked startled at her tone. "Your Highness, forgive our presumption. The only reason it was brought to your attention was because of the young man's father."

Jilana looked sharply at the bejeweled Lord Mashkon, who was sweating profusely. "Just because Lord Mashkon is of a High House does not mean that any infringement of his rights is a matter of national concern."

Prime Minister Shakra cleared his throat. "Your Majesty, I was not referring to Lord Mashkon. When I referred to the young man's father, I meant the father of the accused."

"How wonderful," Jilana said, "Who is he, then? Another lord of one of our many fine High Houses?"

"No, he is merely a charioteer, but, my queen — it is Charioteer Adran."

2

Jilana blinked at the name. "Our family charioteer? *Our* Charioteer Adran?"

"The same."

Jilana looked for the man in the crowd. "I don't see him here."

"He is away, my queen. He drove Princess Karni to Pramankota for the day. Prince Adri and Princess Geldry were also on the same trip. They are scheduled to return this evening. If you so command it, I will send for him at once."

"No . . . there is little point; it would take hours for him to return. Let us hear the matter first."

Prime Minister Shakra regarded Jilana. "That is the entirety of the matter, Your Highness."

Jilana frowned. "I don't understand. A charioteer's son . . . my personal charioteer's son . . . attacked and injured a dozen young men, and a dozen or so city guards, all by himself? Is that what you are saying?"

"It is, my queen."

Jilana looked around, nonplussed. She found Vrath's eye and saw his face was as expressionless as ever, but in the tilt of his head she thought she read his meaning. There must be some reason why he had insisted they hear this matter together. Usually, as regent, Vrath handled all petitions and court matters. This must be important. She felt that he was urging her to consider it fully, yet she wasn't sure why — even if a charioteer's son had, for unknown reasons, gotten hold of a weapon and lashed out at a nobleman's son. No, there was something very strange here. Apart from the fact that a royal charioteer was not some common vagabond going around picking street fights, there was the fact that Adran was a relatively young man. She hadn't even known he had a son. How old could the boy possibly be?

She realized then that she had not as yet laid eyes on the accused himself.

"Let me see the accused."

Prime Minister Shakra spoke to one of the guards surrounding the accused. The guard said something in response. The prime minister looked at the distraught charioteer's wife standing nearby and spoke to her softly. She nodded. The guard gave a terse order to the four quads in the formation, and with impeccable Krushan discipline, they each took a step sideways, then diagonally, then again sideways, in different directions. In just three steps, the box formation opened to reveal the criminal at the center of the sixteen guards. The charioteer's wife said something to the boy, and he stepped forward, guards on either side of him as well as behind him holding spears to his throat, sides, and back. They had to bend the spears very low, pointing them almost straight downward because the boy was so short.

No, not short: small.

The boy was remarkably small. Barely a boy, even. Practically an infant.

Jilana was shocked. "How old is this boy?" she asked.

The mother shuffled forward, hands joined in a pleading gesture that Jilana knew all too well. The mothers, wives, sisters, daughters always clasped their hands together to plead for mercy. "He will be six years old next month, my queen."

Jilana thought she must have heard wrong. But the boy was right there, and he looked exactly the age his mother said he was; yet it was impossible. This whole situation was impossible.

"Prime Minister," she said sharply, "are you trying to tell us that a six-year-old boy, the son of a charioteer, attacked over two dozen young men, including a dozen armed and armored city guards?"

The prime minister nodded unhappily. "I am, Your Majesty. I did not believe the report myself, so I asked to see the victims. They are all being treated by the healers, and while none of their injuries are fatal or particularly severe, they do appear to have been caused by a person of very short stature. And there were witnesses."

"Witnesses," she repeated, wondering if she was going mad or if everyone else was.

"Apart from the thirteen guards who were injured, there were another five or six quads who arrived on the scene and viewed the last part of the skirmish with their own eyes. All their accounts concur in detail and broad description."

"And what were those accounts? No, don't start reciting parva and mantra to me, Prime Minister, simply summarize concisely and tell me the overall gist. What is it that they saw happen here? How could a six-year-old infant possibly assault two dozen people?"

"With great skill and mastery, Your Highness. It appears that despite his age, the boy is already a master of martial craft. He was able to fight and overcome all these opponents using only one weapon, a practice sword." The prime minister gestured to an aide, who stepped forward and bowed, presenting a wooden practice sword. To Jilana's eye, it looked like any similar practice weapon. Not quite a child's toy, yet not a real weapon either. This made no sense at all.

"Was Young Master Mashkon armed?"

Lord Mashkon started to say something but was cut short by a sharp order from the prime minister. He glowered and continued sweating but remained silent while Shakra went on. "He was, Your Highness, and so were his bodyguards and his companions. As were the city guards, of course."

"Of course," she repeated. This was growing more and more curious. She looked at the little boy. He looked quite ordinary except for the strange armor and jewelry he sported. The earrings appeared to be pure gold, as did the necklace, the chest and shoulder armor. Perfectly fitted too. Curious possessions for a charioteer's son. "How did the boy come by his armor and accoutrements?"

Prime Minister Shakra looked to the mother.

She raised her clasped hands to Jilana. "They came with him, my queen. They have always been part of him. They grow larger as he grows."

What an odd choice of words: "they *came* with him." Not the usual "he was born with them" that a mother would have said. She supposed it meant the same thing, but still, the odd usage bothered her. But she was distracted from the vocabulary by the sheer novelty of the fact: the earrings, necklace, chest armor, shoulder guards, back protector . . . It was all a part of his body? Flesh and bone? How was that possible? It looked so real, like actual armor, sculpted and shaped and burnished a deep, reflective golden hue. This case was growing curiouser and curiouser.

The boy himself was handsome if unformed. Except for the parts which were covered by those odd growths that looked like golden armor, the rest of his skin was dark, a deep dark brown that verged on ebony. Even his hair was curled. Overall, he resembled the travelers and ambassadors who visited Hastinaga from the distant kingdoms of that fabled continent across the ocean, land of the great river that rivaled their own Mother Jeel. She realized that even his jewelry and armor resembled the accoutrements those tribal emissaries wore.

The boy's mother — still bent over with her hands clasped — was dark too, but nowhere near as dark as her little son. As for the charioteer Adran, it was true he was dark, almost as dark as Jilana herself, and she supposed it was not that unusual for children to turn out lighter or darker skinned than their parents. After all, she herself was jet-black in appearance, but her mother was of a much lighter hue, and her father was at least a shade lighter than Jilana. She saw nothing unusual in the difference in coloring, or features. But those odd growths? That was unique.

And there was something else about the boy, too.

He stood with legs slightly apart, hands by his side, gazing up at her with utter calm. His eyes were clear, his face and body unmarked. He did not appear to be injured or even bruised at all. He looked barely old enough to pick up that wooden sword, let alone wield it with mastery enough to defeat a dozen armed city guards, as well as a dozen other armed young ruffians.

Yet there was something about him that made it clear he was no mere charioteer's boy. A sense of quiet confidence. An attitude of perfect patience. He looked as if he could stand there all day, waiting. Jilana noticed a beam of sunlight falling on his side and feet. The late afternoon sunlight had reached its long arms farther into the sabha hall. The boy turned his head very slightly, just enough to allow the top of the beam of sunlight to catch his chin, and as the sunbeam touched his face, Jilana glimpsed something strange: the sunlight seemed to diminish where it touched his body. She looked around the sabha hall. Sunlight was streaming in everywhere, falling on courtiers, nobles, guards, ministers, even the palace cat in the corner, now dozing. But where it touched the charioteer's son, it seemed to vanish, like water into a sponge.

There was more. As the sunbeams stretched across the sabha hall, they appeared to bend slightly, to veer *toward* the charioteer's boy, as if they were literally attracted to him.

Or he is attracting them to himself.

Jilana frowned and shook her head. It must be a trick of the light. But she knew better. She had seen enough such oddities before to know when she was looking at something not quite natural.

The boy had power.

She turned toward Vrath and found him gazing back at her, as if watching her arrive at this conclusion. He nodded once, and she knew he had known all along; this was the reason why he had wanted them to hear this matter. He had known the boy was special. Was he a demigod too, like Vrath? She had no way of knowing that for sure, but based on what she'd seen and heard so far, she believed it was a possibility. Either a demigod or something equally powerful — that was the only explanation for what she had just seen and the circumstances of this case. She could not imagine how exactly a little boy with a wooden sword could have fought, injured, and disabled so many opponents — a dozen of them heavily armed and armored fighting men of the highest caliber — but he *had* done it, and here he was, untouched, unblemished, beautiful, perfect, and calm as any average little boy. There was no fear in him, no nervousness, not even the normal deference of a child visiting the royal court for the first time. He stood as if he owned the sabha, the palace, the city . . . indeed, the world itself. As if everything belonged to him, and everyone ought to defer to him. It was not the arrogance of the noblemen's young sons and daughters she saw every day; this was simple self-assurance. The boy knew his place in the world was secure and had no fear of any creature, man or beast. His confidence was that of someone who was neither mortal nor subject to mortal laws.

Jilana looked to Vrath. "Do you have anything you wish to ask?"

Vrath considered the question. "I have a question for the pradhan mantri."

Shakra nodded.

"Did the boy attack first, or was he defending himself?"

Prime Minister Shakra looked immediately at Lord Mashkon, who glowered but said nothing. He looked at the guards, who looked back at him and nodded once. "Prince Vrath, the Young Master's claim was that the charioteer's son attacked unprovoked, but on further investigation and after questioning all parties, including the Young Master's companions and the city guards, it is my conclusion that the attack was provoked by the Young Master Mashkon and his bodyguards. The charioteer's son was only defending himself against their assaults, and thereafter, from all the others who attacked him."

Vrath considered this for a moment, then regarded Lord Mashkon. The nobleman quailed visibly, fresh sweat bursting out on his face and neck like a rash of hives.

"Go home, Lord Mashkon," Vrath said. "Go home, embrace your son, and perform a sacrifice thanking the gods that he still lives. The reason he does is because the boy was only defending himself. If he had been attacking, then your son, and all the others, would now be dead."

Karni

～

1

"HALT! HALT!"

The charioteer's cry echoed through the quiet glade. The thundering of hooves and rumbling wheels briefly interrupted the idyllic calm, sending a flock of cranes rising up, wheeling and crying plaintively. Bison bathing in the shallows glanced up but continued their frolic. A baby elephant, her mother, and her aunts paused briefly to watch the new arrivals from the opposite shore of the river, then trundled on their way, curling their trunks to inform the rest of the traveling herd that humans were within eyesight. Deer, chital, rabbits, squirrels, foxes, even a well-fed cheetah lying lazily on a branch, all scattered as the dust cloud raised by the arrival of the human procession settled over Pramankota.

The charioteer drew the chariot to a halt with expert flicks and tugs on the reins of his horse team. The other chariots and horse riders also drew to a halt and dismounted. The guards took up positions, flanking the main chariot, while outliers rode through the grove, ensuring the area was clear of predators and any other potential threats. Once certain the area was secure, their lieutenant gave orders to take up sentry positions. The rest of the entourage — mainly maids, cooks, and serving boys and girls — began to set up camp. They unloaded enough food to feed a dozen queens and began lighting and stoking the earth ovens maintained here for the royal visitors who frequented the place.

Pramankota was only a few hours' ride from Hastinaga, an idyllic grove on the banks of the Jeel, with plenty of fruit trees, game, shade, and grass slopes overlooking the river. A small waterfall and rock pool within easy walking distance provided a safe bathing spot for those inclined, and the great jungles known as Krushan-jangala were only a couple of hours' ride from here, providing more game than all the kings and queens of Krushan could hunt down in their combined lifetimes. It was the royal family's official picnic spot.

Karni loved coming here. It was her favorite place to get away from the hustle and crowds of the capital city. She loved the river and the grove and the sense of timelessness here. Though she was a princess of Mraashk by birth and Stonecastle by adoption — and well accustomed to the politics and public life of a royal — she found the imperial politics of Krushan too loud, too shrill, and too aggressive for her liking. It was a far cry from the court of her adoptive father's kingdom. Hastinaga was like a thousand Stonecastles, all crammed into one enormous palace sabha hall, all speaking at once in a thousand different tongues, each with its own agenda, every one constantly pushing that agenda. In contrast, the leisurely pace of King Stonecastle's court seemed like a nostalgic memory now, even though it had been only a few short years since she had come here.

"Thank you, charioteer," she said, as she dismounted from the chariot.

The elegantly mustached charioteer bowed low.

The compliment was heartfelt. She genuinely liked the way he drove. That was why she had asked for him today. He treated the horses kindly, almost never using the whip, and he took care to groom, feed, and wash them whenever possible. She had hated the last charioteer who drove her only because of the way he had treated his animals. She had requested that Princess Geldry allow her the use of her charioteer on this trip and was pleased when her sister-in-law had agreed to let the man drive her. She was slightly less pleased when Geldry expressed a desire to accompany Karni on the journey but had not wanted to seem rude, and so of course she said yes.

She watched as her sister-in-law and brother-in-law both dismounted from the chariot, each guiding the other. Adri's milky white pupils left no doubt about his blindness; he had been born with the condition, after all. It was Geldry's habit of binding her own eyes with silk scarves that Karni didn't quite understand. But she had been raised with impeccable manners and was too polite to ever question or critique anyone's personal choices, especially when it came to such sensitive matters. If Geldry wanted to feign blindness to show sympathy for her blind husband, that was her choice. To Karni, it seemed like a denial rather than an acceptance: if Adri was born blind, then Geldry was also born sighted. How did disabling herself alleviate her husband's disability?

Karni watched now as Adri dismounted the chariot easily, stepping down to the ground with the natural ease he always displayed. There were times when she could almost forget he was blind, so graceful and confident was he in his movements. In sharp contrast, Geldry stumbled as she misjudged the height of the chariot and overstepped; ironically, it was Adri's hand that steadied her.

"It smells horrible," Geldry said, wrinkling her nose and making a face. "What *is* that smell?"

Karni glanced at the chariot horses. Tired after their hours-long drive, they were now relieving themselves copiously. It was only natural, and anyone who traveled by horse or chariot regularly was accustomed to it. But of course, Geldry *would* presume that the smell was native to this place. Karni had only known her a short time but was already beginning to tire of her sister-in-law's habit of belittling people and criticizing everything she encountered.

"It's only the horses, Geldry," Adri said pleasantly. He turned his head away, toward the river. "I can smell the river. And jambun trees. Come, walk with me."

"Trisha," Geldry called to her harried handmaiden, "see to the food. I'm starving! Don't make us wait all day." Geldry then issued several more instructions before finally letting her husband lead her through the grove.

Karni walked a few yards ahead of them, trying to stay as far out of earshot as possible without seeming rude. She came here to Pramankota to get away from the constant squabbling and bickering of court and palace. But bringing Geldry along was like packing a basket full of bickering along as well; the woman found something to fault in everything.

Karni found a spot by the river and asked her own maid to fetch her some fruits and light refreshments, none of the heavy meats and rich foods that Geldry had her servants scurrying around to prepare. The whole point of a picnic was to relax and enjoy the natural surroundings, the solitude, to commune with nature. Geldry had brought musicians along to entertain herself and her husband, and of course, she found reason to criticize their playing as well as their choice of songs.

Karni kept to her own spot, within sight of Geldry and Adri's elaborate site, sipping on some juice and eating lightly. A curious doe and then a squirrel came up to her blanket, and she shared some of her repast with them, glad for the company. They were startled away by Geldry raising her voice to complain about the roasting of the meat and the temperature at which it was served. Karni finally tired of the fuss and rose to her feet, strolling farther away, making no pretense of her desire for solitude. Her personal guards accompanied her, keeping their distance to give her the privacy she desired, but remaining within sight and earshot in case they were required. Karni had only brought two maids along, and she told them to stay put and help themselves to the ample food while she took a stroll.

As Karni wandered closer to the river, the sound of the water rushing over the little rapids and the waterfall that fed the rock pool drowned out the last irritating traces of her sister-in-law's grating tones. The sound of rushing water was peaceful, and the afternoon sun was bright, but the wind off the Jeel was cool and refreshing, and the air smelled of apples and jambun.

The water looked so inviting, Karni had a sudden desire to take a swim. Glancing around, she saw one of her sentries and beckoned to the woman. When the guard was close enough, she told her what she intended, and the woman nodded. "I will keep all at bay, Princess Karni. You will not be disturbed."

The sentries backed away to give Karni a wide area of privacy. They were all women, so there was no real concern of male lechery, and Karni had never been particularly shy about things like nudity, anyway. But now that she was a princess of Hastinaga, there were protocols and matters of royal etiquette to observe, and she had no desire to receive another lecture on the topic of queenly behavior from Queen Mother Jilana. Once was quite enough!

Karni experienced a moment of perfect bliss as she entered the water. It was both warm on the surface and cool below. The combination of the warm afternoon sun and cool river breeze felt wonderful. She immersed herself fully in the rushing waters and felt a sense of freedom she had almost forgotten. It recalled her younger days when she had frolicked and dived into the lake near her father's palace at Stonecastle with her friends. Where were they all now? she wondered. All married and at their husbands' houses, raising children and managing the endless work of building a family, no doubt. She knew she ought to cherish these precious years after marriage but before she was blessed with child; they would pass all too quickly and then she would be raising children of her own, spending her days swaddled in maternal responsibilities.

Pushing such thoughts from her mind, Karni splashed about, relishing the feel of the moving water against her naked body. She swam out against the current, enjoying the challenge of swimming upstream against the rushing Jeel, using muscles she used far too rarely these days. She swam almost a mile upstream before finally turning back and allowing the current to carry her downriver. She floated, lying on her back and letting the river do the hard work. The sensation of weightlessness, the sensuality of the water on her bare skin, the sleepy glade, the idyllic surroundings, the absence of metropolitan hustle and bustle, all carried her into a dreamlike state somewhere between waking and memory.

Something brushed against her arm.

She pulled back her arm instinctively but wasn't initially alarmed; she assumed it was a plant or a flower, or perhaps even a fish. The lake back home had been filled with fish. They hadn't bothered her, though when they brushed against the soles of her feet, it would tickle.

She opened her eyes languidly.

And lost her balance.

She splashed and went under the surface, swallowing some water, and emerged, coughing and flailing. She regained control of herself, looked around at the shore to get her bearings, and saw that she was almost back to the place where she had entered the river, the quiet patch of the grove near the rock pool and the waterfall. Her guards were keeping their distance, their backs turned to her. Her maids were a little further up the bank, stretched out in the shade of a tree, napping. She could glimpse the smoke from the sunken earth ovens and cookfires of Adri and Geldry's entourage about five hundred yards further downstream.

She turned her head slowly, certain that all she would see now was the river, sunlight turning it into a field of sparkling gold, the lush green tops of the forest on the far bank. Nothing more. Nothing less.

There was a basket in the river.

Her breath caught in her throat, and she forgot to cycle her feet, starting to sink again. She controlled herself in time, remaining aloft, but her heart was pounding louder in her ears than the rushing of the river, and the sun that had felt so pleasant earlier now felt oppressively hot. She felt sweat burst out on her face and neck and under her arms. The breeze had died out, leaving an uncomfortable stillness. Somewhere in the jungle, a predator roared, and its prey screamed, even though no predators usually hunted at this time of day. The death cries of the unfortunate beast continued shrilly, far longer than ought to have been possible.

Karni felt her head spin. The river blurred around her, and the water began to feel clammy and cold against her skin. She forced her eyes to focus, to see the object that she knew could not possibly be there. A basket woven from bamboo strips, lined with soft cloth thickly piled inside, with a blanket on top, concealing and protecting its contents.

Her hand touched the basket again. She felt the weave of the bamboo, the smooth flat strips interwoven tightly. Good craftsmanship. The soft flannel of the blanket brushed her fingertips. She moved her other hand and brought it up under the bottom of the basket, floating inches deep in the river, and pressed her palm to the base. The basket was wet at the bottom but still watertight, even though it had floated downriver several yojanas, over a hundred miles in fact. It was a wonder it was still intact, that it hadn't gone over a fall or struck a rock and been overturned, spilling its contents, drowning . . .

She heard a sob and looked around, startled, to see who had made the sound.

There was nobody else in the river except she herself, and the basket.

Another sob.

This time she recognized it as her own sound. The sob of a woman unable to believe what she had done, had had to do. Six years. Six years ago, she had been a different woman, a young girl, really, knowing nothing of life, the world, the future.

She opened her mouth and water rushed in at once, the Jeel tasting bitter, sour, acrid, even though she knew that the water itself was sweet, pure, delicious. It was the taste of regret in her mouth. Guilt. Remorse.

She grasped the basket with both hands, pressing against it from opposite sides as she and it floated downriver together.

She felt its weight, the burden bundled within those blankets and soft cloths.

She felt the life within stirring, moving . . . kicking.

She recoiled and let go, pushing it away, shoving it.

It's a lie, an illusion, it has to be.

"No!" she cried. "No!"

Her voice was shockingly loud, even to her own ears. It seemed to drown out the sound of the water.

She turned her head and swam away ferociously.

She reached the shore and pulled herself onto dry land.

The mud sucked at her feet, pulling her back inside. Drawing her in. Refusing to let her go. Memory, pain, and sorrow, grasping her ankles with both hands, pulling at her, unyielding, unforgiving.

"I had no choice!" she said, softly this time. Hot tears spilled from her eyes, scalding her chilled skin. They felt like drops of hot oil from a burning clay lamp. She brushed them away roughly, smearing mud across her chest, her face, as she addressed the goddess of the river.

"I was young, unmarried, a princess. What would people think? What would I say? How would my father bear the shame? I did what I had to, I cast it away. It is a woman's lot in this man-dominated world. We fight, we birth, we cook, we clean, we do everything men do yet enjoy only half or less than half the rights and privileges. We are judged at every moment of our lives, in everything we say and do. If it had been up to me, I would have kept him, raised him, loved him. But it was never up to me. Not even the boon he gave me, that wretched mantra! Who asked him for it? I didn't want it. I never asked for a mantra to summon the gods! I did not want to take Sharra as a lover. I was not ready to be a mother at that tender age! And once the god Sharra left my bedside, it was as if almost no time had passed. I slept, and when I woke later the same night, my child was birthed. There was no gestation, no time to prepare my adolescent mind for such a momentous life event. And early the next morn, I birthed the child, alone and afraid, terrified and in pain, because the heat — the heat was indescribable! I saw him and knew that nobody would ever mistake him for an ordinary mortal child. How could I explain him to anyone? How could I live as an unwed mother? So I gave him away. I put him in a basket, bathed him with kisses and love and good wishes, and sent him to your care."

The river murmured softly.

"Yes, *your* care. Jeel Mata! You are Mother of Rivers, and mother of our land. I entrusted him to your care, knowing that you would not let any harm befall a demigod, son of another god. Whatever happened to him after that was his fate and your responsibility."

The river gurgled softly, the sound of a baby absorbed in its own dreaming.

"Forgive me," Karni said. "Forgive me, forgive me, forgive me."

She fell silent, lying back on the muddy bank.

The river continued its eternal song, neither judging nor accusing. Simply flowing as it had flowed for a thousand years and would flow for a thousand more.

2

In her distressed state, Karni had come ashore on the wrong bank. She was a stone's throw from the campsite but on the other side of the Jeel. She could see the cookfires of Adri and Geldry's picnic from where she stood, and because it was late summer, the river was only a few hundred yards across. She was a strong swimmer; she used to swim thirty times that distance every day just as exercise back in Stonecastle. She didn't think twice before pushing herself off from the bank and striking out. The current was steady, and by taking a diagonal angle, she would hit the other bank just about where she had started out.

The emotional outburst had drained her, but in a way it had also refreshed her. She had purged something from her system that she had been carrying inside for a long time. Was it the cleansing waters of the Jeel? Mother River's powers of purification were legendary — even mythical. Or perhaps it was just being able to shout out her pain and regret aloud for the first time.

She was always surrounded by people day and night; that was part of being a princess. It had meant suppressing her anguish and sorrow for years.

She had never told anyone about it, never even spoken about it aloud. That silence had taken its toll. She had become a subdued, quieter version of her younger self. Hastinaga only knew this quiet, subdued Karni; they had never seen the vivacious ebullient Karni who could turn cartwheels on a whim, perform somersaults in midair while plunging into a lake from fifty yards high, dance and play a dhol drum at festival time with total abandon, and laugh — oh, how she had laughed back then, anything and everything made her laugh, or shout, or sing. When was the last time she had whistled or even hummed a favorite tune? Back in Stonecastle, she would imitate birdsongs well enough to dupe the birds themselves. She had been a prankster, a tomboy, an entertainer, and a know-it-all, all wrapped into one bouncing bundle of energy.

Now she was just Karni, wife of Prince Shvate. Daughter-in-law of the House of Krushan. Princess of Hastinaga and the Burnt Empire. To millions of people, she was a symbol rather than a person. And with the one person to whom she should have been close enough to confide her secrets, she shared a warm but not intimate relationship. She liked Shvate a lot, perhaps she even loved him. She had liked him well enough to have chosen him from among several score suitors at the swayamvara in Stonecastle three years ago, but she had only agreed to the swayamvara because she had given up on relationships and no longer expected or desired to meet a man she liked enough to spend the rest of her life with.

Her father had been concerned — anxious, really — about her growing older and staying unmarried, and she had given in at last because it simply didn't matter anymore: nothing seemed to matter anymore. All the joy, the pleasure had gone out of life after the death of her first love, and those miserable months serving Guru Pasha'ar. The accident of her unwanted pregnancy and abandoning her child had left her in a fog of depression and self-recrimination from which she had never recovered entirely. She had agreed to a swayamvara as a compromise between her principles, which still saw arranged marriage as backward and barbaric, and choosing her own life mate, which she no longer had any real interest in anymore.

The late afternoon sun was warm on her back and face and arms as she swam steadily. She was more than halfway across already, and the current was strongest here, pushing her farther downriver than she would have wanted. She was going to miss her picnic spot. She could see the maids looking around anxiously, concerned about her long absence now. There were sentries also looking for her, scanning the river upstream and downstream intently, but for some reason, none of them were looking at the point where she was now. She thought of waving and yelling, but the river was so loud and choppy she doubted they would hear her, and if she stopped swimming for even a moment, the river would bear her even farther off course.

With each yard she swam, she was being pushed three or four yards downriver. At this rate, she would reach the other bank a good half mile away. Oh, well. She could run the distance in a few minutes, and it would still be daylight for another hour yet. Let the maids and sentries worry; it was their job.

Karni concentrated on swimming strongly, feeling muscles and tendons that she hadn't used in years starting to ache. This was a good thing. She ought to come here to swim more often. She liked the sense of freedom, the open, clear landscape, the cool water and warm sunshine, the large flocks of birds sweeping overhead, calling out, the sounds of animals in the woods, the raw, earthy odor of river and grass and flowers and dirt. It made her feel closer to her body, more rooted in her own self. And the emotional confession to Mother Jeel had helped. She felt purged and cleansed. And hungry. Goddess, she felt hungrier than she had felt in years! She would send her maids to Adri and Geldry's picnic and ask them to bring back some roast meats; it had been a while since she had felt such a craving for some spicy roasted flesh. Swimming had always given her an appetite, and it seemed, so did crying.

She continued to make her way toward the shore, and when she felt the first tug at her ankle, she assumed it was just the current. The second tug was hard enough that she went under for a moment, water flooding her nose and mouth. She emerged, choking and gasping, and struck out again. She had experienced strong currents before while swimming, and had always been able to break free of their grip by changing her angle.

But it was not the current; there was something actually grasping her ankle and tugging it downward.

She scanned the bank ahead. It was less than two hundred yards away, but she was now several hundred yards downriver from her campsite, and none of the maids or sentries were even looking for her this far down — not yet anyway. Besides, shouting or waving now would be pointless. There was a strong wind blowing from the west, and her yells would only be blown back in her own face.

The strange thing was that she was still moving downriver, even though her ankle was snagged. As if whatever her foot had caught on was also moving with the current. An underwater plant that had been ripped loose, maybe?

She took a quick deep breath and dove down to see what it was. She had to double over, like somersaulting. She bent over, straining to see what was snagging her ankle. The water, through relatively clean, was cloudy from the sheer force of its current, and she could barely make out a murky shadow that floated deep down, reaching up a long tendril-like appendage which ended in her foot. A weed of some kind? She dove down further, forcing her head down against the current, trying to see the thing itself but the water kept pushing her upper body aside. The force of the current was so intense, it buffeted her face hard enough to feel like someone was kneading the flesh, making it impossible to focus her vision.

All she could make out was that the thing arresting her movement was very long and thin. From the way it felt around her ankle, it was soft but firm, like a tubular plant. A weed, then, or a clump of weeds. What else could it be? But why was it not moving now? If it had been ripped from its roots, the current ought to be pushing it along. She tried swimming downriver, under the water, kicking her legs and spanning her arms as hard as she could, but the grip on her ankle tightened further, until she felt her right foot starting to go numb.

She emerged at the surface, gasping for breath. The daylight was fading fast, the sun already near the horizon. In a very short while it would set. The maids and sentries must be searching frantically now. Even Adri and Geldry must have been alerted. But somehow during her efforts to pull free of the weed, she had drifted downriver to a place where a rocky outcrop blocked her completely from view of the north bank. Unless someone climbed that rock and leaned over the river precariously, they would never spot her. The river was louder here too: a roaring torrent that drowned out the cries of the cranes flying overhead.

She started to realize she could be in real trouble soon. The current was buffeting her to and fro now that she was anchored to the weeds, and the strain was starting to hurt her left leg. She could feel the nerves pulled tight and the circulation around the area almost at a standstill. Treading water with just her right foot was awkward and tiring. Once her left leg went numb and her right foot tired or cramped, she would not be able to keep her head above the surface. Ridiculous as it seemed, there was a real possibility she could drown here, within a few hundred yards of threescore royal guards and a score of maids and servants. And how fitting that would be: to end up in the same river into which she had lowered the basket six years ago.

Except that she had never meant for her baby boy to die. Only to float downriver far enough to be well away from Stonecastle, where he would hopefully find some kind soul to adopt and care for him. He was the son of a god after all; surely, he had not drowned in the waters of Goddess Jeel?

Could it be Goddess Jeel herself doing this to Karni? To reprimand her for abandoning her son? To make her experience the fate her son could have suffered? But surely he *hadn't* suffered such a fate. Her little armored sun god *couldn't* have drowned in the Jeel.

"Is that it, Mata?" she said. "Are you punishing me because he died? Tell me that isn't what happened!"

And what if it was? What if he *had* drowned in the river? It would be her fault. Perhaps that was the only way a demigod could be killed, by drowning in the Jeel. What did she know of such things, after all? She had used the God Mantra, as she now thought of the Mantra of Summoning to summon Goddess Jeel and had been intimidated when the river rose up like a statue carved from water. Karni had offered her newborn babe to the river goddess, beseeching her to take him and give him to a family that would cherish and raise him as their own. Karni had been unable to think of anything else at the time. And Jeel had taken him, wrapping him in a bubble of air and carrying him away downriver. Karni had cried with remorse and regret, but knew she had no choice at the time.

But now, with the hindsight of time and experience, she felt a pang of guilt. What if she had condemned him to a watery death, and now, six years later, by stepping into the Jeel for an afternoon dip, she had condemned herself to the same fate? She imagined her little babe floundering in this rushing torrent, his tiny lungs filling with the pure blessed water, his little heart slowing, his little arms and legs hanging limply as he floated in the water, face-down, lifeless. Had she murdered her baby?

"If I did cause his death, then I deserve to die," she said, her words echoing in her own head over the sound of rushing water. "If that is my crime, then I surrender to your sentence, Jeel Mata. Take me and do with me what you will. I deserve the worst fate you mete out."

There was an instant when the river seemed to grow still. She felt the current slow, then halt completely, the rushing torrent fall silent, she could hear the cranes calling to their family to come home for the night, the sparrows chirping, the crows cawing, elephants trumpeting in the distance, even the faint sound of human voices calling out . . . calling her title and her name: "Princess Karni!"

Princess Karni. What use were titles and kingdoms when you had failed your most fundamental Krushan law? Yes, she deserved to die, to be pulled deep into the murky depths of the Jeel, taken to the bosom of the river and held there forever, as sentence for the crime of infanticide.

She felt the grip on her ankle tighten further, the pressure growing unbearably, and the weeds yanked her down suddenly. She gasped in time, instinct causing her to take one final breath. Then she went under the surface completely.

Something took hold of her other ankle, the right one, and pulled hard at that one too. With both her ankles caught, she was completely trapped. Her feet were pulled downward suddenly, the force startling. How could weeds pull her down so quickly? She saw the surface rise above her head, the sky fading, blurring, then disappearing completely. Down she went, the force on her legs too strong to even think of resisting. If someone had tied ropes to her ankles and had a horse pull the other end of the rope, she couldn't have gone faster. She was several yards down now, perhaps twenty or more, and descending very quickly. How deep was the Jeel here? Thirty yards? Deeper? She tried to turn her head, to see if there was something she could grab hold of, use to stop her downward descent. But there was nothing except water and the occasional fish. There were plenty of fish here, deep below the surface, fish of all sizes and colorings. Even river eels swimming in a group, undulating as they crept through the water. She saw a huge turtle the size of a chariot floating tilted at an angle, as if riding a current. She thought she saw the large silver shapes of porpoises, but surely there were no porpoises this far downriver. They lived in the colder heights of the Jeel, far higher than Stonecastle even.

Thirty yards now, and still no ground in sight. Her lungs were emptying of air quickly, soon she would be unable to breathe. She had barely gasped enough air for a short dive. The force with which she was being dragged down was incredible. It felt like not just one horse, but a whole team of horses was pulling her. Her body was stretched out vertically, her arms thrown up above her head by the sheer force of her descent. She felt as if she were being stretched out. Her body arched and undulated like a fish as the force pulling her veered in a slightly more upriver direction. She wondered how it was that weeds could adjust their descent, yet she already knew that it was truly no clump of weeds that had hold of her; there was something sentient about the things that had gripped her ankles, a sense of great strength clutching her tightly, strong enough to snap her feet like dry twigs if it desired, but careful to use only as much force as was necessary to pull her without actually causing her harm.

Out of breath, she felt herself starting to black out, and her vision began to blur. The bottom was in sight now, about twenty yards further down, a small forest of vegetation, weeds, underwater flowers. There were river crabs there, scrabbling over the bottom. An entire school of turtles, marching along slowly together as if on a mission. Large shoals of tiny silver fish darting between tall weeds and plants. Brightly colored fish traveling in precise underwater patterns, crisscrossing underneath and over each other. An entire world of different underwater fauna and flora spread out before her, as rich and diverse as any jungle aboveground.

The water was cold here, colder than she could have imagined. A deep, penetrating cold, down in these murky depths where sunlight never reached and hot-blooded two-legged creatures did not belong.

She summoned the last of her reserves of energy and forced her neck down, pushing her face down as well, and tried to see directly below her feet.

She saw it then. The thing that had taken hold of her and was dragging her down to the river's bottom: it was not human, but it was not aquatic either; it was neither of the land nor the river. The shock of seeing it was intense: whatever she might have expected, this was not it. This was not Mother Jeel's doing. This was not Karni being punished for abandoning her newborn child. It was something else entirely.

Everything was going dark around her, like her bedchamber in Hastinaga when she told the maids not to relight the lamps after they went out, and she just lay there in the darkness, listening to the sounds of the palace and the city, the constant thrum and throb of a jungle of humanity, all those lives and lusts, ambitions and dreams, hopes and desires, conflicting and intersecting, like chariots clashing at night on a dark plain. She liked it when Shvate came to her at such times and would accept his embraces more willingly than at the unexpected moments when he became amorous in the middle of the day or early morning. She liked dusk, and the soft, easy light at that hour, the way she felt, soft, languorous, the cares and responsibilities of the day past, the night of respite ahead, these hours of peaceful solitude all to herself to do with as she pleased.

She felt herself slipping into unconsciousness as her descent reached its end. The muddy bottom of the river, teeming with life, an underwater metropolis no less populated and busy than great Hastinaga, rushed up to greet her. But just as she thought she would surely collide with the floor of the riverbed, something opened beneath her — a portal of some kind — and through it she went, and her descent continued.

She was barely conscious as she looked up and saw the portal closing above her, the river and the distant, remote light of the upper world far above her now, just a pinprick of memory in the fading sunset of her mind, and then she was embraced by a darkness more than night and welcomed by oblivion.

Shvate

~

1

GETTING IN WAS THE easy part.

Though the city of Reygar stood on its living tentacles of flesh, when it was at rest, its lowest extremities sagged only a few yards above the desert floor.

Shvate ordered a company of the tallest elephants in his command to cluster beneath the city. It took some effort and much coaxing by the mahouts to make the great beasts move so close to the unnatural phenomenon, but once they were gathered together, it was possible for the three adventurers to climb onto their backs and, from there, clamber onto the base of the city.

The city had uprooted itself from a foundation of bedrock, tearing a large chunk of the rock with it. It was onto this rock that Shvate, Mayla, and Vida climbed. From here, they made their way up to the base of the city itself. It was not unlike climbing a rock face, and while Shvate and Mayla were both strong climbers, Vida had some trouble. Credit to his spirit, he managed the climb, and a short while after deciding on their plan, the three stood on a street strewn with rubble. Cracks ran zigzaggedly along the ground, up the sides of the houses. The scene resembled a city that had experienced an earthquake of the highest magnitude, which in a sense, was what had actually happened. Except that after the earthquake, the city had gone for a drunken stroll!

The thing that was notably absent was any human presence. There were no people anywhere in sight. Shvate and Mayla searched the houses on the street quickly, swords drawn. Vida was handy with a bow and kept an arrow nocked at all times, but no target presented itself. After combing through a half dozen deserted houses, they returned to the main street no wiser than when they had begun.

"Where could they go?" Mayla asked. "People can't just disappear."

"We know where some of them are." Shvate pointed down to the tentacles that extended from under the city to curl onto the desert floor. The three Krushan were currently about a hundred yards above the ground. Even from here, they could see the living faces and limbs of the people who had sacrificed themselves to form the grotesque human chains. The tentacles undulated and stirred from time to time but did not move from their places. Was it too much to hope that it had exhausted itself and could not continue the battle? That would be expecting too much. "Perhaps that is the entire population?"

"That doesn't make sense." Vida was emphatic. "Reygar is home to over one hundred thousand people, but what about the *armies* of Reygistan? We know that they number over a million strong. A substantial portion of that is certainly deployed at the far borders of the empire, fighting rebellions and even our own carefully timed attacks designed to divert their attention, but at least a third that number ought to be here in the capital city. That is the information I received from our spies, and it was on the basis of that information that we marched from Hastinaga with two million." Vida pointed at the tentacles below. "I attempted an estimate of how many poor souls were sacrificed to create those living chains. Those terrible things, all told, could not number more than fifty thousand. And we know that most of those definitely came from *outside* Reygar, climbing in through the tunnels."

Shvate shook his head impatiently. "Never mind the count. Where are they? Hundreds of thousands of men cannot simply disappear."

"Who knows what Jarsun is capable of?" Mayla said. "If he could make those *things . . .*"

"Princess Mayla may be right," Vida said. "Nobody knows the full extent of Jarsun's powers. He displays new talents in each encounter, adapting his resources and magical abilities to match the circumstances. What he did here with the human chains is something he has never done before. I know because I have read the history. For instance, on one occasion during the fifteenth siege of Mraashk —"

They never got to hear what Jarsun did at the fifteenth siege of Mraashk. The ground tilted suddenly underfoot, first one way then the other, then the entire city began to shake and tremble around them. Plaster and brick dust crumbled from the broken walls, loose stones rolled from the cracked streets, and debris from the houses began falling from all directions.

"It's on the move!" Mayla cried, hooking her elbow and one foot around a pillar and offering Shvate her free arm. He grasped her forearm and used the support till he could find something more solid to hold on to. Vida exclaimed and grabbed on to a half wall just in time. The street began shaking from side to side as the city raised itself high on its tentacles and began moving around in huge strides that spanned a dozen yards at a time.

Shvate looked down and saw the tentacles lashing out at his forces, knocking entire companies of infantry and cavalry down like they were wooden toys. He saw his brave soldiers fighting back as best as they could, using arrows, spears, javelins, even flaming missiles. It was strange to be watching the slaughter of his own army from the enemy side. It made him feel sick.

"We have to find a way to stop this wretched thing," he shouted at Vida above the noise of the city and the battle.

"Our best chance is to keep moving upward, to the top of the city, as I said before. I am certain the brain is up there somewhere. That is where we shall find its most vulnerable point."

Shvate craned his neck to look up at the top of Reygar. The street they were on was the main street of the city, the kingsroad as it was called. It wound its way around the city-mountain for an entire mile before ending at the peak. The street was built on a very gradual incline, with buildings constructed on natural ledges of mountainside, to make it easier for men and beasts of burden to climb all the way, but it was still a steep gradient. And with the city moving and tilting constantly, it was a challenge just to keep themselves from being thrown free of solid ground. A fall from even a hundred yards high was enough to kill anyone; if they fell from up here, General Prishata wouldn't even be able to reassemble their body parts.

"Let's stop talking about it, then, and do it," Shvate said.

He made the first move, climbing upward along the street, using pillars, walls, even the cracks in the street to assist in the climb.

The three climbed for the next hour, often forced to stop as the city swayed and shook like a bucking bull trying to free itself of unwanted riders. Shvate was furious at the toll being taken on his forces, but as Mayla reminded him, they were already taking the most effective action possible. All that mattered was stopping this monstrosity by any means, and Vida's theory was the only one that offered any possible solution.

All through their long, arduous climb, there remained no sign of any of Reygar's denizens. Not so much as a single human being, man, woman, or child. Not even a dog, a cat, nor rodents of any kind. There was something very strange about the experience of climbing through an entirely deserted city of such size and scope. They passed hovels which must have housed the very poor and mansions that housed the very rich, great estates and tiny tenements. All equally deserted.

There was little to be gained from talking — the noise and movement was so great that it required every ounce of their strength and concentration simply to ensure they did not fall. Climbing was a challenge akin to climbing a mountain which was shuddering in the throes of an earthquake.

Hours of climbing later, they stood, exhausted and bathed in perspiration, a full mile above the ground.

The sun had risen high in the sky during their climb, and the heat was scorching hot. Mercifully, the houses and the city itself blocked most of the sunlight, though even the occasional flashes and reflections were torturous to Shvate. From time to time, when the city turned and was directly facing the sun, he was forced to seek shelter till they were in the shade again.

The brightness at such moments blinded him near totally. He relied more and more on Mayla's eyesight and grit to keep them going. She was a staunch ally, always warning him just in time to avoid being blasted by direct exposure and quick to tell him when it was safe to move on. He cursed his condition more than once, but Mayla reminded him that they would have had to pause from time to time for respite anyway. His heart filled with love for her. He kissed her on the lips, unmindful of the coating of dust and sand that covered them both.

"What would I do without you?" he said.

She grinned at him, her bright green eyes the only clear spots on her grimy face. Even her eyelashes had dust on them. "You would be kissing your other wife, Karni," she said with her usual spirit.

He laughed. "I love you both."

"We love you too," she said, giving him another quick kiss. "That's from my sister wife."

When they turned back, they saw Vida staring at something.

"Brother?"

Vida looked back at Shvate, holding on to a doorway as the city shuddered and shook. "I think I have the answer," he said.

There was no need to shout anymore, as the noise and falling debris were far below them now. They were cocooned above the clouds in a pocket of quiet. Even the shaking and moving of the city was not as intense as it was lower down.

"The answer to what?" Shvate said.

"To *everything*," Vida replied. He pointed above their heads. "It lies in there."

Shvate peered up at the structure Vida was pointing at, on the street just above the one they were standing on. It was less than ten yards further up the mountain, but a good hundred and fifty yards from the actual peak.

It was a squat, nondescript building with a large ungated entranceway. There were no sigils or markings anywhere on the front that Shvate could see, and it was unusual only in that he could not make out its function. It looked neither like a domicile nor a place of business. Simply a rectangular structure of indeterminate purpose.

"Are you sure?" He was doubtful. "That doesn't look like a palace."

Vida's voice was very quiet now, but firm. "I am certain. That is what we seek. The answer lies in there."

Shvate nodded. If Vida said that was their destination, it was good enough for him. "All right, then. I'll go first, you stay close behind me. Mayla, you bring up the rear."

"To hell with that," she retorted, and before Shvate could object, she began running up the street, leaping from pole to wall to tilted house, using whatever was at hand to climb the last several yards to their destination. Shvate sighed and followed her. "Come on, Vida."

They entered the structure cautiously, weapons drawn and ready, moving in a triangular formation, alert for anything that might await them.

2

The darkness that greeted them was absolute. Shvate looked back at the entrance they had come through, but it had disappeared behind them, only a few yards after they had walked through it. How was that possible? Unless night had abruptly fallen outside, they should have been able to see the square of light marking the doorway. But there was nothing. Just pitch-blackness in all directions.

"It's too dark," Mayla whispered beside him. "I can't see."

"Nor can I," he replied. "But we have no means to light our way. Vida?"

"Yes, brother," came the response from his other side. "Give me a moment."

They waited in the darkness. Shvate noted that the interior of the structure felt noticeably cooler than outside. But it was more than the mere absence of sunlight. There was a chill in here that sank into the bone. There was also an odor, something very familiar but uncommon. It reminded him of the tunnel under the desert, and he braced himself for more horrific sights of supernatural monstrosity. But Shvate was also very conscious of the numbers Vida had reeled off earlier, of the army of Reygistan and the population of Reygar. All those people had to be *somewhere*. He sniffed the air, expecting to smell carnage, blood, sweat . . . something indicating the presence of people inside this dark stone box. But there was only the same odd odor, maddeningly familiar yet somehow also strange — definitely not the typical smells of human exudation.

A light appeared ahead, surprising Shvate. It seemed to spark out of nowhere at first, illuminating himself, Mayla, and Vida. It was not a flame from a lamp or a torch, but a faint greenish glow that provided a smoky illumination that was just sufficient to make out the shapes and outlines of objects, but not enough to reveal much detail; he could see Mayla's outline and make out the curves of her body and the lines of her angular face, but he could not see details of her anatomy or features.

Vida was better illuminated, but the reason for that turned out to be because he himself was the source of the light. Shvate's half brother was holding something that looked like an ordinary stone, flat and about as broad as the palm of his hand, but the surface of the stone itself gave off some kind of greenish glow; this was the source of the illumination.

"A rock that burns!" The awe in Mayla's voice was matched by the amazement in her face as she peered at the stone in Vida's hand.

"It is a natural phenomenon," Vida said, "found in many underground caverns. The light is caused by some manner of radiation, I believe. I found a piece of it while exploring subterranean caverns. It has stayed in my pouch ever since. I thought it might be of use on this expedition."

Shirrrrrr.

"Quiet." Shvate raised his sword, turning to face the direction from which he had heard the sound. He had whispered the admonition, but his voice sounded louder in this black space. "Give me the light."

Vida handed over the stone. Shvate took it and held it out as far as his arm would reach, in the direction from which the sound had come. The stone's light faded to a dullness at two yards that made it impossible to tell even shapes or outlines. But Shvate saw something ahead that was moving, and that was enough for him. He took a step, then another step, then a third and fourth, his sword held ready in his left fist, right hand holding out the stone at an angle away from his face to avoid getting its light in his eyes directly.

He could glimpse something in the darkness ahead. A swirling like a person wearing a large thick cloak.

It moved again, and he was certain this time that it was a person. It wavered before him, hanging in the air, as the light caught only the edges and outline of the cloak without illuminating the person within the garment. But as he had experienced in the thick of battle, it was the movement that mattered more than the details. One did not need to see an opponent's face, handsome or otherwise, to know that they had violence in mind.

The apparition before him was preparing to attack, he was certain of that. Shvate took another step, preparing to strike at the moving shadow.

"Shvate, stop! Look down!"

Mayla's voice brought him to a halt. He kept his eyes on the swirling cloak before him, then quickly flicked his view down. What he saw made him catch his breath.

The ground fell away beneath his feet, yielding to an abyss that stretched on seemingly forever. Of course, the light of the stone could not illuminate it entirely, but there were pebbles underfoot, and his foot had dislodged them, sending them falling into the abyss, and he could not hear them striking ground. That meant a very long fall. As high as the mountain itself, perhaps.

He swallowed and stepped back, one, then two steps. He felt Mayla's strong grip take hold of his arm, gripping the muscle of his right biceps with both hands. His left hand was still free, and he had kept his sword upheld, a soldier's instinct. But when he raised his eyes to look at the enemy he had sensed earlier, he now saw nothing except darkness, and he felt a wind from below, blowing upward, cool and redolent of moisture. There was water somewhere below, far below. And it was icy cold.

"You almost fell," his wife said, holding onto him hard enough that his arm, where she clutched it, ached. "I thought —"

"Vida," Shvate said, interrupting Mayla. "What is this place? Where are we?"

Vida's face swam into focus as he stepped closer to Shvate, into the reach of the light. The green illumination lit up his features, shading half his face in shadow, painting the other half leaf green. There were dark sockets where his eyes should have been, only a dull greenish gleam reflecting from the eye in the strange light. "In the heart of the mountain city. The heart of Reygar. This is where we shall find our enemy, and only by finding him and killing him can we stop the city-beast from rampaging and destroying our forces. Brother, you have to find Jarsun here and kill him if we are to win this battle. It is the only way."

Shvate studied Vida, trying to see his face clearly and failing. Vida's half-shadowed face and the strange way his voice resonated here in this place made him sound very different. There was something about his voice that made Shvate's hackles rise. "How are you so certain?"

"The heart of the city is in here, I am certain of it."

Shvate raised his head and tried to look around. He could see nothing except endless darkness in every direction. Now that he had stepped back from the edge of the abyss, even the little patch of ground beneath his feet seemed solid rock. All he could tell for certain was that they were inside some kind of cavern. He sensed that it was the inside of the mountain, a natural cavern carved from eons of ice melt dripping from the peak down through the center. He had seen similar places before. But there was no sound nor sign of any living being. Even the floating cloak he thought he had seen was just a trick of the darkness, his own warrior's instinct warning him of possible danger even where there was none. What did Vida see or sense that Shvate could not?

He reminded himself for the thousandth time that Vida thought and analyzed information differently than anyone Shvate had ever met. This was why he was a genius, and, indeed, even Vrath had said so in open sabha.

The city-mountain was still now, undergoing another period of rest. But soon enough, in an hour or two, it would resume its relentless assaults. How much of the Krushan army was already dead or maimed? A third? Half? He sensed that Reygar would not cease attacking until his army was either wiped out or had withdrawn. And if he withdrew, that would mean surrender. It would mean that Hastinaga had failed to overcome the might of Reygistan. That Jarsun had triumphed. The implications would be terrible, the consequences monumental. It could lead to another uprising, another alliance against them. And it would almost certainly mean the end of Shvate's ambition to be a future king of Hastinaga.

If Vida said he was sure, then Shvate was sure too.

"Very well, brother," Shvate said. "But how do I find our enemy in this darkness? Where do I go?"

Vida took the stone from Shvate's hand and stretched his own arm outwards, in the direction of the chasm. "You must go down into this abyss to seek him out and end this battle. It is the only way."

Mayla swore into Shvate's ear. She had relaxed her grip on his biceps but was still holding it lightly, and at Vida's words he felt her fingers tighten again as if preparing to hold him back. "Are you insane, Vida? All that lies below is death! How dare you give my beloved husband such cruel advice?"

"I am sorry, sister Mayla. It is the only way. Otherwise, we will surely lose this battle and who knows what else besides, and if we do, it will be the beginning of the end, as Vrath said. Once Hastinaga begins to lose, it will continue to do so. We cannot back away from a challenge, however deadly. We are Krushan. Whatever the odds, we stand and fight. It is our Krushan law."

"Vida is right," Shvate said. "If that is the only way, then into this abyss is where I must go."

Mayla squeezed his arm hard enough to hurt, surprising Shvate again with her strength. "If that is where you must go, then it is where I go as well. Where Shvate goes, Mayla follows — always."

Shvate turned his head to look at her. Her face was a faint greenish smear against the darkness but he could feel her pulse beneath her palm as she held his arm tightly. He felt her life and resolve and strength, her love for him beating strong in her heart. "So be it." He reached with his hand, touching her hip, her waist, and the arch of her back. He found her hand and grasped it in his own, squeezing it lightly. "Come then, my love, let us embrace the darkness together. Whatever dangers it holds, we face them together."

With that, they stepped forward together, seeking a way into the abyss. Shvate held the stone before him, searching for steps cut into the rock — any means by which they might descend. Here at the edge, the light from the stone seemed to glow brighter. Shvate was pleased because he could now see the ground underfoot more clearly, even the way ahead for several yards. The downside was that he could also see the edge of the abyss, which even for a man as brave as he was a terrifying thing to stand beside. The light grew even brighter then, now illuminating the entire chamber. He frowned, and thought that surely all that light could not be coming from a single stone — and then looked up and saw that it was not the stone at all: this new illumination was coming from elsewhere.

An oval of deep crimson light had appeared in midair, suspended above the abyss. It hung there, throbbing, pulsing with light, brightening then darkening, brightening again and darkening again. This pulsing became a steady rhythm, and each time it pulsed, the light grew brighter yet, until it was so bright it could barely be looked upon, forcing Shvate and the others to raise their arms to shield their eyes. The illumination cast by the oval shape was reddish, but at its center it was hot white light, so bright that it was not possible to stare directly at it. That core blazed like a fire yet the waves emanating from it were not hot but cold. An icy chill pervaded the space, and Shvate saw his own breath condensing into mist as he exhaled. He glanced at Vida and Mayla, seeing puffs of mist emerge from their lips as well.

"*Shvate!*"

He was looking at his companions when the voice spoke. Neither of their lips had moved. They were both staring raptly at the oval light, and Shvate did now as well. There was something mesmerizing about its steady pulsing rhythm. Brighter. Darker. Brighter. Darker. Brighter . . .

"*Shvate!*"

Shvate saw now that there was someone standing *inside* the oval light, dressed exactly the way she always dressed, looking exactly the same as the last time he had seen her.

His mother.

She stood on solid ground, on some surface in another place he recognized well. The oval light formed a passageway between that place where she stood and the place where Shvate was standing. He could see the floor beneath her feet, the walls to either side, the statuary, the palatial furnishings. He knew that place well. It made no sense — for her to be there and him to be here, both able to see and hear each other — yet somehow it was so.

"Shvate, come to me. I need to speak with you."

He tried to turn his head to ask Vida how this was possible, if it was really happening or some kind of urrkh maya, an illusion caused by demonic sorcery. But he could no longer turn his head or look away. The oval light kept his gaze trapped. He was transfixed by the light and the woman standing inside it.

"Shvate, please. We do not have much time. Come to me now."

He wanted to go to her. He wanted it more than anything else in the world. But still he hesitated, some part of his brain cautioning him, reminding him that he was in the lair of his enemy, that Jarsun was known for his sorcery, that demons were capable of elaborate, convincing illusions, that this could be a trap.

"Are you afraid that this could be Jarsun's sorcery? It is not, I assure you. Jarsun is far from here. He is occupied with another crisis of his own. That is why you could not find him in Reygar. This portal you see here is only meant for you to cross over, to come to me here, in Hastinaga. It is perfectly safe. Trust me. No harm will come to you here. Come to me now, my son."

That last word caught in his heart like a hook in the mouth of a fish. He was struck by emotion. How long had it been since his mother had sent for him? Too long. Even when he was a child, when he needed her, wanted her, she would shun him. When compelled to hold him for a moment on royal occasions, to present the appearance of a devoted mother and child, she could touch him with the tips of her fingers, just enough to keep up appearances. He could not recall a time when she had embraced him, hugged him, shown any real affection for him. But now here she was, standing before him, calling to him. How could he refuse? Perhaps this was the day she would finally embrace him, ask forgiveness for all those years of neglect and distancing, hold him tight and weep, or laugh, or show some emotion in his presence. How could he not go to her? He had waited for this day all his childhood, and even if it had come years later when he was a grown man, he could not simply turn away and ignore her.

"How do I come to you?" he asked, feeling foolish at the sound of his own echoing voice. What must Mayla and Vida think? He wanted to turn to glance at their faces but the oval light was too compelling; he could not look away.

"All you have to do is walk to me," his mother said. "It is like stepping on solid ground. Have no fear, you will not fall into the abyss. The portal will bring you safely to me. Come quickly, son, before the portal closes and we lose this opportunity to speak. I have urgent news for you."

Urgent news. What did that mean?

"I am fighting a battle, Mother," he said, though he was already taking the first step forward.

"What I have to tell you will help you be victorious. Come quickly, son. Before it's too late!" She beckoned to him.

Even if this made no sense at all, he had to find out what she knew. Winning the battle of Reygar was crucial to his life, his career, his entire family's future.

Shvate took another step forward, and another. He walked across thin air, over the abyss, and entered the oval of blue light. A peculiar vibration thrummed in his inner ears, resonating within him. He smelled an odd mixture of scents, things he had experienced at different times in his life. His body felt unusual, as if he were lighter, refreshed, stronger.

He walked into the portal and passed through to the other side.

3

It was so bright here. Brighter than it had ever been, brighter than he remembered. Everything was tinged white at the edges, the corners of every object obscured by the white light, smoothed and blended into the whiteness that pervaded all. It was as if the world outside this place were entirely filled with blinding white light, as if they existed in a pocket of solidity in a galaxy of whiteness. The place itself was his mother's private chamber in the palace at Hastinaga. He had been brought here occasionally by his wet nurses, to "spend time" with her. It held a mixture of memories for him: sadness, regret, loss, hope, longing, wanting . . . the childhood he had had versus the childhood he wished he could have had. The mother he'd had versus the mother he'd needed.

"Son."

She was an apparition. A vision in saffron, red, and white. Despite being a widow, the princesses of Hastinaga were required to wear white only on formal occasions. In the privacy of her private chambers, she could wear what she pleased. It pleased him to see her wearing color: he had always felt saddened by the sight of her in white. Seeing her in white reminded him of the fact that his father was dead. But in color, he felt like at least he had her, his mother, and he could pretend that he had a semblance of a normal life, a normal family.

"You look good. Strong. Healthy. I am so proud of you and all that you have achieved."

He bent awkwardly, reaching down to touch her feet in the traditional gesture of respect shown to elders. "Ma, aashirwaad." *Mother, bless me.*

"Ayushmaanbhavya, putr." *Live long, my son.* She touched his forehead with her fingertips. They felt cool, cooler than he recalled, but he supposed it was only because of how cold the cavern was — but the cavern was in Reygar, while he was here . . . in Hastinaga?

"Where are we?" he asked, looking around. There were windows at the far wall of the chamber, but outside, all he could see was blinding whiteness, as if nothing existed outside of his immediate surroundings, just this chamber floating in the cosmos, an island outside of time.

"It doesn't matter, son. None of this matters. What is important is that I have to tell you something very important. Something that will change your life."

"Change my life," he repeated. He looked at her. She looked just the way he remembered her from his boyhood, but on the last occasion he had actually seen her, at his wedding, she had looked older, her pretty face lined with new signs of age, her hair tinged with grains of white. How was it that she looked younger and prettier now?

"Yes. There are moments in life when we are faced with choices that determine the course of our future. This is one of those times."

He breathed in lightly. The air felt cooler too, despite the bright light and her garments, both of which suggested late spring or summer. That same mixture of odors, an amalgam of smells remembered from childhood and other odd, random odors and fragrances, all mashed together to form a peculiar concoction. "I still don't understand how I got here." He looked back over his shoulder, expecting to see the oval of crimson light through which he had stepped. There was only the doorway to his mother's chambers. In the place outside, where the sentries ought to have been, there was only the same blinding whiteness, making it impossible to see further. That was another thing odd about this place: there were no people. No maids, wet nurses, servants, guards . . . nobody. He had never known it to be so empty before. A princess of Hastinaga always had dozens of people around her, for her service and her security. "Where is everyone?"

"Never mind that, my son," she said. "Listen. We don't have much time. You must defeat Darinda."

Shvate's attention returned to her. "Darinda?"

"The king of Reygar, the commander of the city kingdom you are attempting to conquer. He is your enemy. Did you not know this already?"

Shvate frowned. "I know that Darinda is king of Reygar. But like all other Reygistani rulers, he is only a puppet. The one pulling the strings is Jarsun. He is the one I must defeat."

Princess Umber's forehead creased; she shook her head impatiently. "Jarsun is beyond your reach at present. You will have another opportunity to confront him, but now is not that time. Today the enemy you face is Darinda, and only by killing him can you achieve your victory."

Shvate absorbed this. It did make sense. If Jarsun had been present, he would have revealed himself at Reygar by now. And it was true that Darinda was king of Reygar, and thus killing him would mean victory. "Where is he?"

"He is in Reygar, but hiding from view."

"You know where he is?"

"I do."

"Tell me."

His mother made a dismissive gesture that he remembered well from his childhood. She used to make the same gesture most times when his wet nurses brought him to her chambers; he knew it meant *I don't have time for that now.* It had hurt him deeply when she made that gesture, because she was not merely dismissing the wet nurses, she was dismissing him, her son. He felt the same pain now, in his heart. But now, it made him angry.

"Before I tell you where Darinda is hiding, you have to do something for me."

So now we come to the nub. "What is it?"

She smiled at him — a sweet smile that lit up her pretty face, made his heart skip. How he had longed for such a look of love when he was a boy, how he had hoped and prayed for it; yet, for all his effort, how rarely had he actually seen such an expression on her face: almost never. But she was smiling at him now, and it was suddenly as if all those years, all that pain, all that regret, was melted away. He was a boy again, and she his mother, and she was smiling at him, she loved him, she cared about him, and all was well with the world.

"We have not spoken in a while," she said. "It has been too long. We must spend more time together. A mother and son should confide everything to one another."

They should but, when were we ever mother and son? Shvate thought. Aloud, he said, "Yes."

"You must come visit me more often. We must take our meals together as often as possible. How strange it feels to be living in the same palace together and rarely seeing you, my son."

And yet, I spent my entire boyhood alone with wet nurses and maids and servants and guards, almost never seeing you, almost never taking a meal together, and never, not once, not ever, being fed by you, by your own hands. Isn't that strange, Mother? A mother who never fed her own son?

"It is strange," he agreed.

Something of his thoughts must have shown on his face because she looked down suddenly at her hands, a pall coming over her pretty features. "I know I have not been the best of mothers. I did not spend as much time with you as I should have while you were growing. I had my own anxieties, of course: your father's sudden death, the circumstances of your conception . . . I had suffered two great shocks, one after another. It was hard for me to keep up appearances."

What does that have to do with being a mother, with loving your own son? he thought, but listened in silence.

"By the time I had recovered sufficiently, Vrath had taken you and your brother far away to the gurukul for your studies. You may not be aware of this, my son, but I was not permitted to visit you there."

Why would you travel hundreds of miles to the forest to visit me when you never once walked the thirty yards to my chambers next door to your own? Do you know how many nights I lay awake thinking you would come to say good night to me, to kiss me and put me to bed, perhaps tell me a bedtime story, tell me sweet dreams . . . Yet you never came. Not once. Not ever.

"I know you must have a great many regrets, perhaps even recriminations against me for things undone, words unsaid. Perhaps you even hate me for neglecting you during those years."

He looked away. "I don't hate you, Mother."

Was this even his mother? He had no way of knowing for certain. Then again, did it really matter? To his mind, his heart, she was his mother. That was all that mattered. People exist as much inside ourselves as they do outside of us, often long after they are gone.

She touched his shoulder. "I don't blame you if you feel harshly toward me. I know how difficult it must have been for you."

He said nothing. There was nothing to be said. Had it been difficult? *Unbearable.* Some things were beyond the capacity of words to express.

"But you are now at a crossroad, Shvate. The choice you face is crucial to your future. That is why I seek to guide you, to help you make the right choice. No mother wants to see her son fail, to squander his promise, the legacy of his birth, his heritage. You are entitled to so much, my son. It is time for you to claim it, to own it. The world is yours for the taking. You must apprehend it with both hands, or it will slip from your grasp."

He looked at her again. "I don't understand. What are we talking about now?"

"Choices, my son. Decisions. Destiny."

"Do you mean Reygar? I am here to take the city. Tell me where Darinda is hiding, and I will drag him out and fight him to the death. I will not leave without completing my mission."

Again the same dismissive gesture. "Reygar is one city, one kingdom. I am speaking of the world entire. Of wealth beyond imagining. Of power too great to be challenged. Of luxury, pleasure, sensual delights, whatever you desire, it can all be yours."

Shvate shook his head. "I still don't follow."

"Shvate, my son, you can have it all. Everything you desire. Power, glory, adulation, respect, love . . . And I shall be there at your side. We shall walk up the steps of the throne dais together, mother and son. I shall sit behind you, guiding and mentoring you through the years. You shall be Emperor of the World, and I will be the Queen Mother."

He stared at her, astonished by her passion, her intensity. He had never seen his mother display such emotion before. The Umber he had seen as a boy had been reserved, pent, silent — speaking only to vent irritation, anger, or to dismiss.

"How is all this to be accomplished?" he asked. "How does one become Emperor of the World?"

"By doing whatever it takes," she said, her eyes flashing. "By taking what is yours. By cutting out what is unnecessary."

"What does it take? What is it that is unnecessary?"

She started to speak in the same heated tone, then stopped herself. She looked down at her hands, composing herself. When she spoke again, it was still with passion, but her emotions were banked now, under control. He sensed that he had glimpsed a side of her she had not intended to reveal to him. He didn't know whether to be flattered or dismayed.

"There are things you must do, my son. The path to greatness requires sacrifice, but do not think of it as such. Think of it as necessary evils. Things that must be done. Like cutting down or burning a forest to clear a space for a city. How many animals die when you burn down the jungle? And yet, without their sacrifice, there would not be a Hastinaga. All great edifices are built on the broken backs of such sacrifices."

He began to see a glimmer of what she was leading up to. It felt like she was walking him up to the edge of a precipice, preparing him to jump. He knew exactly what she was doing: he did the same thing when making a speech to his army before going into battle. She was rallying him, priming him, preparing him to do something that he would not normally want to do. Instead of arguing the point, he chose to go along with her.

"What is this sacrifice you wish me to make, Mother? How may I achieve these ends? Tell me, what must I do to become Emperor of the World?"

She stared at him, pleased. She beamed. She was delighted that he had acquiesced without an argument. She did not know him at all, despite having birthed him over two decades ago. Had she known him well enough, she would know that he never argued, he simply found a way to get the other party to reveal all his best arguments, then simply cut him to shreds. He felt no sympathy for her lack of knowledge. Had she truly loved him, spent time with him, she would have known this. She would have known better than to try to manipulate him.

"Son, I have seen your future. There is a darkness ahead on your path. Your wives, both of them, are unlucky for you."

"My wives are unlucky for me."

"Yes! I know you love them dearly, but if you stay with them, they will lead you down dangerous byways. You will succumb to things that will not aid you in your path to greatness. They will bring you down, and keep you down."

"You know this to be true?"

"Yes. It was shown to me by . . . by someone of great power."

"What would you have me do?"

"Abandon them."

"You wish me to abandon my wives."

"Yes. You will have other wives. As many as you please. All the world's most beautiful women can be yours. They will fall at your feet."

He almost smiled at that. Mayla and Karni were not the kind to fall at his feet; they were more likely to kick him with their own. They were both proud, strong women with their own minds and self-respect. That was a large part of why he loved them so much. The thought of women falling at his feet as an appealing thing was so contrary to his own nature that it almost made him smile. But he forced himself to maintain a straight face. "Is that all?"

"That and one more thing. You must deny your brother any claim to the throne."

"I must deny Adri's claim to the throne."

"Yes. You are the elder born, yours is the first right. Besides, he is blind. A blind king can never rule Hastinaga."

What she said was not untrue — at least as far as history and custom were concerned. But that did not make it right.

"Is that all?"

"That is all. See? It is nothing really. A few minor sacrifices and everything you desire can be yours."

Shvate walked a few steps away, looking at the whiteness outside the palace. In this entire time he had been speaking with his mother, there had been no other sound or sign of another being. Just the two of them, alone in this facsimile of the palace suspended in a white limbo.

"And if I agree to do this, you will tell me where Darinda is hiding so I can kill him?"

When she did not answer, he turned to look at her.

She was looking down at her hands, staring at her open palms as if she was holding something in them. "It is not necessary to kill Darinda."

"It is not necessary to kill Darinda."

She looked up at him. "Leave Reygar, withdraw your army, return to Hastinaga."

He stared. "And the campaign? My mission?"

She shrugged. "Reygar is only symbolic. It has no strategic value to Hastinaga. Conquering it means nothing politically."

"It means that we marched into Jarsun's stronghold and dealt him a punishing blow for daring to rally our own allies against us."

She made a face. "It still proves nothing. Jarsun is not here. You cannot reach him. Merely killing one of many kings who pledge loyalty to him, taking one of a hundred cities in his vast empire, doesn't end the threat of Reygistan."

"How else to end the threat of Reygistan except to kill one king at a time, take each city, conquer his empire step by step?"

She shook her head. "You are not seeing the larger picture, Shvate. Jarsun is a powerful ally. He is of more use to you alive than dead. In any case, you will never be able to kill him. That will never happen."

"How can you be so sure? If I could reach Dirda, where he was only a short while ago, then it means I am close on his heels."

"You may nip at his heels all you want, but you will never face him in battle and win. You are no match for the God-Emperor himself."

"And you are sure of this?"

"Yes."

Shvate pursed his lips. *Enough. Time to end this charade.*

"It seems to me that you deceived me. You said first that I must kill Darinda, and that you would tell me where he was hiding so I could accomplish that task. But in reality you were only luring me in so you could manipulate me into doing what you wanted me to do all along."

Again that same gesture of dismissal. "You are still such a boy. Immature. Not just pale of skin, but pale of blood, as well. You do not have the stomach or the strength. It will take someone far stronger than you to stand against Jarsun. You are not even fit to challenge Darinda. I was wrong about you. You are every bit the disappointment I knew you were when you were born."

Shvate knew the time for words was past.

He drew his sword and strode forward.

Umber raised her head and saw him coming. Her eyes flared as he approached, and in her grey pupils he saw twin reflections of himself looming, sword raised, and in that instant, as he struck down with all his might —

4

Everything changed.

Hastinaga palace disappeared. The whiteness vanished.

His mother . . . transformed.

He was in the cave, in the exact same spot he had been in when he stepped out over the abyss. Except it wasn't a portal to another place, it was simply an artfully concealed stone bridge leading to a central platform. The bridge was cut from the same black stone as the inside of the cave. It led to a central edifice that rose from the heart of the abyss, which Shvate recognized as some manner of altar. But in place of a deity sitting atop it was a peculiarly shaped rock about eight feet high and only a foot and a half wide, resembling an unusually tall and slender man. The rock hung suspended in midair. This was the source of the light he had seen earlier, through which he had stepped into that other place where he'd conversed with the being who'd claimed to be his mother. But the rock was dark now. And he was back in the shrine in the heart of the mountain.

But he was not alone.

A man stood before him — standing exactly in the same spot as where his "mother" had been — and blocked Shvate's mighty sword thrust with a blade of his own. He was a bearded, hulking brute with large, bulging eyes, clothed in furs from head to foot, giving him the appearance of a very large animal. He snarled at Shvate and deflected his sword strike.

"Ayushmaanbhavya, son! So sad that you could not meet your actual mother. I trust I played the part well?"

He laughed then, at Shvate, and began circling the oval stone above the altar. Shvate maintained his guard, his heart and mind racing.

"Are you still trying to comprehend what is happening? What did you think? That you would march into my lord's empire and simply conquer us? We are not mere Krushan to be bullied by your tactics, Shvate. We are Reygistani. We have fought and won a thousand battles. We eat Krushan for breakfast and shit out the pits!"

Darinda — for it was he, Shvate knew with sudden surety — sprang from behind the altar, lunging at Shvate with a sideways thrust. Shvate parried once, then again after another thrust, then swung back, only to be countered by Darinda again. As they dueled, the steel of their swords rang out and echoed in the enclosed space.

"You didn't fool me," Shvate said. "I knew from the start it was not my mother."

Darinda chuckled as he thrust and then danced away, surprisingly nimble for such a large man. "I don't believe you. You drank in every word as if it would change your life. Jarsun told me how your mother neglected you as a boy. So sad, poor little Krushan prince — all alone and neglected in his great big palace."

Shvate lunged and hacked at Darinda, who dodged away in the nick of time, and Shvate's sword struck the stone wall behind the man, raising a shower of sparks. He recovered and swung around in time to parry a killing blow from Darinda, then kicked his opponent's thigh. Darinda cried out, staggering back, his face twisted.

"Took it personally, did we, Krushan boy? Don't blame me for your gullibility. You were ready to do as Ma said, weren't you?"

"I was just playing along, biding my time," Shvate said, moving sideways, sword held at the ready. "Your poor attempt to manipulate me was too pathetic to even comment on. Abandon my wives, disinherit my brother, leave you alive, depart Reygar? You were so transparent, I had to stop myself from laughing out loud at times!"

Darinda's face reflected his confusion: the Reygistani didn't know that Shvate was only able to say these things now that the illusion was dispelled. Truthfully, Shvate had come close to being duped, not by the illusion itself, but because of the weakness of his own heart. He had wanted to believe it really was his mother, to hear her speak sweetly to him, smile her pretty smile, be kind to him, express affection and love for him . . . He had needed that so badly for so long, it had made him want to succumb to the illusion, to pretend it was real. That was the evil genius of Jarsun's sorcery, not to force a person into seeing something impossible, but simply to make one believe what one *wanted* to believe.

"You lie, Krushan!" he snarled, fighting back now with less reserve. Shvate noted the limp in his opponent's right leg. That kick had struck a nerve. If he could press his advantage on that side . . . "I had you fooled! You would have done anything your mother said. All she had to do was bat her eyelashes and smile at you." A sly look came over the man's face as he sought an opening in Shvate's defenses. "Quite a pretty piece, your mother. I intend to visit her someday. Except, I don't intend to waste time pretending to be a good son! I recall that she has been widowed for a very long time. She must crave the company of a man. Do you get my meaning, Krushan boy?"

Shvate roared and swung out at Darinda, striking left, right, and then left again, each blow pressing the Reygistani a step back.

"Did I strike a sore point?" Darinda yelled. "Don't be so —"

Suddenly, a voice cut through the ringing of their swords. "Shvate, *the altar!* Strike the altar!"

Vida. Shvate couldn't see his half brother but knew he must be on the ledge, where he and Mayla had been standing before he'd stepped through the portal. Except . . . what if it wasn't actually Vida but another illusion?

"Are you sure, brother?" Shvate called back as he continued to press Darinda. The Reygistani had rallied and was pounding Shvate now with hammer-like blows. But his smile had faltered and he was scowling now again, his sword moves more desperate, as if he sought to end the fight quickly.

"Yes, the altar!" Vida shouted back.

Shvate grinned and winked at Darinda. "That's my brother, arrogant know-it-all."

Shvate turned his sword and hacked at the oval stone. As his blade struck it, Shvate felt a peculiar, dead sensation reverberate up his arm. There was no sound of impact, but it felt as if his weapon had struck something solid yet yielding, and his arm went numb for an instant. But Darinda's face went slack with horror, and Shvate looked down and saw that his blade was embedded in the empty center of the oval stone, as if buried in the body of an invisible being.

"No!" Darinda cried.

With some effort, Shvate wrenched his sword free; it took nearly all his strength. He reared back and swung again, striking at the same spot with twice as much force as before. This time he sensed that the blade bit deeper, and then felt a splash of something cold and wet on his chest and the underside of his neck.

Darinda roared and lunged at him.

Shvate released his sword, drew his short knife, and stabbed the Reygistani low, in the place beneath his ribs, pushing the blade upward, into the center of the man's chest cavity. Darinda's sword was slashing toward Shvate's neck, but it lost its momentum and clattered to the stone floor of the shrine. The life began to drain from his face, and Shvate knew he had struck the man's heart a fatal blow.

"You fool!" Darinda said as he collapsed on the altar. "The offer was real. My god would have fulfilled his promise to you. You would have had everything you desired. You would be Emperor of the World. But you . . . you . . . you *Krushan!*"

Shvate took hold of the man by the front of his furs, grasping them in his fist, and lifting Darinda bodily. "Yes. I am Krushan. To hell with your god and his devilish offer."

Shvate let the man drop back. Darinda fell against the altar, his head striking the empty space inside the oval. It made a wet sound as if striking something solid, but if there was indeed anything there, it was not visible. Just the empty oval ring of stone floating in midair — and Shvate's sword stuck in the center of its void.

A deep rumbling began from somewhere far below Shvate's feet, and a dark red glow began to seep from the oval rock — similar to the earlier crimson glow that had blazed in the cave, but a deeper red this time, and now not in pulses but in waves, seeping and ebbing, flowing and fading again . . .

"Shvate! We have to go!"

Shvate looked around. There was nothing more to be done here. Darinda was dead.

He stepped through the stone-cut entrance. The abyss yawned beneath his feet, but thanks to the crimson light behind him, he could see the stone bridge. Across the bridge, Mayla and Vida were standing, beckoning to him anxiously.

"Quickly, brother!" Vida shouted. "You have struck the heart of the city. Soon it will fall!"

Shvate started to traverse the bridge, but when he was halfway across, the entire cavern shuddered. A stone underfoot cracked, and part of the bridge collapsed into the abyss.

Shvate lost his footing and fell —

But Mayla screamed and threw herself forward, catching his hand as he fell, grabbing hold just in time. Shvate heard the thump of her body striking the ground hard, but she held on to his hand with all her strength. Shvate grunted as he struggled to gain his footing, but the side of the cavern was crumbling. The whole city was shuddering and trembling now, not like it had earlier when it was attacking the Krushan army, but as if it was standing still and shivering. He felt Mayla's grip starting to slip, and for an instant, it seemed certain he would fall into darkness, to his death.

Then Vida's hand grabbed his other hand, and Mayla changed hands to get a better grip. Together they began to pull Shvate upward, all of them straining.

"Heavy!" Mayla complained.

Shvate grinned as he came over the top and collapsed beside her. "Man muscle is heavy, my love," he said.

Mayla slapped him lightly, then kissed him. "I thought I lost you!"

"Lovebirds!" Vida shouted. "Talk less, run faster!"

They rose to their feet and began to run.

Emerging from the cave, through the squat rectangular entranceway, into the streets of Reygar, Shvate was shocked to see it was past sundown. How long had they been in there? Surely it could not have been so many hours? But time must pass differently inside one of Jarsun's illusions. He had so many questions, but now was not the time to ask them. Later, he would discuss them with Vida. Now, they had to survive — literally — the fall of Reygar.

5

Some time later, after a great deal of leaping, running madly, and vigorous climbing, Mayla, Vida, and Shvate finally stood on the desert floor again, and watched the giant city-mountain shudder one last time and then collapse like a pile of bricks, crashing down onto the desert in a gigantic heap of debris, as his army watched and cheered. As Vida blinked and grinned in relief alongside him, Shvate thought of what Darinda, impersonating his mother, had said.

You are now at a crossroad, Shvate. The choice you face is crucial to your future.

He had made his choice.

The only question was, had it been the right one?

Karni

~

THE WORLD WAS THUNDERING, and the sky was rolling.

Karni was lying on her side on a heap of fur blankets, another two furs covering her. Everything was moving, the ground was rumbling beneath her. She turned her head and saw a wall of metal. She sat up slowly with an effort and found herself in the well of her own chariot. She had been covered and padded so effectively that even if the chariot had crashed, she would have been well protected by the sheer number of furs.

She was disoriented for a moment. The last she remembered, she had been dragged down into the river's belly and drawn through some kind of portal. Or had that been some kind of . . . dream?

She rose to her feet slowly, gripping the sideboard. They were moving at a fast pace, and from the trees zipping past, she guessed that they were almost halfway to Hastinaga. She saw they were alone on the road, except for her armed escort of soldiers, who rode in front of and behind her vehicle. There was no sign of Adri and Geldry's chariot.

"Adran," she called out.

The charioteer turned his head but kept his tight grip on the reins of the horse team. He saw her standing upright and eased back on the reins, pulling the chariot off to one side. He raised his whip, waving it in the gesture that indicated to the guards that he was stopping. A moment later, he came to a halt on the side of the road. Her escort pulled over as well, resting their horses.

"Princess, you should be resting."

"I am fine, Adran."

He looked at her with concern. The lanterns on the chariot cast shadows, but she could see his face well enough. He looked at her as if afraid that she would collapse at any time.

"You should lie down, Princess. We will reach Hastinaga soon."

"What happened to me?"

He was silent for a moment. She could hear the night sounds of the forest all around, the neighing of the horses, the voices of the guards as they conversed. "You don't remember?"

"I remember going into the river for a swim. I remember swimming to the far bank, then swimming back. After that . . ." She frowned, trying to think back. Sunlight. Water. The sun low on the horizon. The cries of birds in the sky. That was it. "After that, I woke up to find myself in the chariot just now."

Adran sighed. "You should speak with the royal healers. Perhaps the drowning—"

"Drowning? What drowning?"

He looked at her.

"You mean me? I drowned? That's absurd, Adran. I'm an excellent swimmer."

He looked uncomfortable. "I found you in the river, floating on your back, unconscious. The sentries and maids had been searching for you for hours by then. At first, I thought you were—" He shook his head. "There was no water in your chest; you did not cough up or spit out any water. Yet you were deeply unconscious. It was . . . strange. I did not know what else to do, so we put you in the chariot and bundled you with furs, and I am taking you home."

Karni considered all this. "Where were Adri and Geldry?"

"Prince Adri and Princess Geldry had left for the city by the time we found you. The princess received word that her brother had arrived from Geera and wanted to meet him at once. Prince Adri sent word to you that they were leaving, but your maids could not find you. And by the time I located you in the river, they had long gone." He trailed off. "Are you sure you are well enough to stand up, Princess?"

"I feel absolutely fine." And she did, except for a ravenous hunger. She felt like she could eat a whole bull. "What were you doing by the river?"

"Huh? Oh, apologies, Princess. I was offering prayers to Mother Jeel. She has been very munificent to my wife, Reeda, and myself. We owe her so much."

She nodded. Strange that while all her maids and sentries had been searching for her, it was Adran who had found her floating in the Jeel.

"Are you sure you remember nothing else, Princess?"

She shook her head. "No." It was the truth. But somewhere at the back of her mind, there was something she felt she ought to remember. But it didn't seem connected to the river or to this day. It was something entirely different. Something to do with . . . *Shvate, and our five children.* The thought popped into her head out of nowhere. She blushed at the thought. What a strange thought. She had not had any children by her husband yet, and here she was thinking of the five of them!

Adran saw her blush but did not remark on it. He glanced around at the forest. "Princess, it is late, and we are still in the woods. The horses are growing restless. Perhaps we should be on our way?"

"What? Yes, yes, of course. Please, continue. I want to be home as soon as possible."

He nodded, relieved. This was the longest conversation they had had, or, indeed, that Karni had ever had with any charioteer.

Adran took up the reins again, giving the guards the signal that they were resuming their journey.

The familiar trundling motion of the chariot began to lull Karni again, but she knew she would not sleep again. She was still ravenously hungry. And there was something just out of reach inside her memory, some recollection of something to do with Shvate and her future sons. A warning? A threat? A prophecy?

Or all of the above.

She contemplated these strange thoughts as the forest sped by and night drew in closer around the chariot.

They raced back toward Hastinaga.

Jarsun

~

1

THE INTRUDER CAME FROM no direction and all directions.

He was spotted by a corpse-burner near the east gate, by a sentry at the north gate, by a pair of bickering lovers in a field outside the west gate, and a drunk out-of-work mercenary leaning against a pillar vomiting by the south gate.

There were other sightings too, several dozen in all, at different places: some at the city walls, mostly outside the city.

Animals sensed his coming and reacted. The war elephants in the great enclosures behind the city, thousands upon thousands of enormous beasts, battle veterans all, stirred uneasily, raising their trunks and lowing in alarm, alerting their mahouts and masters. The chariot horses whinnied and shied away from shadows. The milch cows mooed, white-eyed with panic. Dogs began barking and would not stop even when ordered by their masters. Babies cried for no reason.

Animals and children unfortunate enough to be birthed that night were either stillborn, though they had been alive and kicking only moments earlier, or expired shortly after birth of inexplicable causes. Strange winds sprang up, blowing dust dervishes into the houses of sleeping priests. Cows gave curdled milk. Chickens laid malformed eggs. A calf was born with two heads. Birds rose in great flocks from the trees where they slept at night and dashed themselves against stone cliffs, dying by the thousands. Food spoiled while it was cooking.

Hundreds of citizens fell ill, and those who were already ill and had been on the road to recovery relapsed and died. An ancient woman, said to be close to two hundred years of age, cried out the names of 107 urrkh demons before collapsing into a comatose sleep from which she never woke. Pundits and astrologers saw the star patterns alter before their very eyes, and could not explain the change of constellations. Other eldritch phenomena proliferated as well — marvels and portents that defied explanation.

This was only the beginning.

A darkness greater than night had descended on the City of Elephants and Snakes.

2

The devil walked the streets of Hastinaga.

Like all demons and gods, he was a shape shifter. He could assume any form or shape he desired. He chose to assume several, all at once, each ansh serving a different purpose, intent on individual missions.

He entered the house of a sleeping priest, stood in the simple bedchamber, and watched the elderly guru and his wife sleeping deeply. The city outside the house was restless and filled with strange sounds. The cries of elephants, horses, dogs, and cows filled the night, but in the mage's unostentatious residence, all was quiet. The old couple slumbered peacefully on their simple cots, unaware of the terror that walked the streets — or the monster that stood within reach.

The fiend reduced himself to a mist, his solid flesh melting away suddenly as if burned by acid. In moments, only fumes remained. They settled over the mage's bed, a cloud that enveloped both priest and wife. With each breath they took, they inhaled the noxious fumes. Both stirred restlessly in their sleep, their bodies sensing something amiss, but breath was life, and they could hardly cease breathing.

In moments, the entire cloud had been absorbed into their lungs, and from there, into their blood. It altered the very substance of their bodies, leaving them exactly the same in outward appearance, but changing them completely on the inside. They went to sleep as two individuals; by the time they woke next morning, they would be completely different people, with very different minds and missions. Yet to the world at large, they would appear no different.

The devil reduced himself to lumps of raw meat that lay in the street. Stray dogs caught the scent of it and slunk down to consume it. They wolfed it down hungrily, but even before it reached their bellies, they knew something was wrong. After eating, the dogs sniffed at each other uneasily, neither growling nor making any other sounds. In unnatural silence, they slunk away to dark corners, the backs of houses, the roofs or pits where they lay in troubled sleep, feverish and racked with chills, their fur sprouting hideous boils. They did not die, but they did not live either. They became . . . something else. Something Other.

Carrion birds swooped down to consume the flakes of meat that lay on the street; their fate was no better than that of the dogs. They slept on tree branches, heads tucked under their wings, racked by strange ailments. Their eyes glittered with manic light. Other birds of their own species avoided them, crying out loudly to alert their fellows of these diseased few.

One ansh of the stranger reduced himself to tiny spores that resembled those produced by flowering plants in bloom, and traveled on a breeze that blew through the city; the minuscule spores were inhaled by people as they slept.

Another ansh turned into a mist that rose up and condensed as moisture, which descended to fall into the water troughs of elephants, horses, camels . . .

In various ways, insidious and subtle, the stranger's many divisions transformed themselves into rain, smoke, clouds, mist, fog, even food, and were inhaled, drunk, or eaten by people and animals in all the different parts of the city. Some of the victims were regular citizens, some rich nobles and merchants, others were midwives, the wives of priests, ladies of the court, but many were soldiers, charioteers, mahouts, archers, war marshals, generals . . .

Through that long dark night, the evil that walked on two feet insinuated himself into the bodies and minds of the people of Krushan in a horrific number of ways.

Many other strange and unnatural things occurred that night across Hastinaga. Dark shapes moved through the night, terrible acts were committed, awful things were done that could never be undone; all night the city was racked by a series of supernatural disturbances. All night the terror held sway. Those who sensed the presence of evil locked their doors, barred their windows, and stayed indoors with their loved ones. Those foolish or ignorant enough to challenge the devil that walked the streets were quickly dispatched to the netherworld of Shima, their bodies discovered the next day, horribly mutilated, faces frozen in an awful rictus of agony. All night the terror walked through the capital city of the Burnt Empire and worked its urrkh evil.

All this was only the prelude.

The real terror was yet to come.

Geldry

~

GELDRY TOSSED AND TURNED restlessly in her bed. It was a hot summer night, and beads of sweat lay on her neck and face. She wiped them off with the back of her hand, accidentally jostling her eyeband. One side of the band shifted, allowing some light to shine into her left eye.

Without meaning to, she opened the eye to see where the light could be coming from at this late hour. It was moonlight shining directly onto her face from the sky above the open balcony. Her side of the large bed was closest to the verandah, and from her position she could see the night sky glittering with stars.

The moon was full and red, larger, brighter, and redder than she had ever seen it before. What did they call that kind of moon — a blood moon? Yes, that was it. She had heard the phrase often but had never seen a blood moon so large. It loomed like a living thing in the night sky, hanging over her verandah and painting the entire bedchamber crimson. It called to her, powerfully compelling. She felt like throwing off the bedcovers and walking out. But she could tell by Adri's breathing that he was deeply asleep; soon, he would begin to snore lightly. She reached up to pull the eyeband back over her eye, thinking she would return to sleep, but paused.

She turned her head slowly, far enough that she could see Adri. He was turned away from her, facing into the bedchamber. The moonlight only touched his back and his curled feet. Not that it would disturb him anyway: unlike some blind persons who could sense light and shapes, Adri was completely, totally unsighted. He could raise his eyes to stare up at the sun and see nothing. And now that he was in that breathing pattern, he would sleep deeply through till morning.

She exhaled soundlessly, releasing the breath through slightly parted lips to avoid making the sound that usually accompanied a sigh. She had learned to do that in the first months after her marriage. Back when she had first come to live with Adri, she would sigh often, and each time he would turn his head and ask, "Are you well, Geldry?" And so she had learned to sigh without making any sound, to cry noiselessly, to laugh silently, to live in darkness.

She reached up, touching the displaced eyeband. She had taken to wearing it since just before her wedding rituals. It had been entirely her decision, even though Jilana, Vrath, Shvate, even Adri himself had all tried to talk her out of doing it. At the time, she had been naive, adolescent, proud, idealistic; she had thought it unjust to be the wife of a blind prince and be able to see when he was deprived of sight. A good wife should share the circumstances of her husband, be they as they may. For richer or poorer, in sickness and in health ... in sight as well as blindness. The last was a logical corollary. How unfair of a wife to be able to enjoy the sights and sounds, colors, and lights of the world when her husband was deprived of those pleasures. She had vowed to wear the eyeband for the rest of her life, to share her husband's circumstances and enjoy only that which he was able to enjoy.

But she had been only sixteen when she made the vow, and the rest of one's life is a long, long time. Now, several years later, she was no longer an adolescent, nowhere near as proud and idealistic, and anything but naive.

She had accepted her life with Adri, limitations and all. She was even content, in a manner of speaking. She was the daughter-in-law of the richest family in the known world, after all. A princess of the great Burnt Empire. Tying a band over her eyes to feign blindness was not as great a disability as many people thought: unlike Adri, she could see lights, shapes, silhouettes, even through the eyeband. She could tell the difference between day and night, morning and noon. And, if she wished, she could always remove the band and simply see with her own eyes. She had taken to doing that more often lately, not always on purpose: she would wake at night and find that the band had been pushed off, either deliberately or accidentally, while she was sleeping. At such times, if Adri was still sleeping, she often left the band off till morning, always making sure to slip it on the next morning before waking up to meet the new day. At first she had felt guilty at being able to enjoy the sighted world, even for these few stolen moments, when Adri could never see anything, ever.

But as the years had passed and the reality of her situation had finally sunk into her bones, she had begun to feel resentful of that guilt. What was wrong with being able to enjoy a gift she had been born with? Even the most devoted of wives was entitled to some time off, wasn't she? Even the most dedicated workers deserved a little downtime from their day jobs. What harm was there in enjoying a few moments of sighted pleasure? She would never dream of doing it in public, or even in the presence of anyone else, most of all Adri himself. But alone in the privacy of her bedchamber late at night, where nobody could see her or know what she did, surely there was no harm in it.

She never told Adri about these stolen glimpses. She had almost told him once, when they had been in one of their rare tender moments of togetherness, but at the last instant, she had stopped herself. She decided that it was something best kept to herself.

Besides, she resented the idea that she might be expected to ask his permission to enjoy the natural pleasures of sight. It enraged her when she met someone for the first time and they expressed sympathy for her condition, assuming, as some often did, that the Krushan had insisted on her blinding her eyes in order to serve as their daughter-in-law. What nonsense! No one told Geldry what to do! She had chosen to blind her eyes of her own accord. It was her decision and hers alone. Such people would always say, *Of course, of course,* and nod sympathetically, as if they knew the truth and were only commiserating with her. So infuriating!

Why was it so difficult for people to believe that a woman would choose to live sightless in order to share her husband's condition? It was not as if she had plucked out her eyes, rendering herself permanently and totally blind. The very thought of such a thing made her squirm uncomfortably. Imagine actually putting out her own eyes! That was grotesque, monstrous. Surely not even Adri would want her to disfigure herself.

But Mother Jilana might.

The old lady was so upright and ironclad about everything, so full of Krushan pride — "Krushan this" and "Krushan that" all day long — as if the Krushan had created the whole world and built everything in it with their own hands. Geldry was a princess in her own right, and her homeland was a place to be proud of too: Geldran was a great nation, Geera a great city. Sure, they weren't Hastinaga, but in their own way, they were looked up to and admired by many nations in that part of the world.

Life was much tougher in the northwest. There was no time or resources to build great palaces and monuments to ancestors on such a scale as Hastinaga had. The City of Elephants and Snakes was truly awe-inspiring, but the Krushan had access to many more resources and governed far, far more people and kingdoms than Geldran or any other nation. Though no nation could compete with the might of the Burnt Empire, she was nonetheless proud to be a Geldran, and her name, Geldry, proclaimed that she was the first of her people, the First Spear of Geera. Yet Mother Jilana looked down at her over her long hooked nose as if she were a goat-eating, mule-riding mountain girl who knew nothing about royal etiquette and politics. It made her so mad sometimes, she wanted to scream.

But what really infuriated her was the fact that she couldn't talk to Adri about these things. That was something that was completely untenable. Adri worshipped the ground his grandmother walked on. The same went for Prince Regent Vrath. He wouldn't hear a whisper of criticism about either of them. Even when Jilana was being a big bee, buzzing and stinging Geldry's ego, Adri would refuse to discuss her. This attitude extended to almost all things Krushan, with one exception: his mother. On that one topic he was sensitive in a different way. He wanted to talk about her — even tolerated criticism of her — but only up to a point. If Geldry went so far as to call Princess Ember a "bad mother" or anything else that could be construed as an outright insult, he would grow very quiet, then walk away. Offended.

He, on the other hand, could speak poorly of Ember for hours, endlessly asking the same old questions, all of which amounted to just one really: Why? Why? Why? Why had she turned her back on him when he needed her most? Why wouldn't she show him any affection? Why was she still so cold and distant, even now? Why did he feel as if it was his fault that he had been born blind?

She was so tired of hearing about Ember, and of comforting Adri when he broke down and cried, as he almost always did during these confessional sessions.

She was tired of Adri. Of this life, their marriage, her minuscule role in the vast enterprise of the Burnt Empire.

Tired of being relegated to an insignificant decorative role: the dutiful wife of one of two princes in the line of succession, the one that was least likely to ascend the throne.

Tired of Adri's continuing descent into inactivity. When they had married, he had seemed so strong, confident, capable despite his sightlessness. The story of his exploits in the Battle of the Rebels had thrilled and inspired her. A blind prince winning a battle! Fighting and killing enemies despite his inability to see! She had imagined him leading the Krushan armies to victory across a hundred foreign kingdoms, crushing the enemies of Hastinaga, and silencing all those who dared to assume that a blind prince could not fight.

But as the years passed, the Adri she had married seemed to slip away, to shrink into a shadow of his former self. His confidence had ebbed, his strength diminished, his capacity reduced to the point where he could barely function some days. While his brother Shvate did everything that she had thought Adri himself would do: lead the Krushan armies to victory after victory, conquering the unconquerable Reygar, then going on to equally spectacular victories in Virdhh, Serapi, Anga, Trigarta, Kanunga, and a number of smaller territories.

Shvate had returned to Hastinaga with enormous wagon trains loaded with treasure, enough wealth to build a whole new empire, and to add insult and injury, he had offered all that bounty to his brother Adri. Geldry knew very well why he had done that: to show that he was the superior one. He had claimed he was offering it to Adri as a sign of respect but she took it as an insult nonetheless. Shvate was reminding Adri that he had done what Adri could never do: conquer a half dozen enemy nations and bring back five thousand wagonloads of treasure. He was asserting his superiority over his disabled shut-in brother.

Even so, Geldry's mind had leaped at the thought of so much wealth. She had swallowed the insult and been willing to accept the gift. She had already begun imagining what she could do with so much wealth at her command. This would be her personal treasure after all, unlike the burgeoning coffers of Hastinaga, which remained just out of reach to her so long as she was only the wife of a prince-in-waiting. With that much wealth, she could support her brother, Kune, in his campaign against their enemies, pay off their father's debts, rebuild the palace at Geldran that had been destroyed in the last rebellion, and fund a hundred good causes in her home nation. She had smiled at that moment, thinking that this was it, her moment of glory, when her years of patience and self-enforced blindness would come finally to fruition, when she would come into her own, a rich powerful benefactress dispensing gold to whom she pleased, when she pleased. She had even pictured herself riding in a great white carriage in the hills of Geera, overseeing the building of great monuments to her ancestors, using her wealth to benefit her people — and punish her enemies.

But even that dream had come crashing to a halt.

Adri had refused Shvate's offering, had joined his palms and told his brother that he could not accept the treasure as it rightly belonged to Vrath, the elder of the house. He had asked Shvate to take it to Vrath and offer it to him with humility and grace.

Geldry had been so shocked at hearing Adri speak those words to his brother she had wanted to grab her husband's arm and say, *What are you doing? Take the treasure!* She had not actually said those words — or anything — aloud, for Adri had already spoken, and his brother was already agreeing with him, saying that Adri was a true Krushan, respectful of his elders and adhering to Krushan law.

To hell with Krushan law! To hell with respecting elders! Geldry thought. She had wanted to tear off her eyeband right then and there and give her husband and her brother-in-law a piece of her mind.

But she didn't — she had somehow restrained herself. Even so, Mother Jilana had seen her trembling and misunderstood her condition.

"Daughter, are you well?" she had asked, then told the maids to accompany Geldry to her chambers as she appeared to be fainting.

Geldry had gone with the maids, not because she was fainting or ill, but because she had been sick with rage. How could Adri have made such a decision without even discussing it with her first? How could he refuse a fortune of that magnitude without even asking her opinion? What would Vrath do with all that wealth? He already had a hundred times, no, a thousand times that much in the coffers of Hastinaga. He was the true emperor of Krushan in all but name, and he didn't even use his power for his own needs. What a waste!

The Krushan didn't need more treasure; they were already the richest family in the world. But to Geldran, those five thousand wagonloads would have meant a historic change of fortune. Geldry could have done so much with it, for the Geldrans, for Geera, for her father, her brother, her sisters . . . and yes, for herself too. So what if she used some of the gold for her own purposes? She had equal right to it, did she not? Wasn't Krushan property supposed to be matriarchally owned and held? And she was the matriarch of Adri's house, and thus should have received that treasure.

After that day, her relationship with Adri had soured. She had never completely forgiven him. She had confronted him afterward, and he had seemed shocked by her anger, her outburst. That had enraged her even more. How could he not understand her emotions? She had a right. She had a claim to that wealth. Yet he had treated her like she didn't even matter. And so it was then that she saw it was true what they said of the Krushan, that they were totally male-dominated, women-suppressing . . . just like so many other nations, despite their claims to the contrary.

"*Geldry . . .*"

She started. In an instant, she removed the eyeband and looked around the room, seeking the source of the whisper. No conscious thought went into it; her hand simply snatched the band off her head. Her right eye was blurry from being shut for so long, and so she rubbed it with her knuckle, trying to clear her vision. Despite the bright moonlight streaming in from the verandah, there were pools of darkness across the large bedchamber. The lavish furnishings, mirrors, statuary, art, and pillars produced multiple reflections, shadows, dark corners. A dozen people could be lurking in those shadows, and it would be impossible to see them unless one walked right into them — or they walked right out.

She swallowed, her throat suddenly as dry as old leather. The palace was strongly guarded, the princely chambers formidably so. There were a hundred thousand of Krushan's finest permanently garrisoned in the city precincts. Only a handful of assassins had ever dared attempt ingress to the royal chambers: none had survived beyond the entrance. Those blackguard efforts had all come decades ago, long before Vrath's time. Under his reign, there had never been any such attempt; the rumor was that those who even spoke of such things were executed on the spot. Hastinaga had a no-tolerance policy when it came to treason and assassination: simply discussing it was grounds for execution. Even the kusalavya bards who composed and sang epic ballads to entertain the populace sang of Hastinaga being "anashya," literally unconquerable, or unassailable.

"*Geldry...*"

She gasped. She had heard it distinctly this time. A whisper calling her name.

She rose from the edge of the bed where she had been sitting and looked around the large chamber. There was no sign of movement, no sign of life. The air was so still, so humid, sweat beads continued to form on her forehead, face, and neck. She felt a trickle of sweat roll down her back. She took a step forward, her vision finally clearing sufficiently for her to see normally. There! Over by the far window, a movement. She took another step forward and saw the shadow make a corresponding move.

She gritted her teeth in frustration.

It was her own reflection, visible in the polished metal surface of the mirror she used to examine herself after her bath each day: the eyeband always got wet and slipped off anyway, so she had taken to removing it before her bath and then replacing it with a fresh one afterward. Sometimes, she was slow to replace it, taking her time examining her own reflection in the mirror, before and after dressing herself: slender, tall, shapely, strong. A fine Geldran figure. A warrior's figure, but also a queen's. Words like "stately," "elegant," "sensual," and "alluring" had been used to describe her by the fire-singers, the roving itinerants who sang for their supper in the rough hills of her homeland. Unlike the kusalavya bards of Krushan, the fire-singers used ribald, lusty language and didn't hesitate to speculate in their songs. She had heard a song about herself that had almost made her blush once — and it was hard to make a Geldran blush, so that was saying something.

The things the fire-singers had said about her — that she was a warrior-princess who loved as lustily as she fought, that the bedroom and the battlefield were both her playgrounds, that men were her rivals and her lovers both at once . . . Those verses, so evocatively described — forcefully sung by the light of a roaring fire on a cold winter's night high in the wild mountains, with a belly full of goat mutton and liquor — came to her now. She was that Geldran. Not merely the blind wife of a blind prince of Krushan. She was a warrior and a conqueror, in a long line of warrior-conquerors. She did not fear shadows at night, or whispers in the dark.

"Geldry..."

She spun around. The whisper had come from behind her. She was sure of it this time. From the verandah.

She started forward, but stopped. *Weapon.* She needed something to defend herself with if it was an intruder.

In Geera, no one was ever without a weapon. Here, in Hastinaga, she had been dismayed to learn that princes and princesses did not arm themselves within the city's walls. According to Mother Jilana, to do so would suggest that they were afraid. *To hell with fear,* Geldry thought, *what about self-defense?* When they had tried to remove her cache of weapons, some of them historical relics handed down over generations, she had almost thrown a fit. Her sister-in-law Karni had come up with a diplomatic solution: keep the weapons in her chambers but mount them as displays. Art. The idea was ridiculous, but there they were, her grandmother's sword and her great-aunt's stabbing dagger, tastefully mounted on marble stands and in velvet cases.

She stood on tiptoe and took down both the sword and the dagger. Now armed, she turned back to the verandah, ready to face whatever threat lay in wait in the moonlight.

Karni

~

THE STONE TEMPLE STEPS felt cold and damp to Karni's bare feet. She could feel the grain of the stone, the pitted and dimpled surface worn away by rain and the elements over time. She held her garment up with one hand to avoid it trailing on the wet stone and getting soiled, and her prayer offerings in the other hand. The light from the torches set at intervals was unnecessary: the moon alone was bright enough to illuminate her way.

This was the oldest temple in the region, said to have been instituted by the great Kr'ush himself, founder of the dynasty. Unlike the newer, more ostentatious temples with their marble pillars and vaulting facades in the richer parts of the city, this ancient shrine was barely visible from the narrow dirt path which was the only way in. Aboveground it looked like nothing noteworthy, just another small ancient shrine, its black stone stippled with age, moss, lichen, and flowers. It sat in a small grove whose trees crowded in so densely, they almost blocked out the city around it. Though within the city precincts, it was surrounded on three sides by thickly wooded or scrubby areas, foraging grounds and preserves which were meant to be filled during times of siege. It was like a little forest within the heart of the city, and once you entered the grove where the shrine reposed, you could almost forget you were the greatest metropolis in the known world.

That was one of the reasons why Karni liked coming here: it felt secluded, remote, private. Especially now, at this late hour, on a day which was neither a day of festivity nor of fasting, there was barely a soul here. Most of the city's residents performed their rituals at their own local neighborhood shrines, usually dedicated to the more popular deities. The few large temples that attracted greater numbers on festive days were in the more

populous areas of the city. A small industry of flower sellers, priests, acolytes, craftsmen, even prostitutes and sellswords, always gathered around
any large place of worship, making those areas the most crowded parts of
Hastinaga. Over the centuries, this small unimpressive-looking shrine had
fallen out of favor with the more fashionable, leaving it without the usual
infrastructure most temples enjoyed. Karni brought her own flowers, which
she had freshly plucked with her own hands from a field nearby, and was
carrying them in a fold of her garment.

She had left her sandals in the chariot. At her request, Adran waited on
the dirt track while she walked the several dozen yards to the stone steps.
The structure visible aboveground was only the top of the temple; the actual
shrine was below ground level, because that was where great Kr'ush had
discovered the stone effigy of the deity buried in the ground. Or so the story
went.

She reached the first underground level. From here, she could still see
the surface, the tops of trees, the large blood moon looming in the sky, and
hear the distant sounds of the city. There was something strange about the
night: odd sounds and disturbances, packs of dogs barking or fighting for no
reason, other animal cries and even screams and shouts. She didn't pay it too
much attention; her attention was directed inward.

That was why she had come here to this favorite shrine: the troubles of
the world at large were too overwhelming for her to deal with; it was hard
enough dealing with one life's problems; she couldn't begin to understand
how one dealt with the problems of an entire city-state, a kingdom, an empire. Even as a girl, that part of queenship had never attracted her. As the
wife of a future king of Hastinaga, she knew she ought to take more interest
in the complex, layered nuances of Krushan politics, but for the life of her
she could not bring herself to even feign interest in such matters.

Shvate was not unlike her. A man of action, he was always happier wielding a sword rather than a scepter. Even now, he was away in Hastinaga Forest, hunting with Mayla. They had both asked Karni to accompany them,
and on the previous such trip, she had gone along. But she hadn't been inclined this time and had begged off. Mayla had been more disappointed
than Shvate; she had enjoyed their woman-to-woman talks by the campfire
during that last hunting trip. Karni had as well, but she enjoyed her time
alone even more. She knew they would enjoy their time alone together as

well: they'd be hunting and drinking and feasting—and yes, making love
—lustily through the night and day, enjoying their time to the fullest.

That was fine with her; she loved Shvate for his physicality, his ability to
get to grips with anything without a fuss, just as she loved Mayla's quick wit
and even quicker hand. She missed both her husband and her sister queen
while they were away, but also needed time to herself. As she always said
to Mayla, only half jokingly, "Better we're apart for a while and miss one
another, than stay together all the time and grow fed up with each other."

Right now, as she continued to descend the stone steps to the second underground level of the temple, she was content to be alone. The moonlight,
the late hour, the solitude of this place, the cool, wet stone underfoot, the
ancient shrine, these things were immensely comforting. She had been uneasy in the palace. There were strange sounds from the city, peculiar odors
in the air. And there was that awful blood moon hanging low in the sky, as
if some gigantic red-eyed demon had opened an eye in space and was looking down malevolently upon Arthaloka with malicious intent. The air had
been too still, filled with strange whispers and distant echoes. She had felt so
uneasy in the palace, alone without Shvate and Mayla, and it was too late to
go to Mother Jilana's chambers, so she had sent for Adran, apologizing for
troubling him at this late hour.

"You need never apologize to me, my princess," he had said graciously, "I
live to serve."

"Thank you," she had said. "I wish to go to the temple."

He had taken up the reins as she got into the chariot. He knew which
temple. It was he who had suggested this shrine in the first place, telling her
at the time that it was the oldest of its kind in Hastinaga. He drove her without further conversation, and when they arrived, he had only requested that
she bring him a little prasadam for his wife and son. Charioteers, like most
lower castes, were not permitted entry into most temples, but there was no
prohibition against high castes sharing their sacramental sweetmeats with
their servants. "With pleasure," she had said, meaning it.

Karni arrived at the second level of the temple. This was almost fifteen
yards belowground. Only the sky above was visible here, glowing with the
eerie light of that ungodly moon. For a moment, she thought she heard faint
screams from the city and paused to listen. But there was only the sound
of water trickling somewhere, and a silence so absolute, she could hear ev-

ery whisper and tinkle of her own garments and jewelry when she moved. Similar to the upper level, it was a large square hollow carved from solid stone, with a smaller square space carved out for the shrine in the heart of the complex.

She approached the entrance of the shrine, paused to touch the bell above the carved stone doorway, sounding it once. The brass voice sang out, enveloping her with echoes. She loved the way the tone of the bell resonated in her chest; she could feel it in the bone cage that surrounded her heart, could feel it penetrate to her heart itself. It calmed something deep within her soul, brought a sense of tranquility she had been craving all day, perhaps all her life.

She shut her eyes, joined her palms together, and uttered the sacred syllable: "*Auma . . .*"

The resonance of the bell merged with the sacred word, filling her with such an exquisite sensation of bliss, she smiled involuntarily. She opened her eyes, amused and a little embarrassed at herself for smiling at worship, but it felt so right. She felt peaceful, at ease.

The stone shrine set into the ground had been carved from a single solid block of black rock. Adran had told her that the great Krushan had put his finest craftsmen to work, cutting the stone monolith, carving out doorways, windows, interior spaces. They had done a magnificent job. The shrine itself was small, barely enough inside for two persons to walk around the central square where the sacred fire resided, but it was beautiful in its very simplicity and perfection. Karni experienced a sense of bliss here that she had never found in the largest, most popular temples.

She stepped over the wooden threshold and into the temple. It was dark here, the stone-cut interior dimly lit by little clay lamps set against the walls. There was no wind to disturb the clay lamps here, and the flames stayed steadfast, but the black stone seemed to absorb their light, leaving only just enough for her to make her way forward a few steps at a time. She bowed to Gnash, in his auspicious place on the right after entering, then to the other deities in turn, spending an appropriate amount of time with each one, before finally moving to the rear of the space. She paused to light the clay lamp in her offering plate before moving on.

Another flight of steps cut spirally into the stone led down to the next, lowermost level. She climbed slowly, careful to hold her garment out of the way and her thali close to her body to avoid jostling it against the curving wall as she descended. The stairs seemed to go downward for longer than she remembered, the only light coming from her clay lamp, which, being on top of her offering plate, only illuminated her own face and the wall above her. She had to feel her way by touch, stepping very carefully and slowly. She wondered how tall, largely built persons were able to navigate these stairs. She couldn't imagine someone like Vrath making his way down them.

She finally felt the flat stone floor of the lowermost level under her bare foot and exhaled the breath she'd been holding. She was not claustrophobic by nature, but there had been an instant when she'd thought the stairs might go down forever, without any end, and the idea had been nightmarish. She paused and turned to glance up, convinced that there had been at least twice as many stairs this time as on her last visit, but the diya's feeble light only showed the curving wall and a few yards of winding stone steps. The rest merged into the black stone ceiling above her, indistinguishable in the dimness.

She sighed and adjusted her garment to cover her head again: it had slipped down to her shoulders during the descent. Her bangles tinkled softly, sounding very loud in the silence of the temple, echoing in the emptiness. Usually there was a priest or two around, or at least an acolyte, but thus far, she hadn't seen a soul since she had entered the temple. *Perhaps there will be someone at the main deity's altar,* she thought, and continued walking.

The floor and ceiling sloped gradually downward, leading to the main shrine. The stone felt cold to her bare feet, but at least it wasn't wet, just a little damp. She ducked her head below the overhang before entering the main shrine, then passed through.

She blinked, her eyes adjusting to the much brighter light. The chamber felt larger and seemed better lit than on her previous visits. There were clay lamps on every surface. On the floor, the ledge that ran along the floor, the little nooks where smaller effigies were placed, on the raised stone square around the sacred fire, behind the sacred fire, and on the floor of the alcove inside which the main deity was placed. *There must be hundreds of clay lamps in this one chamber,* she thought, awed by the spectacle. It was quite beautiful, and inspiring too. She wondered if there was a reason for the lights. Was there a local festival that she had forgotten? Then she recalled the blood moon and wondered if perhaps that had something to do with it.

There was no priest here that she could ask. Not a single priest, not even an acolyte was present. Where had they all gone? It was quite unusual for the sacred fire to be untended, and even the main deity itself to be unwatched.

Whatever the reason, she was here now. The only option she had was to traverse the corridor, climb all the way up the spiral stone staircase, walk up the steps to the surface level and then search for a priest. She had seen nobody there when she began her descent, so returning that way might be all for naught. And it would be rude — even inauspicious — to leave here without praying. Since she had come all this way, she may as well perform her prayer and worship.

The items in her thali had been jostled a little during the long descent. She adjusted them, adjusted her head covering as well, then moved around the shrine, offering prayers to each deity in the correct order.

She reached the carving representing Goddess Jeel and knelt down, putting the steel plate on the floor so she could genuflect. Her forehead touched the stone floor just hard enough that she could feel her skull make contact. The stone felt oddly warm to her skin despite the overall chill of the underground shrine. Perhaps it was because of the clay lamps, she thought. It had felt cold the last time she was here. But now, as she kept her forehead in contact with the floor and recited the sacred syllable, her head began to burn from contact, fever hot.

"Auma . . ."

She forced herself to keep her head on the floor till the last vibrations dissipated from her chest.

"Karni . . ."

She started. Her head rose an inch before striking the floor again. The impact jarred her head, making her eyes water.

She raised her head and looked around. Except for the clay lamps and the deities, there was nothing else there.

She rose to her feet in a single motion, leaving the pooja thali on the floor where she had set it down. She turned around in a complete circle, still remaining in place before the deity. It was a relatively small chamber, only about five yards by five yards, a perfect square. She could see every corner of the chamber, even the nooks in which the deities were placed.

There was no question: she was alone in the shrine.

"Karni . . ."

She gasped, the sound very loud to her ears.

"Who . . . ?" she asked uncertainly. "Who said that?"

The silence grew, looming around her like a living thing. She was suddenly aware that she was deep within the earth, at least twenty or thirty yards underground, maybe more. If the shrine was indeed empty, as it seemed, then there was no one here to call to, to ask for help. The closest person aware of her presence was the charioteer Adran, and he was all the way up there by the gates with his chariot, almost fifty yards from the shrine itself. There was not the slightest chance that he would hear her if she were to call for help, or even if a hundred Karnis were to call for help from down here. She felt the weight of the stone around her, above her, pressing down with its tons of weight, pressing in from all sides, closing in. She was alone underground in a stone cave, and no one to help within hearing distance. She felt the cold, wet stone chill in her bones and shivered. A scream began to grow inside her throat, threatening to burst loose, but instead —

"Enough." The sound of her own voice in this sacred empty space was unexpectedly loud. "Enough, Karni," she said. "Get a hold of yourself."

She was in the shrine of her deity, the most sacred and blessed place in all of Hastinaga.

No harm could come to her *here*, of all places.

It didn't matter if she was alone, if there was nobody within earshot or eyesight, if she was fifty or a hundred or a thousand yards underground, if there were a ton of stone above her or a thousand tons. She was in the shrine of her goddess, and nothing could touch her here. How could she even think that she could be harmed? She was safer here than in her own chambers in the palace, safer than anywhere else in all Hastinaga. This was the place she came to when she sought protection, where she had recited the Goddess Kavach, the ritual mantras asking the goddess for a shield of protection. The Goddess Kavach that protected her from all evil, all harm, all adversity. How could she even think that she could be harmed in this of all places, this place where the devi's power was the strongest, when she stood within the heart of the devi's sanctum itself. Before the goddess herself!

Karni put her palms together. Her hands were rock steady, her breathing calm and measured.

She turned and bowed her head low, touching it to the base of the alcove, the foot of the devi's altar. The stone here was warm, the hard stone meeting her forehead and skull gently enough that it may as well have been made of wool, not rock. She said the requisite incantation of greeting, then raised her eyes slowly to the deity herself.

What she saw there stopped her breath, paused her heart, silenced her voice, and stilled her very soul.

Geldry

~

THE MOONLIGHT WAS TOO bright for Geldry's dark-adapted eyes.

She blinked and lowered her head as she stepped out onto the balcony, unable to look directly into the glare. It beamed down and seemed to her as fiercely bright as sunlight at noon, turning the edges of her vision white. Too bright. Had her vision become impaired somehow? She had never seen moonlight this bright before. It dazzled her and turned every reflective surface into a glittering spark. She actually felt the brightness searing her eyes, burning out the periphery of her view. She found it hard to keep her eyes open at all. For the first time in several years, she missed her eyeband; it would have protected her from this blinding white radiance. But the strip of silk was back in the bedchamber, lying on the bed . . . and there was danger lurking here on this verandah; she had heard the whisper coming from here, she was positive.

"Geldry . . ."

She spun around, sword in one hand, dagger in the other. The dagger was held point downward, the sword up and sideways in a defensive posture. She moved diagonally, taking care to keep turning a little each step, in case danger sprang from behind.

Initially, she saw nothing, but then — *there.* A shadow loomed at the far end of the verandah. It was a dark shape, clothed in black flowing garb. Wind pressed the robes against its tall, slender form, outlining an unmistakably masculine body; the same wind also set the sand underfoot to dancing, rising and falling in gentle waves.

Wind? Sand? Here, on her verandah, in Hastinaga? That was impossible.

The closest desert or sandy beach was hundreds of miles from here. She blinked and squeezed her eyes shut, then opened them again.

The figure was still there, limned by moonlight, a mysterious silhouette enveloped from head to foot in flowing dark robes, contrasting sharply with the white sand dunes that rolled for endless miles behind him. The wind was so strong that the corners of his garment fluttered and flapped. The wind was blowing away from her, but she could smell the desert and the striking male odor of the man.

She looked to her left and saw the city laid out before her like an embroidered carpet. Even at this late hour, a smattering of lamps still shone across the metropolis, a few smaller ones moving through the streets, most still and illuminating crossroads, avenues, streets. Beyond them, miles away, the far high walls of the outer perimeter, marking the boundary of Hastinaga, the first defense against threats from outside. But there were no walls to guard anyone from the threats that rose inside the city. We are all vulnerable to the enemy within, no matter how, when, or where we might be. It was true of emperors, kings, and queens — it was true of all living beings.

Geldry knew that what she was experiencing was supernatural in nature. But was it an attack, and if so, by whom?

She glanced back at her bedchamber, saw Adri had not stirred. The room itself was vast and ornate, a mansion by any definition. Every luxury available on Arthaloka at her disposal. The power and might of Hastinaga, of the entire Burnt Empire. The bed, spacious enough for a dozen to sleep on, where she and her husband slept together. She could just make out the rumpled covers on her side of the bed, closer to the balcony. The glare of the moonlight was so harsh, it blurred out the far side of the bed. She could not see Adri's sleeping form. But he must be there, must he not? When he awoke, the first word out of his mouth was always "Geldry?" Just so, with the question at the end. What was the question? she often wondered. She knew now. It was his way of asking if she was still there, still with him, still in his life.

She turned again and looked straight ahead, compelling herself to see clearly now.

You are on the verandah.

You will see the length of the balcony in front of you, almost thirty yards long, the length of your bedchamber. The verandah runs along the eastern wall of your bedchamber, letting in the light of the rising sun each morning.

In a few hours, it will be daybreak, and the sky will lighten in shades of vermilion, saffron, and haldi yellow. Adri will awaken and say your name. You will answer, and he will smile, reassured.

You will slip on your eyeband and reenter the world of darkness. His world.

And the day will pass, like a thousand days before now, with you always by his side, through the day, listening, being, existing.

Blind loyalty, they call it. That is what your life is now, Geldry. Blind loyalty to a blind husband. See it and nothing else: see it, Geldry.

Now she looked at the verandah and saw something else entirely. She saw a desert of white sand, rolling in waves like a vast ocean. She saw grains of sand dancing and whirling in the wind, dunes undulating and shifting like waves on that vast ocean. She saw three moons in the sky, two wholly visible, one only partially visible: one was red, the other was saffron tinged with red, the third was sickly yellow with patches of green and blue. The moons were different sizes and in different positions in the deep crimson sky.

Closer, a tall, darkly robed man, his features obscured by a flap of his headcloth, fluttering in the wind across his face. A sense of immense strength and vast, supernatural power, the kind of strength that could not be achieved by mere muscle, bone, and sinew. A head as thin and lean as the body it rested on, a sense of a face as thin and long as a hatchet blade. And in the deep shadows beneath the headcloth and cowl, two eyes glittering like hot diamonds.

"Geldry..."

She heard the word clearly now, no longer a whisper but as distinct as if the man were standing right there on the verandah ten or twelve yards from where she herself stood.

Except he was not on there on the verandah, not in the palace, not in Hastinaga, the Burnt Empire, or anywhere else upon the planet. He was somewhere else. Someplace where the sand was as white as driven snow, three moons hung in the sky, and strange alien beasts roamed the unpeopled world. She was certain of this as she had never been certain of anything else before.

The figure raised a robed hand to her.

"Come . . . see . . ."

She drew in a deep breath, clutching her weapons tightly. They were of no use to her, she knew. She could no more fight that being standing on the white sand than she could fight an army single-handed. His power burned from those diamantine eyes, as searing and dazzling as the moonlight. But it gave her comfort to hold the weapons, feel her grandmother's sword and her great-aunt's dagger, to recall the stories she had heard about their exploits, the lives taken by these two blades, the hot blood spilled, the flesh torn, the bones shattered . . . It was power of its own sort, the kind of power that she understood, she owned. The power to take a life with a single thrust or slash. To end an enemy, or silence a rival.

The being summoning her now was possessed of power far, far greater than any mortal weapon. He was capable of facing — and crushing — entire mortal armies. Of battling beings she could not even comprehend, of challenging gods and demons and holding his own against those otherworldly beings.

He was calling to her, inviting her. Not to kill, or to harm. But to show her something. To share something with her that she had never seen before. That she could never see otherwise. All she had to do was step forward, into his world, wherever that might be.

And see.

Her heart leaped. With guilt as well as joy. The guilt was because she was so tempted. To *see*. To do the one thing her husband could not do. The joy was for the same reason: to see because she *could*; Adri had nothing to do with it. She was her own person; her life was hers to rule. She had given him her entire existence, bound her eyes to darkness out of loyalty, accepted his every choice, concurred with his every decision, obeyed his every word. Surely she had earned the right to do this: to explore the wonders of an alien world even if only for a short while. To see things that no mortal being had seen. A place where no mortal had gone before.

It was only seeing. And yet, it was *seeing*. It was both the worst betrayal of all, and no betrayal at all.

She made her decision.

She stepped forward. One step, then another, then another . . .

Suddenly, the cool stone of the verandah floor vanished and her bare foot stepped onto powder-soft sand.

She gasped and took an involuntary step back — and her foot came down on the cool verandah floor again.

She collected herself quickly and stepped forward again, onto sand, and stood that way for a moment, between worlds, between lives, between stone and sand.

She started to look back, turning her head to the right instinctively, to look at the bed, seeking one last glimpse of her sleeping husband —

But stopped herself.

No more, Geldry. This is your life, your choice. He has nothing to do with it.

The words came from within, her own mind. The tall, dark figure before her was silent, waiting expectantly. She gritted her teeth and stepped forward.

She walked on powder-soft sand, felt the kiss of a strangely pleasant desert wind, smelled odors she had never smelled before, under a sky with three moons and a deeply crimson hue.

She walked toward a tall stranger clothed in dark robes waiting for her. He smiled, his eyes glinting like rubies in the darkness. She felt his power even from a distance, the sheer strength of his aura, his presence.

"Come, Geldry, let me show you what you have been missing all your life, what you have been seeking."

"Yes," she said, and walked toward him.

Karni

~

KARNI STARED AT THE goddess.

Not an effigy of the goddess. Not a stone carving. Not a statue. Not an image or reflection.

The goddess herself.

Goddess Jeel stood in the alcove before her.

She glowed so brightly that Karni could barely stand to look directly at her. The brilliance forced her to avert her eyes downward and look upon the goddess only peripherally, but it was sufficient: she could see the beauty of Goddess Jeel, her flawless perfection, her features like water, rippling and shimmering, diamond-sharp, crystal-bright. She shimmered and shone like a liquid sun, like the moon risen from Arthaloka, like a celestial body carved out of pure energy.

There were no words to truly describe her: these were only weak approximations of her greatness. Anything Karni thought or said in an attempt to describe her power would be but a feeble effort, stick figures drawn to represent an image of impossible complexity. There were dimensions and shades and levels of detail to the deity's persona that Karni's mind could not wrap itself around. She could barely stand to glance at the goddess obliquely, through her upraised eyes, so fierce was her aura, her power, her energy; it compared to the one previous divine sighting Karni had experienced in her life — but unlike Sharra, whose effulgence was blindingly, dazzlingly bright, like the sun at noonday, Jeel Ma's aura was cooling, soothing, and calming as the waters of the Jeel River itself.

The difficulty that came in viewing her was not due to the intensity of the light alone, but due to the fact that Karni knew she was looking at a god, at a divine supernatural presence, and as such, the goddess was not made of mere flesh, blood, bone, and skin. She shimmered like a glacier in the highest peaks of the Coldheart Mountains, an ice sculpture with impossible definition, and layers of detail that could not be fully appreciated by human eyes.

Karni ... said the goddess.

Her given name drifted like a cool mist to Karni's ear, dissipating till it seemed like a memory rather than a spoken word.

You are in grave danger.

Karni kept her head lowered, her eyes cast downward, but her heart quickened.

There is a force of evil in Hastinaga that seeks to destroy you and everything you hold dear.

Karni's pulse fluttered. She wanted to exclaim, to react, to ask questions. But she knew better. If the goddess willed it, Karni would ask her questions later, but for now, she understood that she was meant to listen quietly and pay heed. This was a sacred moment, a blessed opportunity. That was why the shrine was deserted, why she was alone. She had come for darshan, and she was literally being given a darshan of the goddess.

This evil force is afoot in the city tonight. It means to cause you grave harm. Already, it is poisoning hearts and minds, sowing the seeds of evil in a thousand unfortunate victims. It has chosen its time astutely. It waited until it knew my son Vrath would be away.

The water that formed the goddess's face churned, revealing the currents of anger that underlay her words, and Karni pressed a hand against her chest, releasing a small gasp. Of course! Vrath was away in Mraashk on an important matter concerning her own brother. She had wanted to accompany him, but both he and Mother Jilana had refused firmly, saying it was too dangerous in Mraashk. Her heart was in turmoil from all the terrible news she had been receiving from her homeland of late: some of it was horrendous, particularly the stories of the usurper Sanka's cruelties. But she knew that they were right to stop her from going: the moment she set foot on Mraashk soil, she would immediately become a potential pawn in the larger political game. The usurper Sanka would like nothing better than to take her hostage and blackmail her adoptive father into ending Stonecastle's resistance to his misrule, as well as to torment her birth parents by holding her captive. She had agreed only for these reasons, but a part of her wanted to pick up a sword and go fight alongside her people who were suffering under the yoke of Sanka's tyranny. It was partly the reason why she had come here tonight, to seek Jeel's blessings and ask her to help end the terror in Mraashk soon.

Vrath is one of only two individuals who possess the power to stop this demon tonight, but even if I summon him from Mraashk and assist him in a speedy return, he cannot reach Hastinaga in time.

One of only two . . . ? Had Karni misheard, or had the goddess implied there was another demigod in Hastinaga? Everyone knew that Vrath was the son of Jeel, possessed of incredible superhuman powers. But who was this *other* celestial being?

Perhaps it is too soon. He is very young to confront this artful demon. I hesitate to ask him to shoulder such a responsibility. If he were my son, I would not think twice, but he is not.

Karni frowned. She was having a hard time following Jeel Ma's line of thought here. She sensed that the goddess was looking at her now, her watery features more composed, though the tide continued to swirl behind her. What was it the goddess expected of her?

Karni . . .

The word was as soft as water, as delicate as dew. The living waters susurrated, gurgling and churning. Karni sensed that the goddess was trying to find the right words to express herself. Why a *goddess* would be cautious about choosing her words when speaking to a mere human, Karni had no idea.

Sometimes we must sacrifice that which is dearest to our hearts to ensure the survival of those we govern. It is the burden of queenship, just as it is the burden of godliness. I loved Vrath's father dearly, more than anything else in the world, yet I had to abandon Sha'ant when the time came. Later, I had to surrender my only begotten son, Vrath himself, to fulfill my promise to Sha'ant and the people of Hastinaga. I set my son to protect this kingdom, and he continues to fulfill his solemn duty, devoting himself completely to the task. He has even forsworn the joy of love and all physical pleasures, committing to lifelong celibacy. What mortal could sacrifice and serve as he has?

That is what it means to be a god or a demigod. All this power, and yet when the time comes, we must use it in service of our devotees; otherwise, what use are we as gods? This is what distinguishes us from demons. They too have great powers, often greater than our own, yet they use them only in service to their own selfish ends. They use them to dominate, torment, tyrannize, torture, murder, commit genocide, perpetrate unspeakable cruelties.

The urrkh that walks the streets of Hastinaga tonight, perpetrating atrocities and evil mischief, is the vilest of the vile, a master of destruction, a bringer of chaos. He means to uproot the very heart of the kingdom, to lay waste to all the good that the Krushan dynasty has done over the years. To poison the well of mortalkind itself. To sow war, rebellion, pestilence, disease, famine, drought, toxic airs and fluids — and these are only his most visible weapons. It is those unseen that are the most insidious. He uses evil methods tonight that cannot be easily stopped or undone except by the most extreme means possible. He is poisoning the very heart of Hastinaga.

And. He. Must. Be. Stopped.

These last five words resounded throughout the underground temple, setting every bell vibrating, jarring even the innermost crevices of Karni's hearing, drenching her with a mist of pure rage. She kept her head lowered and hands joined, but she trembled nonetheless. She didn't fully understand: was the goddess angry with her somehow? These were awful, terrible revelations. Far more than she could have ever wanted to know. Why was the goddess sharing these truths with her? What could she, Karni, possibly do against an urrkh so powerful and dreadful? She kept her head bowed and trembled in helpless confusion.

Karni!

The word resounded like a slap across her face. It assaulted Karni's ears and penetrated into her deepest core. She shivered, feeling the glacial anger of Mother River seep into her heart.

Do what must be done. Mothers, queens, goddesses must surrender their sons for the greater good. You must sacrifice your most precious creation, as did I. Do it before it is too late and the damage is irreversible. Do it now to save Hastinaga and ensure the safety of your own future offspring. It is the only way.

And as suddenly as she had appeared, the goddess began to dissipate, her watery form dissolving into a torrent that bled away into the nooks and crannies and crevices of the rock itself, melting away into the black stone, disappearing from sight and sound. Yet even as the goddess vanished, she called out one last time, whispering a final missive:

When he has done his part, call on me, and I shall come to cleanse the city.

And once again, Karni was left alone in the temple of Goddess Jeel, her garments drenched, her body icy cold and shivering, her senses reeling with the sheer weight of the knowledge and responsibility that had been thrust upon her.

Adri

～

ADRI WAS AWAKENED BY a sensual caress.

From the silence of the hour and the stillness in his bedchamber, he knew that it was still night — hours before dawn, for there was not even the faintest sound of birds chirping in anticipation.

In the distance, he could hear faint sounds from the city: strange, unusual sounds. Was that screaming? It was too far away to tell. He assumed it was some disturbance in the lower city; there was always trouble happening there, and the city guard would handle it if required. Or, if it turned out to be a symptom of some larger problem, Mother Jilana would take note of it, and Vrath would see to it when he returned.

Adri didn't concern himself with matters of administration and city affairs. He was more interested in the larger issues of politics: the complex web of alliances, loyalties, rivalries, enmities, feuds — some going back thousands of years, a twisted, intricately interwoven network that kept growing even as one attempted to unravel its myriad strands. Like a gigantic spiderweb that was constantly being added to by countless chitinous spinnerets. Adri had never actually seen a spiderweb, of course, but he had brushed against a few in his youth, especially during his days in the forest gurukul, and he still remembered the terror and disgust he felt as his fingers and face were caught in the thick sticky threads.

He saw the complexity of politics as a huge battlefield, with himself in the center, and factions on all sides engaging at once in a deafening cacophony of emotions and violence — yet underlying it all, a thread of unifying strategy.

He had never felt more alive, more present in his senses than when he himself had been on the battlefield, and he felt the same thrill, the same sense of peril, the same sense of camaraderie, the same threat of violence and death when he listened to the intense, complex discussions of Krushan politics in the sabha. He knew from Vrath's laconic, rare responses that the prince regent did not care for politics, though he possessed a mind brilliant enough to comprehend it well and recall every detail with startling accuracy. Shvate cared for it even less, preferring to actually be in battle rather than in the royal court listening to men talk. And Mother Jilana could not even bear to endure it an instant more than was necessary, leaving it to Vrath and the very able ministers to handle such matters.

But Adri had a fascination for politics. A passion, even. It was, he had come to realize recently, the one way in which he could govern an empire as vast and complicated as Hastinaga without ever needing to sit on a horse, drive a chariot, fight a battle or a duel, or even leave the palace. If he knew and used his knowledge of politics, he could govern the empire. He could rule. And that, he had begun to think of late, was what he truly aspired to do. What he could do and do well — better than Shvate, better than Mother Jilana, better than even the ministers. Not better than Vrath, but unlike the elder, Adri actually *liked* politics. Surely that gave him an edge.

But right now, it was not politics that had awoken him, or even the distant sounds of disturbances in the city —

It was the sensual caress on his body.

He lay in bed, wondering what had possessed Geldry. She was a passionate woman; he had known that since the first night of marriage. But she had never actually gone as far as to wake him asking to be loved.

He was flattered. It made him feel wanted. Too many times — especially as of late — he felt that there was a divide between them, a gap that he was increasingly unable to bridge. It was not just the difference of sightedness. Even though she wore an eyeband in solidarity, the fact was that she was not truly blind. She could never know what it meant to have never seen, to be completely unaware of what a sunrise looked like, or what the source of some unusual or disturbing noise actually was (the worst being the awful cries from soldiers wounded in battle).

But there was also the difference in culture, in language, in customs and habits, food and clothing, festivals and traditions, beliefs and values. Geera was not Hastinaga, and Geldry's ideas on many things were definitely not Adri's ideas. They differed on many significant points of belief. At times, especially after a particularly frustrating argument, Adri had wondered why she had ever married him — apart from the obvious reasons of court.

There had been one disagreement, after Shvate had returned from his campaign with all those wagonloads of bounty, and offered them to Adri. Naturally, Shvate was not obliged to offer them to his brother, since Shvate was the elder of the two and hence the senior in line of succession. And just as naturally, Adri was expected to refuse and insist that the bounty be offered to Vrath, since he was senior to them both, and the actual prince regent of the empire. Adri had tried to explain to Geldry that the offering of the bounty was symbolic, not literal. That Shvate was only obliged to offer it to his elders in the line of succession and it had to go to Vrath as the eldermost, and Vrath in turn had to accept it formally and turn it over to the imperial coffers for use in the administration of the empire. It was not personal bounty to be used at any one person's whim! He had tried to explain to her how the empire would descend into chaos if every prince, princess, queen, or king simply appropriated all tithes and bounties for their personal consumption; there would be a mass uprising and widespread rebellion.

But Geldry had refused to see sense. She had pretended to agree with him, but he knew from her breathing — the little noises of anger, disgust, and frustration she made, along with the constant sighing — and the scratching of her fingernails on the wooden arm of her chair, the shifting of her feet, and other various signs that he recognized so well as her way of throwing a controlled but furious tantrum.

Things had changed after that day, he knew. He had tried repeatedly to talk to her about it but she would not speak about it honestly or calmly. That was another major point of difference: Geldrans abhorred talk. They favored action. Talk, especially political talk, was the ultimate sign of weakness in her culture. He heard the faint contempt in her attitude even as he struggled to breach the growing abyss, but knew it was hopeless. She had turned away from him, and nothing he did could bring her back.

Now, all of a sudden, in the middle of the night, she had begun caressing him erotically. What did it mean? He lay still and enjoyed the experience. It was pleasant, of course — *more* than pleasant; much more. Touch was a powerful sense for Adri, having been blind from birth. The primary ways he "saw" people were through sound and touch and, to a much lesser extent, by smell. For him, Geldry was the woman he touched — every day at first, in those intense, passionate nights after marriage. He had touched her at all times, whenever possible. He knew the shape of her head, the swell of her skull, the narrow forehead below the hairline, the large, prominent aquiline nose; the high, strong cheekbones; the inward slope of her cheeks; the sharp point of her chin; the hard lines of her jaw; the large ears pressed back close to her head. He loved her slender neck; her wide, strong shoulders; the sharp inward curve of her waist; the flare of her hips and thighs . . . Her skin was not soft, but it had a texture that was both pleasing and erotic to him. In those early nights, he would lie beside her, propped up on one elbow, stroking her naked body with the tips of his fingers, barely touching her, brushing so lightly across the surface of her skin that it felt like his fingers were dancing over the sloping curves and valleys and swells of her femininity. The smooth, soft parts, the warmer hidden crevices, the deep moist place between her thighs . . . He had learned to read these more thoroughly than any scholar could read a treasured scripture. He knew every letter in the alphabet of her anatomy, the language of her body, the secret code of her arousal, the soft poetry of her passion, the raging heat of her climax. Geldry was the one person he felt he truly "saw." He was never more fully alive than when he was with her at such times. She was the secret knowledge he had craved without knowing that it had a name, or that it could be embodied in a person. She was his world and his heart, and he would do anything for her.

We often become the very things that we are perceived to be, even if they are not entirely true. People spoke of Adri's blindness as if it were a curse, a failing, a diminishment of his value as a person. To him it was simply the way he was, nothing more, nothing less. Does a man born with two hands feel diminished because he does not possess four hands — or six, or eight? Darkness was not fearful to him as it was to the sighted; it was the way the world was, all the time. Yet because people displayed ignorant prejudice against him every day of his life, treating the blind as somehow different, diminished, less than human, he had come to think of himself as being these things. So he felt an imbalance between himself and Geldry from the outset. She was sighted, he was blind. (It did not matter that she covered her eyes, just as a person picking up something with only one hand cannot understand what it is like to go through life with only one arm.) If anything, her eagerness to share his condition suggested that she felt sorry for him, and that itself aggrieved him. He did not say so to her because she had the right to show her love for him in any manner she wished, but he felt it only confirmed the difference between them. The imbalance of their births.

But in bed, he felt that imbalance reduced to the minimum. In bed, they met not as a sighted person and a blind person, but as two lovers, naked and entwined, erotically engaged, sensual and charged. Touch *was* sight to a lover. A finger mattered more than an eye. Skin was the primary sensory organ, texture and contact the most eloquent vocabulary. And in bed, Adri found his element; he mastered Geldry and was mastered in turn by her. He conquered her more decisively than any king could conquer another in a real battle and was conquered himself by her passion and desire. He brought her whimpering to the point of ecstasy, held her there on the brink for as long as he thought she could bear, before allowing her to plunge into the deep, cool waters of bliss, then raising her up again, and yet again and again. She responded in turn, and manipulated him just as masterfully. They both clashed on the battlefield of love. And yielded to one another, completely and unequivocally. Here in bed, there was no argument, no disagreement, no misunderstanding, no confusion between cultures or value systems, words, and gestures. It was all pleasure, all joining, all passion.

But now, the balance was gone. No more was this an equal contest. She had gained the upper hand.

The movement of her hands, and now her body, across his own, arousing, titillating, teasing ... He found himself raised up the highest point of pleasure. He felt her mouth on his, her hot breath scalding him, then felt the heat of her nether mouth, and wondered at the fever of her passion. She felt like she had never felt before, like a being made of pure heat and passion. Even her body felt different, stronger, more commanding, dominating even his masculine strength. He groaned, succumbing to her assault. And together they rose to the peak of ecstasy before he exploded in a burst of relief so intense that for a moment, he could see the being mounted above him the way sighted people spoke of seeing things — a sunrise, a furnace, an eclipse at noonday. He wept with pleasure and surrendered to her completely.

Jilana

~

JILANA WOKE FROM RESTLESS dreams. A breeze was blowing through her chambers, an unseasonably warm breeze. Not just warm, but *hot*. The curtains on her verandah were billowing, turning, and twisting, tormented by the wind. A peculiar odor carried on the breeze. The smell of hot sand, unwashed animal fur, and riper odors, the scents of death and war, carcasses rotting in the sun, other unspeakable stenches. It smelled of the desert. But that was impossible. The desert was a thousand miles away.

She sat up in bed, feeling feverish, her vision hazy. She felt as if she might vomit up the contents of her belly at any time. Yet when she had lain down to sleep only hours earlier, she had felt perfectly well. She was not one of those people easily troubled by digestion, and she had eaten nothing amiss for supper. Only fish, and fish was her staple food. The unease in her belly was caused by something else, some feeling of extreme unease. She put a hand to her head and was not surprised to find her forehead burning. So, a fever — perhaps some minor ailment. She rarely summoned the royal healers, preferring to fight minor ailments without the aid of arcane remedies and treatments, but tonight she felt the need for some comfort.

She reached out for the bell by her bedside that would summon one of her maids, who would then summon the healer, but before her hand could reach it, a shadow caught her eye.

There was someone standing by the verandah. Just outside her bedchamber. She could see the shadow behind the billowing drapes. It appeared to be a man: tall, lean, and clad entirely in dark clothing.

"Who is that?" she asked, hearing the weakness in her voice. The act of speaking made her head pound and filled the back of her throat with bile. That awful smelling wind! If only it would stop.

There was no answer.

The wind continued to billow the drapes, rustling the sheets and bed-clothes, even making her hair dance. Beyond the verandah, there was a strange light in the sky. The moon should have been full tonight, she knew, but the patch of sky she could see from here was dark, suffused with strange coloring. Almost like . . . an eclipse. But there was no eclipse tonight. The as-tronomers of Hastinaga were the finest in the world, and they had mapped out the schedule of the planets and stars for thousands of years in advance. The almanac showed every single eclipse, phase of the moon, even the phases of the unseen planets Rohu and Kattu.

She tried to focus on the tall shadow outside her bedchamber, but her vision blurred and swam, the chamber rolling from side to side as she strug-gled to concentrate.

"Who are you? What are you doing here in my chamber?"

Still no answer. Just that festering wind and awful odor, and the strange hue of the sky — deep blue light shot through with threads of crimson and ochre.

There *was* a person on her verandah, she was certain of it, but her eyes would not focus, her head and stomach roiled, and she continued to feel nausea growing in her belly.

"Answer me!" she commanded, summoning up the queenly voice for which she was so notorious. That tone which made even the most powerful nobles, ministers, kings, and ambassadors quail and lower their eyes.

A soft sound from the balcony, carried on the foul wind.

"*Daughter of fishmongers . . .*"

She could not have heard right. Surely that was not what the person had said! Who was this man? She could think of no one that tall, that lean, and what sort of person wore thick black robes from head to toe on such a warm night? She felt her body blazing with fever now, her insides in turmoil, and knew that somehow, her condition was being caused not by any ailment, but by the very presence of this person, this *being*.

"*Mother of whores . . .*"

She had heard enough. She turned back to the bedside table and reached for the bell to summon the maids. "I will have a dozen men here in an instant, and we'll see about your mother then!" she said in irritation and pique.

But the bell was gone. It was always kept in the exact same spot. Yet tonight it was not in its place.

She knew it had been there when she had gone to bed; she had used it one last time to remind her maid not to disturb her until late morning as she wished to sleep in. She had set it back right . . . there.

Instead of the bell, something else lay on her nightstand. She picked it up out of sheer curiosity, and felt cold, wet flesh and prickly scales.

Despite the vile odors from the verandah, the object had its own distinct smell, which she recognized instantly. She *was* the daughter of fisherfolk, after all.

It was a fish.

Still wet and dripping from the river. A river fish — which she knew because she could smell the water pouring off it as if she had just plucked it out of the water. Her father had taught her that if she trained her nose, she could learn a great deal about a fish just by its smell. He could always tell you exactly how long ago a fish had been caught, and likely where it had been caught as well. She was not as gifted as he, and in her disoriented, feverish condition, she could not be certain of her senses, but the fish in her hand smelled exactly like the fish she used to catch in the river just outside her village. Except that her village was a hundred miles away, and this fish had been caught only a few moments ago.

The fish wriggled in her fist suddenly. It shivered and shook, trying to escape her grasp. Still alive!

She dropped it, hearing it slap down on the bed, then flop and dance desperately in its last throes.

How could a fish freshly caught from her village land on her nightstand a hundred miles away in an instant?

"Your father, your mother, your sisters, your brother, your village, your entire clan . . ."

"Maids!" Jilana cried out.

But her voice was hoarse and weak.

"Guards!"

The tall shadow on the verandah leered. She could not see its face, yet she heard the leer in its soft chuckling.

"*I will slay them all, every last one, like that fish that lies dying on your bed . . .*"

"Guards!" she shouted, louder now, yet somehow not louder than that wind, the keening screeching wind that seemed to be blowing at great force from some distant desert battlefield.

"*I took that fish from the river outside your father's hut, while he lay sleeping only yards away. In a moment, I return to take his life just as easily. He will die writhing in my hands like a fish . . .*"

Jilana shut her eyes, ignoring the pounding of her head, the reeling of her senses, the blurring of her vision, the churning of her belly; she shut her eyes and concentrated with all her strength and might, and spoke a single phrase, a mantra she used only when absolutely necessary, for matters of life and death, in times of extreme emergency. This was such a time, she knew, and she did not hesitate to use it.

An explosion of light and sound — and then a tall, dark figure loomed over her bedside, staring down at her with intense eyes that burned like twin suns in the eclipse of her senses.

Adri

⌒

ADRI HAD NEVER FELT so content.

He lay in languorous exhaustion, limbs asprawl, a film of warm sweat on his naked body.

The night was warmer than usual, and had been for a while already, but he was only realizing it now. An unseasonal breeze blew through his bedchamber, bringing with it strange odors, distant sounds... He even thought he could smell and hear elephants, yet that was not possible. The royal elephant enclosures were on the far side of the palace, the opposite end to the wing in which his chambers were situated. Surely, he must be mistaken.

Another gentle breeze stirred the thin garment lying carelessly over his lower body, and he smelled it again, distinctly this time. That was the scent of elephants, no mistaking it. It could not have been stronger had he been in a chamber directly above the elephant enclosures. But he had never even been to that side of the palace. He didn't even know what lay on that side. Was it the palace cooks' quarters? The palace guards?"

A gentle hand touched his cheek.

"My lord."

He smiled.

"May I bring you some refreshment? Something cool to drink? Some fruit to eat? The pantry is not far from my room."

The smile faded from his face. He lay still, staring up at familiar darkness, smelling the scent of elephants, listening to the sound of the female voice, feeling the hand caressing his cheek lightly.

Geldry would never offer to bring him refreshment.

Geldry would never refer to their bedchamber as her room.

Geldry spoke with a very distinct Geldran accent.

He sat up suddenly, gripping the female hand at his face tightly, tightly enough to elicit a gasp of pain from the owner of the hand.

"You are not Geldry."

"My lord, you are hurting my hand."

Adri released the hand and reached out in the same motion, finding the face of the woman sitting beside him, feeling her face, the soft smooth skin, the small snubbed nose, the wide set cheekbones, filled-in cheeks, the broad sloping forehead, the short hair . . .

He jerked his hand back abruptly, shocked.

"Who are you?"

"My lord?"

"Who *are* you?" He felt the urge to grasp her shoulder and shake her, but he did not wish to cause her harm or discomfort. "Answer me!"

"My lord . . . you seem upset. Is everything in order? Are you feeling unwell?"

"I . . ." His head reeled. Somewhere outside but not far away, an elephant lowed softly in its sleep and was answered by several others. He smelled the familiar stench of elephant offal drifting on the warm breeze.

He felt the weight of the bed shift. The woman had risen from the bed. He heard her move about the room, lifting something, and then heard the sound of water being poured from an earthen vessel into a smaller earthen vessel, a cup perhaps. A moment later, he felt her presence by his side, and smelled the water she held in her hand.

"My lord, some water to bring you relief."

He took the cup and brought it to his lips. She continued holding the cup as well, and his fingers covered hers. He drank deeply, the cool water feeling like a blessing as it went down his parched throat and filled his belly. Her hand was soft, her fingers delicate — and he knew these were the same fingers, the same hand, that had caressed him so expertly the night before, had aroused him to such hard passion.

He finished the water but continued holding the cup — and the hand that held it.

"Who are you?" he asked again, but gently this time, with tenderness in his voice befitting a lover.

"My lord," she said, and he sensed her bowing her head instinctively, even though he could not see the gesture. "I am Sauvali, a maid in your employ."

He was silent, absorbing this information.

"Where am I at present?" he asked.

"In my room in the maids' quarters, in the southeastern wing of the palace."

"How did I get here?"

"My lord?"

"I . . . do not recall coming here." *Ever.* But he did not add the last part: it was obvious.

"My lord, I do not know how you came here, I assumed you asked someone the way. I was fast asleep and lying in bed, when suddenly I realized someone else was here beside me. Startled at first, I rose and was about to cry out when you grasped my wrist and pulled me down to you. You whispered softly in my ears that you wished to lie with me. I could not refuse you, my lord. So I . . . I entertained you."

He was silent for another long pause as he tried to recall these events. He had no memory of rising from his own bed, walking all the way to this part of the palace — a distance of almost half a mile through winding corridors, up and down stairways and more corridors, presumably. Nor did he remember grasping her wrist and saying those words to her. But he could hear the truth in her voice. She was being completely honest. There was no deception in her.

He groaned and rubbed a hand across his face.

"My lord? Would you like some more water?"

He nodded.

She poured from the earthen pot and brought the cup back to him. He drank it gratefully.

"Shall I fetch you refreshment, sire?"

He shook his head, handing the clay cup back to her. He heard the faint sound of the cup being set on to the top of the earthen pot. She was a gentle person, her movements, her actions, all very smooth and sensual. He heard the tiny anklet bells she wore as well as the tiny bells on the chain around her waist as she moved. She was wider hipped than Geldry, her rear larger as well, but firm and fleshy. He was shocked to feel himself growing aroused again.

"Is all well, my lord?" she asked, with genuine concern in her voice.

He nodded. Then decided she deserved the benefit of an answer. "Yes, thank you, Sauvali."

"My lord, are you sure you would not like something to eat? You need nourishment to replenish your energies." She paused, and he sensed her blushing as she tried to phrase her next words suitably, "You were extremely vigorous."

He felt his arousal growing.

"You found me vigorous?" he asked, unable to mask the pleasure in his tone.

"Yes, my lord," she said with unmistakable shyness. He knew she had lowered her head and was touching her own breast, her finger circling the swollen nipple. She was growing aroused as well. He smelled the odor of her musk, her yoni dampening in anticipation. "In my village in Saugadha, we had a bull. I watched him cover the cows many a time. You were as vigorous as that bull tonight. Strong and powerful. I was pleased to receive your seed."

Now he was as hard as a rod of metal, harder than he had been in years. Even with Geldry, he had never been so filled with desire, so passionately aroused. With Geldry, there had always been a mask of ego, a keen sense of the difference between them, and a distance within Geldry herself, a remoteness, a form of detachment that kept her removed from even the most physical of acts, as if she retreated to a corner of her own mind, observing but not entirely present in the moment. Perhaps if Adri had not been blind since birth, gifted with other ways of seeing, the ability to see into a person's heart and mind, he might never have realized this about Geldry. But because he *did* realize it, it had saddened him immensely, made him feel somehow smaller, less significant.

It was not a masculine thing; while his ego did enjoy the idea that he was conquering, besieging, "taking" a woman as all men did, it was the fact that she herself was not deeply involved in the act as he was that disappointed him. At its most intimate, lovemaking was a meeting of not only two bodies, but two minds, two hearts, two souls. He brought everything to his moments with Geldry. The fact that she reserved something, held back, was puzzling and somehow a comment on himself, he felt. Even in her wildest moments of ecstasy, crying out with the joy of climax, she still kept a tiny portion of herself away from his reach. He had never understood that. It had made him try even harder at first, thrusting and pounding furiously, using all his newly learned skills as a lover to try to unlock that final gate, and in a way he had never entirely given up on that attempt.

But she had begun to withdraw even further. Especially after their disagreement over Shvate's bounty. And of late, it was as if she was withdrawing farther and farther each day. Lovers can read each other's hearts: even when fully clothed, we are still naked to one another. Adri sensed he had lost another part of Geldry, just when he had thought that he was close to bringing down her last gate, and he had not even known that was possible. If it *was*, then it meant that Geldry might raise new gates in time, one for each time they disagreed or argued or fought.

Over time, she would be unapproachable behind all her many fortifications. And he would be outside, alone and cold and lonely. He could not bear that thought. He didn't care if she conquered and he lost; it didn't matter to him that only he must win. Love was not a war, or even a competition. It was an alliance, the most passionate, intimate alliance of all. How could you build walls and embankments against your own allies? Why would you want to keep out your most intimate friend? He could not understand it, and it hurt him deeply.

And now, here was this maid, a mere girl, judging from the feel of her supple young body and her voice, a low caste from the Daugasya clan, and she was treating him with such warmth and affection, such tenderness. She wanted him. She craved him. He heard the desire in her voice, smelled the lust in her loins, felt the passion in her heartbeat.

Without another word or thought, he reached out his hand to her. Without the slightest hesitation, she came forward, her naked hip brushing against his erect lingam. He grasped her by the shoulders, eliciting a soft gasp from her lips, and pulled her down upon himself, entering and spearing her most tender space with his bull-hard maleness.

Karni

~

KARNI WAS SHAKING AS she emerged from the temple.

She was sopping wet, her clothes dripping onto the black stone stairs as she climbed the last one. She stood for a moment, then lowered herself and sat down heavily on the top step, turning to put her feet on the one below. She bent over double, then hugged her knees for a moment, shuddering with emotion and with cold. The water was freezing, and she was icy chilled, but the shuddering was due to what she had seen and heard.

Finally, she stopped shaking and breathed deeply, exhaling. Her breath felt warm and comforting on her cold knees. She looked down at the temple's first level. It looked quiet and placid, just like it always did. The whole complex was serene and calm. She always liked to spend some time after her prayer, just to commune with the godhead, to allow her thoughts time to gather themselves. It gave her a deep sense of inner calm and strength.

She realized suddenly that she had forgotten the pooja thali. It was probably still in the inner shrine, on the floor before the deity's altar where she had set it down. She had never actually performed the pooja or sung the aarti, rung the little bell and doused herself in the sacred smoke, partaken of the prasadam, none of the usual little ritual things she liked to do every time.

On the other hand, she had never actually been given darshan of the goddess. Somehow, rituals seemed petty and insignificant compared to the presence of the actual deity. The pooja thali was not important in itself. She could get a thousand of them if she desired. The fact that Goddess Jeel had personally appeared to her, and had spoken at such length, was profoundly inspiring as well as startling.

But what did it mean? Her mind was still reeling with the words the goddess had spoken. Still trying to make sense of all that Goddess Jeel had told her. What had she meant when she spoke of sacrifices and sons? Firstborn sons, at that. Surely she could not mean . . .

"*Princess!*"

The shout came from the lane leading to the temple precinct. Karni looked up, trying to see through the foggy darkness. When had this fog set in? For that matter, now that she was aware of it, when had the night grown so dark? Where was that large, brilliant moon that had shone down on her when she descended the temple steps? It had been high in the sky at the time, and that could not have been more than an hour earlier. Even if it had set by now, which was unlikely, why was the sky filled with that strange hue? Why were there dark clouds boiling over the city? What were those strange screams and shouts and cries from all around?

She had no time to ponder all these questions. A new one was posing itself to her as she sought and found the source of the shout.

"Princess Karni!" cried Adran, her charioteer, as he came running down the path. She had never seen him look and sound so agitated before. He was normally a very reserved and dignified man, as befitted any charioteer. It was most unlike him to be so upset, running and shouting like a wild man, in a temple precinct of all places.

"Princess, you must leave here at once! We must return to the palace. Please, come with me now!"

Karni rose to her feet. She had a moment of unsteadiness when she was aware of her empty belly and the supper she had missed that night. She had fasted in anticipation of her darshan. It pleased her to offer the prayers after fasting, made her feel sincere in her offering. One must offer something before one could expect something in return. Then she regained control of her body and her senses with a small effort of will, and she stood firmly on both feet.

"What is the matter, charioteer?" she asked. "Is there some trouble with the horses?"

He halted before her, his mustached face creased with anxiety, and joined his palms in respect. "There is something amiss in the city, my princess. I must take you home now."

"Very well," she said.

They began walking back up the path. He glanced at her once or twice, curiously. Karni realized her wet garments were making a sound. Adran took in her state and frowned.

"Princess, are you well? Your garments . . ."

"I am wet, that's all," she said. "It's only water."

Jeel water, she reminded herself. *A benediction from the goddess herself, blessing me with her sanctified elixir. People travel thousands of miles for a sip of this sacred water. I have been bathed in it from head to foot! I can die and go straight to heaven now.*

A horse whinnied loudly from ahead, and Adran reacted.

He began jogging, picking up speed. Then realized that Karni was still walking at the same pace. She was genuinely unable to run very fast at present, partly because of her fasting condition, and partly because of her wet clothes.

"Go ahead, Adran. I'm right behind you."

Just as he began sprinting, the sound of a horse screaming jarred Karni's nerves. Poor creature! What was happening? She had only heard horses cry out that way when under extreme duress, usually when injured in a battle or a violent accident.

Adran disappeared up the forested pathway, and for a moment Karni was alone. The path was desolate, the area remote. She knew there were some wild creatures in the woods, but they were all harmless ones, the kind that one hunted, not the likes that hunted you. If there were any such predators about, they would have ravaged the elephants and horses in the royal stockades. Yet even though she knew the place was safe, Karni began to feel a sense of great dread. She had the feeling that she was being watched.

Up ahead, at the end of the dark pathway, the horse was still screaming, and now Adran's hoarse voice began to speak, saying something she could not fully comprehend.

"*Daughter of Karna Sura . . .*"

She exclaimed. That was Adran's voice, but was it really Adran speaking the words?

The woods around her were dark. Even the sky above was barely visible. What little of it she could glimpse was obscured by dark seething clouds driven by a great demonic wind. The slashes of sky visible through the rents and rips in these driven clouds were sometimes blue, sometimes red, sometimes jet-black. The moon itself seemed to be still there, still high, but eclipsed by some other body. It made no sense because there was no eclipse predicted for tonight, yet something *was* eclipsing the moon. She wished she had a light by which to see. As it was, she couldn't even make out the path on which she walked.

"*Sister of Vasurava . . .*"

She tried to walk faster.

A wind rose from nowhere, carrying a foul stench. It was surprisingly warm, smelling of strange, exotic odors: sand, sun, salt, and corpses — the rank battlefield reek of putrid carcasses. She covered the lower part of her face with the end of her garment, the damp cloth helping to mask the awful stench. The wind assaulted her from all sides, driving dust and dried leaves into her face. From whence had this ghastly wind risen? She could not hear any leaves rustling, see no trees bowing, yet here on the ground, she was being assailed relentlessly.

"*Wife of Shvate . . .*"

She could not make out where the voice was coming from. One time it seemed to originate from the right, then from behind her, then directly *above* her. She was shivering again, despite the warm wind. The wind driving against her cold garments was causing her to shiver, the foul stench and strange whispers adding to her distress. She tried to walk faster, knowing she must be close to the chariot now, knowing it could not be much farther.

"*Mother of bastards . . .*"

She cried out as if physically struck.

This time the whisper had sounded just behind her shoulder, spoken almost directly into her right ear. She turned and flailed with her right hand, but her hand met nothing but air and driven dust.

Karni stopped running.

Stopped walking.

Came to a complete halt.

Both her fists were clenched, her legs spread slightly apart in a fighting stance, her eyes furious. Her belly might be empty, but her spirit was full of strength.

"Enough!" she cried out. "I am not just a daughter, sister, or wife. I am a woman. I exist in my own right. My name is Karni, and I take abuse from no one—mortal, god, or demon. If you want to speak with me, then show yourself. Show yourself and speak to me, person-to-person, face-to-face. Coward!"

A brief moment of silence.

Then a hissing sound that echoed all around, nowhere and everywhere at once, susurrating through the woods, filling the night with the sound of a thousand serpents.

Then, silence again.

The wind died down as suddenly as it had risen.

The foul stench dissipated.

The miasma surrounding her—she was still not sure whether it was fog or just the lack of sufficient light—cleared to reveal the pathway, the silhouettes of the nearest trees, and on the trail just ahead, the shape of the chariot and horses and a man.

"Princess!" shouted the familiar hoarse voice of Adran. "Make haste! We must not tarry here."

Karni lifted up the wet hem of her garment and ran the last several yards. She reached the chariot and leaped onboard, her bare feet slapping loudly against the metal-plated wooden floor. Adran was standing in his driving position, reins in hand, head turned to watch her climb aboard. She saw a horse lying on its side nearby, and noted that only one horse was now hitched to the chariot, whereas there had been two earlier.

"The horse?" she asked, unable to coherently string words together in a complete sentence.

"Attacked," he said grimly. "Wounded too badly to survive. I had to put it down. Shall we go, my princess?"

"Yes!" she said.

He urged the single horse forward, driving it with a whinny and a thumping of hooves. The familiar sound of the chariot wheels rumbling on the dirt path, the familiar motion of the vehicle as it began to move through the dark woods, carrying her back homewards, toward the main palace precinct—all of these things comforted and eased Karni's anxiety. She glanced back as they passed the fallen horse, and she grimaced as she glimpsed the poor beast's belly ripped open, intestines strung out. What manner of creature could have attacked the horse? There were no predators here in these woods. Were there? Then who was it that whispered to her in the darkness? Who — or what — was it that attacked and killed the horse so brutally?

The chariot raced through the night, toward the city, toward home, toward safety.

Jilana

~

AS THE FINAL SYLLABLES of the mantra faded, the air rippled and Vessa appeared, looming over Jilana's bed.

The twisted locks of his matted hair spread out from his head like the rays of light from the corona of the sun. His lean, hard body was taut from years of subsisting on the bare minimum required for sustenance, his muscles and bones hard from constant feats of endurance, his eyes enormous blazing orbs in the dark sky of his face. His features, shocking and ugly to most women, were as familiar to Jilana as the jungle itself. The wildness of his features; the piercing, intense glare of his eyes; the crow black skin and raven dark hair; the dirt encrusted beneath his nails, his long, gnarled fingernails and toenails; the thick wildwood staff in his fist; the large hands and knobby knuckles . . . to her these were simply the way he had always looked. He was her son; she had birthed him from her own womb, and to her, and her alone, he was beautiful and perfect. Never more beautiful and perfect than he was right now, in her moment of need.

"Son," she cried, "save me from this monster!"

But he was already looking in the direction of her verandah, at the place from where the vile stench and even viler threats had come, at the tall dark shadow that stood there, terrorizing her.

With a flash, he vanished from her bedside.

She turned her head, her senses spinning as she moved too quickly, and looked at the balcony just in time to see Vessa reappear there, his staff already raised to strike, his voice booming with an unearthly echo.

"Urrkh, I shall tear you asunder! You dare threaten my mother. Be gone!"

A flurry of wind, a blaze of blue fire spewing forth from Vessa's eyes, and the shadow screamed and withered before her son's maya and fury. Jilana caught a glimpse of a dark oval that hadn't been there a moment ago, like a tear in the fabric of the night itself, and beyond it, a strange alien vista: a desert landscape with more than one moon in the sky, each a different color. The shadow slipped through the portal, fleeing like a snake into its burrow, and then the alien vista vanished and the night was whole once again. The wind died out, the bedchamber returned, slowly, to a state of calm.

Jilana sat up, blinked, held her head; the fever heat of her forehead was now diminished. The churning in her belly too. And the reeling of her senses had reduced sufficiently to allow her to sit upright without feeling as if she was about to fall. The nausea that had been threatening her also receded.

"Mother." Vessa was by her side again. "Are you well? Did he harm you?"

She started to shake her head, then thought better of it. "No. He kept his distance and threatened. Like a coward. But I feel . . . I felt . . . *ill*. Could he have poisoned me somehow?"

He looked at her with eyes that saw far more than any mortal eyes. "No. It was a miasma caused by his foul presence. It will pass."

He raised a hand and gestured, muttering a phrase in the ancient tongue. At once, she felt her head clear, the fever fade, her belly settle, and her nausea disappear. She sat up, scarcely able to believe that only a moment ago she had thought she would collapse from her ailment.

"*Who . . . what* was he?"

Vessa stared in the direction of the verandah, as if ensuring that the threat would not return. "Jarsun. The Reygistani seeks vengeance for Shvate's invasion of his territories and Vrath defeating him at the Battle of the Rebels."

"By attacking *me*?"

"Not just you, Mother. All Hastinaga is his target tonight. He has eclipsed Krushan law in the city."

Eclipsed Krushan law? *What does that even mean?* she wondered. Her head reeled, not with illness now, but with a thousand conflicting thoughts and possibilities. Then she remembered what the urrkh had said. "My father, my mother. He threatened to attack them."

Vessa raised his head, as if listening to sounds that Jilana herself could not hear, that no mortal ears could hear. "That may well be his aim."

"Then you must aid them! Go to them now. Assist them against this demon. Keep my family safe."

Still, he did not move. He raised his head and frowned. "What of Hastinaga?"

"I shall see to Hastinaga. Go save my family. Remember: they are your family too! Once you are done, you can return to help us here."

He tilted his head, acknowledging her command.

"If I go now, Mother, I must stay on his trail. It is still fresh. If I follow him through the portal corridors, I may be able to intercept him and stop him before he attacks our clan."

"Do it," she said.

Vessa tilted his head again.

"And, my son . . ."

He waited.

"Kill him."

Vessa smiled at her, displaying a mouthful of terrible, misshapen yellow teeth. And with a flash, he was on the other side of the bedchamber, striding toward the verandah. He called out a mantra as he strode, and without hesitating, he walked off the edge of the balcony and into emptiness, fifty feet above the ground. She saw the portal she had glimpsed earlier reopen, revealing the baleful triple eye of those alien moons and desert landscape. Vessa stepped through and was gone from sight. The blue oval hissed shut behind him, and now all that remained was the dark sky and the single blood moon of Arthaloka.

Jilana turned back to her nightstand. She was relieved to see the bell that she had sought earlier. It was right there, only a few inches farther back on the stand than its usual place. She picked it up and rang it loudly, insistently, repeatedly. The sound rang out through the silent palace, echoing and reverberating. The sound of running footsteps came from outside her doors, then the doors flew open and her maids and guards began to pour in all at once. They all seemed dazed and disoriented, some clutching their bellies, some their heads, all seeming out of sorts but recovering. She guessed that they had experienced the same debilitating symptoms she had suffered before Vessa came and chased the devil away.

"Sound the alert. The city is under attack by evil forces. Call out the entire city guard and reserves. Do it at once."

As they rushed to obey her orders, Jilana slumped back in her bed, drained. Her hand fell on something wet and hard and she stared down, confused. She picked up the object that was soaking her bedclothes and stared at it, dumbfounded. It was the fish. It was no longer flopping or gasping. Its sightless eye stared up at her. She prayed all she cared about and loved would not share its fate.

Karni

~

AS THE CHARIOT APPROACHED the first main street of the city, Karni saw a crowd ahead. Adran had already spotted it and slowed the horse, turning his head to search for another route. The crowd was at a crossing point where a larger avenue intersected with a smaller side street. The only other way was to go back, but that would return them to the reserve and the temple of Goddess Jeel.

"The only way out is onward," Adran said.

And then he handed her a bow.

She looked at the weapon, surprised. She knew there was a cache of weapons kept in the well of the chariot, for use by the occupants as well as the charioteer in case of threat. But ever since coming to Hastinaga, she had never had to touch a weapon. There had simply been no need.

She looked at the crowd of people on the crossroads ahead, perhaps a hundred and fifty or two hundred yards away. They appeared to be ordinary Krushan citizens, judging from their garb and the way they were milling about without any sense of order. What threat did Adran anticipate from them?

"We are in the city, the city guard is there to protect us," she said.

He looked at her, an expression on his face that she could not read. "Princess . . . the horse, the one that was killed by the temple, she was attacked by the soldiers who were accompanying us. They were city guard too. But there was something wrong with them. They were acting like madmen, like beasts. I have never seen anything like it before. By the time I reached the clearing, they had attacked the horse and wounded her terribly. The poor animal, my beloved Chhatri, a fine strong young mare who has served me well for the past three years, was still alive, fallen onto her side, screaming in agony while these men, these monsters . . ." He passed a hand over his face, reliving the horror of the moment. "They were feeding on her vitals, literally *eating* her with their bare mouths, their teeth, their hands."

Adran shook his head. "It was the most horrible thing. I shouted at them to stop, demanding to know what they were about. They stared back at me with eyes like blood moons, full of madness and evil. I had already picked up the sword in my hand, and I raised it and cut them both down as they squatted there, filthy with the fresh blood of Chhatri. But my princess, they did not die! They made such terrible sounds as I have never heard from any creature, human or beast, and then they scampered into the woods to escape. I did not know what else to do. I used the sword to end Chhatri's misery. Then, just as I took up the reins, you arrived."

She stared at him, horrified by the story. The thought of men, her own guard, acting in this manner, *eating* a living horse, was unbearable. She knew the men he spoke of. They were healthy, happy men, with families and children. What madness would possess them to do such a thing, to out of nowhere behave like beasts?

With sudden understanding, Karni looked down at the bow in her hand. "You expect . . . more of such behavior?" she asked slowly.

Adran looked pointedly at the crowd ahead. "There is strange evil about tonight. There is a miasma in the air, foul odors, strange occurrences. Earlier, when you were in the temple, the moon was occluded by a strange phenomenon. Something unnatural is happening in Hastinaga, my princess. My responsibility is to escort you home safely, but I have to drive the chariot." He looked at the bow in her hand. "You are familiar with its use?"

In response, she fitted an arrow to the bow and drew the string. "Ride on, Adran. Do not stop until we reach the palace."

He needed no further urging. With a clicking of his tongue and a waving of the reins — Adran had never used the whip in all the time he had driven her chariot — he urged the single horse forward. The going was slower than usual, since the chariot was meant to be drawn by two horses, but the single mare did her job stoutly, trotting ahead.

"What is this one's name?" Karni asked.

"Sreela," he replied shortly, his attention focused on the road ahead.

Almost on cue, Sreela whinnied, shying away from something. Her nostrils flared and her head was turning aside. Karni saw the roan horse's eyes flashing with panic. *She sees and smells something she doesn't like.*

At the crossroads ahead, the crowd had caught sight of the chariot and had turned toward it. Karni could see the men and women in the distance, staring in her direction. They appeared to be simply standing, none of them talking or exchanging glances. This itself was unusual. But there was something else odd about the way they stood, their arms and legs stiff and at awkward angles. Like someone caught in a rictus, frozen at an unnatural pose.

Adran spoke softly to Sreela, attempting to calm her. The horse reluctantly did her duty, trotting on down the road, but seemed hesitant to pick up speed. She kept shying away, making it difficult for Adran to keep the chariot steady.

The crowd began to move.

It happened all at once — the entire group running suddenly toward the chariot. It was like a regiment of soldiers who had been given a command and had begun charging at the enemy. But these were not soldiers — they were mere ordinary citizens; Karni could make out men in dhotis, barechested as if they had woken from their beds in the middle of the night and wandered out-of-doors, women in nightclothes, even children in their loincloths. Why were these people out of bed at this hour? What had possessed them? The hand that drew the bowstring began to ease. How could she harm ordinary citizens? None of them were even armed.

"Princess, be ready," Adran said. He urged Sreela on with more tongue-clicking, but the horse was clearly panicking now.

The crowd broke out into a run. Karni could see a very corpulent man wearing only a loin-cloth running directly at the chariot as if trying to win a race. His body language was all wrong: his limbs flailing in all directions, his head lolling back, his tongue dangling out, eyes bulging. He was breathing so loudly from the effort, she could hear him even above the sound of the chariot and the horse, huffing and panting. Karni had never seen anything like it before. There were others, all running in the same manner. They looked like they might break their arms and legs simply by running. They reminded her of something, but she could not recall what.

Sreela shied away from the approaching crowd one final time, then rose up, kicking and screaming. Karni felt the entire front of the chariot rock. The poor creature was extremely agitated, and Karni could understand her terror; it was obvious to anyone, even a horse, that those people were completely out of their minds. There was nothing remotely normal about their behavior, their appearance, the wild way they rolled their eyes and breathed through open mouths . . .

Sreela screamed and kicked out as the people reached her. The corpulent half-naked man in the loincloth was the first. Karni watched with horror as he ran straight at the rearing horse, not even slowing down or altering course. Sreela kicked out at him, shrieking, and her fore legs lashed at the man, one hoof catching him squarely on the head. Karni heard the sickening sound of the hoof making contact with the man's skull. The man flew several yards backward from the force of the impact, knocking down two or three other people behind him, sending them all to the ground in a heap.

Suddenly, the crowd was on them, all around the horse, the chariot, filling the road on either side.

"Princess, use your bow!" Adran shouted.

Karni saw Adran himself reach down and pick up a lance, holding it in a two-handed stance.

The crazed people began to slam into the side of the chariot. The sound their bodies made as they smashed into the metal-clad vehicle was horrible. She could hear bones breaking, flesh slapping, could see blood spurting. They simply ran till they met an obstacle and collided with it — in this case, the chariot. She watched as an elderly woman struck the side of the chariot and broke her arm and nose. The woman staggered back briefly, blood spurting from her face, her arm dangling at an obscene angle — and grinned up at Karni with a ravenous, insane expression. She bared her mouth, revealing several gaps in her teeth, and snarled at Karni, then started to crawl over the chariot well to get at its occupants.

Adran struck out with the lance, striking the old woman in the throat and sending her falling backward.

"Back!" he shouted hoarsely. "This is Princess Karni's chariot! Stay back!"

No one was listening. It was complete madness, people rushing them at full tilt, slamming into the chariot, smashing their faces, limbs, and bodies into it with reckless force, scrabbling madly at the sides of the well, their eyes filled with rage and insanity, trying to climb into the cab, trying to get at Karni and Adran and pull them apart. She saw the lunacy in their eyes, the unnatural way they moved and breathed, heard the animal sounds they made, and suddenly she knew what they reminded her of: puppets. Wooden puppets on strings, held by an invisible puppeteer. Except these were human beings, bodies of flesh and blood and bone.

Sreela screamed as a horde of people fell upon her and began attacking her. Karni saw people scratching, clawing, and biting, using everything at their disposal to attack the poor creature. She saw blood spurt and heard the unfortunate animal scream as the sheer weight of numbers overwhelmed her.

People now were trying to climb over the chariot well, standing on the wheels, trying to get at her and the charioteer. Adran was working the lance furiously, his muscles straining, face shiny with sweat, as he struck out, swinging the bladed tip as hard and fast as possible. Karni saw necks, cheeks, and eyes, slashed and cut, blood spilling, skin ripping, and yet none of them screamed or cried out or even clutched at their wounds. They simply came on, mindlessly dedicated to their mission. Like puppets, forced to do as the puppeteer made them do.

As if in a dream, Karni saw the corpulent man in the loincloth rise to his feet and come staggering toward the chariot once again. The spot on his skull where the horse's hoof had struck him was staved in, his skull crushed beneath the clearly visible horseshoe imprint, brain matter and blood oozing down the side of his head and neck.

Karni snapped back to her senses. She drew the arrow back and loosed. She saw it strike the chest of the old woman — who was standing on the wheel about to climb over into the cab — sending her falling back, taking two others down with her. Karni nocked another arrow and loosed again. This time a young boy went down — a child! — flying back with enough force to knock a grown man behind him off his feet. The child rose again immediately, the arrow embedded in his chest neither stopping him nor slowing him down.

Karni loosed and loosed again, killing innocents left, right, and center. Surrounded by madness, fighting for her life, not knowing why. Adran fought alongside her, slashing and jabbing, thrusting and kicking, keeping the lunacy at bay as best as he could. Sreela screamed a final hopeless scream and fell onto her side. The crowd swarmed over her fallen body, tearing her open with their teeth, eating her alive . . .

I cannot die here, Karni thought as she continued to loose arrow after arrow. The sounds of the crowd, of the madness, of the meaningless death and destruction all around faded to a blur.

All she could think of was *I cannot die here. This is not the way my story ends.*

Jilana

~

JILANA STOOD AT THE high point of the palace and looked down on Hastinaga.

The city was rioting.

Even at this height, over a hundred yards above the city, she could see the madness in action. Every instant, soldiers brought new reports of more fighting, more horrific reports. Parents assaulting children. Children killing their own parents. Women assaulting other women for no fault at all. Men and women randomly attacking others on the street, in their homes, in places of worship . . . There was no rhyme or reason to the attacks, no pattern, no sense. It was simply ordinary citizens attacking other ordinary citizens.

Another report said that all the street dogs and alley cats in the city had banded together and were attacking humans. Elephants in the stockades had begun going insane, acting as if they were in heat, attacking one another, smashing out their own brains. Horses were impaling themselves on fences, kicking at each other, biting at their riders. Everywhere it was the same story: random acts of madness and mayhem.

From what she could tell, about one in three people had been affected by this insanity. Even some of the palace guards had started attacking one another, cutting down their own comrades, even their own siblings or parents, or children who were also in the service. Cooks, maids, sentries . . . no one was spared. She had heard the madness was afoot in the richer sections of the city as well, yet there were no reports of looting, theft, burglary — it was only murder and violence. Senseless attacks aimed at destroying the sanity of Krushan society.

A sound made her turn at once. Since the attack in her own bedchamber, she was wary of every shadow or whisper. A soldier stood before her, his sweating face revealing his nervousness and exertion. "Dowager Empress Jilana."

She frowned. "I was expecting Captain Manasvati. I told him to report directly to me."

The soldier's throat worked. "The captain was . . . killed, Your Majesty. Eaten alive by a pack of wild alley cats. Several other soldiers died trying to save him." He held up an arm, displaying an ugly wound, a long deep scratch that bled darkly. "We fear lockjaw may be the cause."

Jilana shook her head. "Lockjaw did not cause the entire citizenry to attack each other. No, soldier. This is being caused by supernatural forces."

The soldier gulped. "Supernatural forces?"

She didn't try to explain. "You should get that looked at. The feral creature that did that might well have lockjaw after all."

The soldier nodded slowly. He knew as well as she did that there was no cure for lockjaw. If he had it, he was as good as dead anyway.

She tried to harden herself to overlook such things. *We have to work with what we have, to make the best of whatever we're given; not all of us have the powers of a Vessa, a Vrath . . . or a Jarsun.* "I sent Captain Manasvati to locate and bring back Princess Karni safely. Did he succeed before he was killed?"

"Nay, my queen. The streets are filled with thousands of rioters. Even some of our own number are afflicted with the madness. We are still fighting to keep the crowds from the palace doors. It is taking all the soldiers and resources at our disposal. The squads we have sent out to bring back Princess Karni . . . none of them have yet returned. The reports are that they have all been killed before succeeding in their task."

Jilana's hand covered her mouth. "Holy Jeel. You mean to say the princess is still out there. In *that?*" Her hand flew out, indicating the city sprawled below her, crawling with antlike figures bent on mayhem and destruction.

"Aye, my queen. She went to the temple of Goddess Jeel, on the far side of the royal reserve. We have been unable to secure that part of the city as yet. We are doing our best, Your Majesty."

"*Do better!*" she cried, unable to help herself. "That is my daughter-in-law out there! We must bring her home safely."

He looked down, silent. She immediately regretted her outburst. It was not this poor man's fault. He was indeed doing his best: quite likely, even if he survived this night, he would be dead in the next day or two, frothing from the mouth and shuddering in a fatal fit.

In a gentler tone, she resumed. "And Prince Shvate and Princess Mayla?"

"They are in in the kingswood just outside of Hastinaga, hunting. At least, that is the last we heard of them. We have attempted to send word to the outer city reserves to inform them of the events in the city, but also that they are not to return until further word from you, as you ordered."

She nodded. "Yes, yes, that is good. Well done. And Captain Manasvati had said in his last report that Prince Adri had been located in the palace and he would report back on his condition. Is he well?"

"Aye, my queen. As is Princess Geldry. There was some confusion, because neither were in their bedchamber and . . ." He trailed off, avoiding her eyes.

She frowned. "And what?"

"The circumstances in which they were found were somewhat . . . embarrassing."

She shrugged. "They are husband and wife. Nothing they do should be embarrassing to anyone." *Or even if they're not husband and wife,* she wanted to add, *after all, they're consenting adults.* Why was the soldier even mentioning such irrelevant things?

"My queen, forgive me if I spoke amiss. I simply meant that they were found in . . . different rooms."

"Wait. Did you say different rooms? What does that mean? Were they both not together?"

"Nay, my queen. When the guards first searched the bedchamber, neither was anywhere to be seen. Later, Prince Adri was finally discovered in the southeastern quarters."

"The maids' quarters?"

"Aye, my queen. In the room of the maid Sauvali. They were both in a state of undress and . . . um . . . extreme passion."

"Oh," she said, aware that her mouth had fallen open. This she had not expected, especially tonight of all nights. Adri and a maid? How long had this been going on? Was Geldry aware? She had a dozen questions, none of which she could ask this unfortunate soldier.

"And while the guards were still searching the palace for Princess Geldry, the maids came running to report that they had found her."

"Where?" Jilana asked warily, afraid of what she might hear next.

"In the verandah of her own bedchamber . . . um . . . undressed and also in a state of extreme passion."

"Alone?" Jilana asked.

The soldier inclined his head, still not meeting her eyes. "It appeared that someone else had been . . . with her. Judging by her state and her condition." He cleared his throat. "There was also a considerable amount of sand on the verandah."

"Sand," she repeated, wondering if she were going insane too now. Adri in a maid's room, in a state of "extreme passion." Geldry found at the other end of the palace, also in a similar state, but with no man around. Just sand. Strange, yet no more bizarre or illogical than the other events of the night.

"Is there anything else?" she asked, hoping he would say there was not. She didn't think she could stand to hear any more such reports. Suddenly, she wished Vrath was here, instead of away on imperial matters. He would have been able to go out into the city and fetch Karni back safely at least. Goddess alone knew what the poor girl was going through right now. To think of her out in this madness and mayhem was horrible. But then to hear of Adri's and Geldry's antics, it churned her stomach. Had her entire family gone crazy this night? And why not? It seemed the whole city was.

"Nothing more to report, my queen. We have secured the outer gates of the city in order to try to contain the rioting. As a last resort, if you order, we can take extreme measures."

She frowned. "Remind me. It has been so long since we experienced such a state of unrest in Hastinaga. What is the last resort in such a circumstance?"

He swallowed again. "Burning."

She nodded as if she had been expecting exactly that answer. "Thank you for your service. Dismissed."

She turned again to the city as he left, staring out at the metropolis she had watched grow, rise, expand, and develop into one of the greatest cities in the known world in her own lifetime. *Burning*. If they could not contain the madness, the last resort was to burn it all down. So even if Jarsun failed in his mission to destroy Hastinaga, he would still succeed. The city would still be destroyed, but by their own hands. But what else could they do?

She looked up at the night sky, praying for morning to come quickly, and to bring with it a new, sane sunrise.

And Karni. Keep my beloved daughter-in-law safe and sound. Bring her home to me. And Shvate and Mayla and . . .

It was a long and fervent prayer.

Reeda

~

REEDA WAS SCARED.

She had barred the door to the hut and had refused to open it to anyone, for any reason. She knew the city had gone mad tonight. She had glimpsed the first signs when she was sitting on the stoop, waiting for Adran to return. She knew that he had been summoned by Princess Karni to take her to the Jeel temple. That trip normally only took an hour or so, but he'd already been gone much longer. She had tried to sleep but had soon been roused by a sense of great unease. There were strange sounds and odors in the air, a peculiar light in the sky, the strangest moon she had ever seen. And then she had seen the dogs.

She had gone outside to sit on the stoop, where she would be able to see Adran as he came up the narrow, winding lane to the top of the little hill where their hut was sited. She knew him well enough to recognize his silhouette even in the dark. She had waited up for him many a night. What else had there been to do, when one had no child of one's own and it seemed unlikely the goddess would ever grant her one? Even after she had found Kern in the river and brought him home to raise as her own, she had still kept her habit of sitting out there and waiting for Adran. It pleased her to see his strong body walking easily up the hillside, his proud mane of hair, his long mustaches framing his hard jaw and handsome face. She loved him dearly.

After Kern had come, she had been prepared to stay up till all hours, tending to his needs. But Kern had never followed the norm. Once he lay down for the night, he slept through till morning. Even as a babe, he would sleep until dawn, then wake and demand his feeding. It was uncanny. She had never heard of a child who slept so deeply, so completely, all through the night *every single* night. She had never seen Kern wake even once, for any reason whatsoever. Once he slept, he *slept!* Later, as she came to understand him better, she knew it was somehow related to his obsession with the sun. It was as if Kern needed the sun in order to thrive, and once the sun went down, he went down with it. His energy levels, his enthusiasm, his appetite, his desire for play, everything dimmed as twilight darkened the sky. Like a bird, he wanted only to bury his beak and sleep. And just like a bird, he woke before dawn, eager, hungry, and full of enthusiasm. And once the sun rose, he did as well. That was when he became himself, truly — with sunrise.

So from sundown to sunup, Reeda could do as she pleased. Never did she concern herself with the night terrors, the tantrums, the cranky child, the hungry child, or any other such problems. Kern was always a perfect angel, even by day, but at night he was the easiest child to care for. All he did was sleep! Twelve, fourteen, even sixteen hours at times during winter. The only times of the year when he was less than his usual sunny self was during the monsoons, when the sun often didn't show itself all day, for days on end.

Reeda had still to make sense of the incident with the merchant's son and the other boys. She had always known Kern was no ordinary boy. But for a mother to know and for the world to acknowledge the fact were two entirely different things. The hearing in court, before Queen Mother Jilana and Prince Regent Vrath no less, before the Burning Throne itself, had been a startling confirmation. She was still trying to understand. Adran, on the other hand, had taken it in his stride. Then again, he spent his days in the presence of Krushan royals. He was used to the extraordinary. She had yet to wrap her mind around the possibility that her beloved Kern was . . . what exactly? A born warrior? Gifted with some innate ability? There were things in the world for which there were no exact words or names, not even in the great mother language.

Tonight, she had been sitting on the stoop, waiting for Adran when she saw the shadows lurking at the bottom of the lane. At first she had mistaken them for children, returning from play. Then as they continued to gather, she realized they were animals. Dogs. Dozens at first, then, as they continued to gather, hundreds, and finally, an hour or so later, there were what seemed to be thousands of dogs all surrounding the hill. And all of them seemed to be looking up at her, or to be more precise, at their hut. She had no idea why, but the sight was quite chilling. All those dogs, all those lolling tongues, hanging jaws, pricked-up ears, all directed at her house. Even at that moment, she had sensed instinctively that this had something to do with Kern. The reason they were all standing or sitting at the bottom of the hill and gazing up at her house was not because of her or Adran, but because of her adopted son. She had no idea what the connection might be, but she knew it as surely as she knew that Kern would not awaken until the crack of dawn tomorrow.

When the dogs had begun climbing the hillside, coming up the lane, just walking up the hill in an eerie unnatural silence, thousands upon thousands of pairs of canine eyes staring up in her direction, reflecting the strange reddish moonlight, she had lost her nerve. She had retreated into the house, barring the door.

She stood there, inside the door, listening. There were cracks in the wall, and she put her eye to one of them and peered out. She could glimpse the low shapes moving outside, filling the lane that led up to the front of her hut and the other charioteers' quarters upon this hilltop. They were out there, the hounds, milling about, surrounding the house. She had never seen or heard of so many dogs gathering in one place while remaining so silent. Not a bark, a whimper, a growl, or even a snarl. Just the *tiktik* of their claws on the ground, and the soft sounds they made as they brushed their brindly coats against each other. They kept coming up the hill, until there was no more room for them to move about. They sat facing the hut, tongues lolling, staring. Still not a sound. Thousands of dogs all around her, sitting, waiting. For what? She didn't know. But it scared her. It scared the life out of her.

She didn't know what to do. She had thought of calling to one of her neighbors. But they were all asleep by the time the trouble started. All the charioteers were in bed, along with their wives and families. The only ones in the royal family who were out-of-doors were Shvate and Mayla, who had driven themselves to Hastinaga for one of their days-long hunting expeditions, and Vrath, who had also driven himself to Mraashk a day earlier. And Karni, who had taken Adran to the temple. Everyone else was in the palace: the princesses Ember, Umber, and Geldry; Prince Adri; Dowager Empress Jilana; and the other lesser-ranking cousins and relatives. Besides, even if she had wakened one of her neighbors, what would she ask them to do? Chase away the dogs? How did one chase away a thousand dogs? Or ten thousand? She would sooner not disturb this horde. So she had gone indoors and barred herself in. And waited.

She was still waiting now.

There were sounds from other parts of the city. Strange, eerie, bone-chilling sounds. There were awful things happening everywhere, she knew. Even without seeing, she knew. Something evil was abroad tonight. It was in the air, it was in the moon, in the foul stench that carried on the night breezes. She didn't know what was happening, but she knew it was terrible and that people were getting hurt, dying, killing... She didn't want to know more. Like all Krushan women, Reeda was no coward in a fight. She would fight to defend herself and her loved ones. But she was no warrior; she did not live to fight, let alone *love* to fight. She abhorred violence, unless it was absolutely essential. She had no desire to go out there and save anyone by risking her own life and limb. Besides, she had a son to watch over, and her sweet Kern slept like the dead. Even now, despite all the strangeness abroad in the city tonight, he had not awoken. She had checked on him every now and then, to make sure. He had stirred in his sleep a few times, and that was unusual, but she assumed he was only reacting to the same sense of unease that she herself felt. His eyes had remained firmly shut, his breathing regular, and his body limp. Fast asleep. She could hardly leave him and go out to help others, if there even were others near *to* help.

Perhaps because of the dogs, or because all her neighbors were sleeping, the hilltop where the charioteer quarters were located was quieter than most of the city. There were no screams and shouts here, no sounds of violence or death. Just the soft, steady panting of several thousand dogs. She could hear them even through the closed door, through the walls of the hut. What were they waiting for? What did they want? What possessed them to act in this manner?

She leaned her head against the wall, shutting her eyes for a moment to rest them. She was anxious about Adran now. How would he return home through that huge crowd of dogs? Would they let him pass unharmed? If there was trouble in the city, was he caught up in it? Surely he would be fine; he was with Princess Karni, after all. The royal guard would not let any harm befall her. Perhaps he had been tasked with driving her back to the palace and then decided to stay there till morning, until order was restored.

This was what she hoped, that he would be safe in the palace. Alternatively, she hoped that even if he did choose to come home, he would use the back alley. The lane that went down the hill led directly to the chariot compound adjoining the palace. Adran was usually in the habit of coming around by the main street since he usually stopped to buy something or other from the marketplace on the way home, but at this late hour all the shops would be closed and she hoped he would make an exception and come straight home . . .

Her thoughts were rambling now, she realized, making no sense anymore. She was anxious. She felt tears well up in her eyes and drip onto the back of her hand. She leaned against the wall and prayed for her husband's safe return. He and Kern were all she had in this world. Like Adran, she too was an orphan, her family lost in one of the countless caste feuds that plagued their home district. That was why they had come to Hastinaga and settled here, over two decades ago. Surely they had not survived that violence at home to end their lives here?

No, no, no, she should not be allowing herself to think like that. She wiped her cheek with her hand and took a deep breath, pushing away from the wall. She took hold of herself and opened her eyes, determined to be strong, no matter what this night might bring.

When she saw the yellow light, her first thought was *Fire!*

It was always a danger in the big city. With so many dwellings packed so close together, a small fire could quickly leap across lanes and alleys, growing into a citywide blaze. She had heard that Mraashk had burned down in a single night, although that was linked to the usurper Sanka's cruel regime. She could not imagine Hastinaga burning. It would be a horror to beat all horrors.

The light was coming from behind her from inside the house. She gasped and sprang to her feet. Had she left the fire burning? That was impossible. She hadn't been at the cookfire for hours. It couldn't have remained alight all this while without adding charcoal. And she clearly remembered sweeping up the ashes and banking the embers before leaving the kitchen alcove.

The light was coming from the eastern room. It had always been the storeroom, but ever since Kern came into their lives, it was where he slept as well. It was the first room to get the light of the rising sun, and even as a baby, she would wake in the morning and find that he had crawled all the way there to sleep, so finally she had made him a cot in that room, and it was there that he slept to this day.

She gasped, thinking Kern's room was on fire.

She ran the short distance of a few yards, then stopped abruptly.

There was no fire in the room.

The light was coming from Kern himself.

Karni

~

KARNI WAS FIGHTING FOR her life, Adran beside her.

Both of them were doing everything they could to keep the mob of maniacs at bay. The poor horse, Sreela, had long since succumbed, and now the chariot was surrounded on all sides by people. Men, women, and children, old and young, fat and thin, ailing and healthy and strong and weak — all manner of folk. The one thing, the *only* thing, that they all had in common was madness. Every single one of them was utterly out of their mind.

Their eyes were dilated, bulging from their sockets, their tongues lolling, their limbs splayed, flopping in all directions like the tentacles of some sea creature rather than mammalian bipeds. They seemed to have lost all control of their limbs. Whether running or attacking, they seemingly had no means of regulating where their hands went, how their legs moved, where their eyes were looking.

A middle-aged woman with streaks of grey in her hair was trying to climb over the well of the chariot, but backward, flailing her legs and arms as if that would enable her to get over. Karni winced as she struck the woman's shoulder with the hilt of her sword, knocking her off balance. The woman fell back to the street and was instantly stamped on and climbed over by others seeking to get at the chariot. Disturbing to behold though it was, it was this lack of bodily control that was keeping the mob from overrunning them. Had these same people had full command of their bodies, they would easily have overwhelmed the chariot. However fiercely Karni and Adran might fight, they were no match for a hundred attackers. Or two hundred. Or however many there were surrounding them.

Karni had lost all sense of numbers or time. Her arrows had run out a while ago, and she had picked up a sword in one hand and was using the bow like a staff in the other, striking with the hilt and the flat of the blade whenever possible. Adran was not as considerate. He was hacking and cutting down people without a second thought. She knew that she would have to start doing the same any moment now. There were just too many of these lunatics and only two of them.

But are they really *mad?* Karni couldn't quite understand how so many people could just lose their minds all of a sudden. And why were they all attacking her chariot?

A burly man in a rich noble's robes tried to climb onto the rear of the chariot. Adran's face was turned for a second as he dealt with another attacker, and the man lunged at the charioteer's back, teeth bared in a wolflike snarl.

"Charioteer!" Karni called.

She lashed out with the sword, catching the man's forehead with the blunt side of the blade. A strip of skin tore free, sending blood washing down the man's face, over his right eye. The man turned toward Karni — not even blinking his eye, despite the blood running into it — and snarled at her, lunging in her direction now. She struck out with the bow, but he snatched it and wrenched hard, twisting her wrist to breaking point; she let it fall.

He came at her with the viciousness of a hungry wolf.

The man was twice Karni's height and as wide around as her arms could spread. She cried out in distress and plunged the blade into his torso out of a sense of self-preservation. The sword pierced his chest, and she felt the blade strike bone and catch. The man growled at her, teeth snapping at the hand that held the sword. Karni yanked back the weapon and swept it at his head again as he came at her once more. This time she hacked at his neck — with the edge rather than the flat of the blade — and almost severed the man's head with the blow; he toppled sideways, his weight knocking down several others with him.

Blood spattered across Karni, all over her hands and face and hair. But she had no time for revulsion, so she spat it out and brought the sword about to stave off a pair of young girls in nightdresses climbing over the chariot's side, hitting one with the hilt, the other with the heel of her palm. The blow jarred her funny bone, and her hand went numb for an instant. She used the other hand with the bow to defend herself as the numb hand fell useless by her side.

The strangest thing about the mob surrounding them was how silent they were. Not one person was speaking, or shouting, or saying anything coherent. The only noises they made were snarls, growls, and other animal sounds. It was as if they had all lost the power of speech and all other normal human faculties had been replaced with the single-minded need to attack, maim, kill, and destroy.

"Princess!" Adran shouted. "We must break free of this mob."

Karni used the points of the bow to jab another pair of attackers in their faces, shaking her numb hand to try and restore circulation faster. "How do we do that?"

Adran slashed the point of the lance across several attackers at once. Karni tried not to look at the blood spurting and the ugly gashes caused by the weapon.

"I will draw them upon myself, while you climb over that wall," he said, gesturing quickly with the lance before swinging it down forcefully across the neck of another assailant.

Karni looked in the direction he had indicated; he meant the wall about three yards away. If she climbed onto the edge of the well of the chariot, she could probably climb onto the top of the wall. There were fewer attackers on that side because of the chariot's proximity to the wall. It was a good plan, except for one thing.

"What about you?"

He jabbed the point of the lance into the throat of an attacker. She averted her eyes from the point of impact — it was a young woman in her bridal attire.

"My Krushan law is to serve and protect you, my princess."

Karni felt the tingling pain that indicated her arm was awake again. She hefted the sword, swinging it at an old man struggling to climb over the chariot. The hilt cracked his nose, breaking it, and he toppled backward, disappearing into the mob.

"I will not leave without you, charioteer. We fight together, we leave together."

Adran cursed as three attackers came at him at once. Karni wanted to go to his aid, but there were several on her side as well. Were there more of them coming now than before? It certainly seemed like it. She tried to see beyond the crowd of manic-eyed, frenzied miens lolling up at her from all directions. The entire street appeared to be moving, seething with faces and limbs. Holy Goddess Jeel! How many were there? Was all Hastinaga trying to kill her? What insanity was this?

"Where is the city guard? The royal guard?" she asked, as she fought off attackers with both the bow and the sword. Her arms were starting to hurt now.

Adran was sweating profusely and sucking in air in gulps between strikes. "I fear we are on our own, Princess. We must fend for ourselves."

But just then, a sound attracted her attention. A sound like the ocean tide.

Karni looked up at the street ahead, the same crossroads that they had been headed toward an hour — or was it two hours? — ago, and was shocked by what she saw.

Thousands more people were swarming down the street now. Climbing over walls. Down the side of houses. They were falling over each other, trampling one another, stampeding . . . All rushing toward the chariot.

Coming to kill Karni.

She felt her heart leap in her chest. "Goddess!"

Adran glanced up, and she saw the look of horror on his face. "Surya!"

So dense was the crowd that it actually pushed and crushed the people who were already surrounding the chariot, pressing their bodies against the sides of the vehicle. Karni heard the sound of metal and wood cracking and crumpling, saw the sides of the chariot starting to buckle. The weight of thousands of bodies pushed down the street, cracking the bones of the vehicle. She felt the floor heave under her feet, starting to rise and crack. Her tired arms fell by her sides.

The attackers had mostly stopped now, crushed between the horde flowing down the street and the walls of the chariot. She saw their bodies being pushed so hard, their eyes popped loose of their sockets, their shoulders dislocated, then broke, legs and hips cracked, flesh mashed into bloody pulp like grapes in a press . . .

But Adran had stopped fighting too.

He and Karni both looked at each other, and this time he did not suggest she escape.

There were people coming over the wall as well, literally falling over it in their eagerness to get at the chariot. She could hear the sickening sound their bodies made as they thumped onto those already trapped between the chariot and the wall, bone striking bone, striking flesh, striking skulls. The chariot was crumbling to pieces now, and she felt as if it would collapse upon itself at any moment, smashing her and Adran into the same pulp as those poor unfortunates.

That was when she looked up and saw the sun rise in the middle of the night.

Reeda

~

REEDA HAD, AT FIRST, thought that the fire was in Kern's bed, but soon realized it was not a fire at all and that Kern was, in fact, quite safe and sound.

Still sleeping deeply beneath his sheet, he lay exactly as she had last seen him, several minutes earlier. But now there was an illumination emanating from his body — buttery yellow light leaking from his skin, his head, his toes, every inch of his being. She could see it through the sheet, limning his outline.

He was literally glowing.

She couldn't understand what could be causing this strange phenomenon. It frightened her and made her want to cry out, but she forced herself to breathe and stay calm.

He is no ordinary boy, you know that already, Reeda, she reminded herself. From the very first time she had laid eyes on him, she had known her little Kern was special. The armorlike growths on his shoulders, chest, back, and ears. The way he spent every waking minute under direct sunlight, as if his body craved it, needed it, drank it in the way a thirsty camel gulped down liters and liters of water. Various incidents over the years had only confirmed his special qualities, including that first fight with the rich noble's spoiled son and his mates, ending in open court before Dowager Empress Jilana and Prince Regent Vrath, when he was but six. Other incidents with similar results followed in subsequent years. Now, although a year later, Kern had grown in status more than height or breadth. Still small and relatively puny for his age, his reputation had grown formidably. What was it Adran always said? It's not the size of the hound in the fight, it's the size of the fight in the hound. That was very true of Kern, and every boy in the area knew it well.

Now when Kern walked down a street, most boys — and even grown men — knew well enough to stay out of his way. No one challenged or threatened him anymore — and those who had done so in the past had cried out their stories loudly enough for everyone in the neighborhood to know better. His fighting skills were so prodigious, even Adran said he had never heard of anyone with such ability other than Vrath himself. In his own small way, little Kern was a legend in these parts. Word of him had even spread to other parts of the city, and from time to time Reeda had seen groups of boys or young men, even some sellswords, hanging around the vicinity, waiting to lay eyes on the young fighter who had bested a dozen in his first fight, armed with only a wooden practice sword.

But this was an entirely new addition to his legend.

He was literally glowing with light from within. Not just a dull glow, but brilliant yellow, luminous light that looked like that of the sun god himself. Reeda gazed up at the dappled light on the ceiling, the walls, the floor of the room — if she had not known it was coming from her son, she would have believed it was the light of the sun.

As she watched, Kern stirred in his sleep. This too was unusual. He was moving his legs and arms, adjusting his position, raising his head.

Then — suddenly — he opened his eyes.

The light from his eyes shot up to the ceiling like a single large beam of sunlight. Bright as the glow from his body was, the beams emanating from his eyes were extremely intense. Golden-hued and steady as god-given sunlight.

Kern sat up.

Reeda took a step back. *What are you doing, Reeda?* she asked herself. *Are you afraid of your own son?* Truth be told, she was, at least a little.

Though his eyes were open, Kern did not appear to be awake. He seemed to be staring at the wall with no awareness. He was sitting up, straight and still, barely breathing.

Reeda stepped forward again, tentatively.

He did not react.

"Kern?" she said softly.

Kern did not react to the sound of his name.

"Kern, are you awake?" she asked.

Still no response.

She watched him uncertainly, wondering what to make of this. But then, without warning, he rose to his feet. The sheet covering him fell to the bedding, and Kern stood and turned around to face the doorway. Reeda could see his face clearly now, glowing with the same yellow light, his eyes beaming the brightest. There was no recognition in his gaze, no response. He might as well have been fast asleep, yet his eyes were open and staring dead ahead.

"Vashta?" she asked, with some concern now.

He did not even look at her . . . and then began walking. He walked out of the room and down the hallway. When Reeda realized he was heading toward the front door, she exclaimed and ran after him, her bare feet padding across the floor.

"No, don't open the door, there are dogs —" she said.

Kern opened the front door anyway, ignoring Reeda's pleas, and stepped outside, barefoot and still dressed only in his loincloth.

Reeda gasped and ran to the doorway, then stepped outside without hesitation. Kern didn't know about the dogs. What if they —

She stopped short.

The dogs had all risen to their feet.

Thousands upon thousands of them, filling every available space on the hillside, in the street, between the houses, in the front yards, and even on the walls and every available surface.

They were all now staring at at Reeda's sweet boy.

Kern stood on the stoop, staring blankly at nothing at all. His body glowed with the bright, yellow luminescence. It leaked from his pores, flowed from inside his skin, illuminating the night, dispelling the darkness.

Reeda could see the upturned faces of the dogs caught by Kern's light. They were staring raptly at the little boy standing there. Their animal eyes gleamed and reflected back the light as animal eyes did. Their mouths were shut, their tongues no longer lolling. They were gazing at him as if mesmerized. As if they had been waiting for him to waken and emerge from the house.

Reeda froze where she was. If all these dogs began attacking her Kern, would his prodigious fighting skills be enough to save him from such an onslaught? Other boys or men would attack with weapons, one or two or maybe ten at a time. But thousands of dogs, each with a set of teeth sharp and strong enough to bite a man's fingers off in a single snap — how could anyone hope to defend against such a horde? Besides, Kern was completely unarmed, and he stood there in his langot, apparently still asleep but with his eyes open.

For a long moment, neither Kern nor the dogs moved beyond simple breathing and blinking.

Then Kern began walking.

He went down the steps of the stoop and reached the street level, and to Reeda's shock, the dogs moved aside for him. He continued walking out to the gate, then into the street beyond. As he passed them by, each dog began to turn and follow him with their eyes, watching him intently.

Kern continued walking down the hill. Unmolested.

The dogs that were behind him began to move forward, following him, now. The dogs still ahead of him stayed where they were, waiting. When Kern passed them by, their heads turned, following his progress. Once he had walked by, their bodies turned as well and they began trailing after him.

Reeda didn't hesitate for even a moment. Once she saw that the dogs were not hostile toward her Kern, she went down the steps, following in her son's wake.

Kern walked quickly downhill, moving much faster than Reeda could. The dogs began trotting, picking up speed. The noise of thousands of claws clicking on the ground was surprisingly loud. Reeda followed just behind the enormous horde of raised tails, trying her best to keep pace.

It was the strangest procession she had ever seen. She kept glancing at the houses on either side of the street, but she saw not a single face or pair of eyes looking out. Everyone appeared to be fast asleep. She wondered how a person could sleep through such a night, but then again, it *was* a very strange night — even the moon above was as if in a state of eclipse, yet there definitely was no such occultation tonight, or she would have known. Perhaps that was what was keeping people indoors, the superstitious fear of an eclipse? But that did not explain why they were not looking out of their windows. Even the strange sight and sounds of a young boy followed by thousands of dogs did not warrant their attention — with a boy at the head of the procession whose body and eyes emanated a brilliant bright yellow glow, no less.

The light lit up the dark streets and the fronts of the houses Kern passed by, and reflected off the undersides of the roofs. For the first several hundred yards, they encountered no other people. Then they turned a corner, the smaller side street giving way to a larger avenue, and Reeda gasped: the avenue was packed with people.

It looked like all of Hastinaga had poured out of their houses and taken to the streets. But not just citizens; soldiers, too, were among the crowd. Apart from the obvious strangeness of this large crowd gathered on a city avenue in the middle of an already strange night, Reeda noted several odd things as well.

The crowd was dead silent, for one thing. Not a single person was talking or saying a word. Not even to each other. But there were other oddities too: soldiers and citizens mingled freely, which was not protocol. She could see children, women, older people, soldiers, priests, merchants, rich, poor — all together, literally rubbing shoulders. Many of those shoulders were bare, as the crowd appeared to be in their nightwear, as if they had risen from their beds and come out into the streets spontaneously. Even many of the soldiers were only partially clothed, as if they had been undressing after a tour of duty and suddenly been struck by the urge to go out and wander the streets.

All of them were staring up at the sky, seemingly at the moon specifically, as if hypnotized. Their mouths hung open, dribbling saliva, drooling senselessly. And the way they stood, limbs hanging limply, looked completely unnatural, like puppets dangling from loose strings.

Then Kern came around the corner onto the avenue, followed by his army of dogs —

And the crowd *reacted*.

They turned as one, the noise made by their bodies turning, their clothes rustling, their feet shuffling on the street the only sounds in the silence of the night. Their slack-jawed faces turned to face Kern, their eyes struggling visibly to focus on him, like a walleyed person looking two different directions at once. The way all of them were staggering was rather bizarre, as if all in this crowd were suddenly somehow incapable of moving their bodies normally. In a way, they reminded Reeda of the oddity of the dogs — but only in the perfect unison with which they moved, like they had rehearsed this very moment a thousand times. Except that whereas the dogs had still seemed like dogs, their four-footed bodies moving surely and normally, these people seemed to no longer be human beings, not *normal* human beings at least — it was like they were all afflicted with some condition, the exact same condition, and it linked them into a human chain joined by an invisible thread. The actions of any one of them were perfectly copied by all of the others in perfect synchronicity.

Now they all, as one, looked at Kern. He walked down the avenue toward the crowd, the dogs following dutifully behind him — and the crowd, as one, charged at him.

One moment they were still, staring slack-jawed and walleyed, heads lolling, arms limp, legs loose and uncoordinated. The next instant, they were charging toward Reeda's son, bodies moving so erratically and spasmodically that she thought they must be afflicted with some awful disease, except she knew of no affliction that could work and spread — infecting thousands of healthy, ordinary people — this quickly, let alone cause them to behave in such a crazed manner.

They charged at Kern with mouths open, teeth bared, and now Reeda heard them speaking for the first time, if the noises that emanated from them could be called speech; what Reeda heard was more akin to snarling, growling, roaring, grunting, chuffing . . . a variety of incomprehensible noises better suited to animals than to people.

And then, with a shock that rippled down her spine and raised the hackles on her bare arms, Reeda witnessed perhaps the strangest event of the night: The dogs replied. With words.

"*Protect!*" they cried, shouting with one voice from a thousand throats. "*Protect! Protect!*"

And the army of dogs charged.

Adri

~

"GELDRY?"

Adri felt his way along the bed. His hand found his wife's foot, and he hesitated. She appeared to be still, and from the faint sound of her breathing, seemed to be asleep. He started to rise again, suddenly overcome by the urge to remove himself from her presence, to be anywhere but here. He was not prepared to do this, to meet with her so soon after . . . after committing infidelity. He was too confused by his own feelings. He needed time to sort through them, to make sense of what had happened tonight, what he had done.

He stood up and started to make his way back toward the doorway. Yes, he would leave her be now, spend the rest of the night in his sky chamber, resting, recovering in the serene environment designed to promote mindfulness and healing. Perhaps tomorrow he would come see her. The maids had said she was well, merely resting, so there was no reason to be concerned. He needed some time alone, apart from her.

The worst thing was, he didn't feel guilty. He knew he *should* feel guilty, terribly remorseful and ashamed of himself for what he had done. Slept with another woman. A maid, at that. Someone he barely knew, had never spoken a word to until today, apart from asking for a drink of water or for refreshments, or some such routine request. Someone he had never given a thought to until the moment he woke in her room and found himself naked in bed with her. He had cheated on his wife, defiled the sanctity of their marriage vows, and he ought to feel horrible for having done that.

Instead, he felt refreshed, liberated, more relaxed than he had been in years, perhaps in his entire life. He felt so content, so satisfied, so much at ease. The lovemaking had been wonderful, like nothing he had ever experienced before, but that was only part of it. The real reason had been the way she had accepted him, joined with him, treated him as a lover, a man, an intimate friend, without judgment, rancor, emotional entanglement, or complication. There were no ulterior considerations, no thinking about wealth and power, the alliances between tribes and nations, the state of the empire, no concern about the difference between their peoples, between her status and his, no care that he was the prince of the great Burnt Empire and she a lowly maid. Just two bodies meeting in the night, two souls mating. The heat of passion, the fire of arousal, the mutual quenching of desire. They had been man and woman, nothing more, nothing less.

And it had left him feeling *wonderful*. Like a man, a prince, a king, an emperor. And in that moment of ecstasy, Sauvali had been his woman, his princess, his queen, his empress. It did not matter that she had no title and would never have one. All that mattered was what they were to one another in those most intimate, most private moments in the darkness and privacy of her room.

For the first time in his life, Adri felt whole, complete, desired, needed. Sauvali had needed him at that moment. She had wanted his body on hers, his mouth on her breasts, his lingam in her yoni, his seed inside herself. And he had given her what she wanted, he had aroused her, and he had satisfied her. That simple act, uncomplicated by politics, concerns of wealth, status, family ties, imperial alliances, had been so fulfilling, so satisfying; he had never realized life could have such pleasures.

It was to preserve that feeling that he wanted to withdraw from Geldry for a while, from his marriage.

To savor the pleasure. To enjoy this delicious state of abandonment he was in right now.

Suddenly, none of the cares and worries that had weighed him down yesterday mattered anymore. The politics of the empire, the line of succession, Shvate's military accomplishments, his own lack of military victories, the power imbalance between himself and his elders — the question of who really ran the empire, the never-ending pressure from Geldry on him to wield *more* power, make *more* decisions, exert *more* influence. Urging him to take the throne as was his birthright. The constant harping about how brilliant her brother Kune was as a political advisor, how Adri should take his advice, let the man guide his political career.

But Adri didn't even *want* a political career! He was content to let each person do what they did best: Shvate fight the battles, Vrath run the empire, Mother Jilana hold court. Hastinaga was powerful, wealthy, stable, at peace — or as much at peace as any great empire ever could be. There was no need to change things. Why not simply live? Enjoy the power and wealth they had been given. They were so privileged to be born in such a House, while millions starved, suffering terrible, unspeakable abuse, prejudice, disenfranchisement, and misery. Adri and Geldry had everything anyone could ever want from life already. What had they to fight for? Why not simply live and enjoy the bounty they had been given? Give thanks and blessings for the abundance?

Sauvali, on the other hand, had almost nothing and was perfectly content with her lot. Even though they had not spoken of her circumstances, he had sensed that contentment within her. Heard it in her lack of complaint. Felt it in her ability to give herself over so completely to pleasure and the moment.

Geldry lacked those qualities. She was constantly chasing, wanting, demanding . . . She was the kind of woman who would have everything and then one day see a neighbor with a flower she had just plucked, or a hair color that was different, or anything, the slightest thing, and she would want it too. Demand it to the point where if she did not get that thing at once, she would become adamant, defiant, mean, angry. Adri had known her to fly into rages over something some courtier had remarked about her appearance, or her garb, or a savory served at a feast, and Geldry would simmer and seethe until Adri and she returned to their chambers, then explode with suppressed rage and discontent. She would speak of killing the woman or man who had made the remark, of gouging their eyes out, cutting off their tongue, slaughtering their entire clan, reacting so disproportionately to the single critical remark that Adri often wondered if that was how she had been raised in Geldran: to wreak havoc on anyone who crossed her with even a single misspoken word. He knew Geldrans were proud and fierce to the point of instant violence when challenged, but the Geldrans he had known had also prided themselves on their self-control, discipline, and extreme courtesy. Geldry put paid to that cultural image: Adri realized that her family was the kind likely to start a feud over an unkind word, or punish the slightest offense, even one given inadvertently.

It made Adri uncomfortable in the extreme. At times, he wanted to simply walk away from her when she was in such a mood. He couldn't endure such violent outbursts. As it was, by virtue of being deprived of sight, his other senses were extremely sensitive, and Geldry's emotional explosions were like an *assault* on his senses, reducing him to a quivering bundle of nerves whenever they erupted. It often took him days to recover from one of her outbursts.

So it was with no guilt, no remorse, no shame that he sought now to withdraw himself from her presence, if only for a while. He would see about the future later; the present was still so placid, so beautiful, he wanted to savor the afterglow of his night with Sauvali for as long as possible.

He was almost at the doorway when he heard a soft voice call his name.

"Adri."

The voice was so soft, so unlike Geldry, that he thought that someone else had called him, someone from outside the chamber. It could not be Geldry. But it was.

"Adri . . . are you there?"

He stood still for a moment, weighing his options. Perhaps he could simply walk out, pretend he had not heard. Perhaps she had not actually seen him, had only heard the sound of his feet shuffling. He could walk out, go to his akasa chamber, enjoy the few hours left in the night in solitude, then when the sun rose, feel its warm embrace, bask in its warmth, relive the pleasures of the night over and over. He felt that if he did this, if he withdrew into himself and spent some time alone, he would drift naturally to a place wherefrom he could make sense of his entire existence, see the way ahead more clearly, have a better command of the future and what he wanted to do with his life. He felt more certain of this than he had ever felt about anything before.

"Adri . . . ?"

He sighed, turned, walked slowly back into the room.

Later, in the days, weeks, months, and years to come . . . the decades even . . . he would always remember this moment. This turning point in his life. The one time he was walking away from what was toward what could

be. The moment when he was poised on the cusp of the past and the future. When he felt as if he had some control of his own existence. When
he could change things by changing himself. When he felt himself changing
from within, and all he had to do was go along with it. Let it ripen and grow
naturally, simply nurturing the change and letting what would be *be*.

The moment when he could have changed who he was and become who
he really wanted to be.

And instead, he had stayed back with Geldry.

"I'm here," he said quietly.

He stood there, closer to the doorway than to the bed, waiting.

"Come to me," she said.

He shuffled forward, finding his way back to the bed, then stood beside it.

"Sit," she said.

He sat.

"Give me your hand," she said.

He gave her his hand.

"Adri, what happened tonight was wonderful. It was so beautiful and incredible, I don't have words to describe it."

At first he could not understand what she was talking about. He thought
she was speaking of something that had happened earlier, before they had
gone to bed. It made no sense at all, because he could barely remember anything before waking up in bed beside Sauvali. It was as if, for him, a curtain
had divided his life: Before Sauvali and After Sauvali, a life in two acts.

"When you made love to me, it was like nothing else I've felt before."

A strange sensation began to chill his spine. He felt his hands grow cold,
the blood fleeing them to return to his heart.

"Your passion, your strength, your virility . . . You were the man I always
knew you were, the man I wanted you to be. My man. My Adri."

He wanted to pull his hand away, to rush from the room, to scream, to
cry out, to rage. Instead, he sat there, letting her hold his hand, listening to
her voice in the night-shrouded bedchamber.

"And your virility was so masculine, so intense, I am certain that tonight,
your seed flowered in my womb. I am sure that you impregnated me tonight, Adri. I can feel your child inside me. I am going to be the mother of
your offspring. I am so certain of it, I cannot describe it in words. It is like
a living thing already, alive and aware inside me, growing and flourishing.

That is what I wanted you to know, Adri. That your seed has taken root inside my womb. Soon, I will bear you an heir. Many heirs. And together we will rule the empire."

He listened without saying a word. There were no words to describe what he was feeling just then. Even the most honey-tongued court bards could not compose a poem that would express the emotions roiling inside of him in that moment.

He sat and listened as she talked and talked. Until she tired of talking. Until she fell asleep at last, breathing calmly, contentedly, leaving him the extreme opposite of calm and content.

Karni

～

KARNI SAW THE LIGHT at the crossroads and thought it was the sun. It was bright as the dawn, honey golden in hue, and it suffused the entire street, lighting up the entire neighborhood and that part of the city. But as it came closer, she saw it surely was something else, for it was moving along the street. She saw the mob around her stop, reacting to the light, and then, as if with a single hive mind, every one of them turned to face it. This was no more eerie than anything else about their strange behavior until now, but there was something different about it. A sound rose from their open slack mouths. A sound like a groan or a sigh. An inhuman, incomprehensible sound that was like no word in any human language that she knew. But its meaning was clear. The mob was angry — and scared.

The light continued down the street, coming toward her. Now she could see it a little more clearly. She raised one tired arm, the sword still held in her fist, dripping blood, to shield her eyes from the full glare of the light, and by doing this, she was able to make out the source. It looked like . . . a boy! A human boy, a mere child, walking down the street. Aside from his glow, he looked perfectly ordinary, unlike any of the crazed mob who had been attacking Karni and Adran these past hours. Except for the radiance — that bright, golden sunlight — emanating from every part of his body.

Not perfectly ordinary, however, were his companions. Behind him came a group of animals — dogs. A crowd of ragtag canines of all sizes, colors, ages, breeds.

The dogs followed the boy who glowed like sunlight, filling the street with their numbers; there were hundreds of them, perhaps a thousand or more. Many of the dogs at the rear of the pack were limping, some visibly struggling to walk, others collapsing and lying down on the street, unable to take another step, but still trying to crawl bravely, pulling themselves forward inch by inch, as if they were determined to be loyal to their little human master to the very end. Karni sensed that there had been more dogs, that many had been hurt or killed and had fallen along the way, and these were now all that remained.

It was one of the strangest sights she had ever seen — a boy who shone like sunshine walking down a city street with a thousand dogs following loyally at his heel. But then stranger yet, the mob, as one, began shambling toward the boy.

Slowly, by degrees, they picked up speed, eventually breaking into a loping run, their limbs still flailing, their mouths open, heads jerking in every direction, bodies spasming. The sound from their throats grew louder, too, becoming an angry growl.

She was startled when the dogs began to shout.

"Protect! Protect!"

She gasped and covered her mouth. She had seen it with her own eyes and heard it with her own ears, but she couldn't believe it. Dogs shouting! While humans growled incoherently.

She turned to Adran. He was staring at the street with a peculiar expression on his face — not the surprise or shock that she knew must be visible on her own face.

It was pride.

"Kern . . ." he said softly.

The word pierced her heart.

"Protect! Protect!" the dogs called out again, and she saw them swarm forward, tails raised and stiff, eyes shining and alert, muzzles parted to reveal their fangs. Many of them were bloody from earlier fights, and she realized that the boy and his pack must have fought their way across the city to reach this place.

Karni thought, then, of Jeel Ma's words: *If he were my son, I would not think twice, but he is not my son . . .*

Just as it seemed the mob and the pack of dogs would meet in a bloodbath, the boy stopped in the middle of the street. The maniacs were charging toward him, murder in their eyes, while he was unarmed and defenseless; yet still he stood there calmly, gazing at them without fear.

That is what it means to be a god or a demigod, Jeel Ma had said. All this power, and yet when the time comes, we must use it in service of our devotees; otherwise, what use are we as gods?

"Kern," said Adran proudly. "My son."

The dogs began surging forward, snapping their jaws, waving their tails, ready to attack the oncoming mob, to fight tooth and claw, to lay down their lives to protect their beloved leader. But the boy raised his arms, and they suddenly went still. He raised his head, and they fell back, retreating behind him.

Karni saw the dogs slink down till their bellies touched the street, lowering their heads till their muzzles touched their forepaws. They lay flat on the street, like dogs who had been commanded by their master. Their tails went down, their jaws closed, and they obediently waited and stared at the oncoming mob.

The maniacs roared with fury, running full tilt now at the boy. From Karni's point of view, it was like watching a tidal wave about to wash over a tiny snail. In another moment or two, they would reach him and surely engulf him with their fury, tearing him apart with their hands and teeth, ripping his little body to shreds, devouring him.

The boy spoke a single word.

"Enough!"

The word echoed like the voice of thunder, booming not only through the street, but throughout the city, the entire valley, resonating off the Krushan hills yojanas away. It reverberated in Karni's chest, striking the center of her pain, her guilt, her shame. It brought a smile across Adran's face. It made the woman standing far behind the pack of dogs and watching gasp with awe and grin with amazement. It made every single person in that great metropolis stop whatever they were doing and look in the direction from where the sound had come.

More powerful than the word and the voice was the light from the boy. Now it was bursting forth in an unrestrained explosion brighter than the flare of the brightest sunlight on the hottest summer day.

It blazed forth from the boy's every pore like the purest power itself, the power that created and destroyed universes, that made and rebuilt worlds, that ended and began creation. Like the flames of the sun. The destructive power of an exploding star. The brilliance of a solar flare.

For an instant, all Hastinaga was as bright as day.

Karni and Adran and the woman trailing behind the dogs were all forced to shut their eyes to protect themselves from the glare. Even the dogs lying in the street shut their eyes.

Only the ones afflicted by the devil's poison dared to stare, transfixed, gazing at the boy exploding with radiance like a sun in fury. They stared and felt the pure, intrusive energy of the light filling the cells of their bodies, purging them of the poison that they had been infected with, cleansing them.

Then the light faded —

And the boy returned to being a boy again.

The dogs rose to their feet, wagged their tails once, and became mere dogs again.

And the infected blinked and became human once more.

And with an explosion of emotion in her breast, Karni learned for the first time in years that the child she had placed in a basket and put into the loving arms of Goddess Jeel was still alive. Still alive and right here, in the very city where she herself lived.

Vessa

~

VESSA MATERIALIZED IN THE forest. He arrived striding with his usual long-limbed pace, not slowing an instant. A pair of foxes feeding on a rabbit they had hunted down were startled by his appearance and fled barking, but otherwise the jungle absorbed his presence without a flutter. He was as much a part of the jungle as the foxes, the rabbit, the trees, and the insects. In a sense, he *was* the forest.

He was also angry. His tall, lean body shook with rage. It took him several miles of brisk walking before he was able to calm himself.

He'd failed. He'd been unable to apprehend the Reygistani when he chased him through the portal on the verandah of Jilana's bedchamber. It had led him on a journey through time and space, taking him to other dimensions, strange alien worlds, to the future and back again. It had taken him decades before he finally realized he was being led on a wild, aimless chase. Jarsun had anticipated that Jilana would summon her son and that Vessa would then come after him, and thus he had laid down false trails for this very purpose — created not just one or two, but an infinite number of false trails, all in the hopes of keeping Vessa infinitely occupied with his pursuit. Vessa could have spent eons chasing after Jarsun without ever finding him. But he could not afford to spend an eon hunting the Reygistani — there was mischief abroad here on Arthaloka, in this age and time, and if good would prevail, he would need to be present to prevent further damage.

Vessa was not easily tricked, and he had come within finger's breadth of apprehending Jarsun, but still the Reygistani had eluded him somehow. It did not matter how. What mattered was that the Reygistani had outwitted him by anticipating his actions, and Vessa must not allow that to happen again.

The next time he went after the devil, he must find a way to get the upper hand. He would meditate on it. All solutions presented themselves through meditation.

He started toward his hermitage. Before he could reach it, he felt a ripple in the wind. The grass shirred. The leaves rustled. The insects chittered. The animals called out. The jungle was telling him something, passing on a message.

He listened.

It was not good news.

Mayla

~

MAYLA CAME TO KARNI'S chambers, trembling and on the verge of tears. She forced herself to breathe deeply and regain control of herself before entering. The sentry at the door tried hard to remain stoic and stare ahead as always, but he could see her distress and could not help but be moved.

"Princess . . ." he began, sounding concerned.

She raised a hand, cutting him off.

She shook her head once, firmly. She was not willing to bandy words with a sentry right now. With anyone.

He shut his mouth and returned to attention.

She breathed in again, counting to ten slowly, then released the breath. She repeated this twice more, slower each time, until she felt her pulse steady. She was a warrior. A warrior had to remain calm and in control at all times. It could make the difference between life and death: not just one's own life, but the lives of one's fighting comrades as well. She was a warrior; she knew how to regain control.

Her breathing calm now, her face composed, she shot a glance at the sentry. He looked straight ahead, avoiding her, but his lip trembled slightly. Her temper was notorious, as was the strength of her arm. She nodded and passed him by, entering her sister queen's bedchamber.

Karni was standing by the verandah, staring at the risen sun. The morning was hours old, and the city was slowly limping back to normal. Mayla had seen the aftereffects of the rioting and destruction that had taken place the night before as she rode into the city. It must have been quite a night. But it was what had happened to her and Shvate that she was here to talk about.

"Karni," she said, softly but clearly.

Karni did not respond at once. She remained standing as she was, staring out at the late morning sky. She looked as if she had been crying, though her eyes were now dry, her face clean — as if she had wept and then freshened her appearance. She was bathed and dressed in clean clothes, as beautiful and regal as always. Whatever was troubling her, she remained the image of queenly perfection. That was one of the many qualities Mayla admired about Karni.

Mayla herself had been raised as a fighter, by brothers and father and uncles, all of whom had been fighters as well. To her, keeping her sword spotless, sharp-edged, and shining was more important than what she wore or how she looked. Besides, she had never had a problem turning men's heads, even when she was at her most scruffy or soiled with the dust of the field. Shvate had even commented more than once that he preferred her that way; it made her more desirable than if she were all dolled up and prettified.

But that didn't stop Mayla admiring women like Karni, who were beautiful in that exquisitely feminine way, immaculate in their appearance, their toilet, and their accoutrement. They reminded her of her mother, whom she had lost much too soon, when Mayla herself was barely eight years old. Her mother had died fighting of course, like almost all the women of their clan died, but she had been one of those rare women who could walk both roads: the one of feminine beauty as well as the one of warrior queen. Mayla had heard that Karni had fought for her life last night, and fought as bravely as any warrior in the field. She had no doubt about it: Karni was the complete woman, beautiful wife and warrior queen. She was the sister that Mayla had always desired, the mother she had lost too soon.

"Sister," she said now, still keeping her distance till Karni responded. Finally Karni seemed to realize someone else was in the room and turned her head slightly. "Mayla."

Mayla came forward, taking Karni's hand. She saw the cuts and bruises on the hand and the arm attached to it, and handled it tenderly. "My sister, I am so sorry for what you had to go through last night. I am glad you are well and that you survived the dark challenge of those terrible hours."

Karni did not meet her eyes. "Thank you."

Mayla searched her mind for a way to soften what she had to say next, but she could not find any. "I must tell you something."

Karni glanced at her now. "Must you?" She sighed. "Can it wait?"

Mayla swallowed, feeling terrible for pressing Karni at such a time. She was obviously exhausted. "Forgive me, but I must. It cannot wait."

Karni was silent, sat on a divan without saying anything further. Mayla took it as an invitation to sit beside her and speak. She sat next to Karni, still searching for the right words. Finally she decided that the only way to say it was to say it plainly and quickly.

"Last night something happened to Shvate and me in the forest."

Karni looked at Mayla squarely for the first time, genuine concern in her eyes. "Is Shvate well? Are you all right?"

"We are fine. Well. Physically unharmed. But what happened in the forest . . . it has changed things."

Karni looked puzzled.

"Changed things? What things?"

"Everything."

Karni stared at her. "I don't understand."

Mayla nodded. "I'm no good at explaining, you know that. I'm no storyteller, but I have to tell you a story now, and you have to listen very carefully. It's very, very important, perhaps the most important thing that has ever happened in our lives until now."

A strange look came over Karni's face. "The most important thing in our lives until now . . ."

"Yes. You have to believe me, Karni. I will tell you exactly what happened, and you must prepare yourself. Our lives are about to change completely from this day onward, but there was nothing we could have done to prevent it. We had no idea this was going to happen. If we had known . . ."

Karni stared at her. "You're speaking of Shvate and yourself?"

"Yes, yes, about what happened last night in the forest."

Karni nodded slowly. "Tell me what happened."

"I don't have your gift with words. If I'd spent more time with scrolls than with swords growing up . . ."

Karni shook her head slowly, frowning. "Never mind. Just tell me as best as you can. Start at the beginning and go through to the end. I'm listening."

Mayla nodded, relieved. This sounded more like the Karni she knew, the Karni she needed right now. "Thank you, sister. I'm so very fortunate to have you as my sister queen. You have been such a treasure in my life since I came to Hastinaga. I don't know how I ever managed without you. Your wisdom, your grace, your elegance —"

"Mayla," Karni said gently but firmly, "Stop rambling and tell me what happened in the forest."

Mayla nodded, breathing again, regaining control. "We had been hunting all day as we always do. We had a good hunt, a *very* good hunt. More carcasses than we could carry back in the chariot. More than enough for a full feast. We should have left it at that. My grandfather always used to say it's bad luck to hunt more than you can eat before the meat spoils. But Shvate and I were drinking all evening after the hunt and then we made love and then we drank and ate some more. Round about the time that you would have told us both to shut our gobs and go to bed, we got it into our heads that we should hunt more still."

"At night, after feasting and drinking all evening?"

"Yes, yes, it was stupid, I know. We both knew it even then. But we couldn't help it. It was as if the forest was different somehow. I thought it was because we had been drinking. But after we came back to the city this morning and heard about all that had happened, I started to think that maybe it wasn't just our imagination. I think there was something in the forest last night. An evil force. And *it* was hunting *us.*"

Karni was gripping Mayla's hand so tightly, Mayla could feel the bones in her knuckles creak. Karni's lips were pursed tightly, white with pressure. "Go on."

"We were too drunk to hunt, but we were also too drunk to know better. Shvate had this bright notion that he could hunt by sound alone. Every hunter can, of course, but only in the right circumstances, and these were definitely not the right circumstances. He was talking about Adri and about how amazing Adri had been during that battle they fought together."

"The Battle of the Rebels."

"Yes, that one. And he was describing how Adri shot down, I don't know, thirty, forty, fifty, a hundred enemies? All just by following the sounds they made. In the thick of battle, with chariots, horses, elephants, all around! I have to say, that does sound amazing."

"So Shvate began to hunt blind last night," Karni prompted.

"Yes. He made me bind his eyes. I couldn't find a strip of cloth that was the right length, so I tore off a strip of my undergarment and used that. He made some cracks about how nice it smelt and the softness of the fabric and... Anyway, finally we were in the woods, both with our eyes bound tightly—"

"You bound your eyes too?"

"Yes, we were both hunting together, but Shvate was going to shoot first, because I didn't feel right killing more animals when we already had so many carcasses."

Karni looked as if she was about to say something but then seemed to think better of it. "And then what happened?"

"And then we both heard an animal moving in the bushes. We began to track it."

"You both heard it?"

"Yes. But, Karni, you have to remember that we were both very, very drunk."

"I've seen you two get very, very drunk very many times before."

Mayla nodded and looked down for a moment, feeling her eyes tearing up now. "Yes, yes, I know what you're going to say. We drink too much, and we don't know when to stop. But it's how I was raised, how I grew up. Everyone around me, my father, my uncles, my brothers, even my aunts and sisters and grandfather, they all drank heavily. We were raised to be warriors, and warriors eat and drink."

"Until they pass out, vomit, or fall sick," Karni added. "Is that what makes them warriors?"

Mayla sighed. "I suppose not. I know it's wrong. I know we shouldn't have done it. I know all that. I swear I'll never drink again as long as I live. I know I've said that before, but I mean it this time, I really do, Karni."

"Don't make the promise unless you're willing to undergo the penance," Karni said. "Go on, finish your story."

Mayla sniffed and nodded. "So we tracked this noise through the bushes, and then Shvate said he had the prey, and I was giggling and making some stupid comment about how it sounded like the prey was mating or something because we could hear this strange snuffling and some other sounds. And then, and then"—she passed a hand over her face—"and then he loosed the arrow. And it struck its mark of course—you know Shvate never misses."

"He never misses," Karni agreed.

"I heard the sound of it striking home, and I laughed out loud, and I clapped my hands, I couldn't help myself. And I put my arms around his neck and kissed him and said he was the greatest warrior I had ever known and my grandfather would have been proud I had married such a man. And then Shvate and I went over to the prey, and when we went behind the bush, we saw, we saw —"

Mayla stopped, unable to continue. She was hitching in her breath, tears rolling down her face now.

"Easy, easy," Karni said softly, putting her arm around her and bracing her. "Here, drink some juice. Calm down." She held the cup up, but Mayla didn't take it.

"I have to finish," Mayla said. "I have to tell you the whole story."

Karni put the cup back down. "Go on."

"We went around the bush, and we saw that the prey he had hit with the arrow, what we both had thought was a stag and a deer in copulation, was actually not a stag and a deer at all. It was —" Mayla shook her head, her face twisting and distorting with pain. "Oh, Karni, it was a man and a woman, naked. They had been making love!"

Karni looked shocked. She sat still.

Mayla saw the look on Karni's face — the color had drained from it, and she was simply staring at Mayla. "I know what you're thinking. You think that we made a mistake. That we were so drunk that we mistook a man and a woman for a stag and a deer. But that wasn't what happened, Karni. I swear it wasn't."

"Then what did happen?" Karni asked.

"It was a sage and his wife. They had the power to transform themselves into deer. They had turned into a stag and a deer, and they *were* copulating at the time. That was how we heard them so clearly. And Shvate's arrow had gone through both of them, pinning them together — it was a fatal wound, because, as you know, Shvate always shoots to kill."

"'A quick and merciful death,' he always says," Karni said.

"Yes, exactly. They were dying, and there was nothing we could do to save them. The wife was already dead, the arrow had embedded itself in her heart, her eyes wide open. The sage was also pierced through the heart, but somehow he was still alive. He was staring up at us when we found him, and

— Karni, oh, Karni, I don't know how to describe it. There was this rage in his eyes, this fury. Like he wanted to turn us into ashes right there and then. Shvate and I stopped laughing the minute we saw them, and Shvate fell to his knees and started begging his forgiveness. He wanted to do something to help them, but the sage was so angry. His name was Kundaka, and he had practiced severe austerities to achieve his level of accomplishment. Now his life and spiritual efforts were all in vain. He could barely talk, and he was already half dead, but he told Shvate that he should be ashamed to interrupt even a pair of deer when they were making love, and what we had done was a sin and that he would suffer for it. And I was feeling so embarrassed because they were both naked and still joined together and the wife was dead, and I was crying, and Shvate was sobbing, and the sage was so angry, and I didn't know what to do, or what to say . . ."

Mayla held her head in both her hands, tears flowing freely now. She couldn't help it, all her self-control and discipline were gone now. She could still feel the dregs of last night's drinking in her body, and it made her feel sick. She had meant what she said to Karni earlier: she would never drink again as long as she lived. Never.

"Mayla, is that all?" Karni asked gently. "Is that the whole story?"

Mayla raised her face and looked at her sister queen. "No . . . no it isn't."

Karni looked at her and an expression of pure dread came over her face. "The sage said something, didn't he? Before he died?"

Mayla nodded. "Yes," she managed. She looked down at the floor.

"What did he say, Mayla?" Karni asked, her voice faltering.

Mayla sniffed, still looking down at the floor. She couldn't look at Karni anymore. "He cursed Shvate."

Karni's hand flew to her mouth.

"He cursed both of us. All three of us, I guess. Because he said that since Shvate had killed a pair of animals while they were making love, so Shvate and his wife would suffer the same fate."

Karni's hand gripped Mayla's shoulder, squeezing it hard. "Did he say anything else?"

"Shvate begged him — he was crying now, we were both crying — saying sorry, begging his forgiveness. Shvate said, 'Please don't be so harsh. Curse me, but not my wives.' But the sage was dying, I could see the light almost faded from his eyes. He looked at Shvate and said, "Very well, since it was your hand that pulled the arrow, it will be your fate alone. You will die as I died, in the arms of your lover at the peak of your passion." Those were his last words. His eyes closed and then he was gone."

Karni sucked in a breath and shook her head. She covered her own face in her hands.

Mayla wiped her face with the back of her sleeve. "Karni, I am so sorry. We never meant for this to happen. It was the worst night of my life."

Karni sat with her face in her hands, not saying anything.

"Karni, that isn't all. I came here to tell you something else, too."

Karni slowly raised her face, removing her hands. Mayla saw Karni's face and was heartbroken. Karni was not just crying, she looked as if her world had ended.

"Karni, Shvate asked me to come and fetch you. You have to leave with us right away."

Karni looked at her without reaction, as if nothing Mayla could say now would shock her any further. "Where are we going?"

"To the forest," Mayla said. "We will live in the forest the rest of our lives. We are going into self-exile, the three of us: Shvate, you, and myself. We leave right away."

Adri

~

SHVATE STOOD BEFORE ADRI.

"Brother?" Adri asked. "Can we speak later? I am . . . tired."

Shvate heaved in a breath and heaved it out. Adri heard everything in that single breath: the pain that was cutting Shvate's heart to shreds, the anguish, the remorse, the guilt, the shame. He heard it, and he understood it in some small part, because his world had cracked open like an egg this past night and day, and he had come to believe that anything was possible now, anything could happen. The sky could break into pieces and fall, the earth rise up and turn into clouds, the ocean turn to solid stone, and ice boil and become lava. The world had changed overnight and nothing would be the same again. Anything was possible. Even the worst possible thing.

"Adri," Shvate said in a broken voice, "Adri, you know I love you."

Adri was touched. It had been a long time since Shvate and he had been close enough to bare their hearts to one another. At one time, he had felt as if he could tell Shvate anything and everything. But ever since their respective marriages, and perhaps even before that, things had changed. Life was one long slide downhill from innocence to cynicism, and there was no way to climb back up again to the very top. But there were moments when he had felt willing to bare his soul to his brother, if only because he trusted Shvate, because he knew Shvate would understand, would care. He understood now that this was that same Shvate, in as vulnerable a state, about to bare his own soul to Adri. Adri understood this, and he listened.

"I love you too, brother," he said. And he meant it. "You are the eldest of us both. You were born before me."

"Barely," Shvate replied. "But the elders declared us to have equal claim to the Burning Throne."

Adri was puzzled. He didn't understand this part — what did this have to do with loving each other?

"By Krushan law, and by tradition, we are both equal in the line of succession," Shvate said.

"Brother," Adri said, thinking this was some kind of discussion about ambitions and wives and politics. He had had a similar discussion once with Shvate and was not prepared to have another one right now. He needed time to come to terms with the madness that had already spun his life upside down, the fact that his wife believed she was pregnant with his child, yet he knew that he could not possibly be the father. Too much had happened in one night. "Let us not talk politics now."

Shvate shook his head. His hand was on Adri's shoulder, and Adri could feel him shake his head. He knew his brother's every gesture, every mannerism. Shvate was deeply troubled. He was crying. What was the matter? Adri couldn't comprehend what was really happening.

"There is no more politics," Shvate said. "Politics died today. Ambition died today. The line of succession ended today. All that remains now is penance and reparation."

Adri was very confused now, so much so he wondered if Shvate might be drunk. He could smell the drink on his brother's breath, in his sweat, but it was not freshly consumed wine, it was the stale, rancid smell of wine consumed the night before. There were other odors on Shvate as well: the odors of death, of shame, of something else that he could not identify. Something acrid and sour and very dark. It echoed the foul odors Adri had smelled the night before.

"Adri, my brother, I am abdicating all rights to the throne of Hastinaga and to the line of succession. I hereby give up my right to inherit the throne forever, from this moment forward."

"Brother!" Adri exclaimed. But Shvate continued unabated.

"You, Adri, and you alone are now king of Hastinaga, emperor of the Burnt Empire. I am leaving home today and taking my wives, Mayla and Karni, into the forest with me, to live out the rest of our lives in self-imposed exile. I want you to know that I am doing this of my own free will, under no duress or coercion, and that I willingly and gladly bequeath to you, your family, and your future heirs all that belongs to me. My wealth, my holdings, my titles, my share of the family property, my rights, and my options. Everything is yours from this moment henceforth. I do this because I love you, brother. I have already told Mother Jilana of my decision and asked her to convey my decision to Vrath as well. I have also conveyed it to the ministers, so that none can doubt the veracity or the legality of this succession."

Adri's head whirled with the enormity of what had just happened. He tried to come to terms with the implications of this momentous event. "Brother . . ." he said again, trying to make sense of it as well as ask the question — why? — but Shvate concluded with the same single-minded determination with which he had done everything in his life.

"Adri, I say it again so there is no doubt — you are now the king of Hastinaga and sole ruler of the Burnt Empire. I know you will be a great ruler. I wish you well, my brother. Rule long, live long, and rule wisely."

Vessa

～

1

VESSA MATERIALIZED IN THE west courtyard.

Dogs set to barking, horses reared and kicked, elephants trumpeted. Even the sentries on duty sensed the disturbance in the air and smelled the odor of fresh pinewood forest. A blast of wind swept the yard, carrying the chill of the high mountain reaches and a flurry of snowflakes.

A young novice guard was crossing the yard carrying an armful of weapons when he was startled by Vessa's sudden appearance, the sage already striding as he materialized; he cut directly across the path of the young novice, causing the lad to cry out and drop his load. Swords, bows, and daggers went clattering across the cobbled ground, scaring the pair of mares attached to Dowager Empress Jilana's chariot; one mare kicked the front of the chariot, denting the gold plating and sending the queen's signature ornament — a leaping fish — flying. The other mare whinnied in distress and tried to calm her running mate by nuzzling her neck.

Other horses, as well as elephants, dogs, and men and women around the courtyard, all reacted to the appearance of the great sage. All sages were regarded with fear and respect for their power to use stonefire shakti, but among them, Vessa ranked highly. Up to now, his comings and goings had been a closely guarded secret, always occurring behind closed doors. This was the first time he had entered Hastinaga in such spectacular fashion, in the clear light of day, and it sent a ripple of rumors cascading through the metropolis within moments of his arrival.

The subject of these rumors, meanwhile, strode across the courtyard, up the steps to the western entrance, and into the palace proper, leaving a flurry of excitement in his wake. The startled novice gathered up his fallen load and continued with his task, carrying also a story that he would embellish over the years and narrate again and again, well into his last grey hairs. It was a time when persons of power, myth, and legend walked Arthaloka far less frequently than in earlier ages, and any such appearance occasioned much debate.

Vessa strode through the palace, leaving a flurry of startled witnesses in his wake. Through the vaulting entranceway with towering statues, past the lush murals, rich tapestries, brocades, carpeting, marbled floors and sweeping balustrades, polished surfaces and mirrors. He did not slow when he reached the enormous carved and inlaid doors of the great hall. The sentries saw him coming and exchanged startled glances before opting to quickly open the doors and step out of his way.

The great hall was packed with a full court today. The usual assortment of ministers, courtiers, nobles, visiting dignitaries, ambassadors, commoners in the viewing galleries, and the serving staff and sentries on duty were all regaled by the unexpected appearance of this celebrity visitor. A land dispute between two wealthy senapatis, one retired, the other still serving, was on the center court today. Dowager Empress Jilana and Prince Regent Vrath were presiding as usual. The minister of land resources and taxes was arguing with the minister of war about the respective claims of both parties. The entire Senate was listening with varying degrees of attentiveness to the arguments, neither enraptured nor completely bored.

Vessa burst into the great hall with the fury of a blizzard invading a warm, quiet inn. The reactions to his intrusion ranged from startled to terrified to stunned. Once they recognized him, many of the women present eyed him with keen interest. The salubrious talk over Vessa's impregnation of the princesses Ember and Umber, over two decades earlier, had never lost its spice, and many a young girl in the High Houses had spent hours debating just how horrific the sage must be in person to cause one of the princesses to shut her eyes in terror and the other to turn pale and faint from fright, resulting in their offspring, Prince Adri and Prince Shvate, being born blind and albino, respectively. This was the first time most of them had ever laid eyes on him in person — and he did not disappoint. Sage Vessa was as imposing, fearsome, and shocking at first appearance as his reputation claimed. To see this man striding into one's bedchamber at night, with a solitary intent, would startle any woman.

Among those startled, but for a different reason, was Dowager Empress Jilana. Vessa sensed her startle, her dark eyes widening in surprise when she saw him approaching the throne dais. She had never been visited by her son in a public setting, ever. From his aspect and his approach, he saw her grasp at once that this did not bode well.

The ministers and nobles arguing before the dais broke off abruptly, startled into silence as the towering figure walked past them. A giant in stature and width, Vessa resembled a tree in many ways, and the first thing many thought of when seeing him go by was that a tree had uprooted itself from the deepest forest and gone walking away on some urgent business.

He stopped before the dais, his eyes flashing with fury. His wildwood staff was the thickness of a strong man's arm, overgrown with creepers, flowers, fungi. He brought it down on the marbled floor with a resounding crack, shattering the slab and sending a spiderweb of cracks splintering outward.

"I warned you," he said, "that we were planting the seeds of war by taking karma into our own hands."

Dowager Empress Jilana looked at her prime minister, who was transfixed by the sight of Vessa with his staff. "Clear the court at once."

The pradhan mantri began to gesture at the court criers, who opened their mouths to deliver the necessary command in their usual singsong ululating style. But before they could begin their delivery, the visitor raised his staff even higher and thundered a response.

"Stay! It is time Hastinaga knew what is at stake here!"

The sentries had already begun opening the large doors, and people had started moving toward them. At Vessa's words, the doors swung shut of their own accord, pushed by the invisible hand of stonefire. The resulting boom reverberated throughout the vast chamber.

Silence followed.

Every pair of eyes was fixed, wide-eyed, on the tableau at the throne dais.

Vessa lowered his staff, gently this time, and turned his head. His eyes swept the assemblage, striking a variety of emotions, none pleasant, in the hearts of the several scores present. "Stay, Hastinaga, and hear what I have to say. My words are intended for every citizen of this metropolis and this great empire. Yatham rajanam, tatham prajanam."

The Krushan phrase struck a chord. *As does the king, so do the people.* It was a reminder that even the monarchs of the world's greatest empire were governed by a higher power — their own citizens. While accountability was at best a token phrase in a monarchy, emulation was a reality. An ordinary person in the street could not hope to personally hold his or her ruler directly accountable for every decision, but by taking a certain action, or issuing a certain diktat, that ruler then made it permissible for his or her citizens to do the same. *Lead by example* was another way of interpreting the Krushan phrase. By speaking a word or performing an action, the monarch made it legally permissible under Krushan law. True, many wise men would argue that this was not to be taken literally, as Krushan law was individual and not a general law, but it was hard for any king or queen to question the deeds of their citizens if they themselves had committed those same deeds with impunity.

Those who had been about to leave immediately turned back. Most came closer to the dais, the better to hear what was being said. The sage's entrance had already intrigued them; his words had sealed the deal. Every person, highborn or low, royalty, noble, aristocrat or citizen, wanted to hear what Vessa was about to say.

Dowager Empress Jilana was still silent. She glanced in the direction of the pradhan mantri, then at Prince Regent Vrath. The prime minister looked lost; Vrath looked interested. This was a change from the tedious repetition of the court's usual hearings, and anything that was important enough to bring Sage Vessa out of the deep forest and striding into the Senate of Hastinaga with such purpose was of interest to him. Jilana's brow was furrowed; Vessa knew she did not like him taking over her court in this manner, or his tone, but with so many people watching and listening, she could hardly offer any rebuke. Not that they had ever had such a relationship as mother and son. Vessa had grown from infancy to full adulthood within the space of as many hours as it took most humans in years, already imbued with the four vidya, the complete repository of all human knowledge. All she could claim was that she had birthed him.

She sat back down.

Vessa inclined his head to her and to Vrath, acknowledging both and showing the customary respect to their thrones and crowns. Both acknowledged him in turn.

The great court of Hastinaga waited with bated breath to hear what Vessa had to say.

2

"Mother," said the sage. "A mother is creator, preserver, as well as destroyer to a child. You gave me life, and for that I am eternally grateful and respectful to you. Pray, accept all that I now say as my attempt to redress what I see as a misstep on the long road of karma. I seek not to criticize you, but merely to inform you of a larger perspective that you were not aware of at the time that you made certain decisions. Had you been apprised of this larger perspective at the time, I am certain you would have made a different choice. However, I myself only recently came into possession of certain relevant facts that helped me perceive this larger perspective, without which I could not have apprised you at the time in question. I do so now in the hope that even today we may yet be able to take action and prevent further damage from ensuing. Please accept all my words here in the spirit of positive action. My sole intention is to do good here, and to ensure the peace and prosperity of all Krushan."

Jilana seemed guardedly pleased with this long opening in high Krushan and replied mellifluously in language that matched her son's eloquence. "My son, your knowledge is unsurpassed, your wisdom unrivaled, your spiritual power unchallengeable. I know you have only good intentions. A mother's greatest happiness comes from seeing her offspring go forth and flourish in the world. Your heights of achievement have given me more cause to be proud of you than almost any mother in the history of humankind. Whatever brings you here today, away from your life's work of transcribing the sacred vidya, must be of supreme importance to all of us. If I have indeed committed any errors in the past, whether through deeds or misdeeds, action or inaction, I too wish to be enlightened in order that I may avoid such errors in future, and if possible, redress those past errors and make reparations. Pray, proceed."

Vessa bowed his head, straightened, then paused. When he resumed, he addressed his words to his mother, but in truth, they were intended for everyone present, since Jilana herself was already aware of all that he was about to recount.

"Over two decades ago, the Krushan dynasty faced a crisis of inheritance. Both the sons of Sha'ant and Jilana, princes Virya and Gada, died untimely deaths, leaving no heirs. Their widows, Princess Ember and Princess Umber, were left childless. Without an heir to ascend the throne, the Krushan dynasty would perish. Its enemies, always seeking a reason to stoke rebellion and unrest, were already using the lack of heirs as a point of argument to justify rising up against Hastinaga. Without an heir, the Burnt Empire would disintegrate in time, they argued. Better to detach oneself from the sinking ship before it took them down with it. Many with their own political agendas listened and stoked the fires of unrest using this argument. Vrath's relentless war campaigning successfully prevented these fires from spreading, but effective as his campaign was, it could not extinguish the source of those fires. So long as Hastinaga lacked an heir, new uprisings would spark sooner or later, somewhere or other. It is a large empire, and even a man as powerful and indomitable as the prince regent has his limitations. An empire constantly fighting its own people is an empire in decline. Something had to be done to address the issue itself, and end the source of the arguments once and for all.

"To this end, my mother, Dowager Empress Jilana, first went to Vrath, urging him to use the age-old precedent in such a case and father children upon his half brother's widows. This is acceptable under Krushan law, as I'm sure you will all agree."

Many heads nodded, some grey, some not grey at all, concurring from personal knowledge or in acknowledgment of the universally accepted practice. More than one great House of Hastinaga had been extended through the centuries by such means, thus ensuring that the accumulated wealth, property, and name of their ancestors remained within the family rather than being lost in the inevitable squabbles over due shares.

"However, due to his vow of lifelong celibacy, Prince Regent Vrath declined. Even my mother's most persuasive arguments could not sway him. His word was his bond, and he could no more unspeak his vow than the sun retreat into the east at dawn, or an old corpse rise up and become a newborn babe again."

Jilana and Vrath did not exchange a glance: Vessa knew that each could see the other in their peripheral field of vision even while looking directly at him. But they shared an instant of awareness as they listened. He could empathize. Vessa had just recounted, exactly, Vrath's own arguments to Jilana from over two decades ago. Those words had been spoken by Vrath to her in private. She had never recounted them in those exact words to her son. Yet neither was surprised at the accuracy of the quotes: Vessa was gifted with knowledge of past as well as future events. This was only one of his several gifts. They were both Krushan; extraordinary abilities and beings were an integral part of the lineage.

"Vrath could not be faulted for his refusal. His word was his Krushan law, and he adhered to it. Praise his greatness!"

"Blessed be!" the Senate responded, uttering the appropriate response.

Vessa acknowledged them and continued.

"Jilana summoned me next. I appeared before her at once, for a mother is as a god to a child, and my mother's call is no less than a summons from the gods themselves to me. She told me of her quandary and asked me to step in to perform the necessary duty. I was reluctant because even then, I could see, through the shadowy fog of time, that on that path lay many treacherous twists and turns, and even the slightest misstep could lead the entire Krushan dynasty astray. My mother can be very insistent, and she convinced me that to leave the empire without an heir would bring about the certain destruction of the Krushan race in time. I mused upon this and concluded that she was accurate in her assessment. A House without heirs was a House without a future. So long as Vrath lived and continued to suppress the forces that rallied against Hastinaga, the empire would stay intact, but it would be held together by war, and at a terrible cost to its kingdoms. What good an empire that has to fight itself constantly? It would be akin to a person suffering from so many diseases that over time she was forced to cut off parts of her body until finally she lay in bloody fragments.

"Historically, no family that lacked heirs has continued to flourish. This is even more true of ruling dynasties. 'Yatham rajanam, tatham prajanam,' I said at the outset. This is true of families as well as empires. If the ruling family dies out, how can the civil family prosper? A ruling dynasty is creator and preserver to her citizens. In order for Hastinaga to survive and continue prospering, the House of Krushan must survive and prosper. Even a child understands this simple truth. With their husbands dead, the only way for the princesses Ember and Umber to bear progeny was for me to seed their wombs.

"My initial reluctance to my mother's request was not for lack of understanding, but because I sensed the many possible missteps ahead on this new pathway. I urged her to speak with her daughters-in-law to prepare them adequately for the task. For even the flutter of a butterfly's wings can set off a storm, given the right chain of circumstances. It was crucial that Ember and Umber receive my seed with positive acceptance, for every action or inaction would cast its mark on the future of the Krushan race."

Everyone listened raptly. This was the very topic that had set so many young ears and tongues on fire for so long. To hear it discussed in open court by the very man who was at the center of all that gossip caused intense excitement. Some more prurient minds perhaps hoped for explicit details that would reflect the steamy fictions of the plays that claimed to depict the events of those nights. They were about to be disappointed.

"Sadly, while my mother was wise in years and understanding, and did her best to make her daughters-in-law aware of the importance of their roles in this crucial time, the young princesses Ember and Umber were themselves immature and lacking in self-control. Their reception, and one attempt at deception, led to the two young princes Adri and Shvate being born with some limitations. My third child conceived in this time, the good counselor Vida, was the only one of the three offspring to be possessed of all faculties, but as per the laws of succession, he lacked the genetic authority to be considered an heir.

"As a result, the House of Krushan was left with a blind prince and an albino prince. This caused further unrest among the opponents of the empire, particularly the one who has been a bane of all righteous human beings in the Burnt Empire. I speak of course of the vile and vicious Jarsun of Reygistan."

A rustle of unease passed through hall. The name of Jarsun was rarely if ever spoken aloud in Hastinaga since the incidents of the unnatural eclipse. Many of those present shuddered, gasped, or displayed similar reactions. They or someone they knew closely had been afflicted by the events of that night. Many had yet to recover fully. Their faces reflected their discomfort, even pain, at the name of the Reygistani.

Vessa surveyed the hall, taking in these reactions.

"All of you have been subjected to his evil. The night of the eclipse was his doing. This was not his first attempt at harming the Burnt Empire. Earlier, he had gathered a conspiracy of our most disgruntled allies and used his urrkh powers to coerce them into rebelling openly against Hastinaga. This culminated in the Battle of the Rebels. His shameful loss at that venue left him enraged and frustrated. The night of the eclipse was his response. Resorting to the terrorizing of ordinary citizens rather than daring to attack with military means, he struck a blow to the very heart of the empire. I myself was summoned here that night by my mother, and I chased the devil out of the city, forcing him to flee before he could wreak total destruction upon us. What transpired next is the reason for my presence here."

Vessa began to walk slowly along the crowd of patiently listening spectators as he continued. He carried his staff with ease, using it not to facilitate his own movements, but bearing it like a cudgel, a rod, a king's scepter. His searing eyes took in every face, every person present, shining like a light of Krushan law on their souls, promising to expose anyone who displayed even the slightest sign of affliction.

Suddenly, without warning, he raised his staff high, gripping it in two hands, and recited:

Andham tamam pravishantiam yeham avidyam upasteriyam
Tatham bhuyam eevam teyasta tamor yam udh vidyayam rataham

At once Senate Hall was plunged into pitch-darkness.

Jilana

~

1

EVERYONE IN SENATE HALL screamed.

Jilana and Vrath both rose to their feet. Vrath started forward, but Jilana raised a hand. Despite the darkness, Vrath saw her gesture and stopped. Jilana saw that Vrath's eyes were glowing intensely with deep blue light. Her raised hand reflected a similar glow, and she brought the hand closer to her face to confirm that she too was exuding blue light from her own pupils, though the light from her eyes was much less intense than Vrath's. She looked around and saw that most people in Senate Hall had a faint blueish tinge in their eyes, most too faint to be seen individually but visible as a group. But there were many dark patches in the hall, and in some places, a garish red glow was pulsing. Red eyes glittered in the crowd here and there, visible only now in the pitch-darkness.

Her son, however, was glowing brightly. Both Vessa's eyes were glowing with a paler blue light than that of Vrath, and much less intense. But there was a blueish smoke pouring from the tips of his fingers and the palms of his hands, and his staff was leaking blue light as well. Vessa moved the staff violently in one direction then another, as if pointing to various spots around the chamber.

North. South. East. West. The cardinal directions. He's . . . he's purifying the room!

Vessa's voice rang out through the hall, chanting protective mantras over the strange sounds coming now from the crowd.

Jilana realized that the red-eyed people in the gathering were starting to growl and make other strange animal sounds. She saw those around them move away, exclaiming in fear, as the red eyes began to drop their pretense of being human and display their true, demonical natures. Their noises grew, like the sounds of predators preparing to attack.

Vessa's hands and staff were swirling with thick blue-tinted smoke, the illumination from it bright enough to light up his face, casting his intense features into sharp relief. His wild hair and flowing beard caught highlights of blue, giving him the appearance of a saptarishi, one of the Seven Seer-Mages of mythology, depicted in one of the frescoes on the ceiling of the great hall. Stonefire showed beings of power in their truest forms, burning away all artifice and masks.

Now all the red eyes were converging on Vessa as he continued his Kru-shan chanting in that singsong pad-a-pad way that priests practiced to perfection. The others in Senate Hall had backed away to make room for their urrkh-afflicted neighbors. Those who did not move quickly enough were greeted by threatening growls and in some cases, a vicious blow, a kick, or a slash or a swipe. Before they could cause serious harm to the unfortunate victims, Vessa's chanting distracted them, drawing their ire and their mindless violence to focus on him instead.

As they approached, the others backed away, leaving Vessa now in an island of darkness ringed by a circle of red eyes.

There were several dozen of them, all on hands and feet now, crawling like beasts, growling and snarling with fury. Ministers, nobles, courtiers, even beautiful daughters of wealthy aristocrats, all now moving like animals. Vessa had drawn them out so suddenly, so expertly, they had not had a chance for subterfuge or escape.

Jilana understood now why Vessa had wanted everyone to remain in Senate Hall: so that he could expose them. But she had seen the effects of Jarsun's evil that night of the eclipse. What if the devil had gifted the possessed with enough of his urrkh maya that they could harm even Vessa? Perhaps she had been too quick to restrain Vrath. Perhaps she could still appeal to him to go to her son's aid.

Now the red eyes were preparing to leap, to attack, to kill. No longer thinking, functional human beings, they were now minions of Jarsun, mindless tools of his evil. They would either kill their prey . . . or die trying.

Believe, Jilana. Believe in him. He has never let you down yet.
Vessa continued to chant:

Asuryaham namaham teyam lokam andhyena tamasavratyam
Tanam astheyam preytyabhigshanthiam yehaam keycham atmaha-
nahso janaham

With a blinding flash of blue light, Vessa's staff and hands flared with stonefire shakti, blasting outward in every direction. The blue smoke exploded, booming throughout the chamber. Jilana felt the power of a great wind blast her, billowing outward from the center of the circle, causing everyone to stagger back a step or two—everyone except Vrath, of course, who remained standing steadfast, unshakeable as Mount Coldheart itself. The blue light lit up every corner of Senate Hall, illuminating even the dogs and cats nesting in the eaves and corners under the scalloped walls. A huge gasp was forced from the mouths of everyone present—except, again, Vrath—and then, as suddenly as it had flared, the blue light of stonefire was extinguished, leaving the chamber once again in pitch-darkness.

2

Pandemonium ensued.

The Tainted Ones now lay on the floor sprawled in a jagged circle around where Vessa stood. At first glance, they all appeared to be dead, but as Jilana watched, she saw a hand twitch—then a leg, then a head move. So, they were alive, just knocked senseless. She realized she was holding her breath and exhaled, feeling the blood leave her head. She stepped back, found the throne, and sat. Vrath was in the thick of things, issuing quiet, firm instructions; ordering guards and sentries; telling ministers what to do. He took command of the situation in seconds, restoring calm to the unnerved gathering. Those whose relatives, friends, partners, or associates had turned into red eyes were asked to come forward and assist them.

Vessa walked away from the circle, and people parted hurriedly to let him through. He stood at the foot of the throne dais, looking nowhere in particular, calm now that his work was done. Behind him, a young woman and her father were hesitating to lay hands on a middle-aged woman dressed in fine robes, who lay on the floor in a semiconscious state. Clearly, they were afraid that the mother and wife was still possessed and potentially dangerous.

"They are unharmed and harmless," Vessa said, even though his back was turned to the crowd. "I have exorcised the last remnants of Jarsun's evil from their bodies. They will be disoriented and forgetful for a few days, but in time they will be as they were before; however, they will remember nothing of the events since the night of the eclipse. Whatever they may have done in these intervening days since that night, you should know that it was under the influence of the adversary's evil power; it was not their doing. They are victims, not culprits. Treat them with compassion and kindness, and they will recover fully."

This seemed to ease the minds of the crowd. The young woman and her father who had been hesitating now went ahead and helped the middle-aged woman to her feet, supporting her as they moved her to sit on a bench in the lord's gallery. She held her face and cried, shaking her head as she tried to understand what had happened. Jilana felt some sympathy for the woman, and for the others who had been possessed by Jarsun's evil, but her sympathy was overshadowed by the anger she felt for the Reygistani himself. How had this gone unnoticed for so long? The night of the eclipse was weeks ago. Jilana shuddered to think how many others were afflicted in the city, or in the kingdom at large, and couldn't help but fear what other damage they had done in the intervening weeks.

When Jilana snapped out of her reverie, she found Vessa looking up at her. As always he knew her mind and thoughts even without her speaking aloud.

"Fear not, Mother. I have cleared the city already," Vessa said. "These were the last. They were sleeper agents, planted by Jarsun for long-term use. He has not used them since the night of the eclipse, so that no suspicion would fall on them. They were to be activated and used at some future point. That day will never come now, so whatever plan he may have had, he will be disappointed when they fail to respond."

Jilana sighed in relief. "Thank you, Vessa."

Vrath finished speaking with the last of the ministers and returned to his throne on the dais.

"Great One," he said, using the correct, respectful form of address for a sage of Vessa's stature, even though he was the elder of the two men, and, in a manner of speaking, his older brother, since Jilana was his stepmother. "We thank you for the service you have done Hastinaga today. Hastinaga and the Burnt Empire are in your debt."

Vessa inclined his shaggy mane. "The time has come for us to have words in private. Mother, Vrath, let us excuse ourselves."

3

"Let Hastinaga think that the display in the Senate marks the end of Jarsun's evil," Vessa said once the doors were shut.

Jilana glanced at Vrath, who was as usual impossible to read, his handsome, craggy features inscrutable, even his almost translucent eyes revealing nothing of what he thought or felt. "But you rooted out the last of his evil, did you not?"

Vessa sighed. "Would that I had been able to do more. I fear that what I have done is much too little. I have spent the past weeks since the night of the eclipse scouring myriad realms and multiple worlds in search of the Reygistani. Each time I smell his foul trail and think I am close to apprehending him, he leads me to another dimension, another universe. I have exhausted all my knowledge, all my powers, even now resorting to the most arcane methods as well as the most advanced sciences of the future. Yet he continues to elude me. I had hoped to complete my mission and only then return here to clean up the last vestiges of his evil, but I must admit defeat at last. His sorcery is devilishly powerful. I hesitate to say it is beyond my means to defeat, because until I am able to confront him directly, I cannot test my limits against his own."

Vrath said, "He avoids confrontation until he is certain of victory. It was the same with me the day of the Battle of the Rebels. When he was unable to overcome me with his urrkh maya, he fled the field. Since then, he has played this game of hide-and-seek, attacking from the shadows, using puppets and spies. Yet you seem to have come close to cornering him."

Vessa frowned. "To me it seemed as if the closer I came to him, the farther he fled. Each time I thought I was within moments of apprehending him, he turned out to be someplace — or somewhen — else."

"He roves the vastness of time and space like a bird on the high currents,"

Vrath agreed. "His powers are great, his tactics shrewd, but he is not indomitable."

"If you cannot catch an enemy or face him long enough to kill him, then what else can you call him?"

"Uncatchable?" Vrath shrugged. "No man or god is uncatchable. It is only a matter of time."

Vessa shook his head. "Time is one resource we may be in want of."

Jilana studied her son's face. "Do you foresee another attack on the city?"

"He knows better than to come here again," Vrath said. "He was wise to pick the one time I was away, because had I been here . . ."

He did not need to finish the thought.

"He does not need to come here again in person," Vessa said. "He has already corrupted the heart of Hastinaga in the most damaging way of all."

"What do you mean, Vessa?" Jilana asked. "What corruption you speak of?"

Vessa looked at her. "You already know. Or you suspect. You have known since the night of the eclipse."

Now, it was Vrath's turn to furrow his large brow. "What does he mean, Mother? Is there something that you did not tell me about that night?"

Jilana sat on a satin couch, suddenly tired.

"I told you everything I knew . . . but there were things, other things, that I did not wish to speculate on. I could not be certain, so did not want to speak in guesses and rumors."

Vrath exchanged a glance with Vessa, who returned his gaze without response. They both waited for Jilana to continue. She sat, staring at a vase filled with fresh flowers from the imperial gardens, a beautiful arrangement of shades ranging from a faint dusky lavender to a deep crimson, resembling a giant pink-red flower when viewed as a whole. She loved the arrangement, and adored flowers in general, but at this moment, she derived no pleasure from either. The anxiety that had been growing within her for weeks had flowered into full-blown maturity.

"That night," she said at last, her voice heavy with sadness, "when I did not find Adri and Geldry in their bedchamber, I sent guards to search them out. They found Adri in a maid's quarters in the far end of the palace. He had been . . . cohabiting with her."

Vrath took this news without reaction. "I know of this already. It was reported to me even before I returned to Hastinaga."

Jilana nodded slowly. "I thought that might be the case. I did not speak of it only because it caused me some pain. Adri was a good boy and has grown to be a good man, despite the many obstacles life threw in his path. But since his marriage to Geldry, I have begun to notice signs of stress and unhappiness. I thought these were to be expected with any marriage in the early adjustment period. I hoped he would grow out of them, and so would she. But when I heard this news, it hurt my heart, because it told me that things were far worse than I had suspected. To push a man of Adri's upstanding morality to the point of infidelity must have taken a great deal of strife and stress. I do not blame Geldry because a husband's infidelity has nothing whatsoever to do with his wife, and everything to do with his own irresponsibility."

"Forgive me for interrupting, Mother," Vessa said, "but do not overlook the fact that this happened on the night of the eclipse."

"Certainly. I know that this was the effect of Jarsun's evil sorcery. Only just now in Senate Hall, we witnessed the extent to which his powers can drive people even weeks after the event. But even urrkh maya must have some limits. Why drive Adri to infidelity? Why cause him to lie with that particular maid? And if the guard's telling, and the accounts I received from other maids, are to be believed, then none of his actions that night were forced or wholly involuntary. Unlike those poor possessed souls in Senate Hall today, Adri appeared to be in full possession of his faculties, operating of his own volition, and not only indulging in the act of infidelity, but wholeheartedly . . . enjoying it. Repeatedly."

Vessa and Vrath had no response to this new revelation.

Jilana took a single flower from the arrangement, a deep crimson one, and without being fully aware of her actions, began to pluck the petals from the flower, one by one, dropping them on the polished tabletop. "Not only that, but since that night, Adri has had multiple assignations with the same maid. *Enthusiastic* assignations. He has been heard speaking affectionately to her and confessing intensely personal revelations about himself, his marriage, his anxieties and doubts as a king since Shvate's abdication — things he does not speak of to anyone else. I doubt all this was the effect of Jarsun's sorcery too."

Vessa shook his head. "The Reygistani's power could cause him to go to the maid's quarters, perhaps even drive him to priapic lust. But to go back to the same woman time and again, to open his heart in such a manner, no, Mother, that would be beyond even the reach of urrkh maya in my opinion. But there is something else you should know. I observed Adri discreetly before arriving here today."

"You did?" she asked, surprised. "But he is away at Riverdell."

"Indeed, and that is where I visited him. I made myself invisible to the human eye, to avoid being observed by his entourage — and by the maid of whom we speak."

"She was there too?" Jilana was less surprised than disappointed. She had finished removing the petals from the flower and moved to take another one from the arrangement. "That is bold and audacious of him, to take his lover along for a picnic."

"Perhaps it is his way of being discreet," Vrath said. "After all, it is less scandalous than going to her within the palace at odd hours, or holding trysts in various inappropriate places."

Jilana proceeded with the destruction of the flower. "Perhaps. And what did you observe there at Riverdell, my son? If it is too sordid, then spare me the details."

"He loves her deeply and genuinely," Vessa replied, "in a way that he has never loved Geldry and, I fear, may never love her in future. This is no passing fancy or wayward lust. Adri has given his heart to this dasi. Today I heard him speak of marriage."

"Marriage!" Jilana exclaimed, tearing the flower into shreds. She threw the remains on the table, staring up hotly at her son. "What impudence! A king of Hastinaga, ruler of the Burnt Empire, marrying a mere low-caste maid. It is unthinkable!"

"As unthinkable as Sha'ant, king of Hastinaga, marrying a low-caste fisherman's daughter?" Vessa asked softly, without any accusation in his tone.

Jilana sat back, staring at him.

"Yes, of course," she said. "I see the hypocrisy in my words. I myself was Sha'ant's lover and second wife. And low-caste to boot. But there are differences! For one thing, my father was a king among the Nishadas. And Sha'ant was a widower."

"Was he?" Vessa asked, glancing up at Vrath. "I believe his first wife is still very much alive. Is not your mother still extant, Vrath?"

"I meant in her human form," Jilana said, her face flushing with embarrassment. "This . . . maid . . . was she even a maiden at the time of her first copulation with Adri? Who knows what feminine wiles might she have employed to lure him into her bed, or what her motives might have been?"

"You yourself had had at least one other lover before Sha'ant," Vessa said. "You used your gift of scent to allure him while on that first boat ride . . . You have told me the story yourself."

Jilana stared at him angrily, about to protest, but then looked at Vrath's impassive face and deflated. "You are right, my son. Here I am, sitting in judgment of another woman, holding her to some meaningless patriarchal standard, when in fact, she is no more or less than I myself, or any woman. I have spent too much time in the company of old men; I am starting to think like them. What does it matter what her motives or wiles were? The point is that Adri went to her, he slept with her, he returned to her repeatedly, enthusiastically, and now he is clearly in love with the woman, taking her to his favorite picnic spot, spending days in her presence."

Jilana rose from the seat and walked over to a stand where she poured herself a drink of cool water and sipped slowly. "It is *he* who is straying, who has fallen in love, who is continuing the affair. I am being unfair by focusing on this maid. She is irrelevant in this matter. It is Adri's actions that we must speak of."

"Your wisdom continues to be a source of admiration and worthy of emulation, Mother," Vessa said with genuine pride. "This is true. But I disagree on one point. It is neither Adri nor the maid that is the cause of concern. I did not come here to discuss his affair or the repercussions on his marriage or the throne. My anxiety is over something else altogether."

"What is it, my son?" Jilana asked.

Vessa's dark eyes turned steely. "Geldry."

"Geldry?" Vrath repeated. "What of her?"

"She is with child."

"Yes," Vrath said, "She conceived on the night of the eclipse after a tryst with Adri."

"So she says," Jilana said.

"I have heard the rumors too, and the reports of the guards," said Vrath. "They found her in her bedchamber in a state of undress, still bearing the signs of recent passion . . . while Adri was in the maid's chambers. But that does not rule out the possibility that Adri could have ravished her and then gone to the maid's quarters. Under the influence of Jarsun's evil eclipse, of course."

Vessa inclined his head. "That would account for the state in which she was found, and for Adri's remarkable prowess as a lover, but alas, I do not believe that is what transpired."

"What do you believe happened then?"

Vessa sighed, stroking his beard. The unruly growth sprang back each time he released it. "I believe Jarsun somehow lured her into one of his other dimensions, another world somewhere far from here, while her senses were occluded, and . . ."

"And?" Vrath asked, glancing now at Jilana, who remained silent.

"And seduced her," Vessa said, "and impregnated her."

Vrath sucked in a long harsh breath. "Then you are saying that the child in her womb is not born of Adri's seed?"

"He is saying much more than that," Jilana said quietly, still looking down as if Vessa was only voicing what she had suspected and feared all this while.

"I am saying that the thing in her womb is not human," Vessa said. "It is the spawn of evil, seeded by the urrkh Jarsun himself in the ultimate attempt to corrupt the very heart of the Burnt Empire. It is Jarsun's bastard child, and it must be removed at once. That is why I have returned to Hastinaga today, to rid the city of the last of Jarsun's evil sorcery, and that includes ridding Geldry of his spawn. We must abort the child at once."

Jilana held her head for a moment, as if preparing herself. Finally, she raised her head, showing her proud aquiline features to her son.

"No. We will not lay a hand on Geldry or her unborn child."

4

The sun was dawning over Hastinaga. The three elders of the House of Krushan were still in conference. All night they had debated the issue. Vessa had remained stubbornly insistent that Geldry's child must be aborted. The future of the empire depended on it. The safety of the House of Krushan. The sanctity of the lineage. He had many strong, compelling arguments in favor of purging Jilana's great-granddaughter, and, in a manner of speaking, his own granddaughter, since both Adri and Shvate were his biological offspring.

Jilana took the complete opposite view, and she held to it just as stubbornly and insistently. As the morning sunlight poured in through the windows of the chamber, she summed up the gist of her argument:

"Everything you say, my son, I have considered. But consider this in turn. Shvate has abdicated all claim to the throne. He did so with due protocol, informing all the necessary ministers, including the minister of Krushan law and the prime minister, as well as myself. As dowager empress, widow of the last reigning emperor, Samrat Sha'ant, and seniormost elder of the House of Krushan, I possess the power to accept or deny his abdication. I told him so. His response was that he had made up his mind, and whether or not I accepted would not sway him. He had failed the House of Krushan, he said. He had failed the people of Hastinaga."

As Jilana spoke, quoting Shvate's parting words aloud, in her mind it conjured the image of Shvate himself, standing in his forest-soiled, hunt-blooded garments, stripped of his sword and weapons, hair unkempt, beard outgrown, face and hands grimy with the dust of the road and the bloodstains of the man and woman he had killed and sought to save. His hands were clasped together, his handsome pale face distorted with emotion, tears spilling from his colorless eyes and running down well-worn tracks in his face.

"Grandmother, I am not taking this decision out of rash emotion or personal desire," Shvate had said. "I do this for one reason and one reason only. For the sake of Krushan law. As a prince of the Krushan line and one of only two heirs to the throne, it is my Krushan law to produce more heirs to ensure the continuity of our lineage. You have told us how this House came to the brink of dissolution when your fine sons Gada and Virya, sadly, died before their natural time. Only with an effort was disaster averted, and the dynasty continued with the birth of my brother and myself. Yet even we were not the ideal heirs such a great House deserved. Still, we tried to rise above our disabilities and prove ourselves worthy.

"Vrath told us once when we were young boys and he was taking us in his chariot to the gurukul for the first time, 'An enemy of Krushan may be the basest, most deplorable, adharmic being that ever walked Arthaloka, but a son of Krushan must be the truest, most immaculately behaved, shining example of Krushan law that ever lived. Remember this, Adri and Shvate. Your peers will be judged by a different standard; they will be forgiven even their worst transgressions, their errors will be overlooked, their faults ignored, their indiscretions brushed under the rug. But you must be perfect, beyond reproach, unimpeachable, the very symbol of goodness, honesty, courage, and Krushan law. You are not expected to merely be good; you must be great. It is not expected of you; it is taken for granted. You must be everything that everyone else cannot be. You cannot fail, you cannot falter, you cannot weaken, because you carry with you the weight, the burden, the responsibility of all Hastinaga. The hopes, dreams, aspirations, ambitions, and safety of millions rests on your shoulders. If you falter, a clan is exterminated. If you hesitate, a village is lost. If you lose courage, a tribe is wiped out. If you fail, an entire empire goes up in flames. There is no maybe, no try, no attempt, for you. There is only succeed, achieve, triumph, conquer.'"

And then Shvate raised his hand in the Krushan salute, pressing his palm to his heart, and cried out with feverish passion: "Yatham rajanam, tatham prajanam!"

Jilana's own hand now rested on her chest as she emulated Shvate's gesture. She looked into the eyes of her son Vessa, dark, stony, and intense as always. "Shvate said that by committing the murder of the sage and his wife under the influence of wine, he had not only proved himself incompetent to rule as emperor of Hastinaga, he had failed as a human being. A man. A husband."

Jilana lowered her hand, keeping her eyes fixed on her son. "And because of the sage's curse, he would never be able to father progeny on his wives. This meant that if he were to ascend to the throne, he could not further the line of Krushan. The House of his ancestors would die with him. He would have failed as a son, a king, a Krushan."

She sighed softly and spread her dark hands, almost as dark in hue as her black-skinned son. "Shvate cannot father heirs. Mayla and Karni are with him in the forest, living out their days in self-exile for his error that night. Adri has strayed from the path of fidelity, lying with a woman other than his own wife. Even if he were to be brought back in line, made to honor his marital vows, respect his wife, lie with her again, and seed another child in her womb, it is too late to do so. Geldry is already with child. If you do as you insist you must and rid her of this child, what guarantee is there that she will then be capable of bearing another? This seed that you say is Jarsun's foul leaving — if this is so, then might it not render Geldry's womb incapable of conceiving again?"

Vessa's beard rustled, and Jilana raised her hand at once.

"I know what you are about to say. You will say that even if Geldry's womb cannot produce another child, Adri can always take another wife. Father an heir upon her. And the Krushan line may yet go on."

She sighed and shook her head. "Nay. Nay, Vessa, my son. As Vrath here recalls full well, I thought this way once myself. I saw my handsome, strong, young sons Gada and Virya with their beautiful young wives, Ember and Umber, and I thought, *They are so amorous, so eager for each other's company, so besotted with one another, they will surely produce heirs. It is only a matter of time.* And yet, in the end, it transpired, time was the one thing they did not have."

She rose to her feet, raising her voice as well. "You came here yesterday saying that time was what we lacked. I say it back to you now. Time is neither yours nor mine to control, nor Vrath's nor anyone else's. Even the most powerful of seers or sorcerers cannot extend time at will. It rolls inevitably on, the great Samay Chakra, the great Wheel of Time, grinding and grinding us all down into dust. It outlasts and outlives us all, the one power that cannot be defeated. Today, what you say makes sense. We root out the evil seed of Jarsun from Geldry's womb. We rid ourselves of this last wretched stain of his sorcery. But what if she is unable to conceive again? What if Adri does not take another wife? He was married to Geldry long enough to have fathered a half dozen children upon her, yet her womb never quickened for him. He is himself afflicted, and with each passing year, I see him losing his courage, his will to live. What if he dies, leaving us without an heir? What then? People will say that the House of Krushan kills their own unborn heirs, that their sons murder sages and then are forced to go into exile, that we are unable to continue our line, unfit to rule, unworthy of this great empire. We will be on the brink of anarchy."

Vessa opened his mouth to speak again, but Jilana gestured decisively.

"No, I say, Vessa, *no!* There will be no killing of unborn children in this house. I will not risk my only surviving granddaughter-in-law's life with such an act. If it is as you say, and the seed that quickened in her womb was indeed Jarsun's, then it will reveal itself after she gives birth. Time enough to end it there. We women are no strangers to stillbirth. We have seen many a mother and child both die in crimson-washed agony in the birthing room. If there is murder to be done, that will be the day to do it." She gestured again. "Stay your tongue. Hear me out. I will summon you at the first sign of birth pains. You will be present here again when Geldry's time comes. We will see the results of her pregnancy, and if need be, we will convene again, the three of us, and decide what our best course of action is at that time. But not now. Now we will let sleeping babes lie. Let the seed grow and come to term. Let us see this through to the end of the play. Time enough to call down the curtain then.

"There. I have said what I had to say. As your mother, and your elder, and as the conscience of the House of Krushan, that is my final word on this matter. I have heard all your points and considered them, and this is my decision. Let us speak of it no more. I will summon you again when the time comes. Now, go and continue your search for the culprit behind these crimes himself — the evil urrkh Jarsun!"

And with those words, Jilana ended the discussion.

Honoring her decision and her authority, despite his own opinion to the contrary, Vessa took his leave of her and likewise Vrath, and strode away, vanishing before he reached the doorway of the chamber.

Vrath had been silent through most of the discussion. Only once toward the end, during the course of Jilana's long monologue, his eyes flickered, as he reacted to something she said, just before she began recalling what Shvate had said to her when he abdicated. He appeared to be about to speak at that moment, whether to contradict her or to question her on a point of law.

What he intended to say then remained unspoken that morning. He was a being who only spoke when it was absolutely unavoidable and essential. He held his silence that day, but the words he would have said and chose not to would someday have bearing on the entire course of the Krushan dynasty, though it would be decades before this would become apparent.

Part Five

Mayla

~

1

"KARNI."

Mayla called out softly. It was the morning meditation period, and the hermitage was tranquil. Except for the chirping and tweeting of small birds and the cawing of crows in the jungle, the clearing was quiet. All the acolytes and hermits were engaged in their rituals. The chores and tasks of the morning had all been completed, and not a soul was stirring in the hermitage.

Mayla came around to the rear of the hut and found Karni. She was sitting cross-legged on the back stoop in a meditative posture, her hands resting on her knees, her face composed, her eyes shut. She looked so serene, so calm. Mayla stood silently, watching her for several moments. She admired Karni's ability to compose herself. It was as if she drew on deep inner reserves of strength that fortified her even in the worst crisis. Mayla lacked that ability. She only had three modes: fast, faster, fastest. Whether it came to thought, word, or action, that defined her range. During a crisis, she needed to act, to keep moving, to fight back, strike out, run, leap . . . kill. She was a warrior by nature; it was who she was.

Karni, though she could hold her own in a fight, needed to be backed against a wall or put into a corner in order to rouse her inner warrior. Her first choice was *not* to fight, but to reason or talk her way through a conflict. Talk made Mayla restless.

Even as a child, she hated going to gurukul, being schooled in subjects that she felt had no relevance to her own life or anything she was going through on a day-to-day basis. Why did she need to recite mantras? Why did she need to know about Aravidya? Surely a warrior need not know the names of all the possible trees, plants, flowers.

Shastravidya was the only type of knowledge that she enjoyed learning, because it covered the types of weapons used in warfare, the use of the weapons, the tactics and stratagem of war, the use of akshohinis . . . She also loved hearing tales of legendary battles and warriors, the great campaigns of ancient times. Stories in which people did something heroic, fought against evil, loved, lived, died.

"The Exiled Prince," for instance: now, *that* was a great story. She had come to think of it more and more of late. She wished she could be more like the prince of the epic, able to obey his stepmother's wishes even though it meant sacrificing everything he had, giving up his claim to the throne, the kingdom, his princely life and belongings, to go live in the forest for fourteen years. It was always the exiled prince that Mayla compared herself to when she thought of the epic, never the princess. Because the princess had merely followed her husband into exile, while she, Mayla, had *chosen* to accept exile as punishment for her part in the events of that fateful night.

Because Mayla had felt responsible for what had happened in the jungle. She too had been drinking heavily, more than was good for her. She too had been hunting while drunk, encouraging Shvate and shooting off arrows in the jungle without any thought to where she was aiming and whom she might hit. She shared in the blame for his irresponsible behavior. She had even held his arm when he aimed the killing arrow, the one that had pierced the chest of the sage and his wife. They had been in the form of a pair of deer at the time, so she had only been encouraging Shvate to shoot a pair of deer. But they had been human, and when they changed back before Shvate's and Mayla's eyes, naked, bleeding from the fatal wound, still locked in each other's arms, she had felt the shock of having committed murder.

The crime was as much her fault as Shvate's. And the punishment was as much hers as well. The sage had cursed Shvate, saying that he would die copulating with his wife. The only wife the sage had seen at that time was Mayla, standing right beside Shvate. The curse was meant for her just as much as it was for Shvate. They were both responsible for the murders, and both cursed.

Now here they were, in the deep jungle, living among hermits and acolytes, dressed in the same vastras that they had been wearing when they left Hastinaga, washing the woven cotton garments each day in the river and wearing them again, shorn of all jewelry and armor, gold and accoutrements. She had not touched wine since that night. Nor had she used a weapon.

They subsisted on herbs and roots and vegetables grown by the hermits in their own little garden. They slept on straw pallets on floors washed with cow urine in mud huts with thatched roofs. She had not seen anyone other than the hermits and priests of the hermitage in over a year; she had not eaten a feast, or drunk anything other than water, or made love to Shvate. Her life was reduced to sleeping, praying, foraging, helping out with chores around the hermitage, and listening to the evening talks around the campfire about issues of philosophy, morality, or mythological tales. She often fell asleep while these talks were droning on, most of it going totally over her head, while later at night when she lay down on her pallet in the hut she shared with Karni, she found herself unable to sleep for hours, tossing and turning restlessly. She would listen to the sounds of predators and animals in the jungle and ache to be a lion, a bear, a doe, a monkey. Anything but human. Free to live wild, unchained by Krushan law, the expectations of society, the demands of human responsibility.

"Mayla? How long have you been standing there?" Karni rose to her feet and came forward, taking Mayla's hands as she peered up at her face with concern. "Are you well? You look—"

"I look like cow dung," Mayla said. "You don't need to tell me. I know it."

Karni touched Mayla's arm gently. "You are troubled. Tell me, what is the matter?"

Mayla cried out and impulsively hugged Karni. "Karni, oh, Karni. I don't know how to do this anymore. I . . . I can't. I just can't."

Mayla's head felt as if all blood had suddenly left it, leaving her whole body feeling drained, as if she had been sucked dry by vampire urrkh. In a sense, she had. But not by vampires, by life itself.

She felt her legs stagger as the will to stand left her.

2

Karni caught Mayla as she reeled, her arms surprisingly strong. She helped her to the stoop and sat her down slowly, then sat down beside her.

"Calm yourself, Mayla," Karni said in her firm, no-nonsense way. "There is no need to lose hope. We are all in this together."

"Yes," Mayla said hoarsely, voice thickened by the tears that were forming. She cleared her throat. "Yes, and thank the gods for that. If you were not here with me, Karni, I don't know what I would have done. I think I would have jumped in the river and drowned myself in the first few days alone. I felt so awful, so guilty, so ashamed, so miserable at playing a part in what happened in the jungle with Shvate and that sage and his wife. I wished I could have died rather than seen such a sight. I still wish I could die! Perhaps I *should* die. Just go to the high point over the waterfall and jump and let the river wash me away to the sea because—"

Karni placed her hand over Mayla's mouth, cutting off her last words. "Enough. No more talk like that or you'll get one tight slap from me."

Mayla looked up at Karni's pretty face and saw the first signs of age lines starting to appear faintly around her mouth and eyes and on her forehead. Karni's eyes were hard, and her lips tightly pressed. Mayla knew that she meant it: on at least one previous occasion when Mayla had lost her self-control and begun ranting and babbling, alarming the young acolytes of the hermitage and upsetting the hermits, Karni had hauled off and slapped her hard across the face. Mayla had been struck in combat before, during battles and skirmishes—even during practice sessions by gurus while she was growing up—and so she could attest that Karni had quite a hand on her. That slap had shocked Mayla . . . and also shocked the hysteria out of her. To underline the action, Karni had slapped her again, on the other cheek. A one-two punch combination couldn't have been more effective. Mayla had been rocked back on her heels, almost knocked off her feet, and from that day to this one, she had never lost control again, more than a little afraid of Karni's iron arms and wooden hands.

She cringed now at the reminder and reached up to take hold of Karni's wrists. "Please. No more slaps. I can take a bear's claws, but not another of your slaps, Karni."

Karni smiled at the comparison and lowered her hands, taking Mayla's in her own. She massaged and played with Mayla's fingers as they talked, using the action to relax and set her at ease. Mayla loved it when she did that. Mayla's mother used to play with her fingers when she was very small, pushing each fingertip, rubbing the pads of her fingers against the tips of Mayla's fingernails, twisting and bending the fingers as if pretending to break them but then letting them snap back, never actually hurting her, just teasing and toying; it had brought goose bumps to Mayla's arms, and she felt goose bumps rise now.

"That feels so nice," she said. "Don't stop. My mother used to do it."

Karni smiled, pleased at the change of tone. "You were lucky, then."

Mayla frowned. "Lucky?"

"You had a mother. I didn't. I never knew what it meant to touch or be touched by my mother, to feel her fingers on my face, her lips on my forehead, hear her laughter, smell her hair."

Mayla felt her throat catch. "Yes, of course. You were given away by your father to your uncle. He raised you as his own."

"And raised me well. But a father is not a mother."

"No, they surely are not." Mayla found herself recalling all her most cherished memories of her mother and was about to speak them out loud, then thought better of it. She had come here in the hope that Karni could make her feel better, not to make Karni feel worse.

"Would you like me to braid your hair?" Karni asked.

Mayla felt her cheeks split as she beamed. "Please!"

Karni knelt behind her on the stoop and began cleaning out her hair with a wooden brush. "Whatever do you do with yourself, girl? There are so many leaves and twigs in here!" She held out her hand in front of Mayla's face to show evidence of her findings.

Mayla shrugged. "I go wandering. I don't care much about where I climb or how I get where I want to go, so long as I get there. I've always been like that. My mother used to call me a little vanar, climbing trees and cliffs and anywhere and everywhere. She was always yelling at me: "Mayla! Come down from there!" Whenever I did anything to upset her, which was all the time, she would yell, "Mayla! Climb down from your castle in the sky!"

She felt Karni's body vibrating with laughter, pressed against Mayla's back. "You were quite a tomboy, I'm sure. You still are."

"But that's where you're wrong. I'm no tomboy, Karni, I'm a tomgirl. I was one then, and I still am. You see, I always liked boys, liked being with them, liked playing and fooling around with them, liked kissing them —"

"Stop! Stop!" Karni giggled, slapping Mayla's back lightly to admonish her. "You are such a hot chili! You'll say anything that comes into your head. Remember, I'm your sister wife, and your elder. I don't need to hear about all your youthful indiscretions."

Mayla twisted her head around to look up at Karni, and winked. "Are you sure? There were some very *handsome* indiscretions."

Karni slapped Mayla's back again, laughing and covering her mouth to stifle the sound as she always did. "Behave yourself, woman! You're too much!"

They were quiet for a few moments, still grinning and basking in the afterglow of the brief banter. Then Karni pressed Mayla's shoulder with her strong fingers and asked, "What brought you down today? When I opened my eyes and saw you standing there, I thought you were about to collapse."

Mayla sighed. "I probably was. It's harder for me than for you, Karni. You somehow know how to endure this, how to live here" — she gestured at the jungle around them — "how to *adjust*. I don't."

"You've managed for a year," Karni said gently from behind. "That's quite an adjustment in itself."

"Yes, but today I woke up and realized that it was a whole year since we came here. It's exactly a year today since we left Hastinaga. And I realized that this is only one year, that we're going to be here not for six or seven or fourteen years, like Amara and Siya and Armanya in the legend of the exiled prince, but *forever*. For the *rest of our lives*. And when that dawned over me, I thought I would scream and go mad. I couldn't take it. I *can't* take it. I don't know how I got through one year, let alone how I am going to get through two, or three, or ten."

Karni's strong hands continued braiding Mayla's hair, holding it firmly enough that she couldn't move her head more than an inch or two. "The same as you got through the first year. It'll get easier as it goes along. You'll see."

"How do you know that? Have you been in exile before? How do you know what it's like to live like this forever, to be able to do nothing, go nowhere, eat like a hermit-muni, wear the same garment every day, to have none of the comforts, luxuries, powers, things that you once had so much of? How is it even possible to go from being a prince or a princess one day to living like a jungle hermit the rest of your life? It's impossible!"

Karni sighed, paused in the braiding, and leaned gently against Mayla's back and shoulder. "I don't know about exile; this is my first time, in case that wasn't clear," she said, the irony a familiar part of her conversation, "but I was young and impetuous and impatient too, full of life and energy — too much energy perhaps — always up to mischief and getting into tight scrapes from which it seemed impossible to get out."

"*You* were impetuous and mischievous?" Mayla said, starting to shake her head, then regretting it. "Ow. I don't believe that, Karni. I can't imagine you *ever* doing anything naughty or irresponsible. It's impossible!"

Karni smiled; Mayla heard it in her voice as she replied. "It seems impossible now to you. But it's true. People change, Mayla."

"Why, Karni? Why do people change?" It was a serious question, one to which Mayla genuinely wanted the answer.

"Because we have to. Because life changes, circumstances change, the river flows in different directions, grows hot and cold, goes over rapids and falls, slows and roars down furiously, and we're like little boats bobbing on the great river. We have to adapt and adjust according to the river's flow, or else we capsize and sink."

"So we change to survive."

"Yes. But also because we need to change in order to grow. A cub can play with her mother's ears and tail and tumble over her snout, but when she grows old enough, the mother makes her hunt and kill and fend for herself, because the mother knows she won't always be around, and the cub needs to be able to live without her."

"I don't know about you, Karni," Mayla said laconically, "but my mother never had a tail or a snout. Are you sure you weren't raised by wolves?"

Karni laughed softly, in politeness, but her tone was still serious. "I went through something when I was very young. Something that changed me, forced me to grow up quickly, maybe too quickly. In the course of a single summer, I had to change from being a young fun-loving, mischiefmongering girl to a grown woman."

Mayla was silent. She had never heard Karni speak of such things before. Karni rarely spoke about her childhood or youth, and then only in the broadest terms, keeping her purview mostly to politics and general matters. This was the first time in years that Mayla had heard her reveal something so personal. She decided to bite her tongue on the quips and smart witticisms and listen respectfully.

"What happened?" she asked soberly, trying to encourage Karni to reveal more.

Karni sighed, a long, deep sigh that Mayla felt through Karni's chest and belly and thighs pressed against her back. "A great sage came to visit my father, and I was given the responsibility of serving him."

"Is that all? I mean . . . I'm sorry. I didn't mean to suggest it was nothing. It's just . . . well, I've waited on sages too, and they were difficult, scary people mostly, but they make a lot of demands and keep you up at all hours for a day or two, and then they're gone. Besides, there are always cooks and servants and maids to do the real running around."

"Mostly, yes. But in this case, it was only me doing everything, and it wasn't just a day or two, it was all summer and autumn as well. It felt like a year, or a lifetime."

Mayla recalled the few times she had been forced to serve the priests at her father's palace in Dirda. It had been excruciating service, and it had never lasted more than a day or two. She couldn't imagine what it must have been like to wait on a single priest all summer long, for months on end, and to do everything herself? Impossible!

"I can't imagine how much worse it must have been for you with that horrible sage," she said, reaching up and touching the back of Karni's hand. "It must have been excruciating."

"It was," Karni admitted. "What made it really bad was that I lost someone that same summer . . . someone I cared about very deeply at the time."

"Oh, gods," Mayla said, mortified. "That's so awful. I'm so sorry, Karni."

"It was a long time ago," she said, then was silent for a moment.

"But it feels like just yesterday," Mayla said softly. "Doesn't it?"

"It does," Karni admitted, looking surprised at Mayla's insight.

Mayla nodded. "I can understand. I was thinking of someone I lost when I was very small. An older brother, my eldest, actually. He died in an accident during a chariot race. I was very small but I still remember how I felt. It hurt. It still hurts."

"Yes," Karni said. "It's like a wound that never truly heals."

They sat in silence for the next several moments as Karni finished up the braid. She patted Mayla's back. "You're done."

Mayla swiveled to swing her braids over her shoulders and looked at them. "Lovely. Thank you, Karni. You're the sweetest."

She saw Karni standing on the stoop, gazing out at the forest, a faraway expression in her eyes and went over to her. "That person you lost meant a great deal to you, didn't he?"

"Yes," Karni said at last, wiping a single tear from her eye. "But when we lose something, life often gives us something else in return. That's what grief is, Mayla. It's life's gift to us in exchange for our loss. It teaches us to be wiser, more mature, more responsible, to change and grow. It teaches us that change is inevitable, so the more readily we accept it, the better we adapt to it. That's what I want to tell you, Mayla. Accept the change. Accept it and adapt. It seems hard at first, it seems unbearable or even, to use your favorite word—"

"Impossible!"

"Yes, but in time it will get easier. You'll see. Give yourself time, and you'll do fine."

Mayla nodded. "At some level, I understand that, Karni. But that's not what caused me to panic today. It was Shvate."

Karni frowned, her expression changing. "What about him?"

"As bad as I have been finding it of late, I think he is finding it much harder, Karni. He keeps it from you. He hides it because he feels responsible and guilty for making you have to go into exile for no fault of yours. So he doesn't tell you anything or share his darker, deeper thoughts with you. But I know. I know what he's going through. It's bad, Karni. It's bad, and it's getting worse. And I'm worried now that it could make him do something rash. Something terrible. That's what really scares me. I'm struggling—that's hard enough. But Shvate is reaching some kind of a crisis point, and today being the first-year anniversary, I am worried that he might do something."

"Like what?" Karni asked sharply.

"I don't know," Mayla said. "I don't know, Karni. But I am sure he will do something. He's like me in that respect. He can't not do anything. His anger and frustration and guilt have to be expressed somehow. And I think he's at his breaking point now. I'm afraid he might do something . . . drastic."

Shvate

~

SHVATE STOOD AT THE edge of the cliff, looking down at the valley far below. For as far as the eye could see, every surface of the land was covered with dense, impenetrable jungle. The rolling hills to the west, the mostly flat plains to the north and east, and behind him, there was nothing but yojanas of close-growing ancient forest in every direction. There had been a time when he had loved the jungle, had considered it his true home, a home of the heart.

He still recalled the first time Vrath had driven his brother Adri and himself to the jungle. They were on their way to the gurukul where they were to spend the next several years of their lives in the care of the gurus, learning the vidya, scriptures, and the essential subjects necessary for any future king. It had been a gloomy time for both of them. The first time either had been away from home, from the comforts and security of Hastinaga palace, and neither had known what to expect. When Vrath had made the unexpected detour, driving the chariot off the main marg and into the jungle, weaving his way between close-growing trees over a rough, barely visible pathway, Shvate had thought they must have reached the gurukul already, for what else could be out there in such wilderness?

Shvate remembered the thrill that had coursed through him when Vrath had stopped the chariot and asked them to step down, telling them that they were going to spend the next few days there in the jungle, then asking them both what they would like to do first. Over the following days, as Vrath taught them how to hunt, how to track spoor, stay upwind of prey, read the tracks of different species, bait a line, learn where the most fish were to be found — and the thousand other little insights that were essential to becoming a good tracker and hunter — Shvate had felt as if he had never lived until then. The sheer joy and beauty of the jungle itself, this canopy of green beneath an endless sky, this palace of wonders, this kingdom of beasts, had awed and inspired him to an extent he would never have believed possible.

He recalled the moment when he had known that the jungle was the place he most loved in the whole wide world, that instant when he had smelled the mulchy swampy odor of dead trees, animal urine, wet earth, dewy leaves, freshly blooming wildflowers, breathed the cool, damp air that enveloped him like a living breath, listened to what Vrath called the "voice of the jungle" — which to a city dweller would sound like a single droning hum but that Shvate now knew was composed of a thousand different sounds, the chittering of insects, the calling of birds, the sounds of different animals, even the sounds of water, leaves, trees, and bushes: the orchestra of life primeval — and knew in his heart that he would never again in his life be as happy as he felt in that moment, in that place.

He sighed now and lowered his head, grieving. He mourned the loss of that Shvate, that young boy who had his whole life ahead of him, for whom anything was possible. Despite his infirmity, despite the naysayers, he had succeeded against great odds — only to crash his chariot against the stone wall of karma.

He had lived and relived that night over again a thousand times, and no matter how he reviewed it, he was the one at fault. Not Mayla, not the sage and his wife, not even the wine, it was just he, Shvate, who had made the one mistake any entitled young person should beware of: he had taken the world for granted. He had become arrogant in his privilege and his position, over-confident in his strength and hunting ability, cocky of his masculinity, and had thought he could do anything, anytime, anywhere. It was that which had been his downfall. The wine had clouded his judgment and impaired his senses, not his inherent character and wisdom. He had been raised to be better than that. He had been raised to be the best among the best. And yet he had failed.

Now, a year into his exile, he had come to a new realization. Punishment was not enough. Punishment only served himself. It served as a rebuke to himself for his mortal error, not a true, fitting judgment. Had he been passing sentence upon himself as a king, he would have been far harsher. He would have condemned himself to death. For any person who had been as well educated as Shvate, as well groomed for kingship as an heir to the Kru-shan throne, as well advised and mentored by the likes of Vrath, should have known better, should have done better, should have not acted the way he had.

He had woken this morning with the cold realization that exile was only an escape, not justice. It was his selfish way of evading his own just fate. By sending himself into exile, by abdicating the throne, by declaring his brother to be the unopposed claimant to the Krushan throne, he had performed the most selfish, privileged error of all: he had removed himself from the judgment of his elders and his peers. By punishing himself, he had avoided their punishment. By exiling himself, he had sought to avoid the all-seeing eye of Krushan law.

Krushan law demanded a much harsher penalty.

Krushan law did not compromise or bargain.

Krushan law demanded that like be paid for with like.

Krushan law required that Shvate's crime be given the penalty that *Shvate* deserved.

The punishment in proportion to the crime.

This was not merely some drunken youth who had been sojourning in the woods that night; this was the prince and heir of Hastinaga himself, a sophisticated, educated, mentored young man of prodigious skills, knowl-edge, and talent. The emblem of Krushan morality. His mistake could not be punished as any wayward youth might be punished. He deserved the harshest judgment of all.

Death.

That was the conclusion he had come to, on awakening this morning.

He must die.

And because he had removed himself from the judgment of all others, so he himself must see to it that this final judgment was delivered.

And so he sentenced himself to death — declaring that the penalty be carried out at once, without recourse to appeal or reconsideration.

He would die today, right now, right here.

He stood at the edge of the cliff, a narrow outjutting lip of uneven black stone hanging out over the valley like a wooden board over a swimming hole. All he need do was take a single step further, and he would fall two or three hundred yards. That would mark the end of Shvate the White. And with him would end his ignominy, his shame, his dereliction, his felonious act and its consequences.

Time, he told himself.

He looked up at the deep blue sky one last time.

He saw a ragged V of cranes flocking southward. He heard their distant, mournful calls.

He smelled the familiar enveloping odors of the jungle he loved so dearly, and beneath whose green canopy he had committed the act that had ruined his life. He inhaled it all one final time.

And then he took the last step into darkness.

Karni

～

1

KARNI THREW HERSELF AFTER Shvate.

He was already at the edge of the cliff when she had emerged from the trees. She had taken in the scene in a single glance and sprinted forward without thought or hesitation. He was already stepping off the edge when she ran out onto the ledge, the rough stone pricking and hurting her bare feet. She saw him step off and saw his body falling as she threw herself at the lip. She might well have slid right off the edge and gone falling after him, and she would not have regretted that. Better that she die than let him die without even attempting to save him.

She felt the stony ledge rise and strike her in the chest, the ribs, the hip with stunning force. She gasped and cried out involuntarily. Her chin struck a slightly raised spot, and her teeth snapped together, her jaw cracking audibly. She saw stars in the afternoon sky, the world swirled, and the forest darkened. She knew she was about to pass out from the blow and bit her lip hard, hard enough to draw a spurt of blood. The pain revived her and kept her from unconsciousness.

She lay there on the stony, uneven ledge, her entire body still vibrating from the shock of the fall, and looked over the edge.

Her arms were outstretched, reaching over the lip into empty air, as if trying to grab hold of the sky itself, of emptiness, of hope, of life.

She had something in her fists. It was not sky, or emptiness, or hope.

It was life.

She felt the strain on her wrists, her fingers, her elbows, her shoulder joints, her back.

And she felt her body starting to slide, pulled toward the edge, toward the emptiness.

"Mayla," she groaned, her voice choked out of her.

She turned her head, rubbing her cheek harshly against the ledge, and tried again.

"MAYLA!"

She heard footsteps come running behind her. Mayla could not have been far behind. She was a better, faster runner than Karni. But on this occasion, Karni had taken a lead on her. The instant Mayla had told Karni about Shvate's state of mind that morning, about some of the things he had said to her, the thoughts he had voiced, she had risen from the stoop of their hut and begun running. She had run all the way to the cliff, because it was their favorite spot at this time of day, and because it was the place she herself had often stood and contemplated dying: how easy it would be here to simply step off the ledge and let Goddess Artha, the Great Mother, claim her in her heavy embrace. If Shvate had not been here, she would have gone to the glade, or down to the waterfall, but she had felt instinctively that this was the place he would if he were to think of killing himself.

"MAYLA!" she screamed now, feeling her body slide toward the ledge. She was already at the thinnest part, the very tip, and she could see the valley on either side of the tapering lip of rock, yawning darkly below. In another moment, she would slide all the way over, and then she would know at last what it felt like to simply let go, to abdicate her claim to life, to love, to everything. She could feel Great Mother Artha calling to her, whispering like the sound of the insects at dusk. **Come**, she was saying, **come to me, child. I will take you into my heart and keep you safe. No more worry, no more cares, no more responsibilities. Only cool, blessed darkness. Eternal sleep.**

She felt her eyes starting to tear, from the pain of the impact, the jarring blow to her ribs and hip, but also from the realization that she was close to the end now, the end of everything. This must be how Siya had felt when Artha had opened her arms and invited her in. When she had preferred to return to her mother's womb rather than accept the dominance of a broken god.

Mayla's hands grasped her ankles. "I have you!" Mayla cried hoarsely. "I have you, sister! I will not let you fall!"

Karni squeezed the tears out of her eyes and forced them open again, blinking rapidly to clear them. She was at the very edge now, her arms stretched over the emptiness up to the elbows.

"Pull me back, Mayla," she said, speaking slowly and clearly. "Whatever you do, do not let go. Pull me back inch by inch, and make sure you are well anchored and do not slip. There is gravel on the ledge, take care."

She felt Mayla look around her, getting her bearings, then felt the younger woman's hands grasp her ankles even more tightly and start to pull. Karni's bruised ribs bounced against the uneven ledge, and she wanted to cry out with the pain, but she bit her lip again and suppressed the cry. She did not want to distract Mayla. Right now, Mayla was all that stood between Karni and certain death. And widowhood.

As she slid backward, she saw her forearms retreat onto the ledge, then saw her hands come into view, bent with the weight of their burden. Her knuckles were white with strain, fists bunched tightly as manacles around two pale white wrists.

Shvate's wrists.

She had him.

She had her husband in her hands.

He was her life, and she held her life in her hands. She was not going to let go, for anything in the world.

She felt with her feet and found a protruding lip of rock, sufficient for her to hook one foot over, giving her some leverage.

"Mayla, stop pulling me," she said, "I am far enough back now. Now come here and lie next to me, face-down. We must both help Shvate climb back over the top."

As Mayla moved to comply, Karni saw Shvate's head lift up. The top of Shvate's face came into view, contorted with the effort of being held and with something else, some emotion she had never seen before on his face. His eyes found her eyes, and she saw the desolation in them. He could not speak, but his eyes spoke to her eyes, and she knew exactly what he was saying.

2

"Why?" Shvate asked.

They were sitting in the shadow of a tree near the cliffside where Karni and Mayla had just pulled him back up over the edge. Karni could see the cliff from where she sat and shuddered at the thought of how close she had come to losing her husband. Her ribs, her hip — her whole body — throbbed and ached. Her lip, too, felt swollen, and a patch of skin on her cheek was abraded. She had contusions and bruises all over the front of her body. Her ankles ached from the force with which Mayla had gripped them. Half a toenail had been torn off, and the toe was now encrusted with dried blood.

Mayla had fetched them some water, and Karni had taken a small sip but left the rest for Shvate to drink, knowing he needed it more than she. They were all three sitting on the cool grass beneath the tree, facing each other. Both she and Mayla were alert and watchful, unable to take their eyes off Shvate for more than an instant, as if fearful that he might get up and run for the cliff and jump again. She knew he would not do that; Shvate could be driven by emotion to do foolish things at times, but he was not cruel.

He had been looking at her since he had asked the question, still awaiting an answer.

"What do you mean, 'Why?'" she asked fiercely. "You are my husband. I didn't want you to die. What other answer could there possibly be?"

He looked at her then, in a way that broke her heart. Hopeless, lost, desolate. It was the same look she had seen in his eyes when she had held on to him, as he had hung over the ledge, on the cusp of death. She had never seen such a look in his eyes before. It was the look of a man who was at his life's end, as if nothing anyone did or said would ever matter again to him, as if something within him was already dead.

"You don't understand," he said softly, his voice barely audible over the omnipresent sounds of the jungle. "After I was gone, you could both have returned to Hastinaga, rejoined the family."

Karni looked at Mayla, then back at Shvate. "With you gone, Shvate? What life would we have had?"

"I would have jumped after you," Mayla said matter-of-factly. Tears spilled from her eyes, but she brushed them away roughly, almost surprised by them. "I wouldn't have been able to live a single day without you."

Shvate shook his head. He was sitting with his knees raised and his arms clasped over them. "You could have gone back. Everyone would have accepted you with open arms. The curse would have been lifted. Once I was gone, there would have been no stricture on either of you marrying again, bearing children."

They exchanged another glance, then looked at him as if he was insane. "What?" Karni asked, shocked that he could even contemplate such a thing.

"Don't you see, Karni, Mayla? The sage's curse was for *me*. It predicted that if I lay with my wife, then we would both die. At the time I knew he only meant Mayla, since only she was with me. But if it did extend to you as well, as my wife, it would still have to terminate with my demise. He did not forbid my wife to mate again. Only us together. So you both could have gone on to marry again and bear heirs to the dynasty."

"And this is why you tried to kill yourself?" Karni asked. "So that we would return to Hastinaga and marry again and bear heirs to the Krushan dynasty?"

Shvate looked at her sadly.

"I . . . I want to come over there and slap you," she said, gritting her teeth to control herself from actually doing it. "I want to punch you and pummel you for daring to suggest such a thing. Let me tell you clearly, Shvate of Hastinaga. If you die, I am not going back to Hastinaga! Not even if they tie me to a rope and drag me behind a chariot! I would rather die here in the jungle than go back and become a baby bearer for your dynasty. That is not why I married you. I chose you as my husband because I loved you, and I love you still. Not to rent out my womb as a surrogate for any Krushan man to seed for the continuation of the lineage!"

"I would kill myself rather than let another man touch me," Mayla said, staring at Shvate with such hostility that Karni thought she might actually attack him next. "I would die within a minute of you dying. I would kill myself by any means possible. Do you hear me, Shvate?"

Shvate raised both his hands, trying to calm the two women shouting at him. "Very well, very well. I hear you both. I understand your pain, and your loyalty. But don't you see? I am in pain too. I have a loyalty as well. Not only to you both, but to my family, to my House, to my people."

"To hell with your House and your people," Mayla said. She picked up a stone and threw it at a fallen tree trunk, striking it hard enough that some bark was chipped off. "If you care so much about them, then fight like a man. Don't jump off a cliff and kill yourself. That's just another kind of running away!"

Shvate nodded his head. "Perhaps. But it is the only way left. I have thought it through, and there are no other options. This is the only way to circumvent the curse and compensate for the dishonor I have brought upon my family."

"Then I will jump from that cliff right now!" Mayla said, getting to her feet. "You only care about the honor of your family? What about the honor of your wives? If that is your final word, then I will go and leap off that cliff to my death this very instant!"

Karni saw that Mayla was out of control. She was much more closely attached to Shvate because of their greater physical intimacy; they were soul partners. She was afraid that Mayla might actually do what she threatened, and then Shvate would be irrevocably lost.

"Mayla," she said strongly, grabbing her sister wife's arm. "Sit down."

Eyes flashing, for a moment Mayla looked like she would say something back, but then she saw the determined look on Karni's face and subsided. Without another word, she slumped down again in a heap.

"There will be no more talk of jumping from cliffs," Karni said firmly but gently to Mayla.

Mayla's eyes glared up at Karni, but she said nothing.

Karni turned and looked at Shvate. "That goes for you as well, Shvate."

Shvate sighed. "What good am I to you two? What use am I to anyone? I am a burden on this world. Better I rid you both of my presence."

Karni raised her hand, wanting so badly to slap her husband. To hit him hard enough to rock his head back, the way Siya had slapped Amara—thrice, if she recalled correctly—when he had been in a similar state, saying that he would go into exile alone because it was not fair to deprive Siya of her comfortable life as a princess in Aranya. But she restrained herself. Shvate was not Amara, and she was not Siya. They were already in exile together. Shvate's ego needed to be boosted, not corrected.

"Enough," she said, pointing a finger in warning. "There will be no more talk of that kind. Do you hear me? No more talk of suicide and futility from either of you."

Shvate glanced up at her, saw her withering look, and shrugged. He said nothing. She took that as acceptance. Men could be so weak at times. Correction: all the time. That was why they built their muscles, wore their armor, engaged in all that bluster and man talk. Because inside they were just little boys quivering and scared of everything.

"We don't threaten to kill ourselves. We don't act as if we have no other choice but suicide. Since when is taking one's own life a solution to any problem? Is not our battle cry '*We are Krushan! We fight!*'?" Have you forgotten that, and all your training, and the teachings of your gurus, and the wisdom of your mentors? Is this what Mother Jilana and Vrath raised you for, to throw yourself off a cliff and end your life? Surely there enough enemies out there who want all of the sons and daughters of Krushan dead. Are you now aiding and abetting your enemies by giving them what they want? *Wake up*, Shvate. Wake up and accept the reality of our lives. This is all we have, *we* are all we have. Each other. This jungle, you, Mayla, myself — that's our entire world. We need one another more than ever now. How dare you presume to absolve yourself of your responsibility as a husband, as a man?"

Shvate held his head in his hands, listening to Karni. He said in a mournful, pleading tone, "What would you have me do, wife? Do you not understand how impotent, how useless I feel? Can you not see my pain?"

She sank to her knees, lowering her voice, gentling her tone. "Of course I do, my love. You are a strong, proud man. A prince of Krushan. For you to want to take your own life must mean are at your wits' end. But you can't give up hope. You can't just end your life. It will not solve anything."

"It will solve one problem at least. The problem of progeny."

She felt the urge to slap him again and closed her eyes, willing the urge to pass. When she felt it was safe, she opened her eyes again. "That is not a solution. You heard Mayla's response to your suggestion. She was willing to kill herself rather than let another man touch her. Does that work for you? What if we all three hold hands and jump together? End it all together? Will that resolve the problem of progeny?"

He shook his head and pressed the heels of his palms into his eyes. His voice was hollow. "No. Of course not. But what else can I do? As you say, I have reached my wits' end, Karni. If you have a suggestion, then say it. All I know is that we must do something! I feel responsible for my family's future. It has been a whole year since we came into exile. There has been no child born to Adri and Geldry either in this time."

"How can you be so sure?" Mayla asked.

Karni nodded. "Yes, how can you be so sure? We have had no word from Hastinaga in the past year."

"Exactly." Shvate sat up, looking more animated. "Had they borne a child, word would have traveled to us. News of an heir to the Burnt Empire will spread like wildfire. The acolytes in the hermitage are constantly traveling to other ashrams. Mages from far and wide come and visit occasionally. If they do not find out, then surely Mother Jilana would send word. The only reason we have not heard from Hastinaga is because there has been no news yet. And if Adri and Geldry haven't given the House an heir, then who else will? Everyone was counting on us. By now, we would surely have produced at least one heir, if not more."

Karni shook her head. "I don't know, husband. It isn't that simple. We have been in exile for a year, unable to have intimate relations because of the curse, but we have been married for much longer. You and I for several years, and you and Mayla for some years too. If our wombs have not quickened yet, it could mean that we might not have had a child this year as well. You can't assume that this would have been the year we produced heirs!"

"It would have been. I am sure of it." Shvate took some water from the clay pot and splashed it on his face. "The past several years, we have been campaigning, at war, constantly traveling, on the move, fighting . . ."

"None of that affected our ability to mate," Mayla said softly. She had moved closer to them both, sitting within arm's reach now. She gave Karni a sisterly look of support. "If anything, we were more amorous in camp than we were back home in our bedchamber."

"Mayla's right," Karni said. "You can't just assume that this past year was the crucial one. It takes time. In the legend of the exiled prince, King Ratha and his three wives didn't produce any heirs for several years. Finally he had to call Mage Yaranga, who presided over a special sacrificial ceremony, after which he gave the eldest queen —"

"A sacrament to eat, and she shared it with her sister queens, because of which they all conceived. Yes, I know the story of the epic, Karni," Shvate said. "But you do know that most scholars today regard the sacrament as being apocryphal."

"Meaning . . . the sacrament wasn't real?" Mayla asked, sounding shocked.

"Yes, Mayla," Karni said. "It's symbolic."

Mayla looked confused. "Symbolic . . . for what?"

"Mage Yaranga was called in by King Ratha for the same reason that Seer-Mage Vessa was called in by Mother Jilana."

Mayla blinked several times, processing this information. "You mean . . . ?"

"The time-honored practice of calling in a learned priest to act as surrogate father," Karni said.

Mayla looked at her, then made a face. "Ew! Disgusting. I'll slap any priest who enters *my* bedchamber!"

Karni laughed. She couldn't help herself. The thought of Mayla dropkicking an old venerated priest as he entered her bedchamber was so vivid, so real, that it hit her in the gut. She laughed out loud.

Shvate stared at her uncomprehendingly, then grinned, then laughed as well. The sound of his own laughter seemed to surprise him. He stopped, but then saw Karni continuing to laugh and laughed some more.

Mayla stared at them both as if they had gone completely crazy, then played back her own words in her mind and understood what they were laughing at. She joined in, laughing with her own rhythm.

For the next few minutes, all three of them laughed and laughed, while the squirrels and deer nearby listened with twitching ears at the strange sound.

3

Later that evening, after bathing in the river, performing their evening rituals, eating a sparse evening meal of fruits and some nuts, they sat by the riverbank to talk again.

"Now," Karni said, "we're refreshed, calmer, more relaxed. Let us talk this over without any more threats or dramatic outbursts."

Shvate and Mayla both nodded. It was a peaceful quiet evening. They were sitting on a part of the riverbank away from the waterfall, whose sound was too loud to talk over. It grew louder if one stood, but when seated on the rocks as they were, it was muted to a dull, steady roar. Dusk had settled on the jungle, and the darkling sky was dotted with silhouettes of the last birds seeking their mates and flocks in the high trees. It was very restful here, the air moist with the spray of the river, the evening breeze cool and refreshing. Farther downriver, in the rocky shallows downwind of the humans, a mother bear and her two cubs splashed around noisily, trying to catch fish. By now, they were accustomed to seeing Shvate, Mayla, and Karni about, and because the humans stayed far from the cubs and never made any threatening gestures or sounds, the mother bear had never bothered them.

"Mayla and I have spoken about it in private," Karni went on. "Neither of us are willing to accept a priest as a surrogate. Our decision is final."

Shvate looked out at the far bank across the river. The trees there were still lit by the deep afterglow of the sun's last light. "Then what are we to do?"

"Must we do anything at all?" Karni asked quietly.

Shvate looked up at her. "It is our Krushan law."

She wanted to argue the point, but decided to let it go. If Shvate considered it his Krushan law — or *their* Krushan law — then so it *was*. Shima was what one *believed* was one's Krushan law. If you did not consider a particular task your responsibility, nothing could force you to do it. Only slavery compelled anyone to act against their will. And even with the typical imbalance between men and women in society, Krushan women were not slaves to their men. But if their husband believed they had a duty to their House to procreate for the sake of continuance, then that made it so. There was no point bickering over semantics and personal differences.

"Very well," she said. "Then there may be a solution."

Shvate frowned. She could see his forehead creasing even in the gloaming light. He had once possessed a fine head of hair, bushy and leonine, but the years of warring and traveling had taken their toll, and in the past year itself, he had lost much of his mane, while more and more of his forehead revealed itself. He was aging before his time. She could see that this existence would not sustain him for long. He was no longer the fine specimen of manhood she had married only a few short years ago; indeed he was naught but a shadow of the great conqueror who had fought so splendidly at the Battle of the Rebels and the Battle of Reygar, and achieved so many other historic victories.

The curse and the year of exile had emasculated him, the inactivity and lack of command structure had robbed him of motivation. She wondered how long he could survive this way, compared to his expected life span had their life at Hastinaga not been so cruelly interrupted. She pushed the thought aside. They had a very big decision to consider now, and she was the only one who possessed the solution to the problem at hand.

Are you sure you want to do this, Karni? she asked herself one last time. *You know what it did to you the first time, the toll it took on you. Are you absolutely certain you're willing to go through that again?*

And the answer came, as it had before: *What choice do I have? I am a woman whose husband tried to kill himself because of this conundrum. If I don't do something to solve the problem, what good am I as his wife?*

Also, the afterthought, faint but persistent: *What if this was the reason Pasha'ar gave me the mantra in the first place? What if he knew, with the prescience of wise sages, that this day would come someday, and the mantra would be my only means of salvation? What if that was why he came to Stonecastle, why he spent that long, endless summer, why he put me through such hell? What if he was training and preparing me for this life, this moment, this decision?*

Karni did not believe that everything in life was a foregone conclusion, that everything we said and did was decided by karma. Karma could only determine our future lives in the broadest possible shape. It was up to each of us individually to determine how to live those future lives on a day-to-day basis, the thousands of little acts performed, kind or cruel, gentle or violent, caring or uncaring. Karma could cause us to be reborn as that mother bear in the river a few hundred yards downstream, but whether Mother Bear chose to attack humans for no reason and kill them or simply to fish in the river with her cubs, then go back into the jungle to sleep, was up to her. Karma could put you down in a certain body, a life, a place and time. It didn't give you an exact script of everything you did and said in that body, that lifetime, that place and time.

"What solution?" Shvate asked.

Mayla looked at her curiously too. Karni had not told her sister wife of this part; she had known that Mayla could not keep a secret for more than a moment or two — especially not from Shvate — and she wanted to be the one to tell them both, to control how the information was revealed, and what part of it remained unshared.

Karni took a deep breath.

"Many years ago," she began, "a sage named Pasha'ar came to my father's palace in Stonecastle while I was still a young girl . . ."

It was dark when she finished. Mayla had taken a moment to light a small fire using a piece of banked charcoal. The fire was in a circle of rocks; it gave off enough heat to keep them warm despite the falling temperature, and provided enough light to see each other by. Karni saw both Mayla's and Shvate's faces change as she narrated the story of her time serving Pasha'ar while artfully editing out all mention of the boy with whom she'd had a relationship and the events of his death. She did not even mention her trip to Dirda, knowing that it would elicit a flurry of questions from the eternally curious Mayla, who might well put two and two together and link her visit there with the death of her elder brother in the chariot race around the same time.

Close as she was to Mayla, she had chosen to keep the God Mantra a secret all this while only because of her earlier encounter with the sun god in his avatar as Maheev. She could hardly expect Mayla to understand that she, Karni, had lain with her dead brother and borne an illegitimate child from that union. There was also the issue of the illicit child having a claim to the thrones of all three kingdoms! Even now, as she explained her grueling months of service to the visiting Guru, she found herself glossing over any mention of her former suitor Maheev entirely. When she came to the part where Pasha'ar was leaving and gave her the mantra as a "gift," Karni explained what it would do when recited. Both reacted. Shvate's eyes widened, and he rose to his feet. Mayla exclaimed, and her eyes glinted, twinkling in the firelight.

"How do you know the mantra works?" Mayla asked breathlessly. "It sounds so far-fetched! Imagine it. The power to summon gods!"

"It works," Karni said simply, careful not to elaborate.

Shvate came over to sit beside her, looking at her as if she had just revealed the secret to life itself. "Karni, Karni, my Karni," he said.

"Yes, Shvate?" she replied.

"Why didn't you tell me of this earlier?"

"I had all but forgotten about it myself," she said. "As Mayla said, it seemed so far-fetched at the time, I scarcely believed it. I was just relieved to be free of his service. I resumed my normal everyday life, and soon I forgot about it entirely."

"You forgot the mantra?" Shvate asked, shocked.

"No, not the mantra itself. I forgot *about* it."

Mayla was still staring at her, the wheels of her mind spinning like racing chariot wheels. "If I was given a mantra with the power to summon gods, I wouldn't have been able to stop myself from trying it out! I would have done it right away. I couldn't have waited."

Shvate ignored Mayla. His attention was focused entirely on Karni. "My love, this is the answer to all our prayers."

"What were we praying for?" Karni asked.

"Progeny!" Shvate said, then realized that Karni was teasing him. "Seriously, Karni, imagine the progeny of the gods! We would birth the greatest Krushan king ever born!"

"Or queen," Karni replied.

"Of course," Shvate admitted. "The sex of the child is less important than her or his capabilities. I always dreamed that you and I, and Mayla and I, would produce beautiful, strong children, each capable of ruling the Burnt Empire."

"I did too," Karni admitted, this time quite serious. She felt a tinge of sadness at the realization that such an event would never come to pass. How ironic. How sad.

"I would have used it that very night," Mayla said, pacing up and down now, excited by the fire that Karni's story had lit in her imagination. "Maybe more than once!"

"But since we are prohibited to procreate together by the curse, this mantra could still ensure the survival of the Krushan race." Shvate's eyes reflected the firelight, twinkling and dancing with more enthusiasm than Karni had seen in the past year. Even his colorless face displayed two spots of mottled heat on his cheekbones, something she hadn't seen since his drinking days. "Think of it, Karni! We could summon the greatest of gods, fathering the most powerful demigod children upon you and Mayla! Our children would rule Hastinaga with power and glory. Hastinaga would be unbeatable among all kingdoms, all nations, throughout the world. No one would dare challenge our authority. Even Jarsun himself would tremble when he heard that demigods sat upon the Burning Throne!"

"One moment," Karni said, frowning. "*Children,* plural? Demigods? Won't one heir be sufficient?"

"Of course, of course," Shvate said. "One demigod would be equivalent to a hundred strong sons. A thousand!"

They talked late into the night, with Karni increasingly wondering if she ought to have brought up the matter in the first place, but it was too late to unspeak what she had already spoken.

Vida

~

KUNE MOVED THROUGH THE Council chamber of Hastinaga like a leopard through a herd of bison.

Conversations ended when he approached, resumed when he went by. Smiles faded, frowns deepened, anxiety levels rose, pulses skipped beats. A minor secretarial aide who was known for his gossipmongering and who had been sharing several choice anecdotes about the Geldran prince, abruptly turned pale and skittered out through a side entrance as quickly as his sandaled feet would carry him. Several councilwomen of varying ages, some married, others currently single, watched him slide through the crowd with guarded interest. The brother-in-law of Prince Adri had gained quite a reputation for his cocksmanship in the bedchamber, and some of them were curious as to whether this was gossip or based on some semblance of truth; several men looked at him with as much interest, wondering the same thing, and whether his tastes in the bedroom also included other cocksmen.

Within moments of his entrance, the Council chamber was aflutter.

The brother-in-law to the crown prince was an important and mysterious figure, much talked about, rarely seen. His exploits in the Northwest had preceded him. He had a reputation for several things, none of them pleasant, yet his rakish good looks belied his notoriety. In person, he looked young, devilishly handsome, with finely sculpted features and a strong perfectly balanced physique. There was a look of god to him, resembling the statuary of the Northwestern cities. His looks alone set off a round of speculation about his likely ancestral influences.

Vida watched Kune work his way through the crowd, meeting new people for the first time, greeting those with whom he had corresponded before but was now meeting in the flesh, reestablishing old connections he had built through mutual acquaintances. He was masterful to watch, a perfect specimen of charm and wit, always saying just the right things to each person, making lasting impressions and clarifying his positions in a few well-chosen words, leaving no one in doubt about his ambitions or his intentions. He was here to stay, and Hastinaga was his permanent hunting ground from now on: hear him roar.

Shvate and Adri's half brother, Vida, happened to be close enough to hear one such conversation, about an upcoming vote regarding an administrative matter concerning land taxes and other dry stuff — details of economics and policy that most men of action would yawn and turn away from . . . the kind that Vida was sure Vrath only *pretended* to listen to even on his best days. Kune, however, listened with great interest, his handsome features and piercing eyes focused intently on the speaker, an elderly councilman who was rumored to own the most mineral-rich mountain ranges in the empire, filled with enough gold and other precious metals to keep his descendants immensely rich for several lifetimes. Though the speculations about the size of his fortune were fascinating to many, the man possessed a dreadfully boring personality, yet Kune heard him out to the very end of his tedious argument, added a few choice words of approval, then surprised both the councilman — as well as Vida, who was eavesdropping discreetly — by decisively refusing to support the councilman's tax proposal. With a flawlessly polite apology for his contrary position, smiling handsomely all the while, Kune then took his leave of the stunned councilman and moved on.

Soon after, Vida felt a presence by his side and glanced over to see Kune standing next to him, displaying a perfect set of gleaming white teeth and a smile that could not have looked more charming on a portrait of Kr'ush himself.

"Minister Vida, it is such an honor," Kune said, bowing low in greeting.

"Actually, it's just Councilman Vida," Vida corrected him. "Although I have no objection to being invited to join the chamber of ministers, if you're offering!" He tittered nervously, cursing himself for the slip. *Vidu, be on your guard, this is not a friend!*

Kune looked at him solemnly. So riveting was his focus, so flattering his attentiveness, that even Vida felt the magnetism of his charm. No wonder half the men and women in the Upper City wanted to take this man to bed!

Just having him look at you that way was enough to make anyone feel a little weak at the knees, man or woman.

"We shall just have to see to that, then, shan't we?" Kune said. "A man of your considerable talents deserves to be at the very top. Yes, of course, we'll make it happen."

Vida was taken aback by the sheer confidence, the brazen assurance with which Kune spoke of moving him up the hierarchical ladder. "Um, well, yes, of course, I'm flattered, but, I hope you know I was just making a joke!"

Kune smiled with his lips closed, his hair curling over his forehead adding a certain enigma to the expression. "Vida, Vida, my good man Vida . . . there are only three kinds of people in this world. Do you know what they are?"

"Krushan, mortals, and animals?" Vida said, then immediately began to giggle uncontrollably at his own joke. He stopped himself abruptly. *Get a hold of yourself, Vidu.* He could see how this man was already gaining such a reputation: Vida's tastes favored only women, but he could well imagine the kind of impact Kune must have on men who went with men or enjoyed the company of any gender.

Kune didn't acknowledge Vida's comment: not a flicker in his eyes nor a twitch of his face muscles. He continued to look at Vida till he stopped tittering and straightened his own face.

"Sorry," Vida said, self-conscious now. "I tend to make silly jokes when I'm nervous." *There. You just apologized to him and admitted you're nervous. Great, Vidu. You're impressing him by leaps and bounds. Get a hold of yourself!*

Kune raised a hand gently. He had large, smooth hands, Vida noted, beautifully shaped and manicured fingers. He was, in fact, the complete opposite of the cliché archetype of a Geldran. The ones Vida had met so far were all rough-edged, gruff, bearded men who rarely bathed, dressed like steppes horsemen in winter, and lacked even the most basic etiquette and social graces. Kune, in contrast, was a stone god with the manners of a Krushan aristocrat. A startling combination.

"May I?" Kune asked politely.

Vida blinked, unsure what he was being asked. "Um, of course, sure." He hoped he hadn't just given Kune permission to slap him. A direct blow from that large, strong hand would probably knock him halfway across the chamber.

Kune placed his raised hand on Vida's shoulder with surprising gentleness. He kept it there the way a brother or close friend would. It reminded Vida of the way Shvate and Mayla touched him on the shoulder while talking. Except that Shvate's grip was strong enough to hurt, and Mayla was more likely to slap or punch than actually touch — and she was almost as strong as Shvate. Kune touched his shoulder with great care, while making it seem flattering and intimate. Vida was aware that several pairs of eyes were watching both him and the Geldran now, no doubt burning with curiosity to know what they were discussing. He found himself greatly flattered by the intense attention he was receiving from this man, and realized that the hand on the shoulder was a shrewdly calculated move designed to suggest they were already far better acquainted than they actually were. To those watching, it would seem like they were old friends and allies. While the truth was they had only just met for the first time, and if anything, Vida would assume they were on opposite sides of any political divide, since his personal loyalty lay firmly with Shvate, whereas Kune's lay with Geldry. With a flash of insight, he realized that was the very reason Kune was doing this: he wanted everyone watching — which was basically everybody who mattered in the Council — to *assume* that they were friendly, perhaps even allies. To paint the picture he *wanted* them to see, rather than the real picture.

"There are three kinds of people in this world, Vida," Kune repeated, still acting as if Vida hadn't spoken at all. "Doers, talkers, and obstacles."

Vida raised his eyebrow. He couldn't help it. Another retort sprang to mind, but he bit it back. Despite the politically savvy part of him knowing exactly what Kune was doing, another part of him — the bookish, scholarly part of him — admired *how* he was doing it. The Geldran was demonstrating power, familiarity, and influence, all in a single visual tableau. He — the brother-in-law of Crown Prince Adri, soon to be king — posing with the chief advisor of Adri's only political rival, Prince Shvate, in an apparently friendly private conversation about, presumably, some important matter of administrative or imperial significance.

Kune used his other hand to point to himself, then flicked it to indicate the room in general, and finally pointed a finger at Vida and looked questioningly at him. He didn't say anything further. Just locked eyes with Vida and smiled slowly; the smile of the leopard preparing to feast. Then, as suddenly as he had appeared, he was gone, the impression of his fingers still lingering on Vida's shoulder, the impression that his powerful personality and presence and shrewd political tactic had made on Vida's mind stamped permanently.

That's one to watch out for, Vida told himself. He had a powerful urge to dust off his shoulder but resisted. Everyone was watching him now. Every single person in the chamber. Kune's shrewdly calculated tactic had been a complete success.

Kune

～

"SISTER."

Geldry looked up with a delighted expression. The eyeband on her face concealed her eyes, but the smile on her face was clearly visible. "Brother! When did you return?"

"Just this minute. I came straight to you."

Geldry rose to her feet with a considerable effort. She had to push down on the bed and keep her feet splayed wide, then take the support of two maids: only then was she able to gain her footing. Both maids continued to support her, holding her elbows while standing behind her, as if presenting her. Kune accepted the present, turning his cheek to air-kiss his sister on one, then the other cheek. He had to bend from the waist to do it because of the considerable impediment.

He looked down at her swollen belly. "What do you have in there? A whole flagon of wine?"

"I wish!" she said sourly, making a face. "Then I could simply drain it out. The damn thing just keeps growing and growing. I feel like I'm going to burst any day."

She struck her belly with her clenched fist, the frustration and anger visible in the force she used. The action threatened her balance, and the maids had to use all their strength to keep her from toppling sideways, crying out in horror at her actions. Their distress was contrasted with her utter lack of maternal consideration. Though she had been like this for weeks, they could not comprehend any mother-to-be behaving so brutally toward her unborn child. The word around the palace was that Geldry had gone insane.

Kune stepped in close and slipped his arm around her waist, grasping her tightly. He caught hold of her opposite arm and jerked his head at the maids. "Leave us."

The maids continued to stare at him — whether to make sure he meant it or because they were so enamored of his looks, it was hard to say. One maid blushed and smiled when his hand inadvertently touched her fingers.

Kune's grey eyes narrowed as he looked at the maid.

"Out."

The single word was like a slap. The maid lost her smile and left the room at once. The other maid retreated, bowing, and left as well.

Kune put both his arms around his sister and helped her sit on the bed again. She heaved a sigh of frustrated relief as she was seated without mishap.

"I feel like an elephant!" she said. "Look at how heavy I've become! I can barely stand, let alone walk. I haven't left this bedchamber in months."

Kune walked over to the bedside table and picked up a silver cup. There were juice and water beside it. He poured some juice and brought the cup over to Geldry.

"Here, sip some juice," he said.

Geldry's eyes flashed at him, and she struck the cup from his hand. Juice splattered everywhere, some of it landing on Kune's face, arm, and his spotless white anga garment. The silver cup clattered on the marble floor, rolling noisily all the way across the chamber till it struck the base of a statue of the great Krushan ancestor, Yayati.

"I guess you aren't thirsty, then," he said, with no hint of anger.

"Juice? Really, Kune?" She waved in the direction of the wine jug across the chamber. "Get me wine! I need *wine*, not juice."

"Sister, in your present state, you can barely stand even when sober. Wine isn't a good idea."

She picked up a small pillow and threw it at him. He caught it easily in one hand. "That's the whole point. I can't walk anyway. I can barely stand. All I do is sit and lie down all day and night. I may as well drink wine! I may as well get stinking drunk. What difference will it make?"

Kune raised his eyebrows at her volume and her tone. He shrugged. "When you put it that way . . ." He walked over to the jug of wine and poured a cup. He walked back and offered the cup to Geldry. She snatched it from his hand so roughly, a third of the wine spilled, splashing on the floor and on the bedclothes.

Geldry gulped down the wine in a single swallow. She held the cup out to Kune. "More!"

Kune looked at her without any expression.

Geldry shook the cup at him, shouting, "MORE WINE NOW!"

Kune didn't take the cup from her. He walked over to the jug and picked it up. It was a heavy jug, filled with at least two liters of wine, the jug itself weighing as much as its contents. He held it with one hand, easily. He brought the jug over to the bed and held it out in a pouring angle. Geldry raised the cup and Kune filled it with wine.

Geldry drank again, greedily, wine spilling from her lips and trickling in red rivulets down the sides of her jaw and neck, staining her garments.

She finished the cup and held it out again.

Kune filled it a third time without comment.

She drank it down less hurriedly this time, then wiped her mouth with the back of her hand, no longer looking as harried. "I needed that. I needed that so badly, I can't tell you. Adri forbade the maids from giving me any wine because I happened to have had a little too much and slipped and fell. *Once!* I fell once! He acted like it was a national calamity. The only reason that jug is even here in the chamber is because I told him that I must have some on hand for the times when you visit. He's such a hypocrite. He himself quaffs wine by the skin, and he's blind! But he suddenly decides that I can't have any. Who gave him the right?"

"He is going to be emperor of Hastinaga soon," Kune said.

Geldry raised her head at a sharp angle, frowning above the eyeband. "Are you being sarcastic?"

"I'm simply stating a fact. He's crown prince now. He's going to be emperor. The auspicious date has been set already by the pundits."

Geldry's mouth twisted in a mutation of a smile. "I don't give a damn what he does. He can go directly to Nrruk, for all I care. He doesn't have to sit in this wretched bedchamber all day and suffer like I do. He's off gallivanting with his whore." Suddenly, her hand arched back, and she threw the cup forcefully enough to strike a porcelain vase filled with rare white orchids.

Kune bent his head to move it out of the trajectory of the cup. The vase shattered, spilling perfumed water and expensive flowers. Kune glanced at it as he straightened himself. "I guess you won't be needing more wine, then," he said. He started to walk back to the table to replace the jug.

"I hate that man!" Geldry said, snarling the words. She hawked and spat a wine-colored gob of phlegm on the polished marble floor.

"He is your husband," Kune said as he set the jug of wine down. "And the soon-to-be ruler of the world's most powerful empire."

Geldry spat again.

"I see that things are not rosy hued between you and Adri." Kune walked over to a carved wooden chair, picked up one end, the muscles on his back working, and set it down near the bed. He sat down on the chair, making himself comfortable.

"What do you expect?" she asked harshly. "He's off whoring with his mistress, never here with me. And I'm stuck carrying this ... this thing." She struck herself on the belly again.

"When is it due?" he asked. "I thought when I was here last you said it ought to come in the winter, but winter's come and gone, and it's early spring now. Isn't it late?"

"Late?" she repeated, then grunted. "It's much more than late. I think it's dead!"

"That's a little harsh. Why would you say that?"

"Because it doesn't move, it doesn't kick, nobody can seem to hear a heartbeat; I've asked five different maids and wet nurses to listen, and they say all kinds of comforting things, but none of them are able to find its heartbeat. It hasn't moved once since I became pregnant. Not once in over a year! How is that possible? And it feels solid, like a lump, not like a child, a living thing."

"And yet you said it grows. It does grow, doesn't it? It looks much larger than when I was here some months ago."

"Yes, it grows and grows. I don't know how much bigger it can possibly grow. I can't carry it anymore. I can't do this anymore. Kune, do something. Help me get rid of it."

"Get rid of it?"

Kune rose to his feet, looking alarmed, and sat by his sister on the bed. He took her hands in his hands. "Don't speak like that, Geldry. There are maids always about. That kind of talk will spread faster than you can control it. People will look at you as a traitor to the Krushan race. It is treason to want to abort an heir to the empire!"

She leaned her head against his shoulder. "Kune, I don't know what to tell you. My body hurts. My head hurts. I can't sleep. I can't eat. I can't walk. My husband has left my company to spend his days and nights with a whore of a maid. My belly is weighed down with a lifeless lump that keeps growing. I can't take it anymore. Please, do something."

"What would you have me do?"

"Anything! First, give me more wine."

He patted her hands. "Let's hold off on the wine for a while. Geldry, you're pregnant and overdue, it's a trying time. But think of it. Soon, you'll deliver the child, the heir to the Burnt Empire. Adri will be crowned emperor, and you will be empress by his side. You will rule alongside him, over the greatest empire in the known world. Think about that. What power! What wealth! The world will lie at your feet!"

"And my husband will lie down with a maid, and the whole world will know it!" she said. She was crying now. "Think of my shame and my sorrow."

Kune nodded slowly. "That must stop. It's true, kings and monarchs have always enjoyed the freedom of conjugal rights with whomever they pleased. Even the great and honorable King Ratha of Aranya had three legitimate wives, and three hundred and fifty concubines. He was in the palace of the concubines when he summoned Amara to inform him about his exile."

"Shut up about your old legends and fairy tales," Geldry said, wiping her nose and cheeks on his chest, staining his anga garment further. "Go fetch me more wine and tell me you'll do this much for me."

"Do what for you?" he asked. But he got up and went over to fetch the wine jug and another cup.

"Kill that maid," she said, showing him her teeth. "Kill her and make sure that Adri never looks at another woman ever again."

He stopped short, holding the wine jug and the cup.

He smiled, the smile transforming his face, lighting it up.

Geldry raised her hand and removed the eyeband from her face. "Why the hell should I wear this anymore? I'm the fool to play the good wife while he's off doing as he pleases." She threw it aside.

Blinking, she looked up at Kune's face, squinting and frowning to adjust to the light. "You look like you just thought of something clever. As handsome as ever, brother. Come here. Give me that."

He came over, handing her the cup and pouring out more wine for her. She sipped it more leisurely this time, still frowning up at him. "So? What do you say? Will you do what I said?"

He grinned at her. "Sister, my sister. Have I ever refused you anything before?"

She sipped wine and smiled back at him.

Adri

~

ADRI LAY HIS HEAD down and pressed his ear on the swollen belly. He listened intently for a moment, then smiled. "I hear it," he said with delight, "I hear the heartbeat. It is so loud, so strong, so quick!"

His smile faded, and he raised his head, peering blindly. "Is it supposed to be so quick? It sounds much too fast for a heartbeat!"

Sauvali smiled down at him, caressing his head gently, ruffling his hair. "Silly, baby's heartbeats are always faster than grown people's heartbeats."

"Oh," he said, "I didn't know that."

"There's a lot you don't know, Adri of Hastinaga."

"That is why I depend on you to teach me, Sauvali of Saugadha," he said.

The breeze from the Jeel was gentle and fragrant with the perfume of spring blossoms. They were lying in the shaded pavilion. Their attendants stood at a respectful distance, far enough to give them privacy, close enough to hear should they call. The majority of the servants, maids, cooks, and guards were eating their meals now that Adri and Sauvali had finished eating. The guard contingent was considerable now and seemed to increase each time they left Hastinaga. Adri knew it was because of the impending crowning ceremony, but it still felt like they were under siege. Still, it was a small price to pay to get away from Hastinaga and all its cares, and especially from Geldry.

But you won't think about her now, Adri, you promised yourself. Thinking about Geldry only makes you angry. Don't spoil this beautiful spring afternoon with your lover.

He kissed Sauvali's belly and sat up. "Your time is soon, is it not?"

"Any day now, my lord."

"Don't call me that."

"Even wives call husbands 'lord.'"

"They shouldn't. We are married to each other, we are the most intimate friends anyone can possibly be to one another. Why should we be so formal and call each other 'lord' and 'lady'?"

"It's a sign of respect."

"I don't like it. It makes me feel as if you're acting like a maid and treating me as your master."

"My dearest one, I *am* your maid, and you *are* my master."

"Not anymore. You are my wife now. We exchanged garlands at the temple, in front of the deity and the priest. It is recognized as a forest wedding."

"Even so, my love. You have a wife already, and she was wedded to you in front of the whole city, not just a small deity in a tiny temple, and a single priest. For your other wedding, all the royal family were present, and the aristocrats and all the gurus and preceptors and pundits and purohits. There were thousands of priests alone. It was the finest procession I have ever seen in my life. I should know. I was there, walking behind your chariot, tossing flower petals from a basket into the crowd."

He was silent for a moment. He didn't like to be reminded of the differences in status between them. Even though he knew she was not trying to press the point, he still felt the sting. "We will have a royal wedding too, you and I. It will be grander and more elegant than my first. All the family and priests and nobles will be there. The whole city will celebrate. I will declare a national holiday."

She sighed and stroked her belly gently, in a familiar circling motion. He could hear it as clearly as if she were stroking his own belly. "You don't need to promise me things like that, Adri. You know I don't care about ceremonies and displays. You love me, and that is all that matters."

"What's so wrong with that?" he asked. "Shvate took a second wife. Why can't I?"

"It's not the same, and you know it. Mayla was princess of Dirda, a powerful kingdom."

"And you are Sauvali of Saugadha."

"Exactly, Saugadha . . . a tiny hamlet in the back of nowhere. Besides, my family isn't among the foremost of families there. It's only one of three hundred in the village, and one of the poorest. We have no land, no possessions, barely any food to eat. That's why my sisters and I came to the city to seek work, to feed and clothe ourselves. You can't compare me to Princess Mayla, people will laugh!"

Adri was silent again, trying to imagine such poverty. He couldn't. "I will declare you the queen of your own kingdom. There are always kingdoms that fail to produce heirs or commit some transgression against the empire, and we declare eminent domain over them. I will crown you queen of a kingdom, then you shall be the equal of Mayla or any other princess. No one will dare laugh at you."

She sighed. "Adri, my lovely Adri. You are a wonderful, sweet, great man. You will be a great emperor. But you dream of things that are not meant to be. No matter what title you give me, no matter what throne you seat me on, people will never forget that I was once a maid in this household. That I used to serve and wait on you and clean up after you. They will never accept me as anything but a former maid. The problem is not in Saugadha or any other place where you crown me queen. It's in Hastinaga. The people will never see me as anything but a maid."

He was silent then, because he knew she spoke the truth. Yet he could not accept it. He loved her, and she loved him. They were husband and wife. Why should it matter who they had been before? Yet, deep down, he knew that it did. Just as it mattered to people even now that he was blind, that he could not see as they could, that a sightless person would be on the throne of the empire and would rule them all.

He had heard the voices in the crowds that said rude things about him, about his blindness. Vrath had said to ignore them, that they had a right to their opinion, but that did not mean their opinion was right. Adri tried to ignore them, but still it hurt. Just as it hurt him now to think that even he, Adri, soon to be crowned Emperor Adri of the Burnt Empire, could not marry the woman he desired and have her accepted as his wife, his queen, his empress.

Sauvali was right: no matter what title he conferred upon her, people would still see her as a maid, a low-caste, a servant, a backwoods villager. They would find a dozen ways to discriminate against her, find her inferior, lacking, wanting, undesirable. That was the thing with sighted people: they saw too much. They saw things that weren't even there. He perceived Sauvali as a beautiful, gentle, kind, passionate, strong, and resilient woman. He saw the goodness within her, not the labels or social attachments. But they saw caste and race, skin color and ethnicity, height and weight — things that didn't matter — while failing to see the things that did.

"We will teach our son to be free of these prejudices," he said, "to regard all people as the same, neither inferior nor superior."

He felt her catch her breath and then felt her hands on her face. "You are such a good man, Adri; you will be a wonderful ruler of Hastinaga. I am so proud of you."

He was about to respond with a lighter comment, something self-deprecating and nonchalant, when he felt a vibration through the ground.

He sat up suddenly.

"Adri?" he heard her say, concern in her voice. "What is it?"

"Something is coming," he said.

Prishata

~

GENERAL PRISHATA HAD LEARNED from long decades of experience to read the size of an approaching force just by listening to the vibrations in the ground. The instant he sensed the tremors, he tossed the leaf of food he was eating into the drum provided for trash disposal and moved away from the rest of his men. He was seeking a clear spot of earth, and when he found it nearby, he dropped to the ground and pressed his ear to the grassy mound. He listened, shutting his eyes and letting his mind translate the vibrations and pattern into specific details. There was a difference between the vibrations produced by a two-horse chariot, a four-horse or six-horse wagon, a horse with an armored rider, and so on.

After several minutes, he rose to his feet, his aging face grim. "Everybody to your positions. Full alert! Alert!"

Shouts broke out. Men and women began running to and fro, leaping onto horseback, climbing onto chariots, snatching up lances, spears, javelins. A company of archers took up their weapons and rigs and sprinted for their assigned positions.

Riverdell had been a favorite picnic spot of the Krushan family for generations, and over the decades, numerous generals and captains of the imperial guard had mapped out all the terrain surrounding the riverside. An occasional attempt at banditry and a brief ill-intended attempt at abduction had further informed their understanding of the best tactical positions, and a plan had been devised and perfected to allow for the possibility for a major strike against the family.

It was logical to expect such an attack, and for this very reason, Prishata had been personally entrusted with crown prince Adri's security and given free rein to commandeer whatever resources he desired. A military commander of the old school, he believed there was always strength in numbers. Today, for instance, he had two thousand men and women on duty, and access to a reserve contingent of forty thousand within two hours' ride. The full alert protocol required riders to be sent immediately to summon the reserve, and their horses were already kicking up dust as the general mounted his horse. The archers, elephants, chariots, and cavalry were taking up their allotted positions exactly as assigned, thanks to his systematic regime of drilling and tactical maneuvers.

The security contingent assigned to Adri was no small one. These were dangerous times. Even though the war against Reygistan was no longer ongoing, there were always retaliatory strikes and skirmishes. Ever since the night of the eclipse, Jilana had demanded that no member of the imperial family go anywhere without a full escort, and if they traveled out of the kingdom, then a reserve must always be within easy riding distance to provide backup. The enemies of Hastinaga were manifold and powerful. Jarsun was still at large; his attention may have been diverted, but he still a major threat and not an enemy to be taken lightly.

Prishata rode his horse along the edge of the grove of trees that covered the east bank of the Jeel, checking that all was as he had rehearsed. Elephants who had been dozing in the shade after bathing in the river for most of the afternoon were trundling reluctantly past him, raising their trunks in protest at one another. Their mahouts whispered into their ears and fed them sugarcane treats to motivate them; they would take up positions a hundred yards out, forming a curving wall that would block any chariot or mounted ingress.

Beyond them, the chariots were already rolling out, cavalry leading them. Both were much more effective at offense than defense, and Prishata had assigned them their positions accordingly. His entire tactical plan was based on depriving the enemy of their main advantage: surprise. Anyone seeking to attack the imperial family at this idyllic spot would be expecting everyone to be relaxed, sleepy, well-fed, and well-wined, clustered in the comfortable shade by the river. They would be in for a rude surprise when they found chariots and armored horses charging *at them!*

Another company of riders, archers, and lancers remained in positions around the grove itself. They would form the inner line of defense. And finally, if the attackers got past the outlying archers, the defensive line of chariots, the cavalry, the wall of seventy war elephants, as well as the archers and lancers, they would still have to contend with himself and his hand-selected company of one hundred elite soldiers. Even if they did get that far, the reserve would be there by that time, forty thousand fresh warriors who would crush them to pulp.

Prishata paused his horse alongside a thick banyan tree, slipped off his left glove, and pressed his palm against the bole of the tree. He could again feel the vibrations. About two miles out and approaching fast. They were coming in strong, then, probably hoping to use the elements of speed and surprise to shock the Krushan defenses.

His most trusted subordinate, Captain Karnaki, sidled up on her mount alongside him. "General, all our forces are in position."

Prishata nodded, pleased. That was smartly executed, considering that only minutes earlier they had all been filling their stomachs with wine and good food. "Report on the crown prince."

"Prince Adri is safe and sound. The inner circle is established, and he is aware of the threat. He is sequestered within the pavilion as per your instructions, along with his . . . erm . . . his wife."

Prishata nodded, pleased to hear that as well. The tent pavilion would make it impossible for the attackers to lay eyes on Adri, which would make it that much harder for them to be sure he was actually there. As there were several tent pavilions set up along the riverbank, all identical, it would be impossible from the outside to know which one contained the crown prince. To make it even more confusing, Prishata had arranged men outside each of the tents, suggesting that they all contained imperial family members, even though there was only one currently in his protection today.

Correction: two. Even though his captain had just fumbled her title, the fact was that Sauvali was as much their responsibility as Adri. Prishata grimaced. He didn't approve of the crown prince's relationship with the maid, nor the fact that he seemed to have all but broken ties with his legitimate wife, Princess Geldry. Especially at a time when Geldry was bearing the future heir to the empire and Adri himself ought to be keeping his behavior impeccable prior to the crowning ceremony. But this Sauvali girl was here, and she was with him, and she mattered to the future emperor, so that was all Prishata needed to know. That made her his responsibility and by the gods' lightning bolts, he would ensure that she was as well protected as was possible.

"Companion," Prishata said shortly, in response to Karnaki's verbal stumble.

Captain Karnaki blinked at him. "Sir?"

"The correct term for Madam Sauvali is 'companion.' Or 'imperial companion' if you wish to be formal."

Captain Karnaki blinked again, absorbing this information. "Sir."

"What numbers do the outlier scouts report?"

"General, sir, they have conflicting reports."

Prishata frowned. That was never a good sign. "Explain."

"The northern scout reported an attacking force of some five hundred riders, all well-armed, riding fast. The western scout reported seven hundred riders, two hundred chariots, and two hundred longnecks."

Prishata frowned. "Longnecks?"

"Sir, the western scout wasn't sure of the correct term for those long-necked beasts they use in the desert areas. The ones with the big humps in the middle of their backs. They move with a funny rocking and rolling kind of motion."

Prishata sighed wearily. "Camels. They're called camels."

"Sir, permission to continue calling them longnecks. It's what all the soldiers call them. Except for the few desert warriors, and we don't have any of those in our company today."

"Yes, yes, go on." Prishata gestured at him to continue.

"Sir, the southern scout has the strangest report of all. He says he spotted *two thousand riders*. No elephants, longnecks, chariots — just riders, all riding light, no armor, and moving very fast."

Prishata didn't like the sound of that. "A vajra."

Karnaki nodded. "What I thought too, sir."

A vajra was a lightning force, named after the lightning bolts of the king of the gods. It was a force of riders stripped down to the basics, riding horses bred for speed on short rides, not endurance or weight. They were of little use in a pitched battle against a large army of armored cavalry and elephants, but in a sudden strike like this, against a relatively small force in a single location, they could be devastatingly effective. More than just the tactical deployment, it was the number that worried the general.

"Two thousand, you say?"

Karnaki nodded. "I slapped him on the back of the head, telling him he was lying," Karnaki said, then hesitated, as if realizing her words would sound amiss. "He's a third cousin on my father's side, sir, and I thought perhaps he was trying to impress me by exaggerating. But I believe he's telling the truth."

That was distressing news. Prishata tried not to let his dismay show. "Two thousand vajra horsemen from the south, eleven hundred from the west including two hundred chariots and two hundred camels — longnecks — and five hundred heavily armored and armed from the north. Are all the reports corroborated?"

"Sir, I'm waiting on corroboration as we speak. They should be reaching us at any moment."

Prishata nodded. "And the couriers are well on their way to the reserve regiments?"

"They should be almost halfway there already. Allowing another hour or so to reach, then about two hours more for the backup to reach us. However strong these attackers may be, sir, forty thousand Krushan are an army! They can't possibly withstand those numbers. If you ask me, sir, the instant they get word of our backup arriving, they'll light out of here like arrows from a nervous bow, and that's if they survive even that long."

Prishata did not comment on that assessment. Karnaki was right to be confident in their numbers. But three hours was a long time when arrows were flying, and the deployment of those attackers worried him. It was not a simple abduction; these weren't opportunistic bandits hoping to kidnap and ransom a royal prince. This sounded like a military operation, well planned and well executed. There was also something about the specific deployment of those different cadres that reminded him of something he had seen before. But he had been in dozens of battles and overseen dozens more, and right now, he could not recall exactly where or when he had seen this particular deployment used. It probably didn't matter; all that mattered now was that they had to hold out long enough for the backup to arrive. And the only way to do that, as he had always taught his students, was by taking the offensive.

"Very good, Captain," Prishata said. "And —"

He was interrupted by the arrival of a rider, coming in fast, bent over his horse, arrows in his back and leg and an arrow in the horse's flank as well. The rider was a young woman, and from the blood on her garments and dripping from her wounds, she looked as if she had almost bled out, but she was still somehow mounted and alive. He admired the woman's courage.

Captain Karnaki dismounted and went to her at once, helping her down from the horse. Before she touched the ground, another horse came charging in from another direction. This one collapsed as it reached the clearing, raising a small cloud of dust. The horse screamed, kicking out in its death throes, the rider falling with the animal; Prishata leaped off his own mount and ran to the man's aide. He was riddled with arrows, one sticking out of his chest that appeared as if it had struck within an inch of his heart. He was bleeding profusely and sputtering blood from the mouth and barely coherent. His horse was thrashing around in agony and Prishata shouted to the soldiers who had drawn near to end its suffering. One of them drew her knife and bent over the poor horse as Prishata bent over the dying scout to try to hear his last utterance.

A third horse came in while he was trying to catch the gurgled half-coherent message. This one was itself unharmed but riderless. A large splotch of blood on its saddle marked the end of its rider, his third scout.

Prishata had stationed over a dozen scouts in pairs at intervals several miles out, ensuring that no attackers could come at them from any direction without being seen. The instant a pair of scouts spotted an approaching force, one of them was to ride back to Riverdell with the first estimate. The second scout waited for the attackers to get close enough to corroborate the initial estimate, then followed. The second scouts had clearly been hard-pressed to race ahead of the attackers, judging from the state in which they had arrived.

The scout died with a final exhalation of breath through the blood bubbling up in his mouth. Prishata shut the soldier's eyes gently and rose to his feet.

Karnaki was approaching, looking harried.

"Captain?"

"Sir, it is very bad!"

Prishata was expecting that.

"The northern scout says it's not two thousand, it's *three thousand* riders. The vajra." Karnaki swallowed. "The western scout says something similar.

Fifteen hundred — not nine hundred — horses, five hundred chariots, three hundred longnecks."

Prishata gestured at the riderless horse, which was now munching on grass, unconcerned by all the two-legged beings in a flurry around him. "I don't think we're going to get any corroboration from the southern scout, but let's assume the same, considerably higher enemy numbers than we initially expected."

Karnaki nodded, looking troubled. "Sir, there's more bad news. The western scout saw the courier riders en route to the backup regiment. She says that a section of enemy horse broke away from the main force and went after the couriers."

Prishata took the news in grimly. "So to sum up, our couriers will probably not get through to the backup, which means we have to contend with an attacking force at least twice our numbers, perhaps thrice."

"That's right, sir." Karnaki glanced around the clearing, swallowed hard. "General, what are our orders?"

Prishata didn't need to think about it for more than an instant. *When the enemy is strong, be stronger,* he always told his trainee officers. It was time to put his own advice into action, and not for the first time. He had been in tougher quandaries before, some much worse than this.

But never with the emperor of Hastinaga's life at stake.

"Captain," he said, "our Krushan law is to protect our emperor. That means Prince Adri. We follow our plan, execute the strategy as rehearsed, and whatever happens today, *no matter what happens,* we protect Adri with everything we have. Send the word out: *Stand to the last.*"

Captain Karnaki saluted him smartly. "Sir, yes sir!"

Karnaki turned and mounted his horse. Prishata heard her call out to the other soldiers within hearing as he rode away: *"Stand to the last! Stand to the last!"*

They took the order and passed it on down the lines in all directions: *"Stand to the last! Stand to the last!"*

Prishata heard it echoing into the distance, then fading out even as the rumbling of the approaching attack force grew and grew until it filled the clearing from all sides.

Vessa

~

VESSA WAS DEEP IN meditation when he received word. The jungle itself whispered to him in his transcendental trance.

"*Adri...*" she said.

At the mention of his biological son's name, Vessa pulled himself partially from the trance, moving a part of his consciousness sideways. The bulk of his attention remained on his primary quest, which was to search all possible worlds and dimensions for a clue to Jarsun's whereabouts. The search was an ongoing one and had already been on for well over a year. No matter what Vessa did in his day-to-day existence, that part of his mind continued searching and would continue to do so endlessly until it found its quarry. A master of deep meditation, he was able to compartmentalize parts of his conscious and unconscious mind to focus on different tasks, different functions in parallel. He would not let that part of his mind rest until he found Jarsun, but there were other key phrases he was monitoring that set off alerts if required. Two of those were "Adri" and "Shvate." He was aware of Shvate's near escape from death by suicide, but had not gone to the young man's aid because he had anticipated the situation and known that Karni and Mayla would handle the problem. Karni in particular was competent enough to handle far greater challenges, and in time, he knew, she would rise to the task of managing those as well.

Adri was another matter. His karma was foggy of late. His fate could go in a number of different directions, not all of his own choosing. So he was a topic of concern. That was why, when the jungle alerted Vessa, he turned his attention to Adri at once.

He sent his consciousness out, moving through the cellulose of the leaves, the trees, the water, the moss and the undergrowths, rippling through the body of the Great Mother Forest that was home to all life on Arthaloka, all the way to the banks of the Jeel outside Hastinaga, to the idyllic spot called Riverdell. There, he switched to the viewpoint of a flock of cranes flying overhead to get a better assessment of the situation.

Looking down through a bird's eyes, he saw the grove of shady trees by the Jeel, a patch of green alongside the great river. Within the shade of the thickest trees, he spied the colorful pavilions flying the krtha-dvaj of the House of Krushan: those would be the tents where Adri and his party were enjoying their picnic. He leaped out of the bird's consciousness and into an ant crawling on the inner wall of the largest tent and, inside, saw Adri and Sauvali. She was seated, watching him, while he paced in a circle, clearly agitated. They were safe for now; that was the main thing.

He leaped out of the ant's mind and up to the cranes again. He saw that the pavilion was heavily guarded by strong-willed, well-armed men and women. He saw also the configurations that General Prishata had set up for the defense of the crown prince. It looked adequate for now. He saw Prishata himself riding fast, shouting orders as he went, his captain Karnaki passing on orders to her subordinates in turn, the chain of command carrying down the instructions with quick, practiced efficiency. These were Krushan's best, and that meant they were the world's best. Vessa felt reassured. Whatever the threat, there was no immediate danger to Adri's life.

Then he saw the dust clouds.

He urged the bird to fly higher, flapping his wings to rise and catch a wind current that lifted it high enough. This gave him a much wider overview of the region, reducing the riverside grove to a hand-sized patch.

There were attackers coming in from all sides.

He didn't bother with estimates of numbers or the different cadres. Such things had never concerned him much. He was able to see even at a glance that the attacking forces outnumbered the defenders by a considerable margin. Twice or thrice as many. And the aggressive speed with which they were attacking suggested a well-planned assault. There was a battle ferocity to the charge of those riders and chariots: these villains meant business. That told him they were no mere brigands or bandits looking for a quick profit. They were enemies of Krushan, and any enemy of the House of Krushan was an enemy to Vessa.

He bid thanks and goodbye to the cranes and leaped a few hundred yards down, falling into the mind of a crow flying over the attacking forces. The crow protested by cawing harshly, its cry lost in the thundering of the hooves and wheels of the attackers below. Vessa flapped his wings harder to match their frenetic pace, swooping overhead. He could see just enough to know that they were all hardened soldiers of varying ages, sexes, and ethnicities, with a jumbled assortment of weapons, armor, horses, and chariots of different construction and design. It was an odd mélange for any kingdom and most Houses of the Burnt Empire would not stand for such an admixture. That itself told him that these were not warriors of any specific loyalty; they were mercenaries for hire, sellswords available to anyone who paid well and wanted dirty work done without concern for cost or consequences. Such bands of mercenaries were cobbled together from every manner of lowlife, criminal, bandit, thug, disavowed soldiers from various kingdoms, even foreigners who were exiled from or fed up with their own nations and offered their services for hire. The worst of the worst or the best of the worst, depending on how you viewed it. This was troubling: whoever had cobbled together this force had money to waste and intimate knowledge of the House of Krushan. Even catching and torturing such mercenaries would yield no fruits: very likely they had been hired by a series of intermediaries who themselves did not know the identity of the client.

It also told him that this was not Jarsun's doing: the Reygistani took too much pride in claiming credit to resort to such anonymity.

This was no mere enemy; it was an enemy from within. Someone within the House of Krushan itself, or close enough to it to know many significant private details, such as when Adri would be at Riverdell, what defenses would be present, the lay of the land, the deployment of the defense troops and cadres, and enough military knowledge to know the most effective way to break those defenses and get to the target: Adri himself.

The crow cawed again, wings tiring from the strain of keeping up such a pace. Vessa spied a sparrow flitting about thirty or forty yards closer to the ground and leaped down to her mind. The little bird was startled, then awed, then delighted. She chirped merrily and fluttered her little wings rapidly, happy to do whatever he pleased. He brought her down, close enough to the charging mercenaries to see the sweat on their beards, the stains on their bared teeth, moments before they clashed with the defenders.

Karnaki

~

KARNAKI WAS AT THE flanks of the southern defense when she saw the attackers clash with her soldiers.

In a charge, the attacking cavalry always had the advantage of speed and impact: the sheer force of their charge often broke the spine of any defensive formation, driving them through the lines and into the heart of their target. In a pitched battle, that might not matter as much, since the whole field was filled with battling soldiers of both sides, but in a situation like this, it made a huge difference. The attackers were seeking to get past the defenses and into the grove of Riverdell, where they could achieve their main intent of killing the crown prince. That made the task of the defenders doubly hard: they had to not only stop the attackers from getting past them, they had to drive them back, as hard and as quickly as possible.

General Prishata's solution was brilliant yet controversial. He had trained his defenders to *attack* the attackers. This was why the scouts and the positions mattered so much. Armed with that forewarning, the southern company of defenders had been instructed to begin their charge when their enemy was within a certain distance. They had begun racing at the approaching enemy, matching their approach with their own full-frontal assault.

Now, as Karnaki watched from the sidelines, staying well away from the main body of the defensive forces, she saw the attackers clash with the defenders. For some odd reason, a small bird was flitting over the heads of the attackers, wheeling about and tweeting as if alarmed by the madness of the humans below.

She forgot the sparrow in the next instant as the two forces clashed.

Both attackers and defenders, riding flat out toward each other, met in a deafening clash of armor and weapons, horses and leather, shields and swords, flesh and bones, and all the rest of the vulnerable, breakable things that armies are made up of.

The sound was as awful as anyone might expect. It made Karnaki's hair curl and her spine crawl. She saw weapons and body parts flying through the air — saw soldiers and horses ramming full tilt into one another, smashing skulls, shattering bones, breaking bodies apart like ripe fruit. Animals screamed, people howled, and the air where they met was saturated with blood and dust and pain.

It took several more minutes of what looked like utter chaos and insanity before anything made sense again. It was only Karnaki's practiced, battle-experienced eyes that could tell, even in those minutes, that the charge was going favorably for one particular side, and favorably only for them.

The attackers were prevailing.

The charge had smashed the brave southern defenders into pulp. Several hundred remained alive, but there were many more attackers still living, and they were already hacking and chopping and skewering the defenders with wild purpose. The defenders fought back bravely, sacrificing their limbs and their lives to defend their crown prince, but the weight of sheer numbers was telling. They could hold out for a while longer, keeping the occasional attacker from getting past them, but it was only a matter of time before they broke and were rubbed into the dust, into oblivion.

Karnaki rode westward, moving into a full gallop to get to the second point of intrusion. Due to the natural declivity and curvature of the landscape, these were the three most approachable points near Riverdell for any large-scale attack to be made. General Prishata's deployment was perfect, in Karnaki's opinion, and his tactics brilliant — but even the most acute knowledge of one's theater of battle and the most astute use of one's resources could not overcome the most basic advantage of war: numbers.

Vessa

~

VESSA HAD SEEN ENOUGH of the clash on the southern side to know that the enemy were going to be victorious. He leaped out of the poor sparrow's little brain and to the mind of a bat hanging upside down from a tree on the western side of Riverdell, about a mile away from the grove itself. The tree was tall and set upon a hillside, which gave it shade enough to attract the bats. From here, he had a good vantage point to view the second clash of the day.

The poor sparrow's close view of the gore and carnage of the first encounter had given him his fill of close-up bloodshed. Now, he only wished to gauge the progress of the overall assault without seeing the individual suffering of the soldiers. Whoever they may be, villains or Krushan, defenders or attackers, they were all men and women, living breathing beings, and the damage that war inflicted on the human body and mind was not something to be viewed with glamor or glory. It was a sickening, brutal act of human insanity, the culmination of all the worst, most violent, cruel tendencies of human beings and if he had possessed power enough, he would have banished it forever from existence. *Banish all violence too*, he thought grimly, as he hung upside down from the shaded branch, bracing himself for the next clash.

This was somehow more brutal and yet different from the first: there were camels and elephants in the frontlines here, deployed because of the hilly terrain, and the ungainly longnecked beasts as well as the affectionate lumbering giants were not natural enemies, or even meant to live together. That was what made it seem so perverse, so unnecessarily cruel to see them both used and abused by their human riders, for the sole purpose of gaining a tactical advantage over their opponents.

He watched as a camel screamed and tried to break away from the elephant it was charging against, trapped by its rider's merciless grip on the reins as well as the tight formation that hemmed it into the larger attacking force. The poor beast, colliding head-on with the oncoming elephant, smashed its brains out and broke its neck and most of the bones in its body, even as the elephant itself suffered grievous wounds to the trunk, eyes, head, and forelegs. Both animals collapsed together in a jumble of mangled limbs, their blood mingling, faces lying beside one another. Vessa saw with a breaking heart how the camel's tongue reached out of its shattered jaw to lick at a deep cut on the dying elephant's head and heard the mournful last cry of the elephant as it breathed its last. The camel died a moment later, both beasts victims of a cruel human sport called war, in a game called battle, where all players lost.

The fighting continued, the screams of elephants and camels vying with the yells and shouts of men and women, the shrieking of horses, the rumbling of chariots, the sound of arrows plunging into flesh, bone, metal, leather.

Vessa watched grimly for a few more moments. This clash was more chaotic and difficult to predict than the first: while the camels provided height for the enemy bowmen to attack the defending elephant mahouts as well as other defenders, it was the enemy chariots that were doing the most damage. The attackers were shrewdly using the chariots as battering rams to shatter the cavalry charge of the defenders, deliberately taking their own cavalry around the defenders' flanks to push past and into Riverdell. He saw General Prishata's second in command on his horse, shouting orders, and saw a fresh company of defending cavalry riding to thwart the intrusion of the attackers who had slipped past so cleverly. Horseback fighting broke out, sword striking sword and different languages and dialects shouting curses while the Krushan defenders silently performed their duty. Again, the weight of numbers was stacked against the defenders and it was only a question of how long it would take the attackers to break through.

The situation on the northern front was just as troubling. Brave Krushan defenders died by the scores as the enemy rammed and battered at their defenses, sacrificing animals and humans without mercy in a desperate bid to shatter the defensive lines.

Already, Vessa could see, General Prishata was being forced to thin his own inner circle of defense by sending more soldiers out to bolster the crumbling lines on all three sides. Fortunately, there was one side he did not have to worry about: the Jeel provided a natural barrier to attack, making it impossible for any enemy force to invade from that direction. The river was wide and fast here, and even an armada of boats or barges would not cross easily; even still, Vessa was relieved to see that none were visible. That was one thing less to worry about.

The sight of the Jeel reminded him of something else. Something that had been gnawing at the back of his mind since he had arrived here at Riverdell — arrived in spirit, if not in body.

He took flight, forgetting for an instant that he was in the body of a night-dweller. The sunlight blinded his senses, and the heat of the late afternoon sun seared his sensitive black hide, as he heard the poor bat shriek its silent call of protest.

Apologies, little one, he said, returning the bat to its roost on the tree branch. It trembled with alarm, and he took an instant to calm it down, breathing a soothing *Auma* into its mind. There was always time for kindness. *Auma,* it repeated silently, calming. In an instant, it had retreated back into its deep dreamless sleep. He leaped out of its tiny brain and threw himself into the nearest available form at hand: a dolphin leaping through the waves of the river.

Jeel, he called out as his snout broke the water's skin and caught the light of the sun. *Why do you not alert your son Vrath? His half brother Adri is in desperate need of him. Go, summon him at once, or must I do it myself?*

He did not have to wait long for an answer.

As he splashed back into the river, the water beneath the surface rippled, forming into the shape and features of the goddess herself. As beautiful as ever, yet stern and coldly commanding, Jeel looked up at him.

Son of Jilana, do you presume to command me now? Beware of your insolent tongue.

He sighed and dipped his dolphin snout, squeaking in submission. *Apologies, Great Mother. I meant no disrespect. But Adri is part of your bloodline as well. I was merely expressing my surprise that you had not sought to inform his half brother of the threat he faces.*

She seemed to relent, her features softening. A turtle swam through her left cheek, while an eel darted underneath her chin. Below her face, a large school of silvery fish shimmered, their scales catching the sunlight streaming through the water, and through Jeel's features.

I did not see any reason to trouble him, she said. **He has concerns of his own. My son has done much for Hastinaga already. He cannot be there to help like a mere sentry or guard every time a Krushan is in trouble. Besides, he is dealing with his own problems. The troubles in my sister river's kingdom are far greater than these little mishaps.**

Mishaps? Vessa knew better than to react to her choice of words. He let that slight go. But he could not simply let the matter go entirely. *I understand that there are other crises to deal with, but Adri is my blood, the son of my body, and I cannot simply let him be killed by these villains.*

Then defend him yourself, Jeel said, looking weary and old. **I have business elsewhere now.** He thought the conversation was over and was about to leap out of the dolphin's body, but then she paused, and he saw a frown ripple her watery face. **Besides, he is in no danger physically.**

The dolphin kicked his tail in surprise. *What do you mean?* Vessa started to ask —

But the water was just water again, rippling and flowing by, filled with the abundant fauna of the upper Jeel. The goddess had left his presence.

Prishata

⁓

KARNAKI CAME RIDING UP to Prishata, her horse's mouth lathered with the foam of effort. "Sir, they are breaking through!"

"On which side?" Prishata asked.

"All sides!" Karnaki said, then shouted, "Sir!"

Prishata saw the arrow whistling toward him and inclined his head a few inches to the right, just enough to let the missile zip past his left ear. He did not believe in ducking and hiding. A general led by example, and it made a poor example if he was constantly dodging arrows and spears. He could see the bowman at the far end of the grove, one of several riders who were making their way through the trees. Captain Karnaki had already dispatched several of the inner circle to hold them off, and fighting broke out a minute later, swords and arrows flashing through the grove as both groups engaged.

So it had come down to this, Prishata thought; they were going to have to stand and fight with their backs to the Jeel. He wondered now if he ought to have made arrangements for a boat in which to send the crown prince downriver. He had considered it, but just as he had the policy of not bending or ducking to avoid arrows, so also the House of Krushan had the policy of never retreating. Even Queen Mother Jilana, normally the most anxious about the safety of her family members, had staunchly refused to even discuss it. "The day a Krushan has to flee a fight is the day he abdicates his claim."

Prishata touched the hilt of his own sword. It had stood in him good stead for a dozen battles, including the memorable one at Reygar, where they had fought the supernatural evil of Jarsun. He would have to draw it soon, but not yet. For a general to draw his sword meant that he would not be able to sheath it again unless he won a victory or it was cut from his dying hands.

These rules, these principles, these policies, he thought, with no bitterness, *they are the marks of our honor and privilege, but they are also the signs of our downfall. We humans will kill and wage war for such symbols as a flag or an ideal, but when it comes to saving lives, we can never seem to put our shoulders together with half as much enthusiasm. What is it about killing that fascinates us so?*

There was no more time to think. He shouted to Karnaki, "Last line! Call last line!"

Karnaki nodded and passed the order on.

In moments, a line of horses encircled the imperial pavilions. Behind the horse riders stood a line of soldiers on foot. Both horse and foot soldiers had their swords drawn and were ready to fight.

Prishata took his place in the horse line. The soldiers to either side — one male, one female — both glanced at him in surprise. It was not a general's place to stand in the front line. His place was at the rear, behind his soldiers.

"Last line is last line," he told the curious warriors to either side. "We stand as one."

The others heard and exchanged glances. He saw the pride in their quick smiles and felt gratified. *At least you lived a good life and led your soldiers well enough that they feel proud to have you stand alongside them in the last fight. That is as close as a warrior comes to earning true glory.*

The fighting in the grove was more intense now, the attackers continuing to pour in from all sides in a never-ending stream. Even elephants and camels were visible, their riders pushing the reluctant animals through the close-growing trees. His defenders were dwindling, barely a hundred or so left, apart from the twoscore who stood now with him.

It would soon be all over. The hope of backup was long forgotten. In a few more moments, the attackers would swarm them on all sides and they would be fighting for their lives, destined only to die fighting here.

There were worse places to die. Riverdell was beautiful, and dying here meant one's blood mingled with the Jeel's sacred waters. Prishata had been wounded and near death in some awful spots, in distant, foreign lands. If he was to die here, then he would meet his death with pride and honor.

But before that, he would take a few enemies with him.

"*We are Krushan!*" he called now, raising his sword high. "*We fight!*"

A roar of voices echoed him. *"We are Krushan! We fight!"*

The fighting grew fiercer and closer. Defenders were falling like sheaves of corn hacked by a traveling scythe. There were just too many attackers.

The clearing was filling up rapidly, archers and horsemen and even camels and elephants all pushing in. He saw an elephant brutally prodded, bleeding profusely from a gaping wound behind his ear as the vicious rider forced it to rear up and crush a mounted Krushan. The elephant trumpeted in distress and turned to try and dislodge its cruel mahout, losing its balance and toppling over the horse carcass. It landed on two other Krushan fighting bravely on foot after their horses were killed. The elephant thrashed about madly, upsetting the other elephants and horses and camels, and pandemonium resulted, causing a minor stampede and several more deaths and injuries from kicking animals and accidental deaths.

Prishata had been in battles where this kind of thing happened, dozens or even hundreds dying from some unfortunate turn of weather or geography. He had seen a whole regiment lost to a snow avalanche once, and of course there was the historic Battle of Dasarajna, where King Sudas had cleverly dammed then released the river Parusni to flood the valley and eliminate the army of the Ten Kings; every general since then had studied that battle in depth. This struggle in Riverdell was by no means the most memorable or the most brutal he had seen, but as he always told his junior officers during training, "Every death is the first because it is the first time that person is dying, and every battle is your first, because it is the first time you are experiencing *that* battle."

There was a brief lull in the battle as the confusion caused by the panicked animals dissipated, then the attackers renewed their efforts. Prishata estimated that there were at least a thousand or more of them already in the grove, pushing their way in against perhaps a hundred of his defenders, all told. No, make that three- or fourscore at best. A lot of his defenders were wounded and in agony, but still fighting to the very end.

He saw a half dozen attackers driving spears into the body of a defending soldier still holding her sword. She cut the ankle of one of her attackers as she died, and the man squealed like a rabbit and fell, clutching his foot. An elephant trod on him, crushing his right shoulder and chest, and his squeals ended there and then. The attackers were not even caring who they killed; Prishata saw some of them cutting down their own fighters by accident, something that happened often during sword fights in close quarters when animals were involved. They didn't care or stop to check; mercenaries had no loyalty to one another or any cause; they were each here because they had been paid to kill or die.

He bit his lip in frustration. In a pitched battle he would have made short work of such an enemy force. But in such close quarters, with such unequal numbers, he knew his defenders stood no chance. Already the attackers were only a few yards away. Prishata saw Karnaki fighting against three attackers at the same time, then taking an arrow from a fourth attacker mounted on a camel, and another arrow. Then a third. Then the three attackers circled her, cutting and hewing at will.

Prishata saw bright arterial blood spurt from his lieutenant and sighed and added Karnaki to the long, long list of brave officers lost who had served under him, and the many more lost under whom he had served himself as a young man. Prishata had had a long illustrious career. If he was to die here, defending his crown prince, so be it.

And then it was time.

The attackers were at them and Prishata raised his sword to deflect an arrow, shouting once again, "*Krushan! Fight!*"

"*Krushan! Fight!*" came the response, sounding like it was shouted by several hundred rather than the thirty odd defenders remaining.

Prishata threw himself into the fray, his old muscles remembering timeworn moves as he swung and chopped and stabbed, his horse turning smartly, responding to the years of conscientious grooming and loving care he had lavished on her.

He had taken down four enemy attackers before the completely unexpected happened and the earth exploded in the middle of the grove.

Vessa

~

VESSA POURED HIS SPIRIT into the earth itself, raising it up under the feet of the attackers in the grove. It was like yanking a rug out from under the feet of a dozen men, except the rug was broken into a hundred sods. He raised up the sods of earth, unsettling a hundred attackers and their animals. As sympathetic as he was to the plight of the wretched creatures, his goal was to slay the attackers. Like it or not, he had to achieve that by any means.

For the attackers, it was as if the earth itself had risen up under their feet. Sods and clods of soil sprang up with the force of an elephant, upending horse and camel and soldiers, even throwing an elephant off balance and toppling it onto more attackers. The ground heaved and then slammed down on the men it had thrown down, striking their faces with the impact of a horse kick — shattering teeth and noses and jaws — destroying eyes, and filling nostrils and mouths. Attackers died choking on mud and their own blood and teeth.

Vessa did it again, and yet again.

There was a certain satisfaction to killing such villains, the lowest kind of mercenaries, who had spent their lives raping, killing, mutilating, waylaying travelers, cutting the throats of children while they slept, stealing from defenseless people . . . doing whatever horrific crime enabled them to support their bad habits and existence. Even as he crushed their bodies and spilled their blood, he felt a wicked glee that he was ending their sordid lives. Now that he was doing it, he wished he had intervened sooner. He would have saved many more of those brave Krushan.

But as the minutes passed and he continued killing attackers by the score, he began to remember why it was that he was always careful not to engage in the business of human warfare.

He was starting to enjoy it too much.

To relish this blood lust, this feverish state where crushing and breaking and smashing and killing was all that mattered, when existence was reduced to the simple act of violence. When ending life, even evil, perverse life, brought such satisfaction that one wanted to continue doing it over and over again. This was how killers became killers, how mercenaries became mercenaries in the first place, how soldiers degenerated into heartless assassins.

He fought the urge.

He forced himself to try to disengage.

He focused his mind on the sacred syllables *Auma* to calm it.

Soon, the madness abated.

The fever receded.

The blood lust fell away.

And then, he was just Vessa himself.

He took the mind of a caterpillar crawling on a branch and gazed down at the grove below.

The destruction was considerable.

Hundreds of attackers lay dead everywhere, most of their bodies buried beneath layers and mounds of earth and stones and ripped tree roots. Many dozens of animals were dead too, and that saddened him. He comforted himself with the thought that at least they were out of their misery now.

The last line of defenders stood in front of the pavilions, staring at the devastation. He saw from their awestruck faces that they could not comprehend how this had been accomplished or by whom. That was as it was meant to be. He did not wish to show himself openly to people at such times. Had he desired, he could have transported his physical self here in a blink of an eyelid, as he did when visiting his mother in Hastinaga, but he had chosen to act as an anonymous agent. This way, the enemies of Krushan would remain unaware of who had destroyed them and would fear everything and everyone, even the dirt on which they stood.

He turned the caterpillar's body to try and get a better view of the pavilion.

All looked well. The tent was still intact, and he could sense Adri inside, still alive and safe.

Then he saw the boat.

Prishata

~

PRISHATA KNEW HE HAD just witnessed a miracle of sorts.

He had no idea what god or supernatural power had intervened in the battle to help them. But clearly, something or someone had caused the earth to rise up and strike down those attackers. Several hundred of them lay around the clearing, most buried under tons of dirt, others with their mouths and eyes stuffed, lifeless.

There were probably still attackers outside the grove, he knew, perhaps a few hundred, perhaps more. But he could see none of them attempting to enter the grove itself. The fact that their way was blocked by high mounds of loose dirt and the corpses of their fellow mercenaries and animals was only part of the reason why they were probably hesitant to make the attempt.

He guessed that they were more afraid of the supernatural forces than they had been of the Krushan defenders. These were men and women who had committed terrible atrocities in their lifetimes. They had thought nothing of committing a few more today, for the right amount of gold. But to take on forces that were more than human exceeded their mandate. Like all ignorant, violent persons, they were intensely superstitious. Ironic as it might seem, in his experience, the most violent people were always the most fanatical. Be it religious extremism or simply a fanatical devotion to a creed. Mercenaries were more pragmatic, but even they had their fears and cultural superstitions deeply embedded in their psyches. The attackers were spooked out of their skulls by *the way* their comrades had been killed. They were probably riding away from the grove now as quickly as they had arrived.

"General, the attackers are retreating!" said an exuberant young captain. "Shall we give pursuit?"

Prishata smiled at the young man. "We are the last line, Captain. We do not leave our ward. Remember?"

The soldier realized his mistake. "Apologies, sire. I am a little . . . confused."

"No matter," Prishata said. He dismounted slowly from his horse, stroking her neck affectionately. He was happy she had survived the battle. He would have been happier if Karnaki and more of his defenders had survived as well, but that was the price of war. "I shall go now to check on the prince to make sure —"

A wail rose from the tent behind him, startling him and the two dozen last line defenders. Those who had sheathed their swords drew them again at once, while some wheeled around, expecting to see a new wave of attackers approaching from the grove.

But the danger was not from the grove.

Prishata looked in the direction of the pavilion, which was the direction of the river too, and his heart ran cold.

There was a boat floating across the river, carrying several mercenaries, who laughed and pointed and waved mockingly upon catching sight of Prishata.

He roared and began to run down the bank, skipping and leaping down the gentle slope. "Krushan! To your prince!"

Prishata reached the pavilion and burst in, his sword raised and ready, expecting to see two dead bodies within, one male, one female.

Instead, he saw the blank, unseeing eyes of his crown prince.

"Prince!" he cried, lowering his sword and coming forward. "Are you well?"

Adri held out his hands to Prishata, wailing like an animal in pain.

More soldiers rushed into the tent, one of them the young captain who had spoken to Prishata moments ago.

"General, shall we loose arrows at them? They are still within bowshot!"

"No!" Adri cried. "No arrows! You will hit her."

Prishata stared at his prince, at the tears streaming from those unseeing eyes. He looked around the tent and saw that it was deserted apart from Adri. Then he understood.

He left the tent and looked down at the river.

The boat was several hundred yards downstream already, just a thumb-sized brown shape on the water. But he could make out the faces of the mercenaries, still grinning and waving. And the shapeless form of their passenger. A figure with its head covered by a burlap sack. He saw how it had been done, the boat sent downriver at just the right time, when all the defenders were busy fending off the overwhelming number of attackers in the grove, too preoccupied to even notice the river. The tactic of attacking from all three sides on land, creating the illusion that the direction behind the defenders — the river — was a safe zone.

Prishata realized they had been most brilliantly played and outmatched.

"They never intended to kill Crown Prince Adri at all," he said now, as much to himself as to the captain standing beside him. "This was their plan all along."

To kidnap the prince's beloved companion, the maid. Who also happened to be the mother of his unborn bastard child.

Karni

~

KARNI FELT FEAR.

It was pure, naked fear, not the kind of fear she felt late at night when she heard predators in the jungle, or the times when she saw a pair of eyes glowing in the darkness and knew there were beasts all around that would tear her to pieces and eat her alive. Not even the kind of fear she had felt when she had seen Shvate step off that high ledge.

This was the deepest fear she had. It was the fear of death itself. Of the dark, deadly power against which there was no defense, no recourse, no shield or mantra of protection. A power so great, all beings bowed before it —and succumbed.

She stood in the clearing in the jungle. At her request, Shvate and Mayla had retreated to a safe distance, partly to give her the privacy she desired, and partly because she was afraid for their sakes too. They were within earshot, but not within sight. She had insisted on that, against all Mayla's requests and pleas. Shvate had been acquiescent to her wishes; he had been pleased enough that she had agreed to his request that he offer no argument against any of her conditions. It had taken him days to wear her down. He had used every philosophical argument imaginable, including some she had found so ludicrous that she had laughed out loud, to his distress and, once, to his offense. The words "Krushan law" had featured frequently in these arguments, as was common when men were trying to convince women to do something that women did not want to do. In the end, she had agreed not because he had convinced her philosophically but because she had accepted the basis of the whole argument itself.

She wanted to bear children legitimately.

Children she could call her own. Who could call her mother. Whom she could hug and kiss, pick up and swing around, feed and nurse, and put to bed, teach to walk, to run, to play, to share a million little things with, to teach a million things, to guide through the journey of life.

Children who would bear her name and be proud of it.

And if one or more of those children someday sat on the throne of Hastinaga, well, that was not such a bad thing either, was it?

She had been born a princess, was married to a future king, and had expected to birth an heir someday. Fate — and Shvate and Mayla's mishap in the jungle — had intervened and turned her life in a different direction. But now she had an opportunity to redress that situation, to correct her course again and resume the path she had been meant to take. The circumstances were not of her choosing, the method not of her choice, but the goal would be the same at least. She would bear an heir and further the line of succession. She would save an empire, prolong a dynasty. And there was a certain personal pride in that achievement.

Shvate thought he was convincing her to do it for his sake. Men always made that mistake. They saw a woman as their mother, their sister, their daughter, their wife. They often forgot that a woman was also a person. That she existed in her own right. That she had thoughts, feelings, desires, hopes, ambitions, dreams, that had nothing to do with the men in her life. That were *her* thoughts, feelings, desires, hopes, ambitions, dreams.

Karni wanted to birth an heir to the Krushan dynasty. To see her own son or daughter sit on the Burning Throne. To see her flesh and blood rule the greatest empire in the world. She wanted that for herself. Shvate had had his chance, and he had made his mistake. She forgave him the mistake, but it was not her duty (or her Krushan law) to *correct* his mistake. As if anyone could do such a thing. What you did in life, you did alone. That was the essence of karma. Good deeds were nontransferable. She could no more wash away Shvate's sins than he could wash away hers. They each had made their mistakes, and now they had to live with them.

But if he wanted to believe that it was his days of arguing and philosophical eloquence that had convinced her, well, let him think it. She knew the truth. It was in her heart. She wanted to be mother to a prince, a king, an emperor.

That was why, when she told him yes, finally, and after all the shouting and yelling and hugging and kissing and celebrating was over, and they had discussed which god she ought to summon up to father a child upon her, she had said crisply and decisively, "Shima."

Shvate had frowned. "I'm not sure about that, but we can talk about it."

"We can talk all you want, but if you want me to do it, it will be Shima, and that's final."

He had stared at her, surprised at her vehemence. "There are better choices. Sharra, for instance —"

She had looked away. "Not Sharra, definitely not Sharra."

"But he's one of the most powerful. He's indomitable. A son birthed of Sharra would be invincible in battle, he would be able to face any enemy, any army, and easily —"

"Not Sharra," she said sharply, turning to stare at him until he saw her resolve.

He threw up his hands. "I don't understand why!"

"You don't have to understand. You just have to accept it."

He had risen to his feet then, the color showing in his cheeks, his male ego wounded. "If that's how you're going to go about this."

"Shima is the greatest of all gods. He is powerful, more powerful than any other god, because they all have to adhere to his laws. And also, because he is Death."

"Death," Shvate said doubtfully, still upset.

"Everyone succumbs to Death. Even the gods fear him, because if he wished, he could destroy them as well."

"Theoretically, I suppose," Shvate said, "but in reality —"

"You just spent the last several days arguing with me about shima, the Krushan philosophy of duty, and how it's the most important thing in the world. The underpinning of our entire existence. Are you really going to disagree with me on it now?"

Shvate looked at her, defeated. "Shima?" he said, cautiously.

"Shima," she said, conclusively.

And so it had been settled.

But now that it was time, she felt the cold knife of fear twisting in her chest.

Everything reminded her of the last time, the *first* time. She felt an irrational panic because of how that had gone. Even though she tried to convince herself that this time was different, this time it was her *husband* who *wanted* her to do it, she still felt a twinge of her youthful guilt. She brushed it aside with an effort. Once she had made up her mind, she intended to go through with it. That was it.

She shut her eyes and recited the mantra.

The wind roared.

The jungle quietened.

The sky darkened.

A sound like a great peal of thunder boomed in her consciousness, yet her ears heard nothing, not a sound but the absence of all sound.

She opened her eyes and stared up at two dark piercing eyes.

He stood before her, black as night itself, as tall as a giant, as broad and powerfully built as a wrestler.

His hair was long and hung in curls around his shoulders, his eyes looked as if they were lined by kohl, but she sensed that it was natural. His pupils were diamond-bright, pulsing with a rhythm similar to a heartbeat, but also with a strange hypnotic swirling light. She looked at them for a moment and was sucked into them. With an effort, she forced herself to look away, to look down, lowering her head in respect.

"Shima."

You desire a son.

"Yes." She hesitated, then added, "A son with all the qualities of an emperor. Righteous, fearless, powerful, indomitable, a master of weapons and warcraft, a leader of armies and people, a master of strategy, a wise soul, a perfect, ideal man." She was out of breath by the time she finished. She had memorized the litany to make sure that she would not forget or miss a single detail. She had read far too many stories of people who asked gods for boons but were careless about the phrasing and ended up with a trumpet instead of a horn of plenty.

His thick lips curled in a smile, displaying ivory teeth inside his ebony skin. **You know what you want. That is good.**

She kept her head lowered, seeing him in the periphery of her vision, unwilling to chance being hypnotized again by the spiraling diamond light in his eyes.

He took a step toward her. **You are sure this is what you want.**

She nodded. "It is."

Very well, then, Karni of Hastinaga. It shall be as you will.

He came toward her, his body blazing with black light, and she was engulfed by his darkness.

Part Six

Adri

~

GELDRY SCREAMED.

Adri heard her but did not stir. He had grown tired of Geldry's tantrums and outbursts, her rages and furies. Let Kune deal with them. Her brother now lived permanently in the palace, always by his sister's side, in her bedchamber . . . He had a seat at every Council already, and word was that he was a devilishly brilliant politician.

Vida kept trying to warn Adri about him, but Adri was weary of Vida's warnings. If Kune wanted to involve himself in the swamp of Krushan politics, let him, by all means. Adri had no interest in politics — or in anything else. He had lost all interest in life itself since the attack at Riverdell. It would have been better if the attackers had killed him. By taking Sauvali, the only woman he had ever truly loved, they had wrenched his heart itself from his chest. He was bereft and broken. He could summon up no enthusiasm for anything anymore.

Those months with Sauvali had been wonderful, the most blissful time in his life. He had finally found true happiness in a world so full of pain and disappointment, and then it had been snatched away from him. Now all he could do was eat, drink — both as little as possible, only the bare minimum necessary for survival — and breathe. He did not attend Senate, or Council, even though Mother Jilana and Vrath both urged him repeatedly to do so, reminding him that he would soon be crowned samrat — emperor — and the more he involved himself with state affairs, the better it would be for his future. He did not care about his future, he did not care about the state, he cared about nothing. All he could think of was Sauvali and the time they had spent together.

At times, lying in bed, he felt as if he could reach out and touch her. But of course, she was gone. Emperor of the World, and yet the empire of his heart was desolate.

He heard someone enter his chambers, speaking roughly to his guard, who apologized and moved aside at once, announcing the visitor. "My lord, Prince Kune."

Adri forced himself to assume an upright position. "Brother-in-law."

"Adri, Geldry has done something. She needs help at once. Please come."

Adri sighed. "I can't deal with her outbursts, Kune."

"This is something else. She . . ." Adri heard the note of panic in Kune's voice and frowned. That sounded genuine. He had never heard Kune so scared. "She struck herself."

Adri shook his head, not comprehending. "Struck herself?"

"Her belly. She struck her own belly, and . . . something came out."

"I don't understand, Kune. She struck her own belly? You mean the child?"

"Yes, yes. She struck at her belly to make herself birth the child. She was angry at hearing the news about Karni."

Adri was confused. "News about Karni?"

Kune sounded exasperated and impatient. "We just received word from a visiting hermit that Karni and Shvate have had a son, the first heir to the Krushan throne."

Suddenly Adri was alert and awake, for the first time in almost a year. He felt his face muscles move to form what sighted people called a smile. "That's wonderful news! Happy day, Kune. My brother and sister-in-law have produced a son and heir. My nephew!"

"Yes, well, you can celebrate later. Right now, your wife needs you. She dislodged the child, and I am very concerned."

"Dislodged?" Adri started to rise. "You mean she has given birth already? Two heirs in the same day? How fortuitous!"

"Not exactly." Kune sounded harried. "I need you to send for Mother Jilana. I would do it, but she seems to . . . not like me very much. Besides, Geldry is your wife, this is your child too. Please send for her at once."

"But she has given birth to our child, is that right?"

"No," Kune said hollowly. "She has dropped something from her womb. But it is no child. That much is certain. I don't know what it is, but it isn't a child, and it isn't human."

Jilana

～

JILANA FELT HER SON'S presence before he appeared. As wild-haired and wild-eyed as ever. Staff in hand.

"I warned you of this day," Vessa said.

"What day?" she asked. "What are you talking about, my son?"

Vessa indicated the doorway with his chin. "In a moment, you will receive word from Adri. Geldry heard the news of Karni's child and was so angry with herself, she struck her own womb a furious blow."

Jilana was taken aback. "I just heard of Karni's news myself. It is a wonderful thing, to be sure. But Geldry? You mean, she has given birth?"

"It is no ordinary birthing. The thing she has evicted from her womb is a lump of flesh. It possesses life, but not life as you and I would expect."

Jilana stared at him, shocked. "The . . . You called the child 'it'—are you saying it isn't human?" A part of her had known that Geldry's preganancy was not normal—two years of gestation was hardly the norm, after all—but she had still clung to the hope that this was only a sign that the Krushan heir was somehow extraordinary, even touched with divinity. Vessa's manner and words now told her otherwise. *Not again, Goddess! For once give this family an heir without complications.*

Vessa pursed his lips. "It is quasi-human."

"What does that mean?"

"It defies my knowledge and my powers, because I was certain that this thing was the get of Jarsun himself, but it now appears that it may indeed be the seed of Adri after all." Vessa shook his wildwood staff in frustration. "For some reason beyond my ken, even my powers cannot penetrate its composition. All I can say for certain is that the thing she produced can engender sons of great power."

"Sons? Plural? I thought you said it is only a lump of flesh!"

Vessa looked at her. "A lump of flesh equivalent to a hundred sons."

Jilana's eyes widened. "A hundred . . . sons? Of Adri? Krushan heirs?"

Vessa gritted his teeth. "Let me tell you a story. I shall make it brief. Once, when I was traveling through Geldran, I stopped to nourish myself at a local chief's house. The chief's daughter waited on me with great diligence. Pleased with her service, I offered her a boon. She asked that when she bore children, she should bear a hundred sons. I granted the boon, as I have granted countless such requests. I left the chieftain's house the next morning and thought no more of the girl. Until now."

"Geldry was that girl? Years before her marriage and her arrival in Hastinaga?"

Vessa inclined his head. "And this thing she has produced is the culmination of my boon."

Jilana felt her heart fill with joy. "So Karni and Shvate have birthed a son in the forest, and now Adri and Geldry shall be parents of a hundred sons!"

"Karni has already birthed two more offspring, and Mayla two as well. Shvate is now father to five great Krushan heirs. They are strong, powerful beings, each a god in in their own right."

Jilana clapped her hands with delight. "Happy day! There shall be feasting. Celebrations. National holidays. Good times have returned to Hastinaga once more. I wish Sha'ant could be here with me today to share this joy. I am so filled with delight, I cannot express it in words."

Vessa stepped forward, grasping his mother's arm. "Mother, heed me well, I still see dark days ahead for this family, this empire. These hundred sons of Adri and Geldry —"

"Are sons of Krushan. They shall be raised as heirs to our dynasty. Vessa, my son, I command you to go at once do whatever is needed to ensure the survival and good health of those sons of Geldry. I will hear no more dark prophecies and declarations. This is a day of celebration and rejoicing. Do not cloud it with your talk of omens and portents. This family has seen few happy times. This is one of those rare occasions. Go now, tend to Geldry and her babes. Do whatever must be done. They must live. They must flourish. I place this responsibility upon you."

Vessa withdrew his hand slowly. "I shall do as you say, Mother. For your sake, and also because it was my boon that granted Geldry these hundred offspring. They shall indeed live, and flourish and be strong powerful beings, each a great warrior and leader in his own right. But I warn you now for the last time, if these sons of Geldry live, then Hastinaga shall yet see dark times. Celebrate today, but prepare also for the dismal days ahead. For as surely as my name is Vessa and I am gifted with the power to see past, present, and future events as clearly as you see me standing here today, I predict that these hundred sons shall be the downfall of the Krushan race. These are the sons of misrule."

And with these chilling words, Vessa vanished from Jilana's chamber.

Vessa

〜

1

A DARK PALL HUNG over Hastinaga. Word on the street was that something terrible had happened to Princess Geldry. Ill omens were being sighted around the palace precinct. Carrion birds, wild animals, strange sights and sounds, misshapen clouds, unseasonal hail out of a clear sky . . .

A wet nurse who came from the palace told a bizarre story about the princess striking her own belly in a misguided attempt to end her abnormally long gestation, and of the freakish thing that was then ejected from her womb.

"It was . . . not human," she said, before leaving the city for good, taking her belongings and her family with her. Her face was still aghast with the memory of the horror she had seen. She did not wish to remain in a city where such supernatural things occurred in the ruling family's house. She was never seen or heard from again.

People heard strange cries and shouts of terror from inside the palace. Strange lights were seen to glow and shine in windows usually darkened at night. They glanced up fearfully as they hurried past. Even the palace staff and sentries were on edge, nervously awaiting the ends of their shifts, praying that they would survive these last few hours.

Inside the palace, on the highest level of the main building where the great hall was located, there was unusual activity. Those who saw all the guards and maids in that wing were puzzled: sabha sessions were never held at night except in times of war, and no ministers or other Senate staff had been seen arriving.

Yet all the great hall doors were shut and heavily guarded, the sentries refusing to answer any questions and warning anyone who approached to move on. From inside the great hall, and from its many windows, unexpected sounds were heard by those passing by. Some sounded like the cries of wild animals, but nobody could identify which animal. Other sounds were unrecognizable, but sent chills down the spines of any who heard, encouraging them to stay away. Strange lights and flares as if from explosions were seen at the windows, bright glowing lights of different colors all through the night, some visible from miles away.

Outside the enormous doors of the great hall, the sentries exchanged nervous glances and gripped their spears tighter. Their anxiety was caused not by the fear of anyone attempting to break in but by the thought that whatever was inside might try to break *out*.

2

Inside the vast Senate chamber, the great seer-mage Vessa stood on the throne dais. The dais was empty, as was the dreaded Burning Throne and the rest of Senate Hall. Instead of the usual gathering of ministers, aristocrats, nobles, members of the High Houses, and general public, there were dozens of rows of large earthen pots, set a yard or so apart. What lay inside these pots was obscured by the thick greenish mist seeping out, spilling over the rims of the pots. The floor of the Senate was covered with a thick layer of this greenish mist. The mist continued to thicken and rise, covering the entire floor and climbing the walls and pillars of the hall, rising to the ceiling, and finally collecting there in dense clouds.

Within the pots, strange lights flickered and glowed. From time to time, little bolts of lightning flashed inside them, resembling lightning in monsoon clouds, but instead of flashing white, these jags of energy were greenish and reddish in hue. The lightning shot upward, bursting out of the pots and striking the ceiling. These produced the blinding flashes of light and thundering explosions that unnerved people outside the palace and the sentries outside the door.

Vessa stood on the throne dais and held up his wildwood staff, chanting mantras that even the most learned priests would have been unable to identify. They were the Forbidden Mantras, known only to the most powerful seer-mages of the Burnt Empire, handed down directly from guru to acolyte, and only given by the greatest to the greatest.

One had only to watch the seer for a few moments to see that he was causing whatever it was that was happening in the great hall. He had commandeered it earlier that night as it was the only chamber large enough to suit his purposes, the only location secure enough. He had instructed the palace staff to bring 101 pots of a certain size and thickness and place them in a certain pattern in the hall, then leave. When all was in readiness, he had entered the hall carrying a single large object roughly the size and shape of a large watermelon wrapped in a black cloth. The doors had swung behind him before the sentries could touch them, slamming shut with a resounding boom. Since then, no one had seen him or entered the great hall, as were his instructions.

Once inside the hall, Vessa had unwrapped the black cloth to reveal a grotesque lump of flesh that resembled nothing in the human or animal world. Its uneven surface was mottled, reddish in hue, and lined with veins that throbbed and pulsed. There was no doubt that it was a living thing, but what it was, even Vessa could not have said. There was no name for such a thing in any lexicon.

He had uttered a mantra and released his grip on the lump of flesh: at once it rose from his hands, hanging suspended in the center of the chamber. As he continued to chant the Forbidden Mantras, thunder boomed and lightning flashed from the ceiling and mist began to ooze from the levitating lump, bleeding from its surface and seeping down to the floor. Vessa reached a peak in his chanting and raised his staff to touch the monstrosity. Lightning crackled and a flare of light exploded at the point of contact. The resulting boom was deafening, booming like a stormcloud over Hastinaga itself: it was heard all across the city, people looking up from their beds to wonder what new calamity had befallen the City of Elephants and Snakes.

Mist boiled and hissed in the great hall.

The lump of flesh could be seen to have separated into 101 smaller lumps. Each of these lumps floated over one of the 101 earthen pots in the chamber. Slowly, as Vessa continued chanting and lowered his raised staff, the lumps of flesh descended into the empty vessels. They settled at the base of each pot, and at once began to hiss and boil, seething and moving.

They now resembled sacs of flesh within which something moved, kicked, fought, clawed, and struggled to escape its cage of flesh. Each of the lumps screamed, shrieked, cried out, and made its struggle audible to everyone within hearing.

The more each lump fought and screamed, the greater the mist and steam exuded from the pots. The clouds of mist continued to pour out of the pots, filling the chamber, producing dense clouds that then darkened and flashed with lightning. Thunder and rain followed, a treacly greenish-black downpour that did not resemble natural earthly rain in the slightest. Some of the rain fell on the floor of the great hall, flooding it rapidly, but most of it fell into the large pots, filling them to the brim.

Lightning flashed, shooting in all directions, and the storm increased in intensity as Vessa hastened the rhythm of his chanting. He had to raise his voice too, to make himself heard over the sounds of the downpour, the thunder, the explosions, and the screams and shrieks from the vessels. He was shouting now, his powerful voice booming, the acoustics of the great hall carrying it perfectly to all corners. The Senate mascots had been evicted earlier by the palace staff who brought in the pots, and until now they had stayed outside, mewling and whining to be let into their daily abode. Now, hearing the unnatural sounds and smelling the strange noxious fumes issuing from under the cracks in the great doors, they bolted, barking and screeching in terror. They never returned again, forsaking their home for other safer residences still unpolluted by the presence of such evil doings.

The interior of the great hall now resembled a storm-riddled field at night. The pillars were shrouded in mist, the ceiling, walls, and floor obscured by mist and clouds. Steam hissed and shot out of the pots, interspersed with gouts of fire, bubbling lava that boiled out and spilled over the edges of several of the pots. Others produced disgusting swampy green exudations like the vilest vomit. All manner of foulness bubbled out from the pots, spilling over onto the floor of the hall, turning it into a dense swamp. The stench was unbearable, the air unbreathable, the sounds and light impossible to view without being blinded and disoriented.

Vessa stood unaffected by it all, chanting his mantras for hours on end without a pause. He had mastered the art of perfect breath control, able to breathe in, chant, and breathe out, all without pausing for rest even once in hours, days, weeks, months, years . . . even decades and centuries, some believed.

Tonight, it was not his stamina that was being tested. It was his mastery of stonefire . . . but the Forbidden Mantras enabled him to do what needed to be done.

All night he continued to incubate the offspring of Geldry in this manner. All night the city tossed and turned in restless unease, wondering what strange sorcery was being worked in the House of the Krushan. All night the pots seethed and bubbled over like cauldrons of vile broth.

Finally, as day was breaking, the sentries heard an unexpected sound from inside the great hall.

Silence.

3

As the sentries waited in tense anticipation, the giant doors of the great hall swung open slowly of their own accord. No hand had touched them, no one stood anywhere in sight, yet the thirty-foot-high doors swung all the way open and remained that way. Vile-smelling green mist seeped out, causing the sentries to stir uncomfortably. They glanced at each other, then turned to look into the chamber with much trepidation. At first they could see nothing except the swirling mist that seemed to choke the entire room from floor to ceiling. The ceiling was still seething with clouds that boiled angrily and spat out occasional flickers of lightning. Disgusting green slime spilled out and oozed across the floor, bubbling and popping with heat.

The sentries stepped back before the slime could touch their feet, and as they glanced down for a moment, the towering, gaunt figure of Seer-Mage Vessa appeared before them, even though an instant ago he had not been visible walking toward them.

"Summon my mother, Dowager Empress Jilana," he said.

The sentries scurried away to do as he bade.

Jilana

⁓

BEFORE LONG, JILANA ARRIVED with Vrath in tow.

Adri followed shortly after, taking the help of Vida to descend the lavish palace stairway, having lost much of his confidence and self-esteem since the Battle of Riverdell and the abduction of his beloved Sauvali. Before that sad day, he had navigated the corridors and stairways of the vast palace complex as well as any sighted person. Now he rarely went anywhere, even partaking of his meals in chamber, and when he did emerge, looking haggard and weary, he needed the help of a servant or guard to go anywhere.

"Geldry is still abed," Jilana said to Vessa as she approached him. "She is still in considerable pain. The healers say they cannot find anything physically wrong with her. I beg you to look in on her and hasten her recovery."

"When I am done here," her son said shortly. He did not seem to have much sympathy for Geldry. His lined face was even more deeply etched than usual, and strands of white had appeared in his long, wild black hair overnight.

"This night has taken a toll on you." Jilana reached out to touch one of the errant white hairs.

Vessa did not reply. Instead, he turned and strode back into the great hall.

Jilana took a step forward, then paused, unsure whether to follow him or wait there. He moved so quickly . . .

A moment later, Vessa returned, carrying something in the crook of his arm.

He handed the object to Jilana, who gasped and took it with great caution, holding it in the cradle of her arms.

"Behold your great-grandson and future heir to the Krushan line." Vessa stepped back and gestured with his wildwood staff. "The eldest of the one hundred and one children of Adri and Geldry."

Jilana stared down at the robust baby in her arms, as heavy and healthy of limb as a six-month-old rather than a newborn, fists and legs kicking and striking out fiercely. His face was mottled with blood, eyes shut tightly, and nostrils flared as if with anger. He was covered in green slime, and a last few tiny wisps of mist or smoke issued from his ears, nostrils, mouth, and eyes even now.

"Are they all like this?" she asked. She meant the state of the child, slime-covered and overdeveloped, unlike any newborn she had ever seen before in her life.

Vessa's eyes met hers, then passed on to Vrath's steadfast grey-eyed gaze. "All except one," said the sage. "She is a beautiful young girl. I have named her Princess Duhshala."

"Duhshala . . ." Jilana repeated. "Beautiful name. What do you call this one, the eldest?"

Vessa looked down at the babe in Jilana's arms. "I name him Dhuryo."

"A fine, strong name, fit for a king," she said approvingly. "If you have chosen such a name, I do not doubt that he shall grow up to be a 'great warrior' in deed as well."

Vessa's eyes met those of Vrath. "That he most certainly shall. Whether he approves of his given name, only time will tell."

Before she could ask what he meant by that remark, he turned back and pointed with his staff at the interior of the great hall. "In order of their birth, I name them: Dhuryo, Dushas . . ." He recited each of the 101 names.

Priests were summoned and the names recorded for posterity. A hundred and one wet nurses were called to duty and set about the task of bathing and nursing the Krushan children. In due course, they would be anointed and named according to all traditional rituals. From the very first, the wet nurses and attendants all reported numerous mishaps with the newborns: kicking, biting, grabbing, punching. The healthy, exceedingly strong babes appeared to have been born with a grudge toward the world and everyone they encountered. Accustomed to dealing with stubborn babes and aggressive, entitled ones, the wet nurses were nonetheless taken aback at their propensity for violence and the sheer intensity of their aggression. Over time, it became easier to think of them as a single group rather than individual children, and because they were all children of Krushan, they came to be referred to as Krushan.

Karni

~

IN THE TINY HUT in the hermitage in the middle of the great forest for which Hastinaga was named, Karni, Shvate, and Mayla gazed down in pride at the newborn babe. Shvate was happier than he had been in a long time, his pale face glowing with new energy and joy. "Our firstborn son," he said proudly, clasping Karni tightly with one arm, while keeping the other arm around Mayla. They were one family.

Karni kept her eyes averted from his, focusing them on the babe. She felt Mayla's eyes on her. Mayla's fascination with the God Mantra and the mechanics of calling up gods and having them father children on oneself was too intense for Karni. She had successfully managed to avoid all Mayla's probing questions, but she knew that her sister wife suspected something. Karni was sorely tempted to confess to her, but she knew she could not. To admit that she had used the mantra once before, as a young girl, and given birth to a child of the god Sharra would lead inevitably to the admission that that child now lived in Hastinaga itself, as the adopted son of charioteer Adran and his wife, Reeda. Due to the complexity of personal Krushan and inheritance laws dating back to the earliest matriarchal origins of the Krushan tribe, that meant her true firstborn was that boy, Kern. And Kern was therefore the eldest heir to the Krushan line and the rightful claimant to the Burning Throne.

On the one hand, she thought that perhaps this news might gratify Shvate. After all, he had himself pressured her to use the Mantra of Summoning to birth an heir, since he was prohibited by the rishi Kundaka's curse. On the other hand, she reminded herself sternly, that birth had occurred when she was still a kanya, an unmarried girl. She had not even *met* Shvate then. By law, Kern would still be accepted as Shvate's son, but what if Shvate himself rejected Kern? That would complicate the matter considerably.

Karni had a precedent for this case. Mother Jilana had herself done something very similar, lying with a sage while still an unmarried young girl and birthing a son, Vessa. That same Vessa was then accepted as a legitimate son, and went on to father surrogate sons on the princesses Umber and Ember, one of whom was Shvate himself. So it could be argued that Shvate was the son of such a surrogate born out of wedlock. But this was all legal wrangling and nitpicking. None of this would matter in the least if Shvate himself were to reject the argument and refuse to accept Kern as his son. Whatever his grounds, if he did so, then Karni would be in a mess. Instead of helping salvage the situation, she would worsen it. In his emotionally imbalanced state, she couldn't predict how Shvate might take the news.

And now, with this beautiful baby boy, she felt the point was irrelevant. She had birthed a son by using the God Mantra. Shima had been true to his word, as gods were expected to be, and had fathered a perfect child.

"A son with all the qualities of an emperor. Righteous, fearless, powerful, indomitable, a master of weapons and warcraft, a leader of armies and people, a master of strategy, a wise soul, a perfect, ideal man." Shvate beamed at her as he finished the recitation. "You have done us all proud, Karni of Stonecastle. You have given birth to a great emperor of Hastinaga. Shima is the god of both duty and death — and so our son too shall be as righteous as Shima and as dangerous as Death."

Karni looked up at her husband's shining face. "I'm sure he shall be, one day. But at present he appears to possess neither of those qualities, and quite definitely possesses a third, totally different quality altogether."

Shvate frowned. "What is that?"

"Fearlessness!" Mayla said.

Karni shook her head.

"Power?" Shvate asked.

Karni smiled and shook her head once more.

"Indomitability? A master of strategy? Of warcraft? Weaponry? A wise soul? A perfect, ideal man?" Mayla rattled off in a rush, eyes shining.

Karni shook her head a final time, then gestured to the kicking babe. "Hunger."

As if in agreement with her assessment, the little one began to wail plaintively but timidly, as if too polite to make a real ruckus. Both Shvate and Mayla looked at him, then at Karni, then suddenly burst out laughing. The little tyke stopped crying at once and stared at them in surprise, still for a moment.

Karni laughed as well. "He is a baby now," she said. "In time he will be all of those great things and more, but right now, he needs what any baby needs, mother's milk."

Shvate wagged a finger at her. "And if he takes after you, then he will have a sense of humor as well."

Later, after the baby was put to bed for the night, Shvate came to her again. She was weary after the long day and night of caring for the little one. Mayla had been with her, but Mayla was more excited and curious than helpful, and Karni had had to do most of the baby tending herself, which was fine. She felt a great sense of pride and satisfaction at being able to claim the gift of her body as her own, legitimately and openly. *Nothing will part this one from me.*

"He needs a sibling," Shvate said.

Karni frowned. "We asked for a son with all the qualities of an emperor."

"Exactly. And while he sits on the throne and governs the empire, he needs someone to watch out for him. Care for his well-being, his security, and protect the empire's sovereignty as well."

"Can't he do all that?"

"He can, but it would be so much better if he had a companion."

Karni thought for a moment. "You mean, like yourself and Adri? One of you stays back at home to manage the affairs of the empire while the other goes to war and protects the borders and quells uprisings and so on?"

"In a manner of speaking, yes. A great king needs a great right hand. Our firstborn will be better able to govern and administer if there is someone who has his back. And in the event of an unfortunate calamity, he also has someone worthy to succeed him."

Karni had a number of thoughts and questions about the suitability of Adri as Shvate's successor, and all those stories of brothers warring against brothers for thrones and property, but she did not voice any of these concerns. Shvate knew all that. None of it invalidated his desire to have another child.

"Does it have to be a sibling?" she asked. "For instance, Vida has always been loyal to you and Adri, and is an excellent administrative and legislative mind."

"Exactly my point," Shvate replied. "Vida is my brother, after all. Under our law of succession he cannot inherit because his mother was only a maid, and not a wife of a Krushan, but he is still my blood. Our son needs the same reassurance: only blood can protect blood in dire times."

I wish I could tell you that our firstborn already has a brother. My own son, my true firstborn, a magnificent young boy born of the god Sharra, your first choice for the summoning. His name is Kern, and he lives in Hastinaga itself. All we have to do is claim him and bring him into the palace to live with us, and he can be the future emperor you desire. Or, if that is not possible, then he can be the right hand of this little one.

She ached to tell him all, to unburden her heart, to share this deepest, most intimate secret. But she could not. Even if Shvate accepted her earlier lapse as a youthful indiscretion, there were other things she worried about. For one thing, Mayla would lay eyes on the boy and surely see the resemblance to her own dead eldest brother, Maheev, either right away or at some time in the future. Once that happened, Shvate would soon realize that not only had she used the God Mantra and lain with Sharra the sun god, but she had resurrected Mayla's dead brother as the god's avatar. It was before she had even met Shvate, so it could not be infidelity, but the fact that she had a son was a big secret to have kept from her husband. She had no way to be sure of how or how intensely Shvate might react if he found out now, and it was too sensitive a revelation for her to simply tell him. Too much was at stake here and now. *Our lives and the future of the entire Krushan race and empire.*

Instead she pretended to be thinking deeply about his words and said only, "Yes, this is true. He must have a sibling."

Shvate brightened at once. "Then you agree?"

What choice did she have? "Yes."

He jumped up, clapping his hands together. "This time I know the perfect god to summon."

Mayla

~

MAYLA WATCHED KARNI GO into the clearing alone. When she had passed out of sight, Mayla turned to Shvate. "I should be with her. Just in case."

Shvate looked at her with a patient expression. "She will not be harmed. These are gods, not urrkh."

"But still. If she needs moral support . . ."

Shvate shook his head. "Karni is strong. Stronger than both of us combined."

Mayla squinted at him, playfully. "Are you saying I'm not strong?"

Shvate raised his eyebrows. "Mayla, my love, you are capable of besting me in a duel at least two times out of five."

"It would have been three, but the ground was muddy, and I slipped."

He didn't argue or press the point. He was carving a length of wood and continued whittling at it.

"What are you doing?"

"Carving practice swords for our children."

"Isn't it a bit early? I know that children of the gods are born much sooner than human ones. But even so, it'll be months yet before they can even stand."

Shvate looked at her, then glanced at the cot nearby, in which their little champion lay sleeping peacefully. "Our children will be extraordinary. We must prepare them for extraordinary lives."

Mayla was about to say something else when suddenly a wind whipped up out of nowhere. At once, Shvate dropped the wood and the knife and went to the cot, pulling the covering over the top to keep the wind and dust out of his eyes. When he turned around, Mayla was standing with her mouth open, staring in the direction of the clearing.

Shvate glanced that way and saw the wind churning furiously in the air above the clearing, where only a moment ago all had been still.

A grinding sound came from above.

They both looked up at the sky.

A tornado was descending, a thin, tall wind funnel blurring at tremendous speed, dark as night against the clear, cloudless blue sky.

There were no tornadoes in this part of the Burnt Empire. This was no natural phenomenon.

The tornado touched ground precisely in the clearing.

The wind and sound were both deafening and blinding.

Shvate pulled at Mayla's hand. "We have to get under cover!"

Mayla reluctantly broke away and went with Shvate. She continued looking back as she went, all the way until she reached the safety of the hermitage, where all was quiet and peaceful.

Karni

~

KARNI STOOD CALMLY IN the clearing as the tornado descended. It spun even more furiously the closer it drew to land, the resulting dust and debris threatening to blind her. She had placed the edge of her garment over her face to protect her eyes and other orifices. The material was thin and transparent enough to see through. So it was through a pink veil that she viewed the tornado resolve into a man-shaped being.

The voice of the being was the voice of the tornado itself, angry and thundering.

Mortal woman . . . you dared summon me?

"Lord of Wind and Bird, I am Princess Karni of Hastinaga," she said calmly. "And indeed it was I who summoned thee, using the mantra gifted to me by the rishi Pasha'ar."

He was lean and long-limbed, like an elongated man. He moved with strange, fluid actions and gestures, the outlines of his body and face constantly blurred from incessant motion. Wherever he moved, the funnel of the tornado moved with him. He walked around her, examining her from head to foot as if she were an object on display in a royal viewing gallery. Then again, to the gods perhaps all mortal beings were little more than objects in a divine viewing gallery.

I sense that you have used this mantra before . . . twice already. To summon Sharra . . . and Shima?

At the second name, he expressed surprise, even some admiration. She glanced at the pathway, hoping Mayla and Shvate had not heard that first name. She was relieved to see no sign of them: they must have gone back to the hermitage then, as she'd suggested.

567

"I have," she said simply, knowing that the less said, the better. Besides, she hadn't called on him to banter.

He continued to move around her in whirling, blurring haze. She stood her ground calmly, outwardly showing nothing, but inwardly praying she had not pushed her luck. Thrice on a mantra? It was tempting fate, was it not?

You are bold, Karni of Hastinaga. I do not recall a time when the Mantra of Summoning was used thrice by the same person in such a short interval. And to summon Shima himself? He made a sound that could have been chuckling. It sounded like the tornado was chewing through logs of wood and splintering them to chips. **It is unheard of among us higher gods.**

She offered no response. His comment appeared to require none.

He regarded her for a moment, then abruptly appeared inches in front of her without any transition. *Hence the phrase, "moves like the wind,"* she thought to herself. He peered at her, and she had a sense of his gaze penetrating through her veil, through her garments, into her skin, her body, her brain, her essence. He was not ogling her; he was examining her very fiber and soul. It was an unsettling sensation, but she held still and stayed calm, or as calm as was possible for a mortal woman while being examined in such depth by a powerful god.

You are no ordinary woman, Karni of Hastinaga. The tornado buzzed with strange sounds, like voices filtered down through a storm high, high above. She saw a flash of blinding light above and a sound like a deep subterranean reverberation under her feet. **Sharra and Shima both concur. I am impressed. Any mortal woman who can summon two of the most powerful gods of all creation is one with an extraordinary destiny.**

"Thank you," she said, not sure how else one responded to such a compliment.

Presumably you desire a boon from me. That is customarily the reason for a summoning.

"I do, my lord."

Very well, then, I am intrigued by you. Name your boon. Do you desire indomitable victory in war? The power to destroy all enemies in combat? The strength to lift a hundred Coldstone Mountains at once? Or to crush them below your little toe? What great feat do you aim to accomplish, Karni of Hastinaga?

"The greatest feat of all, Lord of Wind. I wish to birth a child."

Silence, except for the whirring, blurring, grinding of the funnel. Then a strange sharp sound, the wind god's equivalent of laughter. **A jest! You are a bold one. Yes, I suppose that is true. Birthing a child is a feat as miraculous as the workings of any god, yet all mortal women possess this remarkable power. That is why Goddess Jeel often says that females of all species are gods in their own right.**

Karni began to realize that the Lord of Wind was true to his title. She decided to hasten this process along before she found herself standing here in this clearing engaged in banter for the next several thousand years. "My lord, by your grace, I would birth a child worthy of your own powers. As strong as a cyclone, as unstoppable as a tornado, as fierce as a gale, as versatile as wind, as omnipresent and loyal to family as air itself, and yet capable of being as gentle and soothing as a sea breeze when required."

You don't ask for much, do you, Karni of Hastinaga? Again the same grinding laughter. **But I would want my child to be worthy of my name. Your boon shall be granted.**

And without further ado, taking her completely by surprise, he took hold of her with both hands and drew her into his stormy embrace, into the whirling dervish of the funnel. Her vision blurred, and she felt her feet leave the ground as she was lifted up, up, high, the ground falling far beneath her as she flew up and the blood rushed from her head leaving her lightheaded and drunk with power.

Mayla

~

MAYLA LEAPED UP FROM the porch as she saw the shadow approaching through the trees. Her first instinct as always was to reach for her sword — that was something that she could no more control than she could control her need to breathe — but she knew at once from the shape of the shadow and the way it moved that it was Karni. She watched with anticipation as her sister wife reached the backyard of the hut, cradling something in her arms.

Mayla sprang forward. "Karni!"

She hugged her sister queen warmly, genuinely happy to see her. "You were gone so long, I imagined all kinds of things. But now you're back."

She saw Karni wince. "Are you all right?"

Karni smiled. "Never better."

Mayla looked down at the bundle in Karni's arms. "You have already delivered Grrud's child? But you were only gone one night and half a day!"

"Time moves differently in the Lord of Wind's realm. Much, much faster. Had he wanted, he could have returned me a year from when I left, or a decade, or even a century or a millennium later. Yet to you here on Arthaloka, it was as if I spent only a night and half a day away."

Mayla's eyes shone as she stared at Karni, trying to see some difference, some sign of overnight aging. She saw nothing that was easily visible, except perhaps that look of strain on Karni's face. "Are you sure you are well? You seem . . . strained."

"I would like to put her down. She is heavy."

"Oh. Let me take her," Mayla said brightly, taking the baby from Karni's arms.

"Careful!" Karni warned, still keeping her hands on the bundle.

Mayla had once been engaged in an argument with her brothers, one of many such arguments that girls and women faced all their lives. This particular argument was about the relative difference in strength between women and men. They had all been lifting wood blocks of increasingly larger sizes and weights to prove their superior strength. Until then, Mayla had succeeded in lifting every block her brothers had lifted. Frustrated, her brothers decided to increase the odds. They had pointed to a wood bole taller and wider than any of them, lying on its side, and demanded that she lift it to prove that women were stronger than men.

The bole was much too heavy for any of them to lift either, but because she had made the challenge, it was up to her to try first and prove her strength. She knew they would also fail when their turn came, but she wasn't ready to listen to their whistles and jeers as she struggled with the impossible task. So she came up with an idea.

The bole was too broad for her to pick up in its current position. To pick it up, she needed to put her arms around it and hug it tightly, so she could use the larger of her muscles — of the legs and back. It would be the same for any of them when they tried to pick it up, she pointed out. She insisted that they help her position it first, so they could all take turns picking it up the right way so as not to injure themselves.

They agreed, grumbling a bit, and she supervised the eight of them as they took hold of parts of the bole and raised it to a standing position.

"There," Mayla said, clapping loudly. "I did it."

How could she say that? they had exclaimed. She hadn't even touched the bole yet!

"Exactly," she said, "I manipulated all you boys into picking it up for me, proving that women are stronger than men — not always in body, but definitely in mind!"

Mayla was reminded of that incident now because the instant she tried to pick up Karni's second child, she felt as if she had finally picked up that tree bole. She was the heaviest thing Mayla had ever lifted in her life!

She exclaimed and would have dropped her had Karni not still been keeping her hands on the bottom of the bundle. As it was, she gasped and bent over double from the weight, forced to use the benefit of her years of fighting and training to even keep her balance. Somehow she was able to stay on her feet and not fall over, but it took every bit of her strength.

"Let me," Karni said, and took the child back, lifting her with a single grimace.

Mayla stared at her. "How? I mean . . . she must weigh . . . well, a lot! How can you just lift her up like that? She's the heaviest child ever born. She must be!"

Karni smiled at Mayla. "I am her mother. I birthed her. I can carry her."

Shvate had heard their voices and emerged from the hut, holding their firstborn in his arms. His face lit up at the sight of Karni — and at her little burden.

"Happy day!" he said.

Karni showed him her bundle. "Our second born."

He kissed the baby, and then the mother. "I am a proud father and a proud Krushan."

"I am a tired mother and tired Krushan," she replied. "But happy as well as proud."

Mayla wagged a finger at Shvate. "Don't try to pick her up. She's too heavy! Karni seems to possess some kind of new maternal powers — otherwise it's impossible!"

Shvate looked at Karni, who smiled tiredly. "What she said is true. Let me go put her down for a minute."

They all went into the hut together. Karni placed the baby with an effort on the cot. Shvate placed the elder child down beside his sibling. Both of them stirred a little, then went back to sleep.

Mayla slipped an arm around Karni as they went outside again. "What was it like? Tell me everything."

Karni looked back at her with her typical enigmatic smile. Mayla could tell from that smile alone that Karni wasn't going to tell her *anything*. It was so unfair. She wanted to know so much.

Shvate was staring at the sky. He had a certain look on his face, that look he got when he had been thinking about something important and had come to a conclusion.

Mayla looked at Karni and found Karni looking back at her. Both of them arched their eyebrows in sisterly empathy. They knew what he was going to say next.

"Karni . . ." he began slowly.

Karni sighed. "No," she said.

He looked at her. "But I haven't said anything."

"I know what you're going to say."

"How can you know what I'm going to say before I say it?"

"Because I'm your wife. I know you."

"At least let me say it before you answer."

"You already have my answer. No."

Mayla tugged at Karni's elbow. "Sister."

Karni glanced at her, brow puckered. "No."

"What?" Mayla replied, indignant. "Don't say you know what I'm about to say too! You're not my wife!"

"I do know, because I know you, Mayla. And the answer is no." She pointed at Shvate, then at Mayla. "To both of you!"

They had been arguing for only a few minutes when there was a sudden loud sound from the hut. They felt the jolt in the ground, as if a tree had just been felled, or something equally heavy had dropped from a height.

They ran inside together, crowding the little space.

The grinding stone that they had cleaned and kept inside as a barrier, to keep the baby cots from toppling over, lay in pieces, shattered as if struck by a boulder dropped from a height. It would take something that heavy to shatter the massive flat stone.

Sitting amidst the shattered pieces of rough black stone was their second born, clutching the tiny fist of her elder brother. She looked up unsteadily at them as they entered. She smiled at them, then returned her attention to her brother. Putting both arms around her brother's pallet, she cradled him and picked up the entire bundle, baby and all. A loud, wet, smacking sound came from the point where her mouth connected with her brother's belly. She kissed her brother and then set him down slowly, carefully, as easily as Mayla might lower a kitten.

Then she rolled over and went promptly to sleep. After a moment, her thumb found its way into her mouth and she began to snore lightly.

They went out of the hut again without saying another word. Mayla wanted to ask if they should pick up the pieces of the broken grinding stone, then thought that if the baby was strong enough to have broken it into pieces by falling out of the crib, she was probably strong enough not to come to any harm lying on the pieces. From the ease with which she had fallen asleep, Mayla thought this might be the case.

"She's strong," she said. "And heavy."

Karni and Shvate looked at Mayla together, then at each other. Karni was smiling. Shvate frowned, as he tried to read Karni's mood.

Mayla understood what Karni was feeling and thinking. She smiled back at Karni. They linked arms and shared a sisterly moment of consonance.

Finally, Karni turned back to Shvate and said, "Only once more. And then I'm done."

Mayla whispered in Karni's ear: *"Please."*

Karni sighed and said, "And if Mayla wishes, she can use the mantra too. But only once."

Shvate nodded, thinking so hard Mayla could see his eyes rolling up in his head. "So that's once more for you, and once for Mayla."

"It's not fair that you should get three turns, and I only get one," Mayla said.

"It's not fair that you're able to consume five times as much wine as I can and still not put on weight," Karni said. "But that's life."

Mayla thought about that and then nodded, smiling. She patted her flat belly, feeling the taut abdominal muscles beneath the skin. "I suppose that's true. Very well, then. I accept."

Karni smiled at her as if Mayla had told a big joke. "Only once, Mayla! No tricks! I know you." She turned to Shvate and pointed at their husband. "And after, we're done. Don't think you're going to get us to procreate an entire clan fathered by the gods!"

Shvate put his palms together and bowed his head in mock submission. "Yes, my lady, I accept your terms."

Karni drew in a deep breath and released it slowly. "Very well, then, let us get it over with, so we can get on with the business of raising our children, before they grow up before our very eyes!"

Karni

~

KARNI HAD BARELY FINISHED reciting the mantra when a bolt of lightning cracked open the darkling sky, landing right in front of her in the clearing. She was too startled to even jump back. The bolt struck ground, and the entire forest seemed to reverberate with the echoes of thunder that rolled and pealed for yojanas. Vast flocks of birds, already settled in their nests, rose again and littered the sky as they cried out in outrage.

A stocky figure that seemed on first appearance almost as wide as he was tall stood before her. Flashes of lightning flickered in his eyes and continued to flicker from time to time. He wore earrings and jewelry and an assortment of accessories on his tight-fitting leather garments and body. He was powerfully built, but also bulky in the way that some muscular men became with time and age, and while she might have expected that the Lord of Storms and War would be as sleek as lightning and as fearsome as thunder, she could only confirm one of the above. That he was strong was not in any doubt; he had the hard look of the veteran warrior, one who had spent his lifetime, or several thousand human lifetimes, doing nothing but fighting. A thought occurred to Karni: *This is what Shvate might look like if he were to live several million years and be at war all that while, with no wives, children, or any other family to soften his hard edges.*

I know of your desire, woman, he said curtly. **You desire a child by my seed.**

He's a direct one, not even a moment to know my name or ask me any questions. He isn't even looking at me with real interest.

Lightning flickered in Inadran's eyes. **I am a god. I already know every-**

thing worth knowing about you, mortal. Let us not waste time. If you want my seed, say so. I have wars to wage and battles to fight.

She was tempted to reply in the negative but squashed the thought even before it could emerge fully. *Be cautious, Karni!* "I do, my lord," she said, inclining her head to show respect. "Grant me the gift of bearing the greatest warrior that ever lived."

He smiled, showing a dark emptiness where his mouth ought to have been. Within that darkness, she glimpsed two great armies of strange, alien beings clashing at night on a battlefield under three suns, the sky a color she could not even name: fires raged and explosions boomed, killing millions at a blast. She looked down quickly, sensing that these were not sights intended for human perception. *Careful, Karni.* **That boon has already been granted, as you well know. By Sharra.**

She swallowed, trying to think of a response that would not sound offensive or foolish. Before her mind could come up with one, he continued.

I will give you the next best thing: a warrior so powerful that he alone will be the equal of Sharra's son. But you know what that means, do you not?

She kept her eyes lowered. His hand, held at his waist, was flickering with lightning, gathering more and more power, building into a ball of pure energy. "I . . . am not sure, my lord. Pray, enlighten me."

The two greatest warriors of all time, both walking Arthaloka at the same time. It is inevitable that sooner or later they will seek each other out . . . and duel. And when they do so, the duel will be historic and conclusive. Only one will survive that encounter. In case I have not made it amply clear yet, let me clarify further. If I do this, then one day, both your children will face each other and fight to the death. One will kill the other.

She gasped and felt a sharp pain in her chest, like a large needle heated, then inserted between her ribs. She had felt the same pain when she had seen her son Kern for the first time, on the night of the eclipse. "Forgive me, Lord Inadran, but . . . is there no way to prevent such an outcome?"

She saw his chest heaving, his body shaking. She knew he was laughing, but he produced no sound from his mouth, just shook silently, laughing at her heartbreak and dismay. *What a bastard,* she thought with a flash of anger.

Nay, Karni of Hastinaga. As you well know! It is too late for second thoughts now. Once summoned, I must fulfill your wish. Here, he said, and slapped his hand low on her belly, filling her with a surge of such bright mind-melting power that she lost consciousness instantly.

Mayla

～

MAYLA WAS TREMBLING WITH excitement and anticipation. And anxiety too. Karni had told her so many things about the different gods she had summoned, but had also cautioned her that each god was vastly different from the others, so not to assume that any of her experiences would have any bearing on Mayla's own encounter.

Mayla had been shocked by Karni's state after the last summoning. They had suspected something amiss when she hadn't returned after a few hours and had gone to the clearing, where they found her still unconscious, sprawled on the ground. The baby beside her had been quite well, already sitting up and playing. He was looking up at something with such intense concentration, Mayla had to look up to see what it could be.

All she could see was the dawn sky just starting to lighten, trees and more trees. After a moment, she saw a bird on a branch high above, so high that she could barely see it in the dim gloaming. The bird was sitting on the branch, its head cocked to one side, looking down. It was almost as if the bird and the child were both looking at each other, the bird staring down with one eye, as if ready to fly should the child make any sudden moves. *But he's just a baby!* She thought. *What could he possibly do?*

Then the baby pointed a chubby finger at the bird and the bird startled, flapping its wings and soaring off into the dawn sky, and she thought, *Well, that was interesting. If he had a bow and an arrow . . .*

Karni had been all right, but clearly exhausted. Shvate had looked stricken when they found her, and his customary joy at viewing the baby for the first time was dimmed by his concern for Karni's well-being. The baby had not seemed to mind, tugging at Shvate's beard and playing with it each time he bent over to check on Karni.

"She just needs sleep and rest," Mayla told him. "Tend to her for a while. When she wakes, make her eat something. She is nursing and needs her strength. I will be back soon."

He had looked up as she rose to go. She thought he might call her back, tell her not to go, but he said nothing, only looked at her the way he used to look at her each time they went into battle together, an expression of caring, strength, and shared succor that always filled her heart and made her feel that she was fighting the good fight. She nodded curtly to him, acknowledging him, and left.

Now she stood in the same clearing, about to recite the mantra.

She had intended to speak the mantra slowly, cautiously, to avoid making the slightest error. But when the moment came, she said it all in a fierce rush, like drawing her sword and hacking off an enemy's head in a single action. She added the name of the god she had summoned and waited.

At first she thought that nothing had happened. Karni had warned her to expect thunder, lightning, tornadoes, storms, and the gods alone knew what else.

The clearing remained quiet and still, the sky bright now in the morning light. Bars of sunlight filtered through the canopy of the jungle, one falling near her foot. It was warm on her toes. She heard the clip-clop of cloven hooves and identified it as a Coldheart Mountain stag. Something as large and as heavy as an elephant calf or a large bison. Except . . . she could make out four pairs of hooves. That meant two stags? Or two bison? That was highly unlikely.

"Mayla devi."

She turned with a gasp of surprise.

Two magnificent beings stood before her.

Their fore bodies were human in appearance, handsome, well-built, with clearly etched muscles and taut, lean physiques. Their nether bodies most closely resembled horses, yet were not entirely equine. She could see tufts of fur and horns protruding from their flanks, which would be very discouraging to anyone who made the mistake of trying to ride them like earthly horses; also their tails were very different, distinct from any horse Mayla had ever seen, elaborately braided and decorated with bright, colorful gemstones.

Their faces gleamed with curiosity and interest. They were both looking at her with tilted heads, an ironic quirk on one's right cheek, a curled eyebrow on the other's face.

"You, you . . ." she stammered. "Are the Asvas."

"Isn't that who you summoned?" asked the one with the dark curly hair and a small bristling pointed beard on the tip of his chin. She saw that he had kohl in his eyes, or perhaps that was just they way they were naturally. He had thick tufts of hair on his muscular chest.

"Unless you were expecting someone else!" said the other, tossing back his light-colored straight hair. He was smooth of cheek and hairless on his forebody, but his chest was just as sleekly muscled.

"I —" She broke off, unsure of what to say. She could scarcely believe it had actually worked. I am in the presence of two gods! The Asva twins. "I seek a boon."

Both raised their eyebrows. "Only one?"

She looked from one to the other in confusion. "I desire a child. A child who will be beloved of all, irresistible, endearing, and affectionate, and capable of engendering great loyalty from all living beings."

They cocked their heads again. "Interesting choice of words," said the one with light-colored hair and eyes. "All living beings? Do you include animal species in that?"

"Of course she does," said his dark-haired brother. "Insects, birds, fish, everything that lives and moves."

"So does that include trees and plants too? Because they do move and live, but very slowly."

She cleared her throat.

They looked at her.

"Yes," she said. "Everything, every species, the entire kingdom of beasts and all else besides."

They looked at her, and smiles slowly appeared on their faces. "I like that phrasing, 'kingdom of beasts.' It is so apt. They have their own kingdom, after all."

"I'm not so sure about 'beasts,' though," said the other, frowning and tapping the side of his head thoughtfully. "Oh, well, it'll do."

She walked up to them, placing her bare hands on their bare chests. Their muscles rippled in tactile response. She rubbed their chests, relishing the difference between them, the sheer maleness of them both, the partly animal smell and look and feel, and beneath all these physical sensations, the power of godhead itself, very much present and vibrant in their magnificent forms.

"Would it be possible to have two at the same time?" she asked in her sweetest, most affectionate tone. "Twins?"

They exchanged a glance and smiled, eyes twinkling.

"Why not?" they said together.

Geldry

～

GELDRY HATED VISITING THE nursery.

The first time she had come here, she thought she had stepped into an animal pen.

The sounds of her 101 children crying resembled the cries of animals more than human babies. She said so aloud, and the wet nurses told her it was only because there were so many of them, and they all tended to cry together, especially when the eldest started up. But she heard the fear in their voices too and sensed their nervousness. She had worn the eyeband as she did in public, so had to rely on her maids to steer her and on her ears and other senses for impressions. Her sense of smell was overwhelmed too. *Animals*, she told herself, *they smell like animals!*

She asked the wet nurses if they permitted pets in here, making it sound like an admonition. The wet nurses hesitated, then said no, that was only the smell of the babies. One of the wet nurses made some remark about how 101 babies defecating and urinating constantly would produce *some* smell. But Geldry had smelled babies before, and babies didn't produce anything that smelled like *this*. She had not said anything further in front of the wet nurses, but she had told Kune later in her chambers that it felt like being in an animal pen or a menagerie, not a nursery.

The same foul odor met her now as she entered. She stopped abruptly, felt her body tense, her breath catch, then sniffed tentatively, trying to confirm that she was really smelling what she was smelling.

She did not spend much time in the nursery. She couldn't bear it. And after her visit was done, she excused herself to the wet nurses and rushed away. She regurgitated the contents of her stomach. But once the sick feeling had passed, she had smiled, satisfied. She couldn't wait for Adri to visit his children. She hoped he would enjoy the visit. They were her gift to him, and to Hastinaga.

Back in her chambers, she laughed and went over the incident with Kune, again and again, drinking wine and having a merry time of it as they waited for their real lives to start, for the plan in the forest to be completed, for the coronation in two days, and for the empire to be theirs to control and do with as they pleased.

Their time was coming, Krushan be damned.

Jilana

〜

1

THE GUARDS OUTSIDE THE chambers straightened up and saluted Jilana smartly as she approached. They opened the doors and announced her: "Enter . . . *Dowager Empress Mother Jilana!*"

The bedchamber was dark and smelled of stale sweat, food, and even wine. Since when had Adri taken to drinking wine? Or had he always drunk it? She looked around the darkened chamber. An air of sadness and self-pity hung in the air. This was not the chamber of a crown prince. It was the chamber of a man who had given up all love for life itself. She cursed herself for not coming sooner. *I thought he would get over it by himself in time.* Quite apparently he had not: judging by the state of these chambers, he was still wallowing in self-pity and grief. *He's a man,* she thought. *What do you expect?*

She went to the verandah and tugged hard at the drapes. She could have called in servants to do it, but she didn't want to intrude on Adri's privacy any more than she already was. The fewer people who saw the crown prince of Hastinaga in this state, the better. With a struggle, she got the drapes to move and pulled them all the way open, letting in an explosion of daylight that turned the dark, musty room bright.

She dusted off her hands — the drapes needed changing and laundering, she would tell the maids to see to that — and turned to face the bed. The lone figure sprawled across the large satin-sheeted expanse was still dead to the world. Jilana put her hands on her hips and waited for the bright light to wake him up, then remembered with a shock of embarrassment that bright light or dim light made no difference to a blind man. She resisted the impulse to slap herself on the forehead and went over to the bed. She saw belatedly that he was stark naked, but fortunately he was lying face-down. His hands were raised up above his head and his head turned aside: even in sleep, his posture was one of defeat.

She watched him sleep for a moment, overcome by a sudden surge of emotion. Perhaps she should let him sleep, leave him be, as he desired. The poor boy had been born sightless, into a dark and dangerous world surrounded by enemies on all sides, a mother who would not even nurse him, embrace him, or comfort him when he cried, people who either pitied him for his blindness or sought to befriend him because of his position in the imperial hierarchy.

What must it have been to have grown up as Adri? She couldn't imagine. She had enjoyed a wonderful childhood and youth, full of energy and vigor; was treated no differently from her brothers and other men of her tribe; had gone wherever and done whatever she pleased, a high-energy lifestyle marked with much athletic play and activity. She couldn't imagine not being able to run, play, jump, or sport simply because of one's inability to see. This, apart from the other obvious sadness of being forever unable to witness a beautiful sunset over the Jeel, where the sun in late summer seemed to almost bow down to touch his forehead to the feet of the river goddess. To lack color, vividity, beauty, aesthetic pleasure completely . . . . Jilana was never one for art or snobbish pursuits, even now in a palace surrounded by thousands of the most exquisite works of art of this age, most of which she barely spared a glance, but she could afford to have such a careless attitude, because if she ever had the slightest whim, she could take a moment, or an hour, to stop and admire the grace of a sculpted dancer or the colors and detail of a great mural — but to never be able to see anything at all?

"You poor boy," she said softly, mainly to herself.

She picked up the fallen silk sheet and spread it over her grandson's nakedness. She had decided to wait until he woke on his own rather than disturb him. She found a stool set back against a wall — all the furniture in these chambers was placed against the wall, to avoid it encumbering Adri when he moved around — and sat down upon it, looking at the sad detritus of several meals and a toppled jug of wine which had dribbled out a large brown stain onto the richly embroidered rug.

How had it come to this? To the crown prince of Krushan passed out dead drunk in his chambers only days before his own ascension?

Jilana wished then that she had intervened from the outset, taken a hand in his upbringing, even become a surrogate mother to him once she realized that her daughter-in-law had washed her hands completely of the responsibility. The only reason she had not done so was because she felt it would set a bad example. Both her daughters-in-law had sons; both needed to take their maternal responsibilities seriously. Jeel knew she had tried time and time again to drill that into their heads: through frequent arguments or tirades, even threatening them with disinheritance and exile. Nothing had worked.

The princesses Ember and Umber were daughters of Serapi; Vrath had abducted them by force from their own swayamvaras to bring them here as brides for Jilana's sons Gada and Virya. If she were to disown them or exile them, they would simply go back home to their father's house, and their powerful father and all his allies would instantly turn against the House of Krushan. The presence of the princesses here was the only thing that had kept Serapi and its allies on Hastinaga's side till now, despite their deep resentment of the manner in which the princesses had been abducted against their will. The suicide of the third sister, Princess Amber, after she was abandoned by Vrath and spurned by her own former fiancée Prince Shalya, had deepened the old wound. Shalya was now *King* Shalya and a powerful force in his own right, and he had sworn lifelong vengeance against the House of Krushan for that transgression. And were Jilana to have made good on her threats and turned out her daughters-in-law, Shalya would be the first in line, leading the rebellion against Hastinaga.

And he would be in the right, and she in the wrong. Whatever their failings, Princesses Ember and Umber could not genuinely be blamed for their lapses. They had been forcibly abducted and made to marry the Krushan princes. Then, when their husbands had died, they had been told to expect a nighttime visit from Jilana's son Vessa, who would be impregnating them in order to create heirs for the House of Krushan. It could be argued that they considered themselves raped and impregnated against their will. There were some who had said so openly, though of course never in the presence of Jilana or Vrath.

But it had been said, and there was some truth in it. Vrath had heard about it and had wanted to declare in court that any persons who had made such comments would be thrown into the dungeons, but she had dissuaded him. It was a short, slippery slope from muzzling free speech to a dictatorship; Vrath, perhaps, would not have any significant objection to running such a government, but as a young girl, Jilana had seen too many ordinary people victimized by the abuse of power to sanction such a regime herself. That was the reason she had ultimately let her daughters-in-law go about their lives when all her threats and rants went unheeded. What good would it to do punish them, except create more controversy and political upheaval?

I should have stepped in at that time and taken up the job of caring for both the boys myself. I should have done it while they were still young enough to be molded.

But that was when something unexpected had happened: Shvate and Adri had bonded. The two brothers had found one another and forged a brotherhood based more on identification than on blood. They had several things in common: birth infirmities, the scorn and humiliation heaped upon them for being different, the inability to easily do many of the things other children their age did every day, the painful neglect and failure of their own mothers to be there when they were needed most . . . plus the incessant pressure of their gurus, teachers, and elders to live up to the Krushan name. Not to mention the rigorous training and education they received as Krushan princes, and the usual problems and pains any child has growing up.

She had watched this brotherhood develop and grow, to the point where she was astonished by how much potential these two boys had. Her father, the fisherman, had always told her that the strongest fish were those that faced the toughest odds. Salmon — he was always talking about salmon with such admiration. Swimming upstream while pregnant, all the way from the estuary to the high mountains, to lay their eggs. She had thought then that perhaps Adri and Shvate were like salmon in reverse: babes who had to swim upriver in order to find their true strength.

Jilana had decided to watch and wait a while longer before intervening. And then, when she had thought to insert herself into their daily lives, it was too late: Vrath carted them off to gurukul to receive intensive training in the business of kingship. And they were not quite done with their studies, still barely out of boyhood, when the Battle of the Rebels had demanded their presence.

The Children of Midnight, she used to call them, because both were born at the midnight hour. Doomed to a long, dark night ahead. In Adri's case, that had been literally true. She had seen how badly the Battle of the Rebels had shaken him. His performance was stellar: she had personally witnessed his and Shvate's extraordinary fight against impossible odds during that chariot maneuver. But that was also the day that the brothers had started to drift apart. Shvate had thrived and flourished as a warrior — and found his calling. While Adri had distinguished himself in battle, he had also realized he'd had enough of warfare to last a lifetime. She suspected his decline had begun then.

When Shvate took his first wife, Karni, Adri lost his brother forever. No more did Jilana see the two brothers walking, eating, laughing, playing, practicing together, in fact she rarely saw them together at all except at official functions, and even then they barely spent any time in each other's company. She watched her blind grandson sleeping and thought of how the past year or two had brought even more sorrow and loss: Shvate in self-exile, his lover Sauvali abducted. She couldn't imagine how much pain and anguish he must have in his heart. She felt deeply sorry for him. But whatever had happened in the past did not change where they were today, here and now.

Adri stirred.

He moaned and reached up to his head with the typical gesture of a heavy wine drinker. Her late husband, Sha'ant, had been fond of wine too. The age difference between herself and Sha'ant had meant that she was able to shake off the morning hangovers and get on with her day while he often needed to sleep in to recover. As he had aged, she had tapered off her own drinking, then begun discouraging him from drinking as much. It had worked, mostly; from time to time he had overindulged and always paid the price. On those mornings, he had always begun by holding his head in just that way. Even though she knew that Adri was not a direct blood descendant of Sha'ant, she felt a tremor of emotion at the gesture.

She rose from the stool and stood.

"Rise," she said in a quiet but firm voice.

2

Adri turned his head so that his left ear was in Jilana's direction. "Sauvali?" The uncertainty and emotion in his voice was heart-breaking.

Stay firm, Jilana. Remember why you are here. "It is I, your grandmother."

Adri reached down to the sheet, checking if his modesty was covered. "Grandmother, why are you here unannounced? I am not properly attired to receive you!"

"I was properly announced when I arrived hours ago. It is you who seem to be improperly attired for your duties. Is this the usual hour at which you are accustomed to rising, Adri?"

"I . . . am unwell."

"I suspect a malady of excess, nothing more."

"I may have drunk a little wine last night."

"Last night? From what I hear, it has been a very long night for you, Adri. One lasting several months!"

"Things have been difficult since . . . It's been difficult."

"Difficult or not, grandson, you are the crown prince of Hastinaga. You have responsibilities and duties. I learned today that you have not been to see your own newborn children nor their mother. Why is that?"

Adri did not answer her. He had risen to a seated position, the sheets gathered around his midriff. His head hung down, hair falling over his face, partially obscuring his unseeing eyes.

"Rise at once. Bathe and attire yourself. Visit your wife and newborn children and pay them your due respects. It is a proud day for the House of Krushan. You have fathered the future heirs of our great lineage. You must hold your head up high, be seen by the people, celebrate, feast. Not skulk alone in your chambers, drinking yourself to bed each night and lying abed all day."

Adri raised his head, turning it toward her again. "I have no desire to do these things. I have no desire to do anything. I do not even wish to live."

"Enough. No prince of Krushan will speak like that. Get hold of yourself. Bathe and dress. The city awaits, the people gather outside, the empire watches."

Bitterly, he said, "What do I care about the city, the people, the empire? The only person I cared about was taken from me. My life is meaningless."

She stared at him, lips pursed tightly.

She leaned over the bed and stretched out her arm. She administered a sharp quick slap to his cheek, just hard enough that it shocked him, nothing more. The sound was loud in the empty chambers. Adri recoiled. She knew that for all that he had borne in his life, corporal punishment was never among the litany he had suffered.

"Enough!" Her words and tone were as sharp as the slap. "There will be no more of such talk. You are a prince of Krushan, crown prince of the empire. You are to be anointed in days. You will rise and assume your role in the House of Krushan and administer to your duties. I will not hear another word about your complaints and your troubles. Do you understand me?"

He sat holding the sheets with one hand, his own cheek with the other, staring unblinkingly at the bright verandah behind her. "Shvate has a son."

"What did you say?"

"We received word just before Geldry delivered. That was why she struck herself to hasten the birth. A hermit from the jungle brought the news that Shvate and his wives had produced a son."

"Yes, I am aware of this news. They have produced five children in all. What of it?"

"The eldest child was born before Geldry's children."

She observed the fact that he referred to his own children as "Geldry's" but chose to refrain from commenting just yet. "And so?"

"So Shvate's firstborn is the eldest heir. By Krushan law, that makes that child the heir to the Krushan throne, not Geldry's firstborn."

She folded her hands across her chest. There would be no more need for slapping: she could handle this with logic and words. "Shvate abdicated the throne to you and went into self-exile. You will be crowned samrat days from now. Your children will be the heirs to the throne, not Shvate's. The line runs from father to son. It doesn't jump to a nephew unless you have no more sons. As it so happens, you have one hundred and one heirs, so there is little chance of that possibility."

"I do not wish to ascend."

She unfolded her arms. Perhaps there would be need for another slap after all. "What did you just say?"

"I have no desire to rule. I have no wish to sit on the throne."

"I see. And what would you have us do?"

"Call Shvate back from exile. He only abdicated because of the rishi's curse. Now that he has fathered an heir, he can reassume his place in the lineage, ascend the throne. He is much better suited and more fit to rule than I. He is also the eldest, which means he is the legal heir by Krushan law. And after him, his eldest child can inherit once he or she is of age."

Jilana's palm itched, but she resisted the impulse. Slapping her blind grandson was not one of her prouder moments; she justified it by blaming herself for having failed to take a role in Adri's upbringing years earlier. But to repeat the act would be cruelty. *He's only feeling sorry for himself, as men do at such times. He just needs to be talked out of it.*

"Shvate abdicated. He named you. It was legally done and witnessed by all relevant parties, including myself. You were announced as the crown prince. Your ascension is scheduled, your wife has produced heirs — one hundred and one of them! There is no question of rolling back these events to cater to your self-pity. These are your responsibilities under Krushan law. You cannot simply wish them away because you are mourning a dead lover."

"She was my *wife!*" Adri cried, with startling vehemence. He lowered his voice. "Forgive my tone, Grandmother, I mean no disrespect. I am not saying these things because of Sauvali's . . . abduction. I was going to abdicate in any case. I have no stomach for politics. I simply wish to live my life in peace and quiet."

She took this in silently, but she was already shaking her head before he finished speaking, even though he could not see her. "Stomach or no, you were born into politics. That is your legacy, your heritage. It is your Krushan law to accept your responsibilities. Assume the throne. Embrace your wife. Raise your children. These are your given tasks. Accept them without protest or complaint."

"Like my mother accepted hers?" he asked, in such a hurt voice that it pierced her heart.

She was struck dumb. For a moment, she felt his pain, shared his deep, dark vision of the world, saw the bleak, unrelenting prospect of the years ahead, married to a wife who loved power and wealth far more than she loved him — if she loved him at all — living in the same palace as the mother whose loving touch he had never experienced even once in his life, abandoned by a brother who had once been his greatest protector and ally, grieving for the one woman he had truly loved and cherished, grieving for the unborn child he would never hold in his arms while being forced to father 101 children, ascend a throne he cared nothing for, make himself the target of every ruthless warlord in the world, only because it was Krushan law. She understood his bitterness, felt his pain, identified with his disgust at the political life and its endless compromises.

But she was Queen Mother, the widow of Sha'ant. The future of the House of Krushan lay in her hands, and her role demanded strength, not sympathy. She had to stay strong. Had Adri's mother done her job, she would have been the hard one here, while Jilana could have played the doting, indulgent grandmother. But there was only she, and she could not afford to let him feel, even for an instant, that this weakness was permissible.

"Just because she did not fulfill her Krushan law does not justify you failing to fulfill yours."

Adri was the silent one now.

After a long pause, he said finally, with resignation, "Kindly wait outside while I prepare myself."

Then, with a tone of rancor, he added, "Just because I can't see you, doesn't mean I give you the right to see me. In future, if you wish to see me, Grandmother, I suggest you send for me in the proper manner. Do not simply walk into my private chambers."

Jilana departed without further comment. Her cheeks burned at his last words. She knew that she had hurt him by not showing more sympathy, or even empathy. But she had accomplished what she had sought to do. Those last comments of his had contained enough anger in them to satisfy her. Anger was heat. Heat kept one alive and moving forward. She would make a king of Adri yet.

Whatever it took.

Vida

$\sim$

VIDA ENTERED VRATH'S CHAMBERS cautiously. There were no sentries posted at the doors, and the doors themselves lay wide open. It was the first time he had actually entered the prince regent's private chambers, and at first, he thought he had made some mistake, this could not possibly be where Vrath lived.

The chambers were in the center of the palace complex, surrounded by a mass of architecture — buildings, stables, compounds, hundreds of other chambers, quarters, offices, hallways. But when Vida walked in, he found himself in a vast open space. Above him was the sky, bright clear blue, filled with a variety of clouds of different shapes and forms at different heights. There was green grass underfoot and trees on both sides, where he would have expected there to be walls, and ahead was the riverbank, sloping down genially to the great Jeel herself. Vida stopped and looked over his shoulder at the entranceway he had come through. He took several steps till he could see the pillars just inside the open doors through which he had entered. Beyond those pillars was a long hallway leading back to the entrance of the building itself. It was inconceivable that there would be open fields, forest, grass, and the river here, in the heart of the Hastinaga palace complex. Impossible.

But as Vida had learned over the years, growing up in Hastinaga, impossible was not a concept that applied to the world he lived in. If there was one thing he was certain about, it was that *anything* was possible and *nothing* was impossible in Hastinaga. He had learned to keep an open mind and simply adapt.

He did so now, not turning around and gawking like most people would do, or exclaiming and calling out nervously. He simply walked down the riverbank to the riverside, where he presumed he would find the prince regent. Why there? Well, because Vrath was Vrath, son of the late Sha'ant and Jeel, the goddess of the river herself. It was only natural to expect to find Jeel's son by the Jeel itself.

He came around a bend in the Jeel and found what he sought.

Vrath was standing on the edge of the riverbank, talking to someone.

The person he was speaking to was a gigantic mass of living water, shaped and sculpted by invisible forces to form the shape and aspect of Jeel Goddess. The goddess herself stood before her son, risen from the river, its water forming to sculpt itself into a living moving being. Vida could see the water rippling and flowing through the "body" of water that stood several yards taller and larger than the flesh-and-blood man on the riverbank. He marveled at the sight for a brief instant, then, as the goddess's eyes flashed and turned toward him, Vida dropped his gaze and knelt down in respect.

"Forgive my intrusion, Goddess Jeel, Prince Vrath, I did not mean to interrupt."

Jeel's liquid form observed Vida for a moment. Even with his eyes lowered, he could feel the power of her gaze.

It is just as well, son of Vessa, for this concerns you as well. Come, join us.

Vida rose to his feet again, his heart pounding, and walked toward Vrath. The prince regent looked as regal and imposing as ever, his hard, handsome face and powerful body chiseled and carved with muscle and character: he appeared as solid and marbled as his mother appeared fluid, but both shared the same aura of immense, unimaginable power. Vida swallowed hard, nervous at being in the presence of such greatness. He had expected to bring his news to Vrath, speak for a few moments, and then be dismissed. He had not expected a darshan with the Mother Goddess herself.

"Good Vida," Vrath said with his booming, kindly voice. "I see you have brought news of Shvate."

Do I even need to speak it aloud? Surely he already knows everything there is to know already. What a fool I am, to think that I could learn information that a demigod and one of the greatest goddesses of the pantheon could not glean through their supernatural abilities.

Do not underestimate yourself. You too are a son of Vessa. You have gifts of your own that shall be revealed in time.

Vida was startled. He stared at the towering cascade of water in the shape of a woman. The water's movements perfectly imitated the flowing windblown garments of a woman and her open hair. He could even feel the genial breeze blowing across the river, ruffling his own hair and cooling the sudden patina of sweat that had sprung up on his brow.

Both Vrath and Jeel were looking at him expectantly.

"My lord, my lady," he said, hoping he had used the proper form of address. It was his first time meeting a goddess in person, after all. "I am pleased to inform you that Shvate and his wives, Karni and Mayla, have been delivered of five children."

The rushing, rippling water and wind rustling the leaves of the trees nearby were the only sounds for a moment. Then both Vrath and Jeel turned back toward each other. They exchanged a look that suggested they had no need of words to communicate to each other. Vida could clearly see from the way they looked at each other that they were *talking* somehow, but he was not privy to their conversation.

He waited patiently.

When several moments had passed, he began to wonder if perhaps he ought to take his leave. After all, he had come to deliver a message and that message was delivered now. He felt completely redundant.

He was just starting to work up the nerve to take a step backward when Vrath turned toward him again.

"Vida."

Vida said nothing, waiting for the prince regent to continue.

"There is a storm coming."

Vida's first instinct was to turn and look across the river, at the open sky. He could see no storm brewing there, though some of those clouds at the far western horizon were dark and brooding. But he knew that was not what Vrath meant.

He turned back to the prince regent, nodding once. "I understand."

"You must go to your brother Shvate at once. Warn him."

"What shall I say, my lord?"

"Tell him to expect danger. A violent assault. Perhaps even an army."

"An army?" Vida was alarmed. "But Shvate is alone, with just Karni and Mayla. The only people nearby are the hermits and novices of the hermitage where they live. There is no one else to help them — not for many miles. How will they face an army?"

Jeel regarded him, turning her head for a better look. Vida saw her in his field of vision quite clearly, even the large watery eyes in her watery face, but kept his own gaze fixed on Vrath's reassuringly human features.

They are strong fighters. Shvate is a son of Vessa. His wives are warrior queens. They will not yield easily.

Vrath regarded his mother. "Perhaps Vida has a point. They are only three, with limited weapons, and they have spent a great deal of time in the forest without any active combat."

"And they are burdened with five infant children!" Vida said, unable to help himself. "How will they fight and care for the children of Shvate?"

Burdened, Jeel repeated, a tone of liquid amusement in her words. **Burdened, he says.** A silvery tinkling sound issued from her flowing mouth.

Vida came to the hesitant conclusion that he was being laughed at by a goddess.

"They are babies," he said defensively.

Vrath's rugged features twitched in a ghost of a smile. "Babies. Yes. But they are Krushan."

It is not the *burdensome* infants I am concerned for, good Vida, Jeel said. **It is their parents.**

Vida blinked. "Their parents? Yes, of course, I too am concerned for my brother Shvate and my sisters-in-law Karni and Mayla. They are strong fighters all, but only three. If, as you say, an army is going to assault them, they will need help."

Vrath and Jeel both considered him silently. Again, he had the impression that their conversation was continuing exclusive of his participation. He waited, not wanting to speak when they were speaking.

Finally, when they had just been staring at him for several minutes without further communication, he felt compelled to express himself.

"We must send help," he said at last. "Elephants, chariots, cavalry, foot soldiers, materials to enable them to fortify the position and help defend Shvate, Karni, and Mayla against any attack."

Vrath moved slightly. "Yes, we shall send help."

Indeed. It is vital that the son of Vessa be protected. His survival is the key to preventing the Great War. If he lives, then that calamity can be averted.

Vida nodded with relief, even though he had absolutely no idea what Jeel Goddess meant by a "Great War." He did not expect her to explain it to him, nor did he ask for details. He accepted that the gods and demigods possessed knowledge of future and past and even parallel events that mere mortals could not possibly know. "With your permission, I can muster a full akshohini. Or two, if you deem it necessary."

Vrath looked at him silently for a long moment. "Yes, yes, an akshohini would be adequate, that is true. Two would be even better."

Vida nodded, relieved. "Very well, my lord. I shall use your name to command them to assemble and march for the forest at once."

"No."

Vida stared at Vrath. The prince regent's expression had not changed. "My lord?"

"No." This time there was a softer tone to the single word, an inflection of . . . sadness perhaps. "There shall be no akshohinis. None of Hastinaga's armies shall be mustered to go to Shvate's aid."

Vida's head reeled. "My lord!" He struggled for appropriate words. "But you yourself said that an army was going to attack my brother in the forest!"

A very powerful and deadly army, one without honor or regard for warrior Krushan and the rules of war.

"Yes, an army," Vrath acknowledged.

"Then we must send help!"

"We *shall* send help," Vrath agreed. "But no army, no troops, no soldiers, no weapons."

Vida stared at him. "Then how will we help my brother and his wives? How will they overcome this army?"

Vrath and Jeel both regarded him silently for another long moment. Just when Vida was about to break the silence, they both spoke to him almost at once.

You.

"You, Vida. We will send *you* to the forest to help them."

Kune

~

1

KUNE WORKED HIS WAY through the crowd as he always did, pausing to mutter a few words here, another line or three there, moving along steadily. The important thing was to keep moving always.

Krushan politics was stagnated after decades of politics and ingrained loyalties. Everyone came to these Council meetings and headed directly for their usual group of fellow political allies, then spent the rest of their time engaged with them in conversation, sat together with them, went to lunch and meals with them, and voted and vetoed with them as well. At most, they nodded curtly to their rivals in passing, or smiled phony smiles at the more powerful enemies in other factions, other caucuses. *Everyone in their own pens, like sheep, pigs, horses, chickens, buffalo, all separated neatly and fatted for the reaping. Fools!*

These deeply etched lines were a tremendous opportunity waiting to be exploited. He had seen that the very first time he had visited Hastinaga. All these alliances and caucuses went back decades, even centuries in the case of some of the older more venerated Houses. It made things so simple, so easy. With everything laid out so neatly and clearly, he felt like a butcher walking into a breeding farm. All he had to do was choose his victims and cull them from the various pens.

Slaughtering them was the easiest part and had been accomplished within his first several months at the palace. Whatever was required, he had done. In some cases, it involved gold changing hands. In other cases, it required subtler methods: blackmail, intimidation, late-night visits and threats, warnings delivered with hard fists and harder sticks. And in a few exceptional cases, it required something more decisive: physical violence, sexual assault, a dismembering, even an assassination or two.

In all but the most stubborn cases, his methods had worked. He had made inroads into all the major groups and caucuses, insinuating his influence through proxies, changing the balance of power when it suited him. He did not actually use these new channels of influence very much in the early months. The point was not to take the low-hanging fruit. He was building toward much bigger things, and that required tucking away chits in his pockets and then flashing them at the right time — months, even years in the future. That was why the methods were so excessive: it was important to make sure that the person or persons understood the commitment he required. Whenever he called on them to vote or veto as he desired, he had to be sure they would deliver. The violence ensured that they would not forget and would not dare cross him.

Publicly, he did as he was doing now: working his way through Council, seeming to spend all his time bantering genially and maintaining good relations with everyone, regardless of political affiliation or alliance. To see him like this, glad-handing everyone, smiling, moving through the crowd of important personalities, you would assume he was a good-looking and charming but naive politician. The bumpkin Geldran brother-in-law of the future queen of the realm, using his sister's position to try to ingratiate himself with the High Houses of the capital. Perhaps he hoped to make some coin here and there — a commission on setting up a new trade route, a slice of the profit in an overseas military alliance — or even to snare the pretty daughter of a major House as his bride someday. He was everybody's friend, the Nice Man, happily clueless about the real business of administration and the complex interwoven web of Krushan politics.

That was exactly what he wanted them to think.

Naturally, he was the very opposite of what he seemed.

He finished a full circuit and paused briefly, flashing a bright smile at the middle-aged councilwoman wife of an elderly councilman, both of different, equally illustrious Houses. He acknowledged her discreet wink with a twinkle in his eyes, then met the sneer on her husband's face with the same charming smile. He had bedded the wife three nights ago, under her husband's own roof. The husband's House was the more important one in terms of lineage, but he had frittered away all the family fortune due to a compulsive gambling addiction. Kune had moved in on the wife, convincing her that her best interest lay in voting with the caucus he represented when the time came and convincing her husband to do the same. The alternative plan was to buy out the husband's gambling debts and use them as leverage, but it was much easier — and more pleasurable — to let the wife seduce him instead. Sometimes, it took honey to catch a fly rather than a flytrap.

Kune reached the end of the Council chamber and dropped his smile for a moment.

He had completed his full circuit, exchanging his usual pleasantries and banalities with everyone that mattered, all intended to subtly remind each one of their "deal" and that he was watching, always watching. But he was missing one crucial person.

Vida.

While only a councilman, and not actually a scion or head of any major House, Vida was far more important than his administrative status indicated. He was half brother to Adri and Shvate, which made him a part of House Krushan. Even though he was illegitimate in birth and incapable of ever ascending to the throne, he still wielded influence within the family. Indeed, more influence than even he knew. The man's naiveté had shocked Kune at first. How could someone so well placed not realize what opportunities lay before him? He had been sure that Vida's bumbling, self-effacing personality was an act, a front to cover up his true sinister motives. It was only after weeks of study that he had finally, reluctantly, concluded that it was no act. Vida was in fact a bumbling self-effacing personality. He was that most nauseating of types: a good man.

Kune hated such people.

The world was a cold, cruel, unforgiving place, much like the high plains and mountains of his native homeland. There was no room for kindness, gentility, sensitivity, consideration, humanity, or self-sacrifice.

Yet Vida embodied all these qualities and worse.

He was the one kind of person on whom none of Kune's usual methods were effective. An honest, incorruptible politician.

In earlier instances, other places where Kune had encountered such individuals, he had dealt with them very simply: murder. It was the only way to eliminate a good, honest person. Blackmail led to outrage. Assault, abduction, intimidation, even harming family members, all led only to the good person becoming more stubborn, righteous, determined to bring the "evil man" to "justice." As if such a thing existed in the world of politics! Only murder silenced the threat and removed that piece cleanly from the chaupat board.

Kune loved chaupat; it was the perfect game to exercise one's political talents. Chariots, elephants, horses, foot soldiers — four cadres corresponding to the four cadres of the army in reality. Through an infinite combination of moves between two equally numbered sets of pieces moving across a checkered board shaped like a cross, chaupat was an endlessly challenging sport. It was also the game of choice for all the biggest gamblers, most of whom also happened to be the biggest aristocrats, nobles, and politicians.

Evenings typically found Kune engrossed in a succession of chaupat games at various High Houses. He had an endless series of invitations from all the Houses to visit and play, and had gained a reputation for being the most desirable player in Hastinaga. This was partly because he was always great company: cracking jokes, telling entertaining stories, and sharing spicy gossip.

But mostly it was because he was a profitable loser. That is to say, he played reasonably well — up to a point. Then he lost. And because he always bet large sums, he always lost big. This was what capped his desirability as a chaupat player. Who wouldn't love a devilishly handsome, charming, entertaining, good-natured, and *rich* bumpkin who *always* bet huge sums, and *always* lost. And lost graciously!

Kune had dropped a small fortune on his chaupat games alone. Perhaps even a large fortune, by Geldran standards. But it was all in pursuit of a good cause. He was studying his opponents and learning their techniques and moves. By making himself so popular, he was able to play all the best players in the city, which meant the best players in the world, and in doing so amass a great store of useful knowledge about each one. The variations of game technique were always useful, but the information about the players was invaluable.

Kune had spent much of his youth gambling, and while he had not played chaupat till he came to Hastinaga, his gambling technique was the same: lose, lose, lose . . . then win it all back and *then some.*

When the time was right, he would start winning. Not just gold, not just a few fistfuls of coin; he was after much more than mere wealth. He wanted everything there was to have. He would often stop at random villages while traveling, find out what their favorite pastime was, then lay odds on whatever excited people the most. He followed the same technique, losing lavishly to lure them in, then suddenly turning the table with one massive win, shocking everyone. He had once walked away with the entire grain harvest of a village, leaving the villagers with nothing to see them through the cold, harsh winter. When the villagers "disagreed" with his win and accused him of cheating, taking up their weapons and challenging him to a fight, he had backed off and walked away with his usual handsome grin. That night, while they slept, he had crept back into the village and set their houses on fire. The next time he passed that way, there was nothing left but charred timbers and a lot of skeletons, buried by the heavy snowfall. "You play, you pay," he spat at the burned timbers as he rode by. It was his maxim, his words to live by.

Right now, he was missing a key player in this particular game: Vida. He ought to have been here, but it was almost time for Council to go into session and he was still not present in the chambers.

Kune spotted a clerk in the secretariat hall adjoining Council Hall. The munshis were scribes tasked with keeping records of every Council session, decision, vote, argument, legislation, writ, account, and what have you. The shelves against the far walls groaned under the weight of scrolls, but the real meat was to be had from the munshis themselves: there was always anecdotal information that was more valuable than the written records. Kune hated scribes because their work involved words and language, which made them almost as bad as poets and painters, or musicians and dancers. He loathed art and its makers, considering them the most despicable form of human life. But despite his personal hatred, he had begun cultivating the munshis.

He spotted one of these scribes at work, seated cross-legged on a mat on the floor, writing with a quill pen. He was one of hundreds in the large hall, all hard at work. Kune imagined a company of chariots riding through the hall, crushing and smashing all these useless writers to pieces. The thought made him smile, and he flashed the smile at the clerk as he approached. The clerk, a slight, balding young man with a potbelly and thin, emaciated limbs, peered up at him. He nodded as Kune came close enough for his eyes to focus.

"What news, clerk?"

The scribe spread his ink-stained hands in a helpless gesture, then launched into a tiresome explanation of the current legislation on wheat harvest tithes in the southeastern kingdoms. Kune pretended to listen, nodding and smiling while thinking of how easily the clerk's bald head could be smashed by an elephant's foot.

He had once seen a man executed in that manner. The elephant was traditionally the symbolic beast of the Burnt Empire, considered the keeper of wisdom. When a monarch heard a particularly troubling case in court and was unsure of the party's guilt or innocence, they could call for the Elephant's Justice. This simply meant having the accused kneel down and place their head upon a stone slab, and letting the royal elephant decide their fate. If the accused was innocent, the elephant would do nothing. If guilty, the elephant would bring its foot down on the person's head, crushing their skull. Kune loved the concept: he saw it as a brilliant way to dispense justice to anyone who vexed you, while making it seem as if the verdict was declared by the wise elephant. He was biding his time to propose introducing the method in Hastinaga as well. What a shrewd way to get rid of people: let the elephant decide. Right now, he wished he had an elephant handy to shut the clerk up.

Finally losing patience, he cut off the scribe in midsentence, saying curtly, "Councilman Vida was not in session today."

The clerk frowned at him, peering in that irritating nearsighted way that all scribes had. "Councilman Vida is always present." He looked down at the scroll he had been transcribing. "His attendance record is perfect. Out of two hundred and forty-eight sessions last year—"

"I'm not asking about last year," Kune said, straining to keep his smile intact and his temper in check. "I'm asking about now. Today. It is customary for councilpersons to inform the secretariat if they are called away on urgent business, is it not?"

"Yes, but Councilman Vida has never sought leave before. He was present for every single one of the two hundred and forty-eight sessions last year."

Kune continued smiling at the clerk. "Could you check for me?" He added, with a show of teeth, "Please."

The clerk started to shake his head, then saw something in Kune's smile that changed his mind. He nodded and left his mat to go over to one of the other scribes in the far corner of the hall. The other scribes continued working, the hall filled with the sound of rustling scrolls, scratching quills, and the little sounds that scribes made, coughing, clearing their throats, breathing noisily, scratching. Kune was starting to imagine burning down the entire hall when the clerk finally returned, walking slowly enough for even a lame horse to overtake.

"It appears that Councilman Vida has sought a leave of absence from Council," he admitted. "This is highly unusual. Quite unlike him. Now, according to the scribe who keeps the attendance rolls —"

Kune gritted his teeth and said, "Did he give a reason? For the leave of absence?"

The clerk blinked. "Why? I do believe he may have." He scratched the sparse hair on the side of his head, dislodging flakes of dandruff. "What was it the scribe of attendance said? Ah, yes, something about going to the forest to visit his brother."

Kune clutched the man's thin arm hard. "Are you sure?"

The scribe's face twisted. "Lord Kune, my arm."

Kune squeezed harder. "He went to visit his brother in the forest? His brother Shvate?"

"I . . . believe so. My arm . . . that hurts."

Kune released him. He patted the clerk's arm, smiling again. "My apologies. Well done." He took a small cloth bag of coin and dropped it on the clerk's writing board. "Thank you for your time."

He left the hall, swearing under his breath.

2

Kune found Geldry in her chambers, being tended to by five maids at once. One was working on her hair, two on her hands, two on her feet. A trio of Geldran musicians were playing in the antechamber as Kune passed through it. They paused to greet him, and he nodded in passing. Geldry was lying back, looking up at the ceiling and she saw him upside down as he entered.

"Brother?" she asked, reading his mood at once.

Kune looked at the quintet of maids busy buffing, polishing, painting, clipping, cleaning. "We should talk."

Geldry sighed. "Can it wait awhile . . ." She saw his expression. "I suppose not. All of you, out. Wait outside till I summon you back in. And tell the musicians to stop playing."

They filed out quickly. A moment later, the doors shut and the music ceased.

Kune paced back and forth. "Vida has gone to the forest to see Shvate."

"Is that so?" Geldry asked. She sat up slowly, pausing to sip at a goblet of wine. She was wearing only a robe and nothing underneath. It fell open as she sat up, but she didn't bother to close the folds.

Kune strode to and fro, agitated. "I wasn't counting on that happening. It wasn't in my plans."

Geldry shrugged. "These things happen. Change your plans."

"I can't." He stopped and looked at her accusingly. "You know the kind of people we're dealing with. These are not people you simply send a message to at the last minute and change the plan."

"Why not? We're paying them well enough. Speaking of which, the butcher's bill is mounting day by day. Add to that the fortune you've been losing in chaupat in the Upper City, and the other fortune you've been throwing around in the Senate and the Council, and it's a king's ransom."

"Even if it was an *emperor's* ransom, it would be worth it. This is the Burnt Empire we're talking about, not some little fiefdom in Aranya." The word "Aranya" meant wilderness but was also the collective name given to the forest kingdoms in the remote South.

"The Burnt Empire is ours. What I don't understand is why we need to spend so much when we already have it. Adri will be crowned in two days." She saw his face change and waved her hand. "I know you've explained this to me before, but you know I can never understand all your plots and schemes. How do you even plan a hundred or two hundred moves ahead? I just don't get it."

Kune sighed. "This is about control. About being able to make things happen the way we want them to happen, *when* we want them."

She shrugged. "If you say so."

He looked around the bedchamber. It was filled with the usual piles of new attire, boxes and boxes of jewelry, footwear, accessories, and other accoutrements. "I see you are celebrating the end of your confinement."

"I spent almost two years carrying that . . . thing . . . in my body," she said, shivering as she remembered. She patted her flat belly proudly. "I deserve to pamper myself."

"Yes, you do, sister, but refrain from calling your children 'things.' Krushan who overhear you won't appreciate their future kings and queen being referred to as objects."

She gestured at the empty chamber. "Nobody here but you and me, brother."

"Has Adri been in to see you yet?"

"No, and I don't care if never comes." Her voice and face took on a snarl. "After he shared the bed of that common woman, I wouldn't touch him even if he begged."

"Again, speak with care. You're talking about the crown prince, about to be sworn in as king of Hastinaga."

"You mean emperor of Hastinaga."

"Hastinaga is the kingdom that controls the Burnt Empire. The king of Hastinaga *is* the emperor of the Burnt Empire."

"Or queen," she said thoughtfully.

He looked at her.

She smiled craftily, and Kune returned it in kind.

"Or queen," he agreed.

"Adri has been keeping to himself of late," she said, still thoughtful. "He has been drinking, not taking care of his health, eating erratically. He is grieving, confused, has lost the will to live. If he were to fall off his verandah one night while inebriated, or choke on his food . . ." She looked at her brother again, her eyes shining. "It would seem only inevitable. Kings have died of lesser mishaps before."

Kune shook his head slowly. "Not while they have elder brothers who still have some legitimate claim to the throne."

She pouted. "I thought that was all settled. Shvate abdicated, all parties concur."

"Even so, as long as he remains alive, there are loyalists who may argue that he still has a claim. After all, his abdication was not forced upon him, it was voluntary."

"What difference does that make?"

"What is given voluntarily can be taken back."

She winced. "You mean . . . ? But I thought . . . He won't actually come back and claim the throne, will he? Do you really think he might?"

"I don't think he would, but he has a wife. Two wives in fact." He smiled at her by twitching only one cheek. "And some wives are more ambitious than their husbands."

She made a face. "Karni and Mayla."

"Both princesses, highborn, both strong warrior queens in their own rights. And now, both mothers."

"Ah," she said, understanding.

"Exactly. Where a wife may accept her husband forgoing his birthright and inheritance, a mother may see it as depriving her children of *their* birthright and inheritance."

Geldry rose, walking across the room to pick up a row of gold bangles. Her robe opened wide, revealing her naked body. It was as slender and sleek as it had been before she was pregnant, Kune noted. "So you think they may persuade Shvate to come back and reclaim the throne for the sake of the children?"

"Wouldn't you?"

She tried on a large, heavy bangle decorated with green gemstones, sliding it up and down her slender forearm to admire it. "I see your point. But with your plan, that won't happen. Because your people will take care of Shvate, Karni, Mayla, the children — all of them in one quick blow." She made a neck-slicing gesture.

He glanced around. "Caution, sister. Even walls have ears."

"You took care that the attack will never be traced back to you, to us," she said. "Did you not?"

"Was the attack on Riverdell ever linked with us?" he asked.

She looked at him, smiled, and shrugged. "Why would it be? We had nothing to do with it. Those were mercenaries seeking to abduct a royal hostage for ransom, that's all."

"And they just happened to take the wrong woman, believing that they were abducting you, Queen Geldry," he added, smiling. "Which was proven when the ransom demand was made, asking that Hastinaga pay a wagonload of gold if we wanted Queen Geldry back safe and sound."

"And why in the world would you or I want to have me abducted, risking my life and the life of my unborn children, only to earn a ransom which amounts to a fraction of our wealth?" She batted her eyelashes, mimicking a look of utter innocence.

"Exactly. So in the same way, whatever happens in the jungle to Shvate and his family, stays in the jungle. It has nothing to do with us, my sister dear."

Geldry tried on a succession of bangles, each heavier and more richly decorated with precious stones. "Then the sooner it happens, the sooner we are rid of the threat of Shvate or his wives returning to reclaim the throne." She swung around, the open folds of the robe flying. "Maybe then we can talk about Adri having his unfortunate mishap?"

He shrugged. "Perhaps not. I think Adri staying alive makes a valuable asset. So long as he lives, no one else can claim the throne."

"Who else is there?"

"No one perhaps. But one never knows with royalty. There's always a bastard somewhere, often more than one. Even the high and mighty Jilana had an illegitimate son by Shapaar before going on to marry his son Sha'ant later! Did Sha'ant even know about Vessa? Who knows! In any case, so long as Adri is on the throne, your position is secure."

"And yours, dear brother," she said sweetly.

He smiled. "I live to serve, sweet sister."

"So what are you going to do about the Vida problem?" she asked.

He grinned at her sudden change of subject. "Someone has been paying attention. Yes, Vida is a problem."

"Why? Won't he simply be eliminated along with Shvate and his family —" She deliberately raised her voice, adding, "If anything were to happen to them, Stone God forbid."

"That's just it," Kune said, "I don't want him eliminated. He's knowledgeable, resourceful, and can never be a direct threat to us because as a bastard, he has no legitimate claim to the throne or any position of his own."

"He sounds like a pet."

"A very intelligent, well-connected pet. The kind you want to keep by your side if you intend to rule for a long, long time."

"So you want to keep him alive," she said, "but the dogs of war have already been unleashed, and now you can't call them off."

"Something like that." Kune paced to and fro, thinking furiously while his sister continued to try on an assortment of jewelry. "Why did he go out to the hermitage? Why plan this visit just when this is about to happen?"

"Maybe he went to warn them?"

Kune stopped pacing and stared at her.

"Maybe he learned of the attack somehow and went to the forest to let Shvate know."

"He took no soldiers with him, no weapons. Only a horse and enough food and water for the journey. I checked with the stables and the gate-watch. He can't help them. Even a full company of soldiers couldn't help them now. The dogs of war, as you put it, are just too many and they must be already converging as we speak. By tonight, at best tomorrow, they will be there, and any additional help Vida may want to muster will arrive too late."

"What was it you once said about Vida? He's not a fighter, he's an advisor? Maybe he hasn't gone there to offer a military defense; maybe he's gone just to warn them."

Kune frowned. "But how would that help?"

"Once they knew they were going to be attacked, they could flee the jungle. Escape."

"Escape to where?" Kune shook his head. "And Shvate wouldn't do that. He's a warrior, and so is Mayla. They would stand and fight to the death rather than show their backs to an enemy."

"Even if they're vastly outnumbered? Even if their children's lives are at stake?"

Kune wasn't convinced. "Even if they tried to escape, there isn't time. It will take Vida at least a full day and night to reach them. By that time, they will be surrounded. They can try running in any direction for a hundred miles, they won't get away. This isn't Riverdell, this is a very large-scale attack. And it was planned by an expert at tactics and strategy." He tapped his own shoulder to make the point clear.

Geldry rolled her eyes. "Control your ego, brother. Very well, if Vida knows of the attack, then he must also know that he would arrive too late. So then why is he going?"

Kune shook his head in frustration. "I don't know. I can't make sense of it. That's why I came to you."

She took off the armful of gold bangles, dropping them carelessly into the box with a loud clatter. Several fell on the marble floor, rolling this way and that. "Well, I can't make sense of it either. Let's just wait and see. In another day or two, we'll know. And whatever happens, it will be too late to stop the coronation."

Kune was chewing his nails as he paced some more. "I suppose so."

A maid called out from outside the door. "Princess Geldry!"

Geldry frowned. "I left orders that I was not to be disturbed," she said. "I will have that one whipped —"

"*Enter . . . Crown Prince Adri!*" cried the sentries as the doors swung open.

Adri

~

WHEN GELDRY AND HE had shared this same chambers and bed, Adri had known the location of every item of furniture. After he moved into his own chambers, he knew Geldry must have rearranged everything to suit her own convenience. That was only natural. Now, after all that had passed between them, to walk into this chamber again felt strange, uncomfortable, distasteful. But it was he who had left and had cohabited with another, not Geldry, and so he accepted that it was he who should be the one to return and try to make amends.

Mother Jilana did not have to convince him of this, at least. If Adri had had his way, he would not have done anything. He was content to simply pine and waste away to nothing. Life felt pointless without Sauvali. He did not *want* to go back to Geldry. He did not want to get out of bed, to bathe, to dress, to leave his chambers. But if he was to do so, then he agreed that he ought to start with his wife's bedchamber. It was the right thing to do, and Adri had been brought up to do the right thing, even if others did not always do the same.

"Geldry," he said now, stopping just inside the door. He had no wish to stumble over furniture. "It is I."

He was met by silence at first. He knew she was in the chamber. He had distinctly heard the sound of something heavy and metallic falling and rolling on the floor only moments before he entered. And the maids and sentries had all reacted to his approach and begun whispering to each other that he had come to visit the princess, so he knew she was here.

"Husband," she replied finally. "It is good to see you."

He turned toward the sound of her voice. She sounded as if she was sitting down. He noted her choice of words. Was it literal or merely figurative? In the beginning of their marriage, he would have simply walked over to her and touched her head and face, feeling the soft cloth of the eyeband wound tightly and the surge of pleasure that came from knowing she still wore it. It had come to symbolize her love for him, her loyalty. Skeptical at first, he had come to feel pleased by its constant presence.

Now he no longer felt he was entitled to touch her, let alone expect her to be wearing it. Perhaps she was, perhaps she wasn't. What difference did it make anyway? *Perhaps nothing, perhaps everything.* But he could not do it: it would seem too petty, too insecure of him.

"And you," he responded, throwing her own contradiction back at her with a dollop of irony added. "Are you well?"

"As well as can be expected," she shot back with scarcely a pause. From long experience, he knew that when she was angry with him, she spoke in this rapid-response manner, throwing words like darts at him faster than he could catch them. She was angry now, which was not surprising. He had expected that. She had every right to be angry.

"I have been neglectful of my husbandly duties," he said. "I should have visited you sooner."

"Visited . . ." she replied, leaving the word hanging there without comment, which itself was a comment. "Yes, husbands should visit their wives from time to time. So we don't forget each other's faces."

Again, a barb directed at his infirmity. The first time he had been unsure; this time he was certain. She was deliberately reminding him that he was blind and she was not. So be it. She was entitled to her barbs and darts, her petty show of insouciance.

"I was given the news of your birthing our sons and daughter. It is a proud day for us as parents, and for our kingdom."

"Indeed."

"I trust your recovery is going well."

"Quite."

"Is there anything you require? Anything at all that can comfort you and ease your recovery?"

"If I require anything, I shall ask for it. Thank you."

"Is there anything I can do personally to assist?"

Silence for a moment, then: "I seem to have dropped one of my bracelets. It is fallen over by your foot. Could you pick it up and hand it to me?"

He stiffened. He had not expected *this*.

She had made it clear that she was not binding her eyes anymore. Or had she? How else could she have known that the bracelet was by his foot? By the sound? Well, possibly, after all, he too could tell where something had fallen by the sound. But even if she had detected its location by sound and was still wearing the eyeband, her asking him to pick it up was still a slap in the face. That was something one asked a maid to do. Not a husband, a prince, a king, an emperor. Just as he would never have asked her to pick up something for him, she too ought not to have made such a request.

But she had.

And now that she had made the request, he had only two choices: to refuse outright, which would seem churlish of him. Or to do it as gracefully as possible, which was not easy.

"Of course," he said, trying to make his voice seem casual, unaffected. "Which foot?"

"The right foot," she said, then added coyly, "I think."

So she was still pretending that she had the eyeband on. Perhaps she did, at that. Very well. He bent down slowly, crouched, and felt around his right foot. The marble floor felt cold to his touch. He had been feeling a little feverish after the bath. His head throbbed too. He had drunk a great deal of wine over a great many days. It did not help his balance or sense of hearing.

His fingers found nothing except the cold marble floor.

"It does not appear to be here," he said, still trying to sound casual, but hearing the tone of accusation and a slight touch of anger in his own voice.

"Oh," she said, with careless ease. "Perhaps the left foot, then."

He felt around his left foot, with the same results. "Not here either. You were mistaken, my dear. It does not appear to be here."

He stood up and felt his head reel. He staggered slightly and was forced to take a step sideways to stabilize himself. His left foot came down on something hard and encrusted with sharp pointy stones. Not sharp enough to cut skin, but sharp enough that they hurt when stepped on. He swore and lifted his foot to step aside again.

"Are you well, husband dearest?" she asked in that singsong voice she used when being ironic or truly cruel.

He swallowed a retort that he knew he would have regretted later. Not regretted saying, but having given her the satisfaction of knowing she had made him lose his self-control. He bent down again, even though his head throbbed and his senses swam, and picked up the errant bracelet. It felt more like a very large bangle, something heavy and studded with gemstones.

"I found your bracelet, dearest," he said.

He walked over to where she was seated, hoping that there were no impediments in his path. He arrived without any further mishap. He could hear her soft breathing.

He held out the bangle. "Your jewelry."

She snatched it from his hand so forcefully, he felt the bangle scrape his knuckle. She set it down hard on some glass surface. "Thank you."

He smiled to himself. "Shall we visit the children together, good wife?"

He distinctly heard her inhale and exhale more than once, as if trying to regain control. He heard her gesture as well — the whisper of her robe against her bare skin was a familiar sound to him, even though it had been so long since he had heard it — but could not make sense of the movement. When she did it again, he felt a chill encase his heart.

There was someone else in the room.

He listened carefully, his senses attuned now. But his throbbing head and the other aftereffects of the wine had impaired his ability to "see" accurately. He could not be certain of it, but he thought perhaps — just perhaps — there was a sound from near the verandah that could have been a foot scuffing the marble floor.

"Wife?" he asked, hearing the tremor in his voice.

"Yes," she replied shortly, "Yes, of course. Pray allow me a moment to attire myself suitably."

He heard the familiar sounds of her dressing. The sound of her arms and limbs moving against silk, the sound of her shoe scuffing the floor. *It must have been those sounds you heard, the sounds of her dressing.*

But he knew his first instinct had been correct. There *was* someone else in the room. Yet he could think of no way to find out for certain without inquiring on the matter directly. And he had no wish to do so.

Instead, he waited silently and patiently, until his wife came toward him and took his arm, just as she always had in the past, and spoke softly in his ear, as she used to. "Shall we?"

Vessa

~

1

VESSA ROARED WITH FURY as he emerged from the portal. Behind him lay a strange alien world of islands upon an ocean of lava. The ocean blazed and flared with explosions, sending geysers of steaming lava thousands of yards into the air. The island he was leaving was little more than a heap of slag on the volcanic ocean. The heat was so tremendous that the part of the forest into which he emerged in our world was completely seared in moments: the trees burst into flame, the grass turned to ash, and the blast of hot air killed every living thing for a hundred yards in every direction.

Yet somehow, his hair, beard, long flowing red-ochre robes, wooden shoes, and wildwood staff remained unburned and whole. He roared with frustration and fury, giving vent to the anger he felt from yet another failed attempt at chasing down his quarry. It had been years now since he began pursuing the self-declared God-Emperor of Reygistan, and each time he came within grabbing distance of the urrkh, Jarsun somehow managed to slip out of his grasp. This time, the Reygistani had led him on a merry dance across hundreds of parallel universes, from icebound moons to glass mountaintops so tall that their peaks extended into airless space, to the dark bottoms of dense oceans where no light had ever penetrated and gigantic monstrous creatures ruled through brutal domination, to chemical swamps where strange creatures spat poisonous venom at each other in an endless ritual feud, to lands where the sun was deep red and the people slithered on fins on perpetually wet land under year-round monsoon skies, and finally, after dozens of near encounters and at least one sorcerous skirmish, to the volcanic ocean world from which he had just come.

He uttered a stream of curses that would have turned any mage's ears red, striding through the blazing forest. As a burning tree fell with a crackling impact, he grew aware of the damage caused by his arrival and raised his staff again, uttering a mantra that brought down a sudden rain shower. As the cool downpour doused the fire and prevented it from spreading further, his temper cooled too. One does not become a seer-mage if one is unable to curb one's emotions, and it was rare enough for Vessa to lose his temper, but the past years had tested his patience to the limit.

Jarsun had to be stopped. The demonlord had inflicted much damage on the Krushan already, and his insidious influence was taking a toll on Vessa's own biological children, Shvate, Adri, and Vida, as well as his mother, Jilana, and the rest of the imperial family of Hastinaga. Vessa had made it his mission to stop the Reygistani and slay him before he inflicted further harm, but thus far his attempts had been unsuccessful. Failure was not something the seer-mage was accustomed to experiencing, and he did not take it well.

He gestured again, shutting off the rain to avoid overhydrating this section of the forest, and continued walking. His tall, lanky form, long robes, and great strides made it appear as if he was floating across the forest floor. Animals and insects that marked his passing watched with tense anticipation. His power was palpable, his anger still not entirely doused. Only once he passed by did the birds resume their twittering, did the leaves breathe again, did the insects and animals move about their daily business of foraging, eating, mating. This was one of the world's most ancient forests, its high canopy dense enough in some places that only a few rays of sunlight could pass through to reach the forest floor. Strange exotic species grew and flourished here that were not to be found anywhere else in the Burnt Empire — or anywhere else in this world. Vessa walked through dense green parts where no human had ever set foot before, but he was too engrossed in his contemplation to take notice of all the wonders of the natural world. It was the unnatural doings of his enemy that occupied him.

Hastinaga was not the only kingdom plagued by the demonlord's evil attacks. All lands and people that adored Krushan were equally under threat. Jarsun was no ordinary villain seeking to amass power, wealth, land by any means; he was an urrkh, the most powerful of demon species, reborn in this age to try to end Krushan itself. His minions were legion, his works unspeakable in their horror and violence, his misdeeds legendary. He had built an empire of evil, corrupting the name of the ancient Reygistani Empire and making it feared and hated by decent people everywhere. He commanded great armies of mortal soldiers who were in fact demons reborn in human form. If he were to invade Hastinaga, he would wreak devastation on a vast scale, as he had already done to many inner kingdoms of the continent.

The only reason he was not invading was because his main attention was focused on another city-nation that was giving him great resistance: Mraashk, capital of the Yadu nation. Jarsun's plans for Mraashk and the Yadu people had been staunchly opposed first by the Yadu king Suvaa and his allies, and now by Suvaa's son Avasi.

No ordinary mortal, Avasi was nothing less than a full reincarnation of the great god Vish, the Protector of Worlds, God Himself, descended from the heavenly realms to rid the world of the last of the urrkh. His struggle was ongoing, as Jarsun's seemingly infinite resources of power continued to inflict great loss of life and dignity on the suffering people of Mraashk. But on the other hand, the fierce resistance of Avasi and his half brother in Mraashk kept Jarsun from unleashing his full malice on Hastinaga.

Vessa grew impatient with mere physical walking and transported himself in the blink of an eye — and the utterance of a single mantra — a dozen yojanas away to a point closer to his destination. He disappeared from one place and appeared in the other without breaking his stride. His appearance startled a bustle of hedgehogs who scurried into their holes in panic.

He raised his head, sending out his aura to study the region, in the event, however unlikely, that there might be any trace of urrkh maya here. He found none. That was a relief. He had uttered powerful mantras, performed an ancient fire sacrifice, and created a circle of protection around a wide swath of forest, all to ensure that his wards were unharmed by mortal or urrkh attackers. The stonefire spells he had woven were designed to confuse any who approached with ill intentions: the attackers would simply go around the circle of power and return to the same spot while believing that they were traveling forward. Even if Jarsun or his minions did succeed in making ingress, Vessa would be alerted at once, no matter where he might be at the time.

Despite all these precautions, he still breathed a great sigh of relief as he saw the clearing ahead, and the silhouettes of priests and acolytes going about their business as usual. A doe and her mother feeding nearby looked up to show him mouthfuls of green leaves, unafraid by his presence because they were accustomed to humans and had learned no reason to fear them as yet. An owl on a branch turned its articulate neck a full half circle as it watched him stride away. Other animals of the woods watched his passage without concern.

Vessa emerged into the clearing, slowing his stride to a brisk walk.

The acolytes and priests all reacted to his arrival.

Cries of "Great Guru!" were heard from the oldest greybeards to the youngest acolytes, all bowing low and greeting the sage with full respect. Admiring eyes watched him as he passed by, hand raised and palm blessing them all.

"Live long and flourish," he said by way of benediction.

The simple blessing was enough to inspire every single one of the young acolytes to dedicate their lives to spreading the word of knowledge and helping dispel the darkness of ignorance. These were all his students, for they followed his system of compiling the sacred Krushan scriptures, a mammoth task that had engaged Vessa for much of his lifetime.

But today his presence here had nothing to do with the dissemination of knowledge or the awakening of young minds. He was here to ensure that his family was safe and that they would remain so.

He walked toward the last hut at the very end of the hermitage, located about a hundred yards beyond the main hermitage to afford its residents the privacy that a domestic household required. The hut had been expanded recently by the acolytes and priests, enlarged to accommodate the increase in the family's size. The original hut had been sufficient for three persons, but now there were five more. The hut still did not seem large enough to accommodate eight persons, especially persons accustomed to regal chambers and palaces. But these eight people had chosen to live here as simply as the other spiritual residents of the hermitage and eschewed all luxuries, comforts, and royal possessions. Vessa was pleased to see the state of cleanliness of the hut and its environs; he could see that the sweeping and cleaning had been done by small hands, for the brushstrokes of the thrash brooms were still faintly visible on the open front yard of the hut and the arcs were too tiny to have been made by adults. That told him that his grandchildren were dutiful and did their chores diligently, which pleased him. Those children were hard enough to raise without their getting any airs about being princes and princesses. Life was hard, and their lives were going to be harder than most; it was best if they accepted their lot and worked without complaint. Starting them young on such chores was the best way to get them used to the litany of hardships that lay ahead.

Vessa stopped in the middle of the front courtyard, looking around and taking stock.

All appeared to be in order. There was no sense of threat from human, urrkh, or any other presence. The jungle was safe and normal for a hundred miles in every direction. He expanded his range to a hundred and fifty miles, two hundred, and still found no sign of human movement or presence. Good. That was as it should be.

He decided it was time to announce his presence.

He raised his staff and was about to speak when suddenly, from above his head, a small shape descended with dazzling speed. At the same time, several more opponents appeared around him, aiming their weapons.

He was under attack.

2

"*Halt!*"

The courtyard of the little hut rang out with the sharp cry. A single word, yelled by five separate throats: "Stop!"

Vessa stood still, not moving a muscle.

He sensed five attackers, surrounding him on four sides, with one directly above, suspended from the branch of a tree. They were all armed, their weapons aimed at his vital organs, except for the one who was in front of him. This one was unarmed, but her stance and aggressive eye contact suggested that she was capable of inflicting as much damage with her bare hands as any weapon.

"I surrender," Vessa said. "You have nothing to fear from me."

"*Silence!*" said the one directly behind him. "You . . . *stranger!*"

"*Stranger!*" yelled the other four, repeating it in unison.

Vessa raised his eyebrows. "I am no stranger. Don't you know me?"

Silence. An exchange of glances between his five captors.

The one directly in front of him curled her hands into fists. "*Fight!*" she said. "*Fight stranger!*"

"*Halt!*" said the one behind Vessa. "No fight!"

"*Fight!*" said the one in front, more belligerently. She pointed one balled fist and yelled, "*Stranger come! Brum! Fight! Stranger!*" Vessa raised his eyebrows in response.

"*Halt!*" shouted the one behind Vessa. "Brum *no* fight!"

Even the one hanging upside down from the branch over Vessa's head shouted, "Listen!"

Brum snarled in frustration, then bent over and punched her fist into the ground. The ground erupted in a small explosion of mud and cow dung, raising a cloud of dust. When the air cleared, the one named Brum was coated in dust, and a hole the size of a large cauldron lay at her feet, with cracks spiderwebbing outward across the front yard.

Vessa coughed as some of the grit drifted in his direction. He was still holding his wildwood staff in his hand. He lowered it to the ground and tapped the dirt once. At once, the cracks closed, the hole filled up, and the dirt was drawn back into the ground, leaving the floor of the front yard intact and pristine as before. Only the grime on Brum's face remained, masking her look of utter astonishment.

The bundle over Vessa's head somersaulted down to the ground, landing on his feet with acrobatic ease. The other three all rushed forward, all four of them staring at the ground where the hole had been just a minute ago.

"Magic!" yelled the one who had stood behind Vessa, the leader of the group.

"Magic!" the others agreed.

All five of them stared up at Vessa, tilting their heads almost as far up as they would go to gaze up at the tall, gaunt figure.

"Guru!" said the leader.

"Guru!" agreed the others.

The leader bowed down, joining his palms together respectfully. "Pranaam."

The others imitated their leader exactly. "Pranaam."

Vessa gestured, causing a tiny rain cloud to appear out of nowhere. The cloud hovered over Brum's head. Vessa uttered a mantra subvocally and it began to rain on Brum, drenching her instantly. Brum stared indignantly for a moment, then realized that the rain was washing the dirt from her face and raised her head, opening her mouth. She filled her mouth with rain and gargled, then produced a spout of water from her mouth. The water splashed over the heads of the other four.

They didn't seem to mind. They were busy staring up in awe at the tiny thundercloud over Brum's head.

The leader turned back to look at Vessa again. "Guru."

The others turned as well, and also said, imitating their leader's reverential tone, "Guru."

Vessa switched off the rain and gestured. The little cloud began to float away, still sparking with lightning as it went. Brum jumped, trying to catch the cloud. A tiny bolt of lightning sparked, striking the tip of her finger. She stopped and looked at the finger, then continued jumping, still trying to catch the cloud. She kept after it until the cloud had dissipated completely.

Vessa heard a sound from the side of the hut and saw two young women come around the corner, each carrying a pot full of water. The water sloshed and spilled as they both reacted to the sight of Vessa standing in their front yard.

"Great One!" the elder of the two women cried out as she set down her pot. "Mayla, go tell Shvate at once." She wrapped her garment over her head and bowed down, joining her palms. "Pranaam, Great One."

The younger woman set down her pot as well, spilling most of the water. She turned to run, then stopped, turned back and bowed low, joining her palms. "Pranaam, Great One!" she called out, then ran away.

Karni picked up her pot and came forward. She bent down and poured water over Vessa's feet, dusty from the road. She washed his feet, using her hands to clean off the dust and dirt. She touched his feet with her fingertips, then touched the same fingertips to her forehead. "Aashirwaad, Great One."

"Ayushmaanbhavya, Karni," Vessa said warmly.

Karni stood and looked at the five little children. "I see you have already met our little scoundrels."

The leader frowned and shook his head. "Not scoundrels. Krushan."

Vessa suppressed a chuckle. "Yes, I have met your Krushan. Their security protocol is quite impressive!"

Karni stared at her children. "Krushan! Were you troubling our guest?

How many times have I told you about that? Poor Seer-Mage Sanathan is still confined to his hut with nervous shivers after the scare you gave him at the riverside last week!"

Four of them looked down with guilty expressions. Only Brum continued looking upward, staring this way and that, as if searching for something.

Karni looked at Brum hard. "Brum."

Brum looked at Karni. "Cloud. Flew." She waggled her arms to imitate a bird flying away.

Karni wagged a finger at Brum. "Brum."

Brum pouted and shrugged, then looked down. But when Karni turned away, she sneaked a quick glance again upward, still searching for the lost cloud.

Karni turned back to Vessa. "Gurudev, pray forgive my little Krushan any rudeness they may have shown you. They are still young and learning."

"No apology necessary. They are fine young children full of boundless energy and gifted with great qualities. It is only natural that they would need to exercise their talents."

The pattering of feet sounded from behind the hut. Shvate and Mayla appeared from around the corner, running. Shvate fell at the feet of Vessa, touching the sage's toes.

"Great One, Father, father of my body and flesh, aashirwaad, Great One."

Mayla also touched Vessa's feet. "Pranaam, Great One. Aashirwaad!"

"Ayushmaanbhavya, Shvate, Mayla. I was just telling Karni here how I encountered your five Krushan and how meticulously they were protecting the sanctity of your humble abode."

Shvate and Mayla immediately turned toward Brum, who happened to be looking upward with one eye closed, her face screwed up with concentration. She suddenly realized that everyone was looking at her and made a face. "Brum! *No* fight!"

Vessa laughed. The sound of his harsh, deep voice breaking into laughter made everyone start. He laughed as he hadn't laughed in years, releasing all his frustration and anger at not finding Jarsun in a long, pealing sequence of amusement. After a moment, Shvate joined in as well, adding his own tenor laugh to the symphony. Karni and Mayla began laughing as well. The five Krushan stared at the adults in astonishment, then joined them. Brum laughed the loudest and the hardest, though she kept stopping to frown and scratch her head, as if wondering what they were laughing at, and squinting up at the sky from time to time.

3

"They are asleep at last," Karni said to Mayla as she returned from putting down the children.

They had finished their meal and were now sitting on the back porch, enjoying the placid afternoon.

Vessa indicated the ground nearby, inviting them to sit. Karni and Mayla sat down cross-legged, joining Shvate and Vessa. Vessa puffed on the chillum that Shvate had offered him, enjoying a smoke after the meal. He passed the pipe to Shvate, who took a puff, then passed it to his wives. Karni declined, but Mayla took a long, deep puff, exhaling the smoke with great relish. The tiny creases on her forehead that had appeared in the past year eased a little.

"It has been a while since I saw the Krushan," Vessa said. "Has it not?"

"You were here last on their naming day, Great One," Karni said.

"Ah, yes, of course," Vessa said. "So much has happened since then, and yet they seem to have grown faster than I recall children growing in such a short time."

"They are . . ." Shvate searched for the right word. "Precocious. It is no easy task keeping them in hand."

"I'm sure. But that is as it should be. As I was telling Karni earlier, they are extraordinary children with great talents; they must explore their abilities and learn to use them to their advantage. How else will they learn?"

Mayla nodded. "That is what I also say, Great One. But sometimes their antics are beyond belief. Why, just the other day —"

Karni touched Mayla's shoulder gently. "Mayla, let us not spend the little time we have with Great One talking about the children's mischief. If he has taken the effort to visit us, he must have good reason. Only something of great importance would bring him to our little hut."

"You are right, Karni," Vessa said, exhaling a stream of smoke slowly. "I come on a mission of great importance."

"Enlighten us, Great One," Shvate said. "How may we be of service?"

Unseen by any of the adults — or so they thought (there was little that a high guru like Vessa would miss) — a small, smooth face had appeared in the window of the second room of the hut, the one from which Karni had emerged a short while earlier. Small hands rubbed the sleep from eyes, and little Arrow, taking care to keep from being clearly seen, peered out at the adults seated on the porch.

"Not you, Shvate," Vessa said. "It is I who wish to be of service to you."

Shvate exchanged a glance with both his wives. All three of them looked anxious. "You, Great One?" he asked.

A second face — broader, rounder — appeared beside Arrow's. Brum grinned as she stuck her head out to see the adults. Arrow shot Brum a stern look. Brum shed her grin and pulled her head back inside, but kept watching.

A moment later, two more heads popped up beside Brum: Kula and Saha. And then of course, there came a fifth: Yudishira. All five Krushan were now eavesdropping on their parents and their grandfather; though they thought themselves undetectable due to their stealth, the great guru knew their every movement.

"Indeed." Vessa set the chillum aside, its work done. "It is time for you all to return to Hastinaga."

Mayla's face lit up at once. Her eyes gleamed. Karni and Shvate exchanged a look which became a shared smile.

"Now, I know," Vessa went on, "you will say that you abdicated the throne and took exile of your own volition. But that was when you feared that the rishi Kundaka's curse would render you incapable of fathering heirs to the Krushan line. That is no longer the case. You have five robust children, each and every one capable of becoming a great leader to Hastinaga and to the empire. All five together are capable of ruling the world — and many worlds besides!"

The five little faces all lit up with proud smiles. Brum started to speak, but the instant her mouth opened, Yudi turned and looked at her sternly. Brum shut her mouth.

"Even so, Great One," Shvate said hesitantly, "I officially and legally abdicated my claim to the throne. I gave my brother Adri my blessing to ascend and even donated all my wealth and possessions."

"Wealth and possessions can be regained. Blessings cause no harm to anyone. Your claim was legitimate and well-intended at that time. But circumstances have changed. And these changes in circumstances now cast a shadow on the validity of your abdication."

"You refer to our children, Great One?" Karni asked.

"Indeed. The very existence of the Krushan changes everything. Your son Yudi was the eldest born of his generation. He came into this world well before Adri and Geldry's eldest son, Dhuryo."

The five little faces at the window all silently attempted to mouth the word "Dhuryo," with varying results.

"We heard of their good fortune," Shvate said. "A hundred and one children is a great gift to the Krushan dynasty."

Vessa's face hardened. "One would think so, normally."

"But, Great One," Mayla asked, "doesn't that contradict Krushan law?"

"What Mayla means to ask," Karni added, "is does the fact that they also have progeny give them a legal advantage over us? After all, Shvate abdicated to Adri, and Adri now has children of his own, so legally and logically, shouldn't the throne pass from Adri to Dhuryo now?"

Vessa brooded for a moment. "Normally, it might be argued. But the circumstances are not normal. Since Shvate now has children, his abdication is nullified. Therefore he alone is the rightful crown prince, and his eldest born is the next in line."

Karni and Mayla exchanged a glance. Mayla gestured to Karni, who then nodded.

"Gurudev," Karni said, "Mayla has one more query. She wishes to know whether all at Hastinaga will interpret the law as you do."

Vessa nodded slowly. "Possibly not everyone. Certainly not Geldry."

Mayla's eyes narrowed sharply at the sound of Geldry's name. Karni sighed softly.

Vessa continued. "But you need have no concerns about any controversy. There will be no arguments over questions of law or succession. I will see to that myself."

"You, Father?" Shvate asked.

"Indeed, my son," Vessa replied. "I shall accompany you all to Hastinaga and take our case directly to Vrath and Jilana. We need not concern ourselves with anyone else. As Krushan elders, we have a responsibility to decide the fate of the dynasty. This is a matter of family and succession, and we are the family elders."

"What about Hastinaga? The nobles, the Senate, the Council?" Shvate asked. "Will they not want to have a say in the matter?"

Vessa shrugged. "I'm sure they will. Everyone wants to have a say in political matters. But it doesn't matter what they want or even what they may say. Hastinaga is not a republic. It is a kingdom and a monarchy, and the Burnt Empire is ruled by the Krushan family. Ours are the only voices that matter in this case. But even if it were a republic, this particular issue is one of family succession, not administration or governance."

Vessa put a large dark hand on Shvate's bare white shoulder. "And if it were to come to that, then be sure that the people of Hastinaga love you far, far more than they do Adri."

Five little faces smiled brightly at the window.

"They do, great guru?" Shvate asked, genuinely surprised.

"Of course they do!" Vessa said, slapping his son hard on the back. "You are the champion of Reygar, the victor of the Battle of the Rebels, the conqueror of Serapi! You won more battles and wars in a short period than even the late Shapaar, your grandfather by law, won in a decade. You are a hero to your people, and they wept grievously when they heard of your abdication and exile."

Karni and Mayla exchanged tentative, happy smiles.

Vessa's face grew serious again, settling into its deep-etched lines. "But make no mistake about it, Shvate, Karni, Mayla. This is not just about legalities and succession. It is about Krushan."

"Shima, Father?" Shvate asked.

Five little mouths confidentially formed the word "Krushan" silently, proud of themselves for already knowing its meaning and how to pronounce it.

"Shima, my son. There is a great crisis coming, and it threatens to engulf all Hastinaga, all the Burnt Empire, and even the entire world in its grasp of evil. It is vital that a strong king rule on the Burning Throne. A king who has the strength and courage to fight the vilest enemy. The past decade has already proven that between yourself and Adri, you are by far the greater warrior and king at war."

Shvate sighed. "At one time, my brother was quite exceptional too."

"*Was.* But *is* no more. The crisis approaches now, not in the past. Adri had a spark of courage once but has since lost it. He is now a sad, broken shadow of his former self. I do not wish to speak ill of my own flesh and blood, but it is the truth. He is my son, and I shall always be proud of his achievements, but Hastinaga will not be saved by excuses and compensations. The times call for a great warrior king. And you are the only one who can fill those shoes. Only you deserve to sit on the Burning Throne. That is why we leave for Hastinaga shortly."

"When?" Shvate asked, looking up at the sky.

At once, five little faces turned to look up at the sky as well.

"It is late afternoon," Shvate said. "It will be dark in a few hours. Hastinaga is several days' walk from here. Even if we are able to find mounts to ride, it will still take two days or more."

"And the children," Karni pointed out, "their little feet cannot walk as quickly as our own over such a long distance."

Vessa smiled an enigmatic smile, glancing over his shoulder in the direction of the window where five little pairs of eyes were peeping out. At once the five heads bobbed down out of sight. "Your little Krushan have yet to show you the full extent of their abilities. But fear not. We shall neither ride nor walk all the way to Hastinaga. As befits a returning king, you shall arrive home in regal style."

Shvate frowned. "But if we neither ride nor walk, how will we travel?"

"By carriage!" Mayla said, flushed and excited from the conversation — and the chillum. "Royal horse carriage drawn by a team of great horses and liveried footmen!"

Vessa chuckled. "You shall have plenty of horse carriages and liveried footmen too when you are home, Mayla. Queen Mayla, I should say! But no, we shall make this journey in a far simpler, quicker manner. I shall return tomorrow at sunrise. You must prepare yourselves and the little Krushan for the return home. Tomorrow morning, I shall transport you there using the power of stonefire shakti. We shall take a single step and arrive at Hastinaga in the blink of an eye."

The five little faces rose up again at the window, eyes wide with wonder. *Guru!* they all mouthed silently.

Shvate's, Karni's and Mayla's faces lit up with joy. Almost at once, the two women looked at each other, then felt their own hair, patting their bodies, and looking down at their hands and feet with dismay.

"Gurudev," Mayla asked, sounding alarmed, "could we not have a day longer to prepare ourselves? We are not wholly . . . presentable as yet."

Even Karni hesitantly suggested, "Perhaps we could go the day after?"

"Presentable?" Vessa frowned. "Presentable or not, my good queens, we must arrive at Hastinaga tomorrow at the very latest. Perhaps I neglected to mention this earlier, but the day after tomorrow is the coronation of Prince Adri, and if we do not arrive before it takes place, then Adri will be crowned king, and that will considerably complicate matters for everyone concerned."

"Coronation?" Karni repeated. "No, of course, then we must arrive in time. Mayla and I will prepare ourselves as best as we can shortly and be ready to depart first thing tomorrow morning."

Mayla looked as if she were about to argue, but Karni nudged her with her elbow and so Mayla nodded as well.

Shvate waved dismissively. "Do not fret, my queens. You can spend all the time you want preparing yourselves once we are home. You will have maids and baths, fine gowns and jewels to enhance your beauty. But what Father says is right, if we are to go anyway, then there is no point waiting even a day longer than necessary. Father, we shall be ready to accompany you tomorrow morning at sunrise!"

Vessa stood up. "Tomorrow we shall take back control of the City of Elephants and Snakes. Not for nothing is Hastinaga named after the wisest of beasts. It deserves a king capable of commanding such a majestic metropolis. I am very pleased, my son. I shall take my leave now and return tomorrow at sunrise."

Together, they all rose to their feet.

Karni turned to glance in the direction of the hut, seeming to sense something with a mother's instinct.

There was nothing to be seen, just the hut and the empty window. The children were all fast asleep still.

Shvate and his wives bade goodbye to the great guru, bowing to touch his feet once again.

Vessa strode away, headed toward the forest, which was only a few dozen yards from the porch and disappeared before he reached the trees.

"Guru!" came a soft excited exclamation from inside the hut.

Cobra

~

THE BEADY EYES OF a king cobra watched from the forest. Only a few moments had passed since Vessa had vanished from the forest hermitage.

The cobra had been watching the hut for the past several hours, unseen. Now he observed that the sage had departed the area and hissed with pleasure, his forked tongue flickering in and out of his mouth. He began to slither away sinuously, making his way over a mound, under a rock, and into the mouth of a hole. He slipped into the hole easily, winding his way down into the earth.

But instead of leading to a typical snake warren a few yards underground, the hole continued descending deeper and deeper beneath the earth. It was, of course, no ordinary snake hole, and no ordinary serpent. Cobras did not dig this far into the earth; no snake did.

After descending for several dozen yards through layers of earth and bedrock, the hole widened suddenly, expanding into a subterranean cavern. The king cobra wound his tail around a rock embedded in the side of the hole and lowered his considerable length down into the cavern, mouth first. He hung down like a shimmering black rope, over five yards long and gifted with a magnificent hood almost a foot wide when fully expanded. His black eyes gleamed in the darkness of the cavern, as he turned and twisted, seeking out the one he served.

"Master," he hissed.

The word echoed in the darkness of the cavern. Somewhere, water dripped with the slow, timeless rhythm of a thousand-year-old phenomenon, continuing to erode the bedrock and expand the ancient cavern. This

entire subterranean cavern had been created by the erosion of slowly dripping and flowing water over millennia. Sometimes, the greatest things are
accomplished only through the gradual application of effort over a great
quantum of time.

The cobra waited patiently, knowing his master did not appreciate im-
petuousness. Sometimes, it took hours or even days before he responded.
The cobra's job was to wait as long as was required. The slow but steady
dripping of the water onto rock was the only thing that marked the passage
of time.

On this occasion, he did not have long to wait.

Only an hour or two after the cobra had called for his master, something
arrived in the cavern. It was as faint as a miasma, barely a thin mist, invisible
in the darkness. Yet the cobra sensed it and woke from his doze, instantly
alert. His tongue flickered as he wondered if it was his master or merely a
cold wind carried by underground air currents.

The cobra hissed again. *"Master, the greybeard has come and left. He returns
again tomorrow at sunrise to take his son and grandchildren with him to the City
of Snakes."*

A period of silence followed, as if the snake's missive was being carried
across a great distance to some other location, ported by supernatural
means. Eventually the response came.

"It is no more called Nagapura, City of Snakes," his master Jarsun said.
"That name was never again spoken after your great ancestor was deposed.
Once your kind roamed freely over Hastinaga in far greater numbers than
the human pests who now populate the region. Soon, it shall be yours to
roam freely again and the name Nagapura will sing out on the lips of the
people once more."

The cobra's eyes glinted and his tongue hissed sibilantly, expressing the
innate hatred of his species for all elephants, for he knew that Hastinaga,
City of Elephants and Snakes, housed them in substantial numbers.

"You have done well to keep watch and pass on this timely message. Now
you must do one more thing for me. It will require a great number of your
kind working in concert to accomplish this task."

The cobra hissed excitedly. "I am Lord of Snakes of this forest. I have an
army of serpents at my command. You have only to say the word, Master."

"It is imperative that the human named Shvate and his family be destroyed this very night, before the greybeard returns. I myself cannot set foot in this jungle because of the stonefire snare set in place by the greybeard."

The cobra's tongue flickered eagerly. "Say the word, and my serpents and I shall strike at them with our fangs until their bodies are black and writhing with our venom."

"No need; my army of assassins is camped in the nearby mountain ranges, awaiting only my signal to enter the jungle and eliminate the Krushan family. But the greybeard's stonefire spells of protection will alert the sage to our forces' presence the instant they set foot there. That too is the reason for us meeting in this dank cavern."

"What would you have us do, Master? We live to serve you."

"And you *shall* serve. The runes the greybeard has placed encircle the hermitage of the Krushan in a very wide, large circle ranging several scores of miles. They are ancient, powerful spells woven into the trees, the leaves, the earth, the air, the grass itself."

The cobra hissed to hear of such treachery. *Priests!* Their stonefire sorcery was the bane of many of his kind. They came into the deep forest, felled trees to clear spaces to build their hermitages, killing many of his species and depriving many more of their natural habitats. He longed for an opportunity to pay them back with venomous vengeance. "How may we remove the spell of protection, Master?"

"There is only one way, and it will be extremely difficult for you and your kind, but there is no alternative."

"Anything!" hissed the cobra.

Jarsun's voice drifted on the cold mist. "Fire."

The cobra writhed. The very mention of the dreaded one struck terror into his cold heart. "*Fire?* It is our mortal enemy, Master!"

"I know how deeply your kind fears the open flame, Lord of Snakes. It has been responsible for the deaths of untold millions of your species since the beginning of life on Arthaloka. But sadly, it is our only option."

"Master, we are snakes! How can we use fire, our most hated enemy?"

Jarsun's voice hardened. "*Because I command it.* Because it is the only way. Only by burning that section of the forest, a complete ring of fire encircling the hermitage where the Krushan reside, can the spell of protection set by the greybeard be broken."

"Cannot your own men do it, then?" the cobra asked, his ebony body trembling with fear at the very thought of those searing flames.

"If they could, we wouldn't be having this conversation, fool," Jarsun snarled, his voice echoing in the cavern. "I am tasking you and your kin with this mission. I shall guide you with my power to the circle where the greybeard has laid the spell of protection. You and your serpents must carry fire to that spot and burn it. The ring must be complete and unbroken."

"So that the Krushan family does not escape?" asked the cobra, still trembling, but whether from fear of fire or his master, it was impossible to say.

"No, fool — once the spell of protection is burned and destroyed by the fire, I shall douse the flames at once so that my soldiers and I may enter the forest."

"Then you too shall grace us with your presence, Master?" asked the cobra, his terror diminished in part by the possibility of receiving the Great One in person.

"Indeed. Tonight will mark the end of the Krushan family and the greybeard sage Vessa's dream of seating his son Shvate on the Burning Throne. Do as I bid, follow my instructions to the letter, and no matter how many of your serpents sacrifice their lives to this battle tonight, know that it shall all be in service to a great cause. Go, Lord of Snakes, accomplish your duties this night, and soon, I vow, a Naga will once again sit upon the Snake Throne of Nagapura. Now go."

The words echoed through the earth as the king cobra slithered up the hole and back toward the surface, shivering with excitement and anticipation.

Kula

~

KULA AND SAHA WERE the first of the Five to wake. Both opened their eyes at the same time, looked up at the darkness and then remained still, trying to sense what had woken them.

Their eyes gleamed in the darkness, reflecting the faint glimmer of moonlight and starlight that came in through the open window. In this, they resembled the eyes of animals, which had the ability to trap and reflect even the faintest light, enabling them to see in the dark. Kula and Saha could see the room in which they slept as clearly as anyone could see it during the day. They saw the shapes of their siblings lying alongside them, all fast asleep. They saw the walls, the pot of water in the corner with the clay lid upside down on top, the doorway that led to the adjoining room of the hut where their parents slept, and the window, which faced west.

A gentle breeze wafted in through the window, carrying the usual smells of the jungle — and something unusual as well. Kula and Saha sniffed the air, then exchanged a glance. As one, they both rose and went to the casement. Saha boosted his sister over the sill and then followed her.

Outside the hut, the twins climbed down from the porch of their hut carefully, instead of jumping as they usually did. They knew their siblings' and parents' hearing was sharp enough to catch even the soft sound their little feet made when hitting the ground and didn't want to wake anyone until they had checked out the situation for themselves.

They walked barefoot across the flat clearing to the forest. The moon was still low on the horizon, at a declination that did not permit much of its silver light to reach the hermitage clearing, but there was plenty of starlight, and this illuminated the twins. The forest around the clearing was shrouded in dense darkness, the thick canopy of close-growing trees barely allowing a sliver or two of starlight and moonlight to reach the ground. But to Kula and Saha, the darkness was no impediment. They could see into the jungle, and what they saw there was troubling: it was filled with the eyes of creatures watching the clearing.

There were thousands of pairs of eyes, all different sizes, shapes, belonging to different species. They were accustomed to seeing some animals at all times, their dark-adapted eyes easily spotting the creatures wherever they might be: on a tree, low on the ground, peeping from behind a rock, or standing tall. But they had never seen anything like this before. At night, when the predators came out, they might see several dozen animals at a glance, or even a hundred or two. Tonight was unusual. There were more creatures in the jungle around the clearing than they had ever seen at a time. And they were all staring at the hut where the Krushan lived.

Exchanging another glance, this a troubled one, the twins continued to walk toward the trees. They reached the edge of the forest, and without hesitation, walked into the jungle, into the forest of a thousand eyes.

Yudi

~

YUDI WAS WOKEN BY a palm gently placed on his shoulder and a soft whisper in his ear. *"Yudi . . ."*

He came awake at once, alert. He could just make out the shape of Kula's face as his sister bent over him. Behind Kula, Saha was placing a hand on Arrow's shoulder and had just started to whisper, *"Arr —"* when Arrow sat up, awake and instantly alert.

"Kula?" Yudi asked. He already knew something was wrong from the way Kula and Saha were waking up their siblings.

Kula glanced back at her twin brother. Saha was about to wake up Brum. Kula looked at Yudi again and jerked her head toward the window. Yudi understood: *Talk outside.*

Saha was still trying to wake up Brum. *"Brum . . ."* he whispered directly into Brum's ear, hitting his sleeping sister on the shoulder with the side of his hand to avoid making any sound. Brum continued sleeping. Saha looked at his siblings and made a helpless gesture.

Kula kicked Brum's foot lightly. Nothing.

Arrow bent down and pinched Brum's arm.

Kula and Saha both put their mouths to Brum's ears and whispered urgently, *"Brum!"*

Through it all, Brum continued sleeping.

All three of them turned and looked at their eldest sibling.

Yudi went over to his sleeping sister. He bent down and put his palm on Brum's chest firmly and whispered over Brum's face, *"Brum."*

Brum opened her eyes and grasped Yudi's hand. *"Yudi? Safe?"*

Yudi put his finger on his lips, making a shush gesture.

Brum glanced around, saw her other siblings awake, and nodded her head vigorously to show she understood.

Yudi gestured toward the window.

All five of them climbed out the window and left the hut.

As they walked across the clearing, Arrow leading the group as always, Kula and Saha explained the danger. "Fire," they whispered.

Yudi nodded. He could smell the smoke — they all could. They could also see in the distance, just becoming visible now, a faint reddish glow that could be nothing else. He guessed that it was what their parents would call a "day's walk" from the hermitage, but for fire itself, that distance meant nothing. It could be here in the hermitage within the hour, if the wind blew this way. He knew this instinctively, even though he had never actually seen a forest fire or been told about them. He *had* seen a fire up close and knew it could kill and destroy everything it touched. The thought of that destructive energy consuming his family's house and the houses of the other priests of the hermitage was not a happy one. His little face set itself in a grim expression as he listened to what the twins had to say.

He looked at the jungle. Not having their ability to see in the dark, he could only make out the dense jungle and the general outlines of the trees, with some upper foliage tinged by starlight. But as they grew closer to the jungle itself, he began to make out the gleaming silvery eyes of animals in the darkness. He did not slow his step, but he felt somewhat troubled by the sight of so many pairs of eyes. It was not normal to see so many, and anything not normal was to be treated with suspicion, his instincts warned him.

Brum must have also sensed the same thing because her stocky little shape stopped at once. Her fists rose up. "Animals! Brum fight animals!"

Kula touched her shoulder, reassuring her. "Friends," Kula said. "No hurt."

Brum reluctantly lowered her fists.

They entered the canopy of trees and were surrounded by the jungle.

As Yudi's eyes adapted to the darkness, he began to make out the faint outlines of creatures all around. There were more than he had ever seen before, predators and prey alike, all gathered together, none showing any aggression toward each other. He could smell them too, their fur and sweat and urine and excrement.

Brum wrinkled her nose, rubbing it hard to try to get rid of the stink. "Ugh. Smell!" Brum said.

"Why animals here?" Yudi asked Kula.

"Fire make animals run," Kula said. "Fire all around. Big circle." She gestured with her hands. "Animals come here. To Krushan. Ask for help."

"From *us*?" Yudi asked, incredulous. "How we help animals?"

"Fight!" Brum said, rubbing her hands together. "Brum fight fire!"

"Fire burn Brum," Arrow said scornfully.

Brum glared at Arrow. "Brum fight fire."

"Can't fight fire," Yudi said. He looked around at all the animals. He could see them now, looking at him, their large soulful eyes, their snouts, their furry faces, their lowered tails. "Krushan can't fight fire."

"Not fire," Kula said. "Soldiers. Bad soldiers come. Kill Krushan. Kill father, mothers."

Yudi caught his breath. "Where?"

Kula made the same circling gesture again. "Everywhere. Coming fast. Many bad soldiers."

Brum slapped her own chest. "Brum. Fight. Soldiers."

For once, nobody corrected her.

Brum looked around at her siblings, surprised. "Brum! Fight! Soldiers!" she repeated, waiting to be corrected.

Arrow's dark eyes gleamed. "Arrow fight soldiers."

Kula and Saha said together, "Kula Saha fight soldiers."

Yudi nodded grimly. "Krushan fight soldiers. Protect father, mothers, hermitage."

Brum grinned, her large white teeth shining in the darkness.

Vida

~

VIDA HAD SEEN THE flames from miles away, lighting up the night sky over the jungle. Now, as the charioteer brought the chariot to a complete halt, he could still see the red glow in the sky above the trees. It extended to both sides for miles in both directions, as well as further ahead.

The charioteer pointed upward. "It is a circle," Adran said. "That is not a naturally occurring forest fire. Someone has deliberately set the fire in a large circle, and from what I can tell from here, it appears to enclose the area where the hermitage is situated."

Vida's hand pressed against his chest. "Goddess! That means the hermitage is now isolated? How do I get there?"

Adran shook his head. "Nobody can get to the hermitage now. Not until the fire subsides. Unless . . ."

"Unless?"

"Unless the goal is to burn them down," Adran said. "Hence the circular fire. It is a tactic used by some cowardly tribes who do not have the courage to engage in honorable face-to-face combat."

Vida exclaimed, "But I must reach Shvate. I have an important message for him."

Adran gestured at the red glow. "We would have to leave the chariot here anyway, as the jungle is too dense from this point onward to travel further. If you wish, I can accompany you on foot as far as we can go. Perhaps we may find a firebreak. But we also run the risk of perishing in the fire. I have seen forest fires before. They are impossible to outrun, and once engulfed by smoke and heat, one can no longer make out east from west, north from south. We risk our own lives if we go forward."

Vida took a deep breath and released it. "So be it. I must reach my brother at all costs. It is a matter of life and death. Vrath and Goddess Jeel themselves have entrusted me with this communication."

Adran stared at him. "Then our path is set. I will hobble the horses in such a manner that if the fire does reach here, they will be able to break free with an effort and flee for their lives. There is no use having them perish with us. But if we survive the attempt, we may have to walk all the way back to Hastinaga."

"Do what you must. All that matters to me at this moment is reaching Shvate and giving him my message."

Adran took a few moments to do as he had indicated, then the two men set out on foot through the dark forest. Within a few miles, they began to smell the acrid fumes of smoke and could already feel the warmth of the fire. The closer they went, the warmer it grew, and the smoke and fumes increased as well.

Adran placed a hand on Vida's shoulder. "The smoke will soon surround us. I cannot guarantee that I will be able to find our way back."

"The way back does not concern me," Vida said. "Only the way forward. If you fear for your own life, you may return, good charioteer. I do not ask you to risk your life as well. This burden is mine alone to bear."

Adran shook his head. "Nay, good Vida. You are an honorable master and a man of Krushan. I will go with you to the ends of Arthaloka. Give me a moment."

Adran tore two strips from his garment and doused them with water from a small lota of water he had taken from the waterskin kept in the chariot. He handed one wet cloth to Vida. "Wrap this firmly around your head and your face, cover every inch carefully. You will be able to breathe through the wet cloth, and it will keep some of the smoke and ash from entering your lungs."

Vida did as the charioteer advised and saw him do the same. Then Adran splashed a small amount of water from the lota over their heads and asked Vida to drink a little as well. He upended the lota over Vida's mouth and dripped out the last drops. Then he put the lota aside and indicated that they should keep moving.

As they continued forward, the smoke increased suddenly, filling the forest around them like a thick fog. The wet cloth around his face helped him breathe, but even so, Vida found it growing harder to take in air. Abruptly, a thick cloud of smoke billowed over them, engulfing them completely and plunging them into darkness more impenetrable than the natural night.

The sound of the fire ahead was loud and intense, but there was also a strange hissing that Vida could not identify. The two men stopped moving, and Vida felt Adran's strong arm on his shoulder, pressing down to indicate that he should stay still. Adran's face appeared beside Vida's ear, speaking to him over the noise of the fire. "We must stop awhile and climb a tree; there is too much smoke."

Vida wanted to protest, to argue that he needed to push on to reach Shvate at the earliest, but the charioteer added, "You will not get your message to Shvate if we both die here in the jungle. Do as I say, and we may yet survive."

Vida still felt reluctant to deviate from his mission, but he saw the sense in Adran's words. He let the charioteer lead him to a suitable tree and bend down to form a bridge with his hands so Vida could more easily climb. And so he did — going as high as he could on Adran's instruction, and as he climbed, he found the smoke reducing until by the time he was at the very highest point of the trunk, some fifty yards above the ground, he could almost breathe normally again. The charioteer climbed up after him, remaining below him to help and support or push when Vida found the going too difficult. Finally, both of them rested on the strong upper branches of the tree, looking out at the tops of the trees.

Vida found that he could see the sky here and even a bit of the forest beyond the fire. The flames had cut down a patch of forest in a large ring, exactly as Adran had suspected, and the break in foliage provided glimpses of the clearing, which gave him hope, because he could see, even at this distance, that the huts of the hermitage appeared to still be standing and untouched by the fire.

But now there was something else that he could see. He squinted, trying to make out if what he thought he was seeing was real or just a miasma caused by all the smoke swirling around them.

"The fire has been put out," Adran said, confirming Vida's suspicion. The charioteer pointed with one hand, gripping the bole of the tree trunk with the other. "That is what produced all the smoke. Someone has put out the entire circle of flame at the same time, producing the clouds of smoke that we encountered. I thought that was the case, but could not be certain till we climbed to this vantage point."

Vida's eyes were watering from trying to stare through the smoky air. "That is good news! Now we will be able to continue on our way and reach my brother very soon."

"If you wish, then we shall," Adran said, "but I must caution you, Councilman, that such an enormous fire would have taken a great number of hands to put out with such precision. And it is to be expected that these parties would not be friendly to us or to your brother and his people. At first I thought the fire was to burn down Shvate and his family, but now I suspect another reason altogether."

"Such as the elimination of a patch of forest," Vida said slowly, coming to the same conclusion.

Adran nodded. "I cannot speculate on why this was seen to be necessary, but it has been done. And there can be no question that something else is meant to follow the dousing of the fire. Whatever that event may be, it will not be pleasant."

Vida was about to respond when suddenly, he felt a vibration through the trunk he was holding on to. It felt as if the earth were shaking. He looked around, puzzled, then thought to look down, at the ground. Even in the smoky darkness, he saw the shapes of many figures moving quickly through the woods. Dozens, hundreds, more and more, they kept on coming in endless waves, running at full speed through the jungle, all carrying arms, all moving with the silent, deadly grace of veteran warriors. His heart sank. "We are already too late, the attack has begun on the hermitage."

Adran was also watching the swarm of soldiers below. From this height it looked to them as if the ground itself were moving or was covered with water flowing in only one direction — toward the hermitage. "I fear it may be so."

"But my message," Vida said in dismay. "I must reach Shvate and pass it on to him!"

Adran gestured at the ground, carpeted with never-ending waves of soldiers racing through the dark night. "Even a soul as brave as yourself cannot fight an army single-handedly, good Vida. I urge you to stay here until the danger is past, or we will become the first casualties of war."

Vida knew the charioteer was right. He had no choice but to stay where he could survive. The worst thing, he thought as he looked back toward the hermitage, was that he had a prime view of the battle that was about to commence yet could do nothing now to influence its outcome.

Shvate

~

SHVATE WOKE TO THE smell of smoke. His first thought was that the hut was on fire. He sprang up, looking for any sign of flames.

Mayla jerked awake beside him. "Shvate! Fire!"

Karni came rushing back from the children's room. "Shvate, Mayla, the Krushan are gone."

"Gone?" Shvate asked. "Where?"

"I don't know," Karni asked. "Something very strange is going on."

All three of them picked up their weapons and rushed outside at once, alert and ready for danger. All three had bows as well as swords, while Mayla also carried a fist-sized clutch of metal darts and spears. The moon was just high enough for them to see by its light. The folk of the hermitage were also waking up now and peering out of their huts.

A white-haired hermit saw them and called out, "Is it an attack?"

"We don't know yet," Shvate called out. "Stay indoors. We are going to investigate."

"Have you seen the Krushan?" Karni asked the priests.

Several shook their heads. Others were still staring around in bewilderment.

The smoke appeared to be coming from the forest. They could see thick plumes of it rising from several miles farther away. Mayla swung around as she walked, turning a full circle. "It is on all sides. A fire lit in a circle around our hermitage. A war tactic."

"But it has been doused now," Shvate said. "That means they did not intend to burn us out."

"Then they have something else in mind," Karni said grimly, notching an arrow to her bow as she ran. Though Shvate and Mayla both had bows, neither of them had used them in a while, the weapons still causing both of them painful memories due to the association with the accidental killing of Rishi Kundaka and his wife. Shvate had his sword in his fist, and Mayla was pulling a spear from the clutch, holding it in her free hand, ready to throw at the first sight of an enemy.

The three of them ran across the clearing to the forest, calling out the names of their five children as they went. But there was no reply.

They entered the dark woods and slowed, letting their eyes adjust to the greater darkness. Shvate was the first to adjust, his albino vision better able to handle low light than high. He waited for his wives to be able to see as well.

No sign of their children. Nothing that caused concern. They stood for a moment, getting their bearings, trying to listen and smell and sense what was happening.

From deeper inside the forest, then, they heard sounds. At the same time, they felt the vibrations. Shvate pressed his palm against the trunk of a tree and listened. "Soldiers," he said grimly. "Many hundreds, perhaps thousands — it is difficult to say because they are moving with great skill and stealth."

"An army, then," Mayla said. "Who is it? Which of our enemies has come to seek vengeance?"

"What difference does it make?" Karni said, "Whoever they are, if they come to harm us, we fight back. But first, we must find our Krushan. Where could they be?"

Shvate tucked his sword under his arm for a moment and raised his hands to his mouth, shaping and funneling his lips to produce a low, piercing bird cry that carried a long distance in the night. He waited, then repeated the cry twice more. After the third time, an answering cry came to their ears, then repeated itself.

"Kula-Saha," he said, smiling briefly, "They are only a few miles away from the sound of it. Let us make our way toward them." He took up the sword again and pointed. "This way."

They began running into the jungle, their weapons ready and senses alert. As they approached the place where the fire had burned and been extinguished, the air became smokier and more pungent. Their eyes began to sting from the smoke and ash, and they were forced to slow to a near-walking pace. Shvate's eyes were watering, but he kept going, as did Mayla and Karni — his wives as stubborn and determined as he. Finally, eyes streaming freely, they came to a place where they saw the forest ahead thick with dark shadows and shapes. At once, they raised their weapons, ready to fight.

It was Shvate who swore and took a step forward, rubbing at his eyes to stare. "Impossible," he said. "Those are not soldiers . . . They are . . . *not human.*"

Mayla and Karni stared as well.

"You are right," Mayla said. "I can see tusks, and antlers, and the ears of a wolf, and of foxes, and . . . a lion? Yes, several lions!"

"And birds in the trees, and smaller creatures clinging to the branches and trunks . . . They are the animals and birds of the jungle," Karni said. "Great numbers of them, all gathered together!"

"The beasts of the jungle do not simply gather together!" Shvate said, "For what purpose would they gather? And predators and prey side by side? It is unheard of!"

"They would join together peacefully to race away from a forest fire," Mayla said. "I have seen animals fleeing a forest fire once. All different species together, just like this . . ." She paused. "But no — not like this. They were not simply standing together in one place."

"It is as if they are waiting," Karni said.

"But for what?" Shvate asked.

Yudi

~

YUDI RAISED HIS HAND, gesturing to Kula, who nodded and passed on the message to Saha with a single silent look. Saha and Kula both looked at the lioness nearest to them. She was a magnificent old beast, her fur faded white with age, but her stance still proud, her eyes still fierce. She was enormous by lion standards, her head huge, her withers twice as high as Yudi, who was the tallest of the Krushan. Her haunches were still strong and powerful.

"Pashupati be with you, great mother," Saha said softly.

The lioness growled softly in response.

Then she raised her head high and howled.

Around her the rest of her pride howled as well. Other lions took up the cry. There were several scores of them, all ages and sizes, with different colored coats, from several different prides.

The wolves howled.

The foxes barked.

The elephants lowed.

The buffalo grunted.

The boars snorted.

The bulls stamped their hooves.

The great stags crashed their antlers against the trunks of trees.

Soon, the entire kingdom of beasts had added their own voices to echo the war cry. Even the tiniest squirrels and hedgehogs made their own noises, acknowledging the clarion call of their commander.

The five Krushan siblings exchanged looks and nodded.

Brum grinned and slapped her fist into her palm. "Fight!" she shouted. "Brum fight! Animals fight! Soldiers fight!"

Arrow sighed.

The army of animals began to move, running forward into the jungle, toward the great ring of ash where the fires had raged, away from the hermitage and the people they were fighting to protect.

They picked up speed gradually, their movements various and of a wide range of gaits. Galloping, leaping, trundling, skittering . . .

Their momentum built until they were all one mass, an army charging as one being.

The great mother lion roared again, letting the enemy know what terrors lay in store for them.

The army of beasts again echoed her, filling the dark jungle with their horrific cry.

Vida

~

VIDA AND ADRAN WATCHED in astonishment from the top of the tree.

"The beasts of the jungle," Adran said, his charioteer's eyesight keener than the sight of Vida, who spent too much of his time poring over scrolls in poor light. "They have risen up and joined the Krushan to fight their enemy. I have never seen anything like it . . ." He paused, as if recalling something. "Except once before, on the night of the eclipse. But that was nothing like this. This is the entire jungle of animals, all united for a common cause."

"Yes," Vida said solemnly, "and the cause is Krushan."

They watched as the army of assassins, all with weapons drawn, charged forward, racing into the circle inscribed by the extinguished fire, while the army of beasts raced outward, rushing to meet the enemy.

The two armies met with a clashing of bodies, human and inhuman.

Fangs met swords.

Claws met arrows.

Tusks met bellies.

Trunks grasped necks.

Paws struck faces.

Teeth slashed throats.

Swords hacked fur.

Blades pierced hides.

Through the smoke of the extinguished fire, the battle was visible in glimpses. Bears swung vicious blows, separating human heads from torsos with a single slash of their long claws, ripping open bodies to spill out steaming organs. Great cats sprang upon soldiers, tearing flesh, rending bodies, crushing bones. Elephants ran down hundreds of men, stamping their bones and skulls into the mulch of the forest floor. Owls flew through the darkness, ripping open faces, crows plucked out eyes, eagles slashed scalps and raked faces. Even the small creatures slipped up sleeves and down yokes into the assassins' garments, nipping sensitive parts of their anatomy, distracting the humans long enough for the larger animals to do their grisly work.

But the enemy fought back viciously. Trained, veteran killers, they were not easily overcome. They used their weapons as easily against these animal attackers as they would have against fellow humans. They jabbed and cut, slashed and stabbed, wounded and maimed in every way possible. Even though they died by the dozen in the wake of the animal onslaught, they inflicted great damage on their furred attackers, giving no quarter, charging a heavy toll for their own casualties. They did not retreat, because they were not paid to retreat: they were paid to kill and die. And so that is what they did, even if the enemy they were faced with was not the one they had expected.

All night the battle continued; hundreds, perhaps thousands of animals died or were injured. But thousands upon thousands of assassins also died, and by the time the first faint light of dawn was creeping across the eastern sky, the corpses lay across the forest, human and animal alike, all intermingled.

Those animals who had survived the battle and were still able to stand, rewarded themselves by feeding on the corpses of their enemy. Those who were not meat eaters made do with a well-deserved meal of leaves, herbs, fruits. Or, in the case of the bears, honey from honeycombs hanging from trees: rich, dripping, full of nourishing sweetness, they consumed it with great relish, the golden treat washing away the blood around those great jaws and massive teeth.

Mayla

~

SHVATE, MAYLA, AND KARNI found the children soon after the battle began. They joined the Krushan and watched in wonderment the charge of the beasts and the clash of the two armies.

A few assassins who succeeded in making it past the animals alive had the Krushan family to contend with. Barely a few dozen succeeded in making it that far, and those poor souls were dispatched easily by the two mothers and the father.

The children were not permitted to fight, on the strict orders of their parents.

"What you have done, summoning the beasts of the forest and enlisting their aid, has already ensured the safety of our hermitage and the survival of our family," Shvate told them, "but you are still too young to fight your own battles. As your parents, it would shame us if we permitted our own little children to risk their lives while we yet stand able to protect you."

Four of the Five accepted their parents' decision. Only Brum took it sourly.

"Brum fight," she said, her eyes filling with tears. "Fight!" she said, stamping her foot.

Karni raised her finger in warning. Brum subsided, hanging her big round head. "Brum," she said in resignation.

Karni patted and then kissed her on the head. The girl sulked but accepted the decision.

The Krushan were forced to retreat to the clearing, to wait there till their parents returned. Finally at dawn, the three adults returned, their clothes and bodies marked and stained from the battle, their arrows depleted, their spears all gone, their swords nicked and scored. They themselves were un-harmed, barring a few scratches. Shvate had a cut across his chest that had become encrusted with blood, Karni a slash across her back and one shoulder, but Mayla was unmarked and proud of it.

"Battle? Finish?" Brum asked, turning her hand this way and that to indicate "finish." She sounded hopeful even now.

Her parents took turns kissing her and the other Krushan. "All finished," they said. Then they embraced as a group, savoring the joy of still being alive together, still able to breathe and feel one another's warmth, see each other's faces and smiles, to press hands.

They were alive. They had survived. They were together. What else mattered?

They walked together through the battlefield, the jungle strewn with corpses for scores of miles all around the clearing in a large concentric circle. They marked the passing of the brave beasts who died fighting for their cause and noted the great number of assassins who had been sent. Mayla felt that even if the animals had not intervened, they might still have managed to fend them off. She was still riding high on the aftermath of the victory.

"Yes, we might have," Karni said sharply. "But at what price? A single casualty? Two? Three?"

Mayla looked at the little heads of their children, and her bravado faded at once. "None," she said softly, "none at all." She said no more about fighting a thousand assassins. Even heroism had its limits. They all knew that without the beasts of the jungle rising up on their behalf, they would surely have failed. Especially when even a single casualty meant failure.

They were about to start back to the hermitage when two figures appeared out of the still smoky jungle.

Brum raised her fists at once. "Men!"

The two men came into sight, raising their arms to show they were not a threat.

"Vida!" Shvate said with pleasure.

Karni recognize the familiar mustached face of Adran, her former charioteer, and felt a twinge of guilt. She glanced behind the man, her gaze low, as if searching for someone else following. Mayla noticed and frowned, wondering whom she might be seeking.

"Brother!" Vida cried. The two siblings embraced with warmth.

Adran bowed his head in greeting to the two princesses and prince. "You are well, Princess Karni?" he asked.

"I am. And your family?" she asked. "Are they well?" Her voice had a trace of some emotion that Mayla had never heard before.

"They are well," Adran said, "by your grace and Mother Jeel's blessings."

Vida cleared his throat, attracting their attention. Everyone looked at him. "I regret that I come bearing dire tidings."

The Five

〜

LATER THAT SAME MORNING, Vida sat with the others in their hut. They had all taken time to bathe and change their garments and feed themselves. All were tired but also jubilant from the night's success, though the deaths of so many brave creatures had been devastating. They honored the beasts that had volunteered to lay down their lives in service of the Krushan; they were the true heroes of the battle.

"It will be sunrise in a few moments," Karni said. "Guru Vessa will be coming to take us to Hastinaga. You and your charioteer can come with us as well, surely."

Vida shook his head. "I cannot say, sister-in-law. I was sent here on a special mission. Jeel Goddess herself, and her son Vrath, tasked me with delivering an important message. I come to deliver the message. Whatever happens after that is up to you to decide."

In their room, the five Krushan sat in an array of postures, all listening eagerly to the conversation of the adults.

"What is the message?" Shvate said. "Speak it now and deliver yourself of the burden."

Vida took a deep breath. "A great threat approaches. An army unlike anything you have encountered before comes to ensure your destruction. It will be upon your household within the day, perhaps even within the hour."

Shvate stared at Vida, then turned and looked at Mayla and Karni. They looked back at him, equally nonplussed.

"An army?" he said. "Attacking us? Vida, my brother, did you not see the battle in the jungle last night?"

"I did," Vida said.

"What was that if not an army?"

"It was an army," Vida agreed.

"And it was hell-bent on destroying us all," Shvate said.

"It was," Vida said.

Shvate sat back, smiling, and spread his hands. "So the threat that you come to warn us of has already been thwarted. Our house is saved, our family survives this crisis, and we are all whole of body and mind. We thank you for the warning, but it is no longer relevant. The crisis is past, the danger averted, the threat demolished."

Mayla nodded. "Soon the great Vessa will be here, and we shall all go home together to Hastinaga. To reclaim Shvate's birthright."

Vida frowned. "You mean . . ."

"Yes," Karni said, "Guru Vessa persuaded Shvate that Hastinaga deserves a king of his talents. Now that he has produced heirs, the stigma of his earlier mistake is erased. The responsibility of leading the empire once again lies on his shoulders. He is to return to Hastinaga, rescind his abdication, and ascend the throne. Guru Vessa himself has said he will ensure this happens, and to that end, he has told us to be prepared to go with him when he comes to fetch us at sunrise this day."

"This is wonderful news, my brother, my sisters-in-law. Truly I could not think to hear of anything better. It will be a grand day again in Hastinaga when you return and reclaim the Burning Throne. If ever there was a Krushan destined to greatness it was you, brother Shvate! This is the happiest day of my life. I am privileged to be here on such a great day."

Vida paused, then continued, "But I fear that all may not be as well as we believe it to be. For one thing, there is still the threat of the army that approaches. Now even the beasts of the jungle are all slaughtered. How will the Krushan defend themselves against yet another great enemy?"

Shvate and his wives all frowned and looked at each other.

"Vida, what are you saying?" Shvate asked. "We have already told you, the army came, it attacked, and it was destroyed. You saw the corpses yourself. They are finished. We won the battle. There is no more threat."

Vida looked at him soberly, then shook his head slowly. "I wish it were so, brother. But Jeel Goddess and Vrath cannot have been wrong. A god knows things that we mortals can never even hope to learn or understand. They tasked me with this mission, saying quite clearly that the threat that comes will not be of a human nature. And those assassins that came last night, though they were of a demonic aspect, were in fact all quite human. I examined their corpses afterward, to be sure of it. They are all too mortal."

"What do you mean, 'not of a human nature'?" Karni asked, alarmed. "What are you saying?"

In the room next door, the five small faces were all screwed up with concentration, listening intently. Brum was chewing on her lower lip as she listened.

"I am saying, sister-in-law Karni, that the attack last night was a different attack altogether. It is not that of the army that I came to warn you of, but another one altogether. Goddess Jeel and Vrath's instructions were quite clear and precise. The attack will be of a supernatural nature. And it will be very powerful and nearly beyond human ability to defend against. I fear that threat is yet to come!"

Shvate and his wives studied each other's faces, aghast at the implications behind Vida's words. The five Krushan stared at each other as well, all silent for once.

Mayla rose to her feet and went to the doorway. "Sunrise came and went while we were talking. It is now several minutes past. Yet there is no sign of Guru Vessa."

Vida sighed and released his breath. "So that is what they meant."

Shvate, Mayla, and Karni all looked at him.

Vida saw their faces and nodded. "Goddess Jeel and Vrath said one more thing. They said that though they both would dearly want to come and assist you in repelling this demonic threat that approaches, they are unable to do so."

"Unable?" Karni asked. "But Jeel is a goddess and Vrath a demigod!"

"Even so," Vida said heavily, "they are forbidden from taking part in this conflict. It is the same with Vessa and any other elders of the family. Whatever this terrible crisis, you must face it as a family and endure it as best as you can. That is the complete message I was sent to deliver. I have told you all that I know. Forgive me for bringing such terrible tidings, but tragic as it is, I felt that the sooner I brought it to you, the sooner you would know what to expect."

"Then even Guru Vessa will not come to our aid?" Mayla asked.

Vida spread his hands. "I do not know if he will not or cannot, but Vrath said that there are powerful evil forces aligned against you, and Vessa may well be occupied battling them in some other realm. Perhaps that is why he has not arrived here at the appointed time. As Shvate knows well, Guru Vessa never arrives late or fails to keep his word."

"Never," Shvate agreed, his voice hollow.

Karni rubbed her forehead with the heel of her palm. "Then we are isolated and alone. Not only are we not to go to Hastinaga today, we are still to face an even greater threat. A new army. A supernatural, demonic one. And this time we will not even have the beasts of the jungle to fight with us. We stand alone."

"No," Shvate said, rising and embracing both his wives. "We stand together, as one. We are family. We are Krushan. We are Krushan. We shall fight."

And with those words, he took up his sword.

"The time for fighting is past. It is time to celebrate and claim your true heritage."

The voice came from the doorway of the hut. A tall figure loomed, his wild hair and unruly beard unmistakable even in silhouette.

"Guru Vessa!" Shvate put down his sword and went to his biological father, paying his respects. "I knew you would not let us down. Even when Vida said you had been detained elsewhere, I knew you would keep your promise."

Mayla and Karni paid their respects to the guru as well. "Great One, we are so pleased to see you. It has been a night of terrors."

"Indeed," said the seer-mage. "You have survived a veritable invasion. Though I know the Krushan are legendary warriors, I would not have believed it had I not seen the mangled corpses of your enemy with my own eyes. Just the four of you against that horde? Incredible."

"We were aided by the beasts of the animal kingdom," Karni said, "summoned by our intrepid young rascals."

"I see," said Vessa. He was silent a moment. "So the next generation of Krushan are already proving themselves. If they can accomplish such feats as mere toddlers, barely three years of age, one can only imagine what heights they will attain when they come of age."

"Each of them alone is an army," said Mayla proudly. "They are gifted with great powers."

"Great Father, we have already prepared ourselves for the journey," Shvate said. "We should leave for Hastinaga at once. Vida has informed us that there is another army coming to attack us."

Vessa glanced in Vida's direction. He sat silently in the corner, glancing up at the tall mage, with a crease lining his forehead. "Good Vida. Friend and advisor to the Krushan heirs. Whatever would they do without you?"

Shvate paused, looking from Vessa to Vida and back uncertainly, then regarded Karni and Mayla, both of whom watched curiously as well. They sensed as much as he did that the guru was in an uncharacteristic mood.

"Vida," Shvate asked slowly, "will you not greet our great father? He is as much your sire as mine and Adri's."

Still, Vida remained seated, staring up silently at Vessa with the same frown on his face. He didn't seem to have heard Shvate's question at all.

"Vida?" Karni said, now starting to look anxious. "Is all well?"

Vida rose to his feet suddenly, pointing at the seer-mage. "That," he said in an odd tone, "is not Guru Vessa."

Mayla gasped, then covered her mouth with her hand. "Vida! Show some respect."

Shvate's eyes widened. He looked at Vessa, then at Vida again. "What do you mean, brother?"

Vida swallowed nervously. "It cannot be Vessa. He is a thousand dimensions from here. Besides, the scar that ought to be on his right shoulder is on his left forearm." He paused, looking agitated. "This is an imposter."

There was complete silence for a moment.

In the adjoining room, the Five stared at each other, eyes as wide and alert as their father's. Brum's fists clenched as she mouthed her favorite two words silently. Yudi got to his feet, the others following his example.

Vessa glowered at Vida for another moment.

Then he began to chuckle softly.

He ended the chuckle with a small sound, like that of a man clearing his throat.

He took a step forward, coming from shadow into light.

In that fraction of a second, he transformed, as easily as a liquid ripple, from Guru Vessa into the even taller, hunched form of Jarsun.

Still moving, he continued taking the next step, directly toward Shvate.

Shvate lunged for the sword he had put down only a few moments ago.

Karni moved in another direction, going for her own blade.

Mayla stood still, gaping with shock.

Vida took a step back.

Even as Shvate's fingers touched the hilt of the sword, the five Krushan infants burst into the room, ready for battle. Karni reached her blade and turned in the same motion, moving toward the imposter. Mayla broke out of her stupor and snarled, throwing herself bare-handed at Jarsun. Only Vida hung back, knowing better than to join in.

They were all too slow to respond.

Jarsun's fingertips reached Shvate's throat even as the Krushan prince's fingertips touched the hilt of the sword.

Except Jarsun's fingertips were not fingertips.

They struck at Shvate's throat with five undulating snake heads, each barely the width of a fingernail. The most venomous snakes are often the smallest. Five snakes sank their fangs deep into Shvate's throat, injecting their venom into his blood.

By the time Shvate's hand closed around the hilt of the sword, the venom had already reached his heart. He fell to the floor, mouth foaming, eyes bulging, skin turning blue, feet hammering a death tattoo.

Jarsun took another step — Karni's shortsword swung toward his chest — and stepped into a portal that opened instantly, engulfed him in its dark embrace, and closed immediately after. The faint odor of stale rice wine lingered briefly, then dissipated.

Karni's shortsword passed through empty air, catching only a few threads of the robe that Jarsun had been wearing, producing a single drop of his blood, and meeting no resistance.

Mayla struck at nothing.

The five children of Shvate, Karni, and Mayla cried out in rage and despair.

Jarsun was gone, leaving only a sudden gust of wind through the hut and an odor of strange fruit and alien flowers.

Then everyone's attention turned to Shvate.

But it was too late.

Shvate was dead.

Adri

~

"ADRI?" A VOICE CALLED softly.

Adri sighed. "Are my chambers now a part of the city thoroughfare? Can a prince of Krushan no longer enjoy any privacy in his own palace?"

"I beg your forgiveness. I only came because I thought you would want to hear the news immediately. I will withdraw at once."

"Vida?"

"Yes, my liege."

"Brother, why did you not say it was you? Please. Come in. You will excuse my shortness of temper. It has been a difficult morning."

The visitor came a few paces into the bedchamber then stood, waiting patiently. That was just like Vida. A half brother, biologically speaking, and his most trusted advisor and confidant, yet he behaved as if he were nothing more than a clerk.

"Why were you not announced? I will have to dismiss whoever is assigned to my door. They are supposed to announce every single visitor."

"I . . . I requested them to let me enter unannounced."

"Vida, please, come in. Sit with me. You are my brother in blood, a Krushan in all but name. It is an injustice that you are not recognized as an heir in your own right. These obsolete traditions and customs are so unfair. If we lived in a just society, you would have undergone the test of fire at the same time as Shvate and myself. But enough of my blathering. You said you had news for me. It must be urgent for you to come to me unannounced. Pray, tell me. What is the news?"

"My lord, it concerns Sauvali."

Adri was dumbstruck. He felt for a moment as if his heart stopped beating.

He rose from his bed and went toward the source of the voice. He found his half brother seated on the same stool where Grandmother Jilana had sat not long before. He put his arms on Vida's shoulders, almost as thin and underdeveloped as his own, and pressed them tightly.

"Where is she? Have you found her? Take me to her at once!"

"My lord, please calm yourself."

"Enough of this 'my lord' nonsense. Talk to me, Vida! What have you found out? I've sent spies in all directions of the empire, searching for months. But I know that you are the master of analysis and intellect. If you learned something new, it must be important. What have you found?"

Vida sighed deeply. "Adri . . . brother. Brace yourself. The news is not good."

Adri felt the darkness behind his eyes grow heavier, denser. "Is she . . ."

"Yes," Vida said softly, with genuine concern. "I'm sorry to be the one to tell you."

"You are sure?"

"Yes. The person who told me had no reason to lie. He had no idea who I was. He was present when they . . . when they killed her."

Adri released Vida's shoulders and turned away, trying to find something to hold on to in his anchorless world. The past months had been terrible, unbearable, but through it all, there had still been the tiny seed of hope. The possibility, however remote, that she was still alive. Somewhere. Somehow.

After a long silence, Adri regained control of his voice and asked, "What were you about to say, brother?"

"It doesn't matter."

"Tell me anyway."

"They . . . tortured her. Before they killed her. She suffered for a very long time. They did . . . terrible, unspeakable things to her."

For the past months, Adri thought he had endured the worst grief imaginable. Now, he felt as if he had been struck by a wave of such intense misery that it seemed as if he had never felt pain before now.

"What about the child?" he asked in a voice that surprised him with its coherence. In his mind, there were only the echoes of screams. "Did they spare the child?"

"No, my brother. The child was the reason they took her from you. He would have been Krushan, a potential heir. He died with his mother, still unborn."

Adri shook his head. But there could be no denying what was true. Had anyone else brought this news to him, he would have ranted and railed. But this was Vida. He trusted Vida to tell him the truth and nothing but.

Finally, he turned back to his half brother.

"Who?"

He could feel Vida hesitate, even though there was no sound from the man.

"Tell me," he pleaded.

Still, Vida said nothing. That was so typically Vida, to think through every angle, examine every aspect of a piece of information and the possible consequences before sharing it. This also told him how genuine the information had to be. It was not some carelessly gathered and hastily shared bit of gossip. It was real.

"*Tell me!*"

"Brother," Vida said, "I am so sorry. It was your own wife, Geldry, and her brother, Kune. They conspired with your sister-in-law Karni in order to deprive you of your inheritance and depose you from the throne. I have yet to unravel the entire web of the conspiracy, but as far as I can tell, Shvate's wife and Geldry came up with this evil design. Shvate himself knew nothing."

Adri probed toward Vida with every nerve in his body. He felt as if his mind and blood were all ablaze, as if he were seated on the Burning Throne at this very instant.

"Karni I can understand. She would resent Shvate for walking away from the throne. I have heard the news of her and Mayla's offspring. If she was already pregnant at the time, she would have resented her unborn children losing their inheritance. But I don't understand about Geldry. Why would she conspire against me? Her children are already in line for succession."

"Which wife would accept her husband's bastard or his mistress?" Vida said. "Her reason was simply jealousy and revenge. To her mind, she probably didn't see it as conspiring against you at all. She probably thought she was asserting her right as a wife and a queen, by eliminating her husband's lover and bastard child, and avenging the dishonor of her cuckoldry. The alliance with Karni was only to keep her own hands clean. By letting Karni organize the attack at the picnic, Geldry would not arouse your suspicions, while still getting what she desired. Perhaps she led Karni into believing, incorrectly of course, that she would let their children share the empire."

Something about that did not ring true. Geldry was not the kind of woman who would share anything with anyone. But that hardly mattered right now. The conspiracy itself was painfully plausible. Geldry had known and resented Sauvali's very existence. She would have wanted her dead. As for Karni, she had probably been desperate to have done this behind Shvate's back. And he recalled the many occasions when he had scented or sensed Kune in Geldry's bedchamber at inappropriate times, a fact that Geldry herself seemed determined to conceal from him. No wonder. Mere incest would have been sickening, but it was infinitely less sickening than their conspiracy to kidnap, torture, and murder the woman the future emperor of Hastinaga loved.

Adri knew there must be more details and logistics to the treachery, such as how, in the middle of a jungle, Karni had managed to hire so many sells-words to attack the picnic without Shvate finding out. Or had Shvate known as well? But none of that mattered now. All that mattered was that Sauvali was dead. His own unborn son — a son — was dead too.

And Karni and Geldry were the ones responsible.

He felt the heat rising within him, the banked fire of his bloodline, the raging volcanic inferno of the throne hissing in his veins.

"They will pay for this," Adri said. "They will pay dearly."

He felt stonefire, several floors below him, respond to his rage and reply with an answering surge of its own power. *Burn,* it said to him in its own secret song.

Burn.

Acknowledgments

After a lifetime (half a century) of knocking, someone finally opened the door to American science fiction and fantasy publishing and let me in.

His name is John Joseph Adams.

He's far from the first good editor I've worked with; over my long career, I've had the pleasure of working with over a hundred editors, if I include commissioning editors, editors, and copyeditors, on over sixty books in multiple editions.

But he is the best by far.

After over a hundred editors and over sixty books, I say that with great conviction.

I've known no editor as quick, friendly, kind, generous, sensitive, incisive, precise, exacting, rigorous, diligent, in touch with the zeitgeist, able to see the big picture as well as home in on the finest detail. As if all that wasn't enough, he's also a nice person, and a really great guy.

Many US editors and publishers these days talk about welcoming diversity, #OwnVoices, multicultural perspectives, secondary-world settings, marginalized perspectives. Very few actually mean it. John does because he doesn't talk or think about "diversity" as something to add to a publishing list; he simply accepts other cultures, other ways of seeing, no matter how foreign or individualistic, as equally valid. He doesn't "other" the stories, the characters, or the author.

As you probably know already, not only is this not the norm in SFF in the US; it's an extremely rare exception.

I'm lucky to have been discovered by him, inasmuch as it's possible to be discovered after almost forty years of publishing over sixty books, selling over 3.2 million copies, translated into twenty-one languages and sold in sixty-one countries. All that wasn't worth a damn to the several dozen editors and over three hundred agents in the US and UK. They didn't even look at the pages I sent them; I know this, because not one rejected me for cause: none of them even replied!

John did both; he read the pages, and he replied.

Then he bought the book you now hold in your hands.

John is the only reason I'm an American author of SFF today.

This book exists because of him.

My US publishing career exists because of him.

John, you made it all possible.

You opened the door. And then you held it open and welcomed me in.

I owe you everything.

Thank you.

I'd also like to give a big, warm shout-out to Bruce Nichols, who backed up John, signed on an unagented debut author and a 250,000-word book for a generous advance, and has been nothing less than awesome ever since: please stay awesome. The rest of the team at HMH has been equally awesome as well. It takes a publishing village to raise a book as beautiful as this one, and I can't thank them enough for their support and enthusiasm.

Ana Deboo made copyediting a 234,000-word manuscript seem like a walk in a short story park! This was the most amazing job of copy editing I've seen in my career. Whether you're an editor, publisher, author, or even an aspiring author, I urge you to walk, run, leapfrog, or fly to get her to copyedit your book. She wrangled this massive book using real as well as fictional words, a made-up language resembling Sanskrit as well as some real Sanskrit, Indian as well as fantasy cultural and word references, and she did it all so masterfully that I can only pray that she copyedits every book I write from here on. Thank you, Ana!

Hubris is what it takes to attempt a book this ambitious, the first of a series.

Humility is what's required to carry it from idea to final publication.

The book you've just read (or are about to read, if you're like me and skip to the acknowledgments to get a sense of the author) and the series you're beginning was birthed over twenty years ago. That's when I actually set fingertips to keyboard and began typing the first words of what is now the Burnt Empire Saga. The spark of that story began long before that, and in a sense, the writing of this series parallels my entire life.

It's impossible to thank only the people involved with publishing just a single edition, or even a single book, when the task entailed decades of growing, living, struggling, nurturing, dreaming, before the physical act of writing could even begin. So please excuse me as I set down this epic recounting of names and expressing of gratitude and make a long book even longer:

John Joseph Smith and (Siobhan) Kelly, my great-grandparents who sailed away into obscurity a century ago and were never heard from again: the family intrigue, mystery, drama — and ten abandoned children — that you left behind on the island of Sri Lanka (then Ceylon) laid the template for a lifelong fascination with family sagas to which the Burnt Empire Saga is the inevitable culmination.

Agnes May Smith: a brown boy in Bombay, India, raised by an Irish grandmother is, by definition, "different." I wouldn't have had it otherwise. Nana, you were my first patron, sponsor, and fan. From letting me take over your dining table for hours on end to taking eight hundred rupees out of your meager savings to pay for the printing of my first book in 1979, you let me be a writer. I know this isn't a historical novel, the kind you like best, but it's a family saga, and I know you enjoy those. Wish you were here to read it. I miss you and love you.

Sheila Ray D'Souza: as if an Irish grandmother weren't enough, an Irish-Portuguese mother with more attitude and progressive ideas than most "woke" women today, you were far ahead of your time. Enormous India was too small to contain you, cosmopolitan Bombay wasn't sophisticated enough to understand you, and the men in your life sure as hell didn't do right by you. I love you for doing so much more than seemed possible, against impossible odds. You were the best mother anyone could want. If you were still around, you would have read this book and given me notes, I know. I can only hope it's up to scratch! Love and miss you.

Polycarp Joseph D'Souza, Brian Xavier D'Souza, Yvonne D'Souza, and all the cousins and relatives who've drifted away over the decades or just plain died out. Thanks for the time we spent together, brief as it mostly was.

The extended Jain family: Indrakumar, Prakash, Vivek, Vaibhav, Usha, Pragati, Prakhar, Saumya, Mauryansh.

I've worked with many, many publishing professionals over my career. I'm grateful to every single person who played a role in the life of every book I wrote. You make it possible for authors to pursue careers. Thank you.

A few names stand out:

Arun Shastri, who was responsible for my first print byline, and Miss Sheila (whose surname I've forgotten in the fog of forty-plus years ago), the editor who gave me my first edits and praise.

The brothers at St. Francis, Bangalore, who wrote such a warm letter of praise for my poem "The Kingdom of Beasts" and then published it.

Joyce Aranha, for giving me a love for history that has endured all my life. It was good speaking with you last — was it ten years ago or fifteen? — and being able to thank you personally. You were more instrumental in my becoming a writer than any English teacher.

Ezra Aboudi, who saw a twelve-year-old boy scribbling on the back of his exam question paper and, instead of reprimanding me, praised my writing talent. Your encouragement was exponential in its effect!

Miss Sophy Kelly, a great educationist, a pillar of the community, and one of the greatest people I ever had the pleasure of knowing. Not only did she create a great institution, Hill Grange High School, Pedder Road, but she fostered the arts, theater, dance, music, and deserved far, far better than she received. Her sponsorship of my work — she gave me ten thousand rupees to write, mount, and produce my first theatrical production, "Are They Guilty?" — and her embrassingly effusive praise and support made me believe I *was* a writer, not just a boy trying to become one.

Kelly Cohen, who was right there at Hill Grange during those final golden years of that great institution, head boy to my assistant head boy, producer to my writer-director, fellow organizer of socials and eater of paper dosas on Altamount Road. Those were the days, old friend. Who would have thought two Hill Grangers from aamchi Mumbai would end up in Los Angeles and Cleveland around the same time? Shalom, pardner!

Randhir Khare for mentoring a very raw young writer, opening his bookshelves and his home, and for sharing the invaluable gifts of time, advice, camaraderie, and the first real drink this fifteen-year-old had ever taken (a Screwdriver with freshly squeezed orange juice). Randhir, thank you for everything and wish you well.

Menke Katz of *Bitterroot*, the editors of the literary journal of the University of Texas at Dallas and other literary journals in the US and UK for publishing the work of a teenager (without knowing he was a teenager), and all the other editors (*Atlantic Review*! *TLS*!) who wrote me personalized rejection notes with such warm encouragement.

Zamir Ansari, who took the time and trouble to write back to and then meet with an eager young novelist (all of fifteen years old in 1979) carrying a backpack filled with an entire science fiction trilogy (*The Man Machine, The Ultimatum, The Last of the Robots*) and for giving me gentle, useful advice on how to approach international publishers.

Aughie Dalton, who believed that a junior undergrad was capable of tackling a postgrad course, and gave me the encouragement I needed sorely at that crucial point in my budding career.

The sisters at Daughters of St. Paul, who published my first book — and paid me my first book advance. Sister Mary, I'm happy to say it earned out!

R. K. Mehra, who launched me properly as a novelist, published my first bestsellers including my novel *Vertigo*, and paid me what he said was the highest advance paid for an Indian English novel at the time (Rs. 50,000 in 1992), which made me believe it was possible to earn a living as a full-time novelist. It wasn't, but I did it anyway.

Amit Chaudhuri, for sharing a love for literary Bombay, recognizing something that would stand the test of time in a self-effacing twenty-nine-year old in torn jeans, and for including my work in *The Picador Book of Modern Indian Literature*. (Back in print recently.)

David Davidar, for introducing me to the world of power editors and publishers with far more on their minds than books, and for all those wonderful breakfasts at the Oberoi discussing books, literature, Bombay, and publishing. The rest I could have done without, but as time goes by, I've come to accept that publishers, like authors, are at least partly human.

Dom Moraes for all the mumbled but excellent advice and wise suggestions, the good reviews and editorial encouragement. I never did write that literary memoir, Dom, but I will soon, I promise!

Jeet Thayil, who edited and published one of my first science fiction stories — in an anthology translated into Hebrew and released in Haifa, Israel — but it still counts!

Robert N. Stephenson of Altair, Ian Randal Strock of Artemis, David G. Hartwell and Kathryn Cramer of Year's Best Fantasy, Michael Plogmann of Storisende, Darrell Schweitzer and Nick Mamatas of *Weird Tales*, and probably a few more whose names I've forgotten, all of whom published my early short work through the '80s and '90s.

Mr. Shanbhag of Strand Book Stall at P.M. Road, who was kind enough to extend credit to a young writer who promised to pay for the books at month's end when his salary came in. It was my dream to someday see my own books in that small, crowded, but wonderful shop. Not only did the dream come true, my books topped the Strand Bestseller Lists for weeks. The man was an institution unto himself in Indian bookselling!

R. Sriram of Crossword, India's first bookstore chain, who took a bean-head's suggestion to introduce a separate section for science fiction and fantasy, and agreed with me that 250 copies of a children's book by an obscure new author named Rowling would surely sell out overnight because the book was that good. (They didn't; the copies just sat there for most of a year, but when they finally began to move, boy, did they *move!*)

Ravi Singh, Paromita Mohanchandra, V. K. Karthika, Hemali Sodhi, Lillette Dubey, Pallavi Joshi, Hemu Ramaiah, Saugata Mukherjee, Chiki Sarkar, Akash Shah, Mugdha Godse, and all the other wonderful people who played a role, some more significant than others, in a long and eventful publishing career.

Gautam Padmanabhan, the finest publisher any Indian author could ever ask for, and a wonderful human being. The only publisher who came to visit me at home in two different cities, on two separate occasions, to convince me to publish with him. I'm delighted to have been a small part of the great success that is Westland (now Amazon Westland) but am not surprised at the sheer level of your success. The Indian Big Five publishers were content to act (mostly) as import gateways for all the foreign dross flooding desi bookshelves. It took publishers like yourself — and specifically you — to show them that desi authors could achieve videshi sales targets. You made it possible for Indian authors to sign million-dollar contracts just for Indian publishing rights. You changed Indian publishing and my career.

I owe you far more than just books. Thank you, and here's to another several dozen books together!

This list is already long, and I've only just reached the present millennium! Like my literary idol Harlan Ellison (when it comes to forewords and afterwards, acknowledgments, and the like), I offer no apologies, but I am going to do something unusual in an acknowledgments page. I'm going to stop this already very long section here with a promise that epic fantasy novelists are notorious for: To Be Continued. (Soon, I promise!) There are still several dozen (hundred?) more people I have to thank, and I'm out of time and space here, a predicament in which more than one science fiction writer has found themselves. Ciao, for now!

Ashok Kumar Banker
Mumbai, India / Los Angeles, USA
September 3, 2018

The Burnt Empire Saga continues

A DARK QUEEN RISES

Coming spring 2020